MW00610826

|>::<|<<<|>::<| :+: |>::<|>>>|>::<|

The
Murmurings

The 1st Ely Stone Novel

By

David Walks-As-Bear

|>::<|<<<|>::<| :+: |>::<|>>>|>::<|

Based on a true 1953 Michigan Mystery

This book is a work of fiction. Some places, events and situations in this story are the products of the author's imagination or are used fictitiously. Any resemblance to actual persons, living or dead, is entirely coincidental.

THE MURMURINGS The 1st Ely Stone Novel

All rights are reserved, including the right to reproduce this book, cover/dust jacket or portions thereof, in any form without the written permission of the author.

Text Copyright ©2002 by David Walks-As-Bear
Cover Design ©2002 by David Walks-As-Bear
Author Photo ©2002 by Rebecca Snowhawk

Blade Edge Press
Manufactured in the United States of America
Mass Market Soft Cover ISBN: 978-0-615-26142-3
Dust Jacket ISBN: 1-4033-2501-4

Library of Congress Control Number: 2002091575
Cataloging-in-Publication Data: Walks-As-Bear, David, 1957 –

1. Stone, Ely (Fictitious character) – Fiction.

2. Native American – Fiction. 3. Spirituality – Native American

4. Mysticism – Native American   5. History – Michigan.

6. US Air Force – Non-fiction. Michigan Upper Peninsula – Fiction.

Other Works

1. *OLD MONEY An Ely Stone Novel* – The Ely Stone Series

2. *The L.P.* – Military Fiction

3. *How To Become A Swamp Creature* – Juvenile Non-fiction

4. *Mystery of The Medicine Pipe* – Children's Literature

|<<<|>::<|<<<|>::<|<<< |>::<| :+: |>::<|>>>|>::<|>>>|>::<|>>>|

Acknowledgements

Any cop or reporter worth their sand knows that whatever they accomplish is almost solely attributable to their sources. And whether it's conceded or not, they also need to receive support in their efforts. That goes for an author, too, maybe even more so. In the writing and researching of this novel, I have innumerable people to thank. Chief among them is my wife, Maureen. Without this girl's limitless insight, tireless editing and wholehearted encouragement, this book would have never seen print. In fact, without her pushing me constantly, I would never have written this, my first novel. But heck, even my kids propped-up the old man, so I'm very proud to acknowledge my family's backing in my first effort. Now as to sources, well that's a whole 'nother deal.

Just like a cop or reporter's confidential informant is vital to them, a writer sometimes relies heavily on people of vast knowledge and expertise, who occasionally wish to remain on the "QT" too. They have their reasons and mostly, I understand them. There are a number of current and past military folks, who provided historical context, modern applications and overall guidance. I do wish to recognize your nameless contributions to this tome. You know who you are.

But there are others, whose whole "modus operandi" is in the garnering and giving forth of information to the public. They are librarians. A unique and unparalleled breed, seldom given their rightful due. First on my list is Teresa Gray, of the Bayliss Public Library, in Sault Ste. Marie, MI. She graciously found information on a 50-year old missing jet, that was unattainable at much larger libraries. Then there's Meg Goodrich, of the Marquette County Historical Society in Marquette, MI. This lady too, was able to provide me with the unprovidable about this true Michigan mystery.

Then there is the wonderfully talented lady named Laura Zenker that painted the cover for this book. When I first saw the rendering of Muskrat Island, I was amazed. I had written about this place for almost a year and to see it come alive, exactly as I pictured it... well, you know. So, in conclusion, I should state that there are many other folks who had a hand in this endeavor like of Mark Rodeghier of CUFOS and many other book aficionados like John Halloran. In truth, they're all just too numerous to mention in the space allowed. All of them, though are just as noteworthy. To everyone concerned, I'm extremely proud and honored by our association. Thank you so much.

I<<<I>::<I<<<I>::<I<<<I>::<I :+: I>::<I>>>I>::<I>>>I>::<I>>>I

For
Maureen Therese

She's the rhythm of my heart,
The light of my soul,
Without her beside me,
I've no wish to grow old.
She's the mother of my babies,
My anchor in Mother Earth's storm,
My night-long fantasy,
My very breath and form.
She's my essence of being,
My reason for life,
She's my best friend, my girl... my wife.

I<<<I>::<I<<<I>::<I<<<I>::<I :+: I>::<I>>>I>::<I>>>I>::<I>>>I

I<<<I>::<I<<<I>::<I<<<I>::<I :+: I>::<I>>>I>::<I>>>I>::<I>>>I

A papa-quote of an astitute observation… that's applicable to any and all warfare… even that… of the spiritual kind.

"You don't wanna die for your country.   You wanna make the other poor, dumb bastard die for his!"

General George S. Patton Jr, US Army

I<<<I>::<I<<<I>::<I<<< I>::<I :+: I>::<I>>> I>::<I>>>I>::<I>>>I

Prologue
Makings of A Ghost

The War on Drugs,
The U.S. Coast Guard's "Line In The Water"
Somewhere South of Key West, Florida - The Recent Past.

I hang my head out of the door of the helicopter and take one last look at the sleek cigarette boat as it races away behind us, the late afternoon sun sparkling off its creamy white wake. That's the boat I was looking for all right and they almost blew us right out of the sky. Where did they get an RPG? Even better, why didn't somebody tell me they might have one...? Maaaaan, I gotta start listening to those little noises in my head! The door opening is sucking the smoke out, and when I turn back into the cabin the acrid fumes burn deep into my eyes, causing water to stream down my cheeks. I reach up and pull the helmet mounted microphone close to my mouth.

"The door's open, Skipper."

"Yeah, okay, roger that. How's Hookerman?"

I look over at the mangled body that used to be Petty Officer First Class Charles Hookerman. The explosion killed him instantly. His face and shoulders are a knot of twisted glistening red. We really hadn't ever gotten along. I knew he resented me, and that's was partly because my mere presence onboard the aircraft usurped his position as the crewtech. And, well, that always pissed crewtechs off to a degree. But they usually never took it personally. Hookerman just plain didn't like me.

I always had the feeling that he disliked Indians and hated CGI (Coast Guard Intelligence) people in particular. Seems like he was from Montana or someplace out there. It isn't unusual for Westerners to dislike Indians. I'd see him on base somewhere, and he wouldn't even return a hello. Just the same, he was one of the best airdales I'd served with even if he didn't appreciate my companionship. He knew his job and he did it well. Whatever his problem was, he never let it interfere with the job. He treated me as a part of the team for the mission, even if I was a "spook." His helmet lolled from side to side. He was married with kids, if I remember right. I shake my head to clear the pictures it contains and key the mike.

"He's dead, Skipper, killed instantly." I answer as I make my way around the gaping hole in the deck and head for the cockpit. As I inch between the two seats, I look over at the pilot, Lieutenant Mike Antlovitch. He's still wrestling with the controls while talking into his headset. I know what he's doing, but I think it's a lost cause. He's trying to raise someone, but the radio is gone. It's a wonder that the intercom is still operational. My gaze switches to the co-pilot. There's a slight trickle of blood dripping down the side of his mouth, and a very unnatural slant to his position.

I raise my right hand to my teeth, and bite the fingertips of the flight glove pulling it free. I haven't looked at my left hand yet, but I know that it's messed up pretty bad. A lot of pain and some fair bleeding there. I stick my two right fingers against the copilot's jugular. Nothing. His visor snapped down during the impact, and I raise it up to see the eyes of Lieutenant JG. Pete Johnston already glazing over. The smoke is getting heavier in the cockpit, and I look over to the pilot. He's fighting the cyclic, manhandling the aircraft, while calling out MAYDAYS on the dead radio.

I glance back at Johnston and wonder what killed him. I ease him forward, his chest pushing against the harness. The smoke is bad enough that I can't see clearly, and I have to bend over to make out the three small holes in his flight suit - probably shrapnel- and then I see where the fragments penetrated the seat cushion. I gently set him back. The smoke is getting thicker and carries the scent of scorched metal. I turn back to the pilot. I tap him on his shoulder, but he's too busy to notice. I glance at the frequency light and switch my own headset over. The fear in the pilot's voice sends a cold shiver down my spine.

"MAYDAY, MAYDAY, MAYDAY...Coast Guard Aircraft 6578... I have injured crewmen onboard and am losing power...Request Assistance ASAP...Does anyone copy...over..."

He gives our location, but his plea is answered by the sick sound of solid radio static. A growing uneasiness grips me like a bad case of stomach flu as I tap his shoulder again.

"Lieutenant, I think the radio's shot. What's going on with the bird?" I ask as I point to the instruments in front of him. He turns to look at me and the panic displayed on his face is enough to make me piss my pants. I'd flown with this guy a lot over the past couple of years and he wasn't the type to scare easily. I get the nasty feeling that we're in deep shit. He's probably just in shock, but I can't sail a paper airplane much less fly this Dolphin. I need this guy to be alright and he sure doesn't look like he is.

"I've lost some hydraulics and oil pressure is going," he nervously looks out the window and then back to me. "We're gonna go in. I'll do the best I can, but you better make sure those guys are secured when we hit the water. How're they doing?" he asks me in gasps as he fights the helicopter.

He is alternately looking at me and at his controls. He didn't hear me tell him before about Hookerman, and he doesn't know about Mr. Johnston. I sure don't want to be the one to tell him that his whole crew is dead but...

"Hookerman and Mr. Johnston are dead, sir, and there's an eighteen inch hole in the flightdeck. When we touch down, we're gonna sink like a rock."

His eyes lock onto mine, and they change as he gets the message. I know what he's thinking. If it wasn't for me, his crew would still be alive. I can feel the hate as his pale blue eyes blaze into mine, but at least the panic is gone, replaced by a seething scorn. He slowly nods his head.

"Okay...see if we got any survival gear back there, yet. I'm gonna look for someplace to set this tired girl down." He switches his attention back to flying the aircraft. He's the tried and true professional again. His voice is close to calm and his eyes seem steadier. I asked him about injuries right after the hit. He said he wasn't hurt, just a little shook up. That's fine. If giving him someone to hate brought him back to reality, that's tits with me. We can square it once we get down safely.

I make my way back to the tail and pull the netting open. There's nothing but fast-moving turquoise water where the survival raft used to be. The whole rear of the fuselage has been blown away. Oh that's just marvelous. What's next on this fun-filled little excursion?

"The survival gear's gone, Skipper." I say as I start to turn around.

"Yeah, well that makes sense considering where we took the hit," his voice vibrates in my ear. "Make your way back up here, Stone. Maybe we caaaa..."

The helo noses to the right, and I slide toward the open door. My good hand is trying to scratch grooves in the no-skid deck, but gravity is proving more powerful. An all-consuming fear chokes my throat. The bird rights itself as I smack into the starboard side of the aircraft, just missing the opening in the fuselage. Hookerman piles into me. Pushing the dead man off, I scramble forward. The pilot looks like death warmed over. Sweat is pouring off his face like he's standing bareheaded in a rainstorm and outside the world is spinning.

"That's it, the engine seized," Antlovitch grunts while straining to work the dead controls. "I'm autorotating in! There's a reef down there but I don't know how deep it is. Grab something and hang on!" The aircraft spools down in wide circles, and I can't make any sense of anything through the canopied windows. I struggle to the bulkhead behind the co-pilot's seat, wrap my arms through the nylon loop straps and scrunch down. The last thing I hear before my helmet is slammed against the bulkhead is Mr. Antlovich's long and continuously repeated "Hail Mary,... Mother of God!"

The world comes back into focus in a darkened haze. I don't know where I am. After a minute or two, the cobwebs cave in and I remember something about a crash. I start to take inventory. My legs?...Oh please, no...My God, what happened to my legs. I tell them to move...NOW! and they pop up out of the water. Okay, I guess I still have them, but where did all the water come from? It's covering the whole inside of the aircraft and is almost a foot deep. I force myself to think. I realize that I'm in shock. My head is pounding, swimming to and fro. Probably some type of concussion. I use my good hand and pull off the helmet and move my arms from the straps.

I call out to Mr. Antlovich. He doesn't answer. Hookerman's body is floating near the open door, half in and half out, bobbing like a piece of forgotten driftwood. Peering out the door and into the depths, the phosphorescence of a coral reef glows brightly. The chopper appears to be sitting on the very edge of the incandescent mountain. The only light inside the helicopter is coming from the stars, as I start splashing up toward the cockpit.

As I crawl along, a sharp pain stabs at my knee. I roll over on my butt and raise my leg. A slice of meat is hanging from my kneecap, showing through the torn flight suit. It's bleeding, but not bad. I feel around under the water, and my hand rubs across a protrusion of something gritty and sharp. I make my way up forward. Mr. Antlovitch's head is hanging. I reach over his neck, and I already know he's gone. The starlight is casting an eerie glow inside the downed aircraft, and as I focus my eyes I can see a huge dark stain all around the pilot's groin. A piece of jagged coral is jutting through his right thigh. It probably cut an artery so that he bled to death. No two ways about it, this day will not get a smiley face in my diary. Outside, through the cracked Plexiglas, the light is dancing off a quiet sea, the gentle waves appearing like rippled black velvet. I ease against the pilot's seat and the only thing I think or say...is a whispered "sheeeit."

Something out the window catches my eye. I scoot over and look across Mr. Johnston's chest. There. There it is again. Just a fish's fin poking above the calm water's surface. I slowly realize what kind of a fish has a dorsal fin like that. In that instant, I remember Hookerman. Racing back onto the crewdeck, I grab Hookerman's leg and start pulling him back from the open door. His left arm is dragging the water, seeping a steady stream of dark looking fluid. All of a sudden, a geyser blasts forth after it. A hideously huge gray and white toothed mouth reaches for Hookerman. Large black omniscient eyes guide the mouth and push it after us.

A scream erupts from inside me before I have to tell it to. Scrambling backward, my foot slips into the blasted-out hole in the deck of the aircraft. The mouth closes with a "thaawack" onto Hookerman's arm, and the black eyes twist from side to side. I scream at the top my lungs and pull Hookerman, while pounding the shark with my wounded hand. The fish makes a final jerk creating a disgusting splash and crunch. It completely severs Hookerman's arm. The shark flops and slides backwards into the water, the crewtech's dissected arm protruding from it's evil mouth as it sinks into the depths.

I get my leg free and drag Hookerman over to the straps behind the co-pilot's seat, slipping and splashing the whole way. I stare at the open door and my mouth voices my mind's words.

"Holy shit...Hoooly shit!"
I tie Hookerman off to the straps while watching that damn door. My heart is pounding harder than it ever has and I wonder if it will blow out of my chest. I scoot myself along between the pilot seats, my eyes refusing to leave the door and the frothy black water surrounding it. I scooch back up into the dash between the two dead pilots and wait. Sonavabitch! I hate sharks.

My heart is slowing down now, but I can't stop my eyes from flicking to the door opening every couple of seconds. Just for the hell of it, my hand reaches up and unsnaps the shoulder holster under my left arm and eases out the Colt 45 pistol resting there. It adds a certain amount of comfort to my psyche. But other parts of my body ain't so lucky. I can feel the pain setting in again now, and I know that the adrenalin is backing off. With the pain comes the woozies. I can feel reality shifting gears around me.

Somewhere, somehow, I know that the visit's coming, and I don't want it to. But I've been here many times before and know that this bit of social protocol that will have to go on. I would give anything not to do this. But I know that it's God's plan. I also know that it's just. I ask anyway, already knowing that it's academic. "Please Jesus, don't make me do this...please?" But it's no use. I always come back. The Great Good Spirit has his reasons for my torment. For the next 37 hours, I'm going to sit and talk with these men. I'm going to hear about Mr. Johnston's times at the academy and his fiancé. He was going to get married in a month. Hookerman just made the Chief's list and had one more hitch to go until he retired.

Mr. Antlovitch had four kids, and was looking forward to taking them and his wife back to his parents' home for Christmas. Like so many times in the past, I tell them that "It wasn't my fault. No one told me that the pukes in the cigarette boat might be carrying a grenade launcher. The only info I had," I tell them, "is that the baddies were picking up – not chauffeuring the coke. My command should have clued-me-in guys, I swear, I'd never have taken us close if I thought they would be carrying heavy stuff!" The ghosts say that they don't blame me for their deaths, but their eyes…their eyes tell a different story. They always do.

And so it is. Here we go again…Mr. Johnston is telling me about the farm he grew up on when the alarm goes off. The ghosts look at me. It's my call. I tell them I don't know what it is, as we all turn and look at the overhead of the downed helo. Then, it begins to blur and changes shape, twisting and revolving, and slowly… it becomes…a bedroom ceiling. The alarm is ringing on the nightstand and it takes form as a… telephone.

|<<<|>::<|<<<|>::<|<<<|>::<| :+: |>::<|>>>|>::<|>>>|>::<|>>>|

Chapter One
Time for a change

The Lake Superior Coast off Yellow Dog Point,
A Deeply Wooded Lake,
Michigan's Upper Peninsula, Today.

I reach over and pick up the receiver. It's the hardware store in town and the happy guy on the other end tells me that my chainsaw has been sharpened, tuned up and is ready to go. The clock on the nightstand is reading 8:01 am. That seems too early to be jovial for most folks, but people up here are like that. They're a happy group that add an "eh"at the end of almost every sentence and are proud to be "Yuppers", short for UPPER Michiganders.

I mumble a few words of thanks, and tell him I'll be in to get it. After I hang up the phone, I look at my pillow. It's soaked with sweat. There are few things I hate in this world anymore, but sleep is beginning to hold first place in the limited inventory. I really hate that dream, too. I rub the light scars on my left hand and look out the cabin's window. Another beautiful fall day. The trees are bursting with color and the sun's already dancing off the dewy grass.

After pulling out a clean pair of underwear from the dresser, I move into the tiny bathroom. I twist on the shower to get the old hot water heater to begin it's labored function, then pop the lid on the toilet and relieve a bladder that holds it's share of beer from last night. I turn the water off in the tub, and apply shaving cream to a face that is haunted, to say the least.

After dressing and taking another look in the mirror, I'm reminded of why I never became a model. Never mind the fact that I ain't pretty enough, but wearing a suit is something I've never done well. Seeing my reflection staring back, I know why. I don't look half bad in Coast Guard Blues, and on occasion, I can even manage to look decent in a pair of jeans and a t-shirt. But in a dark suit, I look just like one of those guys that does the greetings at a funeral home.

My biggest fear is that I'll be wearing a suit some day at a funeral, and they'll mistake me for either an undertaker or the dead guy. Given the choice between the two…I guess I'd rather be the corpse. I shake my head as I look at the face in the mirror. I've been tentatively offered a job, and it sounds like one I could deal with. I want to make a good impression when I interview, and I think I probably even want the job. But it's not worth this. There's nothing worth being uncomfortable anymore, be it physical or mental. I untwist the tie and slide it off my neck as I open the closet and spy a Western dress shirt. Standing in front of the reflection again in a peach shirt with black piping and a pair of clean Levis topped off by a deer hide belt, turquoise buckle and polished black shitkickers, my appearance is more satisfactory. At least to me anyway.

I bend in a little closer, and see the dark rings surrounding my eyes and the hundreds of little red lines in the whites that make them look like the open page of a road atlas. I don't look so good, but what the hell, sleep is elusive when you visit with ghosts. Being one myself…I ought to know. A half hour later, I sip some coffee and turn my wrist to the black face of a battered old diver's watch. It's ten after ten, and my interview is at four. I've got plenty of time.

As I walk into the kitchen, I grab my cigarette box off the table, and continue out through the back door. I pull my uncle's old Zippo lighter out of my pants pocket and shake out a cigarette. As I suck in the first smoke of the day, I take in the majestic beauty that surrounds me. The maples are a fusillade of reds, oranges, and yellows, and I feel like I'm standing in a monstrous kaleidoscope. The lake wraps around the cabin like a lazy fat snake and a lone blue heron is fishing the shallows for an early breakfast. A flock of mallards are cruising the far shore, their feeding chatter biting the crisp air like mini-machine guns. The center water is rippled by a muskrat, chugging along as he cuts across it's girth. Behind me, in the thick tangle of thorn apple woods, I can hear a bunch of blue jays arguing heatedly over something.

I've inherited this place. It was my uncle's home for eighty two years and his father's and grandfather's before him. The forty acres that the old cabin sits on was part of the original reservation. It's not far from Yellow Dog Point, nestled on the Lake Superior shoreline. In the early 1800s, each family was given a forty acre tract as part of the land deeded in the only treaty that the Pukaskwa ever signed. Originally, there were some sixty-five families living on their own land here. But as time and life moved on, the Black River Band of Pukaskwa sold or lost most of their property.

Contrary to the popular opinion of sociologists, very little of it was stolen. While the scenario of the white man's graft and corruption was true for many Indian nations, it wasn't the case for the Black River Band. Here, it was mostly just plain old greed on the part of the Indians. As a kid, I remember summer trips to this cabin, and my mother's face smiling admiringly at her brother as he sat on the porch and talked heatedly of local Indians that sold their land to the paper mills.

I pull another puff of smoke from the hand-rolled and cut my eyes to the weathered old porch swing. My uncle would rant and rave, but he learned long ago that the land wasn't as important to others as it was to him. He would work himself into a frenzy, and then plead with his sister to come help him try and convince folks that they were doing wrong. But mamma was married to a man that would never leave the hills of West Tennessee again, so she only grinned at her brother and tried to console him. As it turned out, the Black River Band hadn't fared so badly in the end.

But even knowing that wouldn't have changed my father's mind. My Daddy had worked the barges of the muddy Mississippi when the Second World War broke out. He enlisted in the Coast Guard. He'd worked with the Coasties every day on the job and he knew how the service worked. They'd sent him to a world of freezing cold Lake Superior water, tall timber and chest-high snow. He hated the cold. I feel a smile stretch my mouth as I remember his favorite saying. "The only thing I found that I cared fer up yonder was thet little Indian girl, and hell, if'n ever I get 'er mad, she kin be cooler then a dadgum paddle pop, too." Otherwise, the old man didn't even want the memories of Northern Michigan.

My father ended up the war as a beach master on D-Day's Omaha Beach. He took an 8mm round in the hip and the Million-dollar wound sent him back to the comfort of the good old USA. Once back home though, the warmth of the South beckoned him. And my mother followed. Daddy was what was called a "Hill Indian". His people were a mixture of White, Cherokee, Shawnee and Choctaw. His folks had taken to the low-lying hills when the government came through with it's "Trail of Tears" program. They hid out until the party was over. I knew my mother missed her home here, and felt strongly that Uncle Mason was right. The two of them had grown up in this old pine cabin, and, while I think she secretly longed to come back, she never talked about it. Daddy understood though, because we visited often and my brother and I spent many a summer in this majestic place.

A splash down at the water pulls me out of my reverie as the heron snags a small pike. The lake water where the bird's standing looks like coiled molasses with the full morning sun beating down on it. I watch until the heron chokes down the flopping fish, and then turn to the rising yellow orb and say my prayers. When I finish, I let my eyes wander to the old elm stump, littered with cuts. What's left of the old tree stands maybe seven feet tall and is maybe three feet in diameter. It's part of what I've used to occupy many an hour over the past couple of years.

My Daddy taught my brother and I how to throw a knife when we were little. He told us that our folks used to carry hatchets or tomahawks when they worked the Mississippi River in the old days. A throwback to the Indian times. Being good at throwing one and putting it where you had to was sometimes necessary back then. But, now days, a good knife was all you needed. Putting it where you wanted required as much skill as ever though. Knife throwing, he'd said, was how we keep our senses sharp. Over the years, I found it to be true. Some folks whittle a piece of wood to while away time, but I throw my knife.

The knife is stuck on a chunk of wood there by the swing. I switch the cigarette to my left hand as I move over, pulling up the hefty blade. The Coast Guard had issued this aviation survival knife to me. It has a solid hardened black steel blade that takes and keeps an edge. It also has a deep blood trough and a serrated saw on top of the blade. On the butt of the handle is a weighted steel cap, used for hammering. I've had the knife for the better part of eighteen years and during that time, have indeed used it for it's namesake… to survive. I've speared fish, cut trees, killed animals and… other things with it. The handle is wrapped in rawhide, and over time I've worked with the weight of the knife, fine-tuning it for balance and throwing. I can hit where I aim, and bury the blade if I take a notion. I am proud of this tiny talent, even if it is unused and virtually useless in civilian society. Besides, I've used it aptly and well on occasion while in the employee of Uncle Sugar.

I feel a smile slipping over my lips as I recall another thing I used to be able to do with the blade. Whenever in a combat situation, I've always carried the knife sheathed upside down on the inside of my right arm. Time was when I could unsnap the blade, and with a single twitch of the arm have the knife down and sailing threw the air toward it's target in a half-second. I don't practice that little move, anymore. No reason to. I feel the smile enlarge, because if I tried that little trick today, I'd probably slice my hand off in the process. I flip the knife in the air and catch it. I know I have to get going. I am stalling, more or less. I look over at the elm stump, and whip the knife in a fluid motion. I hear it whistle through the air and stick with a loud "thawack" at five feet of height.

Cupping the cigarette, I draw the last of it's smoke, then Half consciously fieldstrip the butt and drop it in my pocket. Old habits Are hard to break. Walking back into the kitchen, I flip off the coffeemaker, drop my cup in the sink and mosey back into the bedroom. Over the bed there's a fairly good reproduction of Remington's "Custer's Last Stand". The picture is kind of an inspiration for me. A reminder that should I ever decide to bring a lady here, Indians can and do get lucky sometimes.

Pushing the large frame over, I reach into the recession I'd chiseled into the log wall and pull out the little holstered gun, it's oil glistening in the fractured light. The tiny pistol is a Glock model 27. The Coast Guard had just phased these weapons in for intelligence work before I retired. I've used it for the past couple of years, and compared to other small guns this little 40-caliber was a sweet weapon. Since I'm a retired Fed, I can carry it with no problem. I would, however, have carried a gun even if there was a problem. That's just me.

Tucking the gun into my back as I go, I move over to the closet and grab my old leather flight jacket from the hook and drape it over my arm. After a final glance around the living room, I walk out through the front door, hearing the knob click shut as I pull it to. Stepping off the front porch, I follow an age-old trail in the tall grass that leads to the ancient barn. Moving around to the two vertical wooden doors that enclose it's front, I know without looking that they'll be a pain in the ass to open. Sure enough, they stick as I try to pull them apart. But I catch a peek inside as the door parts a little. There's just enough of her cleavage showing to set me to smiling. Picking up on the door while grunting, I'm able to pull the heavy old logged structure to the side.

It's a down-right shame to keep something so incredibly beautiful and alive locked up in this decrepit old shack, but I can't leave her outside naked to the elements. What lies behind the porous old wood is a 1972 Dodge Charger SE. From her 383ci Magnum to her hideaway headlights, she's the car I always dreamed of in my youth. I watched cars like this cruising the streets in the '70's as my buddies and I lit-up the asphalt on Friday and Saturday nights with our beefed-up old stockcars. Nothing we had compared to this Charger. She was manufactured muscle, and made for guys with money. And that did not describe my buddies or me.

I got the car the summer before I left the service. I paid the fee of a solemn and sacred promise for a vintage muscle car with 2700 actual miles and the essence of the word "cherry". To this day, I still marvel at God's sense of irony, or maybe…his sense of humor. The Dodge had only spent two months on the road before it was stored. It's twenty-two year old owner died in the brown waters of Viet Nam. I happened to see the Charger's nose through an open garage door, over a quarter century later, in what had once been a respectable middle-class Florida neighborhood. I parked and walked up to an old gentleman who was busy watering a lawn that could never be lush again because of the litter, spilled anti-freeze, blood, and General

human run-off that was now what the neighborhood consisted of.
When I asked him if the Charger might be for sale, and explained how
I had always wanted one, his old eyes switched quickly to the open
garage door and stayed there.

He stared at the opening in the garage for several minutes, neither
of us talking. When he turned back to look to me, the old brown eyes
were filled with water. His voice was jittery as he looked at my
uniform and asked, "You in the Navy?"
I didn't understand what had set the old fella off, and I shook my
head. "No, sir...Coast Guard".

He nodded, and looked back at the garage. "You know, I haven't
had that door open in at least ten years. My boy Larry was in the
Navy. We bought that car for him right after he finished college. First
one in the family to ever do that and everyone chipped in...aunts,
uncles, cousins...everybody."

He shook his head and wiped his eyes, and then turned to look at
me again. "The deal was, he had to take care of it and he did. Until his
ROTC time came. He had to go, but the fool kid volunteered for them
SEALS, or whatever, over there in Viet Nam."

The old eyes wandered back to the garage again. "He parked it
there, covered it with that old tarp and made me promise not to let
anybody drive it just before he left. And I haven't. He never came home
though. He loved that car but I reckon it's time for someone else to drive
it now." He bent down and screwed the hose spray off.

"Well...maybe it would be better if someone else in the family
kept the car, sir. I didn't mean to trouble you." I started to turn away,
but he grabbed my arm.

"No, son, you don't understand. There ain't nobody else who
would appreciate that car. Aw hell, boy, I don't know, maybe you've
got to be a sailor or something to want that old car. But there's none
of my other sons or daughters who will have anything to do with it. I
reckon to us, it'll always be Larry's car. I know that Larry would want
someone to have it that appreciated it. I'll make the same deal with
you that I had with him. You take care of it and it's yours!"
His old eyes had a forlorn pleading in them. The story that he told
caused me to pain deeply for him.

"Do we have a deal, son?...If we do, you go on over there and see
what it'll take to get it started. I'll go see if I can find the keys."
I looked at his imploring face and had to clear my throat before
answering. "Sir, if that car is in any kind of shape at all, it's worth a
lot of money. I'd be happy to pay..." But he didn't let me finish.

"No boy," he said as he stepped behind me and put his arms to my
shoulders and pushed me in the direction of the garage, "Larry's be

proud to know that somebody got his car that loves it like he did, and that son…is all that's important to me."

The car is covered in a factory coated blue-gray metal flake that gives her a ghostly quality in sun or shade It seems like she's not really there. A lot like me I guess. And that's probably why I like her so much. We're the same. The car, his son Larry and a lot of others. Ghosts in the physical, flesh and spirit. Oh, I believe it's irony, but I also can appreciate the Great Good Spirit's sense of humor.
I spent the better part of my Coast Guard career living in shadows, fighting wars that nobody knew or cared about. I learned to be mystical being - there, but seeming not to be. A true shape shifter - Indian to the bone. But like the spirits that have these abilities, a trade-off is mandatory. A little of your soul must be traded for the deal.

The 383 cubic-inch magnum cracks as she lets loose, her factory-Capped headers resonating off the overhanging tree limbs as I ease her down the old logging road. I've missed the pleasure of driving a car, if for no other reason than just driving it. There's a lot I've missed. A sailor too long at sea and all that stuff. All part of the bargain. But I'm out of that contract now, and my deal with the devil, old "matchemoneto" himself, the great evil spirit, is null and void. After I get to the blacktop, I open her up a bit.

I drive the Charger down and around the hilly wooded land that makes up Northern Michigan. The day is meant to be enjoyed. As I top a hill, I can see four deer standing in the road up ahead. The mating ritual is in it's infant stages, and the whitetails are already acting strange. I lay on the horn to get them moving, and they take the hint, busting into a tangle of jack pines. I look down at a small valley and see a red-tailed hawk, lofting in huge circles, searching for it's next meal. The radio's cranking out oldies, and man…if this ain't heaven, I don't know what is.

I head the car down the twisting old blacktop and wonder about the job. I've been living alone for quite awhile now, since putting in my papers. Lately, I've been getting the distinct impression that it's time to move on, whether I want to or not. It's time I guess. But given my druthers, I'd just as soon sit around the cabin: hunting, fishing, and communing. But, being a child of the military, you learn to do what you're told. And God has made it pretty clear. In my heart, I can feel the need to address the living again, so, I'll follow orders and check out the job.

I've got a couple of hours to kill, so I'll drop into town, pick up the chain saw and maybe some toiletries. Maybe even a new shirt or two, some underwear and socks. I've needed all of them for awhile, but haven't had the urge to drive into town to get them. Yeah, it's time for a change. I feel a slow smile cutting at my mouth. Uh, huh. Well, one of the worst things about being a ghost… is the tendency to haunt just one special place. And my cohort in things supernatural adds her two cents to my thoughts. The Charger finishes out my little mental horror scene, as her exhaust cracks loudly, like rolling thunder…on a dark stormy night.

Chapter Two
The Black River Band

**The Pukaskwa Black River Band Tribal Headquarters,
Near Marquette, Michigan's Upper Peninsula,
The Same Day.**

A couple of hours later, the Dodge and I arrive in the bustling
little soon-to-be casino town of Wiitikan. I stop at a gas station to feed
the Charger some premium and to get directions. The folks inhabiting
this new tribal village don't appear much different than any others
spread across Upper Michigan. They look at me and return the friendly
smile I send them. For all intents and purposes, the town folk could
easily be classified as Caucasian. As my eyes switch from new building
to new building and to freshly completed landscaping and brand new
white concrete curbs, I feel my mouth crack a small smile. Human
nature is a fickle thing. Many of these folks would not change with the
arrival of their new identities. They'd go on living pretty much as they
always have, taking the new blessings in stride and being grateful for
the gifts that they actually are.

Many others though, who never even knew they had Indian blood,
and prior to the change, couldn't tell the difference between a spear
point and an arrowhead, would become radical minorities. They'd
rant and rave about how the Indians have been mistreated. They'd
delve into the customs and speak as though they've practiced them all
their lives. They'd become the loudest voices in the revitalized tribe.
In essence, they'll become what only a short while ago…they
weren't. And strangest of all is that while they'd do it, the practice of
political correctness would accept it.

The gas hose clicks itself off and as I add some additional lead to
the tank, and hang the hose back on the pump. I look around at the
small town. A new park is going in across from the service station.
There're huge silver maples that funnel in and out of the swing sets,
slide and green wooded playhouses. With little imagination, I can see
kids running among the huge trunks and busting the sky on those
swings, almost touching the limbs of the massive maples.
The land surrounding the village is indeed pretty. And I sure don't
begrudge the new tribal identity. It's long overdue. There has never
been a race more persecuted than the American Indian people, at least

on this continent. I've always known that. American Indians had their land, customs, language and religion taken from them as cleanly as a filleted fish loses it's bones. Genocide was practiced and whole tribes ceased to exist, right down to the last man, woman, and child. Slavery was tried and tried hard on the Indian, but the culture and essence that makes us what we are, wouldn't allow it to stick.

Indians died by the thousands while in bondage, usually trying to escape. Hell, Indians didn't even have the right to vote until the 1920s – some, not even until the 1950s. Nope, I know it's fair and equitable for Uncle Sammy to give back a little of what he took in the name of God, greed and Manifest Destiny. As I walk through the station door and hold it open for a thankfully nodding old fellow carrying a plastic grocery bag and a half gallon of milk, I spy the cashier at the counter. She's maybe eighteen, with drastically short blond spiked hair and blue eyes. As I walk up and hand her my credit card, she casually licks her lips and smiles brightly. That's when I see that her tongue is pierced.

The theme seems to go well with her pierced nose and lip. I ask her if She could tell me where the tribal council building is, and as she explains, I notice her high cheek bones and probable Indian lineage. She pleasantly directs me around the corner to a "can't miss it" location. She's what the Black River Pukaskwa have evolved into. Uncle Mason would sure be surprised at this revelation. And while this girl may not be one of them, there's plenty of others who'll yell and scream about the Washington "Redskins" and the Atlanta "Brave's" "chop, chop" of the tomahawk. They call it degrading to the Native American. But for the people who were originally wronged and whose descendents are now being repaid for that disservice, the degradation would probably be manifest within their own people.

Indians, no matter what the tribe or nation, all share a common bond. They are a prideful people, living a life of character, respect and dignity. To my mind, a large part of those qualities have been lost, and to that extent, we're no different than anyone else.

I pull the Charger into the freshly paved Council lot. The bright yellow lines marking the parking places are still vivid against the black drive. And the white concrete sidewalks still show the fresh milky residue of flowing cement. My wrist turns over as I look at the watch and realize that I still have a good half-hour until my appointment. I pop the door and habitually fieldstrip my hand-rolled cigarette, allowing the tobacco to float down to the asphalt. Depositing the tiny paper in my pocket, I head up toward the lobby entrance for a look-see.

I noticed the casino, which is under construction on the way into town, but this place is brand new, too. The Council Building can't be any more than six months old. It's a three-story structure combining rough wood and off-white stucco in a rustic pattern. The large office windows are shaded, but reflect the blue fall sky and puffy white clouds even though they're set into the weathered wood. Overall, the exterior is just what you'd expect of a tribal council headquarters. I open one of the double doors to the main lobby and look for a reception desk or counter. There's an office cubical with sliding glass doors to the rear of the lobby. Even from this distance, I can tell that the young woman sitting at the desk is more than a little attractive. She appears to be reading something.

There are numerous displays and artifacts placed throughout lobby and a number of kiosks scattered about. I ease behind one of the walled kiosks before the young lady sees me. Most of the walls hold old photographs, each with a little legend stating who's in the picture and what family donated it. I researched the newly recognized tribe pretty well after Charlie called me. What this group of Indians had garnered from an 1811 treaty did, and still does, boggle my feeble little mind. Charlie Adkins and I go way back. Charlie and I reported at about the same time to our first duty locale, a little Coast Guard search and rescue station nestled into the Lake Michigan dunes called Station Frankfort.

My reverie is brought to a halt as a phone rings down in the little cubical. Easing around the wall, I see the girl holding the phone to her ear as she shuffles through some paperwork. I casually slip across the opening to another kiosk and wander down the rows of photographs. Charlie has always been a friend. Over the years, we've kept in touch, mostly because we have developed a bond of sorts. You don't spend hundreds of hours together in a 44-foot motor lifeboat, chugging along out on the Great Lake in light, dark, fair, and foul weather without getting to know your crewmates pretty well. But that goes doubly for us. Most of the other Coasties working the station had been there before us or come after. But because we came onboard at the same time, we spent that whole tour together. Old Charlie went back home to college after our four year stint at Frankfort, but I reenlisted. He graduated, got married and took a job with the Bureau of Land Management, and has been a career government puke ever since.

It was Charlie that called me about the Black River Band. Since Charlie works for the BLM, which is under the Department of Interior, it ain't too surprising that he hears stuff. Especially since the Bureau of Indian Affairs, comes under the DOI too. But the fact that the Black River Band received the largest cash payment for latent treaty rights in history was amazing. One point six billion dollars.

That's a lot of cash, or in Indian terms, "really heap big wampum". I can't help but chuckle as I tick my fingers against an original Remington hanging on the wall. The painting is one of the few the artist did depicting Woodland Indians. It had to have cost a pretty penny, but the tribe could afford it.

Federal attorneys had known that the Tribe's take would be huge for years. That was why they'd held it up for as long as possible in the courts. The treaty was ironclad. In 1811, the tiny Black River Band inhabited some 20,800 acres of Lake Superior waterfront in the U.P. of Michigan. The U.S. wanted the land and needed the Black River Band as allies against the British in the War of 1812. In simple basic terms, the treaty stated that for relinquishing the land and agreeing to fight the British, the U.S. Government would immediately deed each tribal family a total of forty acres, and that as soon as the war ended the U.S. would pay the tribe for the land at it's fair market value and feed and clothe the tribe forever, blah, blah, blah… as these stories go.

It would have been a good deal for Uncle Sugar, too, if he'd held up his end. But he'd never fed or clothed a single Pukaskwa and he didn't pay that fair market value until some one hundred and eighty-five years after the war ended. By that time, the land had become highly desired prime waterfront by the affluent Wisconsins and "Trolls" or lower peninsula Michigan citizens. They're called Trolls by the Yuppers because they live under the Mackinaw Bridge. Quaint, but true.

Anyway, the land was worth a lot more than it had been when the real estate brokers were wearing pointy little triangle hats. Charlie remembered that my mother had been from the Black River people, and he made sure I knew about it, even before the tribal elders got the word. He knew me better than to expect me to cash-in on the bonanza, but he figured I'd be interested. And he was right. I've always been fascinated by my culture, and I keep tabs on what's going on out of a flat-out curiosity.

I stop by an old, yellowed photograph. On the dog eared and faded parchment, the side wall of a cabin is clear. An Indian man, woman and four children are perched against a wood pile, the kids scattered like they were flung up there along with the protruding pieces of split timber. There's a smile on every face except for that of the man. He's holding an old lever-action Winchester in one hand and the woman's hand in the other. On his face is a look of pride and contentment.

Every picture I've ever seen of my grandfather has a similar expression on his face. My grandmother is looking sideways at Uncle Mason, my mother, Uncle Ely and Uncle Jack. A mother's pride is different than that of a father I guess. I drop my eyes down to the legend. Donated by Amos Reddeer. Oh, yeah, I remember Mr. Reddeer. He used to own the 40 acres next to Uncle Mason's place…well…my place now.

"Can I help you with anything?"

The voice is deceptively light and seductive, and as I turn to look at her, I realize that the girl from the cubical has snuck up on me while I was entranced in family history. She is definitely Indian with some white overtones. She's wearing a pair of faded jeans, a blue and white checked blouse and simple white deck shoes without socks. When topped off by her "no ring on left hand", long, light brown hair and almond-brown eyes, she's enough to stop traffic, not to mention my feeble old heart.

"Uh, yeah…I suppose so. My name's Stone. I've got an appointment with Mr. Hennessey at four o'clock." I wave my hand at the displays. "I was early, so I thought I'd look around for a bit." A smile decorates her face, and in the process, her lovely eyes disappear, hidden by mirth lines all around her face. Ohhh man, move over Miss Universe, you've just been bumped… big time.

"So you're Mr. Stone. We've been expecting you, eh?" She shakes her head in an "aw gee" manner. "My name's Annette Cole. I'm the Tribal Secretary," she sticks out her hand and I take it, squeezing gently and shaking once before reluctantly letting it go. Her smile is mesmerizing as she continues. "Why don't you come with me and I'll introduce you to everyone."

"Okay…uh, I guess I was unaware that there was going to be an everyone. My understanding was that I'd be meeting with just Mr. Hennessey?" As we walk up the staircase she nods her head.

"Yes, that would have been the case if you were just here for an initial interview, but when we offer a position to someone, we usually have all the people there who'll be interacting with that new person." I'm allowing myself to linger two or three steps behind her, mostly because I'm enjoying the view.

"Uh, ma'am, to my knowledge, I've never given you folks a resume or application. Is there a possibility you have me confused with someone else?"

She looks back over her shoulder as we make the landing and her eyes disappear again with her smile. "Oh, I think we know quite a bit about you from Amos, and anything else we might need, you can probably provide today."

My turn to nod my head. "Uh, huh. Umm, who's Amos then?"

We stop at a large oak door with the lettering TRIBAL COUNCIL CHAMBERS. "Oh, that would be Amos Reddeer, our Tribal

Shaman," she smiles as she opens the door.

Chapter Three
The Job

The Black River Band Tribal Chamber,
Wiitikan, MI.

We walk through a doorway that lets into a huge room, windowed all along one side. The walls are lined with solid oak, stained a rich walnut that is highlighted by the champagne colored carpet. Down the center runs a solid mahogany table, coupled with 12 or so large black leather chairs. On the walls are hand paintings, mandellas, dream catchers, and other Native American artwork. At one end of the table sit four people who look our way as we come in. This is definitely one prestigious boardroom. I find myself glancing sideways for the executive washroom key as the people rise to meet us.

The man at the end of the table, a fellow of maybe fifty-five or sixty, gets up and moves around toward me as I hear Miss Cole close the door. He is medium height, graying, maybe five-nine and has the barrel chest and sharply chiseled countenance typical of a Pukaskwa. "Mr. Stone, how do you do? My name's John Hennessey, the Council President." He extends his right hand while clasping his left on my shoulder. I return his handshake as he pivots and introduces me to the others.

Three people take turns reaching across the table to shake my hand. The first is Alan Morse. A very "white" looking guy, standing six-three, he has a beefy build, sandy, blond hair and blue eyes. He may be about my age and he is dressed in the uniform of a Pukaskwa tribal police captain with all the cop stuff: shiny gold badge, Sam Brown, 9-mm Smith, etc. He doesn't smile when we shake hands. The next is introduced as Nancy Morningstar, the Council's treasurer. Now she's smiling sweetly and seems very pleasant. She may be 35-years old and proudly wearing gold wedding and engagement rings. She has her dark hair put up in a pony tail. The next is Paul Schultz, the Tribal attorney. Paul is tall, slim and probably late thirties. There's Indian blood in his background, and out of everyone, he's the only person dressed for the occasion. He's wearing a nice double-breasted suit and gives me the standard limp lawyer handshake.

The third person has walked around the far end of the table and was now standing next to me.

Hennessey looks at the old man standing there. "And I believe you know Amos Reddeer."

I turn to face him and am struck by how much he has changed since last I saw him. This guy is old. I mean if he is less than a thousand, I'll eat my hat. And my hat fell off my head into the septic tank the other day while I was trying to unplug a sewer line.

I stick out my hand. "Mr. Reddeer, it's been a long time, sir." He looks down at my extended hand and then back to my eyes. He then steps up and embraces me in a feeble hug. I hear him whisper,

"It's been a long while for you to see me, young Raining Wolf, but I've been seeing you pretty regular, eh?" He releases me and then reaches down and takes my hand and gives it a shake. He looks up at me with watery old black eyes and the traces of a smile linger at the edges of his mouth.

It's been a long time since I've been called by my childhood name, and it shakes me a little. I don't know what to say and even if I did, I wouldn't be able to. Then, he ambles back around the table to his seat.

Hennessey points to Annette. "And I assume you've met Miss Cole, our secretary?"

She comes up beside me and pulls out a chair at the table. I 'm still a little off balance by being called Raining Wolf. Uncle Mason gave me my Indian name, and he was the only person who ever used it.

"Uh, yeah, I have." I answer as I take my seat and the others follow suit.

Hennessey looks from face to face and finally settles on mine. "Where to begin, Mr. Stone. Well, how about with names, eh?", as he wipes his hands together and smiles. "Would it be okay if I called you Ely?"

"Yes, sir, please do."

"Good and please call me John and...," he looks around the table, "I assume everyone else would prefer first names too?" Everyone nods.

Hennessey clears his throat. "When I called you awhile back, I believe we spoke about a job with the Band. I'm not sure how much we discussed at that time...uh, do you have any recollection?"

My turn to clear a throat. "Well, sir, I don't think we got into specifics. You said that you knew I was retired from the military and that my name had been listed on tribal roles. Uh...let's see...you said that you'd done some checking and found that I had some fairly unusual experience and that the tribe may be able to use a person with a similar background who could work very independently. That's about it, sir, and to be honest, I was only interested in what you had to say. Mostly, that part about working independently was what pricked my interest and that's why I'm here."

I look around the table and speaking of "pricked", old cop suit looks every inch a prick. Most of the others returned my looks with interest but Morse has a disgusted expression painted all over his face. This guy doesn't like me. That's bad 'cause I know I'll just toss and turn all night wondering why. Uh, huh. You bet. What a pity. Hennessey pulls a manila folder up and opens the cardboard page.

"Alright. We've, um…taken the liberty of gathering some information about you from select sources. Please don't take offence, but for the positions of high trust and responsibility, we have no other choice but to go about it like this."

He looks over at me and all I can think to do is shrug my shoulders. Jeez, the suspense is building. What's all this about anyway?

"Okay…it seems that you retired from the Coast Guard as a Warrant Officer and a…special agent?" He looks at me curiously, his eyebrows raised in a question mark.

"Uh, yeah. That's right. I spent most of my career assigned to CGI or Coast Guard Intelligence. I was a federal law enforcement officer and investigator in that capacity."

I look at Hennessey and then to the other faces around the table. Amos Reddeer is smiling and looking at his shoes. Morse is ever so slowly shaking his head while staring at the ceiling. Everyone else seems to be waiting for me to go on.

"Let's see…I also worked closely with other military services and their intelligence arms as well as all other federal law enforcement and intelligence agencies." A few heads nod here and there, but my little spiel still doesn't seem to be adequate.

"Why don't you ask me some direct questions, Mr. Hennessey, because I really don't know what you're looking for."

Hennessey waves his hand. "Please call me John." He picks up the folder and begins to tap it's end on the table as he looks around at his people. Several of them shrug their shoulders and nod their heads. I'm beginning to wonder if the reason their heads nod so much is because they're not screwed on too tight. Hennessey turns back to me.

"Okay, Ely, it's like this. We know a good deal about you and your history. We also know that you've been checking up on us and have undoubtedly learned enough to know that we're a very wealthy tribe right now, if not the wealthiest tribe in the country."

While he phrased his next sentence, I have time to wonder how in the hell they knew that I'd been poking around. What little I'd done was extremely subtle and as far as I knew, untraceable. Hennessey racks the folder one last time and lays it down.

"You know that money buys information and that a lot of money will buy anything. The position we want to hire you for will have so much leeway…so much authority, jurisdiction, and responsibility that we…well, we just had to be sure." He leans forward onto the table and looks directly into my eyes. "Can you understand that?"

What? Have I forgotten to flush the toilet and they've found out about it. What is all this shit? Whatever it is, I am getting tired of the game.

"Yes, I guess I can understand that." My turn to wave a hand. "Please go on."

Hennessey quickly jerks his head. "Very well. As I said, we know just about all there is to know about you. With the exception of Alan and Paul here, the rest of us are ready to hire you right now. But since they have some questions, I thought we would allow them to ask you and hopefully clear up any misgivings they have. How does that sound, Ely?"

Well, I'll be a sonovabitch. I look over at Mr. Policeman, who's already chomping at the bit to ask his first big question. The esteemed counselor has unbuttoned his jacket and is sprawled out in his chair, quietly tapping his pen on the table while looking at me like I am his next ambulance. Ain't this a lot of pomp and ceremony. Noooo…I don't think we'll play it that way, Bubba. I look back at Hennessey.

"No, that won't be okay, Mr. Hennessey." Since the ball's in my court, I go ahead and dribble it a few times. "Like I told you a few minutes ago, I was interested in what the job was. There's no sense in going through a lot of stuff for nothing because if the job isn't something I want to do, then I'm not taking it." I stand up now to make a shot at the basket. "If you want to tell me what it is that I might be doing, and if," I sway my hand to the cop and lawyer, "I can quell these guys' fears, fine. If not, then I won't waste anymore of your time."

Old Amos has turned his chair toward the window and is gently rocking, a smile draped over his wrinkled face. Both women are examining their hands, the attorney has straightened up in his chair and the cop seems to be seething under the surface. Hennessey rises up and pats me on the shoulder while asking me to please sit back down. I think the ball is going to go in.

"You're right, of course, but see…if the fact that we're hiring a person for this particular job were to get out before it was supposed to, it could jeopardize the whole thing. We're talking about millions of dollars here, Ely. So we have to go about it like this. Is it a little easier for you to see now?"

"Aw heck, sir, I can see just fine. My last physical had me at 20/20 vision. Now if you watch close, you'll be able to see my back disappear through that door. It's been a pleasure." I get up and head for the big oak door when I hear Hennessey.

"Okay, Ely...alright!"

I stop and turn back to see Hennessey standing with both palms flat down on the table, and the cop and lawyer both trying to talk to him at the same time. "Enough!" Hennessey says. Morse and Shultz sit back in their chairs and Hennessey waves me back over to the table. Everyone else seems to be slightly embarrassed, but Morse is madder than a wet hen and the attorney seems highly flustered, too. Shucks, I hate it when I piss people off who are as important as these two boys think they are. Yeah...right.

"We'll do it your way, Ely, and hopefully, we can count on your discretion in the matter?" I nod my head "yes" and slowly move back to my seat at the table. Somewhere, I hear the ball swoosh through the net.

"Let's see, I guess we should start with the island, eh?" Hennessey reaches down to a briefcase alongside his chair and pulls up another folder and lays it open on the table.

"Have you heard of Muskrat Island before?"
My memory draws a blank on specifics but I'd heard of it.
"Vaguely...yeah."

Hennessey smiles. "Well, the Black River Band now owns it. I'll let Annette explain about the island because she's done most of the research and she's also our tribal naturalist."

That little fact is interesting. I turn to my right and return her smile. Good looks and brains, too. Scary combination in a girl, but if it's packaged like her, then fear is definitely something to be conquered. Hennessey lays a contour map between us that depicts a small island located in Lake Michigan, about twelve miles off-shore, almost on the dividing line between Michigan and Wisconsin state waters. The island is small, only three quarters of a mile wide and about a mile and a half long. From the appearance, the whole thing is basically one big tall rock. Hennessey asks Annette to explain about the island and she gently pulls the map over between the two of us.

"As you can see, the island is extremely rocky and appears like a swimming muskrat. There is basically no level ground anywhere on the island except this plateau here, where an old lighthouse sits. The lighthouse is structurally sound but still in need of repair. The Coast Guard abandoned it for use in 1927 because of the difficulty of servicing it. The waters are too shallow and rocky for navigation anyway, so with the more modern charts of that time, the Coast Guard apparently figured that it was enough to have these hazardous waters depicted on the maps."

"This whole area," she swept her finger around the shores of the island, "is very shallow, no more than 12-inches deep in places and boulder-strewn with virtually no room for boats to navigate through them. These obstructions, shallow waters and sand bars extend out for almost three miles from the shore. The shores, themselves, are very close to vertical with limestone and granite being the chief substances. There are also some very shallow sandbars located all along this area. There are no beaches because the island's granite and limestone goes all the way down to the water. Mining companies attempted operations in the mid-1800s in hopes they might find copper and several preliminary mine shafts were dug. The eventual inability to load onto ships stopped all efforts cold though. Even rock climbers shy away from it because the limestone is next to impossible to climb."

She takes one hand to draw back her hair, which cascades like a shimmering brown waterfall with golden highlights down over her shoulders. She's wearing small bone earrings, carved with a turtle totem. I hadn't noticed that before.

"Vegetation is scarce, also. Although, the island does host some forty-six virgin white pines. Other than that, all that's there is some small scrubby jack pine, thorn apple and some mixed deciduous. It appears that the white pine found the only available sources of firm ground on the island. There are few hardwoods and very few deer, but thanks to the miners, there's an ample supply of feral sheep and goats on the island. These animals have been a draw for local guides catering to affluent hunters, who're flown in by helicopter. The island is about as uninhabitable as it can get. The main reason the Coast Guard abandoned it was the difficulty in supplying the lighthouse."

She moves a small hand and extends a finger along a dotted line on the map. Her fingernail has no polish on it, and as I glance at her face, I notice that she's not wearing any makeup, either. Most women look better without that junk but for a girl with a natural beauty like hers, the use of female camouflage would indeed be a sin.

"Here is what remains of the old trail that led down to the water from the lighthouse, but falling rock and thorn apple had fairly well closed it off before we came in and cleared it. Basically, other than those I've mentioned, hunters aren't interested in it. There is no fishing activity because of the wave and rock action and the shallow sandbars keep most intelligent boaters clear of the island. In short, the island is and always has been deserted. There just isn't anything there for anyone."

She folds the map sideways and moves it to her left. Then she reaches for another paper in the file that Hennessey slides over. She doesn't have the usual U.P. accent. While I look at her profile, I catch the scent of some type of wildflower. It's a nice fragrance and it goes well with her. I'm again struck by her beauty. She is a looker and watching her chest through flitting arm movements tells me that she is amply sexed as well. She's not super busty but very pleasantly laid out. I sneak a glance at Morse because I have the feeling he's watching me and sure enough…he is. He's also alternately looking at Annette. Might be I'm interested in somebody else's love interest. Oh, good. Me and the Blue Knight have something in common after all. And here I was thinking we might not get along. Annette takes the paper from the file and turns it around to show me.

"We purchased the island from the National Park Service for 1.8 million. They didn't want to sell, but then, they never want to lose land. The BIA forced the Parks to sell. No one else was really interested and once the decision was made, we moved quickly to acquire the island."

She reaches over and places the paper back into the file, and as she did, I noticed for the first time that she's wearing a bone necklace, matching her earrings, that's mostly hidden under her blouse. She turns sideways and faces me then.

"Now, as far as residual problems, we anticipate some trouble from environmental groups, concerns about cutting trees and the impact on wildlife. We'll have to deal with them as time goes on. Otherwise, that's it for my part. Can I answer any questions for you?"

Wow. I could look at her forever. Considering my luck, she's probably married and doesn't believe in wearing rings, or is queer, or…probably thinks I'm as weird as I look and act. Any one of which could easily be true. She is sharp though. Brains and looks are indeed a dangerous combination. I gotta admit, while I ain't a safe cracker, I'd sure love to work this particular lock.

I shake my head. "No, I don't think I have any questions about what you've told me so far, and, by the way, that was really thorough. But I still don't see what my part might be or what you're going to do with the island."

She smiles at my complement and…there go her eyes again. Hennessey speaks from his spot at the table.

"I know we haven't made that clear yet, Ely, but you'll get a better understanding once you see the whole idea and plan. Paul, why don't you go next?"

The lawyer is chewing on his pen, and he looks at me before removing it from his teeth. Then he sits up and leans forward, elbows on the table and hands formed into a tent.

"Our idea and plan is pretty simple. We propose to build a casino and hotel on the island that will cater to more affluent clientele. Group charters are a big draw at casinos and since there's no way to build an airport and helicopters have limited seating, we'll have to devise a form of water transportation. To that end, we've hooked our horse to a Canadian company that builds hovercraft. These hovercraft are capable of carrying up to 35 passengers and will be able to operate both winter and summer. We will, of course, have to hire crews to operate and maintain them."

He waves one flimsy hand around the table. "I believe that everyone here will be looking to you for help with that. As far as the legal problems, there are none. We are well within our rights to build and operate such an establishment and it really is an ideal piece of property for a unique casino. The only concern I can foresee is the possible trespass by the tree huggers and hunters. That'll be your bailiwick too. Three years ago, we hired an out-of-state consulting firm to do the figures and demographics on a fictitious island, located in Lake Erie, close to similar cities, etc."

He smiles like the Cheshire cat in conclusion. "After reviewing all the data, we believe that the casino will be a huge success for the tribe."

Hennessey moves right along and quickly addresses the pony-tailed woman, asking her to go next. Nancy Morningstar seems a little nervous as she shuffles the papers in front of her. She gave an extensive overall picture of a forty-six room complex with all the amenities. She explained some of the problems they had encountered so far and the ones they foresaw to finish. The total estimated costs for the construction are about 2.5 million dollars. That includes the purchase price of the land, boats, furnishings, staffing, insurances, etc.

That's a lot of coin but I guess they know what they're doing. She has her elbow resting on the table as she reads from papers in front of her and at this juncture, she looks up at me and twirls her wrist with a smile. "What else?" she says as she looks down and shuffles through the papers. "Oh yes, the yearly operating costs are estimated at about $600,000 and net income, should be around two to three million. I think that's all I had prepared." She looks over to Hennessey. And Hennessey looks at Amos Reddeer.

"Do you have anything Amos?"

The old man has been sitting forward, paying rapt attention to Pony Tail's presentation. He takes a deep breath and sighs. His face takes on a look of resignation, and I swear, his voice sounds like the ages themselves.

"No. No, I really don't. You see my job here," he looks at me, "at least as I understand it, is to give spiritual guidance to the tribe. I'm kind of the village preacher to this big money-oriented Indian business and..."

"Amos please," interrupts Hennessey.

That same unique smile cracks across the old shaman's face as he raises his hands in mock surprise and turns to Hennessey.
"Well, John, you asked if I had anything to say and I'm saying it. You didn't ask if I had anything to say that you wanted to hear, eh. So, do I go on or do you want me to be still?"

Hennessey looks at the other members around the table. Then he looks at Amos, shakes his head and throws up his hands in surrender. The old man turns to me. "I don't imagine you know this, but I gave your name to the board for this job. You see, I believe that we are doing many things wrong with all this money." He leans into the table and squints at me, "and the se se kwa speak of bad things on this island." He closes his old eyes tightly and quickly shakes his head before opening them and continuing.

"But basically, I'm just a figurehead, somebody they all can point to and say, "see, we have spiritual guidance for the people." I hear mumbled words from the lawyer, cop, and Hennessey, while the girls are again studying their hands. But the old man goes on.

"Most everyone here thinks that the way to help the people is to make them rich. But this is wrong. I've seen...and so have you, what the white man's money does to people. Any people. I think we need to use it in other ways, but then, I'm just a figurehead. They don't think I know what I'm talking about. Now they have all looked at you. They see what kind of a man you appear to be, with all your sailor stuff and police things behind you, and they think that you will be like them. But I told them of your other self... the true self." He motions to the lawyer. "It's just that they don't believe me. I..." This time the attorney interrupts his talk and the lawyer appears hot under his starchy white collar.

"Now wait a minute, are you impugning my character? Because if you are old..."

Hennessey slams his hand down on the table. "Sam, you be quiet. If you don't want to hear this, then leave the room. He's a member of this Council and he can speak. Understood!" He looks at Morse and Schultz, both of whom begrudgingly nod their heads in a assent. "Okay, Amos, please go on."

The old man has a smile from ear to ear now and a small chuckle slips from his mouth as he begins again.

"What I was going to say is this, young Ely. You are of the old world, yet you live in the present. You see things that others do not. I know that I'm telling you nothing that you do not already know, but these people," he spreads his arms around the table, "need to be told this, even if they will not hear. And the leader must be told the loudest." He turns back to Hennessey.

"I told you this before and the Great Good Spirit has pushed me to make you understand. If you want this young warrior to help us you must know that what I've told you is the truth. Can I prove it to you?" Hennessey has been paying rapt attention and I see him swallow hard as he runs all this through his mind. As for me, I'm so far in the dark that sunlight would have to be pumped in for me to see anything. I have no idea what's going on here and all I know is that I'm getting tired of all this crap. Hennessey's eyes haven't left the old man, and as I live and breath, there's honest-to-God fear in them. As I watch, his head slowly moves up and down. The old man isn't smiling anymore as he turns to face the lawyer.

"I have a question for you. A minute ago, you said that I was impugning your character. Now how... could I impugn something that does not exist?'

The attorney's face quickly turns beet red as he jumps from his chair, raises his voice and moves towards Amos. "Hey, that's it! You know what old man? FUCK YOU! I've had it up to here with all your mumbo-jumbo bullshit, OK! You should be in an institution! Who the hell do you think you are anyway?...I ought to..."

Before I know it, I rise from my chair and have my hand over the table and around the lawyer's tie and shirt collar, giving it just enough of a jerk to get his attention and elevate his heels, the plan already popping into my head to pull him over the table if he resists.

"Back off and watch your mouth. I mean it...DO IT NOW!" The anger in the lawyer has switched to fear, and I see the whites of his eyes roll up in surprise. I pull him back from the old man and half-push him toward his chair as I release him. The cop has finally found his feet and there are voices bubbling all around the table as I point my finger at the attorney.

"Now I don't know this man very well, buddy, but he's older than both of us and the way I was raised, you don't speak to an elder like that. There's no reason to lose your temper and absolutely no reason for disrespect. And I don't know or care if both of these women have foul mouths, but until I learn otherwise, I'll assume that they've been offended, too. If this goes on all the time fine. But if it doesn't, then you're out of line. You just settle down and if you've got more to say to me, then let's just take it outside."

The lawyer is fuming and starts to respond to me when he gets a not-too gentle arm grab from Morse, who guides him toward his seat. He looks over at Morse and then at me with a nasty dislike on his face, but he sits down. Marshall Dillon, on the other hand is recovering from his little upsurge of adrenalin and is staring at my waist, where unfortunately, my shirt has receded to expose the butt of the Glock.

"Are you carrying a weapon?" he asks, his face wrapped up in incredulous surprise.

"Yep, I am." I answer, as I pull my shirt down and begin tucking it back into my jeans. "I happen to be a retired Federal Special Agent. I have the right and authority to carry a weapon."

He comes around the table and gets way too close inboard for my comfort and then points his funny looking finger at my face.

"Just who the hell do you think you are, Stone? What gives you the brass to come onto this Reservation carrying a gun? I don't give a shit what you think you have a right to, all police officers check their weapons when they come on this Reservation! You should've checked yours with the Tribal Police!" He half smirks and puffs up a little more. "You're really a cocky bastard aren't you?"

He's beginning to add something else, and while I hadn't backed away from him, I had switched into a defensive mode and was facing him with my left side. Name calling, now that's not very nice. Like I said, he was way too close inboard, and besides, he had dirty fingernails and bad breath. I had the sorry feeling that the game was about to end. Oh, well, this is the way it often goes for "old big mouth me". We were close to the same height and weight and I stared into his eyes for about five beats before I spoke. As usual in situations like this, my voice automatically drops a couple of octaves.

"Have you considered how difficult it's going to be for you to pick your nose without that finger anymore?"

The finger stops it's incessant jabbing and the cop shuts his mouth. Nobody else in the room has had a chance to say anything. From the corner of my eye, I see Hennessey getting up from his chair. Morse turns his finger and hand palm up with a smirk on the ugly face.

"Give me the gun…Now!"

I look at him and already know that this situation has gotten way out of hand, but what the hell, in for a penny, in for a pound. He sure ain't getting my gun.

"I don't think so there…Deputy Fife. If you want my weapon…I guess you're just gonna have to attempt a physical arrest, and I think you should. You probably always wanted your name on that monument in Washington for all the slain police officers killed in the line of duty."

Hennessey is talking now, but Cop Suit and I are already too far gone for anything he's got to say. We'd long ago sized each other up and now, it's all eye contact. It's just a simple question of whether we go…or don't. I can feel my heart pounding and the juices flowing. I know I'm ready and committed, but I can see a change going on in the big cop. His eyes are losing that challenge, just a little bit of panic creeping in. Nope, he ain't gonna do it. Now he's backing off and pretending to listen to Hennessey, while still maintaining eye contact with me, as if he weren't grateful for the reprieve. But we both know better. I let my fist loosen and begin to allow Hennessey's words in.

"What is all this? It stops now, do you hear me?" He turns to me, "Ely, do you have the right to bring that gun here as you say you do, even on Indian owned land?"

I honestly don't know if I do or not but I'll play the cards I have. "Yes, I do, just like any other federal special agent. It could be that Joe Friday here is thinking of local police and deputy sheriffs, who have to surrender their weapons if the Tribal Cops say so. But then again, if he's got any savvy at all, he already knows that I have the same rights as the FBI, who investigate all felonies on reservations. I'd bet on the latter. My advise to you is to check it out. In any case, I'm outta here."

I know when to make an exit after a bad curtain call and I have that heavy oak door already swinging on it's hinges before anybody even gets a word out. But I can't clear it before I'm completely out of earshot.

"Ely, wait please." It's Amos Reddeer, and hell I don't know why, I honestly don't, but I stop. Maybe this whole thing, as secretive, pompous, and strange as it seems, fascinates me. I know I'm really curious about the job now, especially after all this shit so…I turn around. Everyone is standing now and the old man is moving around the table and up to face Hennessey.

"John, I said I could show you and now you have seen. He is as I said he was. He is not like others and you have to be prepared for this. He is the one to help us though."

The old man has all of Hennessey's attention and total respect. I didn't catch that before. Hennessey finally places both of his hands on the old man's shoulders and smiles. Turning to face me, he rolls his finger in a "come'ere" gesture. And like a stupid sheep, maybe being led to the slaughter, I walk back over to the table.

"We do want you for this position, Ely," Hennessey says while raising

his hand at the same time to quiet the protests of the lawyer and cop.
They go silent at his gesture and he continues.

"Please sit down and we'll explain to you what the job entails and
what you'll be doing." I look around the room, then pull up my chair
next to Annette. Hennessey looks at me.

"What the job requires, Ely, is very similar to what you did
before. You will be the only person holding this position and you will
report to Amos and I and only to Amos and I."
I glance over at Morse and now I know why he had an instant
dislike for me.

"You will be the special agent of the Tribe and have the full police
powers of the Black River Band. We've already checked with BIA
Tribal Law Enforcement and there will be no problem transferring
your previous training and experience. Now this is the part that scares
us, Ely. You will also have full access to a fund specifically set-up for
your job in the band. A fund that totals almost one million dollars.
That's a lot of money and a considerable sum to the Band. It will be
your signature that allocates that money to facilitate your position in
regard to your work. Of course, this means that we are entrusting the
peoples' future in large degree to your judgment, honesty and," he
glances quickly to Amos, "to your Indian heritage. I think I can see by
the expression on your face that you're beginning to understand all
our strangeness today?'

I'm too busy picking my jaw up off the floor to answer his
question right away. Then I finally get it back in place and can speak.
"What would I be doing? where? and why...me?"

Hennessey sighs, then continues. "Right now, your job will be on
the island. We need someone to troubleshoot and pave the way. That
someone will have to be a person who can operate independently and
who is honest and smart and a true one of the people. There will be
other places that we'll send you, but right now the island will be your
priority. As to why you, well...," he quickly looks to Amos and back
again.

"We need someone who will be right for the job and we, or at
least most of us, feel that you're it. For all facts and purposes, Ely,
we're a new people. There are too many things out there that we
know nothing about. Too many ways for us to be hurt. Now Amos has
told me how you feel, but believe it or not, I want to do this right for
the people. Amos and I disagree on things sometimes, but I take his
word for things that are spiritual. And my word is the last one on this
Council. So...what do you think? Are you interested?"

This was definitely a lot to chew on at one time. And what the hell
was that stuff about Amos knowing how I feel? I haven't seen that

man for almost twenty years. But overall, the job sure sounds like it's worth following a little farther. They haven't mentioned money yet but it's got to be pretty good, and besides, I really don't care. I think I'll tag along a little longer.

"Yeah, I think I'm interested but I have a few more questions and…"

Hennessey holds up his palm while glancing at his watch. "Good. But I hope it can wait because I have to be at a meeting in Marquette in an hour. Why don't you and Annette get started on paperwork and we'll get a chance to talk later, eh? Amos can probably answer a lot of your questions until then…will that be acceptable?"

"I think that'll be fine but let's hold off on the paperwork until we've talked some more. I can't commit to the job until I know a little more about it."

Hennessey stands. "Very well, then, we'll call this meeting closed for now and I'm sorry for all the fracas everyone. Annette and Amos, would you take Ely and show him around, answer any questions you can, and," looking at his watch again. "I'll be back as soon as I can. We can get together then, Ely, or set up another meeting if that would be better, eh?"

"That's fine, I'll just stick around for awhile."
He nods his assent and turns to Morse and Shultz. "I need to speak with both of you for a moment before I leave."
I get to my feet and notice that the cop and lawyer are shooting daggers with their beady little eyes. Oh, well, if I do end up taking this job, it won't be the first time I've had to work with people that don't like me. In fact, I'm not sure that I've ever worked with too many people that do. And while I know that's not completely true, it sure feels like it sometimes.

"Would you like to take a look around, Mr. Stone?"
Annette's been standing right next to me and here I am looking at two ugly men. I must be getting senile. Amos has made his way over to us.

"Why don't the three of us go and get a cup of coffee or a soda, eh?" he says as he guides us to the door.

Chapter Four
The People

The Black River Band Reservation
"The Band-Wagon" Restaurant,
Wiitikan, MI.

A few minutes later, we're seated in a nice little eatery about a
block from the Tribal building. Our waitress is a pleasant girl who
explains the menu, and since I haven't eaten, I order a cheeseburger
and fried mushrooms. My companions apparently eat normally and
have managed a breakfast and lunch prior to this time. There's a lot to
be said for normalcy, but I'm not the guy to say it. Annette is nursing
a diet coke, but Amos is already accepting a refill on his coffee and,
as he takes a sip of the fresh cup, he looks at me over the rim.

"So what did you think of our meeting, eh Ely?"
I'm still amazed at the man's voice. It sounds so wise and eons
old and he speaks so slowly. I see Annette's interest perk up, too. I
guess they're both curious. Well, join the club. I'm curious too. I'll
get you guys membership cards.

"Well, I can't say that you folks hold dull ones." I move my
coffee so the waitress can place my food, "and I guess I can say that
the job sounds pretty interesting." I thank the girl as Amos rolls his
finger over the coffee cup rim, and then cocks his eye at me.

"I know that you don't remember me so good, but like I said, I've
been keeping tabs on you, eh? Your uncle and I were close. We grew
up together, your uncle Mason and I. Ohhhh," he closes his eyes and
shakes his head, "I even had dreams of marrying your mother before
she met that hillbilly sailor and ran away." He says the last with a
wistful smile. "Mason and I followed you pretty close and he always
gave me your letters to read when we visited. Between talking with
your mother, what we read, and the few visits you made, we figured
you pretty well I think. John Hennessey, he is a modern man and he
even goes to the white man's church. He's a Methodist, I think, but he
was raised with the old ways and he knows, eh? Oh yes, he knows
and he will do what's right." He winks his eye with a slight shake of
his head. "Your uncle and I knew you'd be the one, alright."

I'm just about to take another bite of the cheeseburger when that
comes out. Now what does that mean? I put the burger down.

"What do you mean I'm the one? The one for what, Amos? I gotta tell you, this has been a real confusing day and heck, sir, I'm easily confused to begin with. I'd like to know what's going on. What did you tell John Hennessey about me, anyway?"

Amos studies me for a minute, glances at Annette, then settles those wise old eyes back on mine.

"I told him you were the "Pathfinder". He looks at me, then leans closer. "Do you know that you are?"

These little mysteries are starting to worry me. The U.S. Army has a pathfinder school for it's Rangers, but otherwise, I'm clueless.

"Nope. Unless you're talking about some Army guy that has a perpetually dirty face and plays in the jungle during wartime, I haven't got a clue."

Amos slowly settles back in his seat and from the corner of my eye, I can see that Annette hasn't been privy to Hennessy and Amos' conversations on this topic, either. She is awaiting an explanation, too.

"A pathfinder is a person chosen for the people by God, the Great Good Spirit. He is the person to guide the people down the right path in times of difficulty. Traditionally, he was the person that searched for and found a new place for the people to live when game disappeared or the soil stopped producing good crops. He then led the followers there. He was guided by the Great Good Spirit in these matters and knew what was right. Therefore, he is a protector of the people, a warrior. Today, that definition has changed a little, but..." he shrugs his shoulders, "you are still a pathfinder, Ely."

I look over at Annette who is also digesting what Amos says. I wonder if she thinks it's as crazy as I do. "Look Amos, I don't know for sure what you think you know about me, but I can assure you, there ain't anything special here."

I poke my thumb into my chest for emphasis, "I'm a loner and I really don't care about causes, property or things, so, odds are good that you've got your wires crossed somewhere." He slowly shakes his head as a small laugh escapes from deep inside.

"Oh, no, there are no crossed wires here. You are the one. And all those things you think you don't care about...well, even if they are things you are not interested in, you still have the only thing that makes you a rarity and a true pathfinder. That is the ability to do what is right, no matter the circumstances or consequences. That, and that alone, is what makes you a pathfinder of the people." He shifts in his seat, seeing that Annette and I aren't buying it. "I have not seen you for many years...true?

I angle my head. "Yeah, it's been a long time, at least fifteen or twenty years."

Amos nods. "Then, how did I know you would respond to the wigwam lawyer's remarks to me, eh? I told Hennessey what you would do in such a situation, and to be honest, even you do not know why you were so willing to defend an old man and complacent women over mere words."

As Annette turns to me with a look of curious wonder, I have to admit, I can't answer that question. In today's world, people just don't give a shit about things like that and, by all rights, I shouldn't either. Yet, I often find myself fighting for something that feels so right, when all around me, nobody else cares. Still, that doesn't mean I'm some kind of Indian lead-man. Hell, I don't know. Maybe they're just looking for a hook to hang some additional spirituality on. And, who knows, if it works for them, and works for me, I really don't mind.

After a few minutes thought, I raise my hands palm-up in a "beats me" gesture and the old man smiles. Then he changes the subject and begins speaking to Annette while I finish my food. I have the feeling that she wanted to continue the last topic, but I'm going to talk more with Amos when we're alone. As I cast quick glances over at this girl, I see she's doing the same. I catch her looks every now and then. Amos Is happily chit-chatting away when a young woman comes up to the table and asks to speak with him. The two walk over to a corner and shortly Amos comes back saying that he needs to go and talk with the woman's husband about a family problem. He assures me that he'll see me again before I leave, then he and the woman make their way out of the eatery.

Annette looks at me and begins some small talk about her school days, life growing up, and the like. I can tell she has something on her mind though. She continues talking as I enjoy watching her. She has a small mole on her temple that I hadn't noticed before. Just watching her conjures up a sensation of ecstasy. I'm enchanted by her. She finally puts to words what's been bopping around in her mind.

"You don't believe Amos about you being a pathfinder, do you?"
"No...do you? I mean, he reminds me so much of my uncle and it sounds like they hung around a lot together, so maybe it's logical that he came up with something like that. Shoot, Uncle Mason was always placing meaning to things I didn't understand."

"And that you didn't agree with?" she turns to look at me.

"No, I didn't say that. I just have no way of knowing about a lot of things, but I can tell you this, there ain't nothing special about me and that's a fact."

"Okay, but was he right? Do you often find yourself fighting for unpopular causes or...I don't know... for things that other people don't care about?"

I look out the window. Do I or don't I? Good question, and the truth makes me look like either a boob or some kind of a savior, depending on whether you're a modern politically correct Native American or your basic old tried and true redskinned Indian. I wonder which she is? I'm probably about to blow whatever chance I might have had with her, but that's life I guess.

"Yep. I guess I do or...did...or, still will, but that's just me, ya know. Everybody's different.

She looks at me intently, curiously for a moment, and then says, "If you're ready, I can show you around a bit?"

I'd already seen most of the town, but I wasn't going to give up the opportunity to get to know her a little better. We wandered around the squeaky-clean new village with her playing guide. I was captivated and way too soon, she was saying it was time to get back.

Chapter Five
The Decision

The Tribal Office Complex,
The Pukaskwa Reservation.
The Same Day.

I sit in Hennessey's office, a nice windowed affair with plenty of Indian decor. The major difference between this and most other stuff I've seen on this reservation is that everything he has on display appears original. I mean, the dream catcher is actual bent wood with real sinew woven as the spidery web.

A bow and arrows hanging on the wall are handmade from real wood, turkey feathers and stone arrow points. It's functional. You could take it off the wall and kill a deer. Apparently, Hennessey likes the "real" thing. That's good I guess because I deal in real stuff as a person and "really" speaking, what he has to say will determine whether or not I take this job.

Working for somebody has always been hard for me. I do things my own way and that tends to piss most folks off. Actually, if I hadn't fallen into CGI in the Coast Guard, where I worked independently most of the time, I would never have stayed in until retirement. I've got a lot of questions but chief among them, is "what the heck is the deal here?" If I can get a logical answer to that one, old man Einstein will have some serious competition in the history books. Lord knows, I do need to do something. I can't continue to just "be" around the cabin anymore. My dreams are encroaching more and more into reality.

I need to do something to occupy my time now, to push them back where they belong. The mental and physical parts of me that can be healed have done so. To stay in this mode any longer will be to invite mental horrors in on a regular basis and I ain't about to do that. I may be a ghost…but there's no law that says I have to be sociable about it. I look around the big office and wonder where my lovely guide went. I'm just about to seek her out when Hennessey comes through the door.

"Now, Ely, I hope you got the chance to see the town, eh?" he sweeps his arm toward the window, "such as it is right now. We're growing, but time can't seem to keep up with our anxiousness."

"I don't know, it seems that you've done well so far," I cock my brow and point a finger in the air as he takes a seat behind the desk. "Remember, those poor Romans had a tough time with the labor unions, too. That's why the town never got built in a day."

This solicits a small smile from him as he folds a hand under his face and rubs his chin. He then rests both arms on the desktop, all mirth gone from his expression now.

"I know that you have questions, Ely, and I'm going to answer them. And I think perhaps that the best way to do that is to tell you a little about myself, eh? About why I'm here and what I'm trying to do. And why...we need you for this position. Is that alright with you?"

Well actually, that's fine with me. I'll still ask about the things I need to ask so I tell him sure, go ahead. He does a one-time nod of the head, as if he's made a decision, and I get the feeling that what he's going to say, hasn't been voiced before.

"Yes. Well, where to begin? First things first I suppose, eh? My father and I never had much in common, Ely. You see, he was much like Amos. He spent a great deal of time trying to convey to me and my siblings what he believed was our birthright. From my youth to early adulthood, he tried to drum into me the fact that I was a Pukaskwa and what it meant." He stood and moved back to the window. "When I was little, being Indian was not a problem. My brothers and sisters and I were proud of the fact, but as I grew up that changed. As I'm sure you know, there is prejudice in the world and Michigan is not immune from it, eh. Unlike the Chippewa, who have tribal affiliation, the Pukaskwa had nothing. No reservation. No pow-wows, no college money. Nothing. And the Chippewa weren't too eager to accept us as equals, either. The Pukaskwa were illegitimate in their eyes. So that basically left us out. We were much more the brunt of the Indian jokes than the Chippewa, and," he slowly shakes his head, "since our mother was half-white, we got the half-breed jokes as well. Such treatment by one's peers does not make for an easy childhood or puberty, Ely, and before long, especially as a young teen, I truly began to hate everything Native American, eh?. Can you understand that?"

The man was keeping his face toward the glass as he spoke and I sensed that this was difficult for him. But having been there and done that, I did for a fact, understand. "Mr. Hennessey, I can easily relate to what you're saying. I've gone through those same feelings and times myself."

He turns back and cuts his eyes at me, a small upturned edge of a smile, playing at the corners of his mouth. "Please call me John, Ely," as he pushes his hands into pants pockets and tilts his eyes to the ceiling.

"Yes, well being Native American would affect many others the same way, wouldn't it, eh? My problem was in not realizing that. I was so self-centered when I was younger that being "Indian" seemed only to plague me. But then, such is the influence of the business world…the white man's world.

"Anyway, I shunned the Pukaskwa more and more as I grew older and fought with my father on a daily basis because of it. I was in college when the big problems arouse over the Chippewa's fishing rights." He jabs his eyes over to me. "Do you know to what I'm referring?'

I do. Treaty fishing rights and sport fishing "rights" caused civil unrest in the 1970's. "Yeah, I remember the turmoil from that time. There was a lot of discontent if my memory serves."

Hennessey nods. "My father was killed in one of the fights back then. That was when I consciously decided to no longer be an Indian. I immersed myself in the white world, got my MBA and became very successful. But then my children got into drugs." He harrumphs. "So it was success, that is, if you don't count my failed marriage and the problems my children have because of this denial. I didn't know who I was. And I finally had to find out. Everyone must find harmony. And harmony is found in God. And God…is found all a round." He straightens his back, turns, and peers deeply into my eyes. I think that he's searching for a brotherhood of belief here and…he's found it. I nod my head in agreement.

"I had never seen life like this before, Ely, and it was enlightening. I finally knew what my father had been trying to tell me, eh?. But it was too late for most of my children. I had kept them in a world where this philosophy doesn't exist. A world where selfishness is the rule and harmony is the abnormal exception. An exception to be trounced upon and destroyed, eh?. The white society outside of this village, and even some Native American people inside of it, denounce these beliefs and despise them."

He shakes his head in wonder as he pauses. I'm wondering a bit myself because I sure didn't expect truth in this equation - what with the money, prestige, and the people I met earlier in that boardroom. Hennessey forms his hands into fists as he begins again.

"Amos has been the one who has guided me in looking out for the people and he believes strongly in you, Ely."

He nods his head as if in agreement with his own statement then moves back to the window.

"Well, once I understood these things, I decided to put my every effort and skill to the Pukaskwa, eh?. I might not be able to save my own children but perhaps I could save others. As I said, I was wealthy, and when I told my wife of my plans, she couldn't agree to them. There was no making it work between us, if I was to pursue this course. I had to go on. So she asked for a divorce, eh?. I reluctantly gave her one and we split everything in half. Afterwards, I liquidated everything and put it into the legal struggle for the tribe."

He again spreads his arms wide to the window, then turns back to face me, his face more peaceful now. "And this had been the result, Ely. As I said, I am still learning, but my goal is to further the people, eh?. Since I know so little truth about the group to which I belong, I have dedicated my trust to Amos. And truth is the pivotal word here, Ely. There are few of the people left who know the old ways but Amos is one. And he is a shaman, eh. Amos is the tribe's spiritual leader and he has my complete loyalty and confidence. Now, I have skills in the white world to make business judgments, but Amos rules the spiritual side of things. As a practicing Methodist and a learning Pukaskwa, all of our decisions must be governed by God, or the Great Good Spirit as we also call Him, eh."

Hennessey comes back to sit on the edge of his desk and looks at me. There's a smile across his face now and I know that the painful part for him has passed.

"So, in essence, Ely, I wanted you to know these things about me. I also want you to know that whatever Amos says about you, I believe. He thinks you're the one to guide us in the outside world. Oh, we can make business plans and do all the leg work but whether it's right for the people...that's for Amos to decide. And I will agree."
He straightens a bit and a fanciful grin dances across his face.

"So Amos says that you are our pathfinder, eh?"
He adds the last as a question, but with a fatherly tease included in the manner. And again I'm dumbfounded. How do you respond to something like this. I've got no idea. I raise my eyebrows.

"That's what Amos says alright."
Hennessey smiles. "But you don't believe it, eh?" He says the last as he again takes his seat and continues.

"Well I wouldn't be too surprised to find out that it's true if I were you. That old man knows things. And I mean things that no one else knows, either. But okay then, you know now that you will have my complete backing in your decisions and that the good of the tribe is all that I want or expect you to be concerned with, eh?. All of the particulars will be handled by Annette, but it's time for your questions. So, go ahead, Ely, shoot."

I've listened to this guy for almost an hour now. And while my own character has always been somewhat suspect, I've usually been a pretty fair judge of other folks' integrity. I think I can trust him and have a gut feeling that what he's said and what he's doing is for real.

It's time for me to move a little now, so I stand up and stretch a bit before asking.

"Well, Mr. Henn...uh, John, just what is it exactly that I'm supposed to do on this island. I mean, I'm not a construction guy and to be honest, I'd be surprised if GREENPEACE showed up to cuddle the pines. I really don't see a role for me here."

He bumps his head. "No, you probably don't and I'm sorry, eh. I can see, looking back over what you've been told, that we didn't make our intentions for you very clear. What Amos and I want you to do, is go there and just...be there. Amos says that by your very nature, you'll find the problem, if there is one, eh?" He waves his hand. "All of that stuff about you doing troubleshooting for the building process is for the other members of the board. They would never go along with a spiritual check of the property and the project." He frowns.

"Most of them have a white mindset and I can relate to them very well. In fact, I personally feel that this is a tremendous opportunity for the Band but Amos says that an evil is there and a danger for the people. Since I can't see this or understand Amos' motives here, I'm in agreement that you are to be the spiritual investigator, as it were, for the Band. Now at least two very influential members of the Board would have major problems with that title, eh? So we have to be careful about titles, but Amos and I need you to work as a pathfinder and..."

I'm waving a hand now. "Wait a minute. I wasn't very clear either because I'm not a pathfinder, a book finder, or any kind of finder, keeper, loser, or weeper. Most days, Mr. Hennessey, I'm lucky if I can find my own rear end, okay?"

This actually evokes a laugh from Hennessey.

"Okay, Ely. But Amos says you are, and as I said, that's good enough for me, eh? As for the legality of this subterfuge, should you be worried about that, there is no problem with it. The tribal bylaws make this decision mine and mine alone. I have the final decision power. I just prefer to keep the fighting down as much as possible. But as to whether you are a pathfinder or not, well, that's between you and Amos, I guess. My bet would be that you are, just because that old man says so, eh. In any case, we would want you to go out there and use all of your background and anything else you can find, to lead us down the right path. Then tell us whether or not to proceed with our plans, eh? Amos says that you'll know. When you do, come back and report to us. That's all we're asking you to do."

I'm just looking at the guy. This is nuts. "What does the job pay?" Hennessey rubs his hands together and grins as if we've finally gotten down to the nitty-gritty of the deal. "Well, the Band isn't doing too badly these days, what would you say to a thousand per week, eh?. Would that be acceptable?"

Oh yeah, well maybe. I mean, I'd have to check with my accountant to see if I could work that cheap but what the heck.

"You've got to be kidding? You're gonna pay me a thousand dollars a week to go visit an island? How long do you want me for?"

Hennessey smiles broadly. "Ely, we need you for as long as it takes. But remember, we've got a schedule with the board, the plans and the project as a whole, eh? So obviously, so the sooner you could tell us something, the better it will be."

I really don't know what to say, but then I think of something. A couple of somethings actually. "What's the deal with this million dollars? I've got to tell ya right up front, that I don't like that part of the deal at all."

Hennessey raises his hand in a halting gesture. "No, Amos and I figured that you wouldn't. But I had to do something to impress your importance upon the Board, eh. And sadly, money is what impresses several of the most powerful members of that group. Now you being in charge of those funds makes these people give you the clout that you will need to do your job, eh. I would expect you to contact me through Annette before spending anything major, but like the spiritual part of this…arrangement… if you will, you'll just have to trust me and my motives for doing this."

There is sincerity in his voice and an earnestness in his expression. But being saddled with that kind of change makes me very nervous. Another thought pops into my head.

"So is Annette privy to this little secret? And if she is, what makes you think that the secret will remain a secret?"

"You will have to know Annette to answer that question. And as time goes on, you will indeed know her better, eh? Even though she is young, she was raised as a traditional Pukaskwa. Her views, mine, and Amos's are the same. She will give Nancy, our treasurer, any invoices or bills you acquire. Annette will be your contact with me and the conduit through which your activities will be maintained."

I really don't like the cloak and dagger stuff, but, what the hell. I've spent my life doing it. And what a nice surprise having that pretty girl as a go-between. If I'm not careful, old stupid me will take the job just for the chance to be near her. I again see the sun glistening off her hair as we walk around town. Hennessey pulls me from this warm memory.

"You'll have to deal with Morse for the law enforcement things, and, on occasion, Shultz our attorney. As you probably noticed, neither of them are happy about you being hired, eh?"

"Yeah, well I got that impression. In fact, I don't think I'll be included on either guy's Christmas card list next year."

Hennessey chuckles, "No, quite possibly not, eh. Do you have any other questions?"

Yep, at least one more I guess. "Okay, what about a contract. Are you going to want me to sign some kind of agreement, or what?"

Hennessey shakes his head and a wispy smile flows over his countenance. "No, as I said. I trust you, Ely, and Amos swears by you.

I hold out my right hand. "Okay, John, I'll give it a try, but you do understand that I'm not anything special, right? Amos' pathfinder doesn't exist in me. All I can do is give you my honest opinion on the land, the project, or whatever."

Hennessey shakes my hand firmly. "That's all we ask, eh. Now, we need you to get all the paperwork signed and Annette will help you with that. Then, you really need to get down to that island and start, eh?"

"Right. Uhm, I'll go check out the island and give you my opinion on it, for whatever that's worth. If that's all you're looking for, then we've got a deal. But again now…you understand that I'm not no Mr. Wizard or anything? I'm just a washed-up old Coastie with a bad attitude and a nice car…right?"

Hennessey nods his head and smiles broadly as he picks up the phone. "Right, Ely. Whatever you say."

I<<<I>::<I<<<I>::<I<<<I>::<I :+: I>::<I>>>I>::<I>>>I>::<I>>>I

PART ONE

Chapter Six
The Island

Escanaba, Michigan,
Michigan's Upper Peninsula, Present Day.

Standing on the balcony of the motel, I lean over the rail and pull the Velvet bag and a cigarette paper out of my pocket. I roll the tobacco cigarette while tilting my head to catch a particular squealing sound. I can hear kids splashing in the pool down below. The poolroom has a domed ceiling with a small skylight centered around its top. I cast my gaze sideways at my watch. According to the sign in the lobby, the pool closes in about fifteen minutes. They sound happy. Well, I guess that's no surprise as most kids sound that way when they're allowed to swim in a big heated pool. Mom and Dad are just letting them burn off a little steam before lights out, I reckon.

A seagull's cry grabs my attention and I make my way down the balcony to look out over Lake Michigan. I catch the bird sailing on a current and moving out toward the water. I've grown to really dislike seagulls over the years and while my upbringing taught me to never hurt any living thing unless I had to, I don't ever feel any remorse for a dead 'gull. Watching the white and gray bird shift and sway in the wind, my mind drifts back to that hot early September day when we came upon the Chriscraft.

I was still fairly new to the Coast Guard and we were out in Lake Michigan doing training in the Station's forty-four footer; man overboard or Wilson drills, search patterns, and boarding techniques. That's when we saw the Chriscraft. She was just bobbing along with no sign of life except the occasional seagull, bouncing off her hull. And that was strange. The lake was quiet and virtually desolate at this summer's end and here was a boat that appeared to have nobody onboard. The coxswain swung our big motor lifeboat over, and as we approached the smell hit us. Then the flies. As we came alongside, a flurry of seagulls broke up and out around us, screaming as they went.

There was what used to be an older white man lying on the deck, inside the gunnels. He was very dead and had probably been that way awhile. The body was surrounded by the remaining 'gulls who weren't about to give up their find to a bunch of Coasties. They raised their wings, cawed, sputtered, and flapped about their prize. The first guy to get a good look at the dead man immediately threw up all over the turtled stern of our boat. That made a couple of others, including me, almost loose our cookies. The birds had eaten the dead man's eyes and all of the meat off from his face, arms, and hands. What remained resembled raw ground beef. The Coxswain went below, grabbed a shotgun, came back topside and started shooting seagulls with buckshot as we shooed them off the Chriscraft. It was illegal to shoot them but not one of us had a problem with it.

The Chriscraft was registered in Wisconsin and the dead man was a fisherman from Manitowoc. He had no family and nobody had noticed when he didn't come back to the marina five days ago. He had apparently gone out fishing and died of a heart attack. And while I know that the 'gulls were just doing what came natural, I still disliked them for it. They're like vultures, no different than any other scavenger. As I watch the bird waft in the breeze, I associate it with the lawyer back at Wiitican.

I've always thought that attorneys and scavengers are very similar in the way they eke out their living. I mean, they both rely on someone else's troubles in order to eat and are extraordinarily greedy about the proceeds. As I watch the bird drift from sight, I run back over my last meeting at the reservation. After I left Hennessey, I'd spent way too little time with Annette in her cubbyhole office. She had me sign my W-2, insurance papers, uniform order, and other paper work. She gave me a shiny new VISA credit card too. The really sad thing for me was that my hero, Captain Morse, had had to leave to cover a car accident somewhere. That meant that I wouldn't get to see him again before I left, and well…that really hurt me. Uh, huh. Yep. You bet.

She handed me a folder that Morse had left with my I.D. card, badge, and case. According to the lettering on the badge, I was a Special Agent of the Pukaskwa Tribe. Now see, and I thought that I wasn't special. There was also a little note that said that Captain Morse WOULD be speaking to me at a later date. Oh well, at least later was better than sooner. At that time, I was tired and my patience was wearing thin. That's why when she took me into Shultz's office, I was already on edge.

The little dweeb had made sure that he was protected on his side of the desk. And that was smart. After about five minutes of his talking, I understood that his whole involvement with the tribe centered on his desire to get rich. He left what he called a "thriving practice" to help his newly recognized people…bla, bla, bla…and his only interest was the people…bla, bla, bla…and I knew right then that

the little puke had been dying in his private practice and had jumped
at the chance to suck whatever tit he could off the Pukaskwa.
He was only out for what he could get. Just scavenging off
somebody else. Pretty much your standard model 302 lawyer.

So I told him as much and walked out of his office while he sat there
with his jaw decorating his fancy desk. He didn't say anything or follow
me, and again, that was good for both of us. I looked for the lovely
Annette, but Nancy ponytail, the treasurer, said that she had left for
the night. Hennessey's office had been dark, too, so, since I had all
my stuff, I decided to just head back to the cabin, pack up and get
started on my new job, whatever the hell it was.

I draw in the last of the smoke as I watch the sun setting over the
lake, the sounds of children's happiness singing in my head. The
Great Lake casts a glare that tends to highlight the beach sand in
shades of orange, blue, and red. The whitecaps on the water take on a
roiling gunmetal cast while the trees seemed dark and hung in
suspended time. As the sun sinks slowly out of sight, I field strip the
hand-rolled and again ponder the job.

I hadn't had the chance to see Amos before I left the reservation
either and that still bothered me. I sure had a lot more questions than
answers, but as I squint my eyes down toward the marina, I figure that
I'll get a better notion of what is going on tomorrow.
Right now I am hungry, and even though I have this credit card
and can use it to eat a fancy meal in the Holiday Inn's restaurant, ring
bologna, cheese, and bread sound better to me right now. If I
remember right, there is what looks like a little Mom & Pop market
down the street a ways. I shift my glance once more to the marina.
Somewhere down there is a boathouse and a twenty-five foot boat that
I would use to make my way out to the island. Yep. Tomorrow. I turn
and go back to my room to pocket my wallet. Then I make my way
down to pick up supper.

I awake from a dream again. But it isn't as bad as usual, and I
even managed to get some real sleep between episodes. That is, right
up until about five o'clock this morning. That's when old Amos
Reddeer popped into my night movies. It was weird, too, even
weirder than my usual stuff. All I could see was Amos, dressed in
deer skins and feathers, standing by a huge tree in this forest with his
arms outstretched. He was looking at me and saying "se se kwa", over
and over again, whatever that meant. And that was it. He was there
for that one episode, then he was gone and I was awake. Now as I
survey my face in the mirror, I'm grateful for that. Some sleep is
better than none.

I finish my morning routine and set off for the marina. I see the big

sign stating that I'm entering the Escanaba Municipal Marina.
The boardwalk lets onto a concrete dockage system with
numerous boat slips and a gasoline dock at the outward end.
The Harbormaster's office will probably be there so I move over
to it. The sign in the window says that the office opens at nine am.
There are three boathouses along the dock, but none of them are
identified except by number. And that does me no good. Oh well,
I have a little time to kill, so I decide to look around a bit.

There're a couple of boats getting ready to leave and I can see
some already moving past the marina's pier heads. They're all sport
fishermen, headed out for steelhead action. Other than the boat traffic,
the place seems deserted. All except for one fisherman, quietly
casting off the gas dock. He nods my way as I approach the office but
we didn't speak. I notice him discretely glancing my way a couple of
times and I guess that visitors to the dock are rare at this time of year.
I drop my bag by the office door and mosey over to chat with the old
angler.

"Doing any good?" I push my hands into jacket pockets and look
down at his bobber as it floats against the gentle wave action.

"Naw, it's slow at this time of year."

Looking down into the plastic pail he has beside him, I see a few
speckled bass and several perch swimming, their gills slowly working
in and out.

"Well, you've got the beginnings of a fish fry, anyway."

The old man glances down at the pail, nods his head and smiles.

"Ya vell, I'll probably not do much better zan vat you see. It
seems that ven the watar begins to get cold, the fish decide not to bite
as much…Ya? An vis those boats coming an going, it only slows zem
even more."

I thought at first that old man just had a "Yupper" accent, but I
can tell now that he's German. And as he turns, a pair of faded green
eyes, encircled by a pair of wire-rimmed glasses, look out at me. I put
him in his seventies with a medium build, and he appears pretty
healthy for his age.

"Do you fish here often then?"

"No. Not really. I'm jus here for a few veeks, kin'ov, how do you
say…vacation?"

"Oh, okay. So you've probably got family here in Escanaba, then?"

The old man slowly moves his capped head up and down as he
looks back to his line. "Ya. My dauater lives here."

I let my eyes drift back to the water and his fishing line as well.
"Yeah, well I was hoping that you might know which one of those
boathouses over there belongs to an Indian tribe, but I guess you wouldn't

have any idea about that, eh?"

"Nein…uh no. I can't help you vith that. I'm sorry."

"Well, that's okay. Thanks anyhow and I wish you luck, alright?" I say the last as I gently pat him on his shoulder and move away. I can see a guy walking down the dock with a set of keys jingling from his hand, and if I'm luck, that'll be the Harbormaster, showing up early for work. It turns out to be him alright and his name is Joe Fredericks.

After showing him my I.D., he takes me down and opens the door on boathouse number Two. While he's fiddling with the lock, I casually glance around and catch the old fisherman watching me. As soon as he sees me looking, the old guy turns away. My new friend Joe points out the boat lying in the slip, instructs me on how to get the waterfront doors open, gives me a marine gas card and opens a locker where the life jackets are stored. Then he asks me if I'd like to see the other buildings. I didn't know that there were any other buildings and explain that to Joe.

He casually states, "Oh yeah, the tribe bought these three buildings from the city and even had one of them remodeled into kind of an office and living quarters." It seems that I'm continually finding myself in a state of surprise these days. I'm also wondering if the question mark that's appearing on my face will have to be surgically removed.

Joe takes me over to boathouse number one and sure enough, it's a nice little apartment with a small office space incorporated into it's front. A computer, telephone, fax machine, everything. It turns out that the other building is empty and just used for storage. Then, passing me the keys, he tells me that the three parking places alongside the boathouse belong to me, too. Old Joe makes his exit then and I wander back over to the boathouse with the boat. For a time, the little vessel captivates my attention. She is indeed a twenty-five foot long Boston Whaler.

The boat has twin 75 horse Suzuki outboard motors on her stern, and barring a fifty caliber machine gun, was basically the same boat that I'd operated in the Gulf War. I used these craft often during my career because the Coast Guard swears by them. They're a sound and sturdy vessel and are virtually unsinkable. I spend the next half-hour checking out the boat and the three buildings and finally settle back again at the boat. The Boston seems ready to go, with tribal police logos on her sides, flashing lights, siren and radios. What more could a real-live Indian cop want? Oh, excuse me. I mean tribal special agent. Whatever. I break out my chart, open the waterfront doors and take the Boston out. As I cruise past the gas dock, I look up to see the old fisherman watching me. He lifts his hand and I wave back. Then I angle the bow toward Lake Michigan.

I head southeast down along the Wisconsin coast before turning back to the southwest, in order to avoid the shipping lanes. The big lake is pretty flat today with a fifteen to twenty knot breeze out of the north. That gives me a following wind and sea. I scan the weather forecast and things don't seem like they are going to change too much over the next ten hours. As I turn the boat to the left, I can make out several other boats around, but all of them are a good ways off. I keep a steady turn to port until the compass puts me on course.

From the calls over the radio, I know that most of the boats are sportfishermen, out working their downriggers, fishing for chinook salmon or steelhead trout. As the chart shows good depth, I decide I'll crank the Boston up and see what she can do. I raise my rear end off the seat, take the wheel firmly with my left hand and push the throttles ahead to the bury mark. The boat climbs up on-step in a hurry. On-step is just an old Coast Guard term for the action of a boat gaining hydroplane motion over the water, and the Boston does not disappoint me. She is fast, clean and sweet in her element and I am at home in mine.

I ride for about an hour and just past Dead Man's Point the water depth gives way and begins to shallow. A few more minutes and I can see the island, but I have to watch the depth closely. There are rocks, too. Rocks that protrude everywhere. It takes me another fifteen minutes to get her up to the old decrepit dock. She drags bottom a lot in the process, bumping and scraping rocks the whole way. I tie the boat off and take a look around. The island is massive. Yep. Big and…ugly. At least from this viewpoint. The sheer sides run almost vertical, and, barring an old trail that looks like it has seen better days, there appears no other way up. I suck in some air and heft the bag, looping it over my shoulders. The dock has recently been shored-up with new timbers, but it still looks a little shaky. I climb out onto the rickety dock, walk up to the last piling, and step onto the rocky shoreline.

Almost immediately, I feel something strange. The hair on the back of my neck sticks out stiffly and goosebumps rise all along my arms. "Shinkakee." That's what my mother always called it. She said it was the spirits, just letting you know that they were present. White folks sometimes call the feeling "déjà vu". Whatever. For me it was a "knowing" that things are somehow different at that place and time. I don't like it. But the spirits have saved my butt many a time byflashing me this little warning. I've learned to pay attention to it. Is. Hmm. I brush the gooseflesh away. That's spooky. Oh well, cinching the bag up, I set off to explore.

Chapter Seven
The Ghost is Conjured Again

Escanaba, MI.
Same Day.

The old man watched the young Indian return his wave as he
motored the large boat into Lake Michigan. So, he was the one. The
old man had asked enough questions upon arriving to know that some
new Indian tribe now owned the island. They would be sending
someone to caretake the property. He scratched his whiskers and
looked at the boathouse as he reasoned his next move. He had to get
out to that island and he had to have special gear and equipment with
him for what he needed to do. And time was running out. So,
befriending the Indian seemed a logical move. Still, he must proceed
cautiously. Danger was still a very real possibility, even after all these
years.

The very worst outcome, he concluded, was that he would have to
kill the Indian in order to achieve his goal. That idea struck him as
odd. He hadn't thought in these kinds of terms in many, many years.
Funny how it all came back to you. Hopefully, it wouldn't come to
that, but if it should, well, he would deal with that contingency when
it arose. What was important to him now was getting to that island
and getting what he needed. And he would do that. The old man bent,
picked up the pail of fish, and dumped them back into the marina's
water. He gathered his fishing pole and tackle before he glanced again
at the boathouse. He must be about his business. He had much to do
and time was so very short. He kept his gaze on the boathouse as he
passed it on his way back to town. Yes, he determined, he would find
a way. Even if it meant that the young Indian must die.

A Rocky Outcropping in Lake Michigan,
also known as Muskrat Island.
The Distant Past.

The two men struggled up the stony trail past the old deserted
lighthouse and entered the dense cover of the tall pines. The coolness
of their heavy shade was quickly appreciated by the men. It was the
first Sunday in August, 1973 and the heat hung in the wet air like a

barber-dampened towel. The humidity from the big lake sent waves of wetted air upward to the highest elevations of the island, and both men were sweating profusely in their exertions.

They wore summer dress shirts and bell bottom jeans, but the length of hair and their over-all clean-cut appearance gave away their true identities. Air Force dog tags tinkled from around the necks of their unbuttoned shirts as they made their way through the dense undergrowth. One of them, the older of the two, was definitely the leader. He stopped frequently to check a hand-drawn map he carried. His name was Derrick P. Meyers. He was a master sergeant in the U. S. Air Force. His specialty, was supply. The other man was also in the Air Force. He was Airman 3rd Class Donald Pike.

He was a truck driver, and since coming to the base, his specialty was hauling garbage from the mess halls, barracks, offices and the Post Exchange. It was during one of these stops to check the map that he spoke the first words he'd uttered since leaving the boat far below on the rock covered beach. He wiped his face with the sleeve of his shirt and peered at the barely discernable trail they were following. He readjusted the weight of the bag he was carrying and let his eyes wander to the other man's. He spoke between catching his breath.

"Meyers, how the hell did you ever hear of this place anyway?"

The man holding the map didn't answer right away. Instead, he traced the ink-drawn lines with his finger and looked ahead into the woods. Shortly, he nodded, folded the map and turned to his partner.

"I heard about when I was in Viet Nam. My last tour there, I ran the officer's club at DaNang." He looked around as he, too, took the opportunity to catch his breath.

"There was this Army Warrant, a chopper pilot. Name was…" he scratched his head, "Scary or something like that. No, Scari. That's it, Hank Scari. He was having to fly some colonel in every week there for about four months or so. Anyway, he and his co-pilot always came to the club and they'd sit at the bar for a couple of hours until they had to fly the colonel back. So, we shot the shit and he told me he was born and raised up here in Michigan. He's the one told me about the island and the old mine shaft. His old man used to bring him out here hunting."

The other man just grunted. "Okay, tell me again why we had ta come all the way out here to hide the money?"

This time, when the Sergeant spoke his eyes bored into Pike and he was clearly agitated. "Now look, we've gone through this a hundred times! Once the brass finds out about the theft, there's gonna be a big-ass investigation. Fifty grand doesn't come up missing and not have the shit hit the fan. OSI is going to get called, and the first thing they're gonna do is start looking for the money. They're gonna suspect me, but without the money, they can't do anything. Do you understand that? They can't do anything! Now, the places you and me hangout and the places around the base is where they're gonna look, get it? They ain't gonna look out here 'cause as far as they'll know, neither of us have ever been here." He shook his head.

"Shit, as far as that goes, they probably won't even know that this island exists. Now we agreed that we wouldn't touch the dough for two years. I'll be retired and your hitch will be up by then and the heat should be off. That means we gotta put it someplace where nobody can find it until we come to get it and divide it up. Now, no one's gonna come out here, much less go inside some falling-down mine shaft so... the money should be safe! Now that's why, we're hiding it out here! Okay?"

The subject of the Sergeant's wrath looked up and quickly nodded. "Yeah, yeah. Okay, Sarg. But um... well... I'm just kinda worried that this chopper pilot may come out here, ya know, and be snooping in this mine shaft and well..."

Meyer had his fist up and pointed at the other man. "Damn it asshole! I told you not to worry, didn't I? The man told me he was scared to death of tight places! He isn't going to go in that mine shaft or any other mine shaft. He got caught in this one when he was a kid, that's how-come we were talking about it that day. It was some kind of cave-in, and he was scared to death until he dug his way out. So even if he does still come out to this island, he isn't going to go into that hole! And I'm betting that he's the only one that even knows it's there, so nobody else is going in there either! Shit! The dumb sonavabitch probably got shot down and killed in the Nam anyway. Don't you listen to anything?"

The other man had his hand up in a halting motion. "Okay, Sarg... Okay. I'm sorry, it's just that I never done anything like this before and..."

The sergeant cut him off. "Bullshit Pike! You just haven't ever been caught, is all. And we're gonna do this my way because I don't want to spoil your unblemished record. So let's go. We've gotta be back on base before taps tonight."

With that, the Sergeant turned back to the trail and started off, his follower right behind him. About fifteen minutes later, the two stepped from the cover of the high pines into a small clearing, bordered by a stone face. Meyer walked around the tall grass looking at the ground. Finally, he pointed and quickly moved over to an uneven mound rise. Closer observation revealed a hole into the rock that was once an excavation shoot for a mine. Pike followed and

dropped the bag to help as both men began pulling the old boards off
the opening. Several minutes later, Meyer was crawling into the hole
with a flashlight and ten minutes after that, he was pulling himself
back out.

He looked over at Pike, after he lit a Camel cigarette and exhaled
a cloud of blue smoke. "Well that's gotta be the place alright. There's
an old cot and kerosene lantern down there. The lantern works, too.
There's even an old wood stove with a chimney that goes up through
the ceiling. Shit man, can you imagine them guys living in there?"
Meyers shook his head and shivered. "Remind me to never take up
mining as a hobby." He motioned to the bag. "Let me see that, will
ya?"

Pike drug the heavy bag up and handed it over to Meyers. The
Sergeant unzipped the top and rustled around the inside. He hefted out
packs of money, all wrapped in paper tapes, and dropped them into a
pile. There two were zippered side pouches inside the bag and they
contained numerous empty paper coin rolls and a stamping kit.
Something else caught his eye. He pulled out a book bound ledger,
more paperwork and documents. Pike pointed at the papers. "What's
all that stuff, Sarg?"

Meyers turned several of the papers over and gave them cursory
glances. Then he opened the ledger and flipped through the pages.
"Looks like just invoices, codes for various exchanges and vendor
sheets, stuff like that. Nothing to concern us." He put the papers back
in the side compartments and zippered them closed. Then he began
counting the packs of currency in front of them while Pike watched
closely. When he finished, he sat back on his legs and looked at Pike.
"Fifty one thousand, one hundred and thirty two bucks. That's…"

"$25,565. Each," uttered Pike.

Meyers dropped the last pack of greenbacks into the pile while
reaching over and tapping Pike on the arm. He was smiling hugely.

"That's right, my boy! Now, who says crime don't pay?" He nodded
at the mine opening.

"Let's get this bag back in that hole and get the opening covered
up. We both know how much is here and where it is. So, we'll both
know who to come looking for if anything's different in a couple of
years." Meyers cast a steely eye at his cohort in crime. "We'll meet
back here two years from now. Same time, same place to divey it up.
Now let's get the lead out. We gotta have our asses back on base
tonight and we still have'ta get across that lake and drive north."
With that, both men entered the hole and stuffed the bag into a
crevice, deep inside an interior wall. Then they exited, dusted
themselves off and hiked back to the boat.

Both were back safe and sound at K.I Sawyer Air Force Base, near Marquette, Michigan before the recording of taps blew throughout the military establishment. Two years later to the day, both men met on the Island's beach and made the long trek to the hidden mine shaft. After dividing the money, they tossed the bag onto the floor and exited the man-made cave. The two shook hands and separated, never to speak to each other again.

Peoples' Republic of China
Dictorate of Navel Intelligence, Peking.
Recent Days.

The old Admiral sat behind his desk and reread the documents in front of him. He was small, even for a Chinese man. The heavy gold braid on his uniform shoulders appeared almost as if it might pull him down. Though he wasn't privy to the exact circumstances that had brought the RICTOR documents to his hands - he'd heard rumors of an operative deeply embedded in the Soviet Union. But that wasn't what was important. Finishing the text, he laid it aside. He pondered the whole situation again. His staff had verified the authenticity of the document, and if the information inside was true, then the recovery of such an item would greatly advance his country. And if the Navy brought this object in, then it would be the Navy that benefited the most from its procurement.

He had worked out the details of the mission and while it appeared as if it could be accomplished, the risk was great. The result of failure would be catastrophic, most certainly so for his staff and himself. He had not shared the information with the Air Force, Army, or any of the other intelligence branches. The information was, after all, garnered by a Navel agent. The one thing that remained constant in China, he thought, was the fact that the government was not unified in intelligence matters. As a military man, he knew that this was a major mistake. Intelligence was to be shared if battles were to be won. But that wasn't how things were done in China.

Each separate branch of the military operated on its own as did the espionage and counter espionage agencies. Back stabbing was a way of life. No one shared anything, thinking only of themselves, even if it meant losing the very thing they tried to achieve. The admiral shook his head. Why couldn't they see that it was this type of thinking that helped destroy the Soviet Union. He continued to question, but that was how it was just the same. Like a sinking ship, it was every man for himself or in this case, every arm of the intelligence branches for themselves. Sink or swim, each was on their own. He nodded his head once in commitment, then reached over and pushed the intercom button by his phone. He spoke no words and within a few seconds, a young Navy Commander knocked once, then quickly entered and moved up to the desk. The Admiral waved to a chair and the young officer sat. The Admiral pointed a small finger at the papers in front of him.

"Do you still have faith in this mission?"

The young officer crossed his legs and thought for a moment before answering. "Yes, sir I believe that I do." The young intelligence officer was called Ylan Chin, and his steady gaze at his superior solidified the assessment.

The older man held eye contact for a few seconds, then rubbed a hand through parchment-thin hair while he pushed his chair away from his desk. He stood and began pacing about the room, with his hands folded tightly inside one another behind his back. It was a position and movement he had used almost all of his adult life and which had been perfected on the decks of many Chinese warships. The younger man knew this. And he also knew the dilemma that his Admiral faced, in fact, that he faced as well. But the facts were irrefutable, and required a decision. This was vital to his nation and if things went wrong in the operation, he and his superior would pay dearly. But, he thought, as he watched the Admiral pace about, that was the cost of duty sometimes.

The Admiral stopped and turned to the Commander, "Very well. We will proceed then. What is your assessment of using the "CHEE" agents for this?… Will they succeed?"

The officer uncrossed his legs and leaned forward. "Yes, sir, I believe they could. They have been successful in America, but it has been on a very limited basis. The cosmetics are very good and they are extremely well trained. However, sir, since this mission is so important, why should we take a chance on recognition. We could still use Anglican or Caucasian agents for this operation. They are just as well trained and…"

The Admiral had his hand up to stop him. "No. If we are going to do this then I will have Chinese officers performing the task. I want people who are loyal to me, and to their country. If this information ever gets out, if this thing truly exists and that fact becomes known, then the race to get to it by intelligence groups from around the world will be astounding. And this does not even include the Americans. They will be the most ferocious in their quest.

"No, Chin, something like this will be priceless and we must acquire it for China… for the Navy. There can be no chance of Americans learning of it's existence. If it is real, it will take the country holding it to the extreme pinnacle of science technology. Along with several other countries, we are lacking only this one item. The first to get it will be the first into a new age." He said the last with a hint of weariness.

"The agents who go will have to know this before hand. They must know that they can not fail. They cannot be captured. This means that they must not be taken alive. And should they acquire this thing, they cannot allow it to fall into the Americans' or anyone else's hands. They will have to destroy it before that happens, even if it means taking their life in the process. No. No, my young comrade we will have to have loyal Chinese Nationals who are willing to make this type of sacrifice for their country. I can trust no man of foreign decent for this mission. This is not merely the secret plans for an aircraft or a new gadget that makes a better radar. If this is real and our scientists are right, this thing will change the world as we know it. Any outside operative for this mission might decide to take it for their own people or even sell it. The risk would be far too great of this happening, much less them being dedicated enough to take their own life for the sake of a foreign country. Can you see that?"

The young commander had listened intently to his Admiral and upon the older man's closing question, he again knew why he revered and respected the old sailor so much. "Yes, sir. I think now that I can."

The small man had seen the understanding in his subordinate's eyes. He closed his own eyes tightly and nodded his head in satisfaction. Opening them, he once again took up the pacing. "Good. What of the source in Russia then? Has it been eliminated?"

"Yes, sir. The source was a female, employed at the Defense Ministry. She has been terminated per your order. The agent who garnered the documents has been recalled, and at present is being held in the containment building, also per your instruction." Chin said the last with the raised eyebrows of a question.

The Admiral halted his pace by a large bookcase and ran is fingers over the bound copies of tomes resting there. "Very well. If you are sure that he doesn't know what the documents say, then I see no reason for him to be killed. If he knows nothing of what was in the documents then his association with this operation is limited to the RICTOR element only. But as you know Chin, even this could be enough to cause us great harm. You had better be sure of your man, Commander, because keeping tight security on this mission is essential."

"Yes, sir. I will verify this again, but he is a good man and I wouldn't want to lose him unless absolutely necessary." Chin stood up. "I assume, sir, that you would like to see the personnel files on the four CHEE agents that I've selected for your consideration?"

The Admiral dropped his hand from the books and returned to the desk. "Yes. Let's have a look at them and Chin," the old man looked closely at the younger one, "from this point on, you and I and any of the staff who are involved in this mission, will be under the same guidelines as the CHEE agents. If things go wrong, I expect all of us to do our duty. Are you in agreement with this?"

Even though the military was never a diplomatic entity in any country, much less in China, the Admiral had always chosen to give his staff officers this freedom of thought. It made for stronger more honest opinions and ideas on the issues of a given mission. And often, it was that honesty that meant the difference between failure and success. Years ago, when the admiral was in the Naval Academy, they taught him to use what the enemy had that worked. Well this was something that the West did that worked and while the Admiral had to be careful not let things get out of hand, he did genuinely appreciate his officers' opinions.

The younger man was almost to the door when the admiral added the last. He brought himself to full attention and looked sincerely at his Commanding Officer.

"Sir, I would not have it any other way and I am sure the other officers will feel the same." He saluted and held his hand to his brow until the Admiral returned it.

After the door closed, the Admiral rubbed his eyes with the palms of his hands. He thought of this item, this thing that they would seek. If this item existed and it could be harnessed, then, their old enemies would be nothing. He wondered if his young officers understood that. He doubted it. Unlike them, he had benefited from the learning acquired from missionaries in the orphanage where he grew up. That had been before World War II, before the Communists had thrown out every reference to Christianity. But he firmly believed in God, though he had to keep the belief to himself. He had prayed to Him often while in combat. Thinking of the object he now sought, he silently prayed once again. Because as far as the Admiral was concerned, this thing, this object, was what the Catholic Sisters referred to as a demon, a bad spirit, a ghost. And they... were about to conjure it forth.

U.S. Army Fort Belvoir, Virginia,
U.S. Air Force Section, Office of Special Investigations (AFOSI)
Office of Lt. Gen. Kourn, Commanding Officer,
Detachment 4, 696th Air Intelligence Group.
Recent Days.

The Major and the Captain sat with their bodies enveloped in the large leather chairs. The chairs were monstrous and had the effect of consuming an occupant. And although both men wore pilot wings on their uniform blouses, neither had been inside a cramped cockpit, other than to keep current, for quite awhile. That made the wait inside the massive chairs just a little claustrophobic. Both men wore their new-style Dress-Blue Air Force uniforms, another thing that they seldom did nowadays, as they cooled their heels in the large office. The massive room was the lair of their commanding officer, Lieutenant General Raymond A. Kourn. The office, like the branch the two officers worked for, was a secretive part of AFOSI. The Air Force's version of the FBI, AFOSI investigated threats to United States national security and criminal acts directed at the United States.

The General wasn't in command of AFOSI though. That unit had a Brigadier General as boss. Kourn was in command of a secretive subunit within AFOSI, that dealt with specific types of investigations and security. The unit he commanded was Detachment 4 of the 696th Air Intelligence Group.

Both men in the chairs were classified as AFOSI investigators, but actually, they were primarily intelligence operatives. Routinely, they worked as investigators for OSI, but, occasionally, they also worked on missions classified well above top secret and known to no one except their commanding General. The two officers had met and talked at the BOQ (Base Officer's Quarters) and knew that they had been called back from separate missions that each was intricately involved in. That meant that whatever it was they were here for, was hot. The Major was just standing to stretch his legs and escape the chair when the door opened and in strode General Kourn. The Captain quickly stood to attention with the Major as the General moved snappily around the desk and sat down, lifting his hand as he went.

"As you were gentlemen and...," The General looked closely at the two men in front of him, squinting his eyes as he did so and smiling, "please sit back down."

Both of the younger officers retook their seats. General Ray Kourn was a dogged and determined individual, hailing from Kentucky. Part of that determination had worked to get a Kentucky farm boy into the U.S. Air Force Academy. He possessed a hillbilly wit that was often appreciated by the crowd he worked with.

"For a minute there, I thought I was in the wrong office 'cause I declare boys, in them funny new suits ya'all have 'own, you look just like TWA flight attendants."

The General was referring to the new dress uniforms, designed to make Air Force personnel look more like private commercial airline pilots. The uniforms had been issue for a long time but he didn't like them, and…he had seldom seen these two officers wearing them. Both of the younger men smiled as they adjusted themselves in the man-hungry chairs.

Kourn thought for minute as he sat behind the desk. It was his way. He was a big man, topping six foot six. His height had almost stopped him from getting into flight school and that would've killed him. He had passed all the tests and physicals but was told that he was just too tall. But height wasn't a problem for the basketball team. And they had wanted him to play bad. Very bad. He had agreed to play ball for the Academy if and only if, they would guarantee that he could go to flight school. They had hemmed and hawed, but in the end, they gave in to his wishes. Truth be known, the regulations governing height restrictions were about to change, allowing for a more generous size. But Kourn didn't know that and it wouldn't have mattered anyway. He got what he wanted and that…was what mattered to him.

He had played basketball all through his four years at the Air Force Academy and was flying jets a year and a half after he graduated. It hadn't been easy but he had succeeded and eventually won those silver wings. He had made it happen. And that was the way that Ray Kourn looked at life. It had saved him over the skies of Viet Nam and it had gotten him the three stars on his shoulders, too. Making it happen was what won battles and determined wars. That said, he was determined when he leaned forward and faced the two officers on the other side of the desk.

"Okay Alan… Pete, this here's the skinny. I know that ya'all have already figured out that this is a big one so I'll cut ta the chase. We've got some old foreign-source intelligence on a possible MIAC (missing aircraft) case and maybe even an AFCE with a shooting star, right here in the U.S.

"This intel'was garnered through a Chinese double agent and some part of the information makes reference ta a thing called a Russian RICTOR report. Now, ya'all e'll get the particulars but I'm gonna need you two a working this hard and fast. An I mean this… an this alone. You're not gonna be working 'own anything else and that means that there's nothing 'own your personal agendas, neither. So if you've got leave plans or a hot piece of ass a'waiting, then ya better git a message to 'em alet'n 'em know thet you're gonna be tied up awhile.

"Now", the General eased himself back while still maintaining eye contact, "I want ta make sure that this is clear first of all and thet you're gonna be able to give this mission what it takes? If ya kain't do that, then I gotta know right now. So is it yea or nay gentlemen?"

The Major and Captain looked at each other, then back to their superior and both replied, "Yes, sir", in unison.

General Kourn nodded his head solidly, stood and went over to a safe in the wall. The Major was named Alan Shears. He watched the General spin the dial on the safe door and wondered what the hell this was all about. He knew very, very well what a shooting star was. And AFCE stood for Air Force Close Encounter. Hmm, he thought. This might be interesting. He wondered if Mussenberg had caught it. He turned to look at Captain Peter Mussenberg, who was already leaning forward with questioning eyes directed to him. Nope, he decided. All he could do was shrug his shoulders and wait for the "old man" to clue them in.

So, thought Mussenberg as he watched his partner's shoulder's shrug. Shears didn't know what was going on either. His eyes switched back to the General. Kourn commanded Detachment Four and what he wanted, he got. Mussenberg respected that. The man was only interested in good people and his country. He didn't care what color you were, as long as your views were the same as his. And Mussenberg's stacked up nicely with Kourn's. General Kourn had personally recruited all of the teams assigned to Detachment 4 of the 696th Air Intelligence Group. All members of the detachment were assigned to OSI and worked normal cases for that unit until the General called with a…special one. And those, thought Mussenberg, were the exciting ones.

The General closed the safe and walked back over to the desk. Setting the files down, he reached over and picked up the phone receiver. Both junior officers looked at the folders and the large red lettering "ATS", standing for "Above Top Secret" as the General spoke.

"Master Sergeant Temple, I don't want to be disturbed for the next hour or so… Uh, huh…well if he calls, you tell 'em I'll call 'em back. I don't want ta be disturbed… okay?…Very good, Master Sergeant. Thank ya."

Hanging the phone back onto it's cradle, the General picked up two of the folders and passed one to each of the two officers. Then he reached over, retrieved the third and took it with him as he moved over to a large plot table. "Over here boys, if you please."

Shears and Musenberg got up and made their way to the table as the General was pushing a button on a control box that was attached to the table leg. The hard vinyl cover on the plot table slid forward and rolled down into the end. What appeared was a dimensional relief map of Lake Michigan and the two states' boundaries that enveloped the northern tip of the Great Lake. The General opened his folder as the two younger intelligence officers followed suit, all of them laying the opened folders on the plot board that wrapped around the sides of the table. Shears looked at the mission title heading: "BLUE BIRD RETRIEVAL" as the General grabbed a pointer and laid it down on the table.

"All righty now, if you'll take out this here little ditty on the Soviet "Rictor" project, we should be able ta get started."
The General pulled out a sheaf of papers and set them aside on the table. The other two men did the same then the tall man continued as he tapped his index finger on the sheaf of papers.

"Now, this intelligence was garnered from a Chinese double agent, whose working for us 'own his backside. It took us awhile to decode and make hide nor hair of this stuff but we did, and as ya'all 'ell see… it's scary'ere than hell to know what them Ruskies was doing right here 'own our back forty.

"Now elsewhere in this file, you'll find a copy of the dying declaration of one former Airman Donald Pike. He was involved with another fella, a master sergeant name of Meyers. He's also deceased. Anyways, these two old boys robbed the PX at KI Sawyer Air Force base back in 1973. They got away with over $50,000, and according to Pike's dying words, they hid the money out own an island in Lake Michigan for a couple a years before getting it and living high on the hog." The tall man looked at the map, then picked up the pointer.

"Okay, this here is obviously Lake Michigan and it's a part of the good ole' U.S.A. An' since both you boys are Yankees, I figure you already know that."

Shears and Mussenberg smiled as the General side-stepped a little and raised the pointer again. "But this here little piece….," Kourn tapped the stick on the raised elevation of an island, "is something else all together. Up until a couple a months ago, it too was the home of the free and the brave, and it would've caused us no problems what-so-ever. But now gentlemen, it belongs ta the sovereign nation of the Pukaskwa Indians

The General sighed as he looked at his two best agents, then back to the small island resting in the northern waters of Lake Michigan. "Unfortunately boys, that little 'ole island ain't the territory of the U.S. Government anymore. So, what we're a look'n fer, may just be right smack-dab in the middle a Injun Country."

The General and his two officers looked quietly at the tiny representation of Muskrat Island.

|<<<I>::<I<<<I>::<I<<<I>::<I :+: I>::<I>>>I>::<I>>>I>::<I>>>I

Chapter Eight
"Ghost Riders In The Sky"

Muskrat Island,
Northeastern Lake Michigan
Present Day.

Looking back down the trail, I allow my breath to catch up with
my heart. Man that's a hike. I just stand still a minute as the cool air
blows the sweat off by back, and I wait for a fresh wind to blow into
my sails. The trail is crooked and wearisome to travel, and given my
druthers, I'd just as soon the rich old Pukaskwa Band would install an
elevator. I immediately know that I shouldn't have thought that. All
the money that the Tribe's got is already starting to play on my mind.
I once again make a mental note to control these thoughts as I walk on
up to the lighthouse door.

Then, because I'm feeling pretty close to dead right now, I allow
myself a little groan as I pull the bag off my shoulders and set it down.
It feels like the straps from the bag have cut plow furrows in my shoulders.
Ahh, to be youthful and uncaring again about little aches and pains. Well,
buddy, you can forget that. Those days are long gone for your red hide.
There's a stiff breeze up here, and still catching my breath, I allow my
gaze to float out to the Big Lake that's pictured all around. She is
beautiful – a part of a great seascape painting of God's design.

The day is clear and visibility is close to ten miles or so. From my
vantage point, I can see the rock-strewn shallows all around the island
running out to where the deep water meets them. Out there, the lake is
majestic, with the afternoon sun glinting off her surface. Her blue is
dark and resonant, speaking of its richness and depth. There are no
whitecaps on her surface, just a swirl that brings to mind a louvered
fan. The white cumulous clouds are puffing their way across a sky
that is a color coordinated powder blue, to the lake itself. And from
this elevation, the rock-strewn shallows looks like a painters easel,
with the stones appearing like great globs of brown, gray and black
paint, thrown on a light blue background. What a picture that
The Creator makes. Sneaking a peak at my watch, I know
that I'm going to have to get a move on here directly. I pick up the
bag and enter the lighthouse.

Once inside, I tote the bag over to an old couch, set it down and

undo the jacket that I'd tied to the extra strap-ons. This had been
my first stop when I followed the trail up from the boat a few weeks
ago. And I've got to say, this place ain't half bad. Somebody's
obviously done some repair work recently and I assume it was the Band.
They probably had a contractor come out and do some fixing up here
and there. Actually, the lighthouse is in better shape than my cabin is.
At least everything works in it. I mosey over to the kitchen window
and take a gander out through the glass. I have to wipe the dust from
it with my hand to get a glimpse. From this window, you can see all
the way down to the boat dock. The dock isn't visible from the other
side of the house. Now, as I look down there, I see a boat.

Huh. I wonder what that's about. The boat doesn't appear to be
closing on the dock, just floating near it. Squinting my eyes against
the glare, it looks like just one person is aboard. I decide that a better
picture is in order. Snatching my binoculars from the top of the
refrigerator, I put them up and it seems almost like the person in the
boat has got something up to his face and is looking up here. I try
focusing, but the window glass is too dirty for a clearer picture. I
really ought to have a cleaning person come out and... Seee. There I
go again. This shit has got to stop. I've got to get a handle on this
money thing or else I'll drive myself crazy. I peer back out the
window and feel the curiosity welling. Okay, maybe a higher point of
reference. My heart rate and respiration just about back to normal, I
decide that the best way to accompany that is with a cigarette. I know
it's stupid but I've never pretended to be anything else. Looping the
glasses over my neck, I grab my smoke box from the bag and hit the
stairs that lead up to the old light.

As I come out the door and move outside around the railing, I can
see the boat already moving off into deep water. There's a small
channel that's just deep enough for a boat to travel through quickly,
without bottoming out, and it appears like this one is doing just that.
Swinging the binoculars up and spinning the focus brings the boat
into view. The small outboard is headed out fast and it's already too
far away to get a make on its operator. Yep. Just one person on a little
fourteen foot outboard and it appears like a male. This is a little
puzzling. Now it took me a couple of days to find that channel, and
your casual every day boater would have a rough time finding it on
his own. Funny. I haven't seen another boat close to the island since
I've been out here playing around. I'm pretty sure that I recognize the
boat, too. If I'm not mistaken, it's one of the rentals from a little
tackle shop back in Escanaba.

I shake a hand-rolled out and snap the old Zippo to it's end. The
smoke is quickly blown away in the breeze as I watch the

disappearing outboard. The weird thing about it is, at this time of year, there just aren't any fishermen out except for those working deep water for trout or salmon. And I didn't see any downriggers that would make the outboard equipped for that kind of fishing. The water surrounding the island is too shallow for pan fish at this time of year. And weather is a consideration, too. In the fall, the weather can turn bad in an hour or so. So, why would anyone make a trip in a small boat out to this island given those facts? Scratching my ear, I wonder "why" indeed. Oh, wait a minute, how silly of me. Now I know what it is. It's the old "could've" again, that tricky age-old synonym for coincidence.

More than likely, a man in a boat, that "could've" been rented from Escanaba, "could've" been out salmon fishing and I "could've" just not seen the equipment. Then he "could've" been in this area and "could've" just happened to see the island and "could've" chosen to investigate. And as luck "could've" had it, he "could've" stumbled upon the channel and was able to fly right out of here. Yep. Purely coincidence. As I watch the small boat grow smaller in the twilight, I'm reminded that I don't believe in coincidence, especially that many of them. If too many cooks spoil the stew, then too many "could'ves" spoil the coincidence.

I figure I'll stop over to that tackle shop and check out the rental boats the next time I'm in town. I let the last of the smoke be pulled from my nose and into the breeze, then I strip the butt and drop the paper into my pants pocket. The wind is beginning to take on a chill as I meander back to the door and inside the light tower. Making my way down the spiral stairs, my stomach reminds me that it hasn't seen any food in awhile. I've got two venison steaks in my bag downstairs and they sound mighty good right now. I swing over to the couch as I exit the stairway. Grabbing up the bag and moving into the kitchen, I think about how truly weird this whole thing is turning out to be. The tune bounces back into my head again. "Ghost Riders In The Sky", the song has been a constant since last night.

I empty the bag and flip the venison around as I look it over. I packed it between two zip-locked baggies filled with frozen water, then bundled the whole thing in plastic wrap. With the back roads that exist in the Upper Peninsula, it's about a two-hour drive from the cabin to Escanaba. In September, the days are still warm for a drive that long and I wanted the meat to make it. The water was back to its liquid form, but the steaks appeared cool and as fresh as they were when I butchered the buck deer. The meat seems to have held well. I pulled it out of my freezer at my cabin late last night, and was about to drive back south when Amos Reddeer showed up to visit. And while some strange things had been happening lately, it may have been Amos who brought "Ghost Riders In The Sky" into my little picture.

Southern raising being as it is, I invited Amos in even though I was headed out. I offered him either a beer or a Pepsi and to my surprise, he opted for the beer. The old fellow twisted the cap off the Hamm's bottle with a practiced finesse and chugged a goodly amount down before looking at me and smiling. Then he asked me if I had gotten around the island, how it seemed, etc. the usual small talk until he dropped the bomb. The old shaman leaned forward, looked deeply into my eyes and said that there was evil on the island. Then, still searching my soul with those piercing black eyes of his, he asked if I'd felt it too.

Well, what could I answer to that? Obviously I'd felt something, but heck if I knew what it was. So, I just told him that the island seemed… different. Amos kept his eyes locked on mine, searching for a few seconds more, then he smiled broadly and nodded his head. He said that he could see that I felt it, too, whatever the hell that meant. He swallowed the last of his beer and stood up to leave. That's when he decided to touch my shoulder, open his bomb bay doors and drop the big one.

"Listen to the se se kwa", he told me, "and it will guide you to it."

Then he just squeezed my shoulder and smiled at my open mouth and bugged eyes before saying his goodbyes. Now… I had seen this man in a dream, dressed in skins, chanting that very same thing. And as somebody who's regularly haunted and yet, regularly protected, I immediately went into "Ohhhhboys'ville". My arm flesh pimpled up, a chilled tingly feeling shot through me and well - the whole enchilada. Spooky and spiritual, all at the same time. Us "Injuns", this one anyway, put a lot of stock in dreams. I had to ask myself, "did he know about that dream?" Or spookier yet… "did he send himself to my dreams?" It may sound hokey, but I'm easily persuaded in matters like these.

After closing the door behind him, I'd gone right away to my Uncle's old trunk in the bedroom. He had a lot of Indian stuff in there, and one of the things was an old Pukaskwa-to-English dictionary. It took me awhile, but I finally figured it out. "Se se kwa" roughly translates into, "The Murmuring of the Trees." Well.. isn't this fun. While I don't believe that trees and plants can talk and don't even think they need to be talked to, I've often heard their leaves whisper in a sing-song voice during a light breeze. I also know that the Great Good Spirit speaks in many ways, through many things. That's one reason why all things He created on Mother Earth have value.

As I'd fired off the Charger and headed south, I remember thinking that maybe Hennessey was right to be little disquieted about old Amos. A couple of miles down the road, the delayed fuse-bomb went off. An old Johnny Cash song, "Ghost Riders In The Sky", came over my "Oldies" station. I'd pulled the car off to the side of the road and just sat there. It was probably just coincidence. But like that guy in the outboard I'd seen at the island, there were too many "could've's" in this scenario, too. Now just to show you how weird your imagination can get, I swear that the rustling of some tall pines led me to a particularly interesting spot on the island the other day. And I could have sworn... that the pine needles brushing against each other were doing so to the rhythm and beat of... "Ghost Riders In The Sky".

I hadn't heard the song in quite awhile, so I thought it strange that it popped into my head, right then and there, ya know. In fact, I'd had the tune stuck in my head ever since. After about five minutes, I resumed my journey, but I've been plagued with a lot of questions ever since. And most of them seem to have little rhyme or reason. Uh, huh. Well, to paraphrase Forrest Gump, "weird is as weird does". And this island does have a weird feeling to it.

After I put everything away, I light one of the gas lanterns and get started on supper. I salt and pepper the steaks, roll them in flour, then lay them in a broiling pan. Next, I spread a can of mushrooms over the meat and add a sliced onion to the pan. I decide to toss in a sliced potato and a carrot just for the heck of it. After covering the pan with foil, I dial the old propane oven to two hundred seventy five degrees and pop the steaks in to cook. The outside darkness is full by the time I'm done, and as I move into the great room the chill reminds me that I'd better fire-off the old wood stove.

There's kindling that I bring in and stacked alongside the stove, next to the split wood piled there. Before long, I've got a fire going in the old cast iron heater, it's crackling and popping adding solidly to the silence inside the house. Outside, I hear the ever-present breeze cooing through ridges and valleys of the old lighthouse. The smells of pine burning and meat cooking mingle pleasantly in the room.

The lighthouse has one great room in it with exposed rafters leading from wall to roof. The open kitchenette is off to one side and an enclosed bathroom is off to the other. The room is probably 24 by 30 feet in size and there's a small addition off the back that makes two small bedrooms. Then there's the circled stone column that encloses the lighthouse stairs. The side wall is built into the circle as it protrudes into the room. It kind of acts as a tower in the middle of the wall and adds a feeling of medieval times to the place.

Grabbing my flight jacket from the couch, I throw it on and head out to fire off the power generator. Even though it's only late September, this is still Upper Michigan and it gets cold after dark. The little Honda generator is nestled under a lean-to against the house. It starts with the first pull of the rope and I head back inside. I'm struck by those delicious aromas again as I enter, flip a light switch and stand savoring the cool night air and the interior warmth as the two converge at the doorway. Closing the door, I make my way over and plop my weary body onto the old couch. Lying back, I fold my hands under my head and look up at the ceiling shadows, cast by the newly illuminated room. My mind drifts a tad and I begin to ponder the events of the last couple of weeks.

I made my way around the island and for the most part, what I'd been told about it was true. There were, however, a couple of things they had wrong. Number one was the plan to bring in hovercraft. Oh, it was do-able, but a lot of those rocks were going to have to be removed in order for it to work. A hovercraft floats on a cushion of air and for the most part, can usually blow right over normal obstacles. But on a day when the weather is bad and the seas are intense, the craft would be barred from traveling over those rocks. The craft are durable, but not that durable. Some of the rocks are huge and would tear the bottom out of the vessel on a day when the wave action was just right. That's because the water is so shallow that large waves would create uneven voids in the surface, that the hovercraft has to count on for a cushion. So the cost of clearing a large enough channel through the rocks is definitely something to consider. My guess is that it won't be economically feasible. But then, this is the opinion of a guy who can't balance his own checkbook, either.

Another thing that they missed here was the wildlife. Yeah, there are the wild goats that they mentioned, but there are whitetail deer, too. Not many of them, but a small herd. There's also at least one black bear on the island. I found his tracks the second day of my scouting. Not only that, but I saw grouse, rabbit and squirrel sign, too. So, I wouldn't be too quick to say that there is little wildlife here. I have to admit though, that for the acreage, terrain and timber, I am also surprised at the diversity that I've found. The logical conclusion leads you to believe that the deer and bear had to follow that one known trail up here to the relative flats of this plateau. And that's unusual.

It seems rare to have so many species utilizing the same path. But then, that conclusion leads to some other things the pretty young Annette might've missed. The stand of white pine that I was told about is indeed virgin and appears older than any on the mainland. They're the dominant tall timber presence. But there're a few maples and white oaks mixed in here and there, too, probably just enough to support the small deer herd present. So even though scrub pine does finish out the island, there's still enough of an ecosystem to support a healthy and diverse wildlife population.

That's also where the other stuff comes in. I'm not sure, but I think I may have found another avenue of approach for the wildlife that have trekked across the frozen lake to find this island. Maybe something that nobody else has noticed yet. I stumbled across it last week, on the north side. At first, I'd assumed that the land below the plateau dropped off and went basically straight down to the water. I'd circled the island with the boat and confirmed that this was pretty much the case. In hindsight, nobody could tell otherwise because the pines and their shadows are so thick in this particular area. The needled boughs of the pines form an interlocking cover, way too dense to allow light through. And with the terrain and angle on that side, shadows obscure anything else.

Last week, I was walking below these pines when the dumb song popped into my head. I began softly singing the words to the melody as the cooing wind whispered through the pines to the beat of the song's melody. I entered the forest canopy before I even realized that… I thought the bristling of the pine needles… seemed to be keeping tempo with the song. I remember thinking it was just my senility acting-up again. Yet, when I stopped to contemplate this little oddity, my attention was drawn to a hidden trail.

The ground here gave way to solid stone, and while it was difficult to see it, an animal trail wheeled its way over the hard surface. Odds were good that if you weren't looking in that exact spot, you'd never see the trail. No doubt, it was just a goat trail. And as anybody who knows wild goats can tell you, they can basically walk upside down on the slipperiest substances known to mankind while juggling three china plates and chewing bubble gum. And those are just the run-of-the-mill goats, not the circus kind. My curiosity got the better of me, and for the moment, I forgot all about the sing-song voice of the trees. I inched closer to the slippery trail. Yeah, it was a goat trail alright, and it leveled out after about an eight foot, angled drop. There was some dirt in the trail down there and although it was dark, something looked strange. I could have sworn that the tracks in it looked like deer tracks. Goats and deer are in the same family, but there are differences. I pulled the binoculars out of the pack and brought the area into a shaded focus. Sure enough, there were deer tracks mixed in with the goat. At least, it looked like it from my vantage.

The trail continued downward past the dirt to disappear into a tangle of thick brush. Earlier, I'd seen the shore where the water formed a small cove. That had been quite interesting. I really wanted to go down the little drop, but I hadn't brought a rope. A deer or bear could probably jump or navigate this eight foot section of slippery stone, but I knew I couldn't. I was kind of excited about the prospect that I might have found another access to the plateau. If deer moved on this path, then odds were good that men could. Goats could easily move up and down steep trails, but it's next to impossible for deer. That was what made me think that maybe the trail was not quite as steep as you'd expect. In any case, I'm planning on going over there to take a closer look in the morning. I've brought some climbing rope up with me this time and should be able to check it out before I have to be back in Escanaba.

I have to meet up with my old pal Morse and Annette at the boathouse tomorrow night. And while one of these people causes me some nausea, the second one really sets my head to spinning. Makes you wonder about someone who hangs around people who cause these flu-like symptoms, eh? Oh well, now is not the time to ponder philosophy. I unfold my hands from behind my head and roll off the couch. Now's the time to eat venison. I move into the kitchen while humming the same old song made famous by the "Man in Black". As I'm taking the steaks out of the oven, the cell phone rings.

I've hardly used the thing and it takes me a second to remember out how to turn it on. It turns out to be the nausea-causer. Morse states that Annette just received a call from the Escanaba City Attorney saying that he has papers ready for her to sign. So we're going to meet early afternoon instead, so she can take care of that while in town. I tell him no problem, and that one o'clock will be fine and we hang up. As I peel the foil off my supper, I remember that I was planning on roping down to that trail tomorrow. Oh well, I'll get to it. Sitting down at the table listening to the gentle whistling of the wind outside, I think about Annette. It'll be real nice to see her again. As I work the knife and fork over the meat and potatoes, I think of Morse, too. Now you'd think that after speaking with that guy I'd have lost my appetite. But I'm a strong believer in mind over matter. And right now, I'm being reminded that I'm hungry, and Morse… doesn't matter.

|<<<|>::<|<<<|>::<|<<<|>::<| :+: |>::<|>>>|>::<|>>>|>::<|>>>|

Chapter Nine
The Chat

The Boathouse,
Escanaba, Mi.
Present Day.

My gloved hand slips on the boat's steel wheel as I hold it tightly against the rolling waves and enter the Escanaba pierheads. With my free hand, I throttle back the outboards and let the backwash push me on. The wind and waves are back to their normal southwesterly action and I logger the boat in the following sea. It's been a wild and cool ride in from the Island and I'm pretty glad to see shore. It rained last night and I pumped water out of the boat's bilge for a good ten minutes before starting off this morning. Then, with the cold front passing through, it was a bumpy ride and the spray was cold.

I pull off the water spotted sunglasses and squint over a shoulder to look at the sparkling sun and fuzzy blue sky. It's going to be nice today, but I know, without a doubt that going back against those waves isn't going to be fun. Maybe it's not such a bad idea to stay in my little boathouse for a week. I do have stuff to do and…as quickly as that thought manifests, I know that it won't work. So far, we've been blessed with mild weather, but it can't continue to hold. It's late September, and even though it's been unusually warm, it's still upper Michigan here'bouts. Odds are good that it's going to get worse…not better. And I've still got things to do on that Island. I'll see how it goes, but I better get my ugly red butt back to that rock ASAP. Once inside the breakwalls, the wave and wind activity drops off and control of the boat eases. I unzip the flight jacket and pull the wet wool collar off my neck. I slowly cruise down past several out-bound sportfishermen and one little fourteen foot Coast Guard boat, loaded with an ATON (aids to navigation) team. They're busily checking the light on a navigation buoy in the channel. They all wave, "watercop to watercop", as I pass by.

Turning into the marina's access channel, I can just make out the front ends of two Jeep Cherokees, parked in the lot by the boathouses. They're two-toned dark green and gray and have overhead flashers, spotlights and Tribal Police logos on their doors. They look new. And best of all, they come with an ugly hood ornament too. No wait…my mistake. That's not a hood ornament, it's my old pal Captain Morse, leaning against the front of one of the Jeeps. Oh, well, for a nickel and no other reason, I'd probably be willing to make him a hood ornament anyway. I know…I know…be nice.

I allow my gaze to drift to the marina dock as I idle the Boston toward its slip. There are already a lot of people out and about, but then, it's a Saturday and there won't be that many nice days left. That sets me to wondering why a lawyer is working on the weekend. It's not like them. Could be, that this one's sick or else the more logical answer is that he's making big bucks off the Tribe, too.

Getting closer to the boathouse, I casually glance around for the old German man. If he's into fishing, he won't get a better day than this. But he isn't around. I'd seen him every time I was back here and his presence has become normal. Maybe he had to get back to the Fatherland. Soon I'm pulling up to the button that raises the boathouse door. I get a quick look at the scowling face of Morse as I wheel the boat into the slip, and for the life of me, I think a boy like that really should look into cosmetic surgery.

After shutting down the boat and tying her off to the dock cleats, I go through the door into the little office. My eyes dart over to my duffle bag because right away I see that it's been disturbed. I feel the heat rising as I make my way toward it. If he's gone through my stuff, then that's it. I'm gonna rip his head off and pull his spine out through the hole! By the time the stream of curse words are forming, I see that someone has just moved the bag out of the small closet so that they could hang up some tribal uniforms. Feeling like an ass, I realize that they're probably "my" new uniforms. The duffle still has the same old padlock on it and it hasn't been messed with. I swish the uniform shirts back and forth on their hangers. They're the same gray shirts and green pants that Morse is wearing. Not too terribly ugly. Well, okay then… I walk toward the door and notice a briefcase sitting on the desk as I pass. I turn the knob, being thankful that only I… saw my own foolishness.

Morse is still leaning against the front of the Jeep as I approach. He casually turns and looks at me as I walk up and nod a greeting. He has the same old smirk on his face as he looks over my wet jacket.

"Well, you're wet enough, but I see that you didn't drown." Then his smirk turns to a crooked smile, "That's too bad, ya know?"

I give him my number-six deadpan look and respond, "Yeah… but at least one of us did, you look kind'a splotchy and bloated."

His face and eyes grow dark and the smile disappears. He didn't like that, but heck, I thought it was cute. Besides… if you're jousting with words…then you better be wearing some armor. He pushes himself forward from leaning on the Jeep and digs around in his pants pocket. His hand comes out with a set of keys and he looks over to me.

"We just picked these two up at the dealership this morning," he tosses me the set and I manage to catch it with my left hand.
He nods his head to the keys and points his finger while patting the other hand on the Jeep's fender. "This one will be yours and I expect you to take care of it. There's a Chevron card over the visor. Use it to fill-up whenever you can. The dealership here in town will service it."

I drop the keys into my jacket pocket and move over to the building. I pull out the silver cigarette case and snap open the lid, drawing one out. Morse looks closely at the case, which has turquoise inlaid in the engraving, and watches me fire off the hand rolled. I think that he's wondering if it's marijuana, as he leans into the cloud that billows his way. After a second, he's satisfied that it's not reefer and watches as I return the case to my pocket.
The case was given to me on the island of Grenada back in 1983. I happened to be standing outside the lounge at the airport and had just lit a cigarette when a slew of college kids came hustling out the door to board a prop-airplane that was warming up on the runway. One of the young medical students saw me, stopped, jogged over to where I was and extended this case. "Here", he said, "if it wasn't for you Marines, we'd a never got out'ta here."

I had taken the case and was about to tell him I wasn't a Marine when he yelled "Thanks!" and ran over to the plane. He was the last one on and they buttoned it up as he went through the door. I'd watched the plane taxi out while I finished my smoke. I'd been accused of worse than being a Marine, maybe not a lot worse, but still… I guess I looked the part. I was dressed in filthy Tiger Stripes and had a squiggly green, white and black painted face. It was hot and I didn't smell good either. As I watched the plane take off, I guess I also figured that I liberated them just as much as the Army Rangers and Marines did, so I kept the case in the spirit it was given. Of course, my friend the copsuit here didn't know any of that.

I put the cigarette in my mouth and let it hang as I leaned back against the building and looked down at a lone weed growing through a crack in the asphalt. I cast my eyes up and let them roam while I waited for Morse to say something else. Foot traffic was picking up on the dock as more people made their way to their boats. We were drawing a lot of looks as the procession made its way past. My exhaled smoke was quickly snatched by the freshening breeze.
The town seems alive on this pretty, fall morning. Traffic is steady

on the street parading past the Marina. There is a red Mitsubishi parked in the lot with a blond-haired guy sitting in it. He appears to be reading a book and eating a paper-wrapped sandwich. Seems like a strange activity for a Saturday, but maybe he was waiting to pick up a fisherman. I still don't see the old German guy, either.

Morse adjusts his stance and folds his arms. I notice that he is wearing a different sidearm when a small commotion on the boardwalk draws our attention. A short stubby man, kind of athletic looking, is telling a small group of people that he will be just a minute. Then he makes his way over to Morse and extends his right hand. Morse sees him coming and stands up straight, and I swear, an amiable smile even appears on his face.

"Hello there, my name's Hank Scari," Morse takes the offered hand and shakes it.

"I run Scari's Guide Service and I'm da one dat takes some hunters out ta da Island, eh?"

Morse releases his hand and maintains a pleasant posture. "Nice to meet you, …Alan Morse." The little man nods his head with a big grin.

"Ya well, I been wanting ta meet ya and maybe talk about my being able ta still take hunt'n parties out ta da Island, eh? I mean, now dat you Indians own it an all."

Morse never loses a beat. He points to me and returns the man's smile broadly, "Well, Mr. Scari, the man you want to talk to about that is right here," he points over to me. "This is Officer Stone and he'll be in charge of those kinds of things on the Island for right now."

The little fellow turned his focus to me as I kicked myself off the building and leaned over to shake the offered hand. "Ely Stone, Mr. Scari. How do you do?"

The man continued his grin and I had the impression that smiling was something he did a lot of. "Ya, it's good ta meet ya too, eh. Uh, listen, my boat's da "Mary Jane" down in slip 24. I'm taking these people," he jabbed a stubby thumb over his shoulder, "out on'a charter right now. But I was wondering…if maybe we couldn't get tagether an maybe talk some, eh? About hunt'n on da Island."

He has a pleasant face and a gentle manner. I figure him to be an easy-going guy. "Uh, sure. We should be able to do that. But right now, I'm really not sure about the likelihood of that working out. I'll be in town for a few days though, so you can drop back over here or call…," I looked at Morse for a phone number but Scari was shaking his head.

"Naw, it'd be easier for you ta call me, eh, if ya don't mind, an just let me know when's a good time, eh? I'll be out late with dis charter an I gotta fly a some people over ta Green Bay tomorrow morning, eh, but I'll be back tomorrow night… if dat'ed be okay? Maybe we can talk after dat? It's kind'a important ta me, eh?"

My turn to nod. "That'd be fine. Are you a pilot then, Mr. Scari?" He nods his head while handing me a business card. "Ya, a chopper pilot, eh? I gotta Hughs 500 helicopter dat I use ta ferry hunters out ta da Island and odder places, eh?" he smiles broadly.

The three of us shake hands again and Scari is off to his waiting charter group. The little meeting, though, has inspired several other folks to come up and inquire about our undoubtedly strange presence. I am mildly surprised to watch Morse deal with the public in a friendly and professional manner as he explains the Tribe's new existence here in Escanaba. When a brief lull finally comes about, Morse turns to me.

"Let's go inside and get away form all these people. We need to have a little chat. But I've got to get some stuff first." He moves over to the other Jeep, pops the rear hatch and pulls out a medium sized cardboard box, then secures the door. Walking past, he motions me to follow.

As we walk around front, I see that the mailbox has its door partially open and is jammed with a large manila envelope and other mail. I stop and take it out, carrying it inside with me. Morse goes over to the desk and sits down behind it. He waves at the door, indicating that I should close it. I push it to, while he pops his briefcase open and draws out a cop's notebook. I casually move over to the small couch and sit down. I am mildly surprised that I have so much mail. I put in a change of address, but normally the only stuff I get is junk mail and bills. I thumb through the mail while I know he's watching. He probably thinks I have a lot of nerve, not standing at attention in front of the desk, but shit… I kind'a figured that he was sitting behind my desk, too…ya know?

After I think he's waited long enough, I set the mail down on the end table. My eyes linger on the vaguely familiar writing style on the large manila envelope. Then I switch my eyes up to Morse. He's holding the notebook in the air with his right hand while his elbow rests on the table. When we make eye contact, he gives a little shoulder-shift as if saying, "Are you through now?" and I just continue my gaze. He clears his throat and lays the notebook down.

"Okay, I put your uniforms in that closet over there. I need you to try'em on, make sure they fit. If they need to be altered, there's a drycleaners in town that can do it for you. Either way, when they're all set, I expect you to wear them. Understand?"

I have the feeling that this is going to be a lecture so I slump down on the couch and allow my head to rest on the side of my upturned hand. "I think I can assure you that anyone I meet will know that I'm a fine upstanding member of the Pukaskwa Tribal Police Department."

Morse grunts. "Uh, huh. Well you just wear 'em. Now," he reaches into the cardboard box and pulls out a set of leather Sam Browne gear and places it on the desk, pushing it toward me. Then he retrieves a smaller box that has the Colt Firearms logo on it, four magazine clips, some type of printed form and two boxes of .45 caliber ammunition. He focuses his attention back to me.

"Alright, this is your issue weapon. I hope you ain't got a problem with a .45 because that's what we're carrying. I was chief of police downstate in a little town called New Era and the city council made us carry .9 millimeters. That's a crappy round as far as I'm concerned, but I had to use it until this order came in. Now, I've made arrangements with the P.D. here in Escanaba to let you qualify on their range so until you get that qualification, I don't want you carrying a weapon. Get it?"

I am moderately interested in the gun until he says that. I like the .45 and I wouldn't count on a 9mm to splat a fly. I'm from the old school where one shot, often, is all you get. And I prefer that one shot to knock the person I am shooting at down… not just piss them off. Still, I'm not going to go to a shooting range to prove to this guy that I can hit what I'm aiming at. This is probably pushing my little position too far, but what the heck, I really don't want old Barney Fife here thinking that I worked for him, either.

I shrug my shoulders in a show of "who gives a shit" and sigh. "You can keep it then."

Morse's mouth hangs open. "What the hell do ya mean I can keep it? You will take this weapon and you will get qualified with it on the police range here in town!"

I just smile at him and glance to the mail on the table again, shuffling through it as I speak. "No, I'm not going to go to any range and get qualified anywhere unless I decide to. So, you just keep the .45 and I'll carry my own weapon."

Morse was incredulous. "Ya know, Stone, you think you got my ass over a barrel but you shouldn't be so quick to jump to conclusions. I ain't done with you yet and the fat lady… ain't sung yet either. Alright," he pushed the form over, "have it your way, Super Cop. I need you to sign and date that where I got it x'ed."

I wipe the smile from my face, stand and move over to the desk. The paper is just an BIA Tribal Police form stating that I received this firearm. It has a serial number for the gun listed and after opening the box and verifying that the number matches the one on the .45, I sign and date it. Then I look down at him. "Let's just keep your sex life with barrels and your mother's singing voice out've this, okay?"

Morse's face reddens as he turns his head sideways, temper flaring, jabbing that ugly finger at me again. "And another thing, you need a haircut. I expect my officers to look like policemen, not Sitting Bull. The only way you can keep your hair that long is if you're doing that hokus-pokus bullshit with old man Reddeer. I already got one officer doing that and I don't intend to have any more!"

I just put the pen down and look at him. That's when the phone rings. Morse looks at it then to me. Then he reaches over and picks up the receiver. "Tribal Police, Captain Morse."

I move over to the window and scan outside while Morse talks on the phone.

"Yeah, Jason...what's up?... Oh, yeah, an unruly bastard, huh?... Well you got'ta nightstick don't'cha?... As soon as the asshole starts acting up, just pull off and put'em to sleep."

I decide to change into dry pants while I hear Morse being transferred to the to the jail nurse. His voice is getting steadily louder.

"Look," Morse growls into the phone, "Why can't you just sedate him?... I've never heard of a policy like that...Yeah, well I can't tie up two officers just to transport a... Yeah, I guess that's right... Okay, it's my problem. But you tell your Captain that we'll extend the same kind of courtesy for you guys, too! ... Can you put my officer back on?"

I move back over and take my seat on the couch. Morse's face is flushed and he's hot. I'm keeping my amusement under control, but I gotta say it's a struggle. Morse begins with the cop on the other end. "Yeah, Jason... it's a bunch of bullshit!.. Why don't you just head back over here to the substation and I'll send the new guy Stone with you and the two of you can go back and get him."

I'm shaking my head, but it takes a few seconds for Morse to notice and he continues to talk with a question mark directed my way. ..."Because I can't... I'm dropping Annette off at her grandmother's on my way back, remember?... Yeah, okay, I'll see you." Morse hangs up the phone and looks to me.

"I'm going to need you to ride with another one of my guys to transfer a prisoner back up to the Soo." Morse glances at his watch, then back to me.

"He'll be here in about a half hour or so, and ...," I'm shaking my head no again when Morse stops.

I give my most sincere expression. "Look, I can't help you with the transport because I've got things to do. And we might as well get the lines defined right now Morse. And the number one line is," I hold up my hand with the thumb pointed straight up. "I don't work for you. Number two," I rolled out my index finger, "I didn't apply for a job with your department, I was invited to a specific job by the Council. Number three," another finger.

"I will do the job I was hired for and that's all I'll do, unless I choose to do more. And number four," my ring finger pops up, "I don't like you any more than you like me. Now, you take those four lines and they form a box that you and I are going to have to work with. I won't be messing with you and…," my pinky rolls out, "I don't want you messing with me. I'm not going to quit just to make you happy, either. You leave me alone and the package will be alright. You don't… and it's going to be like opening Pandora's Box."

I finish with a look of query directed at him. Morse listens, but he isn't pleased. He rocks back in his chair and taps a finger to his jaw while studying me from across the room. He has a sardonic look as he clears his throat and gently rocks in the chair.

"Okay, smartass. You're right. I really don't like you. I think there's a lot wrong with you. And whether you know it or not, I care about how this department and the tribe are viewed. So, I'll play your," he twiddles his fingers in the air, "box game but I want some answers first. Fair enough?"

I look at him with surprise. Actually, I do wonder what he wants to know because if I am going to keep this job, we will have to find some medium ground. "I'll tell you what I can, but for the most part, you seem to know it all."

He leans over the desk and picks up the notebook. "No, I don't think so. Not hardly." He pulls another police writing tablet and opens it. "You're a hard man to find out about, Stone. But", he waggles a finger at the notes, "I got some stuff anyway. I researched your ass. I can't get any hardcopy, yet, but I will." He lays the notebook open on the desk and glances down at it. Even from across the room I can see handwritten entries on the open page.

"It seems that they call you the "Ghost", huh? And apparently, you were involved in at least three operations where you were the only one to come out alive?"

I just keep the same expression on my face. It was a lot more than three operations. But he doesn't need to know that. He's fishing, but I'm not biting. Just the same, I don't like him poking his ugly face into my record anymore than they already have. So, before this little pow-wow is done, we'll have that much settled, too.

He taps his finger on the file while scrutinizing me over the desk.

"Also says here, that you received the Legion of Merit? Now that's a pretty hefty decoration for a Coast Guard guy, don'cha think? And low and behold, that little tid-bit don't appear in your regular service jacket, either."

I feel my eyes go to slits but say nothing. The lack of response on my part is starting to irritate him. He returns my stare for a few seconds and then exhales a sigh. "Ya know, it's been my experience over the years that often, when a big medal is pinned on somebody, they usually don't deserve it. And something else, too... a name like Ghost could be given to a guy because he's lucky ta be alive or... maybe it's because he's a chickenshit?" He leans forward over the desk to make his point as he adds the last. All I can think of during this whole little interrogation is how childish it seems. And maybe how dangerous. Besides, he's got it backwards – you don't drop a bare hook in when you're fishing then try... baiting So, I answer in the same vein while keeping my eyes locked on his.

"Maybe you better "eeni-meenie-mini-mo" it then."
He maintains eye contact for several seconds before looking away and murmuring a "shit" in the process. Then he slaps the tablet with one hand and looks at me while jabbing his other finger in my direction.

"Look, you may not know this, but I got 30 years in the Army. I retired as a Command Sergeant Major in '98. Now my whole career was in the military police, and I've still got a few connections... ya know? Now I'm guessing you were a spook... right? Maybe CIA, huh?"

I still just look at him, but I must say I'm impressed. I didn't think that he was smart enough to make it to E-9. He's getting more frustrated as he rails on. And the chips are getting higher, too. I'll have to go along to see just what he has now. He's not getting any response from me and it's getting to him. He swings his hands in accusation.

"Are you trying ta tell me you weren't a spook?"
I look at him incredulously, "You can't be that dense, Morse. What makes you think I'm trying to tell you anything?"

He leans back in the chair and studies me, then shakes his head and continues. "According to this, you also did some kind of mission in Viet Nam back in '79? Shit! we weren't even in Nam in '79!"

He says the last as a question with raised eyebrows and a curious face. "And it was some kind'da covert thing because I recognize the code that comes after the notation here."

My neck is beginning to flush and I know that I'm close to losing it. Control, Ghostman. Get a handle on your ass, I tell myself as he rambles on. Morse rolls out his hand. "What the hell was the Coast Guard doing in Viet Nam in 1979?"

He shouldn't have that information. Nobody should. I can feel my ears getting hot and know that my temper is following suit. I hunch my shoulders in an "I dunno" attitude, trying desperately to keep a handle on this situation. I answer, "Maybe Ho Chi Minh had a hole in his rubber ducky."

Morse rolls his eyes and pushes his hands out in an angry motion. "You're not gonna tell me anything, huh? Well look, asshole, whether you like it or not… I gotta RIGHT ta know and I'll keep digging until I find out! And you can bet your ass I'll find out, too! So you might as well come clean here and now! I did a tour in CID and I still got connections there." He says the last while jabbing a finger onto the notepad.

Morse is taking on a red hue in my vision and that's…not good. I tell myself to settle down and take a few breaths. I stand and walk over to the window. If he was an E-9 with 30 years in the Army, then there's no doubt he has contacts that could dig up bits and pieces on my background, even though it's classified as top secret. The only problem is that that would automatically dredge up other people connected to me, too. And I ain't about to have anybody else exposed just because this cockbite has a power complex. After a minute, I think I'm ready so I move over in front of the desk.

"Okay. If you're done with your questions now and want some answers, then I'll give you some." Morse looks at me for a beat, and then rocks back in the chair again with a satisfied expression as he rubs a hand under his jaw. I am looking for an opening and feel lucky to have this one so quick. As fast as I can, I reach over and snatch the notebook in a continuous motion, returning to my previous stance. Morse's chair bumps forward as he reacts to the move. He watches me and an artery begins surging furiously on his temple. But he doesn't say anything as I look at the pages. I hold the tablet with my left hand and use my right to flip around. There is only one page making mention of me. The other pages are accident notes and similar cop stuff. Morse moves his right hand to the gunbutt jutting from his holster, his face beet red.

I feel the Glock begin to vibrate against my back as I let my eyes travel to his hand, then slowly back up to meet his expression. I make sure he knows… that I know… what he is thinking. Sound and the outside world stop for me. The air becomes as thick as cream and the mood in the room turns dark. Tension bounces around like a sparking electrical wire. We both feel it. We both know it. A wrong move here and one of us…maybe both…could die. I can feel the adrenalin flowing freely in my veins as my mind computes time and distance, the distance to his gun in his front holster - the distance to mine in the small of my back. Then as quickly as it began… Morse releases the pressure.

He slowly eases his hand off the gun and brings it up to meet his other and folds them together on the desktop. Inside, the walls of my head are pounding as the blood that had just been coursing explosively begins to slow. I tear the one page out, dropping the tablet and pulling the lighter from my pants pocket as Morse looks on, incredulously. I snap open the Zippo and strike the flint, allowing the flame to touch on the paper. It flares up quickly and I twist it to keep the course of the fire burning upward. Then, I allow the chunk of ash to drop in an empty wastebasket next to the desk. I return my thoughts to words. My voice comes out as almost a whisper and I wonder if he can even hear me.

"Now, I said some, and SOME answers are all you're going to get. You think that you have a right to know… but… you do not have a NEED to know. It was DIA… not CIA and with you fuck'n around like you're doing, other peoples' names…people who have nothing to do with you or this tribe, are going to be brought into this."

I caught the surprise on his face when I said DIA (Defense Intelligence Agency). I'd given him that much, but that was all he was going to get. I try to elevate my voice because I know I'm still speaking too low.

"Now that'd place their names in the open and…definitely… place them in jeopardy… just because of their past connection to me. I won't let that happen. So, just so we understand each other… you do any more digging about me and I promise you… I'll smoke your contacts and I mean, "burn'em" proper. Whatever happens to them, well that'll be on your head. And as far as you and me… well anymore," I picked up the notepad, "of this so-called research and I come after you. No shit, buddy. Honest Injun, I will… until I can't come anymore. It ain't a threat… it's a promise."

I drop the pad on the desk, take a couple of steps back and point at the wastebasket. "Do you have anymore of that type of information? I have a NEED to know because peoples' lives depend on it!"

Morse thinks for a moment, maybe trying to make up his mind before he shakes his head no. I wait a few beats then feel my head nod once.

"Now, if you've still got questions, you go ahead and ask them. But I wouldn't count on getting answers every time. I'm going to finish the job I was hired for, and you and I can work together or not… that's up to you. But either way, I ain't quitting until I… feel it's time."

I more or less back my way to the couch and sit down. Morse's expression has changed. A look of satisfaction or maybe it's "ease" is displayed now. He pushes the chair away, stands and walks over to open the door, probably as much to clear the room from the heaviness in it as anything else. I know I'm glad for the freshness that comes in. He leans against the jamb and hooks thumbs over his gunbelt as he peers outside at the bright day.

"I knew you were a spook." He shakes his head while looking off. "Too much shit covered up in your background to be a normal military retiree. And… okay, the DIA does a lot of good out there. But I didn't know that they had regular military operatives back in the '70s?"

I look noncommittal. "They didn't."

He's turned his head in my direction but I don't add anymore. "So I guess you're saying "Ghost" doesn't mean chickenshit either, huh?"

I let my eyebrows form question marks until he looks back to the outside. He sighs deeply. "I was drafted in '67 and was in Viet Nam two days after my nineteenth birthday. I was a green-ass Spec-4 in Saigon in 1968." He pulls up a hand and rubs his nose. "You ever hear about Tet?"

"Some." I knew that it was the Chinese New Year and that in '68 Saigon got hit hard during the Tet offensive. Army M.P.s did most of the fighting in that town and it was bloody. If he was there, then he'd seen his share of action.

"Yeah, well the Army gave me a bronze star for staying alive for those few days. I never figured that I deserved it, you know? I had guys die all around me, who were a hell'ava lot better soldiers than I was." He turned back to me again. "You ever feel that way?"

I give a shrug. "Only every time I think about it."

He shakes his head in a gesture of futility. And something passes between us… warrior to warrior… then it's gone. But a sort of bond is still there… in the recesses, somewhere.

"Either way, Stone, I still don't like you. To me, a spy is a spy. It may be better that you were a DIA spook but your kind of people have a way of fucking up other people and things. And in spite of what you may think, I ain't scared of you." He looks down at the floor as he seems to search for his next words.

"I've got something you don't have and that's kids… without a mother. I'm all they got. That makes me tread lightly when I know you're a dangerous sonavabitch. But being a badass will only go so far with me so… I wouldn't push it. I'll leave you alone and like you said… you leave me alone and maybe… we can get along. Deal?" He raises his expression to meet my eyes and I return his gaze.

I look at him and see a different man than what I had figured. He deals with the public better than I'd thought he would, he seems more professional than I'd expected and he'd made E-9 in Uncle Sugar's Soldier Machine. All of those things were moderately impressive to me. But I didn't like him either. He was a "by the book" coloring type and I was a "color outside the lines" type. You never find those two happily sharing the same box of crayons. But I do respect him and that's a lot more than I'd done before we had this little chat. I cross my legs and answer, "Deal."

Morse nods in assent, but points a finger at me in conclusion about the same time another tribal patrol unit pulls into the lot. "One other thing, though. You stay away from Annette! I don't want her near you because like I said, people that are around you … can get hurt. I care about her and that's all there is to it."

I puff up my cheeks in a farcical smile and tilt my head. "Now remember our little four sided box, Captain. I don't work for you, and… I don't follow your orders, either."

He is about to respond when an officer with coal black hair, tied in a ponytail steps up to the doorway. My old heart flutters as I catch sight of Annette coming up beside him.

"Hey, Jase. What's happening?" Morse drops our dialog and addresses his officer while he keeps his eyes on Annette, who is coming to a stop.

"I'm sorry, Cap, but they wouldn't give him the shot and he's a mean sucker, too. He kicked the back window out've a one of their new cruisers."

Morse tells him not to sweat it as he smiles at the young woman in the doorway. "And I see you've already got picked up, too?"

"Yeah, well we wrapped it up and I called your cell but got no answer. So, I tried Jason and he swung by to get me." She seemed tired. Lawyers will do that to you. She tilts her head and goes on. "I never thought of calling this office though."

Morse drops his hand to feel for the phone, and then apologizes for leaving it in his Jeep. Nobody has seen little old me, tucked inside the room, so I decide to stand. Annette makes eye contact then, and that captivating smile appears forcing her almond eyes to vanish. I really enjoy seeing that happen. She lets out a, "Hi, Ely."

I smile back at her and nod at the younger cop. "Hello, there." I stick out my hand to the ponytail. He is quick to return the shake as Morse introduces me to Officer Jason Treebird. After we drop our hands he takes an appraisal of me. I notice his eyes sway for a moment on my hair and a slow smile appeared on his face.

"So you're the new detective we've heard so much about, eh?"

"Yeah, I guess so… special agent or I guess detective, if that's what it is."

He nodded his head and the ponytail bounced reactively.

"Yeahhhh. Amos has talked about you a lot. I've been looking forward to meeting you, eh?"

So this must be the "one" officer Morse has who's got long hair. And supposedly, he's working with Amos in some spiritual capacity. That is interesting. He has intelligent black eyes and a confident manner, topped off by the typical Pukaskwa physique. We drop into small talk as Morse shepherds Annette to the Jeeps parked along side the building. Treebird asks if the Charger under the tarp is mine and I tell him it is. He asks what year it is, what engine, the usual stuff. But I am trying to overhear Morse, who is explaining that they would have company on the way to her grandmother's. The prisoner was the company, but she didn't seem upset about it. Jason Treebird goes on to say that he'd owned a '74 Road Runner when he was younger. He asks if he can pull the tarp back and take a quick look at the car. I tell him sure. He trots that way as Annette and Morse come back to the doorway.

"Yeah, Annette… I'm really sorry about this. I have ta have my unit in the morning so I'll be sending Ken and Marvin back tonight to pick it up. And, hey," he points to me as they come to a stop, "I even asked Stone here, but he's busy today, too." She reaches behind her and pulls a barrette out, and then shakes her long hair until it cascades like dark-spun honey. It glistens in the sun and the mere sight startles both Morse and myself. It's beautiful. But then, so is she. She has on a pair of khaki pants and she pulls off her light jacket, underneath of which is a red turtleneck. Red is a good color on her.

"Don't worry about it, Alan. I'm sure it's not a problem," she cooed in that voice as a soft chuckle escapes her lips. Then she folds the jacket over her arm and looks toward Morse as he continues to make his excuses. I think that now would be the perfect time to help the old boy out, what with our new-found understanding and all. I look over at her as she continues her smile.

"Well, I didn't realize that it was that important, Morse," I glance quickly from him and then back to her, "so you can count on me. Annette, I can drop you by your grandmother's, if that would be Alright? I'm sure it's on my way and I understand Morse's position, you know… having a civilian riding with a criminal and all."

Morse appears dumbstruck. I like that look on him. It fits. Annette, meanwhile, turns to Morse. "Oh, no, Alan, I didn't understand that my riding along would cause you problems. I'm sorry." She snaps her head back to me and says that she will be very grateful for the ride. The whole time, Morse is fuming and stammering. He finally gets the words out.

"It's no problem… you riding along with us, Annette…," he shoots daggers at me with his eyes, "and if you want to help out, then ride with Treebird. Besides, you don't even know where she's going, Stone!"

I turn to her with the question on my face. Her smile gets broader. "It's a little town north of here called Bruce's Crossing."

I turn back to Morse with my arms wide and palms splayed open. "See there, Captain. It's right on my way. No problem at all. And while I wish I could ride with your prisoner, I do have things to do today."

Morse looks like a guy with bladder problems because he's stepping from foot to foot in quick procession. Annette makes her goodbyes to him and hollers a farewell to Treebird, too. Then she asks me if we have time for her to speak quickly with the Harbormaster. I say we've got all the time in the world, while Morse continues to pass me the dead man's stare. His voice is hot and low after she's down the boardwalk a little ways.

"Maybe you didn't hear the last thing I said in there?" he stabs his thumb toward the office.

"Oh, I heard it alright. Maybe you didn't hear my answer," I reply as I tilt my head, inquiringly.

Morse takes a deep breath and his eyes go hard. "I thought you have stuff to do today?"

I smile greatly and wink with a slight nod. "Yep. And this… is on my list."

A few minutes later, Morse and Jason Ponytail are pulling out of the lot. From the expression on Morse's face, the prisoner had better be a real good boy. I look down at the cracked concrete of the dock. Well… hasn't this been fun so far? The closeness of the call runs quickly through my mind. One move either way and today would've gone down in history as "The gunfight at the Pukaskwa Boathouse". Sheeeeit!

I glance down to the gas dock to see if Annette is coming yet, but there's no sign of her. I habitually scan the whole area again and the thought passes through my mind that I… had thought that I was done with all this death and dismemberment crap. Since I've taken this job, I've had a couple of run-ins with people that could've got me in deep trouble. And today…could've gotten my ass killed.

The air smells of big lake water, seaweed, and wetness. It's a pleasant and familiar aroma to me. The place seems fairly quiet now. The blond guy in the red Mitsubishi is gone. But there's a jogger running in-place over on the grassy hill by the parking lot now. I noticed him arrive about the same time that Annette and Treebird showed up. Two minutes later, the blond guy had gone.

It almost seems like it was tag-team surveillance. Kind of sloppy too, if that's what it is. I have to physically shake my head to clear the nonsense out. What on earth would anyone be watching here? It was all that crap earlier with Morse, stirring up old thoughts and actions. It's best forgotten, especially those deadly modes of things past. Still, I feel a smile stretching my mouth as I recall Morse's face when I said I'd been with DIA. Most career military people really dislike the CIA and other intelligence agencies. But as a rule, they appreciate the DIA because, unlike its peer group, it only gathers information pertaining to military forces and their respective ability to fight, stay alive and win wars or conflicts. That still makes them spies but for the average G.I., at least a better kind of a spy.

I light a cigarette and move over to a picnic table where I hike my boot up on the board seat and continued my survey of the marina. I catch her coming out of the Harbormaster's door and walking toward me. Her chest bounces pleasantly with her gate as she walks along. Her hair flows lightly behind her and the smile that adorns her face does make me feel giddy. I can hear the clacking of her sneakers as she grows closer and another thought breezes into my mind. It wasn't nice…that little go-round with Morse… but we got the boundaries established in that little chat. And jeeze, I am going to get to spend the day with this girl. As she arrives at the picnic table, the smell of her fragrance floats in with her, and I know that it is all worthwhile.

Chapter Ten
"Honest Injun"

**Michigan's Upper Peninsula,
Present Day.**

The old man pulled his driver's license out of the wallet and laid it on the counter. The woman on the other side picked it up to begin copying information onto a boat rental form. She held the license up and squinted at the name. She was born and raised in Escanaba, and, as such, didn't usually go in for frills. She had just started wearing contact lenses and had a heck of a time remembering to put them in before she left the house.

"Uhh, is that Veeter? I don't have my contacts today."

The old man slipped back into his accent. "Ya, it's Herman Veeter. Can you zee the address okay?

"Oh yah, the words just kind'ov ran tagether there, with yer name, eh?"

She continued to write as the old man waited. Shortly, she was done and passed him back the license. She then walked into another room and returned with a life jacket, placing it on top of the counter.

"Okay, ya've got boat number six and it's all gassed up. Uh, ya've got the weekend rate on da boat and it's got'ta be back here on Monday morning by eight o'clock or you'll be charged a late fee, eh?"

The old man took the life jacket and thanked her before walking out of the Sport Shop. He moved to his car and opened the trunk. He took out a large hiker's pack and a long length of coiled rope, then gathered up everything and toted it over to the rental boat. After stowing the gear onboard, he went back and took a five-gallon can of gas from the trunk before closing it. This, too, he placed in the boat before getting in, starting the outboard and casting off from the dock.

As he guided the boat past the entrance to the marina, he looked carefully to see if there was any activity around the boathouse. There was none. That morning, he had watched the two Indians from his room window at the motel with binoculars. He had watched the other Indian male and female arrive and had waited. Soon they all left and the old man knew that this was his chance. He had tried to get on the island several times before, but the Indian was always there or showed up at the wrong moment. He was running out of time and could afford to wait no longer.

His daughter had said on the phone last night that Carrie was getting worse. So this had to be it. Once he got the thing out, if it was still there, he would still have to arrange other things to get the money he needed. As he entered the rolling waves of Lake Michigan, he zipped his coat up tighter. In his mind, he cautioned – So, if that Indian knows what's good for him, he'll stay away until I got what I came for. As the wind off the lake blew that thought away, the old man turned the throttle up on the little fourteen-foot aluminum boat and it began bouncing over the water toward Muskrat Island.

The two men sat in a back booth at the Ponderosa restaurant in Escanaba. As instructed, they were seated in the smoking section and blue clouds floated aimlessly about. The good thing about the area was the lack of people opting to sit there. The men were eating scrambled eggs, sausage and fruit, gathered from the buffet bar. The place was busy, but then it was late Saturday morning, too, the tail end of the breakfast all-you-can-eat time. People paid them little attention as they traveled back and forth to the buffet tables. The two men still worried. Theirs was a dangerous business and caution needed always to be a consideration.

They looked normal enough. Both wore work shirts and dirty blue jeans, complete with Stanley tape measurers hooked over their belts. To most folks, they appeared as laborers or contractors and that… was exactly what they wanted. A closer look though, would have showed an unusual tweak to their builds. Both men were slight of stature, unusually so for Michiganders. And that was true for the Oriental man that walked into the door just then, too. He wore a tan dress shirt with clean Levis and carried a black briefcase. He paid the cashier and proceeded to the booth to sit down. Chin looked at the two agents and was still amazed at how "white" they appeared. He spoke in perfect English, a bit too perfect, and kept his voice low.

"I've just spoken with Tran. He said that the Indian who is staying on the Island met with another Indian policeman this morning." He halted his speech as a very large man with a heaped plate passed the booth. "Then a third policeman and a woman came also, but Tran said they have all left at this time." He opened his rolled napkin and pulled out the eating utensils, then arose and went to the buffet table. The two CHEE agents remained seated and continued to eat. Shortly, Chin returned to the booth and slid in with a plate of fried potatoes, eggs and bacon. The two other men had finished and a busboy had already taken their plates. Chin spoke between forks of food as he ate. "You two will go back to the Island today. We must find this opening because time is of the essence." The two other men said nothing but nodded as they watched him.

He raised his fork for a final bite, pushed his plate to the side and pulled up the briefcase. He snapped it open and pulled out a map depicting Muskrat Island. He kept the briefcase situated so as to shield the map from passers by. The trio hoped that this all looked as if a boss was just showing his workers something about a job they had. Chin pointed to the paper.

"Look here, in this area," his finger traced the northeastern part of the island, "as this is the only section we have not covered yet. It should be easier as Tran said that the Island Indian may go back at any time or perhaps not for several days." He flipped his hand. "It matters not. Either way, you can search during daylight tomorrow. Look only after darkness today." He made sure that the two men acknowledged before he put away the map and closed the case.

"The listening device that Kuan installed in the Indian's building by the boatyard also picked up something else," Chin swept the room with his eyes before going back to his men, "and that was the visit of two American Air Force officers to the boatyard office last night. Kuan said that he heard the men speaking of the Indian "Stone" as they probably stood by the front door of the office. As the device is planted inside, he could not hear specifics. They knocked and said they were of the Air Force, but the Indian was not there. That is why time is of the essence now." Chin looked into the strange eyes of both men. A secret, any secret only had a fifty percent chance of remaining so. That was the rule in the intelligence game. Neither Chin nor the other men were surprised that the US Air Force now knew about what they were after. The reddish-haired one swore under his breath and looked down.

"Shit! That's just what we need! The fuck'n Air Force!" Chin was still astonished that they could seem so…so, American. Their speech and mannerisms were quite good, even down to the slang. And the doctors had engineered the surgery around their eyes so that unless one looked closely, the scar tissue appeared to be age lines and wrinkles. It was truly amazing. He shook his head.

"Yes, indeed, just what we needed. This now changes some things. I have sent Tran to dispatch the Indian. If luck is with us, perhaps that will quell the American Air Force's activities long enough for us to complete our mission. He is following the Indian as we speak, so regardless of all other things, you should be safe on the Island for tonight."

Chin made a cursory check of the room, and then continued. "It is too dangerous for me to be seen with you anymore, now. I have taken a room in Marquette City, up north," Chin slid a piece of paper with a phone and room number on it over to the darker-haired man, "and this is where you can reach me. I want you to call every night at 10 p.m. sharp. We must get this thing done quickly or we will possibly have to kill more than the Indian. I do not think I have to tell you how much that would diminish our chances of a successful mission or… of leaving here alive… do I?"

Both men shook their heads, with solemn expressions upon their faces. Chin sat back into the padded bench and motioned to them. "You had better be going then. Find this opening. It has to be there somewhere!" he whispered. And the two CHEE agents took their leave with little cordial nods, almost but not quite… bows.

Chin watched them exit the restaurant door and then reached over and picked up a piece of sausage from his plate. He popped the meat into his mouth and reached into his shirt pocket while he chewed. He pulled out a pack of Marlboros and ceremoniously tapped the pack, extracted a smoke and lit it with a Bic Lighter. He sucked the smoke deep into his lungs and looked at the burning cigarette lovingly. He hadn't had any of these since he was a midshipman in Viet Nam, serving as a military advisor.

He fondly remembered taking packs of Marlboros from the pockets of dead American soldiers and smoking the wonderful things. Chinese or Vietnamese cigarettes just couldn't compare. Well, he mused, if things didn't go right on this mission, then some American could probably pay him back. Because if they didn't find this thing before long, he knew that he would die here. The American Air Force was now involved and his team had searched almost the whole island under the cover of darkness, at night when the Indian was sleeping or away. And they had not found this cave or mine shaft, mentioned in the RICTOR report. And now, time was running out. As he looked over the brown filtered cigarette, he smiled at the irony. Odds were good that some American soldier, might be taking his pack of Marlboros…very soon.

**On the road to Bruce's Crossing,
the interior of Michigan's U.P.**

The First twenty minutes of the ride are filled with a narrative of the tribe's immediate and future plans and goals. She points out that everything that's been achieved – from Federal recognition to Wiitikan to Muskrat Island - has been because of Hennessey. I agree with her

assessment, but find I'm a little nervous about her admiration of him.
I ask, "Are you two involved?"

She laughs lightly, "Oh no, I think of him as a father figure."
I throttle the Charger up to pass an old Chevy pick-up truck that is
barely doing 30 miles an hour. She "oo's" appropriately, either out of
honesty or consideration for me. When I'd asked her before leaving if
she had a preference as to whether we drove the Charger or the patrol
unit, she'd opted for my car with a certain amount of enthusiasm. The
girl did keep winning smiley faces with me. We come to a stop sign
and as I brake the old muscle car, she turns to me with a taunting
smile.

"Okay, Missster Stone. I've rattled on for an eternity and I think
it's your turn for awhile."

"Oh you do, huh? Well, okay then... what do I say?"

She ran a hand up above her eyes to brush the hair back that
wafted there from the open window. "I don't know. What about the
island? How's that going?"

I shift in the seat before answering. "I really don't know for sure
yet, but I kind of doubt that what you folks want to do is workable."

She sits forward in the seat and looks over at me intently, one
hand holding back her hair. "Oh, no... you're not serious, are you?"

I click my tongue and keep my eyes on the road while doing a
slight head motion. "Well, yeah, I guess I am, but you know, that's
just my opinion right now. I mean, there're some substantial problems
making the thing work as far as I'm concerned. That's all."

"Such as?"

I glance over and see a worried expression on her face. "Hey...
Don't go thinking I'm any expert on the subject." I look back to the
road then shift my gaze back to her. She's frowning now.

"Well, Ely... are these small problems or... are they big problems
or what?"

I let my fingers all flip outward on the steering wheel in slight
frustration. I really don't want to upset her. "Jeeze, Annette, I guess
I'd call them pretty serious." I take a quick look at her, "Because
you're probably not going to be able to use hovercraft for transporting
folks out there. At least as far as I can see right now, anyway."

She moves the hand from her hair to place over her mouth as her
eyes drift to the windshield. "Are you sure, Ely?"

"No. No, I'm not and I won't be until I can get a hold of someone
at the company on Monday who can answer a few questions." Quick
glances over at her tell me she's not taking this well and that disturbs
me. A lot.

"Look...maybe they've got something new out now that will

work. But from what I know of these craft from a couple of years ago, the waters around the Island are going to pretty much stop their use. I'm really sorry." I wait a few seconds for her to say something and when the wait gets too long, I ask. "Was it your idea then, for the hovercraft... I mean?"

She twists her head and worries a hand on her jaw. "No, not mine. It was Paul's."

"Paul? Paul who?" I shoot her way.

She glances over to me and then back out front. "Paul Shultz, our tribal attorney. You met him, remember?"

Oh, yeah. I nod my head. The seagull. I remember him alright. As I roll the Charger into a tight curve, I start to turn to her again but she's already talking.

"If you're right, then this is going to be bad for us. The hovercraft idea was all Paul's and he supposedly has some friend, who's a salesman for hovercraft company or something like that," she blinks her eyes and twists her wrist, causing her fingers to twirl as she goes on. "Anyway, Paul told us that he had contacted the company and they'd sent out an inspection team, and well... supposedly the company said everything was a go. That's the primary reason why we went ahead with the acquisition of the Island. So if you're right, then we've got major problems."

She kept looking ahead after she finished. As for me, well I already knew that Pauly was... the major problem. "Didn't Shultz submit the hovercraft company's findings to the Board?"

"Nope, we were just getting started five years ago and we all pretty much had to trust each other. But Paul's had some other problems." She looks back as she shifts and brings up her knee. "He went through a divorce and his law practice suffered, too." She squints her eyes in memory, "Something about improprieties with a client or something like that. Anyway, he left his private practice and came on with the Band full-time."

"Uh, huh. So, nobody ever double-checked Shultz's assessments, then? Morse didn't ask about'em either?"

"No. No one did. And I guess, that's just as much my responsibility as any of the other members."

I open my palm and stretched it out. "Why?"

"I guess just because I've always felt a little uneasy about it, and well... a little uneasy about Paul, too. Everyone else who had a part to do in this project submitted their findings, but I guess since we all knew that Paul was an attorney, and that he was holding everyone's paperwork, that it was alright, ya know?" She reaches over and squeezes my arm lightly, then releases it. "So, if your observations are correct, Ely, then we've got a major problem because I don't have any idea as to how we could get visitors out to that island unless we used the hovercraft. I guess we were pretty dumb, huh?"

I'm wishing she still had her hand on my arm. "Well, I wouldn't say that it was anymore your responsibility than anyone else's. I mean there's Hennessey, he's got a lot of experience in stuff like this, right? And Morse, shit… sorry,. I mean shoot, he should know lawyers by now and there's…what's her name…uh, Mrs. Morningstar too." I take a peek at my watch as road sign saying, BRUCE'S CROSSING comes into view. Annette shakes her head no.

"Alan wasn't even hired when we started all of this on the island so he really wasn't involved back then."

I take that in. "Yeah, well anyway, I've seen dumber. And it ain't over yet. I'll give the company a call Monday and we'll see what they have ta say. Until then, though," she looks back at me, "you don't worry about it and you don't say anything to anyone about it…okay?" She leans over and rests her hand on my shoulder and this time, she leaves it there. "Okay, Ely, but you'll let me know right away won't you?"

A smile flits around my mouth as I reach up and squeeze her hand. "Yes, ma'am, I sure will." The Charger cracks as she downshifts for the one blinking traffic light that Bruce's Crossing boasts.

The Municipal Marina,
Escanaba, Michigan.

The two CHEE agents worked steadily as they carried the gear from off the dock. It had barely been a half hour since leaving the restaurant and while they knew they had to go, neither of them looked forward to the bumpy and wet ride over Lake Michigan. The boat was a 20-foot Sullivan with a small cuddy cabin. They had rented it from another marina to the south and had used it several times to venture out to the island. They were just finishing when the tribal police Jeep pulled to a stop in front of the boathouse. Both men froze as the big, sandy-haired policeman exited the passenger door. Was it trouble or, had they simply forgot something? The bigger policeman addressed another man who was sitting in the rear seat. Even from the distance, they could hear the words. He pointed his finger at the passenger and both CHEE agents could clearly hear his words.

"Alright, now I'll be right back, but you remember what happened in the jail parking lot don't'cha?"

The CHEE agents could see that the man in the back seat was a prisoner because he was holding a pair of handcuffed hands to his mouth. Inside the hands, the prisoner held a blood soaked napkin and he looked at the big policeman with fearful eyes and nodded his head.

"Okay then, anymore trouble out'ta you and I'm putting your ass ta sleep for the rest of the trip! You hear me?" The prisoner nodded his head vigorously and the policeman went over to the boathouse. He stopped there momentarily and removed something from the door before entering. The driver was a longhaired Indian who was watching the boat interestedly from the vehicle. But none of this mattered much. The CHEE agents had already decided that it was a very good time to leave.

The two men quickly cast off the lines but the wind had shifted and was now blowing the boat back into the slip. Neither of them were very experienced with small boats, and in a setting like this, it became very evident. The red-haired Quang pushed diligently from the boat's stern, only to have the boat blow back in from the bow. His partner, Fat, couldn't apply enough power, for fear of hitting one of the other tied-up boats or the dock itself. They were still trying to get the boat out when the longhaired Indian stepped out of the Jeep and began walking toward them. Quang saw him coming and dropped the attempt, ducking straight for a bag lying on the deck. Inside the bag, there was a pistol and he had the gun out when his partner hissed at him to stop. The Indian was coming down the dock but not in a threatening manner. He was actually smiling as he approached and raised his voice over the hefty wind.

"Can I give you guys a hand getting out of here?" Quang stood up and waved, holding the small automatic tight to his leg in the other hand. What else could he do? "Yeah, thanks. The wind just keeps pushing us back in here."

He moved to the back of the boat but kept the pistol close to his body. Quang was thinking quickly. Fat didn't have his weapon and couldn't leave the wheel of the boat. If it came to a shooting, his mind raced, it would have to be a head-shot because all American policeman wear bullet-proof vests. The Indian said something to Fat about straightening out the boat, and then Quang saw the bigger policeman exiting the building. The man was carrying a briefcase and looking down at the boat. He sat it on the vehicle's hood and bent in to say something to the prisoner. Then he began walking toward them, too.

Quang and Fat exchanged quick glances as the other policeman approached. But this one, too, seemed amiable. He was smiling as well. The larger policeman took a position in front, stretching his arms to the boat to push. The long-haired one came to the middle and did the same. Quang slipped the pistol into his jeans jacket pocket when he saw them do that then, and held-off the boat from the rear.

The bigger, sandy haired policeman began counting "one, two and at "three", they all pushed together as Fat applied power. The boat backed away and was clear in seconds. Quang smiled genuinely and waved yelling "thank you" over the gusty wind. The two men on the dock returned the wave and watched as the boat cleared the marina and headed out toward the big lake. Treebird looked at his Captain. "Hey, Cap', some people I know would say that was "Mighty White" of you."

Morse looked at his officer and smirked. "Ya know, Jason, with some of the people you know, that don't surprise me too much.," he said as he patted the younger man on the back, and then turned and began walking back toward the Jeep. "But the next time you see them, you tell 'em that I ain't white, anymore. I'm just as red as you are, even if I don't wear my hair longer than a Shetland pony's!"

The Cole residence,
Bruce's Crossing, MI

We eventually pull off the pavement where she points. Then, we motor down a winding driveway and come to a stop in front of a small house. The yard is shaded by tall hemlocks and hardwoods, which shimmer in colors that are already fading with the fall. The home is covered in brown fake-brick asphalt paper and there's a weather-checked old tire swing swaying in the breeze beneath a large maple. I switch the Charger off as Annette clears her throat. "Do you mind waiting here a minute. Gram usually changes for bed early on Saturday because she's going to church in the morning with me. She'll be in bed tonight by 9:30 and if I bring you up to the door and she is in her nightgown…she'll die. But I'd really like you to meet her."

I look over and laugh, in spite of myself. "Heck, no. I don't mind waiting at all. Whenever I'm by myself at home, I loaf around in my underwear."

Annette grins in return, and then opens the door and trots up to the house. I climb out my side and light a cigarette to the tune of snapping and popping as the Charger cools. I can feel where the sweat has beaded on my back and so I reach around and pull the Glock from my pants. I lean into the open window and put the holstered gun in the console between the seats, snapping it shut. I let my eyes travel around. She said that she grew up here with her grandmother, and, as

I watch the tire twisting in the air, I envision her as a little girl, swinging and laughing on that black circle. It's pretty here and would've been good for a kid.

Five minutes later, Annette is summoning me to the front door. I fieldstrip the cigarette butt and start toward the house. Dropping the paper in my pocket, I make a mental note to find a trashcan somewhere as there are quite a few papers in that pocket already. Inside, the house is clean and tidy with crocheted doilies on the coffee and end tables. Annette turns as I enter and an old woman steps out of a bedroom door, fastening the top button of a sack dress. She is kind of bent and wizened, but she has a kindled fire of intelligence in her eyes.

"Gram, the is Ely Stone... Ely, this is my grandmother, Vivian Cole."

I walk over and take an aged hand in mine, "How do you do ma'am. It's nice to meet you."
She peers at me as she fumbles with a pair of reading glasses before answering. "Ya, ya, hello," she turns to Annette. "I taut you said es name was Stillwater, eh Nettie?"
Nettie. So, that's what her grandmother calls her? It is pretty too. My thoughts are broken by Annette's voice.

"Yes, Gram, his last name is Stone, but his mother's maiden name was Stillwater. Um, you said that you knew his uncle..." she looks to me and I caught on.
"Mason Stillwater, ma'am. The family has a cabin up on the old treaty lands by Yellow Dog Point?"

The older Cole lady has her glasses on now and brings a hand up to her cheek, smiling warmly. As she does this, her eyes do a disappearing act, much like her granddaughter's.

"Oh, heck ya. You bet'cha I remember him. He an my husband usta cut trees back in da old days, eh? Dat was when lumberjacks was still lumberjacks, eh?" She steps closer to me and peers into my face. "Darn if you ain't da spitt'en image of 'em too, eh? Boy, he was a handsome devil." I feel my face flush as Annette chuckles over by the door.

"Well, you kids c'mon," she motions with her hand as she turns and heads toward the kitchen, "It's time ta eat. I got pasties galore, eh? I always fix a bunch fer dem old men at church 'cause dey ain't got nobody ta cook fer 'em ya know. C'mon now, we'll jes set anuder plate, eh?"

Annette smiles at me and hunches her shoulders. "Can you stay... I mean, I don't know if you like pasties?"
I don't. Pasties are a "Yupper" specialty, a kind of heavy crusted

pie with beef, potatoes, rutabagas, carrots and other vegetables in it. It's one of the few foods in this world that I don't care for. Just the same though, I've eaten bugs and snakes before and didn't especially like them either. Pasties are a heck'ava lot better then those. And the pleasure of these ladies' company sure beats dining with a couple of smelly military types. I sidestep and hold out my arm to Annette.

"Ma'am, I'm right honored and I appreciate the offer." She grins and those lovely eyes disappear. Then we walk into the kitchen. The pasties aren't bad at all, much to my surprise, and we have a very nice visit while we eat. I learn more about "Nettie" and find that my attraction to her is based on sound reasoning. Her grandmother talks of Annette's youth, often to the embarrassed "Graaaams", emitted by Nettie, until the meal's end. Now I know, for instance, that Annette just graduated last summer with her teaching degree. I feel there is something else there, too, maybe an old boyfriend, but whatever it is, the woman won't let on.

Annette and Mrs. Cole shoo me away when supper is finished, even though I offer to help cleanup. After they're finished, Mrs. Cole bids me goodnight then wanders into one of the front bedrooms. Annette tells me that she'll be a few minutes. She has to put things away and stuff. I tell her that I'll just head outside for a smoke. I grab my jacket and head out the door. I shrug into the old leather flight jacket and light a hand-rolled. I smoke as I wander around the yard. The jacket has dried out nicely draped over my seat during the trip. Now, standing out back, I glance down at the gurgling little stream which courses behind the house.

The water is as clear as air and the myriad of multicolored stones that it swishes around, add a surreal quality in the fast fading light. The hemlocks hang heavy here, their branches drooping to touch the stream in places. I'm looking at an old bird's nest built into the crotch of a laden branch when I hear the back door close. I turn to see Annette meandering from the house. She's barefooted, carrying an old pair of sneakers in her hand. She's taking her time, allowing her toes to sweep the deep grass that's probably beginning to dampen with the onset of evening. As she arrives, she motions to an old porch swing dangling from beneath two elderly maples. "Shall we sit?" she inclines her head and steps in its direction, glancing to see if I'm following.

The swing is old but it appears solid enough when Annette sits on the boarded seat. I ease in beside her and the overhead branches tilt losing a flood of yellow leaves that float downward all around us. Well, too fat me, I guess. But it's a pretty sight anyway and as I look at her beside me I know what "pretty" really is. The sun is filtering its last rays through green pine needles and reddish orange maple leaves to allow shafts of yellow light to illuminate her face. I've been under the impression that she's saintly anyway, but poor old lovesick me just stares at the beauty displayed in that angelic glow. She's not just pretty… she's gorgeous!

We gently sway back and forth as the chains creak with the unusual weight they're carrying. Annette pulls back her hair and retrieves a small gold cross from under the turtleneck, allowing it to fold over her front. "Sooo, Mr. Stone. You've certainly heard plenty about me this evening, haven't you?" Her toes lightly brush the grass under the swing as we glide to and fro.

"Yeah…reckon so, but it's not enough. To tell you the truth, Annette, I believe that I could hear about you… for just about forever."

She drops a foot and it drags us still as she looks at me with a question on her face. Her eyes momentarily search mine, and then she smiles shyly and inspects the side of the swing for her shoes. She raises a knee and brings up her foot to meet the shoe. Her feet are small, dainty and perfect. Even her feet are pretty. That figures. She finishes putting on the sneakers and pushes us off again.

"You're sweet, Ely. Do all the girls tell you that?"

"Oh geeze, how would I know? You're the first girl that's ever even told me the time of day, for crying out loud!"

"Oh hooo, I'll bet that's true alright!" she chuckles. She's quiet for a second. Then she uses her fingers to flip away a gold maple leaf on her leg as the swing creaks along.

"I know you're not married, but… is there anybody special in your life… a girl, I mean?"

Uh, oh. Now here's where I'm supposed to say something like, "only you, my dear" and she falls passionately into my arms. The only problem with that is, I'm not too good at making it come out right. Besides, I learned a long time ago that honesty is the best policy, especially if you ain't a smooth talker. I turn sideways enough to see her profile.

"No. No girl, anywhere. Not for a long time."

I'm probably mistaken, wishful thinking being what it is, but… I could've swore I saw just the slightest hint of happiness at that remark. My turn now. The only problem rests with the answer. If it's yes, I'm going to really hate myself for asking, but it's gotta be done. So I gather nerve and form the words.

"What about you? Is something going on with you and our illustrious Captain Morse? or… maybe … one of the other hundred or so suitors that're after you?"

I actually get a guffaw out of her with that one, and seeing her laugh out loud makes me smile, too. After a few seconds, she wipes the mirth from her eyes and looks up into the trees, her hair wafting around like angels breath.

"No, nothing serious, with even a one of those hundred suitors," she smiles at the treetops, "And as for Alan... well he would like there to be, but... well, he's different." She turns to me then and her face is beginning to be shaded by the coming darkness.

"Why is that anyway, Ely? I mean you and he are so different. Both of you are about the same age and speak in that...," she rolled her hand, "short, quick, military manner, but Alan is so... so demanding, I guess... is the only way I can put it. I don't mean that derogatively because he does have a good heart. He can just be very pushy sometimes, that's all. And you don't seem to be like that. Shouldn't you both be similar? I mean since both of you had a career in the military?"

A dozen smart aleck remarks pop into my head at once but I sense that she really wants to know this answer. She's looking at me, waiting for a reply, so, I train my sight up one of the tall hemlocks and give it that old college try.

"Well, I guess the short answer is that for a lot of guys the military is their life...ya know? And in my case, well... I kind'a figure that I got out with my life... if you can understand that?" I drop my gaze back to meet her almond eyes as we sash-shay back and forth in the swing.

She slowly nods her head while contemplating my answer. "Yeah, you know, I think I do understand now, but," she points her finger at me teasingly, "I'm seeing more and more that what Amos says about you being unusual, too."

I'm about to answer with a smart quip, but the black of night is closing fast now, and I can feel her shiver a bit every now and then. I put my foot down and stop the swing, stand and remove my flight jacket. "Here, stand up a minute," I motion to her as she begins shaking her head.

"Please, don't tell me no. Your grandmother will never invite me to eat again if I have to beat you up just because you won't put on this jacket. Now get up please?" She giggles and stands.

I swing the jacket out and behind her, catching it with my other hand. She faces me as she folds her arms into the sleeves and the sexual tension begins to sizzle like water on a hot griddle. We stand close that way for several beats. She turns her head down and doesn't raise it. Then, I guess she figures that she should be doing something, anything other than what she is doing, so she pulls at the jacket bottom. She fumbles with the zipper before making the connection and pulling it up. I step back before I go any further and get myself in serious trouble. She returns to the swing as I pull the box from my pocket and take out a hand-rolled. The Zippo snaps open with that famous G.I Joe "click" and I fire off the cigarette.

"You know, I usually can't stand cigarette smoke but that honestly smells kind of pleasant." She's swinging alone now, peering up at me in the low light while I ponder my beating heart and the sexual discomfort that is plainly visible. I'm glad that the light is fading. I take another drag and examine the cigarette as I exhale the smoke.

"Yeah, well I guess it's a little different. I roll them myself out of Velvet pipe tobacco. That probably accounts for the aroma."

"Mmmmm. Wait a minute, I almost forgot what we were talking about. Tell me, Ely, were you married before?"

"Nope. I came close once but she died." I push away the memory. "It was a long, long time ago."

She murmurs an apology and asks, "That's it, then? You've never been married or... even lived with someone?"

"Oh, sure. I lived with sixty-eight other guys on a Coast Guard Cutter once. But seriously, I didn't have a love interest in any of them, except maybe the cook. The guy made the best cherry chocolate cake I've ever tasted," she's snickering again, "no honest... he did... really." I offer a stick of gum and she shakes her head, a small laugh playing at her mouth.

"Okay, okay. I get it... Boy you are something."

"Well if I'm something, then what about you?" I drop the ember from the butt and twist out the dead tobacco. "What are the somethings about you? Was there someone special at one time?" She stops the swing and I reach out and take hold of one of the chains to steady it.

"Someone special?... yes or... Actually, no. I don't think that turned out to be the case. Not someone special. I um... I mean, I was married right out of high school, but it... uh... didn't even last a year. We were young and he just wasn't ready to settle down. He just walked away from our marriage and it never bothered him at all. But ... it's... well, complicated I guess. It didn't work that way for me."

Ahh, says the sleuth in me. She was hurt badly and it didn't heal for a long time. Catching a glimpse of her face in the burgeoning starlight, I get the notion that it was a reaaaal bad hurt, too. I bend over and take her chin in my hand and look deeply into her eyes.

"You got hurt real bad on that one... didn't you Nettie?" She swallows and her light eyes flicker about my face. "Yep, I did. But I've been over him for a long, long time. I've come to understand that he was never what hurt me... it was the end result. He was a part of those painful feelings. I still remember them." She clears her throat before going on.

"When I was a little girl, my Dad used to talk a lot about Hawaii. He was stationed there when he was in the Army. It sounded like the most wonderful place in the world and I grew up dreaming of going there some day. We didn't have much money and I knew if I were going to ever get there, I'd have to do it on my own. So, I worked hard. I was the typical geek girl in school. I didn't date, didn't go to the prom. I studied and when I graduated from high school, I had a full scholarship to the University of Hawaii on the Big Island." She sighs and looks down at the leaves around her feet.

"I had my life all set and then it didn't turn out that way." She shakes her head. "I got married and didn't go to college. I met him, and probably because I'd always kept my emotions in check, I fell head over heels in infatuation with him." She looks back up at me.

"And infatuation is the word, too, because it sure wasn't love. I was just pretty naïve for my age and it took a long time for me to realize and accept that about myself. For a long time, I remembered that pain of that loss, and… well, I was scared of reliving it again."

I stroke her cheek with my hand as I look down at her. "Why not go to Hawaii now? Move there, see the place and live your dream?"

She laughs lightly. "Oh, maybe some day I will. But land is so expensive there. Homes and the cost of living can be horrendous. And besides, I have Gram to look after now, and the Tribe to think of. And…" her eyes sparkle in the shaded light, "perhaps you, Ely."

She takes my hand in hers and brings it up to touch her cheek, clinching it tightly. Then she stands, the swing bumping her legs, as she unzips the jacket. Releasing my hand, she puts her arms over my shoulders and looks into my eyes.

"Yes… I think you're another reason. Maybe the truest of all."

Her eyes dart over my face in a searching mode, then they close and she leans her head sideways as her mouth beckons wantonly. I bend down and my lips touch hers, cautiously at first… then passionately as we hold each other in the new starlight. I feel the desire of lust swell deep in my extremities, and I know that she is feeling the same thing as she responds to the arousal.

My hands begin to rove over her back, to her rear and along her sides as we kiss. She begins more hesitantly, but shortly, she is caressing my arms and shoulders as the intensity of the moment builds. I allow my hand to lightly touch one of her breasts inside the jacket and I hear her gasp, and then feel her drive her hip into mine. The passion is tremendous and invigorating… all at the same time. I can tell without a doubt, that she is mine for the taking… right here…

right now... totally! Her breath is hot and enticing and I feel myself seek her body.

Before I know it, my hand has dropped to her khaki pants and the v that forms between her legs. I massage gently, then with a more steady action as I feel us moving closer to a conclusion. A moan escapes from her lips as we move in this heated trance. Reality is a million miles away as she responds to my touch. But somewhere, somehow... I know we have to stop this. We have to live in that reality, and I know... I desperately hate the fact... but I still know... that if this goes on even a second longer, we won't stop. Good old stupid me... has to be the hero... again. I know it is the right thing to do, but Sweet Jesus, my Lord... it is the hardest thing I've done in awhile! I kiss her hard, one last time, and step away from the embrace as her eyes open questioningly. Her voice is husky with sexual tension.

"What is it?" her voice whispers, "Please, Ely, what's wrong?" I still hold her, but at arms length. I look into that beautiful face and wonder to myself, yeah! What is wrong with me! I reach over and wipe the light sweat from her eyebrow and my voice is hoarse when I manage to speak.

"Nothing, Nettie... nothing at all. But this may not be the right place or time... do you think? I mean, I want to continue... you gotta believe me... I'd like to keep this up real bad but I want to be sure that you're not getting caught up wrongly in this thing. I care for you and..." I look at her as she tries to make sense out what I am saying, "you don't know me that well, Nettie. I carry a lot of baggage with me and some of it isn't pretty."

Her eyes are wide with disbelief, as if she is pleading for an answer. Then she drops hold of my arms and moves back by the swing. She turns her back to me and lowers her head. The blood is slowing it's pounding in my temples and I watch her bring a hand up to her mouth. She is crying. I move quickly to her but she pushes me away.

"No, don't. Please, Ely...just leave me alone a minute." Her voice is choked and I rack my brain for a way to fix this mess I've inadvertently caused. Damn! I feel like a piece of shit!

"Nettie, please... I don't mean to hurt you. I'm trying not to do that... don't you see?" I plead with her. After a minute that seems an eternity, she nods and faces me again, her eyes red and watery.

"Yeah, I hear you... but I don't believe in white knights anymore, thank you very much! You think I'm some kind of a whore, don't you?... well I'm not! I haven't been intimate with man for a long time... not since I was divorced! So, you're wrong about that!" she says in a heated voice, "in spite of how I acted here just now!"

I try to move toward her again, muttering the word "no" over and over, but she has her hands up, pushing the air in a "stay away" manner. "If you think that I would've made love to you here," her hand jabs down to the ground, "on this grass, then you're right! I would've! But that doesn't mean that I do it all of the time or even... for a long time... with anyone! I'm not a one night stand or a slut, Ely!" She says the last as tears well up in her eyes and roll gently down her cheeks.

"Jeeze, Annette, I know that!" I switch my eyes toward the house, then back to her, lowering my voice. "I know the kind of girl you are. Why do you think I'm here? I know who you are and what you are and I know that... or at least I feel that... you probably have feelings for me, too." I search her face for a clue to that question and feel good when she nods. "I just can't let anyone I care about get hurt. And until you know everything about me, getting hurt is a possibility... okay?"

I close my eyes tightly and then open them. "I'm not interested in one night stands either, Nettie. Those girls are a dime a dozen and that lifestyle doesn't appeal to me a bit. In fact, I decided a long time ago that I'd never fall in love again. Then I met you and for the life of me, I haven't been able to get you out've my mind since. Nettie, I care for you a lot. An awful lot, so you can't think I would ever think badly about you. You just can't, Nettie...?"

She looks at me for a minute, the emotions mixing over her beautiful face, then she tilts her head. The oversized jacket makes her appear even smaller than she already is. She seems little-girlish. A curious expression is on her face as she searches my eyes. Then her hand comes up to her mouth and her eyes become large. "My gosh... maybe you are a white knight after all."

I'm busy shaking my head. "No, not hardly. And after you learn more about me... I may seem a lot closer to the black knight than I do the white one. Trust me on that. And another thing, if God hadn't caught me when He did back there," I point my thumb to where we had embraced, "a team of wild horses or maybe even you, yourself... couldn't have stopped me from completing that act with you. So, keep that thought in mind when you think of me as a white night. I can be very dark sometimes. Scarily so, Nettie."

She let out a light laugh. "Well, you know, at first I thought you found me unattractive and weren't interested when you pushed me away. Then, I thought the reason was because you considered me a whore and now... you're telling me that for all practical purposes, you could've just raped me." she slowly shakes her head, "I just can't win with you, can I?"

A smile dominates her face now and her mood is lightened. I say a silent prayer of thanks as I cautiously move toward her. "You can. I mean, I've gotta notion that you've already won my heart, little girl," I extend my hand to hers and she takes it. "But you need to know me better than you do now before you consider letting loose of yours, I think." I squeeze her palm, "You and I have a lot in common. Like you, I lost something once that I couldn't afford to lose. And maybe like you... I think it's time to try life again. But while you've been spending your time learning how to look at life... I've spent mine, learning how not to look at it. Big difference there, ya know?"

She brings my hand up to her mouth and kisses it lightly. "It may be too late, Ely, about not losing my heart, I mean." Her eyes roll upward, "Are we nuts, Ely?... to be acting like this when we hardly know each other? I feel like I'm seventeen again."

It's my turn to laugh now as I sweep my other hand through her long hair. "Well if it's nuts, then I finally understand why the squirrels are so big on 'em, I'll tell ya that."

She smiles coyly up at me and asks, "So...where do we go from here, then?"

I glance over to my watch. "Well, I reckon I better be heading back and you'd better be heading inside." I'd learned that she tried to make it home every Saturday to go to church with "Gram" on Sunday. She usually caught a ride with one of the local townsfolk who worked in Marquette three days per week.

I look into her face. "I think we just take it slow and easy Nettie."

She nods and then twists her head and the grin gets larger. "I guess I knew, but I didn't really realize it until now. You've been calling me Nettie all night, haven't you?"

I shrug my shoulders. "Do you mind?"

"No, I think I like it. You're the only person except for Gram and my Dad who's ever called me that."

"I really like it. It seems to fit you." I stroke her hair again then she begins guiding us up toward the house. I voice a thought I'd had earlier.

"I hope we didn't get so loud that we woke up your grandmother?"

"Ha, that would only make her day." She swings our hands as we slowly move along, "You know what she told me while we were doing the dishes?"

I tip my head over, "No, what?"

"She said that that if I had any sense at all, I'd be after you like a dog on a bear," she glances up at me, "because your probably twice the man that white cop is and you're at least five times better looking! So, what'da think of that?"

"Oh five times better looking may be pushing it, I'd say only four… at the most." She chuckles as we reach the back door. Then she pulls off my jacket and hands it to me.

"About the Island, Ely… and the hovercraft. You'll let me know as soon as you find out anything, won't you?"

"Yeah, I will. Like I said, I'll call Monday. I have some mail at the boathouse, but I never got a chance to go through it." I tilt my head. "There may be something there," I add while shrugging my shoulders. She reaches up and runs her hand through my hair, letting her fingers float down my neck and shoulders. Then she sticks out her hand as if to shake, takes a deep breath and looks up at me.

"Well, Mr. Stone, I've had a very enjoyable evening. Thank you so much." I close her hand in mine and lean into her. She turns her mouth to mine and I kiss her, gently, passionately and adoringly. When we part, her eyes float up to me. I take her face in my palms and roll my thumbs over her cheeks, beneath her eyes and down both sides of her jaws. I try to speak, but the words are just whispers.

"You know, Nettie, I've known some pretty women. I've loved one of them and been with many others, all over the world. But as God is my witness, you are the most beautiful creature I've ever seen!"

I have to clear my throat because of the emotion that floods over me then. "We'll talk more and when you get to know me, if I'm lucky, maybe you'll still want me. But as for you winning, well… you've got a lock on my heart. Honest Injun… you do. Now get in that house before we start this all over again."

She opened the door, flipped a light switch and stepped inside. She looked at me with wide eyes and her voice was quiet.

"Good night, Ely, and… thank you."
I have to go quick as a stream of deep affection floods through me. "Good night, Nettie. I'll call you." I'm already turned around and back to the Charger that waits jealously in the front yard, when the porch light goes out.

Chapter Eleven
"You Go First"

Bruce's Crossing, Michigan.
Same Time.

Tran jammed the keys into the ignition and started the Mitsubishi. He eased out of the two-track and kept the lights off as he drove onto the road. Up ahead, he could see the Indian's lights. Tran was breathing heavily after running through the woods to get back to the car. Using his sleeve, he wiped the perspiration off his face. He squinted at the dark road as he pushed the accelerator down.

He was tired. He had been relieved at the marina by Kuan that morning. He had had the marina under surveillance since midnight. Then he had spoken to Chin. That ass of a water buffalo, Chin. He had once again reiterated to Tran that if the mission failed the whole team would have to sacrifice themselves. He meant die. Well fine, Tran thought. He'd agreed with the consequences of failure like all the others had, but Tran had no intention of dying.

He knew too many ways to survive, and although he loved his country, he just didn't seem to love it as much as the others did. If things went badly, Tran had long ago decided that he would just fade into the woodwork. Besides, think of what a smart man could accomplish in such a foolish and godless country. Think of the women, most of them hungry for sex. He would not die if he could help it.

He saw that he was gaining on the car ahead. He had trailed the two Indians all the way up here from Escanaba. Then he had driven past the policeman and found a small drive just large enough to back the car into. Then he'd crept back to the house.
He had weaseled his way close enough to the house to see that the Indian, his squaw and another old woman were eating dinner in a small kitchen. Tran had backed away from the window and surveyed the land around the building. He had just found a suitable observation post in front where he could see the Indian's car when the Indian appeared way over by a small stream. The bastard Indian must have exited out a back entrance.

So, Tran had had to work his way over there. He had to know what the Indian's plans were so he could complete this mission. It took

Tran a long while. And by the time he was close enough to hear, without being seen, the Indian and his squaw were sitting in a swing beneath the trees. Tran had listened to all of it. And he had watched as the two almost began screwing right there under that tree. But the stupid bastard Indian had stopped. Tran was amazed as he remembered it while following the Indian's car. The Indian squaw was very pretty and Tran had entertained fantasies of just going up and killing the Indian and then taking the squaw himself. But that could have gone wrong, too.

Maybe, when this mission was over, he would come back and visit the Indian squaw. After retrieving the package, they were all supposed to leave the country on their own. Yes, he thought, if things went well on the mission, he was coming back to see the little squaw. And, he decided right then, even if they didn't go well, he was still coming back. An evil smile rolled over his face as the thought formed in his mind. Maybe he would come back, rape the squaw and let her live. Then, she would tell the police that she'd been attacked by a white man with blond hair, only, nine months later she could give birth to a very unusual child.

Tran laughed out loud as he backed off on the accelerator. He was closing fast on the Indian, now. He had inched his way as close as he could to the house when the Indian Cop and his squaw had bid each other good night. The Indian had gone straight to his car and left. Tran had almost killed himself, running through the underbrush to get to his own car, but now, he was within tracking range. He waited until he saw the Indian's car round a curve, then he flipped on his lights.

Tran's short plan was pretty simple. He had called their contact here in Michigan while the Indian ate dinner. The man on the other end of the cell phone had told him that the roads in this area of the state were virtually desolate at night. There was only the occasional state police or game warden car that patrolled this vast wilderness after dark. While it was risky, it was really the only alternative, too. Tran had learned by listening that the Indian was driving back to Escanaba tonight. So he planned to pass the Indian, get ahead and find a good place to shoot him. He had a one-gallon can of gasoline in the trunk, and after the Indian was dead, he planned to light the car on fire.

If the police did an autopsy, they would learn the truth, but by that time, Tran and his team would be on their way home or not. And Tran knew that his fingerprints weren't on file anywhere in the world outside of China. Either way, he thought, the bastard Indian was going to die tonight. And since the Indian wasn't man enough to take a woman, then Tran would. He was going to fuck that Indian squaw and... he grinned evilly... he was going to hurt her as well. That was the great fun in taking a woman with such beauty. They always thought that they were much better than you, but when their pretty face winced with pain and they begged you to stop, they knew who was really the better! Tran laughed as he slammed his palm on the seat next to him and pushed down the gas pedal.

The Road Back To Escanaba,
The Followed.

A thousand things whirl around in my mind as I drive down the dark road. I realize that it is really dark as I spin my head around the windows. My mind keeps playing the night over and over again. Did she mean this? Should I have said that? There seem to be a hundred of them and no matter what, I can't change it now anyway. I draw my eyes into slits as I try to make out the bluish neon of some small critter's reflected eyes staring back at me up ahead. Boy, is it ever dark out here. I start applying the brake as I finally see that the eyes belong to a possum.

He gets across the road and I continue with my reverie. I remember how she felt in my arms and the curve of her breast, the way her hair was washed in golden sunlight as we're swinging back and forth. I brake for a stop sign, and for the first time, I notice that I actually have company out on this desolate piece of highway. I mash on the gas and the Charger pulls ahead. I'm not even a quarter mile down the road when my companion races up to pass. I see just enough of the other car to be able to say it's red as it blows on by. In the back of my mind, as I look at the fast-leaving car, something tells me that I've got a problem with my headlights. Then, the "white knight" thing pops into my brain.

Was she thinking of my car? You know, white knight driving a "Charger", when she said that? Or was she really saying that she doesn't believe that a man would care enough for her not to take advantage? Yeah, that's what she was saying alright. I see an occasional pair of amber eyes from deer standing on the roadside as I drive on and think. Man. I'm analyzing this too much. Questions. Man, have I got questions.

One of them is, what the hell am I doing messing with this girl? Do I think, even for a minute, that she'll be like Corina and be able to understand the killing I've done, the things I've seen and been a party to? Corina was the only other girl I'd ever felt like this with. Oh sure, there had been infatuations but not feelings like this. Corina had been from a different world than Annette - a culture where abject poverty and violence was often the norm. She'd known and understood what I did and why I did it because she herself, had been a part of that world – a part that eventually killed her. Would Nettie ever be able to do that – to understand? Maybe. She seemed sturdy enough to handle these truths, but shit, I guess we won't know until we sit down and talk, huh?

My next question is, do I want her to know these truths about me? In my heart, I honestly believe that I'd rather lose her than have her think badly of me. Maybe even badly enough… that she won't even want to be around me. I suddenly realize that at this stage, not being near her would probably kill me. Sonavabitch! I pound the steering wheel. I've lost it. I'm in love with her just surer than shit, and it's worse than it was the last time.

This verification of my romantic state is enough for me to force my thoughts away from Nettie and how it'll all turn out. I squint at the abnormal darkness outside. In the evening in Michigan's U.P., the roads turn into an eerie, wooded abyss with flowing strands of mist, hovering in the low spots. There is no ambient light out here and the world is black. But there is some illumination filtering down on the road so I look up through the Charger's windshield. Sure enough, there's a quarter moon resting in the sky.

Well, what the…? Then that thing in the back of my mind clicked, And I know why it was darker than usual. The Charger has hide-away headlights that are buried in the chrome grill. When the lights are turned on, little louvers in the grill are lifted to reveal the headlights. The one on the driver's side sticks. If I'm driving after dark, I always check to make sure that the louver is up before leaving. A little tap on the louver makes it do its thing and I'm on my way. I guess I forgot about it with e verything else on my feeble mind.

I look up ahead and remember this stretch of road. It's got a lot of curves in it, but another mile or so and the road straightens out enough to stop safely. Okay, I'll stop then. Now what do I do to keep my thoughts occupied elsewhere? I reach over and turn the radio on. The first song is almost over and it's Johnny Paycheck's, "Take This Job And Shove It". Then… next up is "Ghost Riders in the Sky". I just stare at the radio in the car's dash as the shinkakee rolls over me. When I look back up, there is a place to stop and fix my headlight. To say that I am glad to leave the radio, even for only a minute, would've been the world's greatest understatement. I am beginning not to like Johnny Cash anymore.

The Follower.

Tran was positioned on the only high ground he could find and it was on the same side of the road from which his target would approach. Not the best locale, but as his sniper instructor had told him, high ground beats level ground regardless of the angle. The rest of the land was flat and surrounded by a marsh. He had the rifle out and had zeroed the scope as much as he could with the low light. Their Michigan contact couldn't acquire them a starlight scope for the rifle but he had provided a low-light spotting scope of mediocre quality. It was better than nothing. The rifle though, was quite superb, a .308 caliber Remington automatic. It had no silencer but he doubted that anyone would be close enough to hear the shots anyway. The contact had called it a deer rifle and a common commodity here. The luxuries and freedoms these Americans took for granted still amazed Tran. He had the magazine loaded to capacity with hollowpoints and he planned to pepper the car's windshield as it came out of the curves below. Then, if the Indian didn't die in the first couple of seconds, he'd finish the job when he went down to burn the car.

Tran's only concern was the small marsh that ran between him and the road. The marsh was on both sides of the pavement and covered a lot of area. He'd had to drive past it to park on another small road, and then walk the dry land to his sniper perch. The distance to his car was at least a five-minute walk, but much less if he was running. Tran was an excellent marksman and that's why Chin had chosen him. His concern was that if something went wrong and the Indian was only wounded, his quarry would be out of his sight for a period of time while he made his way back to the road. Tran firmed up the grip of the rifle against his jaw while he sighted through the scope. He wouldn't let the Indian have that change. He would kill him with the first shots. The Indian should be coming any second now. As soon as he had that thought, Tran saw the single headlight appear.

He readied the gun, but … something was wrong. The Indian was stopping the car. Tran couldn't believe his luck. The Indian had stopped the car and was getting out. The distance was possibly fifty yards further than his chosen site, but surely not a problem. He watched the Indian walk to the front of the car while he quickly adjusted the scope ring for the range. He had the rifle back up and was focusing when he actually let loose a quiet laugh. The Indian had bent down and fiddled with the defective headlight. Now it was fixed, and his head was perfectly silhouetted against the light. Tran controlled his breathing and was still smiling as he began gently squeezing the trigger. This would be quick and easy after all.

The rifle fired but Tran had a fleeting glance of the Indian turning, moving and twisting at the same time. His eye had flinched for merely a milli-second, and then he saw the Indian up and running to the ditch. He followed him with the rifle, firing round after round that had to be coming close, but, suddenly, the Indian dove into the ditch on the other side of the road and was gone! Tran listened and heard splashing for several seconds then… nothing. Nothing but the hollow sounding gun shots as they echoed across the marsh in the darkness.

The Followed.

With that creepy song on the radio again, I begin to wonder if maybe Johnny Paycheck hasn't got it right as I brake the car to a stop and climb out. Most of my troubles began when I took this dumb job, anyway. Now here's this girl that's got me turned inside-out, old Marshall Dillon, the seagull lawyer, Amos the shaman and now, all the bullshit over the hovercraft. I bend down and tap the headlight louver and it begins its rise. Maybe I should tell'em to shove this job?

The light is almost fully exposed when I hear a screech over my shoulder, making me jump and turn involuntarily, my head snapping around. At the same instant, the headlight explodes and I feel pain as glass shatters into my neck and ear. I'm not waiting around to see if I'm bleeding, I drop to the asphalt and roll. Then I'm up and running, assholes and elbows, as the bullets chip and spark on the road all around me. I make the edge of the ditch and dive headfirst into it, sliding down in mud.

Something, a log or stone, gouges the meaty part of my right thigh as I hit bottom. Then I'm splashing in the ditch, moving and flipping over to look up at the little knob where I figure the shots came from. My right hand searches my back for the Glock. It's not there and I remember it's in the console of the car, where I'd put it before dinner.

It's quiet now except for the shots echoing in the distance. Then the heron screeches again somewhere out in the marsh. Whoever is up there is good. If the heron's screech hadn't scared me, I'd be a closed casket, sure as hell. I inch up to peer over at the knob, and then ease back down. My mind starts figuring. I need to get to my weapon. My opponent, though, has a rifle. I don't. Even with the pistol, in this open area, he'll take me out in a gunfight. Nope, I got'ta get my ass out'ta here and do it ASAP. I look all around the marsh and know that I'll get nailed as soon as I move from here.

Only option then…get the bad guy or guys to come to me. Now how to do that? My mind reels as I ponder who it is? how many they are? and what the hell is going on? Quickly, I decide that I can only answer one of the questions and that's how many? There's probably only one, because if they had the numbers, there would've been another one down here in the ditch in case something went wrong. Now who they are may make a difference for my little plan. If they know me, then they won't buy it. If they don't, then shit, it's still only 50/50.

I figure whoever is up there can't move without losing sight of me for several seconds. That means that they'll probably sit on me until daylight or until another car comes past. With tomorrow being Sunday, I know that chances of seeing a car are slim to none before well past dawn. And glancing around quickly, I know I'm toast if I'm still in this ditch when it gets light. He'll pick me off as easy as pinching lint off a sweater. So I've got to get him down here, but I can't stick around to shake hands and say howdy, either. He'll be below the cattails and I'll be out'ta his sight for several seconds, and that's going to be the only chance I have. I can hear the Charger idling on the road above when I start moaning out loud.

"Ohhhh. help… please? Help me. Ohhhh… I'm a police officer. You've hit me bad.. If you help me now before it's too late.. it might all be okay, help me."

I throw in a couple of coughs for good measure and wait. I'll give it a few more seconds, but then I've got to make a break for the car. If he buys it, I've got a chance. If he doesn't, he'll probably cap me when I climb up out'ta the ditch. I've been counting by thousands in my head, and now, I'm up and running for the Charger. Mud flings off my boots as I make the car, grab the handle, fling the door wide and leap in. My hand pulls the slap stick into drive and I jam the gas pedal to the floor while leaning over to the passenger side. The car leaps up and squeals as she gathers momentum on the cool pavement. I'm frantically jabbing at the headlight switch until they go out then I'm peering over the wheel into the darkness at close to eighty miles an hour.

The Follower.

Tran listened for any sound. His eyes scanned the ditch with the spotter scope and he saw nothing. He could've hit him, he thought. He'd had fleeting pictures in the scope as the Indian ran and he was quite sure that he'd connected with one of the shots. He was pondering what to do next when he heard the Indian moan. Quickly then, the moans grew more urgent. The Indian was pleading for his life. "Ha," Tran smiled, so much for the brave and noble American Savage. The bastard was whimpering like a whipped child. Tran was beginning to move down when he stopped. He stepped back up to the perch and looked along the ditch.

Could the Indian be faking? Could he have figured out this situation so quickly? Was he that good? He rubbed a hand over his chin as he looked below. No, he didn't think so. He was just an Indian policeman who didn't know enough to take a woman when he had the chance. That, thought Tran, was evidence enough of the man's ignorance. No, he'd hit the Indian and he was hurt badly. Now, he would go down and apply the coup de grace. Then he would put him in his car, drive it off the road and light it on fire. Time was getting short thought Tran, as he turned and started for the road. He would have to hurry.

As he trotted up to his car, Tran heard tires screeching and a car engine bellowing up on the road. He swung the rifle up in time to see the Indian's car blast past the two-track where he stood. Then it was gone, leaving only the throb of its big engine in the distance. Tran screamed an obscenity in Chinese as he threw the rifle in the backseat and started the car. "You'll die, Indian!" he croaked, "You're a dead man!" And the red Mitsubishi raced out of the two-track and onto the blacktop in pursuit.

The followed.

I finally rise up in the seat and take a firm grip on the wheel with both hands. I have to swerve quickly to miss the ditch as I right the car's course. No shots have been fired that I can tell. I stab my eyes to the rearview mirror and see headlights swarming the treetops behind me. My heart pounds up into my throat as I flip the lights back on. Then I snap open the console and pull out the Glock, unsnapping the thumb-break, shaking the pistol out of the holster and placing the weapon between my legs. The road ahead is misty and dark as the Charger and I shoot through the night. My foot pops off the gas as I brake into a curve and try to figure out what to do next. I can feel blood dripping onto the jacket and a stinging sensation on my neck and ear. My right leg hurts, too.

What the hell is going on here? The radio is still playing softly as I swing the car through the curving road. Okay… enough of this shit! Do I pick a stand, stop and fight? Or do I run? Fight or flight - that old cop axiom. Stopping and fighting was alright except for one thing. He knows who I am and probably what armament I'm carrying. I don't know squat about him except that he has at least one sniper rifle, and it sounds like a 7.62 caliber. Or maybe a .308. Same thing, I lean my shoulders into another turn. What else does he have, say for close-in work? Maybe an assault weapon or a machine pistol? "Shit!" My eyes see in the outside mirror that the sonava'bitch is coming up fast! I can probably lose him. I get out of these curves and to a straightaway, I'll kick her in the ass and… then what? Jump off somewhere ahead of him, then get on his ass and see where it leads?

That sounds like the best plan and I opt for it. I feel the coolness ebbing through me now, back to my old haunting ways. Whoever it is back there, they want me dead and have come close to making it happen. The roadside is a blur. I feel my eyes slant as I look up at the rearview mirror. The prick had his bright lights on, too. Obviously, a very inconsiderate cocksucker back there. And as I watch, he pulls up even closer. The terrain has switched back to heavy timber again and we are flying through the twisty road. Most of the time, there is just inches between his vehicle and mine.

Well, maybe my plan isn't going to work after all. I hear the tires squawk as I gun it coming out of a curve and pour on the power for a straightaway. Glancing at my dash, I see that all the gauges are good. I slap the shifter down into second gear and feel the Charger bark at the adjustment. Then I nail my foot to the floor. The speed jumps up as the Charger responds. I hold the gas pedal down until the tachometer reaches redline, then pop the shifter back into drive. I am hauling ass now! My eyes leap to the mirror and I see that my pal hasn't been able to keep up. I brake for the next curve, a little late, and have too much speed going in. I barely get the car back under control before he is on me again – close-up. Everything is twisting, turning curves. Well, either the prick knows how to drive or he is crazy. I took that last curve at close to sixty. Nope, things aren't working out like I planned. I begin braking for the next switchback. Then the deer come.

Deer, lots of them, are floating all over my car! Two are leaping over the hood, in a weird kind of slow motion. Out of my left eye, I see the white bellies of deer sailing past my window and over the roof followed by a knock on the top! Out of my right eye, I see the white underbodies of the deer as they sail over and down on the passenger side! Simultaneously in the mirror, I see others as they bound over the fast moving car's trunk! Ahead they're illuminated by the lights as they leap across the road. A whole herd is jumping over me as I drive through them and I know I'm going to die after all! Then they're gone, and the road ahead is empty.

My eyes dart to the mirror and the road behind is just as vacant. We were bumper to bumper when the deer crossed and somehow, by the grace of the Great Good Spirit, I'd made it through. As my eyes wander over the darkness in the mirror, I think maybe my pursuer wasn't so lucky. I continue on about a half mile, easing speed as I keep my eyes glued to the mirrors. Still nothing. There is the possibility that he is running with his lights off, but even he wouldn't be that nuts on this road. He also might've given up the chase but the odds say differently to me. It is a miracle that I made through that deer herd. I slow the

Charger even more and start looking for a turnaround. Still nothing in the mirrors as I swing a uturn and head back, listening to the equal explosions of thunder from the car's pipes and my pounding heart.

I don't see him. He could be parked and waiting. So far, he seems smart enough for that ploy. But a gut feeling tells me, "Uh, uh", that's not what's going on here. As I near the spot where the deer crossed, I switch the lights off and slow the car down. Now, I can make out some fragmented light up ahead.

Rounding the curve, I see his car. It is off in the ditch, its right side heavy into a slant, headlights pointed crazily at the cattails. I ease the Charger up slow with my left hand cradling the Glock out of the window. I come to a stop about seventy-five yards from the other car. Keeping my eyes shifting over the area, my right hand pops off the dome light cover and I twist out the light bulb, dropping both onto the seat. I switch the gun to my right hand and open the door, climbing out low into a crouch. Something bumps and I hear glass breaking from the direction of the car. My aim snaps that way. Nothing. Then, someone moaning, someone uttering words. They weren't English, maybe Vietnamese, Chinese or something else Oriental.

My concentration is complete. I've switched back into a think and act routine that I haven't used in a long time. My training guides my moves as I begin toward the wrecked car. My breathing is fast but not too fast. My heartbeat is high, but again, not too high. These feelings are not at all unfamiliar to me. I am at home in this element, just a bit removed. I advance in a weaver style. Left body positioned forward, weapon aimed with my right arm and supported by the forward left, so I can aim right down the barrel. I crouch low as I constantly pivot my weapon, sweeping the area, and side-stepping ahead. My boots squish water as I move. I freeze. More movement and glass tinkling. The sound of metal denting. More moaning, too. I can make out something, a large blob of cattails, or a heavy log, on the vehicle's hood, but not much more. It doesn't seem threatening, whatever it is. I continue on. The agony is evident from the occupant in the car. His low moans are anguished. They mix with the damaged car's hissing radiator and engine tics as the coolant drips noisily.

A branch cracks! My weapon automatically twists to the road behind the wrecked car as I scan the area back and forth, bending lower. Then a blur steps out from the roadside and I fire. It is a deer! Another stupid ass deer! I hit it because it stumbles as it makes the treeline at a run on the other side of the road. My attention snaps back to the car. Still no movement, but the moaning has stopped now. I ease to a kneeling position, the pain in my leg reminding me it is still there. I survey the wrecked car. I've been in the open for way too long now but there isn't any cover. And besides, if they were able, whoever is in that car would've already sent shots my way. Sounds again. As I listen to the low agonizing moans, I'm pretty sure I'm right. I rise up and continue ahead, water sloshing from my muddy boots.

Closer to the car now, I can see a body on the vehicle's hood. It isn't moving. I move up, my weapon swiveling from side to side. The body on the hood is that of a deer, its head lying over the passenger side of the hood. I can also see the driver now and he's hurt badly. There is a lot of blood around his face. The passenger side of the car is deep into the ditch, the window and door secure. The driver is alone. I ease closer and peer in. The deer's body had gone right through the windshield and into the front seat. The deer had frantically kicked while in its death throes. The animal had tried hard to keep living but it hadn't made it. And it had done a lot of damage to the driver in the process.

Both of his arms appear to be broken. His face has deep lacerations where the deer's rear hooves have kicked and sliced him up. He probably has a broken nose, too. The man looks up at me from a deformed face and coughs, foamy blood dribbling down his chin. I lower my weapon and stand up straight, feeling the adrenalin backing off. The car is a red Mitsubishi. I'd seen one earlier today at the marina. Okay, so that's one coincidence. I tilt forward and moderately move the man's arms to a chorus of guttural groans. Yep, broken. Then I tuck the Glock into my pants and lean closer into the car, allowing only my arms to touch the sides of the door. The driver's window is shattered and glass is everywhere. I peer into the backseat and see a scoped deer-hunting rifle half onto the floorboard. The man's eyes follow me as he breathes sparingly. I survey his face. It's very strange, stranger than even his injuries can explain. The skin around his left eye is torn loose, and the flap of hanging tissue reveals a weird apparition. There's still other skin, like scar tissue, underneath that, that was dislodged, giving the guy an Oriental look to the one eye and a Caucasian appearance to the other. It strikes me as bizarre, but I'd seen accidents do some strange things to the human body, so I look back into the abnormal face.

"Why're you trying to kill me?"

The man only wheezes as his eyes remain on me. I notice that he has blond hair. Again, like the guy at the marina driving a red car just like this. Uh, huh. Coincidence number two. I clear the phlegm from my throat, turn and spit, and then look back at him.

"I know you were at the marina this morning. Now, either you tell me what's going on and who sent you or I'm going to leave you here to die. Do you understand me?" I raise my voice for effect, but the brown eyes themselves never change their character as they watch me. I realize then that he has completely stopped the moaning, too. He seems to be controlling it and the pain. That's odd. Then he speaks.

"You won't leave me to die, policeman. You can't and I know this. So, before I get any worse, you had better call someone to assist me."

The words are low and the English is succinct. There is a gun sticking out of a clip-on holster on his belt and I lean over, popping the holster off his pants. He groans mightily as I pull it loose. The pistol is a .380 Berretta automatic. I stuff it in my jacket pocket and look down at him.

"Well, I'm waiting for answers pal!"

The deranged eyes just return my look. I shrug my shoulders.

I shrug. "Okay, cocksucker." Then, lean deeper into the car and over him to pop the glove compartment. He groans as my weight bears down on him. Nothing. I drop the visors and a flurry of paperwork falls from the driver's side. I hold it up to the meager moonlight and see that it is a Hertz rental agreement, registered to a Comstock Corporation. I look back at him as his eyes stay with me.

"What's this Comstock Corporation? Are you working for them?"

He says nothing. I stuff the papers back over the visor and lean back into the car. "Okay, asshole, let's do it the hard way then!"

I search his shirt and jacket pockets. I find a spotting scope, a pack of Juicy Fruit gum and a little flip cell phone but nothing else. The eyes continue to stare out at me and there is some definite malevolence in them, all mixed up with the pain as I pat his pants pockets down. Then I roll him to his side and he yelps painfully. I find the wallet in his back pocket. I pull it out and turn him back. I can see that he's choking on blood, which is flowing down his throat from the broken nose. He shakes his head, trying to get the nasal passages clear again. Apparently, his nose has to remain open in order for him to breath. He's got too much blood dripping down his throat and he needs his nose clear for an airway. The strange eyes are even more pronounced. I adjust his head until he begins to breathe better. He spits blood from his mouth, while giving me a loathing stare. I paw through the wallet while talking to him.

"Kind'a hard ta breath there, eh partner? Well now, it says here that your name is Michael Nesmith. Hmm, weren't you with the Monkies. You know. That famous rock and roll band from the '60s? Boy, I guess it'll be hard for you sing with that broken nose, huh? You'd probably sound like you have a really bad sinus infection, don'cha think?"

He gives me more of the nasty looks. Then my pal finally utters some words. "Fuck you, Indian!" The words croak out as he spits more blood with that frothy texture to it. Maybe one of his ribs nicked a lung, but I don't think so. From my experience, he's not too bad. Shock though, can be a weird thing. People react differently to it. I shake my head and make a clicking sound with my tongue.

"Now, is that any way to talk to man who can save your life?" I point a finger at him, "You know, if you keep making rude comments, I might just go away and leave you here all alone to think about being a good boy and minding your manners."

He goes into a coughing fit, and when it clears, the ugly eyes are watering. He looks at me. "You should have fucked that woman tonight, Indian. You are a fool." He laughs, but the effort causes him pain. "All those things you told her about being sure. Women do not care about such things, Indian. You should have fucked her when you had the chance."

His breath is coming in wheezes and the agony must be increasing For him. It must hurt for him to talk too much. "I was going back to fuck her for you when it was finished here." He snickers again, but it causes him pain. "We will finish in several days and perhaps, when I get out of the hospital, I will then pay your woman a proper visit." He looks up at me and grins. The deformed and scarred face, covered with blood, is evil.

"Then I will fuck that squaw of yours until she begs for more!" He lapses into another coughing fit, then looks at me with those weird eyes.

"And even with casts on my arms, I will still be able to do to her what you could not. So do not threaten me, Indian. Just be a good policeman and go call for help."

He lowers his eyes as if the conversation is over. All of a sudden, I am quite happy to see him in pain. "Mmm, well, looks like that's not gonna work out now... is it?" I tap the hard plastic driver's license on the man's broken nose and he winces as shiny tears run down his face.

"Besides, cockbreath, don't you know that "squaw" is a derogative term. Trust me pal, she's not a squaw." I tap the license even harder and he blubbers distressfully while peering at me through watery eyes. There's also some newly formed concern on his face. I unbutton my jacket pocket and dig around for the ink pen I keep there. Then I reach back in the car and pull the Hertz envelope from the visor, leaving the paperwork there. I copy the license number, name and date of birth onto the envelope in the flimsy light and stuff it and the pen back in my pocket. Then I hold the license by the edges and blow breath on it, like I am steaming up a pair of glasses to clean,

and wipe each flat surface on my damp shirt. "Old habits." I'm
worried about fingerprints. There'll be some on the paper but
moisture will probably claim them. Still holding the I.D. on edge, I
slip the license back inside the wallet then wipe the leather clean
before flipping it to the floorboard. I feel my mood growing dark, and
that's not a good sign.

So, the prick had been watching us tonight. And he was close
enough to hear our conversation, too. I feel my ears grow warm as I
stare back into his tormented eyes. I rise up and cast my sight in both
directions on the road. It's void of everything but darkness. Then I
turn and walk back to where I fired the Glock and lay down on the
pavement, flat on my belly. My eyes use the scarce moonlight to scan
the asphalt and shortly, I see it. I get to my feet and move over,
stooping to retrieve the shell casing, then pocket it. My eyes cut back
to the red car and I am sure of a couple of things. I can hear the
Charger idling softly from here, as thoughts avalanche through my
mind.

One, this guy and that car were at the marina this morning. Two,
he'd followed us up here. Three, he'd tried to kill me and almost
succeeded. Four, he only referred to me as "Indian" or "Policeman"
so whatever it was about, it probably wasn't my colorful Coast Guard
past. Five, he'd said "we", meaning that there were more than him
and finally six, whatever "it" was, "it" was working off a plan. And it
all adds up to a professional plan. And that means that he's a pro. The
control of his pain, the way he talks, the sniper attack, everything.
He's in shock and that probably accounts for most of what he's
already said. No doubt, he wouldn't have said anything if he weren't
so badly injured. And what I've got, is probably all I'm going to get.

He isn't going to tell me anything else. What a dilemma. What he's
said about Nettie both bothered, and scared me. Morse's words from
this morning about people around me getting hurt briefly floats through
my mind. Nope. I sure don't want this cockbite loose and going after
Nettie. And if they tried for me once, they'll probably try again. And
they might be successful next time.

Whatever is going on, it's big. Big enough to kill a cop for. And I'm
going to keep Annette clear of it. Anyway I don't have a choice. It is
probably no more than a 50/50 chance that someone, a state cop or
delivery person, will drive by and find him in the next couple of
hours. And that's betting that he can hang on that long, too. Nope, I
decide, way too much at stake here. I can feel the heat radiate to my
temples as I approach the car again. I let my sight direct down to the
injured man. Finally, he brings his distressed eyes up to meet mine.
Yeah, that look says it all pal. You're a pro, alright. I don't know for

who, or for what, but you've got the look. It's all over your ass. I know that my mood is going black and that it probably shows on my face, but I lean forward anyhow, and my voice comes out in a whisper.

"So you're not going to tell me anything, then?"
He runs his tortured gaze over my face and he knows something isn't right. His countenance takes on a quizzical look as he utters,

"Who are you?" Then he tries to buck up his resolve again. But it doesn't work. I can see an element of terror in his deformed eyes now that hasn't been present before. But he's still going to try. Too bad for you, partner.

"You can leave, Indian. I will make it until someone comes along. I am sorry for what I said about the woman. I am injured and not thinking clearly. But I know you cannot hurt me, so no more threats! You are a policeman and I know this! All I did was to try to scare you, nothing more. Even if you do not help me," he spits more blood, "then I will still survive and perhaps you will only get into minor trouble. But if you are thinking of other things, then remember. I am not alone here. My friends will avenge me!"

He manages to elevate his voice for the last words and they are tinged with an element of fright, making his voice even higher. I lean back, knowing that his alarm is warranted. "If all you were doing was trying to scare me pal, then you need some serious brushing up on Halloween."

He looks up at me and begins to shake a little. His broken arms lay kiddy-wampus to the norm and I feel my eyes slant at him. He's a pitiful sight, but as far as I'm concerned, a very dangerous one. If he's made contact with his partner or partners, he's given them information and it includes Annette. I don't like that. Besides, when I was employed in this line of work, we didn't hurt innocents. But we routinely paraphrased a verse from the Good Book that went like, "Do Unto Others As… They Would Surely Do Unto You". He'd surely tried his best to kill me a little while ago. Being a pro, he should know that verse, especially since he's a player, and by all accounts, the game's afoot.

His abnormal eyes jump out at me again, a mixture of dread and anguish as he stutters. "Did you hear me? I said leave me alone! I will be fine! But remember what I said Indian! If you do more, then they will make it their business to find you", his grotesque eyes bulge with horror, "and you will be a dead man!"

I just nod my head once. "Uh, huh. But you go first, okay?" His freakish eyes go three times the size of normal as I reach in with my fingers and squeeze his nose together.

Chapter Twelve
A Team Player?

The Boathouse,
Escanaba, Mi.
Present Day, the morning after.

I walk out of the bathroom, swabbing myself with a towel and
head straight for the wall thermostat. If I were smart, I would've
turned the heat up before I climbed in the tub to soak. But nobody's
ever accused me of intelligence, so I have an out. I crank the dial up
and pad my way back into the room, shaking off the chill. The steam
has almost cleared from the mirror now and a quick swipe of the
towel does the rest. I turn backwards and push my butt out, staring
over my shoulder at the long grooved wound that crosses the back of
my right thigh just below the tattoo.

The bullet has grazed a quarter-of-an-inch deep furrow, straight
across the meat. I let my eyes wander up to the tattoo. It is simple in
design and appearance. A Trojan Horse placed high on my right leg,
close to the hip. Everyone on the team got the same tattoo, in the
same place, when we were disbanded. It was the Old Man's idea, and
when we entered the tattoo shop in Norfolk, Virginia, he'd been the
first one to have the ink applied.

I maneuver myself around and look down at the old groove on the
front of my other thigh. A bullet wound from another time and place.
That one had almost bled me dry. It's nice though, having matching
bullet wounds on each leg. Sheeeeit. I send my attention back to the
newest addition of my body art. There'd been a lot of bleeding, but
with all the mud and wetness I'd carried away from the ditch, I didn't
even know that a bullet had hit me until I'd undressed and showered
last night.

It's painful, but I figure I'll live. I grab the antibiotic ointment and
gauze bandage I found in a first-aid kit, and dab the salve over the
wound. Then I pull off the plastic tabs and stick the big bandage on,
all the way around the upper leg. Next, I take a gander at my neck and
ear. I'd pulled out several small shards of glass, but the old flight
jacket collar had stopped most of the damage there. The small
lacerations are hardly noticeable. I pull on a pair of underwear and
apply some deodorant. That is about it since I've already shaved and

brushed my teeth, so I flip off the switch and grab the Glock off the sink. I exit and move over to the closet.

I decide to wear the uniform shirt, badge and a pair of jeans. I'm sure Morse won't approve, but what's a little humor between friends, that's what I always say. Besides, those polyester uniform pants might be a little scratchy on my leg today. It takes a little coaxing to get the pants on over the wound without me crying but I manage. I strap the Glock into an ankle holster and look at the box containing the Colt. I decide to carry it, too. An old Gunner's Mate told me once, that the only thing you can never get enough of is firepower. I've found that to be true over the years.

After lacing up the jungle boots I'd pulled from my duffle, I start on the Colt. I unsnap the holster from its duty belt and thread it onto my own deerhide one, along with two magazine pouches. I check the .45, dry-fire it and chamber a round, apply the safety and drop it into the holster, snapping the thumb-break. Then I load ammunition into the two magazine clips and put them into the pouches. After pocketing my wallet, jackknife, comb and pocket change, I step to the mirror again.

A haggard Indian faces me and from the looks of him, his ass is in deep doo doo. Somebody or somebodies, are trying to kill him and he doesn't have the foggiest idea why. He stopped one of them last night but there are more out there... someplace. The dead eyes that stare out at me have that familiar haunted look. The Ghost is punched-in and on the clock.

I shake my head at the apparition and turn away from the reflection. Since I'm back in the game, even though I don't know why, I figure I'd better get started. The wall mounted electric heaters have warmed the place fast and it's hot now. I turn the thermostat down as I move over and open the door to allow some warmth to escape. Then I make my way over to the desk, and ease down gently onto the chair. The leg hurts and even though I keep telling myself it's not that bad, it still hurts. I'd whine if there was anyone around for sympathy. I pick up a card that was stuck in the door last night. MAJOR ALAN SHEARS, UNITED STATES AIR FORCE OFFICE of SPECIAL INVESTIGATIONS. ("AFOSI" for us military folks who use acronyms for everything).

The Air Force's criminal investigation division. The card has the Air Force shield on it and I rub my thumb over it as I flip this stuff over in my head. Now, who the hell is he and why does he want to talk with me? I turn the card end over end as I tap it on the desktop. I have a shit-load of problems here, the least of which seems to be some Air Force Sherlock Holmes. Unless... he's tied in with that little escapade last night.

I'd made it home safely enough last night after leaving the accident scene. And I'm confident that the state cops will rule the Monkey's death an accident. Michael Nesmith should just end up as another car/deer accident fatality on Michigan's rural roads. I'll check on it to be sure though.

I arrived back in Escanaba at about 3:30 this morning. One lone city cop picked me up at the Dairy Queen and followed me because of the single headlight. He stopped at the parking lot of the marina when I pulled into the boathouse parking space. He watched as I slowly climbed out of the Charger and waved at him. He waved back and pulled out of the lot after assuring himself of who I was. I was filthy with dried mud and wet clothes, but the distance and low light was just enough to conceal my appearance.

By this time, my leg was hurting pretty bad. The car's interior is black so I just brushed the mud off the driver's seat and quickly checked the headlight. The round exploded on impact, telling me that my "almost" assassin was probably using hollow points in that deer rifle. The damage to the car was minimal because of that, the steel surrounding the headlight having a hard molecular structure. But if the bullet had connected with my head like Mr. Nesmith intended, it would've been a whole different story. The only other damage I found was a scuff mark where a deer's hoof had nicked the car's top as it sailed over. I covered the car and hobbled up to the door to find this business card. I stop tamping the card and glance over at the flashing light on the answering machine.

There had been at least one call this morning, but I was soaking in the tub and just didn't give a care. I reach over and push the "all play" button. Morse's voice came over the announcement: "Hello, you've reached the Pukaskwa Tribal Police Substation. No one is available to take your call but if you leave a message, an officer will get back to you...beep."

"Mr. Stone, this is Major Shears, Air Force Office of Special Investigations. I'm calling this morning because I still haven't heard from you yet. We left you a card yesterday and called your machine twice last evening. It is imperative that we speak with you regarding an investigation that involves Muskrat Island. Please call us at the cell number on the card 202-936-6651. This is URGENT, MR STONE. Thank you."... Click...beep. Another one starts.

"Uh, yes. Hello, Mr. Stone, my name is Captain Mussenberg, Air Force OSI. It's 8pm and I'm calling again for Major Shears. Uh, we left a card earlier today and also called and left a message. I'm just leaving another. The cell phone where we can be reached is 202-936-

6651. Please call ASAP. Uh, thanks."…click…beep. Then I hear my favorite voice as it begins.

"Stone… this is Morse! What the hell's going on now? I stopped back by the substation today and there's a card from the Air Force CID stuck in the door! I get back to the reservation and find out that they have been here, wanting to know about the Island. Hennessey told'em they had to talk to you and gave them this number. Look I… well I just… I just would like to know what's going on… if it affects the tribe or the department… okay? Give me a call"…click…beep.

And now the Wingnut again. "Hello Mr. Stone. My name is Alan Shears, US Air Force, OSI. I need to speak with you regarding an on-going investigation. I left a card on your door this morning and apparently, you haven't returned yet. Anyway, the number is 202-936-6651. You can call anytime. I appreciate your cooperation." Thank you and goodbye."…click… beep…
A mechanical voice finished with, "No more messages…beep."
and I watch the little light flash while the machine rewinds the tape.

Well, isn't that interesting. So, the Air Force wanted to talk to me about the Island. Now, two plus two gets the answer four. So, if that addition works right, then maybe adding something to something will get me some answers, too. I was thinking last night that all my troubles started when I took this job. Really though, my problems seem to have showed up since I took over responsibilities for the Island. Maybe, just maybe, the two and two here is that my little assassin from last night is tied in with these Air Force guys. Maybe. If I were to add these two together, would I get an answer? The answer to who's trying to snuff me? A chirping sound begins over by the couch and my eyes shoot that direction. It's coming from the cell phone I took off the Monkey last night. I drop the card and raise up as quickly as I can, then head over to the end table and pick up the chirping phone.

"Hello… Mike?… hello?" The voice was that of a white man. My mind races as I try to figure a course of action. Looking down, I grab up a piece of mail and tear the envelope apart and begin wadding it up as I hold it to the mouthpiece. I drop my voice and say "Hello?" The answer comes quick. "Mike… are you there?… there seems to be much static on the line. Can you hear me?"

I drop my voice further, "Lo… I can't …ear …u," My mind is doing the Indianapolis 500, trying to make the next move the right one. Whoever is on the other end of this phone, is a part of the attempt on my life last night. I want to know more without giving the fact away that their buddy is dead. I suddenly remember the Oriental words I'd heard when I approached the wrecked car last night. It's worth a shot. I say the only thing that comes to mind while I continue to crinkle the paper into the mouthpiece.

"Lo… lo… Choy yoy dinki dow!…Du me Mi!" It's Vietnamese and I hope it works. It does.

A stream of Oriental words flow angrily from the caller before he switches to English… "and you will not speak Chinese, either! Tran, we have a bad connection. I will call you later to see if you have accomplished your task! Remember what I have said! I mean this, you must be careful!"… click…the line was dead. I fold the phone up and am still looking at it when a knock at the doorway brings my eyes up to see two Air Force officers. One of them is a black Captain and the other, a majorly pissed-off looking Major.

**The Budget Host Motel,
Room 231, Marquette, Mi
Same Day**

Chin closed the flip phone and laid it on the sink. Then he rose up, pulled toilet paper from the wall and finally, flushed the toilet. His stomach still bubbled as he pulled his trousers up and fastened them. He carefully rinsed his hands in the sink and dried them before picking up the phone and moving into his room. As he did, the phone on the bed stand rang. He moved over past the low-playing television and answered it. "This is Robert," he said, and then waited.
Kuan cleared his throat. "This is Adam. This line is secure. It is a payphone inside the marina. We have a problem. The Island Indian is back."

Chin recognized the deep voice right away. He was also surprised as he looked at the closed cell phone he was still holding. "Are you sure? I just spoke with Tran. We had a bad connection, so I do not know any details. Perhaps someone has only driven the Indian's car back after Tran completed his task."

"No, it is he. I have seen him moving about inside the building and he is wearing the Indian police uniform and carrying a sidearm. He…wait… the American Air Force is just now walking up to his door as we speak."

Chin swore under his breath. "Very well. We must eliminate this problem right away. I will try again to call Tran back. If you hear from him before I do, tell him he lost the Indian somewhere and now he is back there. Tell him to meet you at the park where we first rendezvoused," Chin looked at his watch, "at seven o'clock tonight. I will call."

Kuan hesitated on the other end of the phone, and then began.

"Sir, do you not think that the team on the Island could handle the Indian if he reappears? He seems to be a simple Indian policeman. Begging your pardon, sir, but it seems foolish to risk this task here, so close to our base of operations. We could call the team and alert them to his arrival."

Chin's stomach grumbled and his hand went to it reflexively. "Perhaps you are right, I do not know yet. If Tran had done his work properly, we would not be discussing this now, and thus, would not be plagued with this problem. So, whatever we decide, it will be carried out quickly and professionally this time! Do you understand?"

"Yes sir! And please sir... I did not wish to offend, only to suggest."

"Yes, yes, I know that. Do not worry about it. We will decide tonight." Chin hesitated as a new thought passed through his mind and a decision followed. "We will decide what to do tonight unless... you see an opportunity to eradicate this problem sooner... without difficulty. If that opportunity should avail itself, then take action. Do you understand, Kuan?"

"Yes sir, I will accomplish this task, should the opportunity present itself. I understand, sir."

Chin breathed easier as he hung up the phone and felt a pang go through his belly. It had to be the rich American food, he thought. His digestive tract was not used to such delicacies as pizza, ribs and Burger King Whoppers. His stomach growled and he began heading toward the bathroom again. He'd had a nervous stomach since last night when Tran had failed to call. The last thing he needed was to be sick on a mission. The last time he fell ill like this on a mission was in Afghanistan, when he was observing with the Russians during that war. He'd nearly been killed then. Yes, it had to be the food. But as he walked into the tiled room, he looked at the cell phone still in his hand. And suddenly, he wasn't so sure.

The Boathouse,
Escanaba, Mi
Same Day

I look up and force a smile at the daring young men without their flying machines. I lay the envelope and phone down on the table and stand. "Howdy, can I help you guys?"
The two officers look at me as I stand, trying to hide a grimace. Both are wearing summer weight Air Force uniforms with blue windbreakers and service dress blue saucer caps. The major half raises a pointed finger at me.

"Are you Stone?" I nod my head and reach my hand to the nametag on my right breast, turning it up and looking down at it.

"Yeah, it seems that would be me alright," I smile back at them. The Major looks annoyed as he bumps his head toward the room. "Can we come in?"

"Sure," I make a sweeping motion with my hand, "So, what brings the Air Force to my door this bright and cherry fall day?" Both officers enter and remove their caps. The Major indicates his partner with a palmed hand.

"This is Captain Pete Mussenberg and I'm Major Al Shears. We're with the Office of Special Investigations, Mr. Stone, and...we've been trying to get in touch with you."

I just nod. I do extend my hand when the black guy offers his. We all shake. The major looks around the office while continuing. "Uh, we left several messages and I left my card yesterday. So...," he brings his eyes back to mine, "I assume you didn't get those?"

Well. So, the Major's a little pissed. My, my. I must tread lightly then. "No, I got'em Major. I found the card this morning, when I got in, and just listened to the messages a few minutes ago." I turned to the other officer. "I've got the Major's card, but... do you happen to have one too, Captain?" I grin happily.

The black officer seems a bit taken aback, as he and the Major exchange glances, but he replies, "Yes, I do," and pulls a card from his inside jacket pocket and passed it to me. I take the card and walk over to the desk, laying it down next to the Major's.

I turn back to them. "Thanks. Now, I'm sorry I couldn't get back to you right away, but I was tied up out of town last night." I look over at the couch and point. "You guys want ta sit down?" Both men mouth their assent and go to the couch and seat themselves. I take a painful roost on the edge of the desk facing them. I pull out the cigarette box, tap out one and offer it to both men. They decline. I turn the flintwheel on the Zippo and say, "So again, gentlemen. What's up?"

The major is watching the blue smoke as it swirls up before switching his eyes to me. "Well, Mr. Stone, what we have is a new lead on a very old case that involves Muskrat Island. We're..."

The cell phone begins chirping next to the black officer and he reaches To pick it up but sees me motioning to him "no".

I smile the best I can. "It's just a telemarketer. He's been driving me nuts all morning, wanting me to buy new windows." I snap out my hand. "I'm sorry Major, you were saying?" After about five rings, the phone is silent and the major looks back to me.

"Uh, yes. Well, we're going to need to get a team of airmen out to the island to look over the place and do a little searching." He adds more. "We could just claim governmental need, but…well, it's just better to work with the Pukaskwa Nation, since it's such a simple matter."

I don't say anything, but I have my eyebrows raised as far as they stretch, and finally, the Major senses that further explanation is warranted.

"Okay," he spreads out his hands, "this dates back to 1973. There was break-in at the P.X. up at K.I. Sawyer Air Force Base, near Marquette. The thieves got away with a little over $50,000 dollars and the case was dead. We had no leads, nothing. The case file shows that there were only a couple of suspects and we never brought charges against them. Recently, one of the suspects has passed away." Shears takes in a deep breath and allows his eyes to roam the room.

"This former airman, a Donald Pike, was one of the original suspects. He had been stationed there at the time of the theft and he came forward with a dying declaration. He indicated that he and another service person were responsible for the break-in. He was dying of cancer and according to him, the money is buried somewhere on the Island." He finishes by bringing his hands together as if that… was all there was to it. But I didn't think it was.

These guys have gone to a lot of trouble to impress me. It's rare for military people to wear their uniforms off-base these days, and almost non-existent for military cops. This showing of the flag and esprit de corp is probably just for my benefit.

"Uh, huh. Soooo, you're wanting to take a team of Air Force personnel out to the Island to look for this money?"

The two men smile broadly and the Captain speaks for the first time.

"That's right, Mr. Stone, and we understand that you're the Tribe's police officer in charge of the Island, so we need your cooperation in this matter. Uh," he looked at his partner before going on, "we also understand that there's no one out there and that the place is pretty desolate. So, we would be airlifting in some supplies for the troops, you know, tents, foodstuffs, those kinds of things, to accommodate the search."

Both men seem happy now. I begin shaking my head while looking at the floor. "I don't think you guys realize just how big and how desolate that island is." I drop the cigarette butt into an old coffee can by the desk. It smolders lightly before going out as I look back at them. "Just how long do you plan on this search taking?"

The Major fields that one. "Oh, we should be out've your hair out there within six months, unless of course, we find it sooner." He beams at me from across the room.

I squint my eyes as the room smoke backtracks on me. "So, you've already got indictments ready on somebody then, huh?"

"No, there won't be any arrests in this case," the Major puckers his lips in dissatisfaction, "because all of the suspects are dead, unfortunately. They escaped justice, but... that's life, I guess. Still, they never got the money and we intend to recover it," he rolled out his hand again, "with your cooperation, of course."

I bring my hand up to my chin and give it a good rub. Boy, what a bunch of bullshit. I wonder if I still have turnips in my hair or what. "Okay. So, you say it was fifty grand that was stolen...right?"

Both men nod and the Captain says, "Approximately, yes. That's correct." My turn to nod.

"And you're wanting to go out there now, this late in the year to look for it with..." I roll out my hand, "how many men?"

"I'm not sure, maybe a flight or... ten airmen or so, all of them security police." The major says with a concerned expression, shared by his partner, the Captain. And for my part, their concern is reasonable, because I'm not buying it. I stare at them for several beats and then slowly shake my head.

"Nope. It's not gonna work like this, fellas. So, why don't you tell me the real reason why you need to go out to the island?"

The Major's face turns a pretty shade of red. "What are you talking about MR. STONE? What real reason?"

I ease off the desk and forget to hide my grimace this time. Neither of them seems to notice anyway.

"Okay, look. Let me put it this way. First of all, I ain't in the military anymore so you guys can stop calling me "Mr. Stone" with the heavy emphasis on the "Mr." part, as if I was still a Warrant Officer. I'm not impressed by your rank or uniform. Seriously," I opened my arms, "I could give a shit less. Now...," I turn the badge on my shirt over and point at it with the other hand, "you can call me Officer Stone, Special Agent Stone or hell... a Rolling Stone for all I Care." I nod.

"But you can knock off the military "Mr." crap. I'm not impressed or intimidated. And two, there ain't any way that Uncle Sugar's Air Farce is going to expend upwards of seventy five grand to ferry troops out to look for a measly fifty grand in return. That is especially true if you guys don't need the cash as evidence. This ain't 1973 and 75Gs is about what it'd cost at today's prices. The government may buy hundred dollar toilet seats," I crinkle my face in a "get real" manner, "but at least some G.I.'s going to sit on 'em. Here, you wouldn't even get that for a return. So, it's up to you." I lean back against the desk and fold my arms. "Either you can tell me what's really going on or... I can't help you."

The Major quickly got his color back to normal, but if Mussenberg could show it, he'd be livid right now. Shears stood up and his partner followed suit.

"Okay, Mr...," the Major smiles wanly, "I'm sorry,... Officer Stone... then we'll do this the hard way. We'll just use the might of the federal government. But we WILL be searching that island. I just hope that you don't find yourself in too much hot water over this little matter."

I slowly swing my head from side to side and shrug my shoulders. "Don't sweat it, Major. I can guarantee that any water I get in will be tepid... at best. But I reckon that whatever you're doing may be hotter'n hell for you. 'Cause I know that the reason you're here... is because you had to be. All three of us know that. As soon as you boys walked through that door over there, you left the United States of America and entered the sovereign Nation of the Pukaskwa." I drywash my hands for emphasis while twisting my head. "Way too much publicity over this new tribe for any governmental heavy-handedness."

I tilt my head. "We both know that if you could've avoided it before, you wouldn't even be talking to me. So, it comes down to this. I've got a strong reason for asking why. I need to know. Period. So, if you boys change your mind, then get back to me." I push myself away from the desk and usher them toward the door. "It's been a pleasure, gentlemen."

Shears goes first and his compatriot follows. Mussenberg stops, then steps back inside the doorway. He raises his finger at me. "You know, Stone, just because you're retired doesn't mean you have to stay that way. You might just find yourself called back on active duty. You might want to consider that."

I look at his jutting finger until he quickly drops it. I slowly raise my eyes to meet his. "You need to look up the regs there, partner. A warrant officer is a member of the enlisted ranks, not the officer corp. I can't be involuntarily recalled." I sigh and wave my hand as if shooing a fly. "Don't bother threatening me, Captain. I had a long night... okay?" The Captain backs down and a slow smile appears on his face, almost congenial. He tips his head in farewell as the Major looks back at me.

"Thank you, Officer Stone. Be assured, we'll be in touch." With that, the two men walk from my sight.

Outside the Boathouse

The two Air Force officers climbed into a brown Chevy Impala rental car, parked alongside the patrol Jeep and closed the doors.

Mussenberg looked at his partner. "Well, that didn't go so well... did it?"

Shears pulled off his saucer cap and tossed it to the back seat.

"No." He looked back at Mussenberg. "Who the hell is that son of a bitch?"

Mussenberg hiked his shoulders and he tossed his cap over the seat as well. "I don't know, but I kind'a like the guy. He's deadshit on his business... that's for sure."

"Yeah, well good for you. Maybe you two can date after we clear this mission." The Major's eyes turned hard. "I thought you said he was just retired Coast Guard? Did you see anything in his file to say otherwise, or what?"

"No, Al, I told ya before, all I did was a preliminary background check on the guy. Now that came up with him retiring a couple a years ago as a Chief Warrant Officer, with 20 good years. I didn't do an in-depth... and I told you that."

The Major turned back to the wheel. "Yeah, yeah you're right. Sorry. Well, we fucked up thinking he was gonna roll over for us, that's for sure." He drummed his fingers on the steering column. "And we should've thought that it'd sound dumb to recover the money if we didn't have a case pending. Shit! Okay, I'm gonna find out who that sucker is right now. Crack out your laptop. I wanna know everything about that fucker from when he took his first standing-up piss to when he got his first gray hair!"

Mussenberg stretched over and grabbed a laptop computer from the back floorboard as Shears started the car. He popped it open and looked at his partner. "You gotta find someplace and park, so I can have a steady signal on the cell."

The Major sighed. "Okay, I'll go over to that Seven-Eleven where we stopped yesterday." He backed the car around and said, "This guy Stone knows something's going on."

The Captain looked over at his superior. "Well, one thing's for sure boss, that boy isn't your regular old military retiree... is he?"

Shears shook his head, the sunglasses hiding his eyes as he wheeled the car out of the lot. "Nope. That he isn't."

A few minutes later, they parked the car in the convenience store back lot, next to an overfull trash can. Mussenberg went to work setting up the laptop. Shortly, Shears came out of the storefront balancing two fountain Cokes and a couple of chilidogs. As he made his way over to the car, two kids on bicycles screamed into the lot past him. Shears bent over the driver's door and passed a soda and hotdog to his partner through the open window. Mussenberg took the items and situated them on the seat, while he kept his eyes on the screen. Then he typed furiously for a second. "Hey… you ain't gonna believe this shit!"

Shears unwrapped the chilidog and took a bite. "Try me." he mumbled between chews, while he reached for his soda on the roof of the car.

Mussenberg leaned over the seat and looked up at him. "You ever hear of something called "Trojan Horse?"

Shears stopped chewing as he stared at his partner. "Shit!" he exclaimed as he lightly popped his fist on the car's top. "Oh, well. That's it for now then!"

"What's it for now, Al? What's this Trojan Horse?" Mussenberg turned back to the screen. "I can't get past that … even with our code. There's what appears to be a lot of covert shit in his jacket but it's intermixed with what I assume is regular Coast Guard duty and stations. There're also recent footprints in his files from somebody at the Army's CID section. Looks like they hit the same walls I have but shit, not us. We shouldn't be denied any access. We should be able to get into anything!" He typed some more, and then shook his head. I can't access any of those files." He said to Shears.

"Yeah, and you're not going to be able to either. The Old Man is going to have to get it for us."

Mussenberg opened his door and stood up on the other side of the car, looking at Shears. "Well, are you going to tell me what Trojan Horse is and what's going on with this or what?"

Shears poked the straw in his mouth and took a drink of his Coke. Then he smiled at the Captain. "I can't tell you much. All I know is that Trojan Horse is DIA and that they seem like mean bastards." He took another bite of his dog and spoke between chomps.
"I bumped into one of these guys during the Gulf War," he flung his hand, "before your time…Anyway, I was working a possible retrieval and had to…" He stopped as the two kids on bikes peddled past with snow cones in their hands.

"Anyway, I was going to have to move a company of infantry that was dug-in and… that the Iraqis didn't know about. It was bad because the company couldn't really get out of there without taking some casualties. And if they stayed put, they could smoke the Iraqis once the battle rolled that way. But hey, I had the priority, ya know?" he twisted his hand and shrugged.

"The whole thing pissed everybody off, but this one guy was hotter than anybody else. I didn't know it then, but apparently, he was the one who had guided that company of infantry into that spot, right under the Iraqi's noses. I didn't know who he was. I still don't." He said the last with a look of wonder.

Anyhow, this guy was arguing against moving the troops from clear across the room. And he was hot. Finally, this Air force Colonel pointed at me and said that I was the one ordering the move. This guy started right for me and I mean every one in the room just moved out of his way, too. He was about six foot three and he drew a Kabar knife as he came. I just knew I was gonna die and all these people were gonna let it happen, too. I had my service pistol but that fucker was there before I even got it unsnapped. At the last second, this One Star Marine General jumped between us and stopped him. And I'm telling ya, Pete, he talked nice to this guy, too. This guy, whoever he was, finally backed down but he never stopped looking at me with death in his eyes. I thought he was nuts. But the General turned and told me to get the fuck out've there or he'd turn the guy loose. So... I beat it."

Shears took another swig of his pop as both he and Mussenberg watched three young girls in short skirts climb out of a rusty blue Ford Bronco and head into the store. Mussenberg continued to eat his chilidog now and he motioned for Shears to resume.

"Okay...so anyway, I went ahead and moved the company but as it turned out, that one star Marine pounded the area with an airstrike to cover their withdrawal and they didn't take any casualties. When I got the chance, I asked the Old Man who this guy was and he said that he was a member of the DIA's Trojan Horse Team." Mussenberg's eyes formed a question but Shears shook him off.

"I know, you think that the DIA team didn't exist until 1992, right?"

Mussenberg nodded his head as he chewed another bite of his Dog as Shears went on. "Well, this Trojan Horse team was apparently formed in secret back in 1980. It was thought up and implemented by none other than Ronald Reagan, himself, as Commander & Chief. And secrecy was the big thing. Their only mission was military intelligence. According to the General, they had a lot to do with the final kiss-off of the USSR. He also says that Reagan honestly didn't know anything about Iran-Contra, but he always knew what these boys were up to."

Shears shifted his jaw while clucking his tongue. "I have to admit, I was impressed by that. Anyway, the team was a mix of Army Green Berets, Navy SEALs, Marine Reckon, Air Force Pararescue and Coast Guard Intelligence types. And all of them were dedicated to the military mission and nothing else. They disbanded in '92, when the DIA stood up the team you know about which could be recognized in public. These guys, most of them anyway, probably don't function too well in normal society. The Old Man said that they were the baddest-assed spies he'd ever seen and that included the CIA."

He popped the last of his dog in his mouth as he snickered. "What'd he say exactly... Oh, yeah. He said they were colder than a whore's heart and deadlier that a point-blank 50 cal. round." He looked at his partner. The Old man respects them and that means something to me, I guess, spies or not."

The black man smiled. "Yes, well at least we aren't calling the kettle black. For we... are not spies you know? At least according to the Old Man, we're not. He says we're liars and cheaters with a "spacial twist". I like that. Spacial twist". Mussenberg softly laughed and took another pull on the soda, finishing the drink.

"So you're saying that these guys would cut your throat in heartbeat, if it saved American lives on the battlefield?"

Shears shook the ice in his cup, "Yep, that's about the size of it."

Mussenberg was astounded as he wadded up the hotdog wrapper. "You're telling me... that a covert government team existed with the same clearance we have?"

Shears looked over at Mussenberg with astonishment. "Oh, hell yeah buddy! They don't exist anymore but they did."

Shears and Mussenberg stopped talking while they watched the three girls come back out of the store. One girl, a cute little blonde, stood holding bags for her friend who was climbing in the back. The wind suddenly gusted and blew up her skirt, revealing a pretty pair of yellow underwear. The panties were sheer and a very dark triangle clearly indicated where the girl's pubic hair was formed. She stood frozen with her parcels until the wind died down and the skirt dropped. Even from the distance, the two men could see the embarrassment on her face. "Nice," uttered Shears, "but we know she's not a real blonde...don't we?"

"Yeah," smiled Mussenberg. "I guess we do." He shook his head. "Man I just can't believe that I've never heard of these guys before." He looked back at Shears and the other man moved his shoulders in a what-will-be, will-be attitude.

"It's like that with everything, Pete. Shit, you know that? The Old Man knows all about them, but until we have that need, he isn't going to tell us. The only reason I know what I know is because one of 'em... tried to kill me. We're going to need to know it all now so, we'll get it now." Shears made a "so there" motion with his hands. He had his partners rapt attention.

"Shit man, think about us for a second. We know a lot of stuff that nobody else knows, right? How many of these have we done? A hundred, two hundred? And while we know all of the particulars about each specific mission... we don't really have any more idea than that. Shit man, we don't even know where they come from or hell, what's really going on... ya know?" Shears took a deep breath and exhaled it. "We just do as we're told and trust that when the Old Man says it's gotta be this way for national security, then that's the way it's gotta be. Period."

He shook his head sadly. "And the only way we're able to keep a lid on this shit is by staying covert. And the only way ta do that is the same way that these Trojan guys did it. Take us and our unit for example." He rolled his hand. "We're assigned to OSI most of the time but just like those Trojan dudes, we're really assigned to the 696th, ya know? We get pulled for these kinds of assignments all of the time but as far as the rest of the world knows, we're just Air Force investigators. That's how it's done. We do duel roles so everybody thinks we're somebody different than who we really are." He twisted his face up in a smirk.

"You know that according to all the paper on existing Air Force units, the 696th Air Intelligence Group doesn't exist, right?" he pointed his finger at Mussenberg. "It's as simple as that. Nobody knows about us and what we do and nobody knew about them and what they did."

Mussenberg pondered that while nodding his head in agreement. Shears went on. "Hell buddy, I'm willing ta bet that the General himself don't know it all. All of this stuff's so compartmentalized and sectioned off that half the things you think are going on, actually aren't. And the stuff that you're sure isn't happening, probably is. It's like a Looney Tune cartoon, all of the time." He shook his head in irritation. "That's my opinion anyway."

Mussenberg let out a low whistle while gazing to his friend. Then he said. "Nope, I think the Old Man knows exactly what's going on, Al. Maybe we don't... but he does. Did I ever tell you about that time I saw him dress-down General Powell?"

Shears was bending down and said, "Uh, uh. I don't think so anyway."

Mussenberg continued. "Yeah, well that before I came to OSI. I was an aid to Colonel Fowler at the Pentagon then. Anyways, one day I was walking past the Joint Chiefs conference room as a meeting was breaking up. The door opened and out comes the Old Man. He was a two star then and right behind him, I shit you not, was four-star General, Chief of Staff, Colon Powell, himself. And the guy was livid. He yelled at the Old Man "General, don't turn your back on me! I'm talking to you!" And this is the God's honest truth," Mussenberg held up his palm, "the Old Man stopped, turned around and brought his middle finger up to his mouth and kissed it to Powell! No shit! I swear he did. Then he just turned and walked away... calm as a spring rain… while Powell stood there shaking like a dog shit'n peach seeds."

Shears smiled and uttered, "I'll be damned." The amazement remained on his face as he reached down to his sock and pulled out a pack of filtered Winston cigarettes. Mussenberg watched him and went on. "So I gotta think that the Old Man knows a lot a shit about a lot a things… to have the clout to pull off something like that. Don't you?"

Shears twisted up his face. "Yeah…hell… I don't know. Maybe he does." He shrugged his shoulders, shook the pack and offered one to Mussenberg who shook his head.

"No, thanks. I'm saving myself for marriage."

Shears clicked his tongue. "Too bad, Captain." He flicked a Bic lighter and drew smoke from the cigarette. "You're foregoing the enjoyable things in life for nothing. 'Cause you aren't pretty enough to get any female to marry you, unless maybe you… "black-male" them!" Shears chuckled at his own joke and even Mussenberg smiled.

"You white guys kill me with your feeble attempts at humor. You will never be an Eddie Murphy, Major." His countenance turned serious as he looked over at Shears. "So, what's the game plan? Obviously, this guy is a player and we aren't going to be able bullshit him, today being a good case in point."

Shears blew a cloud of smoke as a noisy Buick drove past them into the lot. "I don't know, but I'm worried about things right now. This Trojan Team's got some high clearance and that means that they're on the Q.T. all of the time. Just like us. Shit Pete, you can bet your ass that some members of the military here and there know who we are, too. And some of them will even have stories. But none of them will ever get past that on us. Never. Not as long as we're an still active unit, ya know?" He twisted his head for emphasis, "They aren't active anymore." He looked thoughtfully at the sky. There was a storm brewing up there. Then he took another pull off the smoke, exhaling broadly.

"Keeping that lid on, may not be the case with them now, if they've got somebody poking around in their past." Shears snapped his fingers. "Hey, remember that ditsy treasurer chick we met up at the reservation? The one with the flat chest and ponytail?"

Mussenberg thought then raised his eyes to Shears. "Yeah, so?"

"Remember what she said about the Cop Captain disliking Stone? Well our search on him said he was a retired E-9… an Army M.P. right?" Mussenberg nodded his head and Shears continued. "I'll bet those footprints are from him nosing around about Stone!"

Mussenberg shrugged. "From what that chic said, this Captain's not Stone's boss though. But, it'd be easy enough to find out if it was him", he shrugged, "if you want to know?"

Shears shook his cup again and the ice rattled. "No, it isn't going to matter. I want you to superglue Stone's file." He sat the cup back on the roof.

Mussenberg looked at the Major incredulously. "You sure you want to do that, Al? This guy'd be screwed if we sealed his file."

"Yeah, well if someone gets into his file far enough to learn that he's connected with this Trojan outfit, it'll make it a lot harder to explain his death…" he looked over and met Mussenberg's eyes, "if it comes to that."

The two held each other's eyes, and then Shears leaned forward and placed both hands on the car's roof, looking directly at his subordinate. He lowered his voice.

"Hey… don't look at me like that, Captain. You heard the Old Man's orders just as clearly as I did. Termination with extreme prejudice, if, when and where necessary! We have a job to do and we will do it, anyway we have to."

Mussenberg broke eye contact and nodded his head. "Yes, sir," he said in a military tone. "I would strongly suggest, however, that we contact the General before we seal Stone's file. It's my opinion, sir, that at this stage, it's his decision… not ours."

Shears took a deep breath and pushed himself away from the car. "Okay, Pete, you win. Let's go back to the room and call him though." He glanced around the lot as the driver of the loud Buick backed out of its parking space. "I want to get out of this uniform anyway." He smiled at his partner. "That was another brilliant idea of yours, wearing the uniform to impress the retiree?" He pointed the burning cigarette at his partner while the smoke wafted away in the breeze.

Mussenberg took in a breath. It was never easy going against a superior officer's wishes and he was glad that his statement hadn't caused problems. "Well, you know. Who'd a thunk it." He gathered up Shears' and his own hotdog wrappers and napkins, then stuffed all of them into his soda cup and walked over to the trash can. The can was full and leaned heavily against a large white birch tree. He glanced around and finally, just sat the cup on top of the pile. He looked over at his partner as he returned to the car.

"The guy's just not a team player. That's all I can say." Mussenberg added as he raised his hands in an "I give up" manner and smiled. Then he sat down in the car's front seat and closed the door.

Shears watched the Buick driving down the road as he stepped over and laid his soda cup next to Mussenberg's on top of the trash. He took a final draw on his smoke and stuck the burning end into the straw of the soda cup. It sizzled and popped as it extinguished itself in the small dots of soda inside the straw. Then he moved back and climbed into the car and looked up through the windshield, letting his gaze settle on the other man.

"Oh I don't think that's our problem with this guy. I think he's probably a star performer and… a team player when he's gotta be." As he started the car and pulled out of the lot, he glanced at his partner. "He's just not on our team… is all." The brown Chevy moved away as the first raindrops began falling.

Chapter Thirteen
The Whole Wide World

The Boathouse,
Escanaba, Michigan.
Same Time.

I stood in the doorway and watched the brown Chevy carrying the
two officers pull out of the lot. Well, well, well. Isn't that interesting.
I took a final drag off the cigarette and put it out, letting my thoughts
tumble on. First, I've got somebody keeping tabs on me out on the
island, and then back here at the marina. Then one member of a
surveillance team tries to "off" me last night. And now… two
wingnut officers are here saying that they need to get out to the island
to recover some stolen money that will cost them more to get back
than it's worth. And they don't even need this alleged cash for
evidence. While I'm not a genus, I ain't that stupid either.

Something's in the wind, and for whatever reason my ass is hanging
out there in the breeze, too. I look up at the clouds moving in and
know that rain is coming. The temperature is dropping and the air's
taking on a chill. Or maybe… it's just my new-found predicament
that's making me cold. I shake my head and close the door. Either
way, I'd better get some intel going or sure as shit I'm going to be in a
world of hurt.

I glance over at the computer that's perched on the corner of the
desk with a dust cover on it. The internet is supposed to be hooked up.
I think maybe I'll drop a line to old Gangues. He'll be able to help.
No doubt. I drop my eyes as I begin making a to-do list. I have phone
calls to make and that boat rental to check out. But first, my eyes
shoot to the empty cardboard box sitting atop the locker. I want to see
something else. I move over and reach up to it and pull the small
handgun out. I'd dropped the realtor's, or would-be killer's, pistol in
here last night and never did get a chance to look at it closely. I turn
the little Berretta over in my hand. The serial numbers are ground off,
and as I hold it to the light, it appears as if acid has been applied, too.

So… at least I know for certain that whatever is going on, the crew
working it has good help. Grinding the numbers off makes the gun
hard to trace, but applying acid makes it almost impossible, even for
the FBI lab. They know their stuff and have the where-with-all to

make it happen. I figure that the guy who tried to kill me last night was a pro, but now I also know for certain that his team has professional or at least very competent support, too. This deal, whatever it is, is a high-class operation.

I put the gun back in the box and move over to the small table, snatching up the envelope and the other mail before going over to the desk. I pull the cover off the computer and push the button on the tower. The machine is new and begins chirping and clicking as it boots up. I sit in the chair and thumb through the mail. The manila envelope is from my buddy Charlie at the Bureau of Land Management.

He got the information I requested on the island. Folded inside were old USGS topographical line maps of the island dating back to the late 1930s. And sure enough, the old geological surveys showed that the northwest part of the island was much different then than it is now. I slowly get up and go over to my duty bag that I brought in on the boat. I take out several maps that Annette gave me from the survey the tribe had recently paid for and brought them back to the desk. As I twist the maps around, I compare them with the old ones and man... what a difference.

It appears as if a huge piece of the island's real estate is missing. Maybe as much as two or three acres were now gone from the northwest part of the island that was present and mapped back in 1937. I supposed that isn't that unusual. The survey taken in 1937 was the most recent until the tribe had one done. So really, who'd notice over that period of time? I scratch my jaw and glance at the rain that begins tapping against the window. Still, this just doesn't make any sense. Erosion would've eaten away the southern end of the island, not the north. There's no wave or wind action there to speak of, and well, this is weird. I checked the southwestern end of the island and the comparison showed only a marginal loss due to erosion. Why would it be so drastic on the northern side?

I finger through the rest of the stuff Charlie sent me and finally find a sticky note attached to one of the maps. I pull it off and hold it up to what light is available. The room is growing dark with the coming of rain. I read the note. Charlie was just letting me know that the Air Force has been asking questions over at the BIA about the island. They want to know who owned it now, about getting access, etc. Just a heads-up. I put everything back in the envelope and sort through the remaining letters.

I find one from the hovercraft company in Canada. I open it up and see the expensive watermark on the stationary. I read that this is in response to my inquiry, then skim down until the bomb goes off. I reach over to a green shaded table lamp and switch it on. Nope. I'm not seeing things. The letter is signed by the President and CEO of the company and states unequivocally that their company had indeed performed a survey and feasibility study on Muskrat Island six months ago.

The company's CEO went on to say that his machines could not operate in the manner we desired without major excavation work. He'd explained all of this to our attorney, Mr. Shultz, and believed that the matter was closed. His company had not charged for the survey and declined any monies for the sale of craft unless the Pukaskwa Nation was prepared to attempt such changes as would be necessary. He added that he'd be happy to help in any way possible, bla, bla and bla. Signed Delfred Goodrich, President & CEO. I look down at the bottom of the page and see that a copy was sent to Paul Shultz, Pukaskwa Tribal Attorney.

Oh, great. I wonder what the odds are of our tribal lawyer not being in the wind. I twist over to the phone. There is a sheet of paper with a phone number list under the plastic desk mat and I punch in the home number for Morse. A young girl answers. I assume it to be Morse's daughter. She's polite and well mannered and asks me to hold a moment. Shortly, Morse comes on the line. I think he's surprised to hear from me. I ask him if he's seen Shultz lately. His responses are definitely cool. The two of them could be in on this together, but I doubted it. I usually have a pretty good feel for somebody's character and while I'm not overly fond of this guy, I think he's probably honest. He's asking something while I'm rolling this over in my head. He spits the words at me again.

"Stone…I said, what's this all about? Why all the interest with Shultz all of a sudden?" So I tell him. I explain what I'd thought of the hovercraft idea once I'd seen the island and the reason why I'd contacted the company. I tell him what Annette said about Shultz paying money to a company that never got it, and finally, what the CEO of that company says about the feasibility of using the hovercraft as the tribe has planned. He's quiet for a minute. Then he speaks.

"So you think he's skimming off the tribe?"

"I can't say for sure. This is your gig more than it's mine. What do you think?"

"Well, Paul ain't no angel. But I'm kind'a surprised. After hearing what you just said, well I guess I think that it's a good possibility… yeah. You're sure about this though, right?"

"Yeah. I've got the letter right here and I'll fax it to you. I'd also appreciate it if you'd bring Hennessey up to speed on this. But if I were you Morse, I'd send a car over to Shultz's house and pick 'em up, if he's still there. This letter I got, well a copy of it was sent to Shultz, too."

That silence again. If I figure it right, Morse and Shultz are friends, strange bedfellows indeed, cops and lawyers. Finally, he speaks up.

"Yeah, I think you're right. But, Paul's not here anyway. He always takes this week off to go grouse hunting with his brothers from down state and he won't be back until late tonight. So, I'm pretty sure he hasn't seen his mail. I'll have a patrol unit waiting to pick him up for questioning. Shit!" The silence again while he ponder the bizarre turns that friendship can take. "And I'll let Hennessey know what's going on, too. Damn, this is bad. You're sure though, huh?"

I waited for a beat or two. "Yeah. Pretty sure."

"Well, okay then." More silence while I wait for him to finish digesting what I just told him. He clears his throat and switches gears.

"So, what's the Air Force CID want with you?"

Next, I explain what the Air Force officers say they wanted. I add the bit about them not having any suspects, indictments or a need for the some $50,000 in cash, supposedly hidden on the island. He's quiet for a couple of beats, and then says, "So these guys don't need the money for evidence in a prosecution?"

"Nope, not according to them. They just wanna go out to the island to recover the cash."

"That don't make any sense. Unless they know exactly where it's at, there're gonna spend more money in man hours and transport than they're gonna get for retrieving the fifty grand."

"Yep, my thoughts exactly." My turn to clear a throat. "I've gotta feeling that there's more going on here than just recovering some cash. So, I'm going to play it out awhile and see where it goes."

Morse grunts on the phone. "Yeah, well those guys don't have any jurisdiction on that island. It's up ta us whether or not we give'em access. He's quiet again and I let the silence go until he speaks. "Okay, well whatever you think, but I'd like to be kept up to speed on what's happening… if that's alright with you?"

"Sure, I can do that. Oh yeah, by the way, I saw a bad accident last night coming back from Bruce's Crossing. Have any idea what it was?"

"Naw but I can call and check. Stand by a minute." I can hear Morse use the radio to call one of his officers out on patrol. He comes back to me. "What time was it?"

I think for a second. "I'm not sure. Another car had stopped and I just kept on going. I got home around four this morning."

There's dead air space again after I say the time. I can hear
Morse's officer answering him on the radio, but I figure he's taking in
the fact that I was out that late with Annette. Finally, he coughs and
asks his officer the question. I hear the answer. A car/deer accident.
One white male, dead at the scene. The state cops took the report.
Morse relays it to me anyway. Then he asks in a weary voice, "So,
how's Mrs. Cole?"

I tell him she seems fine and chipper for her age and thank him for
getting the question answered. Then, as a way of moving past the
awkwardness, I ask him if that was his very professional little girl that
answered the phone.

"Yeah, that's Tanya. She's my nine year old. She does pretty good
on the phone and it helps, ya know, having my job, I get a lotta calls
at home." The line is silent for awhile and I'm about to say my
goodbyes when he starts again.

"Look, Stone, I appreciate you calling. I know you didn't have to
and well… thanks. I appreciate the heads-up on Paul. Look, it's just
that I want ta work with you if I can and well, that's all. Just thanks
for calling."

I know he wants to ask about Annette, too, but he won't. I tell him
no problem and that I'll keep him apprized of the situation. Then we
hang up. I slip the papers on the hovercraft into the fax slot, dial the
number and press the button when the tone comes on. As the fax
feeds itself, I fold my fingers together and crack my knuckles. Well,
so far, so good. My little pal from last night is listed as a car/deer
fatality. I figure that it will probably stay that way for awhile or at
least until they can't find a next of kin. I know I'm not going to do
anything to change it. And Morse is going to take care of the seagull
tribal lawyer so I have a pretty clear field of fire. Now, if I can just
figure out what I'm shooting at.

I'd called my brother when I got up this morning to see if
everything was alright down in Tennessee. We'd chatted awhile, and
from what I could tell, nothing seemed out of the ordinary there. I just
let him think the call was a routine family check-up. So, whatever I'd
gotten myself into, it didn't appear to be family oriented either. I look
over at the computer as its screen swims to and fro with little boxes. I
turn to the machine and clicked the icons for the internet access. What
I have to do is figure out what the hell is going on. I pull up my e-mail
and open a letter. In the address, I type in Gangues@ beltway.com.
Gangues is short for "Gangues the Conqueror".

He's an old teammate and like all of us, Gangues has a nickname
that fits him. There probably isn't a computer system in existence that
Gangues can't get into and defeat. I stood right next to him once while

he breached the Soviet Union's Air Force personnel files. He is the best. After he left the Navy, he tried working for several computer companies but he just had too much savvy to work for someone else. He started his own business and now, has more money than he knows what to do with. The boy is always looking for something different and challenging. I hoped that my request would fill the bill.

In the subject space, I type "5th Rubber". It's another one of our little Team code words. Trojan is an American brand name of condoms and a slang word for a condom is rubber. Hence, Rubber stands for "Trojan". And since I'm the fifth member of the Team to be recruited, I'm called "5th Rubber". Simple enough, but the simple stuff often works the best. In many parts of the world and the European area especially, the phrase might appear to be someone playing a card game over the internet. But Gangues will know that it's me. I begin typing. I go through the basic hellos, but then I let him know that somebody is trying to sell me real estate.

This is another code but an important one. Someone attempting to sell you real estate is trying to sell you "the farm". Buying the farm is a phrase that dates back to World War Two. G.I.s used it to describe anyone that died in combat. Prior to that war, most folks spent their life trying to pay-off or buy the family farm. And most people managed to do that just about the time they died. Hence, somebody who died usually "bought the farm". For our team, someone trying to kill someone of us is trying to sell us real estate. They are called a realtor. If they complete their task, we say that they "closed their deal" or "sold the farm". Plain and simple.

I ask Gangues to run a search on some names. I type in the realtor's information as I took it off the Hertz rental envelope from last night. Then I punch in the two Air Force officers' names and duty stations from the stuff on their business cards. If there is anything out there on these people, I know Gangues will find it. I click the send button and watch the little icons sail across the computer screen. I sure hope that Gangues gets this soon. I need the information.

I pull another cigarette out of the box and light it up, dragging over an old coffee can I found to use as an ashtray. I lean forward and search the phone list again as I exhale the smoke. I dial Nettie's home number up in Wiitikan. I doubt that she's back there yet, but I want to touch base and advise her of the news so she won't be blind-sided. Sure enough, her answering machine picks-up. Hearing her voice sends a slight shiver through me. As I listen to her recorded message, I again face the fact that I'm hooked… but good. When I get the beep, I leave a detailed message about what I've learned about Shultz and what Morse was up to with it. I tell her I'll be out at the island for awhile but will call the first chance I get. I hesitate. I want to say… I love you, but know that I shouldn't. Instead, I tell her to "take care of my girl" and let it go at that.

I hang up the receiver and sit looking at the phone, wondering what this is and where it will lead. My mind slips gently through the events of last night and the warm memories of her in my arms, her scent, her lips, then… it changed. The deformed eyes of my realtor pal filled my mental picture. Sonavabitch. I look out the window and see the rain exploding on the docks all over the marina. I push myself out of the chair and move over to the locker. My flight jacket is full of mud from last night's little adventure so I pull the uniform jacket off the hanger and loop my arms through it. I grab the patrol Jeep's keys off a wall hook, open the door and step into the falling rain.

The Watcher

Kuan reached up and twisted the windshield wiper switch so that the blades took one swipe over the glass. He had parked the car so as to be able to see the front door of the sport shop. The policeman had left the boathouse and driven in the police vehicle straight to the shop. He had entered and was still inside as Kuan sat inside the car, trying to keep the windows clear in the falling rain. The cell phone on the seat beside him chirped. He picked it up and glanced at the caller I.D. then pushed the on button.

"This is Adam."

The voice on the other end came in scratchy. "This is Wayne. I am headed back in from our jobsite at this time. We have found another mine shaft to the north. It is much deeper and we need additional climbing rope to investigate. Daniel is staying at the jobsite and searching the locality for additional rope. I came out here to get a clear signal for the phone. Also, the seas are picking up out here and I may not be able to return this evening if I continue in. I have not been able to contact the boss to advise him of this. We assume it is due to the weather. Do I continue in or return to the jobsite?"

Kuan scratched his eye as the Indian policeman exited the building. He watched the man look up at the heavens while he spoke into the mouthpiece. "Do you feel that this could be the place Wayne?"

"I do not know but we have been around this rock several times and this is the first time we have discovered another shaft. Daniel and I both believe that this is worth investigating further. However, as I said, the waves out here are growing and Daniel and I both think that if I come in to port, then I will not be able to return until the weather subsides, possibly not until tomorrow morning."

"Yes. I understand. I too, have had difficulty contacting the boss." Kuan thought about what to do as the Indian opened some type of food item and took a bite. He then walked over to his Jeep and climbed in. Kuan hadn't been able to reach Chin in several hours and now the team on the island needed specific instructions. He was the executive officer on the mission and so the decision became his. He made it as he started the car to follow the Indian policeman as the other man pulled out of the shop's lot.

"Very well, Wayne. Continue in. Get your rope, and if it is possible, return to the jobsite yet today. If not, then you will go back as soon as it is feasible. Daniel does know you may have to stay in tonight, correct?"

"Yes, we discussed it before I left in the boat. By the way, the Indian has not returned to the jobsite and the place is deserted." Kuan smiled as he wheeled into traffic two cars behind the policeman. "Yes, I know he has not returned. I am following him as we speak." He looked at his watch. "Try phoning me at eight pm tonight. I must go now."

He waited as the other man acknowledged then pushed the off button as the Indian turned into a drug store.

The Watched

I walk out of the sports shop and tear open a package of beef jerky. The gal behind the counter was pleasant and more than willing to help. We flirted back and forth as she ran down the list of boat rentals for me. I heft the climbing rope I bought and rip off a piece of the dried meat as I make my way over to the Jeep. After I get behind the wheel, I look at the paper I hold in my hand and read the name again. Herman Veeter. As near as I can tell, this is probably the guy I saw that day out at the island. He has a Grand Rapids address.

That's a good-sized town down-state. The shop copies their renter's names, addresses and driver's license numbers so I have some more reference stuff for Gangues to chase. The rain is backing off but the wind is now picking up. As I chew the jerky, I let my eyes wander over the sky and out at the big lake. The waves are running maybe four to five feet high. It won't be an enjoyable trip out to the island in weather like this. As I feel a twinge from the back of my leg, I figure that's especially true right now. Oh well. I stick the remaining piece of meat out of the side of my mouth like a cigar and start the Jeep. I tool the vehicle over to the drug store and go in to buy some Excedrin. The first Aid box only has aspirin and the ache in my leg was crying for something a little stronger.

The Watcher

Kuan backed his car up beside a garbage can and got out. He quickly stepped into the Seven Eleven, never taking his eyes from the drug store across the street. He walked briskly back to the cooler and grabbed a pint of chocolate milk while looking around the ad-signs that decorated the windows of the convenience store. He had been following the Indian since he had left the boathouse at the marina. As he stood at the counter waiting behind a woman with two small children, he also picked up a Little Debbie's snack cake. He paid for the milk and cake then walked out into the lot and over to the overfull waste can next to his car. The can rested against a huge white birch tree that afforded some cover. His car however, almost took that advantage away. It was yellow and stood out. Unfortunately, it was all that was available at the rental agency that day. Kuan shrugged it off as he turned to his snack.

He stripped the wrapping from the cake while he watched the drug store. He ate the sweet confection and swigged from the carton as he waited. Whatever the Indian was doing now, it was mysterious. After speaking with Chin earlier, he'd watched until the American Air Force officers had left. The Indian had watched them leave also, then looked the area over well before closing the door to the building. Kuan had ducked behind the bathrooms when the Indian began looking for watchers.

He had no doubt now, judging from the Indian's actions, that the policeman believed that he was under surveillance. Perhaps the officers had made him think that they were watching him. He had listened to the tape of their conversation after the Indian had gone back inside. He now knew that the Air Force wanted to get out to the island. Perhaps, the Indian thought that the Air Force believed him to be involved in this robbery they spoke of. Maybe he thought that the military was watching him because of this. However, Kuan knew the real reason why they wanted to go there. And it had nothing to with any robbery.

He wadded up the cake paper, crushed the milk carton and laid them on top of the full trash in the can. As he did, he noticed that someone had taken a lit cigarette and placed it upside down into a soda straw, sticking from a large cup. The ember had melted the straw into a glob. He shook his head in wonder as he brought his eyes back up to the drug store. These Americans were a strange people, he thought. Why would someone do such a thing. Surely, they must know that a fire could have been ignited by such a foolish action.

Only in America, he said to himself as the Indian walked out of the drug store carrying a small bag.

Escanaba International Airport,
Late Afternoon, same day

Mussenberg and Shears sat at the bar munching on peanuts and sipping beer from frosted glasses in the airport lounge. Shears turned up a wrist and glanced at his watch. "We've got about ten minutes," he said as he looked at his partner.

Mussenberg sighed. "Yeah, well I guess we better head over to the gate then, huh?"

He turned up his glass and gulped down the golden liquid as Shears did the same. Then both officers, now in civilian dress, stood and took their carry-on bags in hand to begin moving. Mussenberg looked at Shears as they walked up to the line forming for the security check. "So... the Old Man didn't say why he wanted us to report back in person and you've got no ideas either, right?"

Shears gave a quick shake of his head. "Nope. He just listened to what we had and said he'd call us back. When he did, he said for us to get our butts back to base, ASAP. If I had to venture a guess though", Shears canted his sunglassed eyes at Mussenberg, "I'd say he's running into problems with the Indian thing. The Department of Interior can't say shit to those Indians about that island now and I don't think the Puka coo coos or...whatever you call them... are gonna let us just go out to that island either. I'm guessing that there's going to have at be some deal'n done on this one."

Mussenberg took a few steps ahead as the line began to move. "Huh. I wonder if any of Stone's people have any idea who he is."

Shears smirked. "I doubt it."

Mussenberg hefted his bag and dropped it on the x-ray conveyor, then passed through the metal detector. He waited on the other side as Shears appeared. "So what'd'ya think. Are we gonna get knocked off this one or what?"

Shears pulled his bag off the conveyor and began walking with Mussenberg toward the boarding gate. "Naw, I think we'll stay on it. The Old Man wants this one bad 'cause he thinks that the device will be there. And that's the whole enchilada right there, my man." Both men gave their tickets to the attendant as they went through the boarding ramp that led to the plane. Shears looked back over his shoulder at Mussenberg, who stepped quicker to hear his partner. "And whoever gets that little baby... controls the whole world my friend. The whole wide-world and maybe... the whole wide universe."

The Boathouse

It's getting dark as I swing the Jeep into the marina lot. The cold
front moving in is cooling things rapidly, too. My leg hurts and the
prospect of riding that boat through heavy seas out to the island isn't
sounding too good. I think I made a yellow Ford Taurus tailing me
too, but I lost the car in traffic somewhere. Probably just paranoia.
But better paranoid than dead. That's my motto anyway. I grab the
McDonald's bag and go into the boathouse. I sit the bag on the desk
and go straight to the bathroom from there. I drop my pants and peer
at the back of my leg in the mirror. I peel off the blood-soaked
bandage that covers the bullet wound. I wash it out and apply more
ointment before re-bandaging the achy thing. Then, I pop a couple of
Excedrin and go back to eat my Quarter- ponders and fries.

As I eat, I listen to two new messages on the machine. The first is
from Hank Scari, the local guy that wants to hunt the island. He asks
me to call him back and he leaves a number. The next one is from
Nettie. She sounds sad as she says that she got my message about
Shultz and that she'd talked with Morse and Hennessey since then.
She says that the whole thing is awful but that God will see us
through it all. She isn't at all hesitant when she ends the call with "I
love you", before hanging up. My eyes get watery when I hear her say
that on the surreal scratching of the recording. I sit still for a long time
after the machine rewinds itself. Then I reach over, pick up the phone
and dial Hank Scari's number.

The phone's picked up on the third ring and a middle aged woman
said hello in a Upper accent.

"Hi, I'm trying to reach Hank Scari, is he in by chance?"

"Hank? Oh ya, sure he is. Jes a minute dare, okay?"

I hear her call his name and him answer. A few seconds later, he
says hello.

"Mr. Scari, this is Ely Stone, with the Tribal Police. I'm sorry I
missed you earlier but I'm returning your call."

"Oh ya, hey tanks fer calling back, eh. Lisen, I still wanna talk wit
ya about hunt'n on da island, eh, but tomorrow, I gatta fly a guy back
ta Green Bay that is one'of'em dat wants ta try bag' a goat off da
island. An well, I was hope'n maybe it'd be okay if I was ta stop on
da island an let'em look around a bit, eh, jes to get a feel fer it. I know
we ain't got no agreement an all but he knows dat too, eh. I told 'em
it'd only be for half hour or so, if ya said it was alright, cause he's
gatta be in Green Bay by one o'clock, eh?"

I was amazed and excited. "Mr. Scari, you're a pilot? I forgot. A

Chopper, right?"

"Ya, I fly a Hughes 500 for da guide service. Been flying since 1971 in Viet Nam, eh."

"Well I'll tell you what Mr. Scari, if you'll take me with you and come back to pick me up later on, I've got no problem with you showing the guy around. The tribe will even pay your fuel for the trip, how's that?"

"Eh, dat sounds like a winner. But we only do dis on one condition, eh?"

"Name it Mr. Scari and I'll see if I can make it happen."
He laughs then, a deep robust rumble from a man who doesn't look as if he's capable of it. "Ya, well da condition is dat ya call me Hank den, eh? An I getta call ya Ely. Fair enough?"

Now I understand what he thinks is so funny. "Deal, Hank. What time and where's your bird at?"

"I fly otta my back yard, eh. Jes come on down here at around eight thirty tomorrow morning an we'll head out from der, eh?"
He gives me directions and we hang up. Well, that solves one problem anyway. I get up to toss the McDonald's wrappers and notice that the computer screen is blinking a "You've got mail" notice. I drop the trash and click up my e-mail. There's one message. In the subject area it simply says, "Tenth Rubber. Gangues the Con". I click the message and it rolls out on the screen.

Ghost Man!
 As I live and breath. How's it hang'n, you shallow water sailor?
I haven't heard from you in a while. I understand that someone's trying to sell you some property. Nuff said. I am on it, like ugly on a woman officer. The two wing nuts you supplied are causing me difficulty but have no fear! I shall prevail. The other one, whom you say appears to be a realtor, could very well be. Records indicate that his company name, was bought back in 1975, when it was five years old. Nothing further on this individual other than a very recent public works search, etc. Knowing you as I do, I'm assuming that you were successful in selling him the piece of property. Good hearing from you and we must, I say again, MUST get together. Watch for further on the other requests. Take care! Gangues.

As I read the message, I decipher as I go along. Getting info on the two Air Force officers was causing him problems which, was unusual. It should be a routine thing for someone like Gangues but I could tell that he was excited with the challenge, whatever it was. What Gangues said about my pal Michael Nesmith from last night was that indeed, he could've been a killer and or player as his name was listed to a child who had died in 1975. He, or whoever set-up his cover, had probably taken the name from the death certificate of a five year old child, then built his identity from it. The mention Gangues made of a public works search was just the state police, making inquiries, trying to find the next of kin for the dead man. And Gangues assumed that I had sold real estate to this guy. Like I said, Gangues is a smart man.

I acknowledge his message and type in the name of Herman Veeter and his qualifiers. I ask Gangues to run a make on this guy too as he could be part of the game here. Then I sign off, take a deep breath and settle back in the chair. It doesn't appear that I have much I could do for the next ten hours so I decide to take another soaking bath. It will do wonders for my sore leg. I stand and move over to the door. I bolt it and allow myself a groan as I limp back and bolt the rear door, too. Then I pull the heavy .45 from its holster and put it away. I keep the little Glock close at hand though, as I start hot water running in the tub.

The Watcher

Kuan hunkered in the darkness of the marina and watched the boathouse. He had parked his automobile far away in order to assure that the Indian didn't get another look at it. He shivered as another gust of cold wind blew through the divider wall between the men's and women's restrooms. He had unscrewed the light bulbs overhead so as not to be silhouetted. From this position, he had watched the Indian's shadow as he moved inside the building. The Indian was quite sharp for a mere policeman. After he had left the druggist, the Indian had walked directly to his Jeep. Then he had stopped and backed up to peer across the street at Kuan's car. Kuan had quickly walked across the lot to dispel the policeman's fears. It seemed to have worked as the man shortly returned to his vehicle and left the store.

He turned his hand up and looked at the luminous dial of his watch. It was close to eight thirty. What had happened to Chin? What had happened to Tran? These were perplexing questions. He had tried to phone Chin all day and had not been able to. He knew nothing about Tran's whereabouts either. In a word, Kuan was worried. Fat had called shortly after arriving at the marina with his boat. He said that he was soaked from all of the waves and wind and had almost lost the vessel on his way back. He had sounded exhausted and frozen and Kuan had told him to go to the motel room and rest until morning. He could get his rope and proceed back to the island at that time. They would speak again before he left the marina.

Fat had not argued and that too, had displayed the man's utter exhaustion. Kuan was trying to figure out what he was going to do next when his phone chirped. He looked at the I.D. and immediately answered in a deep, excited, voice. "This is Adam!"

"Yes and this is Robert. I have just now been able to receive a telephone signal, so I am calling. This is the first opportunity I have had to do so. I tried to phone you after we spoke earlier but was not able to get through."

Kuan tried to maintain the level of respect in his deep voice. "Sir, is your phone working at all? I tried to call you several times today with some urgent news."

Chin sounded agitated when he replied. "It is working fine, but where I was at today, it was not possible to get a cellular signal. What have you to report?"

Kuan explained it all. Everything up to the discovery of the new mine shaft and his observation of the Indian. He took a gamble again and asked, "So where was this place where no signals can go sir?" Chin now sounded tired as he spoke. "There was a news broadcast by the state police over the television today. They showed a photo of a man killed in an automobile accident near a small village named Bruce's Crossing. The picture was that of a driver's license quality." Chin took a deep breath. "It was not good but I thought it could be Tran. They are looking for family or anyone who knows him. The dead man's name, was Michael Nesmith."

Kuan was dumbfounded. If Tran had been killed, then the mission was a failure. They would have to quickly try to get out of the country. He listened as Chin began speaking again.

"I could not reach you, but yet, I had to verify whether Tran had been killed or whether this was truly an accident. So I drove down to this place and investigated. I told the police that I had heard of the news broadcast and might know the man. They allowed me to look at the accident report and photos of the crash."

Kuan asked, "So do you think he was killed?"

"No. I do not. It was truly an accident, although a very bizarre one. One of these wild deer they have here, jumped right through Tran's windshield. He was then beaten by the animal's hooves, in what the police say is a common occurrence. I do not believe that this could have been staged. It was an accident. Tran was probably close to his mission also, as the police say they found a rifle that they think Tran was using to poach these animals."

"So Tran is dead. What did you tell the police then?"

"After seeing the reports and accident photos, I asked to see the television photo of the dead man. When they gave it to me, I simply said no, the man I thought it could be was an Oriental. They seemed to accept that, after looking at me and thinking about it."

"Ahh. So, how do we proceed now, sir?"

"I think that you and I will meet tomorrow and decide what to do about the one you're monitoring. Have Fat go back to the jobsite and investigate this new development as you planned. We must make headway quickly on this project now or else..." He let the words fade off but both men knew what was meant anyway. When the police couldn't find family or a better identity on Tran, an autopsy would probably be performed. What would be revealed, would alert every law enforcement and federal security agency in the country. Kuan watched as the lights in the boathouse went out. He had a thought.

"Sir, perhaps tonight might be the best time to eradicate the problem I've been monitoring? He has gone to bed now and it would be so easy right now."

"What?... There?... Now? No." Chin said incredulously. "That would seriously jeopardize our mission at this point. It may come to that, but not yet. Besides, you do not have a plan of action or follow-through, do you?"

Kuan hung his head, in spite of the distance of his superior. "No sir, I do not. I just desire to make this mission a success and we seem to be finding many set-backs."

Chin could hear the shame in his man's deep baritone voice. "I know you are a good man, Adam. And I respect your opinion. I promise this now. The eradication of this problem, I shall leave to you. It shall be your task, but... there must be planning and follow-through in its implementation. If your charge has gone to rest, then you should do so as well. Get some sleep my friend. It sounds like tomorrow we may have a long day."

Kuan did a quick bow, even though his superior couldn't see it and pushed the off button on the small phone. Then, he stepped from the cover of the bathrooms and stared at the boathouse. So, he thought, Tran died trying to kill you Indian? Well, I am not Tran. But Tran was one of my men. Ten of you Indian, would not be worth one of him. No wild deer will get me policeman. Your luck has just run out. He spit on the wet grass then turned and began walking toward his car, the cool wind whistling through the lines of the anchored boats in the marina's slips.

*

Chapter Fourteen
Double or Nothing

The Boathouse,
The Next Morning.

I stand outside the boathouse on the rear dock and sip my coffee as the sun peeks through the trees and warms my face. The small woods are a mix of birch and white pine that divide the marina from Lake Michigan. The bright gold leaves and white trunks of the fall birch are beautiful when silhouetted against the dark jade green of the pines. I like them. I've been up since dawn and have already said my prayers. I had dreamed again last night, but mercifully, I hadn't awoken in the middle of a nightmare. The dream was about the island again, and for the life of me, I can't remember it. I feel my head shake unconsciously.

For now, I am just taking in His wonders as I finished my smoke. The weather has softened and there is a gentle breeze out of the southwest. It brings the smell of the Big Lake and freshness to my nose. The temperature is no more than fifty five, but it's going to be a pretty day. Yet, I know this won't last. The weather has been freakishly mild for this time of year, and snow has already fallen up by Sault Ste. Marie and the Keweenaw Peninsula. It was coming this way, too. And soon.

I draw the last of the smoke from the hand-rolled, then field-strip the butt and shoot a glance at my watch. I have to go, but first I want to check on my boat rental guy, to see if maybe Gangues had found anything. I move back inside and over to the computer, I circle the mouse and the machine fires-up, allowing me to key in the internet and my e-mail address. I only have one message and it is from Tenth Rubber. In the subject area after it says "In the Clear," meaning that the message isn't in code. I open and read.

Ghostman,

Nothing of major note on your guy Herman Veeter except for a shooting back in 1993. It seems that Veeter owned a specialty furniture building shop in downtown Grand Rapids, MI. Apparently, two crack heads tried to rob him in his store at gunpoint and somehow, he got the drop on them and shot and killed one of them himself. He had a license for a .38

Smith & Wesson for store protection. Just prior to that he had
been hospitalized in a psychiatric hospital and released so that
spooked the cops because they did some kind of investigation
on him. Records of that are on hard copy so you'll have to contact
the GRPD for further.

Prosecutor eventually ruled it justifiable homicide. Nothing
else other than he's drawing social security and was also
drawing on an IRA. He's apparently retired but it does show
that he just re-mortgaged his home and cashed out the IRA.
That seems kind of weird for a retired guy to do unless he
needs money but otherwise, that's it on him.
I've had Boo Coo trouble getting into these two Wingnuts'
files. The Air Farce has all kinds of blocks up and they're
damn good ones! But I'm going to hammer them with my
Dragon Slayer later tonight, when all their keyheads are gone
home. I'll be in touch... hang loose!   Yo bro, Gangues

I smile as I click off the e-mail and heft the Colt pistol. I have no
doubt that he'll get in. Gangues is always devising a new means to
conquer a computer system. It seems that Dragon Slayer is his current
cutting edge innovation for that purpose. For a rich, brainy guy like
Gangues, this kind of stuff is ecstasy for him. That boy does love
these computer games.

So, Mr. Veeter has no criminal record, but has had a violent
incident in his past. That's interesting. It's also interesting that he was
in a mental hospital. Interesting and scary. So's the little fact that he
re-mortgaged his home recently. Why? I holster the gun on my side
and feel the .45's weight tugging downward. It is a comforting
feeling. I am wearing my jungle boots and atop the right one, my
Glock rests in a ankle holster. That too, feels good. I don't know what
I'll find on the island, but sure as shit, everybody's looking for
something out there. The boy scout in me... always likes to be
prepared. Besides, that's the Coast Guard motto too. "Semper
Paratus"- Always Ready. Can I help it if I've been inundated with this
theme via male dominated clubs over my lifetime?

I start to head out when I decide that a quick call downstate might
be a good idea. I move over to the phone and dial directory for Grand
Rapids. After scribbling down the number, I punch it in. It is picked
up on the second ring.

"Grand Rapids Police, Officer Crow."

"Hey, how ya doing?"

"Well, I'm not dead yet. Can I help you, sir?"

Ahhh. Big city policemen. Always so cheerful and jovial. "Yeah. I'm Special Agent Stone, with the Pukaskwa Tribal Police and I need a little information on a case you guys worked awhile back."

"The what... tribal police?"

"The Pukaskwa. We just got our federal recognition so the name may be unfamiliar to you. We're up in the U.P."

"Yeah, I guess so. I know about the People of the Three Fires, but this is the first time I've ever heard of you guys."

"Uh, huh. Well, what'd'ya think? Can ya help me out with this?"

"Yeah, I think so. I don't usually work the desk. I'm just covering for a guy who's on a fishing trip. Uhh, let's see. I'll need your department I.D. and your badge number for the run."

I already have these numbers out from my wallet and read them to him as I listen to him typing on the computer keys. He has to verify me before getting the file. Then, I give him Veeter's name and particulars. A few seconds later, he comes back to the phone.

"Hey, we gotta a BOLO out on this guy. You people have 'em up there?"

BOLO was the cop acronym for "Be On the Look Out". In other words, Veeter isn't wanted on a warrant but they could be looking for him for questioning, as a missing person, material witness or any one of a dozen things.

"Well, maybe, run the description by me." Crow then relays the physical description of Herman Veeter. My thoughts form a mental picture from his words and... I believe that I have talked to the man here in Escanaba.

"Hmm. What're you guys looking for him for?"

"Says here that he walked away from his house and his daughter hasn't seen him in almost ... well it'd be about two weeks now, according to the report. Uh, let's see. Yeah it looks like an infrequent history of 1096 going back at least ten years. So do you have him there or what?"

I decide that Officer Crow doesn't need that information just yet and maybe not at all. 1096 is police code for a mentally unstable person. Whatever Veeter is doing, I've got a notion I'll find out.

"No, at least not by the physical you gave. His name's come up on a case I'm working right now and I'm trying at see how he fits, ya know? What happened with that shooting he had several years ago? What I have now, says that the investigator checked Veeter for past medical history. Your report show anything on that?"

Crow had to put me on hold while he takes another call and I'm trying to apply this latest info to what I already know when he comes back on the line.

"Yeah, the Dic working the case did check on that. Okay, it says we cleared this guy and the shooting was ruled as justifiable by the Prosecutor. It seems that he had a rough time when his wife died some years back and was hospitalized but he was stable and rational at the time of the shooting incident. Is that what you wanted?"

"Uh, uh. I already have that. You have the hard copy of the investigator's report there, right?"

"That's what I'm looking at."

"Okay, what does the investigator say about Veeter's previous medical record?"

"Ahhh. Okay, wait a second… it says… um… down at the bottom of page two, that the subject was admitted to Saint Mary's Hospital in the psychiatric wing for treatment of severe depression and dementia in 1989. Uh, doctor tells the detective that nothing about Veeter's past illness would contribute or make him prone to a violent act now, etc, etc. Let's see, uhm the doctors said that he was basically hospitalized at that time for depression over his wife's death. And so, since the shooting was justifiable in all other respects, the detective on this case recommended to the prosecutor that there be no criminal charges. It says here that Veeter was suffering from delusions concerning UFOs, and aliens taking his wife instead of him. He couldn't accept her death, da da, daa…uh, that appears to be all it says about it. Does that help?"

I quickly ran it all through my mind and found nothing else to ask. "Yeah, I think so. Thanks for going to the trouble." I wonder about something else. "You said your name was Crow. Are you Indian?"

"Yep. Paquina from out Montana way."

"Holy smoke Bro, what'chu doing this far up north?"

"Ya know, I honestly don't know. I came here after I got out'ta the Army and went into the cops. But I've about had with this big city stuff. My aunt passed away a few months ago and left me her ranch back on the Rez so I'm out'ta here in another couple of weeks. I'm gonna try raising sheep for awhile I guess, see how that works out."

"Well you got my number on the caller I.D. right?"

"Yeah, it's here."

"Okay, buddy, well hang onto it and give me a call if I can ever help you with anything. You can always get a hold of me through our Rez in Wiitikan too, alright?"

"Yeah, okay. Thanks. I appreciate it. Oh shit, I gotta another call. You take care Blood!"

"Yeah and you too Bro. See ya." I hang up the phone and briefly wonder about the circumstances that brought a Western Indian from the Big Sky country to the Great Lakes of the Midwest. It is probably a good story but glancing at the time displayed on the digital telephone window, I don't have time to contemplate it. I get moving. I walk out the door, grabbing my jacket as I go. I'd already loaded the climbing rope and duty bag so I just climb in and start the Jeep. I look around but see nothing suspicious as I back out of the parking spot and then tool up to the main drag.

But as I turn onto the street, I see a yellow car roll out of the gas station down the road and fall-in behind other traffic. Uh, huh. Good to know I'm not seeing things anyway. Well, I have no intention of doubling back to find out who it is. I have to make it to old Hank Scari's place to catch a ride. Besides, whoever it is will be waiting for me when I get back. Ten minutes later, I fold the paper directions I'd scribbled out and turn into the Scari's driveway.

I drive through a thick hedge that grows dense and green around the yard. Hank quickly walks up and introduces me to his wife Eilene and his client. In another five minutes, we are airborne. As the helicopter lifts up, I look down at the street and see the yellow Taurus pulled over to the shoulder just past Hank's house. A man is trotting back to it from the hedges that encompass the Scari home as we circle overhead. He looks up and I get a good look at the face. Then we are past him as he climbs into the vehicle.

The Escanaba Municipal Marina

Kuan pulled into a parking space and exited the car, slamming the door. The marina was fairly deserted today, it being Monday and the beginning of the workweek. He didn't worry about anyone noticing his anger as he quick stepped up to the dock and began walking toward Fat on the boat. A few seconds later, Kuan jumped aboard the little vessel and moved up to where Fat sat in the driver's seat.

"This fucking Indian policeman is a very bad prick!" fumed Kuan as he came to a rest on the other seat. He glared at Fat and the other man winced from the rage exhibited from his superior's face. "I make a vow here. I will kill this man slowly and enjoy it very much." Kuan spit into the water and swore in Chinese while turning back to Fat.

"This policeman flew away on a helicopter a short while ago! How am I to follow him when he does this!" He pounded his fist on the boat's dash. "I should have eliminated him last night! He is a major problem for us. This mission is going to pieces because we do not seem to be able to do the right things when necessary." Kuan shook his head in resignation. "We must make momentum on this mission soon!" He brought his eyes back to Fat. "Tran is dead. The boss said that he died in an automobile accident involving a wild deer."

Fat's eyes grew large and to Kuan, they looked very American when he did this. "Is the boss sure?"

"Yes, he said he drove to the place yesterday and verified it. That is why we could not reach him. He could get no cellular signal there." Fat looked down at his hands. "I have known him for a long time. He will be missed." He raised his eyes back to meet Kuan's. "You do not think the policeman had anything to do with it then?"

"No. He is just a stupid policeman but he has become a pain in my arse." At that time, both men looked to the north where the distinctive sound of a helicopter hummed. A small white helicopter was swooning over the town. "Shit!," exclaimed Kuan, "That is the helicopter the Indian left in!"

Both men watched the aircraft until it disappeared from sight. Fat thought carefully before asking, "Why did you not make the elimination last night then?"

Kuan turned his eyes to the weedy water of the marina. "Because the boss said it would have been foolish to do so and… he was correct. This policeman's death will come to pass though. I swear this!" He nodded his head to himself. "Very well, since we do not know where the policeman went and time is of the essence, you must go back out and investigate this new shaft you have found."

He pointed to the deck where a K-Mart bag with a new red and white braided rope spilling out of it rested. "I see you have purchased your rope so I will let you leave here. Have you spoken to Quang?" Fat shook his head. "No. I have not. I can not reach him. He does not answer and all I get, is the voice mail device. This seems odd also because the weather is clear today."

Kuan took this in then gave a quick nod. "Very well. Proceed with your task and call me with any news." He patted the other man on the shoulder and quickly moved off the boat. Fat flipped a blower switch and turned the key, firing-off the vessel's engine. It coughed to life and blue exhaust spewed over the water. Kuan watched as Fat maneuvered the boat through the marina and out toward the Great Lake beyond. It disturbed him that Quang was not answering his calls. He reached into the front seat of the car, pulled out phone and dialed Quang's number. After several rings, he was put into voice mail. He told Quang to call Adam as soon as possible, then pushed off. He stood watching seagulls floating on the breezes above the tall masts of the sailboats. He didn't like this at all. Quang would be answering his calls if all was well. He looked down at the phone in his hand an punched in another number. It was answered on the third ring.

"This is Robert."

"This is Adam. This line is not secure. We have new developments and most of them… are not good."

In the air to Muskrat Island

I sit in back and only half listen to Hank chatter to his client over the earphones. Hank was jogging around over the town, pointing out things of interest, but my mind was running in different directions, trying to put things together. That is why Hank has to call me twice before I hear him.

"Ely, I say, didja hear me dat we're jus gotta drop ya off an be on'are way?"

"No, I'm sorry. I'm daydreaming, I guess. I thought you guys were going to look around the island a little bit."

"Yah, we was eh, but Larry here gotta call dis morning saying dat he's gotta be back by eleven. Dat'd be cutting it too short, eh." Larry turns around and smiles at me with his hands up in the air in a "what can I do?" attitude. I smile back and nod as Hank speaks again.

"But, I can come back an get'ya whenever ya want, eh. Da weather looks so-so for da next couple a days but ya jus gimme a call an I'll head dat way."

"Okay Hank, sounds good. I don't know when it'll be. Maybe tomorrow, maybe tonight even."

"No problem. Jes gimme a call. Only takes a little while from my house, eh," he says. I have another thought as he finishes.

"Okay, will do. Listen Hank, do me a favor and take us in over the north side of the island, will ya?"

Hank's voice fills the headset. "Sure thing. We can do dat alright." Then he and his client begin chatting again.

I sit back and watch out of the port side as the dark blue water of Lake Michigan begins filling the window of the helicopter, the sun glinting off the white painted aluminum of the aircraft. As I look out of the Plexiglas to the left, I can see the island looming in the distance. It is growing larger as we close the distance. A few minutes more and I see the depth of the Great Lake begin to shallow below. We are approaching the island quickly and I again scoot forward in my seat, peering out the window. Hank asks if I want to hover the north side a little bit and I tell him that that'd be great. Hank takes us slowly along the north shore as I study the face of the rock. The massive white pines decorate the highest points of land and run right down to where the land, seemingly, drops off to nothing. Almost as if it were sliced off at that point.

Looking at this side, with the new information in mind, it appears different than it did from a boat. Of course, the appearance could just as easily have been explained by the fact that I was seeing for the first time from the air. I believe that I can make-out a sharp deviation in mass from the island. I also notice that the water in the cove area is all rock. That differs from every other place surrounding the island where white sand is intermixed with large boulders. That is unusual. Hank's voice brings me out of thought.

"Hey, der's a boat down dere. I didn't know ya could get a boat in dere through those shallows. Looks like it washed up in dere somehow, eh?"

I switch over to the right where Hank and Larry are looking out the starboard windows. Down in that little cove, right where I plan to rope in, sits a fourteen-foot aluminum boat, snugged tightly in to shore. There are branches laying across it that almost obscure it from view. And in fact, unless a helicopter were right here, exactly where we were, odds are good you would never notice it. I don't think it just washed up there.

"Hank, can you drop down a bit? I'd like to get a better look at that."

He doesn't answer in words, he just leans the cyclic forward and the bird drops down. I crane my head and see what I think are small ropes tied off to shore from the boat. The little boat itself, looks just like one of the rentals from the Escanaba tackle shop. I can also see what I take to be a possible trail going up through the dense underbrush. I guess I have company here and... I also figure that these guys have seen enough of this.

"Okay Hank, that'll do it for me. I didn't realize the time. I guess maybe you better drop me off, huh?"

Hank looks at his watch and reluctantly agrees. The boat is a mystery and possibly offers a new route for his hunting expeditions, providing we get the details all worked out. A few minutes later, we spool down to a perfect landing right next to the lighthouse.

Lake Michigan

Fat cut a straight line across Lake Michigan as he held the boat's throttle wide open on the way to Muskrat Island. Time was of the essence and he would not take a leisurely route around the shipping lanes this time. The seas were light today and the breeze was gentle. He marveled at how terrible and treacherous this water had been yesterday and how calm it was today. He knew from his briefing that this Great Lake was one of the world's largest fresh water seas. He also knew and understood that before this mission, he had never operated a vessel on fresh water before. Still, how could they be so different? A fresh water sea and a salt water one. It was a wonderment to him.

Even more of a wonderment, was Quang. Why had he not answered his calls. He was worried about his partner. He adjusted himself in his seat as a wave from another boat, a fishing trawler, came into his path. He rode over it with ease. Fat had spent his first few years in the Navy as a torpedo boat officer so he was used to the open sea and such occurrences. He was able to see the island clearly now and also, what appeared to be an aircraft over it. He backed the throttle off and the boat settled in the water to a stop. He scampered below and returned with a pair of binoculars. He brought them to his eyes and adjusted the focus. He cursed in Chinese and brought the glasses down while reaching for his cell phone.

Muskrat Island

We say our goodbyes and I heft the rope over my shoulder, pick up my bag and watch as the "Magnum P.I." looking helicopter pulls up and away from the ground. Nowadays, the Hughes 500 was called a "Little Bird" and is usually a SPECOPs platform. But it was called a "Loach" by the 'Nam Army pilots that flew it because it resembled a big bug. It was primarily used as a scout aircraft in that war but a sturdier, more agile bird was hard to find. In no time, the chopper is a mere dot in the distance. I glance toward the lighthouse door and wonder if my company is in there.

I move quickly to the doorway and gently set the rope and bag to the grass. I pull the .45 out and ease the slide back to see the brassy shine of a round in the chamber. I ease the slide forward and pull the hammer back, cocking the weapon. I hadn't locked the door when I left last time as I figured visitors were an unlikely commodity out here on this desolate rock. Go figure. My left hand turns the knob as I bend down to the left of the door jamb, the big .45 up, in my other hand. The catch clicks and the door swings squeakily on its hinges to open full. I pan the room and find nothing amiss. I enter in a combat stance, moving swiftly, clearing each room and finally the light tower. Nobody is here. But the shinkakee is with me and I am sure that Someone... has been here. I holster the pistol and make a quick, inventory of items, but again, I don't find anything out of the norm.

Not until I go into the closet, that is. The only piece of rope that I'd been able to find when I went looking for it before, is missing from the wall hook in the closet. It was there beside some new cans of white primer spray paint that the contractors likely used to paint the new electrical conduit. The rope was only about ten feet or so and that wasn't what I needed to get down to the trail where the deer and goats were jumping. So, I just left the rope there, planning on bringing a longer piece back from town. It's gone now. Well, well. Curiouser and curiouser. I move over to the kitchen cabinet and rummage around until I find a box containing several little Slim Jim meat sticks. I peel the wrapper back and munch on the dried sausage as I contemplate my next move.

Somewhere by that boat in the cove is probably where my guests are located. Why they need that piece of rope is a mystery but the fact that they were here sure isn't. If I take the rope I'd bought along, it will slow my reaction time to whatever might come up. I sure can't afford that. I decide to leave it here, along with some other "get your ass killed" stuff, too. I finish the Slim Jim and unbutton the uniform shirt and take it off. It is too light in color and the gold badge and nametag have a tendency to glint in the sun. This is a sure-fire way to draw attention and… gunshots to oneself.

I dig in my duty bag and pull out my old tigerstripe camouflage shirt and pants. I put them on and adjust the fit for today's business. I have four extra clips for the .45. I put two in the right billows pocket of the tigerstripe shirt and two in my right pants side pocket. I have two extra clips for the Glock so I just put them in the left pocket of the shirt. I look down in the bag at my knife. Now the smart thing to do is slide the thing onto my belt, but well… I never score very high on I.Q. tests. I strap the sheathed survival knife upside down to the inside of my right forearm and pulled the sleeve down over it. If I have to use the thing, I'll probably cut my hand off with it. Then, I pull out the shorty twelve gauge Western Field from my bag and screw it together.

It is old, but still a good gun. It had belonged to my Daddy and had been passed down to me. I load it with buckshot and fill the rest of the box of shells into my free pants billows side pocket. As a rule, you're given a choice of weapons whenever you're working special warfare. They've got everything from machine guns to miniature cannons. I always opted for a shotgun. I'd grown up hunting with them and was pretty well-versed in their operation. If you had a good one and kept it clean, it'd never jamb and could clear a zone better than any M-16, in my opinion. It was an excellent assault weapon.

The last thing I do is move over to the wood stove and open the door. I take a scoop of ashes in my hand, go over to the sink and pump the handle. I moisten the ashes, mixing them, then put two streaks of black, straight down along both of my cheeks and make arrow points with my fingers at the tops of both lines. Uncle Mason told me this was our family war paint sign. I'm never sure what good it does but I'd done it the same way hundreds of times, whenever I was in similar fixes and had to wear a painted face. Now, I tote my stuff and quietly sneak out the back door

I travel the back way to the cove, and as I move along, that tune bumps into my consciousness. It had been a couple of days since I last heard it, but it still spooks me. I have to stop as "Ghost Riders in the Sky" plays through my mind again. The shinkakee rolls over me like gangbusters and a shiver goes uncontrollably down my spine. It is several beats before I can continue on. Ooooh, man. This shit isn't good. I become an infantryman, moving only with cover and waiting before moving again. It takes awhile to get somewhere when you do this, and in the back of my mind, along with Johnny Cash and his song, the thought passes by that maybe my visitors will be gone by the time I arrive. But then again, I'm never that lucky.

It was only about a ten minute walk from the lighthouse to the cove area but it takes me all of forty five minutes to get there. I work my way up to where the trail led down to the cove below. A rope is hanging there, lassoed around a natural outcrop of rock that formed a perfect hook for it. So here is proof that this is actually a trail of some kind and not just one used by animals. I wait, watch and listen.

Finally, I decide to move. I have been still for almost ten minutes. I'd knelt beside a small sassafras and the pain, while less than yesterday, is still present in my leg. As I pull the shrub back to stand, a ruffed grouse stands there behind the little tree, bent down feeding on wintergreen. It's brown crested head pops up, twisting and turning as it tries to figure out what I am. The bird is only a foot away from me. The brilliant shades of brown, tan, black and white are stark against the red spotted darkness of the wintergreen. The music in my head stops and is replaced by a myriad of questions. I could try to grab the bird, but I'd probably miss. I could stay still and hope... yeah, right. Either way, if it spooks and busts into flight, my position will be given away.

Decisions, decisions. It doesn't matter. The grouse has made-up his mind. It's decided that whatever the funny looking creature next to it is, it is not sticking around to find out. It explodes into flight, its wings beating a drum as it snaps branches and knocks off leaves in its hasty departure. From the time I first saw the bird until it flew away, no more than five seconds has passed. Now, whatever element of surprise I had was gone. Oh well. I figure that the odds are good that whoever is out there has probably seen the chopper and maybe even my landing too. The cup is half full, that's what I always say. Uh, huh. You'betcha I do. I have to move now and change position, regardless of the stupid ass cup.

I finger the safety off the twelve-guage and side-step over thirty yards or so to another tree, this one bigger and of the white pine variety. I linger there another five minutes and still hear nothing. Up ahead, where the game trail comes up from the eight foot drop, I see a broken branch on a jack pine. Looking closer, I see some wild rye grass is mashed down where someone stepped off the game trail. And it wasn't an animal that had mashed the grass down, either. From where I am, it looks like the trail leads over the stone face back into a small clearing. I can see ample light back there through the foliage. I decide to follow this trace and begin moving along, continuing to spot other tell-tale signs of a man's travel. As I go, I continue my stops and starts until finally, I am abreast of a small clearing.

I can just make out the body of a man, dressed in black, lying face-down on the rock face at the edge of the opening, directly across from my position. Occasionally, as a slight breeze would ruffle through the clearing, the man's red hair would waft about in its momentary current. Even from the distance, I can hear the buzz of flies around the body. I scootch in close to a dead log to watch the clearing. The mosquitoes harass me while I sit in the dense shade of the towering white pines but I keep my stillness. I silently chastise myself for not putting on bug repellant back at the lighthouse, but after thirty three minutes, I am pretty sure that there is nobody left in the clearing except its sole occupant. I ease up from the fallen tree and pick my footing carefully, easing to the edge of the opening and peer about.

I am positive that Redhair is dead. He hasn't moved a muscle in almost an hour. I see what I think is an old mine shaft opening next to where he lay. The hole in the ground is framed with old timbers and butts against a steep incline of solid rock that extends almost straight upward. I can make out other old discarded framing timbers surrounding the underground opening and scattered about.

And tied to another section of rope, is the piece that was missing from the lighthouse. So this was my visitor. I keep the shotgun on him as I enter the small opening and walk toward the body. I stop about fifteen feet away and watch for breathing. I don't expect there to be any, though, because there is a dime sized hole in Redhair's back It is just between the shoulder-blades and there is plenty of dried blood surrounding it. The rock face on which he lays sprawled is covered in blood, also. He has been dead awhile. I bend down and, keeping the gun pointed at the head, roll the body over. Rigor is headed out now but the body is still stiff.

I recognize him. I'd seen him at the marina, too. Shit! What the hell is going on. First old Yellow Hair and now this red-haired one, here? And who took this one out of the game? He has a little Berretta in his hand and I have to lay the shotgun down to pry it from his fingers. I sniff the barrel and can smell the powder. It has been fired recently and glancing around, I see at least two empty shell casings from the gun. His cell phone lay broken open on the rock. I slipped the Berretta into my back pocket and as I looked down at him, I wondered. So, I bent closer and peered closely at the dead man's eyes.

They were locked open but not faded in death. That was odd because they should've been. I looked closer yet. He was wearing blue contact lenses. That explained it. Huh. Well, to paraphrase old Forrest Gump, Weird is as weird does. I noticed that the skin around the eyes, had the same little wrinkles around them that my blond haired realtor'd had too. Something was fishy with that. Hell man, who was I kidding? There was something fishy about all this stuff! I rocked back on my heels and stood up feeling a slight stab of pain in my leg. I started to bend down for the shotgun and a voice behind me… stopped me cold.

"You don't want to do that."

I let both of my hands open and slowly straightened up. "Oh booooy… you don't know how really bad I do… want to do that but… I guess I won't."

"I would say that's a wise decision on your part. Now, would you mind turning around very, very slowly for me. I'd hate to have an accident at this point wouldn't you?"

I eased around slowly. Very slowly. "Oh, yes sir. You're sure right about that. I've always been big on safety." I slowly turned my head from side to side for emphasis, looking as I did for a way out.

"I hate accidents. Just hate 'em. Heck, I was even the captain of my school safety patrol." I can't see him. "Now you gotta admit, that's being safety conscious." When I got turned full around, I still didn't know where the talker was. Not until he spoke again.

"Well to be honest, I'm not sure just much how faith I have in this finger doing exactly as I tell it to. This gun could go off without me desiring it. So that's why slow is best for both of us."

I could see him now and I knew why I'd missed him before. He was artfully camouflaged in front of a barely discernable hole in the ground, covered in old rough-sawn wooded framing boards and only his eyes shown through the slats between the wood. The boards were weathered gray and formed a dense picket that was interwoven with grape vines and the branches of several large cedar trees.

The appearance of his hiding place was that of thick brush against Solid rock. But I had the feeling I knew him. The gun that was leveled at me, looked like an old .38 special, its worn barrel sticking out between a slat. If he'd hit Mr. Redhair from where he was at now, it explained why the man died quickly. It's hard to get more point-blank than twelve feet and even a little .38 special will do the trick at that range. I nodded to him behind the wood and decided to try out my guess on our acquaintance.

"So how're ya doing Mr. Veeter? Do you and your daughter come out to the island often to shoot skeet and um… people?"
I saw a smile crack under the broken image of the face behind the boards. The pale green eyes wound up in mirth lines as a small laugh escaped from him.

"Well, good for you. You've done your homework haven't you? But it's Scheel, actually. Albert Scheel. Not Veeter. And no, I'm afraid my daughter doesn't really live in Escanaba."

The deep German accent he had before was barely a memory in his speech now. I hiked up my shoulders. "Sorry. Honest mistake. But your daughter is looking for you. Did you know that? She's worried about you."

The gun was steady in his hand and leveled straight at my chest. And crazy or not, those green eyes never blinked as they watched me. I had the sinking feeling that me and old Redhair here, were going to be sharing this ground in a few minutes. Talking seemed like the only avenue.

"So, Mr. Vee...uh, Seal is it?"

The man used his free hand and removed some of the boards from his upper body area. "No, it's Scheel, like the heel of a shoe but with an "SC" placed before it. So you pronounce it Sha..eel." The gun never wavered as he pushed several of the boards off from him, prying back the hanging cedar branches. When he did, I could see that he was sitting flat on the ground, propped up against a vertical timber, his rumpled-up jacket lying beside him. It appeared to be a timber-framed opening he was occupying. Okay, now I got it. It was probably the opening to the mine. That made sense. The hole I was standing by, was probably an excavation shoot. The old man wheezed.

"It's funny you know. I haven't said my real name out loud in oh..." he turned his head sideways but the gun remained steady, "perhaps close to fifty years now."

He turned his expression back at me and smiled but I could tell something was wrong with him. The old face was haggard and there were several days growth of gray whiskers on his lined cheeks. Maybe Redhair here had pegged him with one of his rounds. I smiled back at him.

"Well see there, it's good for you to bare your soul like that. Look at what it's done for you already, I mean, you don't speak with hardly any accent anymore, do you?"

He laughed again. "Aha. So you do remember me from the marina then, huh Officer Stone?"

"I never forget a kind face." I looked down at the dead man by my feet. "So, are you just up here doing a little target shooting then?"

The old man tilted his head and brought it back. "You might say that. He is a foreign national. An enemy of this country. Today, he presented a good target for me. He has done so on several occasions but today... he gave me no choice and he became a valid target." He nodded at me. "You've been a target on past occasions also. And I'd determined that you too, would have to be a valid one as well."

Well there it was. Game, set, match and I was out of options. I might try a lunge at him, maybe try to take him that way but I'd never get one of my guns up before he drilled me with that .38. I brought my eyes up to meet his.

"Well I'd sure appreciate it if you'd make it another fine shot like that." I pointed my thumb to the body. "Cause I'm not big on suffering, ya know?" I shrugged my shoulders again. "You're holding all the cards."

The old man looked at me with his light emerald eyes as I watched emotions and thoughts swim through them. Finally, he shook his head, squeezed his eyelids shut and lowered the gun to beside his leg. "I've lived here too long. I can't shoot a cop. Why the hell did I ever I think I could?"

I didn't know but I was sure glad he'd been a citizen long enough for it to affect his outlook. I began easing down to a kneel when he snapped his eyes back to me. I froze.

"I haven't played poker in a long time Officer but since you think I'm holding good cards… maybe you would be interested in a game of double or nothing?"

I canted my eyes downward then back to meet his. "Maybe. Depends on the stakes I guess."

The old man's eyes began to water as he stared at me and shortly, a single tear streamed along one wrinkled cheek, fighting its way downward against the gray stubble of his heard. Then he spoke, in a wheezy voice.

"The stakes are a little girls life!" He jutted his jaw for emphasis as he said it, shaking slightly in emotion. For my part, I was just trying desperately to grab a lever on this situation. After a few seconds of silence, he dropped his countenance and then looked up and around. He sighed as he looked off into the woods behind me.

"You know officer… I dearly hate this place. I hate it more than anywhere else in the world and it scares me. It terrifies me actually, more than anything else in the world too."

I begin slowly easing back down again, turning so that my right hand could move to my boot top. The old man kept looking off in the distance and I shortly had the Glock up and laying easily in my hand, a quick point to him. I cleared my throat, just glad once again, to still be alive.

"I'm hoping you're going to tell me what's going on here Mr. Scheel."

He brought his eyes back to mine then down to the gun in my hand. A small smile tugged at his mouth as he returned his gaze to the far off.

"You are a cool customer aren't you Officer Stone? Tell me, do all the cops up here have dirty faces?" He sighed and leaned forward, letting his pistol twirl over in his finger so the gun went upside down. Then he handed it to me. I leaned over and took it, jabbing it into my pocket with the little Berretta.

"You'll have to trust me that I don't have another one because I probably can't get up. I may have had a stroke or possibly a heart attack, I'm not sure." He seemed pretty nonchalant about that little revelation.

"I have pills in my vest pocket, down in the boat." He shook his head as he looked at me. "I can't believe I forgot them down there but I did." His eyebrows arched in a whimsical pattern.

"I was diagnosed with a mild heart complication in 1989 but really haven't experienced any trouble since then. Just the same, the doctor told me to keep my pills handy, just in case I suppose. Just too much excitement, perhaps." He looked curiously at me. "The encounter probably excited my heart quite thoroughly."

I nodded as I watched him. "Yep. It'll make your old ticker pound a little harder... that's for sure. Of course," I jabbed my thumb to the body, "it was a lot harder on his heart." The old man tightened his jaw as he looked at me then easily, let a slight nod pass my way as if to say, "Touché". I had to know how bad he was and I quickly searched my limited medical knowledge before raising my chin to him.

"Are these nitroglycerin pills down in the boat then?"

He brought his hand up and wiped his mouth before answering.

"No, they're for slowing my heart. I can get an irregular heartbeat when I'm under stress and the pills will regulate that. If I continue without them, then I can have a heart attack. I knew I'd never make it to the pills so I just sat here and remained still. I knew the other one would return sometime but instead, you came along. That partridge you frightened almost gave me a real heart attack."

I nodded, a feeling of concern swelling in me. "There's another one of these guys on the island?"

"No. No," he shook his head. "One of them traveled back to Escanaba to procure more rope last night. He was going to return today. You see," he pointed at the hole beside me, "they thought that was the mine shaft I'd reported all those years ago." He smiled again. "They were close but that isn't it. Where I'm at, is where the entrance to the mine is. That hole, is just an old feeder chute."

I let my sight travel to the dead man and the surrounding clearing. Well, whoever Redair was, he and the old man obviously weren't together. And the dead man carried the same weapon that the blond haired Michael Nessmith'd had on him. And there was another one them out there somewhere. All things considered, I thought I'd better trust the old man's words, for as far as I could anyway. I turned back to him.

"Are you still having chest pains or whatever you had?"

"No. They weren't really pains. More like irregular beating of my heart, I think. I became dizzy and disoriented for some time, then it eased. Now, I seem to be very tired is all."

"Okay. Do you think the pills would help if I went and got them for you?"

The old man tilted his head and fingered the lobe of his ear. "I don't know. Possibly." He nodded. "Yes, probably they would."

"Well that's what we'll do then. Look Scheel, don't take this personal but I've had people trying to kill me for a couple of days now and I'm real tired of it. I think this guy," I pointed to the body, "is a part of that. So, if you're fucking with me over your heart, well... you'd better be sure to kill me next time because I that's what I'll do to you if you don't. Okay?"

The old man raised a hand and smiled. "Understood perfectly."

I looked at him closely. "Okay. I hope so. Now I'll be right back. You sit tight."

I stood, grabbed the shotgun and made my way back through the timber to the rope dangling from the rock hook. This time I'd covered the distance in less than a minute. I slung the gun over my shoulder, grabbed the rope and scampered down the eight foot drop. I followed the trail downward to the small cove. The trail was like a covered bridge, the cedars having grown over themselves to form a natural roof that effectively hid the trail from view. The old man's boat was tied up at the foot of the trail. The vest sat on a seat and I rummaged the pockets until I came up with two medicine bottles. One of them was a vitamin supplement. I pocketed both and slid a plastic bottle of water from under the boat into my pants billows pocket. Then made my way back to the rope, wondering if I was going to get shot the whole way. When I finally popped my head over the top, I was relieved.

A few minutes later, I was back at the clearing. The old man was still plainly visible and sitting in the mine opening. His eyes were closed and as I started across the opening I began to wonder if maybe he'd died on me. But the pale green irises became visible as I knelt down and he opened his eyes. The prescription said to take one tablet at the onset of heart palpitation so I handed him a pill and the water bottle. He took it and swallowed deeply from the water container then leaned back and closed his eyes again. He had to get to a hospital. I pulled out the cellular phone and punched the on button. Several seconds later, it tweaked, signaling that it was operational. The old man's eyes popped open at the sound and he looked at me with a face of fear.

"What are you doing?"

"I'm calling for an air ambulance Mr. Scheel. We've got to get you to a hospital."

He lurched forward and sent his hand over to latch onto my arm.

"No, please don't do that," he said with pleading eyes.

I looked into a face displaying turmoil and anxiety and began to worry that he might cause himself even more harm. "Hey, just settle down, okay. Look," I said as I folded up the phone, "I'm closing it up. Now settle down okay before you have another attack."

The old man eased back down but his eyes never left me and the look of worry remained in them

"Officer Stone, I asked you earlier if you wanted to play for double or nothing... do you remember?"

I began to nod, "Yeah, but look we've got to get..."

"No!" His voice vibrated in determination. "If you do that, then all of this will have been for nothing. Carrie will die. Perhaps I can't stop you but you should at least listen to me before you make the call. It could make you a very rich man Officer Stone. What do you say?" The old eyes held a heightened intensity as I looked at him. I wasn't sure what was going on but he appeared determined. I bumped up my head.

"So how're you feeling now?"

The old man seemed to relax a little more. "Better. I need only to rest a little I think. Look, I will explain everything to you but only if we make this deal now. If you take me away before I have the chance... then my granddaughter will die. If this happens, then I may as well die also. I assure you, I will say nothing to anyone if this is the way it goes. In that event, I might just as well be dead, eh Officer? So let me rest a little and I'll show you how I can get what I need and how you... can be rich. Double or nothing, yes?"

"Okay. Double or nothing. Just lay back there and take it easy. I won't make the call yet. We'll give it awhile, alright?"

There was still a little distrust in the old green eyes but finally, they slowly drooped shut. Shortly thereafter, I heard the old man's breathing roll into slumber. I stood up and moved to a more defensible position of the clearing and adjusted myself to wait and watch. I probably should've called EMS but I needed answers. It was a gamble not calling but a bigger one maybe, to call. I cut my eyes to the shaded spot where the old man slept. I knew he needed to rest before I tried to move him but that was about all I knew. I let my sight float to the dead man lying near him. Boy... was this ever a mess of shit.

Back in Wiitikan

Amos and Annette walked in the cool grass, enjoying each other's company at the newly formed reservation's park. It was something she coaxed him to do whenever possible as the old man needed the exercise. Suddenly, Amos stopped dead still and Annette turned to look at him. His face was clouded and his expression severe as he turned and faced south. "What is it Amos?... Are you alright?... What's wrong?" Her curious gaze followed his to the far off treeline, then back to the worried countenance he displayed. "Amos... what is it?" Now she was scared. All of a sudden, she was very scared.

He turned more to the right and squinted, sniffing the air. Then he chanted a quick prayer before opening his eyes and continuing to stare south. His aged black eyes, taking on a wizened glow in the afternoon light.

"I am afraid our young friend Raining Wolf... is in even greater danger now." The old man took a deep breath and closed his eyes. "For now is his time to know. He is about to be told clearly by... the se se kwa."

Chapter Fifteen
Hope Burns Eternal In The Human Soul

U.S. Army Fort Belvoir, Virginia.
U.S. Air Force section, OSI,
Detachment 4, 696th Air Intelligence Group,
Same Day.

Shears and Mussenberg walked down the hallway, their steps echoing off the pictures hanging from the walls. The paintings depicted great moments in Air Force history and added color to an otherwise dreary corridor. They proceeded to a door where an armed Air Force Security Policeman stood. The Airman Second Class said good afternoon to the men, tilting his blue beret then side-stepping so that each officer could place their hands on the palm scanner attached to the wall by the doorjamb. Within seconds, each man got the approval buzz and a green light. The Airman stepped back over and punched in a code of numbers and the heavy steel door clicked. Then the S.P. turned to the door which had the simple wording "Detachment Four" printed on it and twisted the knob, holding it open for the two officers.

Both men stepped into their commanding officer's outer office where an Air Force Master Sergeant, another S.P. and also armed with a service .9mm looked up from his desk. The blue nametag over his right breast said Temple.

"Good afternoon sirs. The General is expecting you." He said the last as he reached over and picked up the telephone, punching in a line button. Shears and Mussenberg both went to the desk and signed in on the admission book. Shears was first and finished as the Master Sergeant spoke into the phone, then hung-up. "You can go right in gentlemen."

Shears was looking at the coat rack standing in the corner. He saw a dress black overcoat with a single silver star on each shoulder. He turned back to the sergeant in a whisper. "Terry, who's he got in there?"

The Master Sergeant shrugged and pointed to the line above his on the book's page as he stood up. Shears looked but didn't recognize the name. He turned to Mussenberg who had also glanced down at the book. He brought his eyes up to Shears and splayed his hands out in an "I don't know either" gesture. Then the Master Sergeant was opening the General's door and both officers marched in through it. Shears and Mussenberg came to attention in front of the desk and saluted. Shears spoke. "Major Shears and Captain Mussenberg, reporting as ordered sir."

Kourn casually returned their salutes. "Stand easy." Both officers went into at-ease as he pointed his palmed hand toward another officer seated in one of the heavy chairs. "Gentlemen, allow me to introduce Brigadier General Juan Sanchez, Army Special Forces."

Shears and Mussenberg did what all military people do in these situations. They quickly and cleanly performed an evaluation of the man based on his uniform and what it displayed. In his lap, the Army General held a folded green beret. The soldier crossed one leg over the other, his bloused and spit-shined jump boots mirroring light in the room. He was a large dark skinned man with thick black hair, graying at the temples. He was wearing Army dress greens with the 5th Group Special Forces patch on his right shoulder. He had a Joint Chiefs unit patch on his left and that meant he was assigned there now.

Over his left chest, in addition to his starred jump wings, he had a combat infantry badge. Both young Air Force Officers quickly read the numerous ribbons stacked below these devices. The first one on the top left, was the Distinguished Service Cross. He also had a silver star and two purple hearts in the mix. This guy had been around. The older officer stood and reached over to shake hands all around then Kourn asked everyone to be seated again.

Kourn eyed his newest visitors. "Now ya'all don't know it but 'ole Juan here, was your man Stone's XO (executive officer) on the Trojan Team. I've asked him ta come up here to give us the scoop on his old team mate Stone. Ya'know, so's ya'all could tell 'em what Stone's doing, how he's a acting and maybe… we could get'ta handle own this situation."

Kourn looked at the other General and sighed. "Unfortunately, he ain't gonna be much help. Seems these here Trojans got'ta lota loyalty ta each other, even though the team's disbanded." Kourn let his mouth crack into a smile as he looked at the other man.

"Well, don't reckon I kin begrudge 'em that. But he says he's gonna help any way he can, short a doing his man dirty, so why don't you boys lay it out for us so far. Start at the begin'en and bring us up to where we're at now. And boys… the General here's been briefed on our parameters of authority and just what we can… and kain't do. Okay?"

Kourn wanted to make sure that his two men understood that he'd already been talking with the Army General and that they could query the man about whatever they needed to. When he had locked his eyesight on each man and was satisfied that they understood, he rocked back in his chair and to listen.

Shears nodded and began talking with Mussenberg adding information and thoughts occasionally until they were through everything and at the present status. They all looked at the soldier and waited. When he spoke, it was in a deep voice with shades of a faded Spanish accent.

"Okay. From what you've told me, it sounds like Ghost has taken a job with his tribe. So if th…"

Shears was sitting forward and motioning with his hand. "Excuse me sir. Uh, you did say Ghost?"

The General nodded his head with hooded eyes and continued. "Yeah, that's right. Ghost. It was his nickname before he ever joined the team. He came out of oh… I don't remember, several real bad missions in the Coast Guard where he was the sole survivor. He made through a lot more with us. By all rights, he should've been dead too, on each occasion, but he just kept walking away. Hence, the name Ghost. But I'll tell you something," he pointed his hand for emphasis, "the man continued to do those same kinds of things the whole time I knew him. As far as we were concerned, the guy was a ghost."

Shears and Mussenberg looked over to Kourn who only smiled and arched his eyebrows mischievously. Both of the younger officers could tell that their C.O. had already heard most of this stuff today. Shears turned back to the Army General. "I'm sorry to interrupt sir. Please continue."

Sanchez took a breath and exhaled it audibly. "Okay, so if Ghost took a job with his tribe then… he's working for them now. That's it in a nutshell for you guys. For this man, loyalty comes hard but once it comes, it's the only way he plays. He'll be loyal to them as long as he thinks they're doing what's right. He'll stand by them, he'll fight for them and… he'll die for them. He's that way." The big man looked at each officer intently before continuing.

"Now, as I understand it, neither of you are too familiar with Trojan so let me start by telling you this. The Trojan Team was, too a very large degree, the brainchild of President Ronald Reagan. That man was gonna kick Soviet ass and he was looking for the boots to do it with. He wanted something like this and the Chief of Staff put it together for him."

Sanchez narrowed his eyes as he set them on each of the young officers. "So, first and foremost, you need to know that this President personally hand selected, interviewed and admitted each member of the team. Now, Reagan may've been mentally unstable later-on but I assure you… he was extremely sharp in 1981."

The Army General switched his eyes from man to man. "So, are you getting my drift here?" Both Air Force officers nod, their mouths unintentionally opened by this revelation.

Satisfied with the look of astonishment on the other men's faces, Sanchez went on. "Stone, like every member of our team, spent an hour alone with the President of the United States, eating jelly beans, discussing his opinions on communism, American culture and who knows what all… before he was admitted to the Team. So bear that in mind as to your opinion of him."

The large man rubbed his hands together before continuing his briefing. "Okay. Every member on the Team had specialties. Stone's were water-borne smuggling, drug trafficking and piracy. Now he knows all of those areas well and he's worked extensively undercover." He flipped a hand toward Kourn.

"The General here asked whether or not he'll deal with you about this island or whatever. He might. But I'd say only if it'll benefit the tribe. I don't know why he took it but he's not in this job for the money or prestige. My opinion of the man was and is, that he's a little different. In fact, I served with several Native Americans in combat and throughout my career. And to a degree, they're all that way. I mean… lone-wolfish, quiet, reserved and really dedicated to their mission. But Stone is a little different than even those guys… if you get my drift?"

He raised his eyebrows to the younger men. "He seems to admire authority when it's given to people who use it honorably. He distains it whenever it goes the other way. He also seems to have some kind an innate compass that steers him, much more so then the average man." The big officer lets his eyes roam to the floor.

"Honor to him, means a great deal. So, bribing won't work and just to clue you in," the eyes went back on the Air Force Officers, "he was one of the best troopers we had on the team. The man knows his craft and his avenues of mission accomplishment." The big man eased back into his seat, apparently finished.

Shears had been thinking and now leaned forward. "So sir, I'm not saying we're even contemplating this mind you, but if it became mission-critical, you're saying he'll be hard to take out. Correct?" The features of the Army General darkened as the big man leaned forward again with fire in his eyes. "You're fuck'n A right it will be Major! Let me tell you a couple of things about this guy." He snapped a pointed finger at Shears.

"You ever seen them old western movies where the cavalry is riding along in the desert and all of a sudden the Indian Scout stops and looks up to this big ridge. The young officer asks old Tonto, "what's wrong?" The Indian just points up and says "Heap many Indians there". The army guy looks and doesn't see anything and says sheeeeeit, there ain't nothing there. Let's go. And about that time, thousands of Indians pop up over the rise?"

Both younger men bobbed their heads in affirmation. Sanchez looked from man to man and growled, "Yeah, well that's a little piece of Hollywood you can count on as far as this Indian is concerned! I was partnered with him once in Afghanistan. This was the old days, okay, when the Russians were fighting the Afghans. It was a nasty-ass war and every bit due its comparison to ours with Nam. Anyway, me and Ghost had a string of ten camels that we had to get across this road, that was heavily traveled by Russian vehicles. We waited until the road was clear. There was no sound. Nothing. And we were just about to cross when Stone says NO, and held me back. I looked and couldn't see anything and was going to go anyway when here comes a whole convoy of Russian APCs (armored personnel carriers). They'd have caught us right in the middle of the road and our ass would've been grass. And that's a fact!"

The man's voice was rising as he became more and more animated. "The Russians weren't taking any prisoners by that time... know what I mean? So, don't go thinking it'll be easy to kill old Ghost. It's been tried before and that motherfucker will kick your ass and haunt your memory if you ain't careful!"

Kourn had leaned forward and was gently pushing air with his hands toward Sanchez in a gesture of calmness. "Now settle down Juan, there ain't nobody gonna try and hurt your boy. They was just ask'n, is all."

Sanchez looked over at Kourn and finally nodded then turned back to Mussenberg and Shears, the menace almost gone now. "Well, there's something else you better think about if you decide to go that route. If he's been in contact with any of the old team members and something happens to him, then they'll all come looking for you." He cocked his eye, "No shit. And," he snapped his eyes back to Kourn, "you may think "no problem, you'll just take them all out. But I know for a fact that at least three of them are out of sight and mind as far as the world goes. But they'll eventually surface and once they find out... well I guarantee you won't get them all before they get some of you!"

The room was quiet and finally Kourn spoke in a low tone. "Now, there's no call for that kind of talk or... threats General. And I'll just forget about that little bit of insubordination 'cause I know you're worried about your man. Okay?"

Sanchez's anger was intense. He allowed his eyes to travel from Kourn to each of the other men before speaking, his voice deceptively low.

"Look the bottom line is this. I'm only here because the Chief of Staff ordered me to come and he got the word from the Chairman of the Joint Chiefs. I've got a year until I retire and I know Ray here," he flipped his fingers to Kourn, "because he and my old Trojan C.O. Tom O'Halloran knew each other. They were friends. But as far as I'm concerned, I don't like you guys. I never have."

I'm a soldier. I protect my country by leading men into battle, not playing Star Trek. You people think this science fiction shit is more important than some trooper's life and I don't." He looked squarely back at Kourn,

"So, you want to tell the Chief I was insubordinate, then go right ahead. I can live without my retirement General. But Stone's a teammate. My teammate. If gets hurt over one of your little "hide and seek" games, I promise… you'll never live to collect your pension either."

With that, the big man stood, filling the room with his size and barely contained rage, keeping his eyes locked onto Kourn. He placed the green beret on his head, squared it off then, leaned over the desk, placing his palms flat down on it's surface.

He whispered, "I promise you that Ray. My word on it… as an officer and gentleman!" He nodded once, shot heated eye contact to Shears and Mussenberg then turned and moved to the door. He jerked it open and went through, swinging it back, the resulting shudder rattling pictures on the walls as the door slammed behind him.

Shears and Mussenberg were both trying hard to keep their eyes in their respective sockets when Kourn slapped his palm down hard on the desktop and sat forward.

"Well, there ya go. If ya'all ever make it ta General officer, don't think that yer days of being threatened are behind ya." He grabbed a planner book and thumbed it open to a page. Then looked up at his shocked subordinates.

"Well put yer eyes back in yer heads boys. He may've been wrong ta of said it front of ya'all but he was sure as hell within his rights to've said it. And you can bet yer boots that the somebitch meant it too. Now I had him here, ta let ya'all get an inkling of what this feller Stone is all about. So, we're gonna deal on this one, if it's reasonable and at all possible. And shit… it may not be. In either case, I'm going back with ya'all ta talk with him in person."

His eyes scanned the planner as the two younger men stole quick glances at each other. "Okay, shit. Well I gotta meeting I have to be at so I can't get out'ta here until tomorrow afternoon." He slammed the planner closed and looked at his men. I can leave anytime after two o'clock so you boys make the plans. They's more. Somebody, probably one of this guy Stone's friends, has been monkeying around with you two's personnel jackets and the bastard got into 'em."

Shears and Mussenberg displayed their shock. The people who do what they do in the Air Force, have tighter security on their personnel records than does anyone else in the country. And that includes members of the CIA, the military Joint Chiefs of Staff and even the President. The people of Detachment Four, are privy to secrets unimaginable. Both men were beginning to show signs of anger but before either of the astonished officers could speak, Kourn was again signaling them with his hand up in a stopping motion, to wait.

"That ain't all boys. Our most recent intel shows that the Chinese are mounting an operation to that island." Shears and Mussenberg, who had just sat back after the last bombshell, now both scooched forward in their seats again.

"We don't know when they're coming or... if they're already here or what. We don't know if they're using oriental agents, whites or mixed breeds or what-have-ya but they are coming... that much is verified. So we'll make a deal with this Indian if we can. And he's gonna ask why. I think I gotta story that'll convince him. But I'm telling ya boys... that thing is own that island...I'm just sure'er than shit it is. And if so... then we gotta have it!"

Lake Michigan,
Seven miles off Muskrat Island,
Same Day.

Fat waved as the Coast Guard boat pulled away and left him momentarily floating alone in the choppy blue water. The Coast Guardsmen on the grayish 47 footer returned the wave and throttled up their vessel, turning so that the red, white and blue flash painted on the bows shown brightly in the late afternoon sun. He had never been so scared in all of his life. He had lost so much time. When he had called Kuan to tell him about the helicopter, Kuan had ordered him to the island as quickly as he could get there. In such a hurry, he ran right into submerged fishing nets. His prop had become completely entangled in the nets. Such helpful Americans – everyone had attempted to assist him. Fishermen, pleasureboaters, everyone. But he had been wedged-in tightly to the nets. So, even though the Coast Guardsmen were the last people Fat had wanted to see, they were the one's who had ultimately freed him. Now, he had to get to Quang and he had to hurry. Once clear and in safe water, Fat laid the throttle wide-open again, and shortly, he was flying once more over the darkening blue water with Muskrat Island growing larger before him.

Muskrat Island

The old man stirred. He'd been sleeping an hour and I was more than ready for him to be up. I hefted the scattergun and stood. I'd had plenty of time to think this situation through and every time, I came to the same conclusion. While I knew I should get the old man to a hospital, I also knew that he had some notion of what was going on here. I needed that information. I needed it bad. And as long as he was requesting not to get medical attention, I had to garner what I could from the old man. As I walk over toward him, I can see him blinking his green eyes and searching the trees that tower above, momentary confusion entering his waking thoughts. I stop at the boards he moved off earlier and look down at him.

"Feeling better Mr. Scheel?" He looks up at me and again, he appears startled. Oh yeah. I forgot. My face is painted in black soot and I'm decked out in jungle tigerstripes. I imagine it would be a little unsettling to be looking at me right now. Probably even more so than usual I mean. Especially if you've just woke up in a strange unknown place and have had some kind of a heart problem. I bend down to a knee, leaning on the shotgun.

"Mr. Scheel, are you feeling better now?"
The old green eyes finally begin to lose their semblance of alarm and return to normal. He smiles crookedly and sits up. "Oh yes. Much better now. Thank you for allowing me to rest."
I nod and take in a deep breath. "You had me worried for a minute there. But I suppose I'd be a little scared if I woke up in an unfamiliar place too."

The old man's hat has remained on the ground and the strands of his silvery hair are tousled about his head. "Oh no my friend, you misunderstand." he says as he looks around, "You see, I know this place very well. I've dreamed of it almost every night for close to fifty years now. And in those dreams, I'm always right here and they're coming for me. But just when they are here, just when they are about to get me… I always wake up and I'm no longer in this place, you see," he turns he sight back to me. "But this time when I awoke… I was still here."
He looks at me like I should have some kind of clue as to what he's talking about. Problem is, I don't. He searches my face and then he knows. He raises his finger into the air as if he's checking the weather.

"Yes Officer, I know, Of course you really don't know what I'm talking about do you? Well, I'll explain it to you. That is to say…," he looks at me earnestly, "we do have a deal don't we. The one we spoke of earlier? There are no medical personnel or other police coming here, are there?"

I just look at him. "No, I haven't called anybody yet. But," I pointed my finger over at the corpse, "I have a dead man here on my island and that's going to have to be explained and resolved somehow. I'm willing to hear you out before taking other steps but I need to know what's going on and I need to know it now." I tilted my head for effect. He smiles at me and waves a hand. "Yes. Understood."

The old man fussed with something behind him then he stood up and he seemed to do it quite well. I could see that what he'd been messing with behind him had been his jacket. It was lain carefully over a large expandable canvass bag behind where the old man had hidden. I sent my sight back to him. He seemed fit. He didn't sway and his nerves appeared solid. His eyes seemed normal too. Overall, his actions were healthy enough. I gestured to him with my chin.

"So do you think your heart's okay?"

The older man glanced down at his jacket, then looked quickly away. "I don't know, to be honest with you. As I said, I have arrhythmia which is just an irregular heartbeat. The condition is aggravated by stress and," he turns and looks at the corpse lying on the ground, "I suppose I had a little stress today." He twists back and a crooked smile cuts over his face. "I do feel fine now though. I think the pills helped. Thank you again for getting them." He turns his face back to me with the last.

I stand up, laying the shotgun across my arm as I do. "How long's it been since you've eaten?"

The old man scratched his nose and bent down for his cap, placing it on his head as he raised back up. "It was last night, I suppose. I was not far from taking the time to eat when those men came along this morning." He nodded at the dead man and I look over. I turn my gaze back to him.

"What did you mean, when you said they were enemies of this country?"

Scheel looks at me and points his finger to Redhair, lying on the ground with one of his bullets in him. "These men are Chinese. Communist Chinese agents Officer. Of this, there can be no doubt."

"Uh huh. Well you won't mind if I doubt it just a little will ya?" I pointed my thumb over, "Just why do you think this guy is Chinese?" Scheel's eyes enlarged incredulously. "Because they spoke fluent Chinese to one another. I lived with the Chinese communist in the

1950s Officer and I know them when I see them! They used code words in their speech and they made reference to a particular mission. That was enough for me."

I was looking at him differently now. This guy was a nutcase. He had to be. Redhair wasn't an Oriental. He had red hair for crying out loud. How could... then I remember the other one. The one that had tried to kill me. I shot my glance back to the body laying on the ground, then move over to it. I bend down and use my fingers to pry open the dead man's eyes. The contacts. I pop one off and the eye underneath, was brown when is was alive. I pull the skin taunt around the eyes and peer closely there. There are little lines in the tissue, just like my yellow haired friend had. And I remembered his damaged eye. It had looked almost Oriental. I scrutinize the corpse's head and can see black roots at the base of the dyed redness. The dead man's frame was medium. Maybe large for Chinese but just about normal for the average American. Man, this was too weird. I look over at Scheel who has found his way beside me. He motions down to the body.

"Here let me show you something else. I need a hand here. Please hold his shoulders."

I took a knee and did as he asked and immediately wished that I hadn't. Scheel bent over the body and undid the dead man's belt and pants. I let go of the shoulders and stepped back.

"What're you doing?" I put a little venom in my question as he shoots me a disgusted look.

"It isn't what you're thinking I'm doing, that's for damn sure Mr. Stone!"

I watched as he unbuttoned the man's pants and folded them to the side. He pulled back the boxer shorts and now I knew that the old man was crazy after all. He looks up at my unbelieving eyes. "He is not circumcised." When this doesn't remove the shock from my face, he begins pulling the pants back up and fastening them.

"Look Officer, what I did was check a simple fact." He points to the body. "He looks about twenty eight years old and if this man was born in the United States, the odds of him being circumcised are better than ninety five percent. He is not, so that adds some credence to what I am saying. Don't you agree?"

Well what the man says is true. For my part, I don't know if he's Oriental but odds are good, that he's not an American. And while I didn't think to do it, I really couldn't fault the old man's process or conclusion. I can feel my face slowly losing its shock as Scheel leans forward on his palms beside the corpse to look up at me.

"This helps prove what I have said. I don't see why you can't just accept my word."

I stood and lifted the shotgun. "Yeah, imagine that. Here you are a man who killed this guy and here I am a cop. You're telling me this red haired, white-looking fella is really a Chinese National and obviously, you'd have no reason to mislead me, would you? What a hardheaded prick I'm being, huh?"

Scheel looked down at the ground for a moment. Then he raised his eyes to mine. "Of course, you're right Officer. Please forgive my thoughts and whatever I may have said to question your motives." He seemed genuine in his words and I finally nodded.

"Okay, let's head back to the Lighthouse and I'll get you something to eat. Then you're going to tell me everything. And by the way... my name's Stone. Every time you say "officer", I find myself looking for military brass. Alright?"

"Yes, certainly. So, my guess was correct then. You are prior military?" he said that as he moved back to the mine opening and picked up his jacket. He reached in deeper and rolled several timbers off the large black billows bag. The bag is coated with dust and grime and I figure it's been in there awhile.

I watch him as he hefts the bag and retrieves his jacket. He seems the picture of health now. "Yeah, twenty years in the Coast Guard. What's in the bag Scheel?"

I had a real hinky feeling when he lifted that bag and I'd learned over the years, to trust those feelings. He walks up to stand in front of me. "This Mr. Stone, is what all of this is about." He tapped the bag and turns to look at the body once more. "It is what he was searching for and," he twisted back to me "what can make you a very wealthy man."

I let off a slight nod. I could give a shit less about his or anybody else's money but he seemed to think I would. The white man's world. What a great place it had turned out to be. "Is that heavy? Do you want me to carry it?"

Scheel thought a moment before answering. "It isn't heavy. However, if you would be so kind, I would indeed appreciate you taking it from me. I would ask only that you do not look in it until I have had the chance to tell you everything?"

I lean forward and take the bag as he lifts it up to me. "Yeah, reckon I can do that."

Before we start out the old man shutters and snaps his eyes to the bag I now hold. "You know," he says as he brings his gaze back to mine, "I wouldn't be surprised if that thing caused my heart trouble."

I look down at the bag and feel a dread sneaking over me. Scheel must've noticed my expression because he patted my arm.

"No, don't worry. It can't hurt you. Most of it is in my mind. I'm sure of this. But my head has had to deal with what's in there for many years," he pointed at the bag, "so I was just thinking that perhaps my body has had to deal with it as well." He reaches over and pats my arm. "You don't have such a dilemma. It will be fine. Shall we go?"

As I follow him down the game trail, I'm trying to get a handle on this. What the hell is in this bag? I gently feel around it as I step behind Scheel. There's no weight to it. Suddenly, the shinkakee rolls over me with the force of a high mountain waterfall. I get the definite impression that it's evil, whatever it is in the bag. My hand that's been moving over the bag, drops like a stone. I need to know what's going on but I don't know man…if curiosity killed the cat, I wonder what it'd do to an Indian? Where's old Amos when I really need him? A few seconds later, we step out onto the main trail. Scheel walks over and looks down at the cove below. He turns back to me and motions.

"Please come here for a moment Mr. Stone."
I set the bag down, glad to be away from it if even for a short time and move over to where Scheel stands.

"Please look down there Mr. Stone and lock this image in your mind." He turned the green eyes to me then. "Because this place plays heavily in the story I will soon recount to you."

I look down at the rippled water below. I remember that it's different in that little cove than it is elsewhere around the island. I'd discovered that today. But you sure can't tell it from here. What difference does that make anyway? I turn back to him. "Okay, I've seen it. Now let's go." I turn sideways, "After you." I motion with my hand and he begins to move past. I don't trust him anymore. He seems just fit as a fiddle and suddenly the shinkakee… is very strong in my spirit right now.

Marquette, Michigan,
The Upper Peninsula.
Same day.

Chin punched in the numbers from the calling card and waited for the connection to make. He was at a pay phone outside a Walmart. People were hustling back and forth to their cars in the parking lot. Many of them were pushing shopping carts. A young woman passed him pushing a cart containing a small blond haired little girl who waved happily at Chin. "Mommy, why's that man's eyes so funny?," she asked, as the mother hushed her and flustered with embarrassment. Chin smiled back at the child and returned the wave. He smiled broader as he pondered little children. Out of all things in this world, children could always be counted on to be honest.

As the mother and child entered the automatic doors, he wondered if he would ever see his own children again. He doubted it. Hence this call. He could sense that things were headed down-hill. He let his eyes wander to the group of small children gathered around a miniature merry-go-round under the overhanging roof. They laughed while awaiting their turn to ride. It didn't really matter, he decided.

His children were all adults and he had long ago missed their growing-up years. He had always been away with the Navy somewhere and now, now it was too late. Even when he was home, they didn't come around. His wife had died ten years ago and Chin was alone. Alone, except for his work. He sighed as he watched one batch of kids exit the merry-go-round and the next climb on board. He heard the phone click several times and a man's voice in Chinese came on. He turned his full attention to the receiver. It was an old man's voice and it belonged to Chin's Admiral.

"Good morning sir. This is a relatively secure line." Chin spoke in English and waited as the short silence echoed through the thousands of miles.

"Good day to you Chi… ahh… Robert.," replied the Admiral, also in English. "Do you call me to advise of good fortune or is it the latter?"

Chin swallowed. "Ah sir, first, I must apologize for calling on your private line but matters here, are not progressing as expected. I wish to advise you so that you may… be prepared for however this job turns out."

Both of them knew what the words "be prepared" meant. The Chinese Communist regime was not tolerant of espionage missions gone awry. Even less so, when it was a mission taken on by one particular branch of the service without the knowledge of superiors and the other branches. This was multiplied by not having other departments notified. Should such a mission succeed, then all of the non-notifications and acts without permission would be immediately forgiven. If the mission failed, well then those involved would suffer dire consequences indeed. That, was Chinese Communism, plain and simple. Both men knew this, long before the mission was ever attempted. There was a quiet stillness on the line as Chin waited.

Then his commander spoke. "I see. In as few words as possible, please bring me up to date." Chin nodded to his superior, even though the other man could not see him.

"Yes sir. We have lost one of our workers to an accident and it does… appear as an accident, sir. As of yet, we still have not found the jobsite. At the present, I am also out of communication with two of my other workers. I do not know their status. The US Air Force has expressed interest in this job and we have ran into difficulty with a particular Native Tribal Policeman here as well."

The Admiral waited a beat then asked, "Hmm. I have many questions, perhaps first among them is, what exactly is a Native Tribal Policeman? However, I will wait for my answers. What is your plan of action now?"

"Yes sir. Well that is our problem at the present. Our window of opportunity for job accomplishment is fast eroding and well sir, I am hesitant as this point to say that success is at hand. I uh... I just wanted you to be advised of this sir. If things continue to become complicated, I may not have the opportunity to speak with you again. That is all sir... except perhaps for your inquiry. A Native Tribal Policeman is an American Indian policeman, much like the films depicting the western Indians we have seen. That is all though sir, nothing more to report at this time."

The quiet was on the line again as Chin squeezed his ear tighter to the phone. Then the Admiral spoke. "I understand. We will hope for the best. Thank you for calling me. You are a good and loyal man and regardless of how this job turns out, I am proud to have serve... eh.. worked with you."

Chin swallowed and felt his eyes burn slightly as he held the receiver tighter to his ear and looked up at the sky. "Sir, it is I who have been honored by our association. This job may yet turn out well, there is still a chance."

The old man's voice was hoarse when he spoke again. "Yes... I suppose that's possible. But as we've discussed before, the involvement of the American military... probably signifies the end result."

Chin knew this and could hardly disagree. Still, a slight glimmer of hope burns eternal in the human soul. Therefore, he said nothing. He merely waited for any new command, such as a recall of the team. However, he was quite sure that this would not happen. When the Admiral spoke again, his assumption was verified.

"Good luck my friend and... good bye."

Chin stood up straight at attention by the payphone. "Thank you sir and... goodbye to you also."

After several seconds, the line went dead. He hung up the phone and nervously looked around. No one had noticed his little display of military bearing. He drew out a Marlboro, striking the Bic lighter to its tip in one fluid motion. He inhaled deeply and blew a cloud of blue smoke into the crisp air. The snow that had fallen was already gone but the warmth of the day was dissipating just as quickly, too. He walked over to his car and climbed in. He had a few hours drive to Escanaba and he had to get started.

Chapter Sixteen
Playing All The Cards

Muskrat Island,
Same day.

Forty five minutes after leaving the mine shaft where the old man had shot the red haired foreigner, I handed him a cup of coffee and a cardboard plate of hot Ham and scalloped potatoes and he began eating ravenously. I'd washed my face and prepared the food quickly because I needed to talk to him and I needed to do it soon. He spoke between mouthfuls.

I am not very hungry so I just munch an apple as I look out the window and eye the area where the trail comes up to the lighthouse. Any approach to us would have to come from there. While the old man's food warms, I take a piece of black thread from my sewing kit and stretched it across the trail about ten inches up from the ground. I tied it to small brush on either side and add small pieces of faded green curtain cloth that I've torn off the thread-bare kitchen curtains. The green matches the ground cover closely and the thread is almost invisible. If someone comes up that trail, odds are good that they'll trip my little warning. It isn't much of a warning, but I know that I can't keep my eyes on the approach all of the time and this, is better than nothing.

"This is excellent Mr. Stone. How were you able to prepare it so quickly?"

Another cold front is moving in, the warm air of the day hitting the cooler on-coming stuff. A slight mist is forming out over the lake as I finger the butt of the .45 and I answer him without looking his way.

"It's an MRE. That stands for Meal, Ready to Eat. It's the military's modern answer to the C-Rations of Korea and Viet Nam. But you can buy them at sporting goods stores." I glance over and watch him finish his food and coffee. Then I walk over and ask if he wants more. He says no but would like a glass of water. I toss the plate in the garbage can before returning back, handing him the water and sitting down on the old couch. I look down at him.

"Okay Mr. Scheel. It's time for you to talk to me but first, you said earlier that one of the men was coming back. When?"

Scheel hiked his shoulders. "I can't say. They split up after they found the shaft. The other one went back to Escanaba to get an additional length of rope. You see, they didn't know that the opening to the mine was right there all of the time. I'd hidden it before I left the island and when I sent my report in all those years ago, I only said that the object was in the mine and ..."

I was holding my hand up to get him to stop. "Look, I don't know what you're talking about, alright? So just tell me first... when do you think this other guy is coming back?"

Scheel leaned forward. "My Chinese is rusty but I think I understood them to say that it would be sometime last night or today." He held is hands up in a "that's the best I can do" motion.

"The other one, the one I shot, he stayed behind here on the island but went off somewhere for a period of time. The mine opening had collapsed over the years and I had to dig rocks away before I'd be able to get inside. I didn't know when he would be back and I still had to get the item I'd came for." His eyes traveled to the bag on the floor and I felt myself look that way too.

I switch my gaze back to him and prod, "And..." He turns back to me slowly.

"Yes, well I had just got the opening cleared and was preparing to enter when the man returned. He had a piece of rope and was going to attempt to climb down the shaft. I couldn't permit that you see, because the first level the shaft comes to, leads right back to the main opening, where I was hidden and the thing I'd came for as well. I was already finding my health a problem and Carrie needs this. She needs it desperately. I just couldn't let them take that thing. Especially since they were communists. Not without a fight. So I aimed and shot him as he prepared to enter the mine."

His eyes were bright with intensity as he spoke. "He fell but was pulling out his gun and shooting, even as he died." The old man's face was holding that far-off look when he stopped.

This wasn't gonna work like this. These bits and pieces were bad. And maybe I had another realtor about to show up. Time was short. I figure the best thing to do is settle him down and let him go from the beginning. I lean forward and fold my hands together.

"Okay. Here's what I want you to do. You want to make a deal, then I need you to start right from the beginning. The very beginning, if you have to... but start where I can understand what's happening. Okay?"

I waited. He tilted his head in understanding and looked down at the floor. His voice is mellow, and I can see him slipping back in time.

"I grew up in the eastern forests of Germany. All of my life was spent in Nazi Germany, and yet, it didn't affect our village. We belonged to a deeply religious group called, The Brethren." He shrugged his shoulders. "It was much like the Amish or Quakers here are. We were furniture makers. I had a wonderful mother, father and sister. It was a pure and perfect life."

I let my eyes dance quickly to the path and I see the little pieces of green cloth flipping in the wind. I turn back as his voice fills the room once more, but this time all inflection is gone. He speaks like a dead man.

"That was how we lived until the SS came. I was but a young boy and not at home the day they raped my sister and killed my family. I found them... Mamma and Pappa and my sister. Seeing them bloody and dead, I swore revenge, all of my up-bringing, forsaken, I signed up with the Russian Army when they arrived and they became my new family. I killed Germans until there were no more Germans to kill. I murdered them, even when they were surrendering, with a hatred you would not believe."

The old man was somewhere else as he spoke, now. "After the war, I became a committed Communist, until I found they were just as flawed as the German Nazis. That was during the Korean War, after I was assigned to the Chinese Army as an observer. I learned first-hand that communism, was no better than Nazism. But there was no way for me by then. Later, I was trained in spying by the Soviets and became a member of the GRU. I was eventually assigned to a new espionage program in the United States. I learned that I was to be a part of the RICTOR project."

He twists back to me. "Have you ever heard of this, Officer?"

My eyes haven't left the man since I'd heard the part about the GRU. Maybe, I begin to contemplate, this whole mess has more to do with this old man than it does with me. I look into his face and slowly turn my head from side to side. The old man sniffs and turns back to the glass.

"Yes, well the RICTOR project was the brainchild of Colonel Dimetri Segren. He was my superior. You see, the Soviet Union had only just acquired the nuclear bomb in the late 1940s. By the early 1950s, the Russians had their own bombers equipped with nuclear bombs. They didn't have many and they weren't very sophisticated but the Soviets did have them. The USSR and the USA both believed that the other, would launch a sneak attack on them with the bomb. Actually, with what resources were available, the Soviet Union couldn't have managed it at this time but the West didn't know this for certain. What was certain however, was that America could do it easily. There were American Air Force bases scattered throughout the upper United States that had B-47 jet bombers at them. These planes were loaded with nuclear bombs and had Russian cities already targeted into their bomb sights. They were just sitting and waiting for the order to go." Scheel thumbed the window curtain between his fingers as he peered out.

"The RICTOR project was a plan that required the placing of agents into strategic locations near these bases to monitor the bombers and send a short wave radio message to the USSR, via stations in the Arctic or submarines, of a nuclear first launch by the USA. The agents were to watch the bombers and when combined with an already developed knowledge of their actions and procedures, alert Mother Russia of an impending attack. RICTOR agents were stationed in Canada, New York, Montana, Oregon, Washington, Idaho, Alaska, North Dakota, Minnesota, Wisconsin, Maine and several other states. And I...," he turns back to me, "was here on Muskrat Island."

Well I'll be a sonavabitch! I just look at the man. I don't doubt for a second that what he just told me is true. Over the years, I'd learned all kinds of stuff about the Cold War. Things our side did and things their side did. But this was the first I knew of this in-depth of an intrusion of US boundaries. And to be honest, I guess I feel violated somehow. I don't know why. Maybe it's the fact that a spy network inside my own country, monitoring our Air Force, just plain disturbs me. And heck, when you disturb an already disturbed person, it's bound to be bad. And now, he's looking at me, awaiting my reaction. I put forth the effort to conceal my astonishment at this revelation and clear my throat.

"Okay. So, just exactly how were you monitoring jet bombers from this island Mr. Scheel?" He moves back to the chair and picks up his glass, drinking down the last of the water. He uses the glass to motion toward the pitcher pump in the sink and I nod. He walks over and pumps the handle a few times, filling his glass. Then he leans back against the counter and looks across the room at me.

"Well each of us was stationed in a remote area like this island where, we could send our urgent message of an impending attack and be able to keep sending for some time before we were discovered and stopped. We were required to live for six months in our location before we would be relieved. We had to be able to hunt and fish to supplement our supply of canned food. I was put ashore here July 13th, 1953. My contact was a Finnish man named Oscar Kriitinin. Oscar had fought with the Russians during the war also and other than the fact that he was dedicated to the USSR, I liked him very much. He was my link with the outside world. He had all of the cursory work of the bomber movements completed. I had been trained on what to look for as far as specific information and new technology and most importantly, how to determine if the bombers were ever headed to the USSR on a bombing run. You see, bombers from KI Sawyer and Kinross Air Force Bases would take off and circle out over Lake Michigan. Their formation and the number of aircraft was what I watched. They were easy to see from this island and that plus its isolation is why is was chosen for a RICTOR location."

He rubs his eyes with the heel of each palm. "You see, Officer, there were different things to look for and I knew what they were. All I had to do, was watch and on certain days of each month, broadcast a short message to a radio station in the Arctic. Oscar would re-supply me with provisions and other than that, it was to be a lonely life on this island." Schell took a deep breath and drank some from the glass before he continued.

"Oscar dropped me, my radio set and twenty cases of canned goods here late in the afternoon. We packed everything up to this lighthouse and then, Oscar took me to the mine opening where you found me today. The island was much different then." His countenance clouded in deep recollection. I could tell he didn't like what he was remembering too much.

"There were never any visitors here. Oscar had fixed the old mine up quite nicely for me as living quarters with a stove, bed and kitchen of sorts. He had worked hard to disguise the opening of the mine and I'm quite confident that no one ever knew I was there." His face took on that clouded look again as he moved on with the story.

"Other than the tall pines you still see today, the area between the opening of the mine and the cove, was all open. With a pair of binoculars, I could look directly out of the mine and see where the bombers would fly in formation over the Upper Peninsula. Of course," he held the glass up as he made his point, "if you think this place is deserted now, you can only imagine how desolate it was in 1953."

He paused, lost in memory and I was still stuck on how this guy and the others might've got away with it. I also remember that this guy has a history of mental illness. This could just be so much bullshit from a warped mind. I lit a hand-rolled at gestured at him with the smoking cigarette.

"Didn't the Air Force track you with listening stations? I mean, if you were broadcasting in the open, they had to've monitored you?"

He tilted his head in whimsical manner. "Perhaps but we were very careful about when we transmitted and how much we said. And obviously, it was all in code. You must remember too, that this was the early 1950s. There were hundreds of American HAM radio operators throughout the USA, all speaking to other countries. It was a new fad. Also, there were no satellites in space yet so, there were no sophisticated tracking devices like those that exist today. Actually, it was quite easy to do this. It was, Mr. Stone, another world at that time."

Humm. I take a drag of smoke and exhale. I reckon that's true. I can see where he's right. I thought of another question. "So, what did you do when you left the island then? More spying?" I tried to keep the nastiness from my voice but I figure some of it still made it through. Scheel smiled and a slight laugh escaped from him.

"Well yes, actually, that was the plan. And, I did do a modification of that plan, sort of." His smile lingered a moment before he looks at me again. "You see, in the 1950s, most average sized cities in this country, especially the Midwest, were broken down by ethnic neighborhood." He twirled his free hand.

"You know, Irish in this neighborhood, Polish in that one, German here, Dutch there, that kind of thing. German and Polish communities were among the largest. That's why Segren wanted Germans or Poles for his RICTOR agents. People with these backgrounds would be able to enter their respective neighborhoods and fit right in. Then, not only would he get current intelligence on the Strategic Air Command's bombers but he would also have sleeper agents, right in the heart of the USA. You must remember, the KGB was only in the beginning stages of power at this time. The Soviet Army was still king in 1953 and the GRU, ruled all spying activity. More importantly, the Soviet Union had no serious network of spies in the United States yet. We were to be Segren's first attempts at establishing such a network."

He said the last wistfully as he stared off into the distance and I wonder what makes this guy tick. I also wonder where the hell this is going. So far, I haven't heard anything that explains the dead red haired guy the blond haired one that tried to kill me a few days ago. I look back outside and run a quick scan for intruders as my mind flips on. Beside the fact that I don't trust this man, I'm also feeling a certain dislike for him and what he did to my country. If he did it. And yet, my gut is telling me that this isn't dementia talking. He's for real. They're conflicting emotions running around in me and to move away from them, I pose another question.

"So all that shit you said earlier about Korea and figuring out that the Russians were wrong was just that, huh? A bunch of shit. You say you learned that the Russians lied and that the free world wasn't such a bad place after all and then, you come over here and spy, in an effort to cripple the very thing you say, was probably the truth? That sounds a little too much like hypocritical crap to me Scheel?"

Scheel had watched me as I spoke and I don't think he missed the fact that I wasn't happy with him. He waited several beats before answering.

"Not that I especially care about your opinion of me Mr. Stone, but I will tell you that I was doing the only thing I could do until I had the opportunity to make my escape. Whatever damage I did to America's defense capabilities was minimal, I assure you. And while you may not think so, I consider myself to be an American." He points his finger at his chest. "You do not know it all yet so please... don't judge me until you do?"

He's earnest in his request and when I add that to my own mixed feelings, I can see his point. I hold his eyes a second then nod while I field-stripping the butt. "So, how did you get off the island in January then? I assume the lake was frozen and you walked to land? Or what?"

Scheel looks at me, then over at the black bag, lying on the floor by the stairway. His eyes turn dead. "Yes, well you see, I left the island in November... not January. And as bad as this has probably sounded until now Mr. Stone, it is about to get worse. Much worse, I'm afraid. Before I continue though, I must tell you that in spite of what you think you know about me, I am not crazy. I know that you found out about my hospital stay in the mental wing." His twisty gray eyebrows matt together, shading the green eyes below.

"My wife was healthy and vibrant one day and dead of a heart aneurysm the next. Her death was just totally unexpected by me and at the time, I honestly believed that they had done this to her. The shock was just too great." He cut his sight to me. "I suppose you'll still find this hard to comprehend. But that was a long time a go and just for the record, I wish to say that I am not insane, regardless of how it appears. Now," he shifted forward, "I must ask to use your bathroom."

I let my eyes travel with him as he steps toward the table. He seems old and fragile and kind of drained. There's a semblance of consternation on his face as if the next part of his story will take something away from him. I stand and motion to the bathroom door off the kitchen.

"Well that's one thing here that probably hasn't changed much since the fifties. The Head's right there and you'll have to pull the chain over the toilet to flush it. It's still hooked up to a water tank outside."

He smiles weakly and moves slowly into the room, closing the door behind him. As the door latched, my eyes travel to that black bag and in radio quality, with the volume barely discernable, I hear Johnny Cash singing Ghost Riders In the Sky. Ohhhh boy. Will the fun never stop? I shake off the shinkakee that was flowing through me like a raging river and step over to the door, opening it and breathing in the fresh air. I light another hand-rolled as this pounded around in my head. I couldn't get a handle on this deal. I was wondering if this old man hadn't stumbled upon some secret that got him and me into some serious shit with the Air Force and some foreign power. My eyes roam the area in a docile search. The small sections of green cloth are still hanging loosely from the thread. A few minutes later, I hear the distinctive whooshing of the antiquated toilet as it flushes and Scheel steps from the bathroom. I remain where I am. He can talk as good with me here as anywhere. I tip my head at him.

"Ready to go on?"

He looks at me and a transformation of resolve goes over his countenance. "Yes. But remember, we have a deal? I need... Mr. Stone... twenty seven thousand dollars, even?"

I can't help but smile. "And you want me to give this twenty seven thousand dollars to you?"

He nodded his head as he moved over toward me. "Yes and in return, I will give you the names of people who will give a hundred times that much for the item. Trust me, you need these names. If the US government gets to this thing, you won't get a dime and neither will I."

This time I laugh out loud. "You do realize that I don't have a clue as to what you're talking about, right? Why twenty seven thousand dollars, EVEN anyway?"

Scheel rubbed the back of his head as he steps past me and into the lighthouse's excuse for a yard. His voice was almost a whisper.

"My granddaughter has a rare form of leukemia. We've exhausted e verything we had that has any monetary value trying to save her. All of that, just to find that it's not treatable. And we," he looks over his shoulder at me, "my daughter and I... were told that she would die in several months. There was no hope. Then God gave us a miracle. Our physician heard of a doctor in Switzerland who has found a treatment that works. It's worked on eight out of ten other children so far. So, we have to get her there!" He swung back to me.

"It's expensive Mr. Stone, it's a new form of radiation and medicine and it's very expensive. We have no money left. I'd already mortgaged my home, withdrew all of my savings and sold my car, long ago. My daughter has done the same. We still need twenty seven thousand dollars to take her there for the six weeks of treatment. So, that's why twenty seven thousand dollars - even. It is for Carrie. Otherwise Mr. Stone, my grand daughter will die. She is only seven years old." He let his sight droop then slowly raised his eyes to mine. "That's too young for a little girl's death... don't you agree?"

Welllll, I've been up and down on this emotional roller coaster all day and now, the old man drops this on me. Don't that just suck the big one! I'm looking at his watery old green eyes as tears drain from them and well, hell yeah... that's too damn young for a little kid to die. Shit! I try to clear my throat but it takes a couple of times before I'm able to speak.

It was getting quite cool out as I broke eye contact with the man and cut my sight to the thread across the trail. It was still there. I look up at the sky which is moving ever closer to dark gray with puffed-up ashen clouds holding plenty of water. I can feel a cold front moving in and the old man's countenance still upon me. I shiver involuntarily and know that it is going to snow soon. Maybe tonight. This old man is dinky-dou and I don't mean just a little crazy either. But, hell if I know. The only thing I can figure... is to continue to try and get a hold on this, anyway I can. Lord knows, I need some serious help. And I'm beginning to feel that I ain't gonna get any from this senile old fella either. I swivel my view back to the old man and meet his eyes.

"Yeah. I agree. Now why don't you tell me what's in the bag and what the hell is going on? Okay?"

**Muskrat Island,
the same time.**

Fat moved cautiously through the underbrush of the island, his knapsack snagging on branches and protruded rocks while he traveled toward the cave opening where he had left Quang. He was close now but his progress had been slow. Much slower than he would liked it to be. However, the distance and terrain he was covering, were both greater and unfamiliar to him. He had weaseled the boat between the rocks and had gradually got it tied up to a spot that they had previously located for an alternate landing location, should anything go wrong. And obviously, thought Fat, things had done so.

Quang was not answering his phone and he had not been on the promontory rock ledge, where he was supposed to visually signal the boat if he had any type of phone failure. Fat had tried calling Kuan but was unable to get a signal on his cell phone. Because of this, Fat had decided that he had to use the alternate landing site in case the One they had been using, had been compromised. That had made it a slower and more tedious process to get to the cave.

Fat was the youngest member of the group of agents and this, was his first mission as a member of the CHEE. He knew that his lack of experience and his youth were a draw-back for such an important assignment. That is probably why he tasted the fear in the back of his mouth like one tastes a bitter, rotten piece of fruit. He lacked the confidence of Kuan, Chin, Quang and Tran. But he loved his country and the Chinese Navy and he ardently hoped that this, when coupled with his training, would carry him through the mission. Fat eased around a rock out-cropping and looked down the trail that lay before him.

He could see nothing amiss on the trail and knew that he was only a short distance from the clearing. The cave was just through the brush in front of him, perhaps another hundred yards. He listened and heard no sound other than that of the wildlife. He looked up as two black crows with thick yellow beaks cawed down at him from the limbs of a giant white pine tree. Slipping it off his shoulders and drawing the knapsack up to him, he opened it and fished out two hand grenades and another loaded ammunition clip for his pistol.

He quickly fitted the hand grenades into his left pocket and dropped the clip into his right. He then tried the on button on his cell phone again but the battery was definitely dead now. He dropped the phone back in and left the knapsack beside the rock to begin quick-crawling through the underbrush toward the clearing. He stopped frequently and listened. Nothing was abnormal and so he continued and shortly, he was at the edge of the clearing, staring with disbelief at the body of his dead partner, laying face-up in the clearing.

Fat had eased his weapon down after scanning the entire area for several minutes. After almost a fifteen minutes of waiting and watching, he decided that it was safe to move into the clearing. He saw the cell phone lying cracked and broken against the rocks. He looked down at Quang, the man's lifeless round eyes staring into the darkening sky above and felt his cheeks water with tears. He angrily swept the tears from his face and felt shame that his own eyes should have betrayed him like that. It was shameful and he lost face because of it.

He was a man and a warrior, was he not? This was war or a semblance of it, was it not? People die in war and that goes for friends too. He stifled a sob as he looked at his dead companion. He would miss Quang. Well revenge might come for those who did this but the mission was the important thing. He had to prioritize the mission. Fat searched the body but found nothing of value. He wondered if the policeman had the object now? Did Quang find it before being killed? Well if the policeman had it, he might still be on the island and if so, he would be at the lighthouse. He could search the cave but that would do no good if the policeman had the object. Time wasted. First he had to be sure the policeman didn't have what he sought. The man might call a helicopter and leave. No, he had to find the policeman first and foremost. So that determined his next action.

The lighthouse was where he was going. Fat left the dead man and quickly covered the distance back to where he'd left the knapsack. He slipped it on as he made his way briskly toward the lighthouse trail. There was only one approach and it would be difficult to manage but time would tell. Fat moved gingerly through the dense growth that pushed itself up from rock and shale of the island floor. He would find the Indian policeman and have a little talk with him, then come back to search the cave if it proved necessary. But in the end, the Indian would pay for Quang's death and that… would be very good. For the first time all day, Fat smiled as fear took a back seat in his psyche. He trucked along quickly, the sweet and savoring taste of revenge replacing the rotten fruit flavor in his mouth.

Chapter Seventeen
The Burden of Life and Death

Muskrat Island,
Same day, Same time.

The cool air was easing its way past the door as I motion to the old
man again. "Okay partner. You wanted a double or nothing game,
what-say you show me your cards, huh? I need you to tell me the rest
of it before I can get us out of here and off this island."

Once he was seated, Scheel began. His old lined and gray bearded
face took on the far-off look of elderly memories. His eyes began to
dance slightly and his forehead dimpled up in wrinkles as he began his
journey. "It was 1953. My days were all pretty much the same from
late July until the snow came in October. For a young man, such as I
was, it wasn't too bad of a life. I missed women but otherwise, I hunted
and fished and did what was required of me as far as my job went.

It was lonely here though. Terribly lonely. But I knew I could get
through it. I had decided that when I was relieved and off the island, I
would go to the closest American State Department office and request
political asylum. I hated the Soviet Union and all communists. I would
have information to trade for my freedom and hopefully, it would all
work out. I was young though. I look back on what happened now and
know how much better it would have been if I would have just gone
to the Americans with it all." He sighed and slowly shook his head,
his eyes recounting images I'd never see or understand.

"Ahh youth. Terrified and frightened youth. Yes, well… things
went normally until the night of November 23, 1953."

He stopped talking and I could see his lips trembling and fear in
his eyes as he stared at nothing in front of him. As he began again, his
voice trembled, the words falling out in disjointed fashion.

"I… uh… was in my regular evening spot at about six forty p.m…
I guess it was. I had an old wooden chair that I sat on in a wind break
right above the cove. I often sat there to do my monitoring but I didn't
expect any bombers to be flying that night. It was snowing and it was
cold. I remember that I was wearing gloves and trying to carve a piece
of drift wood. I often did that. It had turned into my hobby. The night
was quiet and the snow was… gently… falling when it hap…"

He stopped and his gaze locked on the memory. I waited. He kept looking into space and the terror was growing in his green eyes as I watched. I had to get him talking again.

"What is it Scheel? What's happening?"

He turned his alarmed wide eyes to me. "It hit the island. It hit so hard, I was thrown off the chair! The sound was deafening! The ground shook and rumbled under me!"

I wait as he looks at me with eyes the size of half-dollars. "What hit the island Scheel? What threw you on the ground?"

He kept looking at me with a horror in his eyes I hadn't seen on another man since combat. This guy was genuinely scared to death. After a moment, he looked back down to the floor then up and into that nether world again and continued.

"I got up and ran to where the edge of the cliff used to be. It was gone now, all knocked off by that thing." he turned back to me, "I looked over and saw it down there. It was sinking. But the worst part… The worst part was the jet! It had an American Air Force jet attached to its bottom. Whatever it was, it had flipped over on its top after it hit the island but the jet was still caught by it. I could see the pilots inside the canopy as the thing sank. Then the island started rumbling again and I could feel it shaking loose underneath me. So I ran!"

There was spittle on the old man's lips as he recounted his actions. He was animated now, his arms, feet and hands all helping to tell the story. "I ran as fast as I could back to the big pines. I turned around and saw another big piece of the cliff fall off and into the water below. Something squealed down there then, like metal being stretched or twisted. I didn't know when but the ground had stopped shaking so I inched my way back to the edge and looked down. There were lights down there, shining through the rocks on top of the thing. I could just see parts of the Air Force jet and smaller pieces of rock were still falling away from the side of the island.

Then suddenly," the old man sat back and splayed out his arms, "this orangish yellow lighted ball came up out of the water and was going straight up when a big piece of falling rock hit it and knocked its light out. It fell back down and hit the water. It just… floated away out there. More and more rocks fell down on the other thing and then all of the light from down there went out. Then…" he turned and looks at me, "… it was quiet again."

When the old man had begun talking, I had been leaning back in a slouch. Now I realized that I was standing fully forward, my hands wrapped tightly to each elbow. How about that? The shinkakee was slamming around inside me like a million bumper cars. Whatever he was saying, it had meaning to the spirits. Now I had been thinking that this old man had somehow got his hands on a top secret Air Force something or another and all of a sudden... I was scared that, that... wasn't what was going on here at all. But shit... it's gotta be something like that... doesn't it?

I try to control my facial features as I move my eyes around the room. The old man shivers and keeps looking at me. I really don't know what I'm looking for. Maybe it's for Rod Serling to step in and tell me I'd just entered the Twilight Zone. Or maybe some disenchanted voice telling me not to touch my dial, the problem wasn't with my TV set but with the Outer Limits. Sheeeit! How do I get myself into these situations? But hotdamn and even better yet, how do I get my sorry ass out'ta this one? I took a deep breath and blew it out, letting my sight come to rest on the old man again.

"So you're telling me, what? A B-47 crashed into the island that was carrying a smaller jet?" I said that to him because it was the only logical thing to say. Problem was, I didn't really think the old guy meant a B-47. And as he looked into my eyes, he knew I didn't think that either. He slowly moved his head from side to side and his voice was calmer now.

"No. It wasn't a B-47. It was something else. It was large and round and it was silvery black in color. It had strange markings or writing cut into the metal. And the small jet, was an F-89 Scorpion fighter, serial number 5853. I could see the number clearly before it sank. The jet had missiles under its wings and US Air Force markings. I could see it all clearly, Mr. Stone."

I began shaking my head and forced out a fake snicker. "So, you're saying it was a UFO huh? A UFO with a US Air Force jet stuck to its bottom. Is that what you're telling me?"

The old man nods, the edge of fear still present in his being. "Yes, that's exactly what I'm telling you."

I let out another laugh. It wasn't much of a laugh but heck... what else was there to do? I know of this man's mental history but damn... if he ain't convincing. After quickly scanning the area outside again, I move away from the doorway, the old man's eyes following me. This just can't be happening. I let my view take in the room as he watches me intently. My memory goes back to what the Indian cop in Grand Rapids told me on the phone. Veeter, aka Scheel, was put in the nuthouse for seeing UFOs and aliens. I try desperately to push this fact to the forefront but the Shinkakee was running rampant in my soul. Were the spirits were pulling me toward what the old man was saying? I try hard to keep the feelings I have from erupting as I find my voice and turn to him.

"You're kid'n... right? I mean... com'on...a UFO? Ain't you

asking me to buy an awful lot with that one?"

Scheel turns his head downward and tips it once. "Perhaps. The water in that cove was about thirty feet deep when I first arrived here in 1953. That was where the mining company had tried dredging before they stopped operations here. The water is no more than four feet deep now. I am telling you that the rocks directly below it, cover something sinister." He motions with a hand to the bag lying on the floor. "Why don't you look in the bag?"

I let my sight travel over to the bag and back to him. "So, what's in it? A dead alien?" I try a quivery smile with the question but from his looks, it doesn't work.

Scheel slowly shakes his head, his eyebrows forming peaks. "No, something even more valuable than that I'm afraid. Please," he nods at the bag, "look for yourself. It won't hurt you, although it does cause bad dreams. It has certainly done that for me over the years."

My head's shakes way before I tell it to. "Uh uhh. No thanks. I've got plenty enough of those without any extra." We hold eye contact for several beats until I decide that I have to do as he asks. What else is there? I move over to the lightweight bag, pick it up and move to the table, sitting it down there. Stealing another look at him, I pull back on the zipper. It's rusty and dirty. I have to tug gently to get it to release. I snap another quick glance at Scheel and see that he's watching me with rapt attention. For Indians, some of us at least, the spirit world can be spooky place sometimes. This was one of those times. I take a deep breath and look into the bag.

What's inside the main cavity, is a silvery sphere about the size of a very small beach ball, maybe 10 or 12 inches in diameter. As I stand looking down, indiscernible chants of the shinkakee echo in my head. There are two small pouches on the inside of the bag and I can see that the zippers to these are frozen solid in rust. I leave them alone and reach in to remove the silvery ball. As soon as I touch it, the sounds in my head go silent. Hotdamn! I hate it when that happens. I never know what it means! The goosebumps on my flesh are all that remain of the spirits intimate connection now but I know that they're still with me. The ball weighs nothing when I lift it out. It can't be any heavier than maybe five or six ounces. But it's made out of metal. Not aluminum but something similar maybe.

The appearance is that of dull blue color with tiny specks of sparkly white, like minute diamonds, throughout the substance giving it an overall silvery look. I pull it out and move the thing around in my hands. There doesn't appear to be any seams on it. That's odd. How was it put together? I continue to roll it over and can see nothing of the object's origin. If it was something else, I'd say it could've been drop-forged but not any metal this lightweight. Yep. It was definitely Star Trek time. Where's Mr. Spock when I need him to answer my scientific questions, huh? Instead, I twist back to the old man and ask a question I already know his answer to.

"Okay. I give up. What's this supposed to be? The glowing ball you saw get hit by a rock?"

Scheel nods. "Yes, exactly. From what I've been able to learn, this is the device that drives the big craft. It is the power source and no one in the world has this part of one of their ships. That is why… it is so valuable."

Oh sure. I knew he was gonna say that. I set the ball on top of the table and it begins to roll until I catch it and, mashing the billows bag down, place it in the concave formed by the deflated bag. Well blow me down. My head shakes again of its own accord. Man oh man, what a gig. I move over and peer out the kitchen window at the approach. Nobody there but I can see that the mist has evolved into a light fog at water level now. And dark was coming too. I'd have to call Hank with his chopper pretty soon if I wanted off this island tonight. Cooler thoughts are present now as I turn back to Scheel.

"Okay, let's have the rest of it. Go on." I fling out my fingers like a kid shooting a glass marble at a sand hole. "Continue."

Scheel stands also. He slowly twists his torso from side to side, to release the tension from his little spiel, or so I reckon. "You may not believe it Mr. Stone, but I hate speaking of these things almost as much as you dislike hearing of them. That thing," he points at the ball, "has haunted me every day since I left this island in 1953. And as you may think I've lost my mind, try to remember that the man lying dead back by the cove, is a Chinese agent. He wanted that thing bad enough to kill for it."

I rest my weight against the sink counter and fold my arms.

"Okay. Are you gonna go on or not?"

Scheel takes a deep breath and backs over to the couch, sits down, leans forward and folds his hands in front of him like a tent before starting again.

"After the crash and…" he looks at me, "I assume it was a crash. I was looking directly out over the lake where the thing had to come from and never saw it when it hit. Anyway, I was terrified. I went right away to the radio and called my contact station which, on that day, was a Soviet submarine off the East Coast. I was so frazzled that I began relaying the story in the clear. The submarine captain had to settle me down and get me to send it in code before he would accept the transmission. He kept breaking the connection.

"You must understand," he palmed one hand while raising his

eyes to me, "I was simply horrified. I had been to war Mr. Stone and I had done and seen things that had stopped most fear from affecting me but at that time, I was honestly terrified. Do you see?"

He searches my face for solace but I was short on the commodity right then. I bump my head at him. "Go on."

His face accepts the rejection as he clears his throat and continues.

"Yes, well once I had the message coded and sent, I was told to wait for a reply. I did and it was almost two hours before it came. The message was directly from Colonel Segren himself. I was told that I was to collect the driver device immediately and await further instructions. And the funny part was this. While I heard the message and copied it properly, I could not respond. I could not take the chance because the sky was now full of Air Force and Coast Guard aircraft. They were everywhere. I had never seen such military activity in the area and now… it appeared that I would be captured and eventually executed as a spy in the very country I wanted to escape to."

He sighs and sits back, crossing his legs. "I assumed that they were looking for the jet that… that… that thing had taken." he shakes his head, a look of wonder upon his face. I'd been glancing out the window every now and then and decided that I wanted the rest of it. Time was getting short.

"Okay. What happened next?"

Scheel does a quick look over to me then takes his eyes to the floor. "After two more duplicate transmissions, the radio went silent. That was the procedure if a response wasn't received. I didn't light a fire that night because of all of the activity. I wasn't going to make it easy for them to find me. It was cold, very cold in the mine and I shook even with all of the wool blankets on. Then finally, after about two o'clock in the morning, the searching seemed to stop. I went up from the cave and could see that the snow was falling hard now. Visibility was very low. That was probably why they had stopped searching for now. I thought about trying to contact the sub but knew that the captain had dived his boat when I didn't respond to the radio calls. That too, was procedure. I went back down and bundled up to try and sleep."

He has stopped there, while I was looking closely at a perceived movement out by the trail. My green cloth still fluttered silently. I finally determined that the movement was caused by a brown thrush as the graceful bird flitted from branch to branch of a crabapple tree. I turn back to the old man. There, in his face, was that terror again. I don't like that as it brings the shinkakee, knocking at my door too.

"All right. You think they called off the search. So, then what?"

The old man rolls his large eyes to me and his bottom lip quivers as he speaks. "It was about four in the morning I guess. I'd fallen asleep but was tossing and turning due to the cold. When it was evening outside, the mine was pitch black without the lantern going and I could not use it that night. What little light penetrated the darkness below, was almost insignificant. Suddenly, a brilliant white light shot down the mine shaft. I had been caught! The Americans had found me! I grabbed the double barreled shotgun and scrambled for cover in the mine. The gun was my only weapon and I was to pretend that it was for hunting if I was ever questioned about it. The light was coming from the small opening where the Chinese is at now. The old excavation shoot. The light was so bright, I had to hold a hand over my eyes to shield them and then, as suddenly as it had come, it went out."

He looks at me then, eyes monstrously wide and a curious look spread over his face before he slowly swivels his head from side to side. He was lost again in a memory too spooky for me to contemplate. One of those "you had to be there" things but from his expression, I was glad that I hadn't been as he picked up once more.

"So... I assumed they had not found me but were here looking. About that time, light erupted from the other mine opening but I could tell it wasn't directed at the mine, but just outside of it. I remember cocking the hammers on the shotgun."

His hands were acting as if they were holding the gun now and his fingers pulled back the imaginary hammers. I'm just plain flabbergasted. What could scare this man so much? But somewhere, I had a feeling that I already knew. I blink my eyes as he stares at the floor in a trance.

"I am holding the gun in front of me as I go up the tunnel. At the opening, I hide next to a timber. The light has gone off again. Suddenly, it splashes once more!. It is a long cone shaped light, a configuration like I've never seen. I can see that the light is illuminating a buck deer as it walks along a trail. The snow is falling on the deer and it's beautiful in the brightness. The sky hides whatever is shining the light down. I can see nothing but darkness above the light. Then," the old eyes enlarge even more and go vacant, "another cone of light comes down and it lights up a raccoon who sits on its hind legs and looks up. I raise my eyes too and it's there! Another one! Just like the one in the cove below! The light on the deer goes out and then it comes on again, from different places on the thing. The thing is looking for something. It just hovers up there perfectly still.

"No noise, no movement. Nothing but the lights, going off and on... off and on... I am frozen in panic. I remember I can't make my arms move. I am so frightened. I know that the thing is looking for me. I want to bring the gun up to bear but I am shaking so badly then suddenly… all of the lights go out. Then," the monstrous green eyes dart to the ceiling, "it just shoots up into the sky and is gone." He looks back to me.

"A few minutes later, I heard the faint sound of an airplane's engines and saw the outline of a another search plane's spotlight far out over the lake." He exhales loudly and stands, moving over to the table by the orb where his sight travels over the dull object.

"It didn't come back again that night and I didn't plan on being there when it did. The next morning, I went down to the lake and pulled out the rowboat. It was wooden and I knew that my chances of making it to shore were not good. The temperature and snow were falling fast that day. But I also knew, that that thing would come back for me if I stayed. I'd rather die from drowning than be caught by it or they or… whatever."

He stands eyeing the circular ball but doesn't touch it. The fear in him is genuine and I've got to wonder if maybe, just maybe… he isn't too. I scan the approach out of the window again while speaking. "So how'd the ball get in the mine shaft then?"

He smiles slowly. "Yes, well when I was pulling out the boat, I saw it there, just floating in a amongst some newly fallen limestone. I've wondered over the years, if it wasn't the limestone perhaps, that shielded me from them in the first place. Possibly, their detection devices couldn't penetrate the limestone… I don't know."

He looks back at me like I had an opinion on this nonsense. I don't. When he sees that, he raises his hands and goes on.

"Well, I picked it up and took it back to the mine with me when I went back to get my things. I didn't know what it was then but I figured that if Segren was that interested in it, then it was probably valuable." He hikes his shoulders. "Perhaps, if I didn't die in the boat, I could use it to facilitate my asylum with the Americans."

His gray eyebrows form furrows as he peers at the ball. Then I see him shudder and suddenly, he was done with his study of the object. He went over and retrieved his water glass and walked back toward me, motioning for the pitcher pump in the sink. I oblige and move over. He pumps the handle and fills the glass, taking a long drink. I watch as his Adam's apple moves up and down with the swallows. He fills the glass and drinks again before wiping the back of his hand over the stubbly gray beard by his mouth. He looks out the window and bumps his head toward the glass.

"It looks quite calm and serene out there now." His gray head gives a gentle twist back and forth. "But that morning, the water was wicked. The waves were close to a foot and a half when I pushed the boat away and the snow stung when it hit my face and hands. I assumed that I was going to die."

I'm a little disturbed because I can no longer see the approach but what he's saying, has captivated my attention. It took guts to do what he says he did. I know what the weather is like here in late November and if he really did set off in a wooden rowboat like he says, then the man is damned lucky to be alive. I nod at him.

"So how did you make it back to the mainland in a wooden rowboat?"

He does a quick shake of his head and a slow smile appears over his mouth. "I didn't actually. An Air Force patrol boat…," he turns and points a finger my direction, thinking of something else, "did you ever see a film called PT 109 about President Kennedy?"

I hunch up my shoulders and nod. His smile broadens.

"Yes, well the U.S. Air Force had many such boats back in the 1950s. I saw them often when I was on this island. Their job was to search for downed pilots and crews and it was one of these, that picked me up the same night I left here."

His old eyes wane now, drooping to the floor as he reflects on the past. He raises a hand to signal his continuance while still staring at the floor.

"Anyway, when they fished me from the boat, I was almost frozen to death. I told them that I was from Escanaba and that I'd been out duck hunting and got lost in a snow squall. They seemed to accept that. They had to sink my wooden boat as they couldn't tow it in. They told me that they were looking for a crashed Air Force jet." He blinks as he reminiscences. "Judging by their radio calls I heard that night, there were numerous military aircraft and perhaps another ten patrol boats, such as the one I was on, searching the waters between the Escanaba and Green Bay for this crashed jet. The primary search seemed to be centered farther north, in Lake Superior but I couldn't tell them where their jet was. Not yet."

Scheel straightens up and stretches and I take the opportunity to look behind him at the path. The suspended green cloth still hung in place across the trail. As I was turning back, Scheel folds his arms and begins again.

"I remember that as we came into Escanaba, the activity was surprising. Coast Guard patrol boats and military vehicles of all types were all over the channel area and at the dock. There were military people everywhere. We tied up to the shipping dock." He glances over to me, "The marina and most of the things on the water there now, didn't exist back then. Anyway, they dropped me off on the

dock with the blanket wrapped around me, a hot cup of coffee and my belongings. Then they went back out searching. I made my way into town and took the first car I could find with a full tank of gas."
A slight jag appears in the corner of his mouth that eventually plays into a smile.

"I remember it was a tan 1949 Ford Coup. People often left their cars unlocked with the keys in the ignition back then. Anyway, I stopped at the first payphone I found and called my contact Oscar. I told him that the military had invaded the island, searching for a missing military jet and that I had to get off. I said that I'd come ashore in the boat. He knew of the crash and advised me to go on to Minneapolis and await instructions there. I was to call him again after I arrived. You see, Minnesota was where I was going to be sent when I was relieved on the island. Oscar also told me that Segren was dead. He had been killed that very night in a military coop in Yugoslavia.

"So he didn't know how long it would be before I was re-activated. But I knew. It would be a long time because Colonel Segren was keeping the whole RICTOR project secret. He had told us so because the forerunners of the KGB were constantly trying to snatch operations such as ours from the Army. Oscar said that I was to go where I'd been told and acclimate as best as possible. But I didn't go to Minneapolis," he turns to me and winks, "I went to Milwaukee."

I'd been listening so intently, I'd forgot to mind the trail and had to force myself to look away from Scheel and out and see the green cloth, still fluttering there across the path. When I turn back, the old man was still lost in the past again. And I was right there with him too. He rubs both hands over his face and I could hear the beard stubble bristle against the action. He begins speaking while his hands cover his face. His voice was oddly muffled until he drops the hands.

"You see, I made a plan as I drove. And like I told you before, I wanted out and free of the Soviet's grasp. The only way to do that was to die. So, I drove to Milwaukee. Once in the city, I drove around until I found a police car parked outside a diner. It had what I needed lying on the front seat. It was a policeman's hat. I stole it and took the metal badge off from it and pinned it to the inside of my wallet. Then I waited until after three o'clock in the morning and drove down to the county morgue." Scheel was proud of himself and it was showing n his face as he recounted the story.

"I went into the building and told the night attendant that I was Detective Johnson and needed to look at the personal effects of all of the unclaimed male bodies for an investigation I was involved in. The attendant did as I expected and merely glanced at the badge before getting me five boxes with a form and each man's personal things in it. He left me in a room and I quickly went through them. There were two that were scheduled to be buried the next day. One was a 29 year old car accident victim named Herman Veeter.

"The papers said he had no known family. He was older than me but I believed it would work. I took his driver's license and social security card and put mine in the box instead. I pocketed the form, assuming that they would just fill out another form the identification in the packet. I took everything back to the attendant and from that moment on, I've been Herman Veeter. I left the car there and bought a bus ticket to Grand Rapids, Michigan. I knew that this was a furniture making town and that I would be able to find work there. I bought a Milwaukee newspaper along the way and found that the funeral of Albert Scheel, had been administered by the county in Milwaukee, Wisconsin."

He looks up at me with an intense measure of pride on his face.

"You see Mr. Stone. I had done it. I had died and in the process, had garnered my life. Freedom." He swings his head wonderingly. "I soon met and married Heddie and we started our own furniture shop in Grand Rapids. She never knew anything of any of this. I kept a very low profile over the first few years but eventually, I was sure that the Soviets thought me dead. I mailed an anonymous note to the FBI giving them Oscar's name and phone number in Escanaba and that was that. We had only one child, her name is Gretchen. She married and her husband was killed in a motorcycle accident shortly afterwards but she gave us one grandchild and her name Mr. Stone," he turns to face me solidly now, "is Carrie.

Well wonder of wonders. I've been trying to swallow for a couple of minutes now but it hasn't been easy. I mean… holy shit! What a story. If this guy's not nuts and he's telling the truth, at least about how he got off the island, then he's sure got balls. Of course, he's probably crazier that a shithouse rat, this story's phonier than Dolly Pardon's tits and the only balls this guy has, are the silver metal beach type. He's talking to me again about the deal as I turn to look outside. As my eyes set on the path, I can see both pieces of cloth jumbled up together to one side. I thrust my hand toward the .45. SHIT! At the same time I say it, the window in front of the sink explodes outward and I drop, pulling the old man with me to the floor.

Wood is chipping all along the counter above our heads as the sound of gunfire and the smell of burnt powder wafts through the room. He can't zero us because we're behind the table! If the shooter takes a notion though, he can walk fire right up to us and blow us right outt'a our socks. This ain't good!

"Are you hit?" I have to scream over the gunfire, that I think is coming from the side bedroom.

"Yes, but it's not bad. Just a flesh wound in the shoulder I think!" Scheel screams back at me. I dig in my pocket and pull out the old man's .38 and jab it into his side.

"Take this! I'm gonna try and get around behind him. You cover me when I get ready to move, okay?"

I can see his eyes and they appear calm and confident. For some reason, I subconsciously lock that in my memory. Scheel quick-nods his head while taking the gun. I'm about to make my move when the shooting stops.

"Policeman! Can you hear me?"

Scheel and I look at each other. I turn on my side, getting ready to move. "Yeah, I can hear you."

"Policeman. Do not move from where you are at now. Either of you. I have a hand grenade and I will throw it if you attempt to move from your location. Do you understand? Look. I will not fire as you do so. See, I have it here."

Ahhh piss! I flip back over and bring the Colt up as I move. I was pretty sure that the voice was emanating from the second bedroom. The bastard had got past me while I was listening to Scheel's "My Favorite Martian" story and worked his way down alongside the house to a great shooting position. But he didn't seem to be worth a shit as a shot or we'd both be dead. I eased up and quick-peeked over the table, up and down. I'd seen it alright. An arm extended outside the door with a dark green fragmentation grenade grasped in a hand. I look at Scheel and nod. Then turn my voice upward.

"Okay pal, you got the bigger toy so what's it gonna be?" My eyes are darting all around the room, looking for an opportunity. Any opportunity. "I don't suppose you're interested in just giving up, eh? I could put you under arrest and you'd get to sleep in this really cool cell, eat jail food and..."

"Shut your mouth Policeman! Now throw your weapons out by this stove here. And do not take any sudden moves or this will end with an explosion."

I look over at Scheel and can tell that he's okay for now. I jab my chin at him. "These situations never turn out good but I think we'd better do as he says. He has the grenade and these guys, whoever they are, are the type to use 'em."

Scheel grunts then twists sideways enough to fling the heavy Smith & Wesson skidding across the floor to bounce off the leg of the heating stove. I roll in front of him and send the Colt sliding in the same direction. I already have the Glock out and cupping it in my left hand when our friend gives his next order.

"Good. Now stand up and keep your hands raised highly."

I position the Glock on the seat of the chair in front of me and turn my eyes to Scheel. He sees it and knows where it's at. He nods as we both begin to rise and I reach into my shirtsleeve and unsnap the sheathed knife, then send my arms skyward as I stand. Scheel gets up but can't hold his wounded arm very high. The dark haired man steps from the bedroom as we come up and he immediately snaps his weapon's aim at Scheel while screaming.

"I said keep your arms high!"

"Hey look dildo, he's hit in that arm and he can't hold it any higher than that!"

The gun jerks my way, fast enough for me to see my life go before me. I'd hoped that the tone of my voice would do that cause otherwise, this somebitch would've shot first and asked why afterwards. But just because I'd hoped for it, didn't mean I had to like it. I'm keeping my right elbow bent just slightly and praying that the camouflage shirt has enough bulk to hide that fact. Our new friend looks us over and I catch just a slight dart of his eyes to the silver ball on the table in front of me before he motions us out and into the room. The old man begins to move as directed.

"Nope. Wait a minute Scheel." Scheel stops and peers at me from the corner of his eye. I think I've got it figured out. I tilt my head at the ball.

"That's what you're here for…huh buckwheat?" This one's quite a bit younger than the other two. Maybe I have a chance.

The man's eyes grow even harder as he pockets the grenade and stares at me.

"I told you to come away from there Policeman. I will not tell you again!"

"Yeah maybe you won't but us staying put, change's things a mite there… huh cockbreath?"

The dark haired man's eyes narrow as he side-steps for a better shot with his weapon. I mimic his moves, keeping the ball between us.

"Be a shame to have this little ball get all shot up after your buddy got capped for it and all… now wouldn't it?"

A look of pure hatred flows over the gunman's face as he watches me.

"Capped? Ah, shot. Which of you shot Quang?"

I motion with my head toward Scheel. "Oh that would be my friend with the bloody arm there. He likes doing redheads. Me, I prefer to kill blonds whenever I can."

The man's look is incredulous and the gun lowers slightly, surprise sweeping over his expression in the process.

"You say... you killed Tran?" Astonishment as he digests this.

My minds flying down that highway and I think I've gotta plan but maaaaan... this is one hell of a long-shot here. But shit, there ain't nothing else, is there? I kick Scheel's leg beside the table and he sees me nod in the intended direction. He begins to take a step and the man with the gun swivels his aim toward him, expecting us to move as instructed.

"Yep. It was me or him...uh what was his name? Tran? Yeah, well frankly... I thought it would be better if he went first, ya know? Anyways, you went to all this trouble and all so... here, you can take the ball."

I quickly bend over and grasp the ball with both hands, shaking my arm and feeling the knifepoint drop into my palm while drawing the ball up at almost the same time as the gunman switches back to me. It's all going in slow-motion now, one fluid movement where I live or die. I see the surprise and uncertainty in the other man's eyes as it unfolds. He doesn't shoot and I feel the knife point drop into my fingers, a little pain jabbing my finger as it does. Scheel keeps moving and the gunman turns slightly back toward him as I shift the ball to my left hand, roil back my right arm and whip the knife.

The bad guy's in mid-swing toward Scheel but turning the gun back to me when the knife hits him with a solid "thwuck." Scheel and me both drop to the floor, the silver orb bouncing up and down on the table, sounding in all the world like a giant ping-pong ball. I grab the Glock and roll onto on all fours around the table, the weapon out front but our assailant is down and lying in a fast accruing puddle of blood by the stairway. He's clutching his throat, and gasping for breath. I can see the labored breathing of his chest and hear the gurgle of his blood. I quick-glance to see Scheel catch the ball before it rolls off the table then he's stumbling onto a kitchen table chair, sitting down hard. I move over to the dying man on the floor and remove the fallen Beretta from his proximity.

The coppery smell of blood mixes with the sulfur scent of gun smoke in the room. The knife had hit him dead-center and high in between the breastbone, just under the neck, driving up to the hilt. The eyes have that same starkness that his blond partner's did when I'd looked into them. There is a strangeness there. An oddity unlike any I'd ever seen before. I bend down and pocket the little Berretta pistol. Shit man, at this rate I was going to have enough of the little guns to be able to open a used gun shop. I reach in his pockets as he watches me with weird eyes and take out the hand grenade and an extra clip for the pistol and a cell phone. I drop the items into my own pockets as his breath gurgles through the blood that was filling his body cavity and the floor. He was dying fast and we both knew it. I take to my knees bend close to the young man.

"I don't suppose you want to tell me who you are or what you're doing here, do you?"

His mouth tries to form words but it's not easy for him. His eyebrows arch up in question marks and his strange eyes form the inquiry as he finally mumbles the words through the blood.

"Whob areb you?"

I feel a sigh escape me as I look down at him. "Somebody you didn't want to meet kid."

The eyes dance crazily for a second while he tries to figure out what's happening as his body begins to shut-down. They grow large and lock back on me, fear and confusion mixing in the brown irises. Then his eyes roll up and begin to grow dark. In a few seconds, they aren't seeing anything anymore and his chest is still. I sit back on my haunches and feel the adrenalin backing down too. My leg aches and as I look down at my finger, I see a stream of blood leaking down to mingle with the dead man's on the floor. I can hear Scheel's labored breathing behind me. I look over my shoulder at him and he points at the dead man.

"That is the other one. The one I told you was coming back."

As I cut my sight back to young man on the floor I offer Scheel a nod. "Yeah, I figured. How's the arm?" Scheel clears his throat.

"It's just a graze. It didn't even enter the muscle."

I take in a deep breath and pull out my knife from the dead attacker, wiping the blood on his black sweater, before sliding it back into the sheath. I can't stop looking at the dead man as I talk to Scheel. "How's the heart then?"

"Oh, still beating I'm certain of that at least. A bit erratic but still beating." His voice was quivery but I could tell that the stress was lessening. "Uh indeed Mr. Stone, I have the same question that he had."

He motioned with his good hand at the body. "Who are you? Because I don't think you are an ordinary tribal policeman. No, that you are not."

I pretend not to have heard that. I let my eyes wander to the ball on the table. "He could've taken us out easy but I think he was worried about a round hitting that thing."

Scheel allows his eyes to follow mine to the silvery orb. He looks at it a moment before speaking. "Perhaps. Still," he shot his stare back to me, "We certainly should be dead right now. That man had us at gunpoint and was even armed with a hand grenade and yet, we survived. And you killed this opponent with a knife from across the room." He adds the last with a certain amount of awe, as if he never saw a man throw a knife before. "So I must ask as well. Are you some kind of magician?"

I rock up off my haunches and move over to the kitchen cabinet where I have a first aid kit. "I used to be in the circus. You know, throwing knives at pretty babes on a spinning wheel. That kind'a shit."

I spin off a chunk of paper towel and bind it against my bleeding finger. Grabbing the kit, I go back over to Scheel who has watched me intently, waiting for an answer. I hold up the paper toweled finger and waggle it around. "Well it sure ain't magic or I wouldn't have cut myself with the knife?"

I begin taking out a dressing for his flesh wound and feel the adrenalin dissolving in my body. I'm tired of all this shit but... what's a mother to do? Yeah, mother is what it is too. Just a mother...fucker... all the way around. He keeps his eyes on me as I go about wrapping his arm.

"Maybe you are just out of practice, eh? So, are you a wizard or some kind of Indian witch doctor then?"

I stop and look dead at him. No shit Sherlock! I haven't tried sticking a guy like that for at least ten years. Yep, that's out'ta practice alright! What does he think? That I go out walking around whipping knives out of my sleeve and sticking people for kicks? After a second though, I quit. I give up anyway. Who knows. Maybe he's right. We should've been dead but I've come out of a lot deals this way. I do have an answer for him. Amos Reddeer's answer. And it's the only one I have. I don't like it but it's all there is. So I give it to him as I begin wrapping his arm.

"Yeah. I guess that's what I am. Now let it go... alright?" After another second, the old man nods and looks away.

A half hour later, I'm standing by the door smoking. I'd drug the dead man out to the small tool shed that sat near the back of the house and mopped up the blood. Scheel had tried to help but he was exhausted again and I'd told him to rest on the couch. I look over at the rhythmic rise and fall of his chest as he sleeps gently then cut my focus to the metal ball on the table. Whatever that is, that realtor wanted it and he wanted it bad. Bad enough to die for. While I had to admit, the old man was sincere in his story telling, I just couldn't get behind the UFO thing. I honestly thought that Scheel was goofier than Disney's dog. I had no doubt that he really believed this stuff but I just couldn't hop on for the ride, ya know? So, that said, what was it and who was after it? Okay, lets add it up then. I stepped outside and pondered.

As to what it is, well there're a couple of possibilities. I know that the Air Force is in this thing and even money said that that thing, was their reason. It could be a secret type of weapon or any other military secret thingamajig. I had to bet that they were after it and not the so-called stolen money. Now as to who, well we already have the Air Force in the deal and what the old man said about these guys being Chinese could be true. I'd heard the blond realtor mumbling some type of Oriental words and then there was that call on his cellular phone. That voice had answered me in an Oriental tongue, thinking that I was the phone's dead owner, then chastised me for speaking the only Vietnamese I know. So maybe, just maybe, these people were agents working for the Chinese government. The old man swore they were really Chinese with some type of cosmetic alterations on their eyes and bodies. But, I felt myself shake my head, I had to remember that he was a nut too.

I cupped the cigarette and sucked in a deep drag of smoke, feeling it invade all of my lungs before blowing it out. Shit! This was still a mess. My head slowly swings back and forth. Maaaan, if I get my red butt out'ta this one, I'm taking it straight back to the woods and that little cabin. If I'm lucky, I may get a pretty little Indian girl to go with me. But Nettie… well that was a whole 'nuther dilemma. Right now, I had two dead men on this island, another dead one back on the mainland, no idea how many more there are and… a crazy, sick old man to deal with. All of this and no answers. No solid answers, anyway. Count 'em, none. My ass was in hot doo doo unless I found some soon. So, maybe the best bet was to tell my tale to the wing nuts and see what that got me. Maybe they'd fess up and tell me the truth. Yeah. Right. And maybe the tooth fairy was real and owned an ivory business.

First things first though. My sight dropped to my watch and I saw that I had less than an hour before Hank Scari showed up with the chopper. I'd called him for a ride after cleaning up the body. I butted the smoke, field stripped it then went back inside. Scheel was still asleep, his open mouth looking cavernous in the light of the oil lamp. I hadn't fired-off the generator again because I didn't want the noise or extra light. I went to the storage closet, grabbed the tool box off the shelf, the battery powered Coleman lantern and switched the lantern on. Then I picked up the silvery ball from the bag on the table, tucked it under my arm and made my up the stairs to the huge light that gave the house its name.

I hung the lantern on hooks that dropped down from the ceiling just for that purpose. The massive light was ancient. I'd monkeyed around with it when I first came to the island. It obviously hadn't been used since the 1920s. While I didn't understand it all, I had enough mechanical sense to figure most of it out. It was actually a big lantern of sorts with a large wick that was controlled by gears with hand cranks. The wick was affixed to a metal bracket that had flanges all around it. It could be raised or lowered for maintenance.

The wick itself, ran on this bracket inside a metal tube all the way down to a kerosene tank on the ground. The tube was maybe two and a half feet in diameter. The brightness of the light was controlled by the flame height of the wick. Refractions of the light were somehow bent by mirror-like prism glass in-set on the light surface and sides. A mechanical cog turned them so that the prism bent and magnified the light out toward the lake. But this baby hadn't provided any light in a lot of years.

There were five large curved glass panels that protected the wick and made-up the actual light. One of these glass panels was divided and the bottom section that was metal, slid on a track to allow easy access to the wick for lighting. It opened when a small hand wheel was turned. I sat my stuff down and began twisting the hand wheel. It moved slow but it moved. Once I had the door open, I began trying to twist the hand crank that would lower the wick. It was frozen, which made sense. Still, I figured that the system was probably still airtight or else there would've been rust everywhere. There wasn't and I was hoping that the wick was just a little stuck.

I opened the tool box and took out several large sockets until I found one that fit the bolt head on the hand crank. I reached back in the box and extracted the breaker bar. I fitted it over the socketed bolt and took hold with both hands, pulling with everything I had. Several grunts and a bead of sweat on my forehead later, the wick popped loose and spun easily. I lowered it until the bracket was flush with the base. Next, I lowered the wick itself inside the bracket. Then I bent down and took the silver ball and sat it on the wick bracket and bent the metal flanges in to support the ball.

Like I'd hoped, it was a pretty good fit. Then I cranked the thing down until the ball disappeared inside the hole. I bent in and looking down at it, it looked as if it were a part of the light mechanism. Or that's what I hoped anybody else would think if they did this. I closed everything back up and headed back down the stairs. Scheel was in the bathroom. I could hear the water running in there. I grabbed the black billows bag and along with the tools, carried everything back into the little storage room, closing the door behind me. I was about to force the zippers of the pouches inside the bag when I thought I heard the chopper. I quickly pulled open the coal chute door and stuffed the bag into it, hearing it fall with a thump at the bottom. The coal bin had a loading door outside and I'd check the bag some other time. I was just closing the closet door when I heard Hank Scari lowering his Loach down outside the lighthouse. The sound of the helicopter brought Scheel out of the bathroom too. He watches as I began gathering my gear.

"Okay Scheel or whatever your name is, let's go." The old man nods, his eyes going to the table where the silver ball had been and then back to meet mine.

"Where is it?"

I quick-jab my head. "Don't worry, it's safe for the time being. Now let's get a move on okay?"

The old man doesn't move. "Am I going to jail then?"

I shake my head. "Nope, your going to the hospital. And I expect you to be quiet about all of this until I can get a handle on what's going on. Understood?"

Scheel looks me as I heft my stuff and when I open the door, he still has his eyes on me as he speaks. "I checked the dead man…," he motions outside, toward the storage shed, "and he is not circumcised either."

I return his look. "Okay. Good, now let's go, alright?"

Scheel twists his head. "And our deal? What about our deal?"

He's a pathetic sight, standing there like that. A crazy old man with all these things in his head. "Yeah. Okay. If your story checks out, I'll see that you get your money. Satisfied now? Here, put this on." I toss him his jacket from the couch. "It's cold out there. I'll do all the talking from here on out. You just be still okay?"

He laces his arms through the jacket while keeping his eyes on me. Finally, he takes several steps and stops.

"As I said before Mr. Stone, I have to trust you. I have the names of people who will pay a great sum for that device. And as I said, you can have it all but what I need for my little Carrie. A small child's life depends on that money and now, I shift that burden to you. You shall now have the burden of life or death. You will be responsible as to whether she lives or dies."

With that, he walks past me, taking his share of the gear and moves out to where the chopper is sitting, its rotors bending pine branches and whirling dust around in the darkness. I shoot my glance to the storage building where a body lays hidden and think of another one, lying face-up in a clearing. Oh yeah. That's just tits! As if I don't have enough problems in my life right now without that little extra guilt trip. Geeze. I heft my bag and walk to the bird and Hank's helping hand.

Chapter Eighteen
Things Ain't Always As They Seem

The Leisure Inn Motel,
Escanaba, MI,
Same night.

Kuan stood by the window and looked down as the darkness outside erupted with white. The snow came in torrents of gentle flakes, floating aimlessly downward. Chin had met Kuan in front of the place where the policeman left his vehicle earlier that afternoon. The helicopter had finally returned but only the pilot exited the aircraft. The two had waited and watched but neither the policeman's patrol vehicle or the helicopter had moved again and finally, well after dark, the two agents had returned to Kuan's motel room. There was a knock on the door as Chin finished drying his hands and stepped from the bathroom. Kuan drew his weapon and quick-stepped to the door's side, casting a fast glance over to Chin. His leader already had his small pistol out and was leaning back inside the bathroom, using the doorjamb as cover. He nodded to Kuan from across the room.

"Yes, who is it?"

There was a rustling outside the door then a young man's voice came through. "China Star Restaurant. You's ordered… looks like egg drop soup, fried rice and some other stuff, eh?"

Kuan leaned across the door and peeked through the small hole. He turned and nodded to Chin, who pushed the bathroom door partly closed, leaving enough room to shoot clearly but sheltering his presence. Once done, Kuan lowered his weapon alongside his leg, unchained and twisted the lock free on the door, pulling it open. The delivery person was a very young man in his teens. His face was pitted terribly with the red sores of acne. Kuan looked him up and down while the youth rummaged for the bill, that was stapled to the white paper bags. He looked real enough. The boy tore off the bill and after glancing at it, handed it forth to Kuan.

"That'll be $13.50 sir."

Kuan let the small Beretta drop into his trouser pocket then retrieved a twenty dollar bill from his shirt pocket and handed it to the boy.

"Here you are. Keep it." He took the outstretched bags from the him as the kid wrapped his fingers around the twenty with a large smile.

"Hey, thanks man. I appreciate it, eh."

The boy turned and left as Kuan leaned out and watched him walk down the hallway. Then he closed and re-bolted the door. Chin came out of the bathroom and moved over to take one of the bags from Kuan and set it on the small table.

"Have you had any difficulties with the food here? I have found it to be very rich." He opened the bag and looked down. "And what they call Chinese food here, is quite seriously lacking, do you think so?"

Kuan hunched his shoulders and tilted his head. "I suppose sir. Uh, your pardon, sir but what are we going to do? We have had no word from our two other men in over sixteen hours now. Do you agree then, that we must conclude that they are lost or compromised?"

Chin had taken a cardboard box of fried rice over to one of the beds and sat back against the headboard, his legs out-stretched to begin eating.

"Yes Kuan, I believe that you are correct and I agree. Unfortunately, they are either dead or the mission has been compromised or perhaps, both of these things have happened. This, to answer your question, leaves us but one course of action. We must get to that Indian policeman and see what he knows. If our men are dead, then he probably knows why or perhaps," he took another bite of rice, chewed and swallowed, "he killed them himself." Kuan's eyebrows rose mightily at this statement but Chin went on.

"I know that sounds ludicrous but the fact remains that we simply do not know." He pointed his chop sticks at Kuan, "From what we have learned, the Indians are a separate government here and possibly, the American Air Force knows nothing of this whole thing." Chin waggled his chop sticks while slowly shaking his head toward the other man.

"It is possible Kuan, given our information up until now, that this Indian policeman could indeed, have the object we have been sent here to retrieve." He took another large bite of food and chewed as Kuan began eating from a box also. Chin smiled as he swallowed.

"And what choice do we have anyway? So, if the Indian returns tomorrow, you will have a little talk with this man. And when you are finished, he will have a small accident. I have thought it all out and know exactly how we shall do it."

Kuan looked over at his superior. "It will probably have to be tomorrow night then. I saw signs posted all around the marina stating that the American Coast Guard will be there from noon until six pm tomorrow performing safety checks on the boats. So, I assume that there will be plenty of people in addition to the military there then."

Chin nodded at Kuan and jabbed the sticks down into the box, speared a large piece of egg and rice and pushed them into his mouth. "Very well then, tomorrow night is when you shall have your little talk. Of course, this plan assumes that the Indian will return." Chin speared a piece of cabbage with rice clinging to it and held it up to Kuan.

"And if he does not come back, then we will rent a boat and go out to the island." He snickered. "We will probably drown if that is what we end up doing but simply put my friend... we have no other alternative." He pushed the cabbage into his mouth and spoke while he chewed.

"Our time is up and the weather is growing worse every day." He pointed at the window where the snow dropped endlessly, then speared some more rice and continued. "So, for now," Chin pointed to the bag of food, "eat and be merry... as the Anglos say. For tomorrow dear friend... we may be dead." He laughed out loud and a spray of rice escaped his mouth and landed on the blue motel bedspread.

St. Francis Hospital,
Escanaba, MI,
Same night.

I stand outside under the carport looking at the parking lot of the emergency room. I am eating the last of a vending machine roast beef and cheddar sandwich. It's not too bad. I watch as the first flakes of snow drift downward in the light of the streetlamps to quickly become a white lacy curtain falling over the darkened landscape. I crumple the plastic paper and stuff it inside the trash compartment then reach down into the scalloped top of the standing ashtray for my cup of luke-warm vending machine coffee. I bring it up and take a sip. It's nasty but all vending machine coffee is. I finish the muddy stuff and wipe my mouth and hands with a paper napkin. Then I pull out a hand-rolled and light it up.

I watch a city police cruiser slide past the lot entrance on Ludington Avenue, its wipers snapping occasionally to rid the window of snow. The cop spotlights a car parked close to hydrant. Apparently, it wasn't close enough to the fire plug or else the cop felt charitable tonight because he keeps going. The place was desolate otherwise. I take another drag of smoke and exhale as I dig in my shirt pocket for the slip of paper. I'd had Scheel write his daughter's name and phone number but was afraid I'd left the paper inside my tiger stripes.

We'd stopped by the boathouse before coming here to the hospital and I'd changed while Scheel cleaned up. I figured that being in tribal uniform would help facilitate the fabrications I knew I was going to have to make at the emergency room. Scheel fully expected them to keep him overnight. He'd said that he'd been through this before and that's the way they do things. He'd wanted to clean up before checking in, as it were and I understood that. Old helicopter Hank Scari had skeptically accepted the story I'd told him about Scheel getting lost in his boat and having heart trouble. But just the same, I knew that he had his doubts about the veracity of the tale when I was telling it to him. He'd just looked my tiger stripes up and down and nodded his head at me. I had known men like Hank my whole military career. They were good, honest and trustworthy men and I really didn't like misleading him but heck man, I was between a rock and hard place in so many different positions, I longed for the single good old fashioned missionary one… ya know? I mean, just one would've been really nice.

My fingers rove the pocket but the bandage on my finger makes feeling anything nearly impossible. The E.R. doctor was a fairly young guy and had laid in three stitches where the knife had sliced my ring finger open. I normally wore a silver turquoise ring on that finger but it rested in my pants pocket now, sliced in two at the bottom. The doc had cut it off to relieve the swelling. If I hadn't had the ring on, I'd have probably lost the finger. It could've been worse, I figure. I could've lost the whole hand. I'd been lucky and the Great Good Spirit had been strong with me there in the lighthouse. The doc had sent Scheel down for tests and like Hank Scari, had listened to my story with great doubt displayed on his face. He had alluded to the fact that Scheel's arm wound, looked a lot like a bullet graze. And all I could do in response to that was say, "Hmm?" with raised eyebrows for emphasis. Finally, I give up and switch hands for the search. The other fingers are more fluid and I'm able to latch onto the paper in my shirt pocket. Pulling it out, I see it's what I'm looking for.

I look at the snow falling aimlessly and blanketing the vehicles parked in the lot. I'd left the cell phone in the Jeep and didn't feel like trucking through the snow after it. I butt the smoke and walk back inside the hospital and over to a pay phone in the lobby. I shoot a glance at my watch while reading the name and number. It is five after ten and I figure that isn't too late to call. I take out my tribal VISA and apply the necessary numbers for the mechanical phone voice. The call is picked up.

"Hello?"

"Uh, hi Ma'am. I'm sorry to call so late but I'm looking for a Gretchen Cooper?"

"This is she. I'm Gretchen Cooper."

"Oh, okay. Good. This is Special Agent Stone with the Pukaskwa Tribal Police up in Escanaba Ma'am and I'm calling about your father."

"Oh, thank God! Escanaba! Is he okay? Is he there with you?"

"Yes Ma'am, he's fine and he's here in Escanaba. We're at St. Francis Hospital and…"

"Hospital! What's wrong with him? Is he hurt? Is he…" I cut her off to slow her down and ease the hysteria that this kind of news can bring on.

"No Ma'am! Just settle down now!… He's okay, they're just running some tests on him because he was having trouble with his heart again. The doctor says he's fine and that they're going to keep him overnight just to monitor him to be sure…okay?"
There was silence on the line while I assume she composes herself. I can hear her breathing beginning to slow down and shortly, she speaks again.

"Do you know… uh… I'm sorry. Do you kno…"
She's crying now. Softly but I can hear the breaks in her sobs through the receiver. I get the notion that she's been worried sick over the old man and I feel my heart sail down to Grand Rapids. Nothing hurts me quite as bad as a woman grieving. Even if it's in grateful recognition of news such as this. I wait for her to get her composure back and shortly, she does. Her voice is nasal now and I assume it because of the tears.

"Uh… do you… do you know where he's been?"
"Well, I found him out on Muskrat Island. Does that mean anything to you? I mean, with the time of year and all and the island being deserted… well… it's just lucky I came up on him."

"Muskrat Island?" She was quiet for a beat. "I wonder if that's the island he's always talking about when he goes off?" I felt that the question wasn't directed to me and when she began again, I knew it wasn't.

"He…my father… you see he's sick and… I'm sorry. What did you say your name was again?"

"Stone. Ely Stone. I'm with the Pukaskwa Tribal Police and we own Muskrat Island. That's how I happened to be out there today and find your Dad."

"I see. Well my father has some serious mental problems. I didn't think Alzheimer's disease was one of them but maybe it is. I just don't know. I have no idea why he would've been on an island but in the past… he's had dementia and when he had those episodes, he often made reference to some island or another. But that was years ago. Then he just disappeared two weeks ago. He had been fine for years and then… he was just gone." Her voice broke again. "This is the first word I've had about him since."

I could hear her sob softly over the phone and want desperately to sooth her pain. But I know I can't. The best I can do for her is to switch her off the thought.

"Look Ma'am, he's fine for now but you're going to have to make arrangements to come up here and get him. Is that going to be possible?"

She sniffed and adjusted to the new topic. Her mind now functioning in a different realm other than the painful one it had left. "Yes. Of course. I'll have to get my Mother-In-Law to look after my daughter but I'm sure that won't be a problem and I'll drive up first thing in the morning. Will that be okay?"

She asked the last with the trace of a cry still evident in her speech. I've got a feeling that by asking her the next question, I'll put her right back into the pain but I need to know if Scheel's been telling some truths in this whole mess.

"Yes Ma'am. That should be fine. Oh, by the way. How is your daughter? Your Dad says she's mighty sick?"

There's a long sigh before she begins and when she does, the anguish is right back to the forefront of her being.

"Carrie is doing…okay. She is sick though and…" Her voice breaks as she begins crying again. I feel like the shit I am for putting her through this but I need to hear a little more.

"I'm sorry. Your Dad says it's leukemia and that it's untreatable, huh?" I can hear her covering the mouthpiece with her hand and visualize her tears. It's enough to bring water to my own eyes. Finally, she removes her hand and the sadness in her voice is eating a hole in my stomach.

"Yes… I'm afraid we're going to lose her…" Her voice breaks again.

I clear my throat. "Uh, your Dad said that there's some doctor in Switzerland who may be able to help isn't there?"

I can hear her sniffles and imagine her sitting there with a Kleenex as she answers. "Well yeah, maybe there is but you see, I'm a widow. Carrie's Father died in an accident several years ago. And this therapy is so very expensive. And well, even with all of the cancer fund drives and all the money we've been able to scrape up, we're still almost thirty thousand dollars short. The big thing is time. We're just running out of time for her."

She cleared her throat this time before speaking again. "I'm sorry, this call must be costing you a fortune. Can I call you right back and get directions and everything?"

"No, don't worry about it. This is official police business and actually, I have a few things that I need to get cleared up anyway." I felt like I'd put her through enough already but I could possibly kill two birds with this next stone, guised as a question.

"The dementia you said your Dad has, uh… do you think that could be the problem here? I mean, why he walked away from home and all? You know? I was wondering if he will he be okay here alone until you arrive? What I mean is, I've worked with folks with the disease and he doesn't act like people do when they have Alzheimer's?"

There was a long silence while she pondered that one and while she sure seemed to have enough grief in her life, maybe her father not having another type of mental disorder, was a heartening possibility. When she answered, it was in a much clearer voice. And that was good.

"To tell you the truth, I just don't know. He went off the deep end when my mother died and at that time, he was ranting about UFOs, islands, aliens, government conspiracies, black helicopters, crop circles, Russian spies and boy, you name it… he seemed to think they were after him. Of course, since then, he's been pretty stable. But our doctor says that he suffered from paranoid delusions and could drop back into this dimension at any time of stress. I suppose Carrie's illness is to blame for him behaving like this… I just don't know anymore."

She took a breath and continued. "I just assumed that with the pressure over Carrie and all, well he probably just snapped again. But why in the world he'd go way up to Escanaba… well, that's why I thought it might be Alzheimer's disease, I guess."

My leg ached and now my finger was adding to the chorus. I turned and leaned my back against the wall, re-adjusting the phone handle. "Yeah. That is strange unless you folks have some kind of tie here?"

"No. None. I've never even been to Escanaba, much less some island up there."

She was a lot calmer now so I thought I'd push a little deeper, albeit softer too. "Uh, Miss Cooper, your Dad also said his real name is Albert Scheel and that he was born in Germany. Does that mean anything to you?"

She sighed deeply. "No. His real name is Herman Veeter and he was born in Milwaukee, Wisconsin."

"Okay. The reason I ask, is that he swears that his real name is Scheel and that he was born in Germany. The man seems pretty convincing, ya know?"

"Oh yes. I know all too well. But trust me, he was born in Milwaukee. I've been to the house he grew up in and met my father's parents, my paternal grandparents, there for the first time in my life when I was six. I think they'd know if his name was different or if he had been born somewhere other than at Milwaukee General Hospital, don't you?"

"Sure, I'm sorry. It's just that he seems so convincing and I have to have these things right for the report."

"Oh please. No apology is necessary. I know exactly what you mean about him being convincing. I've seen it. And I suppose," worry creeping into her inflection, "that he could just walk away from there again too."

"Okay Ma'am. I think that'll do it for me but here's what I think you should do to help your Dad, okay? You should call the county sheriff down there… uh, what county is that?"

"Oh, um it's Kent County here."

"Okay, call the Kent County Sheriff's Department and tell them that your Dad has been found and is at St. Francis Hospital in Escanaba. Then ask them if they'll call up here and ask the Sheriff to send someone to watch him until you can get here to pick him up. City police chiefs are responsible to a board that hires them and they're not always willing to fork-out expenses for things like this. Sheriffs, on the other hand, are elected and they'll usually do anything to help out a voting citizen – no matter where they're from, know what I mean? I'll call too but it'd be better if we both do it, okay?"

"Yes. Certainly. I call as soon as we hang up. I… want to thank you for calling and for finding him. You've been very kind. Will you be there when I arrive?"

"No Ma'am. I've got to be going shortly but let me give you my cell number and when you get here, give me a call and I'll try to swing by the hospital before you leave."
I gave her the number and she hesitated after copying the information.

"Okay. Well again, thank you so much for all your courtesy and please, call me Gretchen. I feel so old whenever anyone calls me Ma'am."

"Sorry about that. Southern up-bringing. Please call me Ely. Anyway Gretchen, I look forward to hearing from you and I'll keep you, your daughter and Dad in my prayers, okay?"

"Yes. That's very nice of you. Goodbye, Agent Stone…er, Ely."

I head back out and smoke another one then, call the local sheriff. He says he has already been contacted and is sending over a deputy to watch Mr. Veeter. Then, I go back inside and look up Dr. Max Bonner. He motions me in with a wave of his hand. He twists around in his chair to look me in the eye and elevates his hand to shake. I grasp his hand lightly and wince as he clasps mine. I can't stop the wince.

"Oh, sorry about that." He nods as he releases my hand. "How's the finger?"

"I raise my eyebrows. "Well, it's throbbing right along, Doc."

"Yes, well it's going to. That's a fairly deep laceration. It was fortunate you were wearing that ring when the knife slipped out of your hand." He bumps his head at me. "It's nice to meet you. The new tribal police have been all everyone's talking about." His face turns whimsical. "So, have our nurses been hitting on you?"

That surprises me. But then, so had the nurses. They had been flirting with me hard and heavy, a lot of it sexual and none too subtle, either. Then again, I don't get out much. I clear my throat and shrug. "Uh yeah... kind'a?"

The doc chuckles. "Yeah. I figured. It's mostly the young nurses in E.R. There aren't many eligible men up here and whenever a decent-looking single guy shows up, the females around here turn very competitive." His smile wanes before his face switches back to business.

"Okay. First things first. Mr. Veeter is resting comfortably and is stable. However, he has mild cardio problems that can and will result in a heart attack should he become too excited. His arrhythmia is under control at the present but that can change. As I said, we'll keep him overnight to monitor the situation. Now," he rocked back in his chair and cocked his eye at me, "is this man under arrest?"

I shake my head. "Nope. He's a family walk-away from downstate... Grand Rapids. His daughter is en route to pick him up and should be here sometime tomorrow. I'm pretty sure you can talk to her about insurance if your concerned about that?"

The E.R. doctor wrinkled his forehead. "Well that's good to hear but actually Officer, I'm more concerned about the wound on his arm?" He spiked his eyebrows in a question and I just look at him and wait. After several beats, he twists around and folds his arms looking at me in a fatherly fashion. I think this is a good trick because he's at least ten years younger than me. Then he speaks again.

"Let me put it this way then. If Mr. Veeter had come in here on his own tonight with that wound on his arm, I would've been obliged to contact the police and advise them that I had a patient with a probable gunshot wound. But," he splayed out his palm, "since you are the police, I guess I don't need to make that call... right?"

I nod and look down at the floor. "Tell me Doc, did Mr. Veeter say he had been shot with a gun?"

The doctor slowly shakes his head, his eyes searching my face. "No. No he didn't."

I nod again. "Yeah, well he didn't say anything to me about being shot either." I let my sight travel back to meet him.

He looks closely at me a second before speaking then nods slightly. "Okay. Good enough then."

I take a deep breath. "The Sheriff's Department is sending over a deputy to keep an eye on Veeter until his daughter arrives to pick him up. She figures that if he walked away once, he might do it again." I hunch my shoulders in a sign of "who knows" and lean against the door. The Doc rubs his hands over his face and speaks through them.

"Okay. That's no problem." He looks up at me. "Are you heading out of here then?"

I ease myself off the doorjamb and take in a breath. "Yes sir. I think I'll talk a little with Veeter before I go, if that's alright?"

"Sure. No problem. He's in the forth door down on your right." He turns back to the paperwork on his desk. "Not long though because he needs his rest, okay?"

I nod and make my way down the hallway, stopping at Veeter's door. Other than turning the knob, I had no idea what to do next. What to say or... to ask the old man. I was pretty sure that I needed the information from my old team mate Gangues before I could gauge that. The Air Force was the player here, that much I was sure of. And the dead men... they're not normal and somehow... they're hooked together with the Air Force. I was just taking it as it came at this point. I guess, that's was all I have and... all I could do. I feel a sigh escape as I raise a hand to the door, knock and let myself in.

The old man is awake as I enter and looks tons better now. He'd shaved or the nurses had shaved him. Anyway, his eyes were bright and he was scooting himself up on the bed as he saw who I was. I closed the door and turned back to him.

"Well you look a lot better than when I brought you in here. Must be the shave and the good looking nurses, huh?"

He tilted his head and raised his shoulders. "I feel better. As for the women, I'm well passed being interested in the sexual attributes of the opposite sex I'm afraid."

I step over, drag a chair close to the bed and sit down, looking at him. "I called your daughter. She'll be here tomorrow."
The old eyes traveled over me before coming to rest on the wall above my head. "So what are you going to do? Am I to be placed

under arrest then?"

"No. Not right now anyway. Look, Mr. Veeter or Scheel or whatever your real name is... I've got some serious problems here, okay? Now, I'm still working on them and until I have an answer, you're just going to have to sit tight and wait."

The old green eyes dropped down and fixed on my own, his face a mixture of anxiety and questions. "But you know that time is the one thing I do not have! Carrie does not have it! You spoke to Gretchen? Didn't she tell you about Carrie? Can't you understand that time is of the most importance here!" He was leaning forward, his voice picking up in sound and intensity.

I had my hand up and was patting his shoulder, trying to calm and quiet him at the same time. "Now just settle down. If you have a heart attack and die, what good will you be to your granddaughter then, huh? Now sit back and listen... okay?"

The tenseness slowly melted in the old man but his eyes still retained their fierceness as he settled back against the pillow. I begin speaking in a low voice. "Now, I did talk with your daughter and yes, she confirmed what you said about your granddaughter. But she also said that you weren't born in Germany and that your real name is Veeter, not Scheel. She said that she's been to your parents' home in Milwaukee too so..." He was shaking his head as he interrupted.

"No, no, no! I hired those people to pose as my parents! Don't you see? It was all a part of the cover story I created!"

I let myself ease against the chair back. "Well okay, either way, the bottom line is this. Until I figure out what's going on here, I can't help you or your granddaughter, alright... now I've got things in the works that should pay-out soon but until that time... you're gonna just have to be patient." I lean forward and point my finger against his arm. "Do you understand me? Let's just keep this whole mess to ourselves and I'll do my best... Okay?"

He starts to argue but then, seems to reconsider. "I suppose I have little choice, do I?"

I gently shake my head. "Nope, neither one of us do right now..." There's a knock at the door and I push myself up and move over to open it. A flirtatiously smiling nurse stands there with her palm pointing at a man beside her. An older, irritated deputy steps around her and extends his hand, introducing himself. I shake and turn back to Veeter.

"This officer will be outside the door tonight to make sure nobody bothers you, Mr. Veeter." I wink at him. "So, get some rest and I'll see you tomorrow, okay?"

The old man doesn't speak. He merely nods and turns his face to the wall. I pull the chair out into the hallway and close the door, quickly running down the case for the deputy. He nods with that, 'been-here-done-this' before look. Then with a confused expression, he throws a thumb over his shoulder at the retreating nurse.

"Yah, I don't know why dat nurse taught she had'a show me da way – I done dis a million times, eh?"

I watch the nicely moving rear-end of the nurse as she sash-shays down the hall. She tosses a big smile over her shoulder as she disappears around the corner. I shrug then say, "see ya" to the cop before going outside to start the Jeep. As I wait for it to warm-up, I scroll through the calls on the cell phone. There're quite a few. Hennessey, a few calls with Nettie's number and a few others. Several are from Morse and I listen to him ask me to call – no matter what time - on the voice mail. He'd only left the number from the station so I dial as the Jeep's heater begins spitting out warmth. Five rings and it's picked up.

"Pukaskwa Tribal Police, Officer Treebird. Can I help you?"

My mind races and I remember. The pony-tailed kid. Jason. Yeah, that was it. "Jason. How're ya doing tonight? This is Ely Stone."

"Oh…pretty good Detective. How about you? Everyone's been looking for you, eh."

Detective. That's right. He called me that the day we met. I think I like that title better than all the others. My eyes roam up to the Escanaba police officer I'd seen earlier as he exits the emergency door and climbs into his cruiser. I return my attention to the call as I see the car's headlights come on and it begin to move. I drop the selector and back out.

"Just marvy Jason. Just plain old marvy. I couldn't be better. And I know they're looking but I've been tied up on a accident. I just left the victim now and I'm just leaving the hospital, heading for the boathouse as we speak. Hey, I'm looking for Captain Morse. He left this number to return a call. Is he still there per chance?"

"Uh, no sir he isn't. He's meeting with some U.S. Marshals and FBI people in the Soo right now. I assume that you don't know about Mr. Shultz then do you?"

I watch the city cop drive past and return a wave as he goes out of the lot. What would the Feebies and Marshals be talking to Morse about? That was a wonderment. "Yeah, I know some of the deal with Schultz. You guys were going to pick him up. Did you do that?"

"Yes we did and right now, he's cooling his heels in our newly built little jail here, eh."

"Okay, good. But I haven't heard anything about the feds being involved. What gives with that?"

"Ahhh well, that's the most interesting thing of all then. It seems that Mr. Shultz and some other lawyers from down in Detroit had some type of fraud scheme going. Bilking large sums of money out of non-profits and I guess, Indian tribes, too. And it appears that we caught Schultz before the feds caught their boys down-state. The Detroit attorneys all made a clean get-away and are out of the country. So, they want Schultz but we aren't giving him up and well you know, more or less, that's what's happening, eh."

Well, well. So, my premonitions about Schultz the seagull were correct after all. I put the Jeep in drive and pull through the lot, heading for the boathouse. "Hmm. Well that's interesting Jason. Okay, so we have Schultz in custody and the feds want him, huh?"

"Yes sir. They want him bad. Captain Morse is pretty happy about that, too. I guess it makes us look really good, you know, tagging Schultz while the feds miss their guys. Still, it's kind of surprising you know, them all being lawyers and all, don't'cha think?"

I drive down Ludington Avenue and hold the phone to my ear as I work the wheel. "Nah, not really. You know how you get a lawyer out of a tree don't ya?"

"Is this a joke Detective?"

"Only if you find it funny Jason."

"Okay. How do you get a lawyer out of a tree then?"

"You just cut the rope."

He laughed easily. "Okay, that's a good one. I'll use it. Still, just goes to show you, things ain't always as they seem, eh? Oh yeah, by the way. Some Air Force guy is looking for you too."

"Uh huh. A Major Shears or a Captain Mussenberg, I'll bet?"

"No sir. It was a General. I've never been in the service but doesn't a lieutenant General have three stars? I was just curious about that, eh. Anyway, his name's Lieutenant General Kourn."

My foot involuntarily comes off the gas pedal and the Jeep slows to a stop in the middle of the street. Sonavabitch! I can feel my mouth hanging open as deep in the recesses of my mind, Ghost Riders in the Sky begins playing. An Air Force General! Well that tears it. What had the blond said? What had Jason just said? "Things ain't always as they seem". Well no shit Sailor! Maybe they ain't! But if they ain't... then just how the hell are they then? A horn blows behind me and I look in the mirror to see the flashing yellow lights of a city salt truck. Treebird is asking if I'm still there as I resume driving.

"Yeah Jason, I'm still here. But I gotta hang-up." I realize that I really like this kid as a smile comes to my mouth. "Hey, let me ask you though. Are you married?"

There's quiet on the other end as he, no doubt, tries to figure out where those questions are coming from. Then he answers. "No, I'm not married. Why do you ask?"

"No particular reason but next time you're down here, I need a favor. I need you to stop by the St. Francis Hospital E.R. and introduce yourself to the night staff there, okay? If you do that, you'll understand why I asked. In the meantime, I'll be at the boathouse and you can tell Morse he can reach me there, alright?"

"Yes sir, will do, Detective. Have a good night, eh."

He hung up, a little curious I suppose but shit, if he was curious, well… he just didn't what curious was, ya know? Because things ain't always as they seem… are they?

Chapter Nineteen
"Just My Imagination"

The Boathouse,
Escanaba, MI
The Same Night.

I sit at the little table in the boathouse rolling cigarettes and stacking them against the tobacco pouch. I'm in my underwear and a t-shirt and the little Glock sits within hand's reach on the table beside me. I'd had a number of calls on the answering machine and two of them had been from Hennessey. I'd called his house but apparently, he'd gone with Morse to meet with the feds. So, I'd left a message at his home to call me here when he returned. Nettie had left two messages too. There had also been a call from the Air Force General Treebird had mentioned but I hadn't returned it. I needed to speak with Hennessey first, if I could. Things ain't always as they seem. Nope, they sure weren't. Air Force General, my ass. Why would a three star come all the way here to see 'lil ole me? The wingnuts were into this deal deep and that was a fact. It was important to them.

And, from the sounds of things, we had taken a pretty hard hit on The island deal. Funny how I used the word "we". I guess I'm a full-fledged member of the Tribe now, huh? Anyway, if the Band couldn't use the island for a casino, then any only other uses were almost nonexistent. Maybe a hunting preserve, I don't know. That was a lot of money to pay for land that had little or no return on it. But if I was right, the tribe might be able to swing a deal with the government in exchange for allowing them to go after whatever it was they wanted on the island. I'm still trying figure out exactly what, that could be.

What could the Air Force possibly want out on that island? What was so important that a three star was involved in it and wanting to talk to me personally? Was it the funny looking metal beach ball? I doubt it. But then, things ain't always as they seem, eh? Maybe so but I'm pretty sure now, after talking with Scheel's daughter, that the curious little ball was probably something the old man found in the mine. Maybe it was an old tool or part of a tool or something. So given that, I don't think that the Air Force is looking for the ball. Nope, they're after something else on that island. I needed to know what. I'd checked my e-mail but there was nothing from Gangues the

Con yet. I guess Air Force OSI is a tough one. But I have faith in him.

If it could be done, Gangues was the man who'd do it. I'd left another request, asking him to add Lt. Gen. Kourn to the other wing nuts he was researching. It was late now, almost two o'clock in the morning as I finished the last roll and filled my metal case. I tipped up the bottle and drained the last of the beer, then placed the rest of the rolled cigarettes in plastic bag and stuck them in the freezer. Then I opened the bottom door of the little refrigerator and pulled out a piece of Colby cheese. I munched on the cheese and a piece of white bread and washed it down with another beer before deciding to hit the sack.

Taking the pillows from the bed, I situate them and apply the covers so as to make a false impression of a body lying there. Then I take the extra blankets from the closet and make a pallet on the floor behind the desk. I'll sleep there tonight. I'm not being over-cautious. I'm trying to stay alive... period. I flip the light off and cozy up in my impromptu bed, the Glock within easy reach. I'm tired and can feel the day's activities. The floor's hard and it's cold down here too. Still, a sweet vision floats before my closed eyes as Annette, her dark hair flowing around her, walks down the boardwalk of this marina. I miss her. I couldn't call her tonight because I'd got back too late but I'll talk to her in the morning. It's that thought that begins to warm me as

I drift off to deepness. Immersion for a time then, somewhere, the cobwebs begin. They hang like mist from the corners of my mind and catch rays of the sun as the blue-green water of the ocean wafts through the picture. It's the dream world. But where am I now? I don't remember this place. No, that's not it. It's just that I don't want to remember. I don't like this. Please let me think of something else. Please Jesus! I don't want to remember! But it's too late. I'm already back there...

The East Florida Coast,
The 1980s, Everyday War,
The Recent Past.

The next thing I know, I'm standing on the pitching deck of a white Coast Guard utility boat. But somehow... I know that I've been here before. Lots of times. I'm leaning against the starboard side of the vessel as we close on an old wooden fishing trawler. I have an M-16 leveled on the fishing boat as the 41 footer I ride upon, gains on the other craft. The waves are breaking over the bow, splashing me and my weapon. My dark blue utilities are drenched and heavy with the Florida ocean as the boat wades into the troughs. My web belt and holstered .45 are wet too. But that's nothing compared to my insides.

Internally, the shinkakee has soddened my very being, soaked into my soul and I know that this ain't good! I have my hat on backwards, the bill pointing aimlessly to the rear but I'm much better able to keep a sight picture on the trawler like this. Tony Kikes, a big city kid from Philadelphia, stands doing the same from the back cabin on the port side of our boat. The Coxswain yells to me through the window. He has to yell as the wind, waves and engine noise make it impossible to hear him otherwise.

"Okay Ely, it's our call! Group says they don't have any back-up for us!"

I twist my eyes from the other boat to the coxswain's face as he fights the wheel of the boat, then send them back to the trawler. "What about aircraft?," I scream, "They've gotta have some kind of asset they can send us! What about the Navy or FMP?" The FMP was the Florida Marine Patrol. State police who operated from boats and patrolled the Floridian waters.

Chip grimaces as he shakes his head before hollering back. "Nothing! We're it. Everything else is tied up on SAR cases and that collision. So what'd'ya think? Should we keep it up or what!"

I eyeball the trawler as the distance between us narrows. He's a druggy, sure'n shit. We'd tried to stop him a couple of hours ago but he'd refused our hails. He'd dropped his boat into high gear and motored away from us. It was the fourth of July weekend. A freighter had ran into a supertanker and oil and bodies were leaking from both ships, just south of Miami. There were boat races going on in two different locations on this side of the peninsula state. There were thousands of pleasure boaters out and the search and rescue cases were running crazy.

The trawler and us were closely matched in speed but our 41 was just a tad faster. It'd taken us the last hour to get this close to him but we were closing now and already within small arms range. The Coxswain was Chip Connelly, my replacement. I was leaving in two days, transferred to a new job. Chip had come here to the seventh District from Oregon. He had never worked drug interdiction before and I was training him.

I squinted and hollered back, "It's your call Chip but if you decide ta board him, then I'd get us ahead of him a bit. That'll put the sun behind us before we put a few rounds over his bow." I shake my head hard. "That prick's dirty, no two ways around it and he's probably armed too!"

From my side vision, I see his blond head nodding up and down as he turns and talks with Hector Cruz, the other crewman. Hector's holding a shotgun and standing beside him, then pulling the radio mic down and speaking into it, probably notifying Group Miami of our intent. Then we're coming up on the starboard side of the trawler, maybe eighty yards off. I hear Chip scream out "Stand by for a bow warning shot!"

I'm getting ready to fire a single burst over the vessel's bow as we come past when a hail of bullets rip into us. Chunks of metal and paint snap up and off the wheelhouse and glass blows out of the windows everywhere. Some of the chips sting my eyes but as they water, I see fire coming from the trawler's stern and I throw the sight of the M-16 over the trawler's rear, snapping it to full-auto and pull the trigger.

The 16 erupts in my hands as I see wood pieces blowing up around the trawler's stern. The muzzle flashes from there stop but others are now coming from low on the trawler's bridge. Tony is targeting it so I concentrate on the waterline, firing the remainder of the clip into it, blowing chunks of wood off before I lose my balance. Our boat is swinging hard to port and I'm quickly becoming exposed with no cover. I'm scooting along the deck, hugging the cabin wall then I'm down into the gunnels to safety. Now I'm slipping on glass and blood all over the deck as I release the old and snap another clip in my weapon. Tony opens up from his new position, on the starboard side. I put rounds that way, too.

Tony's firing tracers and targeting the trawler's bridge. In a manner of seconds, there's an explosion and puff of fire. Then the top half of the trawler's wheelhouse disappears in a mass of high flying debris and flame! Phoof! And the flames begin to subside. The fishing boat goes dead in the water, its wooden hulk settling as if she's as tired as she looks. We're still careening hard a port. I quickly look into the cabin and see Chip, lying on the deck. His blue ball cap still tightly over his blond head but a huge black hole, is cut clean through both of his temples. Hector is on the floor moaning and holding his lower side as dark red blood ladles out of his shirt and over his hand.

I race over to the wheel and scream back to Tony. But he's already there beside Hector, then yelling to me that Hector's bad. I get the boat under control and throttled back as Tony tries the radio and finds that it's still operational. He's calling the Group as I handle the wheel and inch us back toward the trawler. The firefight is probably over but it's still our duty to look for anyone that's left alive over there.

I'd swung us around and we were on the fishing boat's starboard side now. I could see that the hulk was sinking. Her waterline was quickly receding as we approached. As we near the trawler Tony's beside me holding Hector's 12 guage. He'd need the shotgun for boarding the damaged vessel. His voice sounds raspy as he tells me that Group's sending a helo and we've got a Cutter re-routing for us too. I'd heard it all but nod anyway. Then he moves to the port side of the boat as I maneuver us closer, cutting a wide path and turning bow to stern of the sinking trawler. When we're close alongside, we don't see anyone alive on the deck of the trawler. Tony's looking at me and I shake my head no. He wanted to know if he should board the sinking boat but we can't. It could go at any time.

I have the 41's engines in neutral and heft my weapon, while stepping around my dead replacement. I do a quick-glance at Hector and see that he's still breathing. Then I'm out on the bow of my boat, ejecting the old and snapping in another clip while floating my weapon over the destroyed trawler. There're at least three dead bodies over there. One on the bow and two on this side of the smoking and dilapidated wheelhouse. The boats are parallel to each other as our way pushes us past the other vessel. I hear Tony curse and then get sick over the stern. That's not like him and I make my way aft in a hurry.

When I get to where he's standing, wiping his arm on his sleeve, he points down into the stern of the trawler. There's a boy lying there. Or what used to be a boy before he was torn apart by M-16 fire. My M-16 fire. He had been maybe thirteen or fourteen years old. There's a shiny new AK-47 lying next to his bullet-holed and outstretched arm, mixed with the blood, intestines and empty bullet casings. Then more gunfire blasts from the dilapidated port side of the trawler's wheelhouse!

It's a heavy weapon of some kind. Machine gun! Chunks of our 41 footer blow-up all around me and I hear the boat's engines die as I'm knocked backwards. Tony drops to the cover of the deck as I spray a hail of bullets over there, exploding what's left of the wheelhouse into a thousand bits and pieces! I watch as a body goes sailing backwards in slow-motion, an arm out-stretched, still grasping an M-60 machine gun. It lands hard with a big splash in the water beside the stricken vessel! The firing has stopped and it's suddenly quiet out here. It's my turn to get sick now and I do, throwing-up where I stand. I stagger backwards and sit against the gunnel. Then I begin crying. Just a hint of a tear then, weeping like an old woman. I don't know where it's coming from or why it's started. I can't stop, even when the trawler begins to bubble and sinks. A few seconds later, white packages of cocaine float to the surface like water lilies emerging all over this big Atlantic pond.

The bags keep popping up. They float listlessly with the scraps of wreckage, oil and bodies. I've stopped crying now but I'm still sniffling and looking at a funny piece of jagged metal poking from the inside my left thigh. It must be a piece of the 41's gunnel, blown off the side when the heavy gun opened up. Gunnel. That's a funny name, ain't it? It comes from the old sailing days and describes the inside wall of a ship or boat, where the or guns were mounted. The gun wall. My fractured mind stumbles over this piece of trivia. I'm still pondering this when the big white helicopter is hovering over us and the loudspeaker is calling out. It looks like Tony's waving to the swimmer who's holding an M-16 inside the open door of the HH-52 as it whips overhead. Then things get blurry for a second.

Now, a crewman's down on the deck dragging a litter basket. I see it all through watery eyes, the visions are blurring and smearing together as I slide down and my rump meets the deck of our boat with a splash. Then Tony's bending over me. I hear him saying over and over, "It's not your fault Ely! Don't do this! You didn't know! Okay? Ely, it isn't your fault! Do you hear me?"

I finally get a grip and look at Tony. He looks different somehow. He's kneeling over me, his eyes searching mine, his weapon resting butt-first on the deck, his white-knuckled hand wrapped around the M-16's forearm like it was a lifeline. That's just what the gun was. A lifeline. My sight travels back to the water, then I remember.

"Hector? ... How's Hector?" I can't look at anything but the blue-green water where the trawler sank, taking the little boy with it.

I feel his other hand squeeze my shoulder and a sob escapes from him. "He's gone pal. They're all gone and you will be too if I don't get you out'ta here!" I'm wondering why he's screaming.

"You've got a bad wound on your thigh and it's bleeding bad. Come on now, help yourself up. You can do it. Let's go!" He doesn't sound right. I look up at him and see an orange-suited man with an unfamiliar face kneeling there. He has a huge head that's white and green. He has on green flight gloves now. It's not Tony! Who the hell is it?

"Hey, where's Tony? He was just here!"

"I don't know buddy. Don't worry about Tony, okay? We'll take care of him!" He has to yell as the helo is noisy. He's talking again so I look back up at him.

"Now we've got'ta get off this boat 'cause it's sinking...okay? You've lost a lot'ta blood so help me while you can! Okay, let go of the rifle now! That's it! It's okay. You can leave it here."

I look over and see my left hand tightly squeezing the forearm of the M-16. My knuckles are white with the effort and I order my hand to let it go. My fingers comply and the rifle drops with a splash onto the deck. He's yelling again.

"Good job! Come on! Up we go!"

He's pulling me up and I try to help him. Then, I can see Tony

laying on the deck. He hasn't moved. He's laying right where he fell
with the last shots from the trawler. Tony's dead and I know that now.
I look over inside the cabin as we hobble in red-colored ankle-deep
water toward the wire basket. Hector's dead too, along with the
Chipster. They're all dead and I... I killed a kid. I wish I was with
them. I so badly want to be dead too! I'm going to protest, to argue to
stay here with my crew when the helo crewman drops me into the
basket.

I'm trying to get up when all of my strength fades away like a
snake disappearing down a hole. I can only watch as I'm strapped into
the basket. Suddenly, I'm floating in the air, twisting upward. I look
up and see another orange-suited man with a white helmet and green
visor looking down at me and guiding the basket. I can see his mouth
moving, talking into the microphone, as I swirl upward. Most of his
face is hidden by the green visor and he looks like a large orange bug
with a white head and monstrous green eyes.

Oh well. I'm getting really tired now. I let my eyes wander over
the massive white helicopter as I glide upward. Funny, from this
angle, it looks just like a big white buffalo. What was it Mamma'd
said... the white buffalo is sacred. That's it. It brings wisdom and
good luck to the people. I'm looking at the front of the chopper as it
appears to be the buffalo's head. I can see the thick white fur of the
neck and then, I see the buffalo's eye. It takes shape, forming more
and more, shifting and twisting until now... it's a man's eye. A
wrinkled old man's face, inside the white buffalo's body. Amos
Reddeer! The face turns and the eyes bore into me. They look right
through me and into my soul.

I close my eyelids to a slit and angle my head to hear what he's
saying. "Listen," the old man's face in the buffalo's body becomes
stern. "Listen! Hear the se se kwa! Hear the murmurings... Raining
Wolf!"

Then I'm being pulled into the helicopter and I can't see or hear
him anymore. Someone is jabbing something in my arm. Then I look
down and see them ripping my pants by the piece of metal in my leg.
It's getting darker in the helicopter now and then it's pitch black. All I
can hear, is the whop, whop, whop of the chopper blades above.
Whop! Whop! Whop!... Whop, Whop, Whop!...........

Then, I'm coming up through layers. One at a time, layer after
layer until I'm awake and the Glock is in my hand and I'm scrunching
back into the wall behind the desk, the gun moving in slow sweeps
around the room. I can feel the sweat beaded-up on my forehead as I
blink in the whiteness of the room. It's daylight and someone's
knocking at the door. Whop, whop, whop! "Mr. Stone? Are you

there? We need to speak to you and it's urgent!"

I scoot myself up while subconsciously running my left hand over the old scar on the inside of my thigh. Pissy-assed dreams! Shit! I shoot a glance at my watch and see that it's almost seven o'clock. My hand drops away as I tip-toe over to the window. As I flatten myself against the wall, I realize that I only have on a pair of underwear and a t-shirt. Gently pulling back the curtain, I see three men outside. The two Air Force officers from before and another, older guy. I put the pistol in the desk drawer and go over to open the door, standing to the side to keep myself in my undies out of sight.

"Morning." I choke the word out. The dream is still caught in the cobwebs that are strung in the corners of my mind. I blink hard at the light and the men standing in it. "What can I do for you guys?"

The older guy is tall. He's dressed in a faded pair of Wrangler jeans, black t-shirt and a blue jean jacket. The other two are dressed in casual sports clothes. The older man smiles and cants his eyes down alongside the door where I'm standing before raising his sight back to mine.

"Well I reckon we got'chu up didn't we? I'm terrible sorry about that but it's pretty urgent that we talk. I'm Lieutenant General Ray Kourn and I believe you've met Major Shears and Captain Mussenberg here. We're Air Force, Office of Special Investigations." He nodded inside. "Uh, can we come in a spell?"

I look back over the room and know that I have stuff undone here but shit, what the hey, ya know? I step back and swing the door open for them and they pass, while I look inward, at the dream up there in the corners of my mind. I order it to be swept away. But I know it'll still be there though, just like the cobwebs. A little less noticeable but... still there. Some things... you just can't ever get rid of permanently. After all three enter, I throw a fleeting glance outside. The snow was already gone and the sun was shinning nicely. I close the door to the cool air and move back to the desk, grabbing my pants.

"So what's so urgent General? I mean it's only seven o'clock in the morning! Your men here tell you that I didn't buy that story about the money out on Muskrat Island?"

The General walks around the room and allows his eyes to travel over the blanket on the floor behind the desk before resting momentarily on the pillow trussed-up bed. Traces of the smile fade as he points at the made-up bunk.

"You expecting company last night?"

I zip up my jeans and sit down in the desk chair to pull on a pair of socks.

"Well just like with you boys General, I like to be cordial. So again sir, what can I do for you?"

After I say that, the dream image of the white buffalo with Amos Reddeer's face steps from it's high corner to the forefront of my mind. "Se se kwa," he says, and the shinkakee momentarily floods over me. I mentally take the broom to the cobwebs again, while faking a yawn in an effort to disguise my discomfort. The tall gangly man watches me fumble with my bandaged finger and the socks, no doubt seeing me wince in the process. He points at my hand.

"Looks like you have a mighty sore digit there my friend?" He smiles again as I look up at him and pull on the sock.

"Yeah, well I bite my nails and get carried away sometimes. Now you'll have to excuse me for being rude General but you still haven't said what you wanted. I had a late night."

He chuckles as he makes his way over to the sofa and sits down, his long legs bending stiffly like a large pair of scissors. His two underlings take up positions on either side of him but remain standing. I hadn't offered him a seat but then, he was a General. Reckon he figured he didn't have to be offered one.

"Well I'll tell ya son, it's this a way. What the Major and Captain told ya about the fifty thousand dollars was true but as you might'a suspected, they's more to it than that."

He leaned forward and laced the fingers of both hands around the knee of one of the long legs before he went on. "I've already spoke to a Mr. Hennessey up at the reservation and he informs me that you and you alone, have the final say-so about that island out yonder." The man breathes deeply and cants his head.

"Now at this point, I need ta tell ya that this is a highly sensitive and secret issue that we're a talking about. Now, we know what yer clearance was in the Coast Guard and all but as you so aptly pointed out to these boys," the smile grew even wider, "you ain't in the service no more, are ya? So, that was why they couldn't tell ya all they was to this little inquiry about the island."

He unfolded his hands and sat back sprawling on the couch. Then he raised one hand and pointed it at me from across the room as I fumbled with my bandaged finger to tuck the t-shirt into my jeans.

"That's been our little problem with confiding the whole story to you. But I've read your record and I'm convinced that we can level with you on this, if'n that is, you're willing to abide by the government secrecy act and the same oath you used to hold?" The hand flips and the smile widens to show an impressive row of white teeth. "So, what say you Officer Stone? Can we rely own yer discretion concerning national security own Muskrat Island?"

I move around and sit on the edge of the desk, the sharp jab of pain, reminding me of the bullet wound across the back of my leg. I move my shoulders upward.

"I reckon that depends on what you're gonna tell me General. If it's reasonable, then you can count on me but I'll tell ya the truth sir, if it's more bullshit then I can't guarantee my discretion. I've got obligations," I roll my hand, "ya know?"

The smile was replaced by a look of determination as he nodded his head on a long neck. "Fair enough. That's more'n fair enough. But Officer," he tipped his head toward the bed against the wall, "I believe that maybe first, you should tell us why… you got that bed over yonder made-up so?"

I blow air out and follow his gaze to the bunk. Why not dish-up a mix of truth, flavored with some fiction. "Yeah, well law enforcement can be hazardous. I had a run-in with a guy last night who showed me a .38 special and told me that he had decided that I was a target. He said that he has friends." I hold up my hand. "There were knives involved too. So…" I clucked my tongue, and sent my sight back to the three men, "I guess I just figured better safe than sorry."

That seemed to satisfy Kourn as his head bobs up and down. The two others say nothing. In fact, they hadn't said a word since coming in. Good officers for a flag officer, I'll bet. From what I'd seen in my career, most admirals and Generals seemed to think that good junior officers were like kids. They should be seen but not heard. They should speak only when spoken to and all that crap. It's not bad – just the military way. I look at the older man as he thinks a moment. It's up to him now anyway. I reach over on the desk and grab my cigarettes and take one from the case. I snap the Zippo and draw in the first smoke of the day while looking back at the General. Finally, he fixes his eyes on me and sets his jaw.

"All righty. But let's set the ground rules. Now before meet'n with you here today, I had a tete-a-tete with yer old X.O. Brigadier General Sanchez."

I feel my eyebrows arching and no matter how hard I try, they won't stay down. Kourn notices them rising.

"Yep. That's right. I did. Now, I know quite a bit about Trojan and if I ell you this stuff, the same rules, terminology and attitude all apply… as did when you were a part of that team." The steely fighter pilot eyes locked onto mine. "Agreed?"

He was saying that I could be killed if it threatened national security or the mission and he wanted to know if I agreed to all of the provisions of spy-craft, honor, decency and the American way… doo da…doo da, or so the tune goes. And yeah, I'll do that but only if it's a two-way street. I clear my throat.

"Okay sir, but it works both ways then, right? The same applies to you and," I let my eyes wander to the other men then back, "yours as well. And... I get straight talk, not B.S.?"

The General did a quick-nod. "Absolutely."

I nod too. "Okay General. Agreed." The man seems to rest easier as he crosses one gangly leg over another and begins.

"Okey, dokey, then. Now, what these boys told you before was true. The PX they told you about was robbed and over fifty thousand dollars was got away with. Now we know, that the money was taken from the manager's office and that it was in a black billows bag. But what was also in that case, along with vouchers and vendors addresses and receipts... was a small booklet with a coded listing of all PX and commissary exchanges throughout the world. The codes corresponded to various pay-outs for post exchange charges on a world-wide basis. Now this listing is from the 1970s, mind you, not today. Obviously, many a those places have been shut-down over the years. In fact, most of them was on bases and such but..."

Kourn's eyes snapped up to mine, "some of 'em wasn't. And the some of 'em that wasn't, was secret listening posts, located in the heart of the Middle and Far East. These posts were and are, clandestine. With what's going own over there now, we need 'em bad. The people running them, are in deep cover, working for fake companies and the like. They were and remain, much too valuable to be shut-down or moved."

The General looks me in the eye. "These are active and extremely valuable assets to national security, totally unknown to the outside world and those that they monitor. At the time that little book was written, I was flying combat missions over North Viet Nam, shooting down Migs. I didn't know didley about it." His eyes roll to the ceiling.

"Our people back here in the States were frantic about it being missing though. But finally, after nothing happened to these secret locations," he shrugs, "it was decided that the thieves probably dumped the case and all the codes with it after getting the money out. Gradually, it was assumed the locations were and would remain, secret."

The General sighs and wrinkles his forehead. "Well, that was the way it was until a few weeks ago anyway. Then, OSI got wind of a Chinese effort to locate the case and the codes. And as it stands now, we have reason ta believe that the Chinese are coming here or, are already here... on a mission to get at these codes. And everything points to that damn island of yours as to where the codes ended up."

I place a blank mask over my face as the realization hits me. So that's it! In my mind's eye, I see a black billows bag, laying on the floor of the coal bin at the lighthouse, out on Muskrat Island! As my old pal Popeye says, "Well blow me down!" That guy at the lighthouse wasn't worried about hitting the little ball with a stray shot... he was worried about hitting the black bag! Aha, says the dumb Indian. And what else is new here? Chinese, the man says. Okay, this is starting to tie it up a bit. Chinese. Chinese with white features? Old man Scheel said that much but he's a nut. More than likely, they're whites working for China. Still, there're all those little things like their eyes, the language and shit... who knows? These thoughts race through my mind as the General finishes speaking. The man un-crosses his legs and sits forward.

"So that, is the deal Officer Stone. Now originally, we figured we needed the island for at least six months or so. Now, with the Chinese in the mix, well we're probably look'n at more like a year. We have to make a thorough search and guard against a Chinese acquirement. We may need your island even longer," he panned his palms outward and raised his eyebrows, "I just don't know."

All of their eyes are on me now, waiting for my reaction. And well, the only reaction I have is... Huh? But then, maybe not. Whose to say? I do a chin-jab at the General. "So, what you're looking for... is a black bag, with money and codes in it?"

The General eases back on the couch and nods. "That's right. And accord'n to our information, the money's gone but the bag's still out there somewhere's own your 'lil island." He hunches his shoulders. "Has been I reckon, for near'bouts ta thirty some years now."

Well that sure doesn't sound like a sliver beach ball, does it? Uh huh, things ain't always as they seem. It makes sense now. The Air Force is after these codes and maybe the old man was mixed up in the heist or... is with the Chinese or... Shit! I've got to sort this out and quick - what I'm going to do and how I'm going to do it. I need some time. I let my eyes float back to Kourn, who appears to be sniffing the air and looking at my cigarette, that's laying a lazy coil of blue smoke upward.

"Jeeze General, that whole island's nothing but one solid piece of rock. Just where do you plan on looking for this item?"

He's up on his feet now, the smile more evident than since he first arrived. I've gotta figure it's my use of the phrase, "where DO YOU plan on looking", as if I was going along with the request. He's got his hands in his pants pockets, rocking on his heels as his junior officers crowd upward too.

"Well, info we have leads us ta believe that the thing may be in one a them abandoned mine shafts out yonder. "Course," he cocks his head, "the plain truth is, we jes ain't got no idea really. That's why I said it could be six months ta a year ta find the blamed thing." He points his hand at mine that's holding the cigarette. "Is that thing hand-rolled tobacco?"

I merely tap my head upward in the affirmative. He looks a little put out then says, "Huh, could I... trouble ya fer one?"

I nod and push the metal box over on the desk. Kourn picks it up and opens it, taking out a smoke and setting it to his mouth. I have the lighter up and he leans into it, the flicker of fire igniting the handrolled as he inhales deeply from the cigarette. He turns the cigarette sideways in his fingers as he takes it away from his mouth and exhales the smoke.

"Well I'll be dadgummed if that it purtty good." He looks at me through the cloud of blue. "I don't hardly smoke atall anymore but every now and then, one jes sounds good, ya know? An this 'uns, jes like the one's my Daddy used ta roll. Well now, where was we?"

The black officer has been watching us intently while the white one is looking at me with a zillion questions on his face. I flick my sight back to the General and he's still smiling, rocking on his heels. The good thing about having to use a feeble brain like mine, is it's only capable of doing a minimum of work. The nasty dream, has now been forced into the deepest recessed corners of my thinker. Well, what's say we just put a crimp in General Kourn's good humor, huh? Besides, my little plan is forming up and I need to keep them talking as I try to fine-tune it. I slowly turn my head from side to side.

"Well General, I think we're gonna have a problem with this whole thing. You see, without getting into too much detail, I can tell you that within a couple of months, my Tribe is planning on having a casino up and operating out on that island. Construction is due to any day now and I mean to start soon..." I let the last of it linger off. There goes the General's smile. It's headed down in flames just like one of those Migs he shot down over Viet Nam. I plunge on.

"Look, we've got a lot of money, and I'm talking millions here General, tied-up on this project. I can almost assure you that you're not going to have no six months to look for the bag. You'll be lucky if I can give you a day."

The frown is forcing his face into one big wrinkle as Kourn drops his eyes to the floor and takes another drag off the smoke. The Major has a hot-flash registering on his face though and I find myself wondering if menopause... is hard for him.

"Just how do intend to get people to your casino Stone? You going to fly them out? That'll be hard to do and expensive with the winters you have up here, won't it?"

He'd spit the words and question both at me and the Kourn had raised his eyes to my face to see the response. Okay, we're functioning on the time-honored most quintessential form of bullshit here. The military bluff. This form entails, not whose is bigger but who, will blink in the lying game. I take the last pull off the smoke before dropping it in the can by my feet. Then I fix my stare on Shears.

"Do you know what a hovercraft is Major?" This time his eyes broaden then go mean as he utters a cuss word.

"Fuck Stone! Don't give us that shit! Hovercraft won't work on that island and you know it!"

I quick-jab my arms up in the air like I'm being held-up at gunpoint and allow my eyes to raise in mock-surprise!

"Well I know they won't now! Thanks to you Major! That dirty, rotten hovercraft company that did the feasibility survey and is selling us the machines well, we sure won't be using them now. Not that we have the wise council of Major Shears here to guide us! Ya see, we didn't know you were a hovercraft specialist! But you've arrived to save us now Major and that's all that matters." I click out my index finger at him.

"Hey, since you're a hovercraft specialist, how about "saving" me a little and coming over here to hover on this awhile," I motion to my groin for several seconds until he jerks his angry eyes away from me. I let my arms drop, then fold them together as I lean back on the desk. Mussenberg snickers but quickly recovers when the Shears snaps a angry glance over at him. I can't see all of the General's face but he appears to be smiling behind a hand over his mouth. I nod my head over at the Shears.

"You ever been out to Muskrat Island Major?" The officer looks hard at me. I can feel the man's dislike from where he stands. Our eyes are locked as he slowly shakes his head no. Stupid answer. Maybe. Probably.

"Well okay then, that explains how you're so knowledgeable about what we can and can't do out there then. Boy Major, I'm sure glad I ran into you today!" I say the last with every bit of sarcasm I can add to it while canting my head sideways in an agreeable mode. I can just barely hear Shears uttering a curse under his breath as he turns away. Kourn bends down and flicks an ash into the can by my feet then walks over to the window and pulls back the curtain. As I look around the room, waiting for the other shoe to drop, that is, if there is another shoe, I weigh my position. I figure it's 50/50 that they've been monitoring my phone conversations and may or, may not know about our little problems with the island and the hovercraft.

If they do, then oh well. If they don't, then I'm guessing that the hovercraft idea will sound just as viable to them as it did to me before I'd seen the place. If this works, then I've got a good shot at bargaining this into something. What exactly? I'm still not sure. I heft myself off the desk and feel that my bladder is calling. I ward it off for now and move back over to sit down in the desk chair. The lanky General speaks while gazing out the window.

"I'm sure you already know that we could just take the island by way of governmental necessity." He sighs and looks sideways out onto the dock. "But I'm also sure that you've figured out that it'd be hard ta do politically too. Jes the same," he twists back and shoots a look my way before turning back to the window again, "ya need ta know that I mean ta get out ta that island and find them codes. That's all they is to it."

Mussenberg has been quiet since arriving and now darts a quick glance to the big boss. "Uh General, if I may?" He asks while looking at the tall man and pointing his hand toward me. Kourn merely does a quick-nod and continues to survey the outside. The black officer steps up to the desk and places his hands in his pants pockets.

"So, is it money that the Tribe will need for this permission? I mean to off-set your costs so far? Because if so, we need to have some idea how much Mr. Stone?"

I'm rocking back and forth in the chair, my socked feet bumping my motion from the floor. It had been their turn and I'd waited patiently for them to serve and now, well now they have. They'd volleyed back and they hadn't scored. They haven't been monitoring my phone. Not yet, at least. That means that I win the first round of military bluff. Problem is in making this one shot, win the game for my side. I need a few minutes to hash this out. I look up at Mussenberg.

"I'll tell you what Captain. I've gotta hit the head and while I'm there, I ponder that." I stand up and move toward the bathroom, stopping and turning back to the man. "You guys got me up a little early so just make yourselves at home. I'll be right back." Then I'm walking through the bathroom door and closing it behind me.

I step over to the toilet and relieve my bladder then flush the apparatus. I rinse my hands, dry them and go over to the tub to sit down on its side, grinding the knuckles of my hands into my eyes. Sonavabitch! Okay. What do I do here? The ball's been tossed back to me and I've got to make a play. Okay. Number one. I no longer work for Uncle Sam. I work for the Pukaskwa Black River Band. That's where my allegiance is. I am no longer a Coastie, I am and have always been, a Pukaskwa. Now, the Air Force is caught between a rock and a hard one here. They need to secure these codes and combat a Chinese threat. Granted. But that's their problem, not mine. That means that they will do whatever they have to though, including seizing the island. It'll be damning politically but they'll do it if they can't make a deal with me. Number two. I have no idea where old man Scheel fits into this scenario. He's either a member of the original theft or is in cahoots with the Chinese.

Whichever, that'll have to wait for now. So, my best bet is to get what I can from the Air Force and hopefully, have them tie up all the dead bodies in the process. That's fair. The way I see it, the corpses are theirs by proxy anyway. The Pukaskwa didn't lose these secret codes and they sure as hell didn't take them out to the island or, invite the Chinese out for a visit. We've just been caught in the middle, is all. And that explains why I feel like the meat on this sandwich. So, why not tap a little of Uncle Sugar's reserve. He's sure never minded taking whatever he could get from us Indians. What though? It can't be money. Even if he is a three star General, he won't have the kind of monetary assets I want for giving up the island for awhile. A trade. Yeah, that's it.

I had been pondering this for a while now. The Tribe was screwed over the hovercraft idea. Out a lot of dough. Now Hennessey, is the business man and he likes land. The more, the better. If I could channel this loss into a gain of equal value for the Tribe, well that's my mission, according to what the Great Good Spirit tells me. And besides, I have this creepy feeling that the Air Force still isn't being on the up and up with me, anyway. I know they're getting antsy out there so I get up and head back out to meet them, the semblance of an idea already forming.

They're talking quietly when I walk out but hush upon seeing me. I just go back over and sit down in my chair. I push with my toes and the chair gently bounces to and fro while I try on an air of thoughtfulness. It's hard for me, because by nature, I'm not a very thoughtful guy. I'm aware of all three sets of eyes on me. Shortly, I stop my bouncing and come to rest, looking directly at Mussenberg.

"Well Captain, it's like this. I've already explained our plans and situation to you and to be honest, we can't just stop this. Not, that is, without taking a huge hit on the monetary end. Now…"

"Ohhh fuck me!" Shears has spun around and is looking daggers at me, his face all snarled up in hate. "You people just won the largest amount of money ever awarded to an Indian tribe and now you're going to sit there and hold Uncle Sam up again?" You've got to be kidding?"

So, the little talk they had was about the 'good wingnut – bad wingnut' routine, eh. Okay. I'll play along. I shake my head. "No.

Hell no Major. If you don't want me to sit here, I'll be happy to stand up for you, if that'll make it easier for your feeble ass to follow the conversation without interrupting!"

Mussenberg was caught between the three of us and was, in military terms I guess, the lowest ranking guy in the room. Because while I wasn't in the "Guard" anymore, I was sure holding an equal footing with the two other Air Force officers there. He was keeping his mouth shut. The General motioned to Shears.

"Al, let the man speak." He nods the back of his head my direction while still peering out of the window. "Please go own Mr. Stone. We're all listening."

I watch as Shears becomes contrite and takes a seat on the abandoned couch. Also without having been asked, I note. I splay out my fingers, then fold them together and rest my hands on the desktop, looking up at Mussenberg.

"Okay, as I was saying. We've got close to two and a half million tied up in the island. That's a big chunk of the Tribe's money and the only way we don't lose it, is to continue on with our plans. Now, up until now, I kind of figured that letting you guys take a look around the island wasn't going to be a big problem. I mean, you said you needed six months but I know that the military always requests more of everything than it actually needs, And that includes time. I figured I'd let you guys poke around while we started construction. It wasn't going to upset our construction plans, just inconvenience us a bit, right?" I turn my hands up for emphasis.

"But now, I'm assuming that with this Chinese element added, you're going to want to secure the island for at least a year and lock it down. Correct?"

The General had turned and is facing me now, his weight resting on one shoulder as he leaned it against the side of the window frame. "Unfortunately, that's true. We just kain't take a chance on them Commies getting ahold a these codes." He grunted. "I don't suppose it'd do any good ta appeal ta yer patriotism, would it?"

I formed my hands up into a pyramid, like I'd seen other big shots do in similar situations and tried to look thoughtful. It wasn't easy, I usually just have a dumb look on my face.

"Nope. This ain't about patriotism. It ain't about just me either, General. It's about a group of people. My people. And while Indians have fought in every war this country's had, we're talking about their families and livelihoods here. That island is wrapped up in a long-term investment that has all kinds of monies, deals and other business crap sewn into it. All of it, is dependent on our plans going ahead. So we'll give you the island, lock, stock and barrel for a whole year but it's gonna cost you something. There's gonna be some kind of economic trade-off." I unfolded my hands and pushed myself up out of the chair. Then I step around the desk and stretch, my arms shooting toward the ceiling before dropping them and continuing.

"As it is," I twist my head for emphasis, "the Tribe will be taking a big hit on the money side. Now, you could just pay some kind of rent but I gotta tell ya, it'd be steep and for us, not a sound option to pursue anyway." I again tilt my head at the General and Mussenberg.

"Now, knowing the military as I do, I figure you'd have a rough time getting your hands on that kind of money without Congressional approval." I flipped my fingers at Kourn. "Unless the OSI has a lot bigger budget than I think?"

He smiles wanly and slow-shakes his head. "No sir, I expect you'd be right own that account."

I nod once. This wasn't how I was going to do this but I had control of the island and the authority. And as far as I was concerned, I also had the moral obligation to help my people. Okay then. I'll toss the dice and go for broke.

"Here's what I propose then. The military services have a lot of land in this country that's not being used. You find me a prime piece of it somewhere General, with a commercial value of around a half of a million dollars and agree to turn it over to the Pukaskwa in exchange for a one year lease on Muskrat Island. If I like it, we'll have a deal. What do ya think?"

Kourn laughs lightly and shakes his head. "A half million dollars, huh? That's a might steep but…" He looks down at the floor…Well, shoot," he shakes his head with a smile, "I'll tell ya the truth, that might jes be doable but I told you, we may need that island for longer than a year?"

The General's blue fighter pilot eyes bore into me as I shake out another cigarette. "Okay." I shrug my shoulders, "a year and a half, a property worth a two million even. Two years, find us something worth a three million. How's that?"

The General slaps his leg and guffaws. "Hot damn boy, you are a card! That's higher that an F-15 goes boy!" What the hell happened to that patriotism?" His smile is genuine but guarded.

I wink at him from across the room. "Shit General, this is about as patriotic as a red man gets anymore. The Tribe's already losing a lot of money on this deal. I'll go to bat for you," I roll my fingers, "for patriotic reasons, but my people ain't taking any more of a bath than they have to in the process." I twist my head and quick-nod at him.

"The one year deal is all I have to offer, General. No more than that. If this little bag is out there and you can't find it by then, well…

shame on you. I've got a guy who guides hunts on the island and you'll have to be off it by opening day of deer season next year."

There was more and I had to get him to bite it all, if I was going to save my sorry butt. I cock my eyes at him.

"One more thing, General. Like I said, I'm only doing a little of this for patriotic reasons." I point a finger up. "Mostly, because you say that we may have foreign operatives working this case. Now, that said, I need it understood that you people," I now turned the finger at each of them, "have to be the ones cleaning up the mess when it's all over. As part of the deal, you'll assume the responsibility for any and all wet work that has… or will be undertaken and also, the repair or replacement of any physical damage to the island or it's structures."

I let that one sink in as I allow my eyes to travel from man to man. Make it or break it, this one gets me out of the hotwater. Wet work. A spy term used to describe the death of someone. I want them to think that I expect them to have dead bodies lying around that island. And I've worded it so that any dead bodies, before or after this agreement, will be their responsibility. That old military bluff again. I continue when my eyes come back to the Kourn.

"I spent enough time around the military to know that you've probably already been checking on this. So, what goes on with any of this business, if it has to do with Chinese agents, well, I figure that's government business not the Pukaskwa's." I set my eyes at him with as much firmness as I can muster. "I figure it's your responsibility. Are you agreeable to that too?" I drop my hand, awaiting his response.

Kourn watches me for a beat, his hand stroking his chin. "You wouldn't be holding out own us now, would ya Mr. Stone? Do you know some'thin that we don't know?"

I hike my eyebrows. "Probably. I'd say I know some things that you don't but I can guarantee you that I have no idea about codes or stolen money or all that jazz. And to the best of my knowledge, I haven't seen any Chinese either. My only concern here, is that my people don't get hung-up with dead Oriental agents or a burned down lighthouse." I wink at him from my perch on the desk. "I'd wager that you have more secrets then I'd ever be able to match."

It's dead silence in the room now. Kourn keeps his eyes on me while he scratches his cheek. It's quiet enough, that I hear his nails brushing against his beard stubble. I can see him mulling it over in his mind, trying to gauge what I'd said and… hadn't said, if anything. It's hard to read between the lines especially when the lines are so blurry. Finally, he drops his hand and juts his chin at me.

"So what kind of land is this that we're a dicker'n over then? I mean, you want me ta find somethin' here in Michigan? 'Cause I gotta tell ya, that ain't gonna be too easy nowdays."

I have to stop and think about that one a second. Where? Shit! This was too quick for me. I really hadn't got this far along in my little plan yet. I'd planned on talking to Hennessey before these guys but fate can be a quick arrival sometimes. Where? I look over to Shears watching me closely from the couch. I hadn't noticed before but he's kind of homely. Hmm. Where? Where is property expensive and highly desired? California! Yeah, that's one place but I can't see the Pukaskwa fitting into the Left Coast too well. Doesn't matter. The Band can sell it, right? Yeah, that's right but there's still some crummy land out there too. Without a thorough research effort, I might end-up bartering the tribe into bankruptcy. My problem is, I don't know enough about land and land prices. My mind's racing and I'm about to settle on California... then I have it.

"Hawaii, General. Find us something in Hawaii and get back to me quick. Because I can't hold-up construction much longer if we can't come to terms, okay?"

The tall old fighter pilot's eyebrows push up in a quizzical arch. "Hiwhya? Why the hell..." then he pushes his hand at me in a stopping motion while shoving himself away from the wall, "Nope. Never mind. Hiwhya it is." He moves toward me, extending his hand. "Okay. I think we've got us a deal then. I'll have something for ya ta look at this afternoon."

I take his big hand and return the pressure being applied while shaking my head no.

"Uh uh, I wouldn't say that General. I ain't seen your offer yet. If I was you, I'd have everything there. Pictures of the property, legal descriptions, proper transfer papers... the whole shebang. I've gotta take it to our attorney, so..."

Kourn was beaming broadly and wagging his hand as he and the other two head for the door. "Understood, understood. You drive a hard bargain Mr. Stone but I dare say, a reasonable one. We'll see ya this afternoon, say around three?" I pretend to think about that, then shoot him a nod. His smile grows larger as he turns to leave.

"General!" I call to him as he's about to go out the door. He stops and turns back to me. "Remember. You guys clean-up everything, including any and all wet work and property damage. That's the package, right?"

He's nodding his head but there's a set to his countenance and a question forming there now, shadowing his eyes. "Surely. We will do that. We do have a deal Mr. Stone." He looks at me and I can see the barest hint of curiosity looming on his face. As for me, I figure it's camouflage time. Another big part of the military bluff. I smile

broadly. Very broadly and try hard to act cavalier, never letting on
that I'm more nervous than a whore in church. Finally, Kourn buys
my act and exits. I watch as Mussenberg pulls the door closed, a smile
on his brown face and a wink snapping from his eye. Then the door's
shut and I'm standing there all alone.

I let my breath out in a low whistle and feel the adrenalin backing
off. Well. So much for that. The bait's been set, so I reckon I just wait
and see if they go ahead and take it. I stretch again and rub my hands
hard over my face. I'm glad that I remembered Nettie and her dreams
of Hawaii. If a man couldn't work to give the woman he loved her
dreams, what good was he? Ha. As I drop my hands and blink into the
bright room, I also wonder, what good was the guy… if he was dead
or in prison? Shit man, at this point, either of those two were just as
viable as me saving the Tribe and giving Nettie Hawaii. This little
scam of mine had better work or no two ways about it, my red ass was
grass. 'Cause I was definitely on the down side of time.

I pull off the t-shirt, move over and lock the door then, after taking
the Glock out of the drawer, pad my way into the bathroom. Like
most Indians, I have a rough time shaving. I bleed like a stuck hog
unless I leave the shaving cream on for an extended period to soften a
beard, that never wanted to grow to begin with, much less be cut. I
finish brushing my teeth when the phone rings. I go out and pick up
the cordless phone from the wall, smearing lather over the
mouthpiece. It's Hennessey. He tells me all about Shultz and the
embezzlement ring he's hooked-up with. I can hear the anxiety in his
voice as he relays the expenditures that the Band's laid out and the
loss we've taken. I make a pot of coffee as he talks. It appears, that
our attorney has a gambling problem and the money's gone. Forever.
He asks if I'm sure about the non-feasibility of the hovercraft and he's
depressed even more when I tell him, yeah, I'm sure.

But I can possibly brighten his day a tad, so I tell him about the
Air Force and their need to lease the island. I explain that it's a
national security issue and can't go into details but maybe, just
maybe, we could come out on top in the deal. I lay out the proposal I
made about us getting some land worth a half a million for letting the
Air Force have the island for a year, explaining that this was probably
the only way to make the deal gel. I leave out the parts about the dead
bodies, people trying to kill me and the crazy old man trespassing on
the island. I figure, why dampen his day with too much information?

It can spoil an otherwise happy announcement. Now I hold my
breath. I know he'd told me that I had total authority and control over
the island but he'd also said that I had to clear everything with him first.
I'd done this backwards. But I'm hoping that in light of the situation,

he might be okay with that. He's silent for a beat then asks where the land would be that we're trading for. I detect a definite simmering of excitement in his voice. Without getting too in depth, I explain that I don't know much about land or land prices and that I had to give the Air Force a location somewhere and I had to give it to them on the spot. I take in a breath and tell him that the Air Force is looking in Hawaii.

Again the silence and finally he asks why Hawaii? I say because it's the only place in the country that I'm pretty sure that the land's expensive. He thinks about that a minute and then tells me that I'm right. Absolutely right! He seems overjoyed at the prospect. The enthusiasm is bubbling out of him as he says he'll contact our new attorney here in Escanaba and have him available to check over whatever lease agreement the Air Force provides, as well as the property they supply. He's happy and I'm just hoping that the deal works. The last thing he says before we hang-up is… "Thank you, Ely. If this comes to pass, you don't know what it means to the Tribe." We make our goodbyes and I truck back into the Head. As I lean over the sink stare at the lathered face of the tired Indian in the mirror, I'm sure that Mr. Hennessey has no idea… what it'll mean to me too. The white buffalo up in the very corner of my mind twitches, just to make sure that I still know he's there.

After I've shaved and showered and dressed in my last clean uniform shirt, I grab a cup of coffee and move out to the back deck to pray. It's cold out here and the wind is flecked with tiny snowflakes. I finish my prayers as the breeze begins to thicken even more with cold. I zip the uniform jacket up tighter and thank the Great Good Spirit for hearing me. Then move back inside to the warmth of the boathouse, closing the door behind me. I have a few errands to run but I should get back to the island too. As I'm walking past I look down at the boat, rocking gently in it's slip. It'd be a cold sucker going out there in her today.

I move over and take my leather flight jacket off the hook where I'd left it to dry. It's filthy and I'd drop it and some uniform shirts off at the dry cleaners, as part of my errands. The hair on my neck takes an upswing as I drape the jacket over my arm. Something's not right. I slowly turn and look behind me at the room. The paint-faded walls are hung with ropes, life jackets, oars, paddles and other boating gear. Boat motor stands and oar locks clutter the decked floor. My eyes travel to the supports and chains that guide and raise the boat door. Nothing. The only sound comes from the water lapping gently against the Boston Whaler in her slip. Nothing seems amiss. Still… the shinkakee is strong. But maybe it's just me. Lord knows I'm a tad het-up these days.

Between the old man's science fiction stories, people trying to kill me and those that're already dead, it's probably just my imagination. I feel my head unconsciously shake. Yeah, just my imagination. As my eyes continue to drift around the room, I hear that old Temptations song, "Just My Imagination", taking off in the distance. The beat grows stronger in my temples. Damn! First, it's Ghost Riders in the Sky and now this old Motown song. Shit man, if this keeps up, I'll be nuttier than old man Scheel before long. I squeeze my eyes shut and force the song and whatever meaning it has, up into the my mental cobwebs with the white buffalo. Then I pull open the door and go through to the office.

Chapter Twenty
"Go Figure"

McDonald's,
Escanaba, MI.
Same day.

Chin held the Egg McMuffin with both hands as he took a bite. He ate with relish. He had found that while he cared little for most American food, he did like these sandwiches made by a restaurant that boasted a clown as its proprietor. He and Kuan sat eating in a booth next to the Playland area. Several young children yelled and screamed just inside the glassed-in enclosure beside them. Over their breakfast, the two men had formulated a plan for eliminating the Native American policeman. It would be dangerous, but they no longer had a choice.

They had been unable to contact either of the two remaining members of their team, and, at present, had to consider them lost. They were most probably dead, killed by the Indian Policeman. For what purpose, they couldn't fathom. But most assuredly, the young Indian had been on the island at the same time they were on it. This fact left little alternative but to assume that he was responsible for their loss or, at the very least, was connected to it in some way. Chin looked over at his partner as the man chewed on the last of his sausage biscuit. Kuan was a big fellow, thought Chin, especially for a Chinese. He looked every bit an American, sitting here with his round eyes and large physique but Chin knew that he came from one of the poorest villages in his province back in China. He dropped his eyes back to his sandwich and was about to take another bite when Kaun took hold of his arm and squeezed.

"We have unwelcome company sir," he whispered, his eyes staying on whatever it was he watched. "Three men. I do not know the older man but the black and white younger ones are the American Air Force officers I have seen at the Indian's office."

Chin had immediately put his sandwich down at Kuan's touch and had dropped his hand to the pistol he carried inside his trousers. He had noticed that Kuan's hand was already under the table. Chin could feel the adrenalin flowing through his veins as he swallowed. His voice came out hoarsely when he spoke again.

"They are not coming over here then?" he croaked.

Kuan maintained his visual observation for several seconds. The time seemed like an eternity to Chin, who watched the big man's right eye twitch involuntarily. Finally, Kuan spoke but he did not deviate his eyes as he did so.

"No sir, they do not seem to notice us. But as you know, this could easily be a trick."

Chin wanted desperately to turn, to face his adversaries, but suddenly, he began to calm. He did not think that three Air Force officers, probable security or intelligence types, would risk having themselves be seen by their intended prey in a crowded restaurant. No, they were probably not here after Kuan and himself. He could now feel the emotional juices ebbing inside him. He allowed himself a deep breath as he let a smile work over his face. He nodded his head up at Kuan, who still watched the men closely, and kept his voice in a whisper.

"I do not think they are here for us comrade. Please avert your eyes before they notice that you're so interested in them."

Kuan dropped his eyes back to his leader and pondered the small man. How could he remain so cool? How did he know that they weren't here for them? But looking at his superior and the smile on his face, he was sure that they were safe, for the present, anyway. He too, began to feel the tension in his body subsiding. He was again proud to be serving under this man. Commander Chin was a remarkable operative and leader with a well-known reputation. He was the very best. He was going to ask his superior how he knew that the officers weren't here for them when he saw that his leader was going to speak. Kuan held his tongue.

"What are they doing now?" asked Chin, his eyes still averted from the scene behind them.

Kuan looked back up and his eyes followed the three men as they walked to a table. "They have their food and are going to sit down. None of them have even looked this way, sir. You seem to be right. Perhaps they are not here for us."

Chin tilted his head. "Time will tell. Are they seated, yet?"

Kuan nodded, "Yes," as he looked back down at the table. Chin casually turned in his seat and took a formative glance around the room, letting his eyes rest on the three newcomers before turning back to face Kuan in a whisper.

"I know the older one. I have seen a file on him. He is a General. One of high rank in the American Air Force Office of Special Investigations." Chin's mind raced and quickly arrived at a plan of action. He continued in a low voice to Kuan.

"I think it is time for us to leave here. We will each exit from different doors and take our own cars to the department store. I think it is best if we get the things we'll need and then lay low until tonight. If we do not meet there, fifteen minutes from now, whichever one is still operational shall continue on alone. Agreed?"

Kuan sat up stiffly in his chair and his answer came out in quiet military bearing. "Yes, sir."

Chin nodded. "Very well. I shall use the door closest to us and you will go out the other, by where they have taken seats. It is probably best if they do not see an Oriental face at this stage. Each of us will take our own trash and deposit it while leaving. I will see you in fifteen minutes." With that, Chin stood and moved over to the side door, dropping his wrappers in the can and exiting quickly.

Kuan took the plastic tray and his wrappers over to the trashcan. He was only four feet from the Air Force officers as he scrapped the stuff into the can. He lingered just long enough to overhear a bit of broken conversation as he was exiting.

The older one, a man with a deep Southern American accent, was saying, "… yessir boys! We'll have that Hiwhya land by elem'em o'clock fer him ta look at and… I'll bet'cha we'll be out own that island by tomorra morning." Kuan heard the last as the door was closing behind him. Closing. Just like their window of opportunity was closing.

Escanaba, MI.
Downtown, same day.

I'm pulling into an angled parking spot with the patrol Jeep When my cell phone rings. I pick it up and push the button. "Stone."

"Ely? Ely is..at..ou?" The connection is bad but I recognize Nettie's voice.

"Hi, Nettie. Yeah, I'm here." I move around to the front of the vehicle, trying to get a better signal.

"Oh, Ely, it's so good to hear your voice! I've been so worried about you. Are you okay?" I could hear her better now, but why was she so concerned?

"It's good to hear you, too, Babe. And yeah, I'm fine. Why are you worried?"

"It's som…g Amos…id. I've bee. so scared, Ely! I'm…coming to see you." I'm losing her again.

"No Nettie! You can't come here! It's dangerous! Nettie, do you hear me! You can't come here! Nettie… Nettie!" Her signal is gone. Shit!

My eyes search over the area until they find a payphone by the grocery store. I move over to it quickly and fish around in my pockets until I find the number and my calling card. I dial the myriad of digits. Her voice mail picks up on the forth ring so I leave a message, telling her not to come. Then I call the tribal headquarters. Nancy Morningstar answers the switchboard. After I tell her who I am and that I'm looking for Annette, she says that the lady I'm seeking is not in the office. She had came back to work today because she had had a sick kid at home. Nancy had not talked to her and is not sure where Nettie is either. Somebody said that they thought she was going to Bruce's Crossing to visit her Granny, but no one knows for sure.

Nancy Ponytail says that she'll have her call me right away when She comes in. I thank her, say my goodbyes and hang up. I could call her grandmother's house but decide against it. I'd have to find the number and I'm short on time right now. So I try her cell number again. No service. As I flip the phone closed I decide that I'll try calling her again later. But I have to reach her. She can't come here. Not now. She can't be around me until it's safe. As that thought passes, I wonder if that'll ever be the case. I go back to the Jeep and grab my filthy flight jacket from the seat and set about my chores.

Twenty minutes later, I step out of the cleaners and onto the sidewalk into a bright early afternoon. The sun's out but the air is crisp. There's the hint of snow in it. There are plenty of folks out and about but it's a business day, so I guess that's to be expected. I'm toting a plastic bag with a replacement headlight in it, purchased from the NAPA store across the way. Next on my errand agenda is a visit to the hospital. Scheel's daughter had called while I was in the cleaners and said that they would be leaving by two pm, headed back home to Grand Rapids. She asked if I'd stop by. I'm a tad hungry and could eat something. But I want to call Nettie first so I try her again on the cell phone. No answer. I look at the little window and read the words flashing there, 'The user is out of the service area.' Great! I start the Jeep and head over to the hospital, all thoughts of food gone for now.

St. Francis Hospital,
Escanaba, MI.

As I enter the automatic doors, I can see that the day shift is a different thing altogether at St. Francis Hospital. I go up to the desk and tell an older lady, a volunteer, that I'm here to see Herman Veeter. She checks and kindly advises me that he is still in testing downstairs, but that his daughter is in the waiting room. She steps out and directs me over to the room where she points out a woman on chair in the lounge. Gretchen Cooper sits quietly on a lone seat in the center of the area. She's reading a magazine and sits with her legs crossed and a hand gently massaging the side of her face as she holds the reading material with the other. I make my way across to introduce myself. When she brings her head up, I'm looking into the eyes of her father. They're the same bright green, but the dark half-circles under them combined with the worry on her face, dim the brightness of their aura. Still, she smiles as she stands and offers her hand.

"It's nice to meet you in person. And I... well I wanted to thank you again for finding my father and well... for being so kind last night."

She's what they used to call a handsome woman. Her Germanic features blend well with her build. She's probably five foot four and kind of chesty. She's anywhere from 35 to 40 years old with slivers of gray flecking her shoulder length black hair. Her eyes show the recentness of tears and she wears no make-up on them. I reckon crying would put a stop to that. She is a very attractive woman.

"I'm glad I was there to help. Uh... how's your Dad?"

She chews her bottom lip and slowly shakes her head. "He's not well. The doctor says that he may be going delusional again. I... uh... I don't know."

Well, that would fit with what I've seen so far. I clear my throat.

"Uh, I assume your in-laws are watching your daughter, then?"

She continues her smile. "Yes. They'll stay with Carrie at my place for a few days so she can still go to school and keep her life as normal as possible. That's important for her. I'll have to get Dad to the doctor as soon as we get back home and, well, you know," she bends down and lays the magazine on a table then rises back up, "it'll be a hassle, driving back with no rest and everything."

She swipes a hand across her eyes to push back some hair that's fallen there. "Um, listen. They said that Dad's going to be awhile finishing up these tests and everything so I was just wondering, um... could I buy you lunch?," she looks around. "I assume they have a cafeteria here somewhere." She brings those flashing green eyes back to my face. "I mean...you know... if you haven't eaten, yet?"

I let out a laugh, in spite of myself. I really don't have time for This. I mean considering the circus I'm a part of and all... but I can see that she's a little flustered. I nod my head.

"Sure. That sounds good but it's on us, the Pukaskwa Nation, that is. We've come into a large inheritance as of late." I take her arm and gently guide her toward the door, releasing it as we move along. I know the way to the cafeteria.

A few minutes later, we're seated with our food. I've got a cheese burger, fries and ice tea and she has a chef's salad, ranch dressing and a coke. We make small talk while we eat, about her long drive from down-state, the weather, that kind of thing. But I can tell that she has something else on her mind. She's nervous as she picks at the lettuce on her plate. She points her fork at my hand.

"So, how did you hurt your finger?"

I look down at it and twist my wrist. "A knife cut, believe it or not. You know, fishing can be a very dangerous sport, sometimes." She nods and smiles. Then her face straightens and she finally forms the question she's been trying ask.

"Did my Dad happen to tell you how he came to be on that island, Officer Stone?" I finish the burger and chew the bite I've taken, then I wipe my mouth with a paper napkin before answering.

"My first name's Ely. Why don't you call me that and I'll call you Gretchen, okay?"

She raises her sea green eyes as I take a drink of tea. She watches me as I set the glass down and a shy smile rolls over her face. "Okay... Ely. But, did he? My father, I mean. Did he say why he was on this island?"

I'm hesitant to go here with her but she probably needs to know this stuff, for her and the old man's sake. Elbows on the table, I fold my hands over the plate and look closely at her. "Yeah, he did. And unfortunately Gretchen, most of it was about flying saucers and that kind of stuff."

Her face turns downward to her plate again. I wait to see her reaction, but when it comes, it's not what I expect and I'm surprised. She nods her head while keeping her eyes on her plate and half-chasing a remaining cherry tomato with her fork.

"I know this will be a silly question, but... since you're a police officer... I was wondering if... well, if you believed any of his story?" Her fork stops the tomato pursuit and her eyes meet mine.

I can feel my eyebrows forming incredulous triangles. So, she already knows this stuff. I assume her father has told her his story or at least some of it. I peer at her from around my poked-up hands and ask, "Do you?"

I watch as the uncertainty blows over her countenance, and slowly a tear forms in one of the green eyes. She shakes her head and looks back down at the table. He voice is barely a squeak.

"No, I suppose not." She sniffles and keeps her head down. "It's just that he can be so convincing sometimes, and then... oh I don't know... it's just so tragically sad for him... for Carrie and... for me"

I reach over and take her hand, uttering that it's okay as she turns her head away from me. She squeezes my hand tightly though. Some people are looking at us and I give them stares until they go back to minding their own business.

"You know, Gretchen, God can be a help in this. I have no doubt that you pray but have you talked to a minister or anything like that?" She releases my hand and jerks her head back to look at me. Her eyes are furious and her voice is low with barely contained anger.

"Do you think even for one minute that if a God existed, he would let this happen to my baby! To my father!... Do you? There is no God, Officer Stone! Or if there is, then He's not anything I want any part of!" She's still now, her anger beginning to flow off as I sit across from her, looking into her hurt green irises. When she's calmed down, she speaks again, her voice quivery and just above a whisper. She drops her eyes.

"I'm sorry. I know you're just trying to help." She sighs and wipes at her face with a napkin. I've spoken to our pastor but he just tells me to have faith. He says that that will carry us through." She looks at me again, with heat in her cheeks and fire in her eyes.

"I don't want to be carried through! I want my baby to live! Why can't God see that? Why doesn't He help her if He exists!"

People around us are noticeably uncomfortable as I sit in the chair and look across at her. "I can answer that... if you want me to... but my response will probably seem too simple to you." I raise my eyebrows as she works to regain her composure, hoping that she'll just let it go. Finally, she nods her head. I sigh as I lean forward. Oh, well.

"I'm not what many would call a religious man, but there are some things I know about Gretchen and God... is one of them. I can tell you that you're wrong about what you expect from Him." I ease back and look at her. She's waiting for me to go on but I don't want to. Awww shit! Why do I have such a big mouth! Okay. I rub my chin and point a lazy finger at her from over the table. "Think about it this way. If God is to blame for what's happening to your child, well, then actually, I suppose he's also to blame for ever having allowed you to get pregnant with Carrie, right? I mean, none of this would be happening if you had never gotten pregnant, would it, Gretchen?"

By the look on her face, I can tell that she's seeing where I'm coming from now. I try to cap it up and get myself out of this situation.

"If you had never had Carrie, she wouldn't be suffering and you would've never known her so you... wouldn't be suffering either... would you?" I drive the point all the way home then.

"So was that God's fault, too? Or... was her birth something that you've thanked him for over and over again?"

Her eyes are troubled but there's an understanding there, too. I

think I'm making headway, so I go on." My people believe that life
is a circle. All of the Mother Earth's life forms are in this circle. This
circle is made by God, The Creator. He is our father, a wise and loving
father. How He did it or even why... is way beyond our comprehension.
But the fact remains that He did make it." I point the finger again for
emphasis.

"The proof is all around, everywhere ...you only need to look to
see it, Gretchen." Her interest is peeked so I figure it's worth a shot.
I continue.

"Remember what I said before...about God being our father?"

She nods her head in the affirmative. "Alright. Let me ask you this,
then. Have you ever had to let Carrie be hurt... because the pain she
feels at the time... is for her greater good in the long run?" Her
eyebrows rise.

"Here," I lean forward, "as an example, when she was a baby, did
you take her to the doctor for her first shots?"

She looks puzzled and finally nods. I bend my palm out. "Okay,
she was what, maybe a year... a year and a half old?"

She snatches her hand at the air impatiently. "Yeah, something
like that."

I nod again and twist around in my seat. "Okay. Now how did
you... make that small, unknowing child understand... that what was
happening to her...was for her own good? Were you able to explain
that those terrible painful shots were so that she wouldn't get diseases?"
Her eyes show astonishment at my apparent stupidity but I truck on
anyway.

"And when you were finished explaining, did she know all about
and understand what the mumps and rubella are?"

She shakes her head, the dark hair flinging about. "Please don't be
ridiculous. There's no way that Carrie would've understood those
things at that age! I never tried to explain it to her because she
couldn't have possibly have comprehended it!" Her eyes are fierce as
she speaks, her dark eyebrows bending into me and I... I've settled
back in my chair and tip my chin at her.

"So you're saying that sometimes parents have to do or... allow
things to be done to their children for their own good. Things that the
kids, because of their inability to understand, just have to accept. Pain,
loss – that kind of stuff? The kids have to accept that their parent...
has their best interest at heart? Is that what you're saying, Gretchen?"

I see the realization flood her face as she too, sits back in her
chair. She shakes her head. "You're right. That's too simple. I see what
you're saying, but that's too simple. Waaaay to simple."

I cock my head at her and push the chair out to stand. "Maybe so, but most things in life are actually that simple. There are tears now and she's dabbing at them with a napkin. I reach out my hand, not knowing whether she'll take it or slap it away. I'm relieved when she reaches up and grasps my fingers tightly, pulling herself off the chair while still hanging on, her body weak, as we walk out of the cafeteria. As we exit the room, she leans her head against my shoulder then looks up at me. Her jade eyes are welled with water as the elevator doors open and people flood out. She looks up at me and whispers "Thank you. I think... I think that you're a good man. An unusual man, Ely."

Unusual again. I guess that means weird. We step into the lift with more bodies and the doors roll shut. By the time they open again, I've decided that I'll help her little girl, if there's any way I can.

When we get to the old man's room, he's propped on the bed, pulling on his boot. He looks up as we come in and smiles at Gretchen. When he sees me, the smile fades. I nod to him.

"Mr. Veeter. How are you?" He looks at me, and for a second I detect something. I don't know, some kind of change as his eyes shift to his daughter and he answers.

"I am fine, thank you. Gretchen, when are we going home?" She seems taken aback as she looks at him. "I have to speak with the doctor first. Uh," her thumb points my way, "Dad, you remember Officer Stone, don't you? He's the one that found you and brought you to the hospital."

The old man's eyes dart back to me and a look of bewilderment covers his face. The room is silent until Gretchen turns to me. "He's been like this. I'll just be a minute, I have to talk to the doctor about getting him released." She turns back to her father.

"Dad, you go ahead and get ready. I have to go talk to the doctor and then we'll leave. Okay?" The old man just looks at her, and then barely nods his head. She sneaks a glance at me before stepping out of the room. After she's gone, Veeter hops off the bed and goes around me, closing the door. He turns back to face me and there's a different man looking out of the green eyes now.

"Well, Officer? What is it to be? Are you going back to get the item?" His face is earnest, but I know how sick he really is. "Look, Mr. Veeter, you could be in a lot of trouble. Right now, I think it's best that you just go on back home with your daugh..." he cuts me off, a look of anger forming over his face as he pounds his fist into his hand.

"Veeter now, is it? I told you my real name is Scheel!" he spits the words out, while managing to keep his voice low, "and what about our deal! My granddaughter is counting on that money!"

I have my hand up trying to calm him. "Okay, just settle down. If you prefer Scheel, then Scheel it is… okay?" I don't know how, but I think this guy was a part of that Air Force robbery back in the seventies. I direct my gaze to him.

"But I'm wondering what happened to the money you had, pal? Fifty grand should be enough to go to Switzerland, shouldn't it?" He looks at me while shivering with anger. He is intense and after a couple of beats, I see the fight go out of him. His determination fades like a closing sun on the distant horizon. He keeps looking at me while he moves back and sits down again on the bed. When he speaks, his voice is old and cracked with age. "What… fifty grand are you talking about?"

I tell him I know all about the robbery and the fifty thousand dollars stolen from the Air Force Base, and the whole time I'm speaking he has a disheartened look on his face. When I finish by telling him that I believe that he had something to with it, he just drops his eyes to the floor. The room is quiet and we can hear the hospital sounds outside the closed door. I figure that I am right and that he was a part of the robbery. But that thought develops a shade of doubt when he raises his head to me and speaks.

"Obviously, you do not believe what I have told you." He flings his hand as if that's a done deal. "Just the same, I know nothing of any robbery, and… I care nothing about any robbery. I never had any fifty thousand dollars and if I did… I certainly would not have ventured out to that God forsaken island. All I know, now…," his face turns to the window as his eyes mist, "is that my Carrie is going to die."

I can see that he's defeated. I'm not sure what to think. Just as I was about to decide that indeed this old man is the thief, the white buffalo kicks a hoof out of the cobweb, way up in the corner of my mind. It had been so quiet up there, that I'd almost forgotten that I still carried it. I'm about to say something to the old man when the door opens and Gretchen walks in.

Fifteen minutes later, I'm closing the driver's door on her Ford Explorer as she hooks up her seatbelt. The clouds have covered the sun and a cold front is upon us. Veeter sits quietly on the passenger side, staring out of the windshield. He hasn't said another word since Gretchen joined us. I tap the roof and look down at her.

"Well, you folks have safe ride and be careful, okay?" She turns the key and the engine fires off. She rests her hands on the wheel and looks up to me and over at her father. "We will, won't we Dad?"

The old man doesn't answer, and then, turns his head away and peers out the side window. Gretchen looks back to me. "I'm sorry. He's… he's…," I reach down and touch her shoulder as her eyes come up to mine. She clears her throat as her fingers drum the steering wheel. Then she reaches up and offers her hand. I take it and shake it gently.

"Well, again, I want to thank you for all that you've done Officer... I mean Ely. And well, if you're ever in Grand Rapids, please come and see us."

"I'll do that. And if you're ever up my way, you stop by too, okay?"

Her green eyes dance as her mouth forms a smile, the interior shadows exposing mirth lines around her mouth. "The old Indian who lives alone in a cabin in the woods?"

My other hand thumps the Ford's roof again. "Yep, that's me. Can't miss the place as long as you have a detailed map, a compass and arrive by air, it's real easy to find."

She laughs then, the deep husky laugh of a mature woman. It's the first time I've heard her laugh, and as I look at her, the dark hair wrapping around her smiling face, I'm struck again by her good looks. I start to release her hand but she squeezes mine tightly.

"I'd like that, Ely. I really think I would." We look at each other, and shortly she lets go and turns back to the wheel, pulling the transmission selector down to reverse. I step away as they back up and begin to pull out of the drive. Veeter is facing me now, staring out of the passenger side of the vehicle as it begins to drive by. As I look at him, he nods and the green eyes lock onto mine. It's barely discernable, but it is there. His eyes are bright and rational as the Explorer passes me and exits the lot. What the hell? I shake my head and climb into the patrol Jeep, flip open my cell phone and punch in Annette's number. She answers on the first ring. "Hello."

"Nettie? It's Ely."

"Ely! Oh Ely, I'm so glad you called! I'm at Bruce's Crossing at the Clinic. Gram's got a terrible chest cold and the doctor here thinks it might turn into pneumonia."

"That's not good. What's the doctor saying? Does he want her in the hospital?"

"I don't know, yet. I'm supposed to talk to him in a few minutes."

"Well, tell her I'm thinking of her and will have her in my prayers, will ya?"

"Yes, Ely, I will. Oh, I miss you so much! Are you okay? Amos says that you're in danger?"

"No, I'm just fine and I miss you, too. But listen, Nettie, about coming to see me...," I can hear other voices now, speaking to her, so I wait. A few seconds later she's back to me.

"Ely, I have to go right now. The doctor's standing here to talk to me, okay?"

"Yeah, okay Nettie but don't come here. Do you hear me? It's not safe..." the other voices again then she's back on the line, hurriedly.

"Ely, I'll have to call you right back!" Then the line goes dead. I turn the phone over in my hand and look at it. Well, don't that just suck! I flip the phone closed and slide the key into the ignition, cranking the Jeep over. I let it run to warm the engine and cold interior, as I shake out a smoke and light it up. I crank down the window and exhale a cloud of blue as my mind begins sorting. At least Veeter and his daughter are clear of my situation now. I glance down to the gauges and watch the temperature needle slowly rising. Then I look up at the cold gray world through the window and begin to allow the other objects juggling around in my head take shape, the Air Force, the dead guys, the island, the tribe, Nettie.

Shit man, my head shakes all by itself as I watch the snow flakes begin to land on the windshield. If, by God's mercy, I get out of this in one piece... I'm done. I'm going back to the woods to live as an Indian should. I chew the inside of my cheek as I twist on the wipers and flip on the defroster. I thought I was done with all this shit when I left the Coast Guard, and now... here I am... right in the middle of it again. Go figure. I back the Jeep up and pull the selector down to drive, and head out of the lot, golfball sized snowflakes floating everywhere.

Chapter Twenty-One
"You Should've Seen The One That Got Away"

The Escanaba Municipal Marina,
Escanaba, MI.
Same Day.

The two workers had been going back and forth to their truck carrying pipe wrenches and various tools all morning long as they worked to close the marina's restrooms for the season. The two, a man and woman, were standing by the truck taking a break and drinking coffee while stomping their feet in an effort to keep warm when the official looking dark blue sedan pulled into the lot by the boathouse. Up until then, they had been the only people around the marina and so, the arrival pricked their interest. They watched as a black man exited the rear and walked up to the boathouse door carrying a large envelope. The appearance of a black guy in this town of predominately white Finnish people was a small curiosity all by itself. The man knocked several times and got no answer. The female city employee set her coffee on the truck's hood, cupped her hands and yelled over.

"Hey! He's not here, eh! He left early this morning, after you's did!"

The black man heard her and waved before jogging back to the car and climbing in. Several seconds later, the door opened again and the man came trotting over to them, still carrying the package. He came to a stop by the truck and smiled at them.

"Hey, how you guys doing?"

Both workers said they were fine and the man nodded. "Listen," he reached in his back pocket and drew out his wallet, opening it and displaying an Air Force OSI badge and credentials. "My name's Mussenberg and I've got a package here that I need to get to the tribal cop that works over there. I don't suppose that you guys are going to be around here most of the day are you?"

The two workers looked at each other and when the older male shrugged his shoulders, the female turned back to the Air Force officer.

"Yah, we'll be here 'til about four o'clock er there'bouts, until we head back ta da barn, eh."

The black man smiled and stuck out the manila envelope, jerking his thumb over his shoulder. "Great! Hey, could you give this to that guy when you see him come in? It's too big to fit in his mailbox over there and it's really important that he gets it. We'll be back before you leave so if he hasn't arrived yet, we'll take it back then. What do ya say?"

The woman reached over and took the envelope. "Sure. Dat's no problem, eh?"

The officer nodded his head and thanked them before trotting back to the car and getting in. The vehicle pulled away as the pair finished their break by shaking out their cups and flinging the cold coffee remains onto the dry pavement.

An hour later, they were taking RV antifreeze out of the truck's box for the plumbing fixtures when they noticed a yellow car parking in the lot. The two kept working as a dark haired, well built man came over to them from the vehicle. He smiled brightly as he greeted them. Then he asked them a bunch of questions about where the fishing was good on the Big Lake, if there were anywhere close by, that sort of thing.

The male worker told him of a spot just southeast of town, by a grouping of rocks close to shore, where he'd heard they were catching some nice steelhead. On calm days, he advised that an angler could park in the scenic outlook above and go down the trail to fish from shore. He advised the man not to go out there today, though, as the weather was surely turning worse. The inquirer said that he probably wouldn't but he was just checking around. After thanking them, he left them to their work. As his car exited the lot, the female looked at her partner again. He shrugged his shoulders as huge snowflakes began falling. Neither of them voiced their thoughts, but both knew that the man was a foreigner. He spoke too succinctly and was too precise to be a Yupper. And if you weren't from the U.P., you were definitely a foreigner.

The wipers are flip-flopping from side to side as I pull the patrol Jeep in beside the Charger at the boathouse lot. I turn them off and snap the heater switch closed before twisting the engine off and pocketing the keys. I pop the door and grab the two bags from the seat. I'd stopped by the Radio Shack and bought a cheap cassette player, tapes and batteries before heading back here. Stepping over to the old Dodge, I pull up the snow-laden tarp so that I can open the passenger door and place the NAPA bag on the seat. I'll get around to replacing the light later. As I'm dropping the tarp, I hear someone behind me in the slush. I switch the Radio Shack bag to my left hand as my right hand shoots down to the holster on my side. I swing around easily.

"Hello."

There's a woman in work clothes standing there and I've seen her before. She works for the city. I've seen her mowing grass and those kinds of things around the marina. I nod at her and move my hand off the gun butt. "Hi."

She holds out a manila envelope as I see another man approaching, also familiar and also a city worker. "Dis is for you, eh? A coupla guys was here dis afternoon an asked us to give it ta ya 'cause it wouldn't fit in yer mailbox."

I take the envelope and can tell that it's heavy with paper. "Thanks. I appreciate it. I guess I better get a bigger box, huh?"

The woman waves her hand like she's swatting a fly. "Hey, dat's no problem, eh? Dey was from," she turns to look at her partner as he arrives by her side, "what was dey, Bernie?"

The man was older and he rubs a hand over his chin as he looks at me. "Da Air Force. He was a black guy from da Air Force wid'a coupla odder white guys in a blue Ford Crown Vic."

I nod while looking at the name "Bernie" stitched onto the chest of his Carhart work jacket. The woman's name, according to her jacket, was "Angie." I tip my head at their truck parked over by the bathrooms. "Something broken over at the bathrooms?"

They both shake their heads and Angie speaks. "Naw, we're jes closing 'em down fer da winter, eh?" She looks up into the snowy sky. "Don't guess dey'll be gett'en many more boats dis year."

My eyes search the sky briefly, too, then I shiver. "Nope, reckon you're right about that. It's turning colder too." The man called Bernie grunts.

"Ya it is. An' der waz some odder guy here taday, want'n ta know where's a good fish'n place out on da big lake. I told 'em dat it waz purtty good south a town, down by da scenic out look but if I waz 'em, I sure wouldn't be going out dere taday!"

I shake my head. "No, sir. Me either. Um, did he drive here or walk up in this weather or… what?"

Bernie puckers his bottom lip and glances over at the lot. "Naw.'E drove in'a little yellow car, eh?" his eyes back to mine. I shiver when he says that but it's not from the cold. I nod my head at them and look to the boathouse.

"Listen, I'm gonna make some coffee. You two want to come in out'ta the cold and have a cup? Maybe warm up a little bit?"

Bernie seems agreeable but Angie shakes her head no and swats that fly again with her hand. "Naw, but tanks anyway. We got coffee in da truck and we gotta get dis stuff done taday er da boss will be on're tail, eh?"

I thank them again and they mosey back to their job. I move over to the front door and unlock it while wedging the envelope against the wall behind the mailbox. A good wind will blow it away, but, hopefully, I won't leave it there long. Then, I set the bag on the sidewalk. After looking over my shoulder to check on the city workers and seeing them enter the bathrooms, I unsnap the thumb break and draw the .45, easing the door open. I enter and check all of the rooms. A few minutes later, I've determined that there's nobody here but us Redskins. I reach out to retrieve the envelope and bag and then I shut the door. I drop the package on the desk and make a small pot of coffee. I flip the thermostat up a bit, too. Since half of it is built over water, the cold outside has quickly worked its way into the building.

A few minutes later, I have a steaming cup of coffee and am easing myself down in the desk chair. The back of my leg is still sore when the meat's stretched but it's healing. I start looking at four pieces of Big Island Hawaii property that my General friend has deemed fit for us noble savages.

Unfortunately, I don't know didly about this stuff. There're legal descriptions, photographs, property evaluations and power of transfers. The last is allocated to Lt. General Raymond Kourn, USAF. There's a place for his signature, as well as Hennessey's, our attorney's, and mine. This is out of my area. I scribble out a note, explaining that a decision, as to which property to take, has to be made by 3pm today, in order to make the deal. Then I enter it first into the fax tray. Next, I take all of the other papers and dial Hennessey's fax number up in Wiitikin. When I get the tone, I feed them until they've all passed through the machine. There are a lot of them. I close out that line and punch in Hennessey's direct number. He answers on the second ring.

"Hello, this is John."

"Mr. Hennessey, it's Ely Stone."

"Ely! How are you, eh? What's happening? Anything new down there on the Air Force trade?"

Boy, is this guy ever excited. Well good. If it works, it works. If it doesn't… well, I don't want to think about that. "Yeah, things are moving along, Mr. Hennessy. In fact, I just faxed you the properties they're giving you to choose from. They should be there by now. And Mr. Hennessey, you've got to make a decision on this now. And I mean right now. Quickly, okay?"

"Sure, Ely! Wait a minute…," I can hear his chair scoot across the floor "…yes! Yes, I have them here now. We'll get started on this right away. And Ely, please call me John, eh?"

I sip coffee as I roll up my hand and look at my watch. "Okay… John. But I need an answer by three o'clock. The Air Force is breathing down my neck and I have to tell them yes or no right now." I hear him moan lowly on the other end of the line.

"Ely… we can't possibly make a determination that soon. It's… it's twelve-fifteen now! I don't understand why there's such a rush, eh? If we have a little time we can…"

I cut him off this time. "Look, we don't have time, okay? I'm telling you that we have to do this now or else we'll lose our chance here."

"But, Ely… we can't possib…"

I cut him off again. "Well you're gonna lose the deal then John 'cause they aren't gonna wait. They'll just take the island by way of governmental necessity, under the umbrella of national security, and eat the bad publicity that goes with it. Now you take it for what it's worth… but I know the military and that's what I'm telling you is going to happen if… we don't make our decision today, by 3 pm, when they come back here."

There's dead silence on the phone as I wait to see if the plan is dead or still has a chance to recoup. At this stage, I don't give a damn anymore. As I listen to the phone line crackle in the distance I know I'm lying to myself. I do give a damn. I want to finish this job and get back to the woods where I belong. As I rub a hand over my sore eyes, another thought flashes by. The statement might still be true, if I can't convince Nettie to come along with me. The sound of papers rustling over the phone line brings me back from my reverie.

"Okay, Ely! We'll get going on these, eh? I've talked with Alan Morse and as you may know, he is retired from the U.S. Army, eh? He's told me that what you're talking about with all of these governmental national security things is correct. He also says that we should trust you, eh? So if we can find one worth the trade, then we'll do it! We'll happily do it! I'll have to get in touch with our attorney there in Escanaba and have him meet ya there but I think we can do this. I'll have your answer for ya by three o'clock and I'll fax the paperwork you need back ta ya. I promise! Okay, Ely?"

Well, well, well. Will miracles never cease? My old pal Marshall Dillon says I should be trusted. I turn my mouth to the receiver.

"Fine, John. That'll be good. I'm not planning on going anywhere, but if you can't reach me here at the boathouse, then call my cell phone, alright?"

"Right! Yah, I'll do that, eh? Be talking ta ya soon, Ely! Bye for now."

I give him my tootle-loo and hang up the phone. I'm exhausted and know that I didn't get enough sleep last night. I close my eyes and see the motion of my friend, the white buffalo, up in the recesses of my mind. Hmm. Nice to know that he's still with me. Shit. I grind my hands into my eyes, trying to relieve the ache there, but I know that only sleep will do that. As I drop my hands and blink into the room, I know that between bad dreams and military wake-ups, I just ain't getting my beauty rest. I twist my hand up, exposing the watch to see that it's twelve-twenty six. I figure I'll get set-up and maybe have enough time for a nap before the "Fun with Uncle Sam" show begins.

I take the tape player out of its box, add the batteries and two blank cassettes. The tape recorder is a copier model. You can insert one tape and record the contents of it onto a blank tape right next to it. There's a switch that reads "Mic Volume" so I push it all the way up. Next, I mash the record button and speak into the face-mounted microphone. Then I hit the rewind and play buttons to hear me saying, "Test... one... two... three." I press stop. Okay. So it works. Now to see from where in the room... My eyes wander around until finally coming to rest on the shelves in the corner. On top, is where one of the numerous Beretta pistols hides that I've begun collecting. I take the recorder and rise. Going out into the dock room, I pull a red rag that's loaded with dust off a nail driven into a stud. Then I go back inside, moving over to the table. I drag a chair across to the shelves and climb up. I place the recorder on the top shelf and push it back all the way. Then I drape the dusty rag over it as camouflage, being sure not to cover the microphone. Then I press the record button and step back down.

Looking up at it, I say "testing" as I slowly make my way over to the entrance door. Once there, I begin to sing some words to the first song that pops into my head. Keeping my voice low, I sing out the words to "Just My Imagination" for a few seconds. Then I head back over and retrieve the player. I push rewind, then play and plainly hear my words and singing. It's audible enough, but as I listen to myself singing, I know that I'll never have a gold record, CD or whatever they call them nowadays. Bottom line though, it works. I punch the rewind button and re-configure my little insurance policy before getting down. I leave the chair in place and begin unbuttoning my shirt while yawning. I place the tape player box and all the plastic stuff in the garbage under the sink. After checking the doors to make sure they're locked and then taking the heavy Colt off my hip, I peel off the uniform shirt and lay down. I draw a blanket over myself on the couch. The little Glock rests easily in my hand under the covers as

I close my eyes. I'm not worried about waking up; the military is good at training you to wake up in a split-second. In a matter of seconds my world goes shady to dark to black.

The next thing I know, there's a ringing in my ears and I wake up. It's not a dream. It's the phone and I'm throwing off the blanket and stuffing the Glock in my pants pocket. I pick up the receiver. My voice comes out croaky as I wipe the sleep from my face.

"Stone."

"Ely? It's John Hennessey here. Did you get the faxes? I just sent them to ya, eh."

I twist around and look at the fax machine. There's a mound of paper in the tray and I turn back to the mouthpiece. "Yeah, looks like they came through."

"Okay. That's good. Our new tribal attorney is named Krinshaw and he's X'ed the places where you need to sign and also where this General Kourn needs to sign. I've already signed in the appropriate places." He takes a breath as I skim through the paperwork. There's a new one here that our lawyer must have drawn up. It's a lease agreement, giving the United States Air Force full proprietary rights to Muskrat Island for a period of bla, bla, bla. Too much lawyer junk will make you go blind. But I think I'll be able to handle my end. Hennessey is talking again.

"When everyone has signed, I need you to immediately fax back the documents so that they can be checked by our attorney here and entered into the court tomorrow morning. Then I'll fax it right back to you by nine am. Will this be okay, Ely?"

"Yeah, I think that'll work. I should be able to handle that."

"Good! Excellent! And Ely, you've done a great job, eh! We selected a sixty acre parcel on the southern tip of the island that used to be some kind of radar site. And Ely, get this, eh, according to what we've learned so far, it's worth a lot more than $500,000. We don't know what we'll do with it yet, but it's a good piece of land for the tribe, eh."

I pinch my nose, the bandage on my finger scratching against the skin, and continue to thumb through the papers while keeping the phone to my ear. The printing all seems legible enough. Then I remember something else. This is the only way I can do it and in my mind and heart, I know it's right. I'm going to tap the tribe for this but I figure that in one way or another, it's owed. I needed the knowledge of that black bag and its existence, in order to deal with the Air Force. Veeter may be a sick old man, full of hallucinations and wild stories, but he gave me what I needed. I could've never trusted the Air Force otherwise. They could've been after anything on Muskrat

Island. I had no way of knowing if what they were telling me was the truth. I no longer believe in the honesty of my fellow man, much less the government or its military representatives so the old man's assistance was vital for me. Veeter, his daughter and granddaughter deserve something for that anyway. They'll get what they want, as well as need.

"That's good, John. But I've got something else to tell you and it has to do with this deal. I need thirty five thousand dollars deposited into the Leukemia Foundation in the name of a child. Her name is Carrie Cooper, a white female and she lives downstate, in Grand Rapids. I need you to transfer the money electronically and fax me the receipt down here."

There's silence on the phone and I figure that I better go on if I'm going to make this whole thing jell. "Look John, you don't need to know why and I can't tell you anyway. So, just look at this as a tax write-off or something because this deal will not work unless we do this. Okay?"

"Very well, Ely. I trust ya, eh? You've done a good job for the people so far. Uh, who do we say this gift is from?"

I look out the window as headlights flash across it. "Just say the People of the Pukaskwa Nation. That should be good enough."

"Okay, Ely," he seems more up-beat now, "I'll see to it right now and send you the confirmation in a few minutes."

"Good, John. Good. I think our Air Force friends are here now so I'll talk to you later, alright?"

"Yes, Ely, and again... good job! On behalf of all of your people...thank you. You are the pathfinder that Amos told us would come."

I feel my eyebrows poke up as I take the receiver from my ear and turn it over to look at it. Jeeze. What'd I do to deserve this? I put the phone back to my ear and hear a dial tone. Hennessey is already gone. I hang it up and pull the pistol from my pocket, draw out the desk drawer and put it inside before sliding it shut. Then I scoot quickly over to the chair, climb up and push the record button on the player. Then I hop down and am dragging the chair back as the first knocks sound on the door.

I open the door and see the cherubic faces of my three friends from this early morning's chat group. I step back and swoosh my arm out, ushering them grandly inside.

Kourn snickers as he passes by. When they're all in, I look outside. The sky is dark and the snow's all turned to slush. But none is falling, now. It's cold out there and total darkness will come early tonight. I point up at the clouds and turn back to the men.

"Hey, I can see the "wild" but ain't you guys supposed to bring "blue" with your yonder?"

The General smiles from across the room as I close the door. "That's just in the song, my friend. In real life, we go up in any 'ole weather." He looks to the couch before turning his eyes back and points at my bare chest, "I see that we caught ya a sleeping, again. Don't ya ever get up and stay up fer awhile?"

I fling up my hands. "Hey, what can I say? I told you I had a late night and when you guys showed up here at the crack of dawn… well a growing boy needs his rest." I move over to the couch and pick up my shirt. As I'm doing so, Shears, who had come to light on the couch's arm, points to me as I'm slipping on the shirt. He has a smirk firmly lodged on his face and his eyes have a mean cast.

"I thought Indians didn't have any hair on their chest?"

My eyes go to slits as I button the shirt and look into his face. "Nawww. That's just TV and movie Indians. Us real ones have it, unless we're real traditional and pull it all out." I finish buttoning while staring at him, then slightly nod my head as I tuck the shirt into my pants.

"Hey, don't feel bad, Major." I wink and then feel my eyes go hard. "I mean… I would've thought that Air Force majors had hair on their ass, too."

Shears' face turns deep red and his fists ball up. It's only a second or two but we stand there looking at each other until Kourn speaks.

"Now boys, if ya'all don't behave then we'll just turn the car around and go straight back home right now… heah?"

I give it a second longer anyway, then turn back to the General and nod at his smiling face. "Okay, dad. Whatever you say, but remember," I jab a thumb over my shoulder at Shears, "he started it."

Kourn's smile fades at the disrespect of me calling him "dad" but he lets it pass. Gheeese. Generals and admirals. So easy to offend! I move across the room in an effort to keep the conversation focused close to the recorder. Picking up the paperwork, I swing back around and hold it out. Then I light a smoke.

"Okay, General. Looks like we're going to have a deal. My people have all signed off on this stuff and…" There's another knock at the door and everyone's attention momentarily swings that way. It's the lawyer and the little man comes swiftly in and busies himself at the desk and the fax machine with hardly a glance at any of us. He seems harried, all business and little talk. But then, it's late. Probably well past banker's and lawyers hours, eh and he got a hurry-up call to be here. I get the required paperwork and then look about the room. Kourn and his little friends have drifted over by the shelves and I can hear them speaking quietly right up until the lawyer sends the last page through the fax, gathers up all the papers and puts them in his briefcase. He goes over and puts on the overcoat and pulls on his hat before turning back to us.

"Very well gentlemen. It's been nice meeting you and I shall see you in the morning to sign the official deeds then." He smiles that lawyer smile as I open the door and see him out. After he's gone, I move back over to where the other men are standing. They all look at me when I come to a stop, but I only hold the General's eyes.

"Anything new on the Chinese General?"

Kourn shakes his head. "Nope. Not as yet, anyhow. But we're own it. If they're here, we'll know before long."

I allow my gaze to briefly touch the other two men before Settling again on Kourn. "Okay then, sir. So, tomorrow we should be able to wrap this thing up. I just want ta go over the deal again, General, just to make sure we're still on the same page."

Kourn nods. "Certainly," he rolls out a hand, "By all means... say yer piece."

"Okay, so we've got the land for the island lease... that much's worked out. But again, General, the deal is... you guys eat any collateral or physical damage that stems from this whole business, be it foreign agents, destroyed property or what-have-you. And the people of the tribe stay free from harm on this operation. And that means before today too, General, even if it's wet work... right? Now that's the whole deal, until we get the island back. Are we still agreed?"

Kourn folds his arms and leans heavily on one foot while cocking an eye at me. "Now why do I feel like you're a holding some'thin back own me?"

I give him my best smile while finishing the cigarette and dropping the butt in the can. "Well, General, I don't know. If I had ta guess, I'd say it's because you have a very suspicious nature." I cock my head and point at him, while holding the smile. "It probably comes from a bad Air Force up-bringing."

Kourn continues to stare at me from across the floor, the doubt still evident on his face. Finally, he smiles faintly and begins moving toward the door, his minions following. "Yeah, I suspect yer right own that account." He stops and looks over to me while nodding. Shears opens the door for him as the General sets his eyes on me. "And yessir... that's still the deal but I caution you, Mr. Stone... don't be a doing anything that will jeopardize the safety of this nation or... this mission. Because... I guarantee you... I won't take kindly ta that."

Our eyes are locked as I give him a gentle nod of my head.

"I won't General. For what it's worth, you can rest assured of that."

After a beat, he forces a smile. "Okey-dokey, then. I reckon we'll see ya in the morn'n." He walks through the open door, followed by Shears who is still shooting daggers at me with his eyes. Mussenberg quickly glances at the retreating men and then turns back to me in a low voice as he's pulling the door closed.

"Man, oh man, buddy, you sure like to live on the edge, don't you?" He's smiling as the door closes and I let the air blow out of my lungs in relief.

It's dark outside now and I stand motionless until I see the headlights of their vehicle flash across the window. Then I move over and peer out of the curtains, watching their car and the three silhouetted heads inside the vehicle pull out of the lot. I scan the outside but can see nothing in the obscurity. I move away from window and flip the deadbolt on the door. Then I stretch, letting the tension of the moment dissipate and shake it off before going over with a chair to check the recorder. I climb up, punch stop, rewind and then play the machine back. I can hear everything that was said a few minutes before. I rewind the tape and push the transfer/record button and watch as the reels of both tapes begin slowly turning. The gizmo should shut itself off when it's done copying so after putting the chair back, I make my way to the head.

In the bathroom, I flush the toilet and step up to the sink and rinse my hands, drying them before peering at the face in the mirror. The stress lines on the face featured there are a lot more than I like. I badly want this shit to be over and adamantly hope that tomorrow it will be. Then this Indian is done with this job and on his way back to the woods where he belongs. No more of this crap... ever! Maybe then I can start to deal with Nettie. I know that I'm in love with this girl and more than anything... I want that to work out. I smirk at the mirror and think, 'If it can work out?' My stomach growls as I realize that I'm hungry. I think I'll stop and get a pizza.

The lady at the dry cleaners said that a little place called 'The Saloon', down in Gladstone, makes a good one. That little town is just a short drive east of Escanaba. But that won't be until on the way back. I've got to go and talk to my helicopter pal Hank first. I've got to explain to him about the Air Force deal and what that'll mean for him, and his guiding business. He won't be pleased, but being prior military, he'll understand. I hope he does anyway. I'll give him a call just to make sure he's home before I drive over. I'll drop one copy of the tape in a mailbox, too. But first, I'll try calling Nettie again. Taking one last look at the Redskin in the mirror, I wink at him and murmur out loud, "Man… pal. Let's hope this all works out!" Then I step out of the room to place the calls.

Just outside of Escanaba, MI.,
A Deserted Stretch of Highway.
Same night.

Chin pulled the wheel over and turned the rental car into the shallow drive leading off the highway. He switched the lights off as he made the turn and after a bit, braked to a stop. Putting the selector into park, he kept the engine running and the heater blowing warm air into the interior. The wind was picking up outside and Chin had no intention of getting any colder than necessary. He was very happy that he had traded in the small little car for this large American model. When he had rented at the airport, the tiny Neon was all that was available. So he was happy that he had checked again and picked this one up.

He could have little pleasures like this Buick, especially considering the circumstances. This car was what an American automobile should be, large and spacious. Speaking of little pleasures, he fumbled in his shirt pocket and pulled out a Marlboro to stick in his mouth. He flicked the lighter and cracked the window as he exhaled smoke. He watched as it was quickly sucked outside and didn't look forward to the time when he would have to leave the warmth of the vehicle to stand in the wind. But it was a small matter. He looked at the seat beside him and the bag sitting there. He pulled the zipper back and withdrew a night vision spotting scope from inside.

It was a cheap model, purchased from a sporting goods store. It wasn't very good and certainly lacked the quality of military issue, but then, one must make do with what one could find. He brought the scope to his eyes and peered outside through the side window while adjusting the instrument. The picture slowly came into focus as he adjusted the focus ring. He could see a large grouping of rocks out in the water and several small boats with fishermen aboard, their anchor and navigation lights standing out clearly. Amazing, thought Chin. These Americans will endure this cold and harsh weather to simply catch a fish. And this is not fishing for market. No, the people down there do not do this to survive. This is not their livelihood, it is simply their pleasure. These people are fishing in these conditions as a form of recreation.

Chin slowly shook his head. To freeze and endure such discomfort in pursuit of a single fish that one does not even need for nourishment was simply beyond his understanding. Sport, he thought. They do this for enjoyment. As he watched, he could see the waves beginning to rise around the vessels out there. Then the rain began, gently at first, then coming in torrents. The wind was picking up, too, and as he continued to monitor, he saw that two of the craft had hauled up anchors and were beginning to move off. A wise action, thought Chin. He hoped that the others would do so also. It would not do at all to have Kuan arrive with bystanders still present. The wind began whistling around outside as Chin put the night glass down.

There was little doubt, he knew, that the sea down there would pick up in intensity, very shortly. Those rocks would be a very dangerous place to be when that happened. He did not worry about Kuan. The man had extensive naval experience and could handle the situation, easily. He raised the scope back to his eyes and saw that indeed, the remaining boats were leaving, also. He sat the scope on his lap and smoked again as he tapped his fingers on the wheel to the droning of the rain. How they would proceed after this next function could only be determined by the circumstance as it arose. Not the best way to run an operation, but still, that was all that was left now. For the moment at least, he had nothing to do but wait.

His eyes traveled up to the disappearing fishing boats out on the water. He flicked ashes out the cracked window as he watched the lights fade into the wet darkness. What was that American saying that had to do with fishing? Oh yes, now he remembered. "You should have seen the one that got away!" Chin chuckled to himself. He wished that "HE" were the one that got away. But as he sat there in the car smoking and the rain turned to sleet, he knew deep down inside that, that... would never happen.

Chapter Twenty-Two
Sticks and Stones Break Bones But Names... Can Shatter Your Heart

The Boathouse,
A short while later, the same night.

I crack the door open and peer inside the room before flipping on the light switch. So far, so good. Everything looks fine. Outside, the rain is pelting down and has turned to sleet. I bend back and retrieve the pizza box from the sidewalk with my left underhand, then ease inside, keeping the .45 out front. Water drips from my hair and jacket as I make my way over to the desk and set the box down. Then I check the bathroom and finally, the back of the boathouse. I crack the rear door and snap on the switch as I bend low and sweep the back room with the pistol. Nothing. Nobody.

I take a breath and relax as the Boston sits bumping gently against her ropes in the rippled water. My eyes jump to the rear window as sleet and wind hammer against it in a sudden gust. I step over to the back door and check the lock. It's secure. I turn around and the room is open before me, the bare light bulbs reflecting eerie shadows upward from the exposed rafters. Everything seems okay, but in the back of my mind, something says it isn't.

Then somebody drops some change into the jukebox of my brain because the "Temptations" start singing "Just My Imagination". My eyes wander the walls, taking in the hanging tarps, ropes and assorted gear as the shinkakee has its way with me. There's nothing here and yet... Oh well. I head back to the office door and peel off the soaking uniform jacket, hanging it on a hook to drip-dry. As I scan the room again, I know that something's not right, but for the life of me... I don't know what it is. Huh? Just for the heck of it, I decide that I'll leave the light on. Then, after looking over the room again, I turn the knob and go inside to the warmth as the tune "Just My Imagination" drones on in my feeble little mind.

I open the icebox and take out a Hamm's, twisting off the cap and chug-a-lugging a good drink of the beer. I force myself to turn the volume down on the Temptations and then, make my way to the desk. I pop open the soggy pizza box while setting the pistol down. I tear off a slice of pizza and begin eating it as I sit down and fire-off the computer. The pizza is barely warm anymore, but it's good. The lady had told the truth, by golly. I dab at my mouth with a paper napkin as the machine warms up and comes alive. An image of Hank Scari's face flashes before me as I remember our talk this evening.

As I'd figured, he wasn't real happy to hear the news that he wouldn't be able to guide any hunts on the island this fall. But after I'd told him about the probable Chinese agents and the Air Force documents, he'd fallen right in with the plan. And I was happy to find that it wasn't a mistake telling him, either. He could be trusted. I knew the type. That was one thing about most guys who'd seen combat. Their experiences kindle an appreciation of this country and a knowledge of the costs of keeping the freedoms we have. And even if we lose a few more of those freedoms each year, the USA is still better than anywhere else in the world. I'd assured him that he should have the hunting privileges back by next fall and that seemed to satisfy him, all things considered. He thanked me for taking him into my confidence. Sitting here eating the fast cooling pizza, I find that I appreciate… him saying that. I punch in the command for the internet and in a few seconds, it's there and I have several messages. One of them is from Gangues. I put the curser on it and click.

Ghostman,
I've had a hell of a time getting this stuff but here is what I've gathered so far on your two Air Force zeros.
1) Alan Edward Shears, White male, DOB: 7/16/63.
USAFA, Class of 1985. Present rank: Major
Assigned to AFOSI and detached often to Detachment 4,
669th Air Intelligence Group. (whatever the hell that is)
2) Peter Ezekiel Mussenberg, Black male, DOB: 12/14/71.
AFROTC, UCLA, Class of 1989. Present rank: Captain
Assigned to AFOSI and like Shears, is also detached often to
this Detachment 4, of the 669th Air Intelligence Group. (I
haven't got "jack" on it yet.)

As near as I can tell, these two boys are TDY'd often to this Intelligence Group but I can't get further before they nail my access routes. For what I've got so far, I've had to use my Dragonslayer. And they've almost burned it a few times. I can get more on these two if you need it but these dudes have some heavy security on their files. I have to set up a network of overseas connections before I attempt further on this DET4, 669th intelligence unit or this hot-ass General you gave me. For what it's worth, Shears was in the Gulf War with this Air Intel Group and as of late, he's been in Bosnia and similar hotspots.

Mussenberg was in flight school during the Gulf but he spent some time in Somalia. Primarily though, both of these guys are detached for temporary duty to this intelligence outfit and sent to these little tiny out-in-the-middle-of-nowhere places and towns. It's bizarre. But I will find out why. Count on it. More when I get it.
Gangues.

I e-mail him back telling him thanks, and that maybe I'd be clear of the whole thing by tomorrow. I bend down and take off the ankle holster holding the Glock around my boot and slip it into the desk drawer. Then I sit back and finish the eating as I ponder my new Air Force friends. So, Shears is an Air Force Academy grad. I don't remember seeing a ring on his ugly, bony finger. Huh? And Mussenberg, ROTC from the University of Southern California. Who'd a thunk it? It is strange though, this business of the 669th Air Intelligence Group. What the hell was that? And then, what the heck was this Detachment Four? I'd never heard of either of them. As I chew the last of my pizza, I realize that it's not all that unusual. There're just way too many military units out there and there's no way that I'd recognize all of them. I look in the pizza box and decide that the remaining pieces will be good for breakfast. 'm placing the box in the little refrigerator as the phone rings. I pick up the receiver. "Stone."

"Ely, it's Annette."

I squeeze the phone tight in my hand and roll it around my ear. Just hearing her voice makes me weak in the knees. "Nettie, how're you doll? How's your grandmother?"

"Oh, she's fine. I just left her house. I stayed until she went to sleep. She's very sick Ely but the doctor says that she'll be fine if she gets some rest."

I'm nodding my head in an empty room. "Good, Nettie. That's really good news. So are you heading back to Wiitican now?" I roll my hand and look at my watch, a slight worry threading its way into my being. "It's late Nettie and the weather's getting bad."

"No, I'm almost to Escanaba now. I should be there shortly."

Aww shit! No! "Nettie! You can't come here! It's not safe! Didn't you get my message? I left it on your cell phone no more than two hours ago."

There's nothing but quiet on the line. "Nettie! Nettie, did you hear me?"

"Ely. Ely, what's wrong? I haven't checked my phone messages. Why can't I come and see you?"

I run a hand through my damp hair and squeeze my eyes shut for a second. "It's a long story, Nettie, but you can't come here right now.

It's not safe. I'll explain it to you later. Where are you now?"

There's some rustling and I can almost see her, twisting in her seat, looking for landmarks. "I'm not… sure I… wait. Okay, I just passed a sign that said I was entering the city limits. It's sleeting pretty bad out here right now and it's hard to tell."

I'm nodding again. "Okay, Nettie, just keep coming this way. I'll meet you at the old Dairy Queen. You'll see it coming up soon, okay? Just pull in there and wait for me. I'll be right there."

"Okay Ely, I'll do as you say. But… but are you going to be all right Ely? I'm scared for you now."

"Yeah, I'll be fine. I'll see you in a few minutes. Bye for now."

"Goodbye, Ely."

I drop the phone in the cradle and spin around in one motion. I've got to hustle. In two strides, I'm turning the knob on the back door of the boathouse to grab my wet jacket. As I swing the door open, my eyes are on the deck and the wet footprints there. SHIT! Time winds up into a tornado. Everything becomes a million miles an hour. It's all happening at once! Out of the corner of my right eye, I see movement and naturally begin shifting my weight to my left. I see him, twisting on his right leg and snapping out his left toward my knee, all of it the speed of light! I'm instinctively jerking my leg up, bending it to take the blow. When it comes, the force is lessened because I'd shifted but the jolt connects with my thigh and still knocks me off balance!

I slam into the door and it springs back, helping me push myself off. I see him twisting around in the air like a ballerina to land on his left and bring his right foot up and snap it out and into my right side! The air blows out of me like a volcano erupting! My wind escapes in a rush and my eyes go bright red with excruciating pain! I feel myself dropping to the floor on my knees, making noises like a wounded seal as I try to draw breath from lungs that don't work anymore! I'm dead now! I know that! Then slowly… so unbelievably, agonizingly, slowly… I'm able to take air again. The red begins to fade from my eyes and the floor comes into focus. I can see the individual grains of wood and realize that I'm still on my knees and that… I'm still alive!

I look up to see him, his hands spinning like propellers on the wings of an airplane as he flings his arms from side to side. He lightly steps from foot to foot, a malicious grin stretching his mouth. As I look at his smiling face, I amend that thought about me still being alive.

"What is the matter, Policeman? Is that painful?"

He easily pushes the door closed. It clicks shut as I focus on breathing, something that I've done easily all my life, but now find really difficult to do. Slowly, it's coming back. I try to talk but speech is not a doable thing yet. Each breath I draw is a new torment. I try to

take stock of my options, but unfortunately, there don't seem to be any.
I don't have a gun or a knife and even if I weren't already injured,
this Bruce Lee impersonator would've smoked my ass in a one on one
anyway. He's a little bigger than his friends have been and a tad older,
too. For all practical purposes, this guy is a deadly weapon, all by
himself, as he hops lightly from foot to foot. In the brief moments
before I die, my mind flashes back to what my Daddy always told me
about fighting. "If the man's bigger or better than you, then find a
balancer.

What that meant was… get an equalizer. I start running my mouth
while using my peripheral vision to look for the balancer. I let my eyes
float toward him again. He's dressed in black sweats pants and a black
sweatshirt, water dribbling off as he moves around like a big cat. Funny,
he kind of looks like James Bond in this light. I grunt out the words.

"You know pal… ugh… you've hurt me pretty bad here. What
say you…ugh… just back off before it gets any worse, okay? You do
know I'm a cop… right?" Saying the words allows for new staggers of
pain to erupt from my side. And as my eyes lock on his, the evil smile
he's wearing only grows wider.

"Ohhhh, but for you, "The Noble Savage", it is going to get much,
much worse before it is over! If you believe that you have pain now,
then just think of what is yet to come."

He giggles as he says the last, while side-stepping like Jackie Chan
and locking onto my eyes. I've seen something that I might use but it's
not much. It's a canoe paddle, leaning against the wall, within arm's
reach for me. I rise and he doesn't come in at me again. I half
expected him to. Instead, he's still moving around in a kung fu, karate,
tae kwon do, judo and every other martial-art-like manner you can
think of. Sheiiit! This is scary. He's staying well out've my reach but I
know that he can come charging in like a streak of lightening, and
when he does it's gonna be night-night time. The one thing I have
going for me is the fact that he's confident. All of these thoughts fly
through my head in a microsecond as I try to figure this situation. I
decide that I'll bank on his confidence and quickly stretch over, grab
the paddle and swing it up in my hands like a bat. When I get my eyes
back to him, he's still there! All coiled and ready, still moving silently
with that stupid grin attached to his face but… he's still there! I'd really
expected him to hit me when I moved! Maybe… just maybe! But he's
laughing now as he watches me.

"Do you think that small stick will save you Indian? Ha! The last
thing that I will do before I kill you… is jam it up your ass! Ha, ha, ha!"

He's got a shitty laugh. I've got a plan but like most I come up
with, it ain't necessarily a good one. I'm still holding the paddle up like

a ball bat over my shoulder as I slowly ease my hands downward on the handle. He's within swinging range now, but I've got a notion that he'll move quick enough to dodge a swing should I start one. I'm banking on that as I slowly inch my hands toward the end of the paddle. At the same time, I keep the conversation going to cover my actions.

"Hey! You think you're gonna just kill a cop and not have any problems, buddy? Well… ugh… that ain't too likely there, friend. A cop is a cop, and when they find me dead, your ass is grass!" His grin only grows broader when I say that.

"Ahhhh. That may be true if it were to happen that way. But you see, your body will be found in the rocks a short way from here in Lake Michigan." His face takes on a look of pretended seriousness and wonder. "Yes, sadly it appears that you took your boat out fishing and fell overboard and drowned." He looks up at me. "I know this because we just bought you a new fishing pole and tackle. So it will be a tragedy, don't you agree?" The smile disappears. "You have caused us much difficulty Indian and I shall personally enjoy causing you great pain, in return."

That evil grin comes back to his face now as my hands continue positioning themselves on the handle. Yeah, he's confident but he hasn't lost a bit of being on guard. And I'm sure that he thinks that I'm already as dead right now as he says I soon will be. I slide my right foot into position as he casually shakes his head and goes on.

"That is why, I can have some fun with you first. The rocks will beat you up quite badly, so I shall," he drops his head in a smart ass manner, "how do you say… soften you up for the rocks, yes?"

At this point, I figure I've got about as much wind back in my sore ribs as I'm gonna get. Timing here is gonna be everything. And what the hell, nobody lives forever so…

I quickly rise up while appearing to swing with everything I have! He sees that the paddle is headed for his calves and he's easily jumping upward, folding his knees to miss the swing, as I'm simultaneously pushing off with my legs, checking the paddle in mid-swing, my hands switching position on the handle! My weight is driving into him now, as he's coming down from his jump, the momentum slamming us into the far wall! Then I'm trying to jam the wood into his groin but I'm hitting the inside of his left thigh as he's scrambling, bringing up his hands to chop them together at both sides of my neck!

The pain is bad but he doesn't have enough leverage to put his all into it! Still, the hit almost causes me to black out! I know instinctively that he's still off balance. Once he regains it, I'm a goner! I'm back to jabbing as hard as I can, looking for that magical pouch! Pounding and slamming, driving with all my might and then he screams! I've found the boy's jewels and I fully intend to rob his ass! I keep driving the end of the paddle into his crotch! His screams have lessened to out and out bawls of agony as I ram the wood home over and over again! His body is now reacting only to this pain and I keep it up for him until he's moaning lowly and limp, vomit trickling down his mouth!

I slide myself back and stand as quickly as I can, wavering and staggering as I do so, using the paddle as a cane-like support. He's whimpering and throwing up on his side now. Watery sweat has cascaded down his face, his eyes teary and looking extraordinarily weird in the shadowed light. I feel the adrenalin peeking then... leeching off me and drop my eyes down at the paddle in my hand. A fine piece of equipment, I think, as I look at the laminated pieces of maple. Great for pushing a canoe away from a dead log or... driving a guy's nuts right up into his throat!

Sonavaaaaabitch! My body is informing me of its many hurting spots now that the overriding natural chemicals are leaving it. My left hand slides up to cradle the soreness on the right side of my chest. Then I look down at my throbbing right leg and see that blood has soaked through my pant leg. Shit. I'd taken the first kick right on the site of the healing bullet wound. My eyes travel back to my assailant who is now curled into a blubbering ball on the wooden floor. His side is uncovered, and, as fury blows into me, I shift my weight and send the toe of my left boot as hard as I can into his exposed right kidney while screaming at him! "You kicked my sore leg, cocksucker!"

He yells, the kick adding something to his agony, and personally... I find that quite soothing, my-ownself. I waver around there for a time, too disoriented to do much of anything but breath hard. Finally, I'm able to be thinking somewhat normal again, as he, too, begins to gain a little coherence. I'm not very worried, he's still in bad shape, probably worse-off than me right now. Still, one never knows. I adjust the paddle for a fell-swoop should he get frogfish and decide to jump my way. I'm looking down at him as his eyes begin to focus in a myriad of present pain. But, he's a trooper and once he regains some measure of control, he looks up at me. The eyes are strange, just like his pals. I bump my head at him.

"What is with you and your friends, anyway? You guys all need glasses or what?"

He's trying to move himself up to an arm, but the ruptures he must have seem to make that awfully difficult for him. Awww, too bad. He finally gives up and lies back, breathing heavily, the bizarre eyes searching my face. Then he speaks, the words coming out as a croak. Maybe he is a frog, eh?

"You… uh… you…ah… said my friends? What do you know of…ah… my friends?"

I tilt my head sideways at him and gently rub my side. "Well I know they're dead. What else is there to know? You want to tell me more?"

His abnormal eyes grow large with questions. As I look at him, I wonder if the strangeness of their eyes can only be noticed when their hurt in some way. He points a crooked and shaking finger at me. "Who are..uh… you?"

I just look down at him. "Ya know, I got the same question from each of your buddies, too." I shake my head, breathing raggedly. "You guys really should've got together and pooled your questions before we had our little meetings like this."

My turn to smile this time and I stretch out a big one for old David Caradine here. I'm basking in the glory of still being able to draw a breath, albeit a painful one, when the door opens and we both turn our heads. Nettie is standing there, and out of the corner of my eye, I see him moving, pushing himself to a sitting position in a microsecond! My mind flies back into action mode again, as I know I've got to Finish it now! He figures out my actions at about the same time and he's up and coming at me!

I swing the paddle with a grunt as Nettie yells, "Ely, Nooo!" I see the end of the paddle connect with the side of his head, the wood exploding into splinters and his ear puffing out in a cloud of red mist! Then his weight is hitting me hard and I'm going down, his body on top of mine! My head smacks the floor! And then… everything goes black.

**The Scenic Overlook,
Just outside Escanaba, MI
Same night.**

Chin stands just in front of the car on the passenger side and holds the night vision scope to his eyes. The sleet is falling mercilessly and he is soaked to the skin and cold to the marrow of his bones. He realizes that he is too old for this, anymore. As he follows the green light on the bow of the boat approaching down below, he wonders why he hadn't realized this before undertaking this mission. Too late now. He shivers and drops the scope to mid-length of his waist. He turns his hand up and looks at the watch. Yes, he thought, that would be Kuan coming now. Well, at least the Policeman would no longer be a problem after tonight. Now, if he only knew what had happened to the rest of the team.

They were dead of course. They had to be or else they would have contacted Kuan and himself, somehow. He raises the glass again and monitors the vessel as it nears the shoreline. Actually, he thinks, the mission had gone awry from the moment the Policeman had arrived here. Shortly after, the American Air Force had come, and being an experienced espionage officer, Chin knew that once a foreign military became interested in a mission that was being worked, the odds of completing it successfully were drastically reduced. He... wait! Chin pulls the focus ring around tighter and peers intently at the boat as it becomes more visible in the sleety darkness.

This isn't the policeman's boat! It's a commercial fishing trawler, merely hugging the shoreline as it travels past! He drops the glass away from his eyes and peers at the luminous dial of his watch. What could have gone so wrong? Where...

"He ain't coming."

Chin freezes. But it isn't the weather this time that sends a chill through him. The words were spoken very quietly, but he is sure he's heard them. He slowly begins to lower his hands, thinking of the pistol in his belt, when the voice comes again.

"If I was you... I'd keep my hands right where they are."

Chin nods. "I think that I agree with you. Tell me, if you were me, might you also ask if you could turn around to see the person with whom you seem to have so much in common?"

Silence for a beat. Then, "Yeah, go ahead, but before I turned, I'd drop the spyglass, and boy... I'd sure keep my hands up as I turned slowly. But hey, what do I know. Go ahead and do your own thing. It's alright by me, either way."

Chin flicks his wrist and sends the night vision scope sailing to land on the grass next to a drinking fountain. Then, he carefully eases around, keeping his hands elevated. The sleet is cutting across his vision until he completes the about-face. The wind drives the frozen water into the side of his face and neck as he stops. Now he can see his adversary. And what a sight he is!

Chin's mouth opens and drops. It is the Indian Policeman leaning over the roof of Chin's car and aiming a pistol at the Chinaman's chest. It is obvious he is in great pain! But what is more incredible is the fact that he is even here! That means that Kuan is dead or captured! And Kuan knew that capture was not an option. This Native American Policeman has killed one of the best agents in the Chinese Navy! Lieutenant Commander Kuan killed by an American Indian? Was it possible? Chin had to answer that question in the affirmative. After all, he was standing here with his hands up. So, indeed, it was all possible. But then, this Indian was no ordinary savage, either.

He studies the man holding a gun on him with the bizarre face. "I assume that I am under arrest. As you are a policeman," he tilts his head, "you probably will not understand this, but… I will not be taken as a prisoner."

I stand resting my aim over the car. The white dot on the site of the Glock is centered steadily on the Oriental's chest. The sleet is slashing into my face but it doesn't bother me or my sight picture. And while I should be cold and feeling my injuries, the silent rage inside of me is firing my soul and supplying warmth. I gently turn the gun sideways, then back again before responding.

"Why do think that was ever an option for you?"

I watch as the little man's eyebrows rise in curiosity. He lets his gaze drop down and then brings it back to me. "I assume Kuan is dead?

I look at him for a beat. "Was that his name?"

He seems mystified as he searches my face in the drizzling sleet. "Are you responsible for the deaths of my other men, too, then?"

I'm growing weary of this. "Let's just say that I was there when they passed away."

He stands flat-footed now, a look of wonder all over his face. "Please… who are you?"

I adjust my footing and begin a gentle easing of my stance, settling into a firing position, my finger already applying more pressure to the trigger. "Some people say that I'm from the nether world."

He's slowly moving his head from side to side, his face a question mark. Finally, he stops and juts his chin out. "The nether world. The nether world." I can see his mind searching for something. Then a light bulb pops on over his head.

"Nether world…American Indian? Ghosts! Where do I know this from? I've seen it before… something to do with…Trojan." His face takes on realization and wonder all at once. He smiles smugly, satisfactorily. "You are a Trojan member!"

He eases back now, a look of contentment on him. "I have read a file on you and your team." He twists his head in interest. "But I thought your team was disbanded?"

This time, I don't answer. After a few beats, he inclines his head in my direction. "Yes, well as this appears to be the end, I wonder, do you know?" He angles his head, amazed. "Do you have any idea what you have on that island, my Indian friend?"

The gun remains steady and unmoved in my hand as I shift my head in a "who cares" manner. "Friend, eh? Well I don't know about

that, pal. But I can tell you that I don't have anything on that island.
The Air Force has control of it now. And I'd say it's a pretty fair bet...
that Mother China won't be getting anything from them so it doesn't
matter much, does it?"

The sleet has stopped as he again nods his head, the water gently
flinging off in the motion. "Yes, indeed. I would say that you are
correct in that assessment." He angles his head.

"May I ask... why do you have a hand painted on the side of your
face in such a manner?"

I wait. I wait some more. Then I tell him. "It's an Indian thing and
it's not paint. It's a warrior's blood pledge." I wait a little more before
saying the rest.

"It means that I will take everything from my foe. I will taste the
blood of my enemy and I will give him no quarter."

He takes that in slowly. A look of comprehension and then dread
rolls over his face, usurped by a quiet determination. He nods while
reapplying the smile and then...quickly drops his hand toward his
waist! The Glock barks twice, bucking in my hands. I see the fire
erupt from the muzzle and a startled look jump over the Oriental's
face as the rounds smack high into his chest and he's blown
backwards to the wet ground.

I keep the weapon on him as I move around the car and up to
where he lays. When I get there, I can see that it's over for him. Still,
he looks up at me as his life fades away. I slip the Glock into my other
hand and bend down to take the exposed pistol from his belt and stuff
it in my own. I feel nothing but calmness. I reach to my pocket for a
hand-rolled as I straighten up but the box is empty. I remember then,
that I'd smoked the last one on the way here. I look at the dying man
and bend down to a knee, holstering the Glock as I do. Then I'm
going through his pockets. I find a hard pack of Marlboros in his shirt,
remove it and take one out to fire up. It's always nice to get a little
present for one's efforts. Cupping the cigarette in the cold, damp air, I
blow out the smoke and thank God the Great Good Spirit, for
allowing me to win and survive. When I look down again, there's a
smile on the Chinese agent's face as he looks at me and the cigarette.
I find that odd. Well, okay. Time to show him that it's not all that funny.

I peel the bandage from my finger and move the cigarette to my
left hand. Then I lean forward, pressing my right hand onto his
bleeding wounds. His eyes follow me with a look of curiosity as I
bring the palm, dripping blood, up to press tightly against my right
cheek. When I move it away, a bloody hand print remains, matching
the one on my left side. Then, while looking into his slanted eyes, I
place the red index and middle fingers into my mouth and closing my

lips, draw them back out. There is a horror on his face now as he tries to speak, his voice faint with death.

Chin is consumed with terror. He knew just before the Indian shot, that he would die here, in this place, on this night. He even found it humorous that the man should take his Marlboros, just as he had taken so many other Americans' cigarettes in the past. But these other things, what did they mean? What was this savage doing? Was that Kuan's blood on the other side of the Indian's face! He was dying and he felt that the Indian was taking more than just his life! He needed to know! He had to have the answer to this one question before he died. The blood was spilling from his mouth as he tried and tried to speak, but, finally, he got out the words.

"What are you doing! Why… ah… why do you do that?"

I bend closer, to be sure that he hears. "You sought to hurt innocents in your quest to kill me and complete your mission… and I… have a serious problem with that. So… I have taken your warrior spirit, and now… when you enter the next world… you'll do so… as a nobody. You… my Chinese friend, should've played by my rules."

The terror on his face is evident and as I watch, the light in his being becomes dimmer and dimmer until it's only an ember then… it goes out, his head lolling to the side. I spit then. Yech! Honor is one thing. You do what you have to do. But nobody ever said that it had to taste good. So much for all that training on blood-born pathogens, huh? I scoop up some slushy water, suck it in and rinse out my mouth before spitting it on the ground. I probably should be more concerned about the blood, but honestly, as I look at the dead Chinese, I'm just happy that it's not my blood, soaking into this wet ground. I am resting on my left knee and slowly allow myself to roll into a sitting position on my left side, disregarding the wetness and pain that shoots through my body. I finish the cigarette and strip the butt as my aches and pains become more noticeable again.

Oh, well. I look up at the heavens. At least the sleet has stopped and the sky is showing a few stars. I reach over to a puddle and scoop up a hand full of slushy water and begin scrubbing my face. The cold water stings the stitches in my finger. I repeat the process until I'm pretty sure I've washed the blood off both sides of my face. Then I force myself to stand and look around. I hadn't seen any cars as I'd made my way up to my ambush position, and even now the road outside the scenic turn-around is barren. I'd better get moving.

I bend down and grab the dead man's arm, pulling him around. Then I drag him to the back of the car, my leg and side rewarding me with pangs of woe. I'd seen the keys hanging from the ignition when I'd first crept up to the vehicle. Now I go to the driver's door, open it and pull out the keys. Back at the trunk, I take another survey of the area. Still nothing. Nobody is moving out here tonight.

I key the lock and pop the trunk, my hand quickly covering and unscrewing the light. Then, with my side complaining, I heft the body up and drop it into the cavity. This guy wasn't too bad. Maybe 140 to 150 pounds, but when you've got sore ribs, one or two ounces seems heavy, ya know? I ease the lid closed until it clicks. Then I pull the penlight from my pocket and go back over to where he'd fallen. I snap it on and can only see trace remnants of blood on the wet ground. Most of it has soaked into the soggy soil. A couple of handfuls of slushy water dissipate what little blood is there. Then I pick up the night scope and move back to the car.

I look around until I find both brass shell casings. Pocketing them, I let my eyes wander over the site one last time before getting in and starting the engine. Keeping the lights off, I drive out onto the road, using the emergency brake to slow and stop when necessary. I've got to head south about a mile and a half to an old driveway that peels off. The road is slippery from the slush, and driving without lights makes it all the more delightful. I have to move as fast as I can, though, so I'm tensely peering out the windshield. The drive I'm headed to leads to an old derelict farm, long abandoned. That's where I'd left the patrol Jeep. I'm just about there when I see headlights coming over the rise ahead.

I slam my foot down on the gas! I can't be seen now! Not when I'm this close to making it! I come up on the drive and jam my left foot on the emergency brake while cranking the wheel hard left and pushing the accelerator to the floor! The tires slide on the slush and ice! The big Buick fishtails onto the drive and I almost lose it into a ditch before catching it and making it to the cover of two big old blue spruce trees. The big car comes to sliding stop as I release and reapply the brake hard, bumping the shifter into neutral!

I quickly twist around in the seat, my side screaming "DON'T DO THAT! and look out the back window. I can see the headlights of the approaching car. Then, the dark blue of a state police cruiser with its gold shield on the door, illuminated by the available light, glides past the drive entrance, none the wiser. I watch it as continues on. Then I turn back around and look ahead at the rear of my Jeep, parked behind the run-down farmhouse. I've got another dead body that I have to transfer from it to the trunk of this car. And that somebitch has got to weigh close to 200 lbs. My eyes burn from the night's activities and I put both quivering hands on the wheel, and then lower my head onto them. Shit man! Will the fun never cease?

A half hour later, I back the Le Sabre into a space at the Greyhound station in Escanaba. I get out and walk back to the rear. The streetlight is illuminating well and I can see that there's a smear of dark color on the bumper. Taking some slush, I swipe at it until it's gone. I look up at the sign above the space that says "Seven Day Parking Only". The station is closed, but I limp up to the window anyway and cup my hands to the glass. I can see the schedule on the board behind the desk. A bus for St. Igneous leaves at six am tomorrow. Okay. Good. Then I start heading toward the Boathouse. I'm walking while trying hard not to drag my right leg too much. With my left hand cradling my right side and with the limp and all, I figure I probably look a lot like Chester from Gunsmoke. I gotta say, I could sure do with a visit to the Long Branch Saloon right about now. A shot of whisky wouldn't do me any harm at all.

A short while later, I make it across the boardwalk to the Boathouse front door. I do not come across another human soul. The town is deserted. I pull the Glock from the holster and ease the door open. After making a sweep of all the rooms and finding nothing, I set about cleaning up the mess from Mr. Kung Fu. As I work, I try hard not to let Nettie enter my thoughts. I have to get through this part of my ordeal first. Then I'll deal with the next. I finish scrubbing the blood and vomit off the floor with bleach, and dump the dirty scrub water down the toilet. The tarp that I'd wrapped the body in was new and I idly wonder if the tribe had paid for it, or if it belonged to the Marina. Nettie is a constant interloper into my mind as I work. After I drop the dirty rags into the clothes hamper, I grab a beer from the ice box and ease myself down onto the couch.

I'm tired, I'm dirty, I'm hurt and I'm a monster, or so my girl thinks. The only thing I'm not, is dead. And heck man, if I don't get back to the woods where I belong, that little oversight will surely come to pass, too. This ain't the old days. I don't have a team backing me up anymore. I think, at least, that I got the opposing team's leader tonight. That doesn't mean that's it's over though. There could be more of them. My eyes wander to the door leading to the boat dock. I should've paid attention to the shinkakee. It told me that something was wrong in that room. Nettie's face looms into my memory. The expression she had on it when I came to with the dead guy on me was one of such worry. Yet, once she knew I was alright, that expression changed to one of fear and apprehension.

She just couldn't believe that I'd killed that man. She just couldn't believe that I killed him in cold blood. That wasn't the case but it's what she thinks she saw. The stark realization on her face sends a dagger into my heart as I recall it. Well, shit, man. I knew that this was going to be the rough water with her. I just never thought she'd have to witness it, is all. Nothing I can do about it, now. I roll the watch up on my wrist. She should be pulling into Wittikan in another hour or so. I'd put her on a bus before making the rendezvous with my new Chinese friend, now residing in a car trunk, over in the bus lot. I'd told her how dangerous it was for her to be here. I'd told her that the dead man was a foreign spy. I'd explained about the Air Force and their involvement, National Security and everything I could relate to her. But it didn't matter. I could tell by the look on her face, that it just didn't matter. As far as she was concerned, I was some kind of a monster. And what... pray tell... could I do about that?

Ya know, I'm sitting here, with every bone in my body aching. I'm physically exhausted. I'm cut, shot, bruised and have broken bones and yet, all of it together, as bad as it is, doesn't hurt half as much as the look I saw on her face tonight. Whoever said that sticks and stones could break bones but names could never hurt you... lied. Sticks and stones break bones but a name... can shatter your heart. I finish the beer then make my way into the bathroom. I lay the Glock on the sink, peel the wet Tiger Stripes off and pile them in the corner. Then I take a gander at all my pretty owies.

The bullet wound in my thigh that had been healing so nicely, was ripped wide open with that first kick. It's a nasty looking thing now, with a deep gash split down the leg. I've got to get some stitches in it. No choice. I look up at my ribcage and it's not pretty either. The deep blue bruising and busted red capillaries make it look like a giant purple velvet pincushion with tiny red polk-a-dots. Agh, for crying out loud! It's just too damn cool being me. I mean who else gets to have this much fun, huh? Crap! I turn on the shower and climb in to feel the heat taking the edge off. I sure wish I could wash the look on Nettie's face from my mind. But I know I'll never do that. As I lather up and rinse away the dirt and crusted blood, I have the sinking feeling that it's over between us... before it ever got started. Yep. Sticks and stones break bones but names... can shatter your heart.

Chapter Twenty-Three
I Could Use A Change Of Mind

St. Francis Hospital, Escanaba, MI.
The Emergency Room, The Same Night.

I limp through the emergency room doors and make my way up to the desk. The lobby and waiting room appear empty. The little brunette nurse, I don't remember her name, watches me as I approach. She's wearing a concerned look as I smile at her.

"Hi, there. I… think I'm gonna need some more stitches."

She hustles right around and takes my arm. "You just lean on me, Sugar. Come on now, we'll go right down this hall here, eh?"

Once we're in the room and she's guided me to the table, she goes over and picks up the phone and pages Dr. Bonner to examination room two. Then she comes back over and asks where I'm hurt. I'd looked at the table when I limped in and decided that I wasn't in any hurry to climb up on it. I smile at her as I rest against the table and touch my right side once.

"Well, you can take your pick actually. I've got some sore ribs and a bad gash in my right leg."

She nods and places her hand gently over my ribcage before stepping back. "Okay, Sugar, why don't you take the shirt and pants off and the doctor'll be right in, eh? I have to get back to the desk but I'll come and check on ya in a minute or two."

I nod and she exit's the room. I've stiffened up some and I'm still pulling off the woodland camouflage BDU pants when the doc comes in.

"Back so soon? I thought it'd be a week at least before we saw you again."

I smile as I take off the t-shirt. "Yeah, well I was jealous with you having all the nurses here and all."

He laughs easily as he glances at the clipboard he's holding and speaks without looking up at me. "So, it appears that we've got some sore ribs, huh? And you've got a problem with the thigh, too. Well why don't you pull the shirt off and we'll take a look at that first." He says the last as he brings his eyes up from the board. I see the surprise in them as he takes in my bruised side. Then he steps over and gently probes with his hand. "We're gonna need some x-rays of that. How did this happen?" he asks as he examines me, mumbling, "sorry" when I wince.

"Would you believe that I fell off a ladder?" I say with a snicker in an effort at believability. He doesn't respond. Next, he peels my make-do bandage off the thigh and looks up at me. I've got a feeling that he's not buying what I'm selling.

"No. No, I wouldn't believe that."

I bump my head. "Well, what can I say, Doc, that's what's in my report."

He traces his hand around my side again. "Hmm. Funny, but I can see and feel the distinct impression in this bruise of a human foot." He brings his questioning eyes back to me. "Did you land on another person's foot when you fell off this alleged ladder?"

I let my face go deadpan. "Nope. I just fell off the ladder onto a piece of wire cable and that's what happened."

I get another "Hmmm" from him on that one. He goes back to the wound on my leg and eases the piece of flesh that has been ripped downward back to its original location. When he does that, the outline of the old bullet gouge is clearly visible.

"Funny. But when I worked at the ER in Chicago, I saw a lot of bullet wounds. You know, gang warfare and shootings of all kinds." He straightens up and brings his stare to my eyes. "If I didn't know better, I'd swear that this was one, too. A grazing bullet wound, older and that was beginning to heal before it was re-injured. I've seen a lot of them and this looks just like they did."

I keep my face non-committal. "Huh. Imagine that. And I got this from that wire cable."

We look at each other for a beat, with no words spoken. Then he drops his eyes as the nurse comes back into the room. I hear the intake of her breath as she gets a look at my side. I'm a little too put-out to even be embarrassed about standing there in my underwear. She gets a grip quickly and looks to Bonner. He talks as he writes on the clipboard.

"Okay. We'll suture this gash up on the leg first then we'll send him down to x-ray for pictures of the side. Who's covering the desk?"

The little nurse brushes hair from her face and replies, "Wanda."

The Doc nods. "Okay," he looks back to me. "I'm going to need you on the table and laying on your left side so I can work on the leg." I nod and heft myself on the table with a grunt as he turns to the nurse, who is already picking up a tray with instruments on it.

"Would you please go to the desk and tell Wanda that I need this guy's history from the file?"

She nods dutifully and is out the door in a second. He looks back to me as I watch his face. "I don't know what's going on here. But I'm telling you right now... I don't like this shit. Not at all."

I give my most determined stare. "Trust me on this Doc, I fell off a ladder and that's all you need to know about it. No crime has been committed here. No citizen has been hurt, except me. And I just acquired some minor injuries. Okay?"

He stares at me, the indecision on his face paramount. "Bullshit! I don't consider a bullet wound or kicked-in ribs to be minor injuries, Officer."

We look at each other some more and finally, I see the decision roll over his face. "Since you're a cop, I'll let it ride for now, but I still don't like it." The chesty little brunette nurse arrives back in the room and he drops the subject. I'm breathing easier, in the figurative sense anyway, as the two of them begin working on me.

An hour and a half later, I limp out to the Charger and fold myself behind the wheel. The bandage around my torso is hurtfully tight and the new stitches in my leg are painful, too. It turns out that I have three very badly bruised ribs, just shy the Doc says, of actual fractures. In addition to the forty-five stiches in my thigh, the sore ribs make a really nice package. I feel my face roll up into a smirk. Yeah, you bet! But just the same, I know where God's grace is. With Thanksgiving coming up, I am indeed grateful. If I hadn't ducked a little when my martial arts friend kicked me, I no doubt would've been much worse off, maybe dead.

I start the old Dodge and let it warm up as I sit behind the wheel and shiver. It's cold out here, and the little pain pills the Doc gave me are still residing in my pocket. That's where they stay, too. Nettie. A shaky sigh escapes from me as I think of her. At least Nettie had arrived back in Wiitikan safely. I'd called her as she was getting off the bus. Her voice had been tense and short. Morse was coming to pick her up, and she said... that she would be fine. But I doubted it. I knew I wasn't going to be. The heat-gauge needle arrives at warm, and I tool out of the lot and nose the car back toward the boathouse.

I open the door and enter, following the same routine as before, sweeping each room with weapon drawn. The boathouse is clear so I head back out the door. I come back in and slowly sink down on the couch, feeling little jabs of pain as I breath. The chest bandage is going to be a painful thing for awhile. I twist my wrist and look at the watch. 04:30. I have to be at the bus station in an hour to catch the bus for St. Igneous. I plan on riding it to just about where the old farm is located and then telling the driver that I want off. Then I'll walk over and get the patrol Jeep. It should work. I need sleep, but know that I can't allow that, yet. I'll never wake up on time if I drift off.

So instead, I play the scene with Nettie over and over again in my mind. I'm trying to find different ways to explain it to her, to solve this wedge that's come between us, but an hour later I still haven't found a way to do that. Maybe, I think, that's because there just isn't any way. Maybe there never could've been. I force myself up and move over, dragging a chair to the shelves. It takes some concerted and painful effort, but I finally get up and assure myself that the new tape in the recorder as I'd left it earlier. Then I get down and slowly put on the jacket before hobbling out the door and over to the bus station.

An hour later, I pull the Jeep back into its parking space next to Nettie's car and again, go through my sweeping ritual in the boathouse. All clear. I'm not worried about waking myself up this time. The Air Force seems to be pretty good at that. I snap off the lights and unbutton the shirt, pulling it from my pants. That eases the strain on my taped torso somewhat. Then I lie down on the couch, pistol in-hand, drawing a cover over myself and close my eyes. In the darkness of my eyelids, I see Nettie's face again and the horror on it as she steps into the back room. I'm trying to shut the image from my mind when exhaustion takes over and solves the problem for me. I'm immediately in deep sleep.

I'm awakened by banging on the door, again. I blink painfully sore eyes at my watch. It's reading 08:45. Well, the Air Force is early. I set the Glock beside me and rub my fists into my eye sockets then ease myself up while raising my voice. "I'll be right there!"
I limp over to the chair and drag it once again over to the shelves, climb up and push the button on the machine, seeing the record light come on and the wheels begin turning. Then I get down, drag the chair back and place the pistol in the desk drawer before teetering over to open the door. Too late, I realize that I hadn't buttoned my shirt back up. The door swings open to the four men standing there. Shit!

Kourn, Shears, Mussenberg and the lawyer are all there and shortly after making eye contact with me, their sight drops to my open shirt and the big bandage around my chest. They all funnel in and I shut the door. Kourn points at my chest.

"So, what's happened ta ya now, Officer?" He turns his hand to Shears while still shooting me a serious look. "Did ole Al here convince ya ta start shaving yer chest hair, or what? I mean… you do seem ta have a problem a cut'n yerself, don't'cha?"

I give him a crooked smile. "No, General, of course not. I would never shave my chest. I tried using that Nair stuff and well…," I look down, then back. "I guess I just rubbed a little too hard is all."

He nods but does not return my smile. His face is granite. The
lawyer moves over to the phone and looks at me while pointing to the
telephone. I nod a yes and he picks it up and begins dialing. The room
is quiet as the three Air Force officers stare at me while I button and
tuck in my shirt. The lawyer begins talking on the phone and Kourn
nods his head at me in a low voice.

"Anything you want ta tell me?"

I put on my best bewildered expression and drop my eyes to the
floor. Then I raise them and slowly shake my head with raised
eyebrows. "No. No General, nothing as of right this moment anyway."
I shrug my shoulders and look to the lawyer.

The tall man follows my look then, switches back to me with a
nod. He folds his arms and drops his head, looking at me from over his
glasses, all stern and commanding, as only a General or admiral
can do. "So, yer a telling me that there's nothing new that effects our
little arrangement own that island then? Is that right?"

I nod whimsically. "Yes, sir. That's what I'm telling you. There's
nothing new that effects our arrangement." I maintain eye contact until
the lawyer hangs up and draws both of our attention by saying that the
fax should be coming any moment now. I head over and begin making
coffee as the fax begins growling. The Air Force officers' eyes have
followed my pained movements but the lawyer is digging in his
briefcase. I turn and look at the group.

"Anybody want coffee?"

The lawyer is back at the fax machine as the first paper begins
feeding out. "None for me, thank you. I've had my share this
morning." He's all wrapped up in the business at hand and either
hasn't noticed the tension in the room or doesn't care. I let my eyes
go to the other men. Kourn nods, his countenance still severe.
"Yeah, reckon I could drink a cup." Mussenberg nods, too. Shears
gives a slight shake of his head in the negative.

I get the coffee on and look fleetingly at the refrigerator behind the
officers. Too far to go. I limp back beside the desk, pick up the pack and
draw one of the Marlboros out and flip the Zippo to its end. I almost get
pleasure from the disgusted expression on Krinshaw's face as I blow out
a blue cloud. I would've preferred a hand-rolled but they're in the little
icebox on the other side of the room. And that looks a billion miles away
right now. My leg has stiffened considerably and I'd just as soon not
walk any more than I have to or display any more of the extent of my
injuries. The lawyer makes a satisfied noise then gathers up the papers
by the fax and moves around to the desk and seats
himself. He shuffles the paperwork then looks up at Kourn.

"Very well. We can begin with you first, General." Kourn walks over and the lawyer goes through the language and explains all of the legal mumbo jumbo and Kourn signs. Then he holds up the pen to me.

"If you'll just sign here, on all three of these forms next to your name please."

Kourn looks at me for a second, then begins signing the papers. The lawyer has me sign where indicated then takes his notary crimp and presses it to all of the papers before signing over the stamp. He puts copies in a large envelope and passes them to Kourn, who in turn passes them to Mussenberg, who puts them in a military-issue, aluminum, locking case. Then the lawyer is up and stuffing the remaining documents in his case while telling me that our business is complete for the day. He guarantees that the forms will be sent back to the Tribe and that everything will be filed correctly. He shakes hands all around and is out the door in less than five seconds flat.

This time, I don't see him out. I amble back over to the coffee pot, trying hard to keep the stiffness less noticeable and the pain from showing on my face. I grab some cups from the cabinet and take down the jar of dry creamer and a small bag of sugar. I fill three cups and look at the men. "What do you take in it, General?"

His look is deadpan as he rocks on his heels. "Black'll be fine." I look to Mussenberg who smiles.

"Me too. Just like my women." I smile back at him and nod. Then I set the cigarette down and take the cups before limping over to them. The officers take the coffee and I move back and add creamer to mine, stirring it before looking at my company. I take a sip and look at Kourn.

"I assume that you want ta know what I know, huh General?"

Kourn nods his head. "Yeahsir, I do. That lawyer's gone now and I've just been a standing here... a waiting for the other shoe ta drop. So, if ya got something ta say, then git it out boy."

I turn and take a last drag on the smoke before crushing it out and then look back at them. "Okay, but you won't mind if I sit down first will ya." Taking my coffee, I move over to the desk and ease down in the chair freshly vacated by the lawyer. The other men move in front of me and Kourn sits down on the couch, pushing my blanket out of the way. I clear my throat and begin.

"Okay, I think your Chinese agents are already here, and..."

Shears cuts me off with a low muffled "Shit!"

Kourn shoots him a hard glance, quieting him, then returns his look to me, his eyes menacing. I pick up where I left off. "Anyway, I'm sure one of them is Chinese and I think that the other four might be." I shrug my shoulders. "I just don't know."

Kourn angles his head at me. "What do you mean you don't

know?"

"I can't say. I mean, they look white but have really strange eyes, especially when they're hurt. That's abo…"

"Hurt! Is that how ya got banged up? You been into it with these agents?" Kourn is angry now, sitting forward on the couch, his coffee spilling over the cup. "You better have a damn good reason for not telling me about this before er I guarantee you that I'll see yer ass in Leavenworth! We're talking about national security here!"

I have my hand up in a stopping motion now, my own hair getting raised. "Look! I didn't know that one of them was Chinese until last night… okay? Before that, all I had was a suspicion. I only knew that somebody… was trying to kill me. And the guys I kept running up against… looked pretty white to me. So spare me the anger, General. I told you I wouldn't do anything to jeopardize the nation or… your mission and I haven't."

Kourn's eyes are blazing. Finally, he sits back and takes a deep breath. "I think I'll be the judge of that… not you. Now go own. Finish it. I wan'na hear the rest of it." He motions with his hand like I'm a little kid.

Oh well, I'll indulge him for awhile. He's got a right to be pissed, I guess. "Okay. I'll nutshell it for you. You've got two dead ones out on the island, two in the trunk of a Buick at the Greyhound bus station here in town and one in a morgue someplace up north. Now, out of all of them, only one had Oriental features. That's one of the guys in the car trunk. I met him last night and from what I saw of him, he was probably the team leader here. The others all looked white, but were very professional."

Mussenberg mumbles something while looking at me. What did he say? CHEE? What the hell was that? I take a breath and look at Mussenberg whose eyes are large with the story. I see him swallow before he speaks. "So, you're saying that you… killed all of these men? Five of them?"

Oh, crap. I've got to keep old man Veeter out of this, too, but shit, even if he did get one, I'd bagged the rest. Nope. I guess I am a monster after all. I twist my head around, but know that I can't dodge the answer.

"Yeah, I guess you can say that. But I can assure ya, they had the same idea in mind for me when we met."

Shears has been silently bubbling and boiling off to the side. His voice is hot with annoyance and anger when he speaks. "Just what gives you the right to take national security matters into you own hands, Stone?" He snaps out an index finger at me. "Wasn't it you who pointed out the fact that you're not in the military anymore? Well then why in the hell are you trying to do our job and fucking it up for us in the process! We didn't need these men dead! We needed them alive, asshole!"

I get up then, the pain I'd been feeling strangely gone as heat begins flowing through my body and start my around the desk. Kourn is up too and moving between us. "Okay! Okay! That's enough now!" He's looking from Shears to me and finally settles on which one by lifting his hand my direction. "Did they get the package? That's all that's important here!"

I don't take my eyes off Shears as I respond. "No. They were still mounting their operation as of last night, and like I said," I turn back to Kourn, accepting the intervention for now, "the guy I took out last night said enough for me to conclude that he was probably the team leader and that they still wanted what was on the island. That was present tense, not past. So, I don't think they got the documents, General. That's my opinion anyway. I also think that their team is finished as an operation, but shit... who knows?"

Mussenberg nods at me. "If these other guys looked white, then why would you think that they're Chinese?"

I hunch my shoulders up. "I don't know. Weird stuff. Their eyes, for one thing. One of them was cut up pretty bad in the face and I'd swear that he'd had some kind of previous facial surgery. The others looked funny around the eyes too and their English was somehow... too precise. One of them, at least, was very proficient in martial arts. Oh, and the two that are out on the island have never been circumcised, either."

Shears again. "Sonafabitch, Stone! What are you, some kind of fucking necrophiliac faggot or what?"

I feel my eyes slanting and going hard as I look over at him. "Hell, no, Shears. If I were in your club, you'd've seen me at your monthly meetings. So I wouldn't get too hot, bothered and jealous! Those boys are still laying out there if you want some!"

That gets him. And I enjoy that. The sneer on his face fades into an angry mug, but he doesn't move. I know that the exhaustion and the wounds that are driving my anger and impatience, but I still can't control the urge to fight now. Come'on, Shears! Take the bait! What's the matter! Let's go tough boy! I can feel my fists balling up, so I give him my last effort at a challenge.

"Of course, Major, if you're really that upset over the whole thing then maybe you should just kick my ass!" Still nothing but rage in his eyes. No movement my way. Fine, cocksucker! Mohamed won't come ta the mountain, then the fuck'n mountain will go ta him! I'm moving and talking as I go.

"Or, maybe... I should just rip your head off and pull your spine out through the fucking hole, you little cockbreathed cunt!" I've started to move toward him but Kourn and Mussenberg are positioning between us. Okay, I think, fine! I stop my motion and look around them at Shears.

His eyes have widened as he looks at me from across the room. Then they change and flick away, all the fight apparently gone out of him. Too bad! Mussenberg has started talking to Kourn during this lull and I turn away from Shears, who has dropped his eyes to the floor.

"They've got to be the CHEE agents General. It all fits!" Kourn is nodding. "You could be right. We'll know more when we examine the bodies."

I flip my hand up and into their conversation. "What's a CHEE agent?

Mussenberg looks at Kourn who nods and then turns back to me.

"Chinese Naval Intelligence Agents, code named "CHEE". These guys have had their bodies surgically altered to look Caucasian." He tilts his head. "No easy task for an Oriental. They take pills to change their skin pigmentation and are schooled in the customs and speech of the country they specialize in. We've only just learned of their existence and I'm betting that's what we have here."

Hmm. Well, as I live and breathe. I glance at Shears, who's appearing quiet now. I look back at Mussenberg. "For what it's worth, if these guys really exist... then I think you're probably right."

Kourn sighs and backs up, sitting down again on the couch. "Well, let's get own with the story. Tell us the rest."

I just look at him. "What rest? There is no rest." I fling up my hands. "What I've told you is all there is. I can give you a detailed summary, but that's about it."

Kourn removes his glasses and pinches his nose with a long hand. "Now ya know, Mr. Stone, I don't believe that. You've lied to us and swindled us own this land swap," he moves his hand away and the steely eyes bore into me, "and now... I won't ta hear the truth and I mean the whole truth."

I make my way back behind the desk and sit down, glancing over to Shears who has moved over to look out the window, obviously disassociating himself from the conversation now. Keeping my hands low, I glide the drawer open and see the Glock from the corner of my eye. It's within easy enough reach. I shift my attention to the General.

"Well, ya know, sir, that's just too damn bad. Sometimes, I don't get all that I want, either. Now, as to me lying to you, that's bullshit! I haven't. I told you, I didn't have a firm handle on who these guys were for sure, until last night. I have a fair number of people in my past that might want to kill me, and I really thought that was what was going on with these boys. Period! I might'a had suspicions, but that was all they were... suspicions."

Kourn leans forward. "And just how do you reconcile that with being disloyal to yer country? I mean, since you suspected something about these people being foreign agents?"

I throw my arms up. "What're ya talking about? I told ya before General, my country is the sovereign Pukaskwa Nation. And I've been loyal to them. Now part of that being loyal is looking out for their best interest." I take a breath and look to Mussenberg, who's listening too.

"If I would've told you that maybe... just maybe, I thought I might have foreign agents sniffing around me and the island, you would've snapped it up and shut it down and just accepted the bad publicity because of it. But my people would've gotten hurt badly over that. And it would've all been over my suspicions. And like I said, General, I don't work for you... I work for them. Now I told you, I wouldn't do anything to jeopardize your mission or the USA and I haven't."

Kourn looks at me for a long few minutes. Finally, he stands. "Okay, then. You'll be coming back with us to Virginia for debriefing." He motions around the room. "You may wanna get some things together."

I shake my head. "I ain't going anywhere with you General. Not down the block, not steady and not to Virginia. I'm heading back home after we wrap it up here. I'm resigning my position with the Tribe. So if you want a play by play of the last month, then you better sit yourself back down and I'll give it to you. But it's my turn for guarantees now." I wink at him. "If we get into a tussling match over you trying to take me back to anywhere... there'll be blood spilled... I promise."

I hold up my left hand to stop him before he gets started. "Hey, I'm aware that some of it will be mine... but not all of it. Besides, a dead man is hard to debrief, General. It kind of defeats the purpose of the debriefing, don't'cha think? Now you should consider that before we go down this road because I give you my word of honor, I meant what I just said." I twist my left hand in an "oh, well" manner.

"After today, I'm done and on my way back to the woods where I belong." I raise my eyebrows and wait to see what's going to happen, my right hand resting on the open drawer holding the black pistol. Kourn takes all that in and shakes his head, his eyebrows arched.

"Do you know who you're a talking to, boy?"

"Yep. I think I do."

"Hmm, hmmm. Well, yer either a very dumb man or... I reckon yer a serious one."

I tilt my head. "I'm not all that bright, General, but I am definitely a no-nonsense kind of a guy."

He looks at me from over his coffee cup as he finishes it. He motions over toward the pot. "Can I have some more a this?"

I nod. "Help yourself."

Kourn motions to Musssenberg and speaks from across the room as the Captain pulls a tape recorder out of the metal case and places it on the desk, pushing the rewind button. "Okay then. We'll just record this little talk for future reference. Reckon you better start jawing then, Mr. Stone, soon as Pete gets that contraption set up."

I look up as Shears steps out the door and disappears. I look back to Mussenberg and he hikes his shoulders. "You know when you said that thing about ripping off his head and pulling his spine out of the hole?"

I nod and Mussenberg makes a face as he explains. "Yeah, well I guess some guy from your old team said that same thing to him once during the Gulf War. Whoever the guy was, he was serious and I think it spooked Al pretty good." He shrugs again. "I wouldn't worry about it."

I laugh. "Oh, buddy, I wouldn't worry about me worrying about Major Shears. That's not a likelihood."

The tape stops and Mussenberg punches record, recites the date, time and location, his name and my name. Then he tells me to begin. So I do, beginning with my arrival in Escanaba. I leave out some things that I figure are none of their business, like Veeter, Martians and flying saucers. I don't mention Nettie or her involvement last night, either. Other than that, they get the whole story. Forty minutes and a lot of stops and starts to explain certain things later, I'm done.

Kourn has been sitting quietly on the couch, listening and occasionally interjecting a question during the interview. Now he stands and stretches, as Mussenberg rewinds the tape and puts the machine back in the case. I look over at Kourn while pointing at the silver case.

"So, tell me, General, is that gonna suffice, or do I have to be looking out for a snatch and grab on my ass?" He waits a beat and then nods at me from across the way.

"I reckon that'll do fer now, but," he points a finger at me, "you better be tell'n the truth and not leaving anything out. I mean it, Mr.!" His eyes go dead hard. "Ya understand me?"

I return the same look. "I think I do." My turn to point a finger and I do so fleetingly. "Something else for you to think about, General." I jerk my head. "If you've checked up on me, then you should probably know that I've covered my bases on this situation. I'll take you at your word that we're through here. So, you should take me at mine, that... we'd better be."

I was telling him that to try anything with me now, or later, would undoubtedly come back to bite him in the ass. And, as I look at him, I see that he gets my meaning.

"Fair enough." He nods solemnly as his hands go back into his pants pockets.

I stand and reach into my own pocket and pull out the keys to the Buick, parked over in the Greyhound lot. I toss them onto the desk and nod at them. "Those're the keys to a gold Buick Le Sabre that's parked over at the Greyhound Station. Your clean-up people will need them."

Kourn clucks his tongue and shakes his head. "Oh yeah, I nearly fergot." He turns to Mussenberg. "Pete, you wanna go tell Al ta get own the horn in the car and dispatch a cleaning crew to this location ASAP?" The Captain is nodding and moving toward the door already as Kourn finishes speaking. As Musenberg goes outside, Kourn turns back to me.

"Ya know, I'd fergot about that part of this thing. According ta our little arrangement, you got us a cleaning up yer little mess, don't'cha?" He slips his glasses back on and continues. "Now maybe ya should tell me again why I shouldn't be a feeling like I got flim-flammed own this deal?"

I hunch my shoulders at him. "Hey, that was the agreement, General. We didn't ask anybody to steal sensitive documents and leave them on our island, or... to have the Chinese come looking for them. These guys and this whole situation, haven't been a Pukaskwa problem. It has been and still is... an Air Force problem." I wink at him. "Just be thankful we're not charging you for taking care of some of your little details for you."

Kourn grunts and cocks an eye at me. "Hmm. To a degree, I reckon that's true, ain't it." He begins moving toward the door and swipes up the Buick keys off the desk in the process. He comes to a halt near the door and turns back to face me.

"Ya know, Mr. Stone, I could use a man like you," he sways out his hand, "should ya ever get a hanker'n ta get back in the game again?"

I've moved around the desk to lean against it as Mussenberg steps back inside and walks over to pick up the aluminum case. My hand has moved up to my side in response to the ache. I'm wincing as I shake my head. "Nope. I don't think so, General, but thanks anyway. I've had about all the games I can stand for awhile."

Kourn's looking at me, and I'd swear that it's with genuine concern. He points to my chest. "What's the sitrep own yer injuries?"

I tip my head sideways a bit. "A couple of bruised ribs, a bullet wound in my thigh and," I hold up my hand and wiggle my newly rebandaged finger," a few stitches here and there." I twist my head. "I won't be dancing the ballet for awhile but I'll live, I guess."

Kourn watches me and clucks his tongue again before shaking his head and smiling. "You are an unusual man, Mr. Stone. I reckon that name they gave you... what was it?" He lowers his head and then snaps it up, "Ghost? Well I reckon that fits... don't it?"

I raise my eyebrows, but don't answer. Kourn waits a beat then straightens. "You take care, heah!" Then, he walks out the door. Mussenberg holds the door slightly ajar and clears his throat before looking up to me.

"You know, if these were CHEE agents... well, what we have on them says that they're the best the Chinese have these days."

I nod. "They were good. I can vouch for that. I guess I was just lucky. But I was under the Great Good Spirit's protection, too." I hunch up my shoulders at him.

He smiles and then nods his head and raises his eyebrows. "No, I don't think so. At least, I don't buy the luck. I think the old man's right... you know... about you being a ghost." He's still holding the smile as he passes through the door and it closes behind him.

Uh, huh. Right. You bet. I push myself off the desk and grunt with the painful effort. Then I hobble back around and sit down gently before touching the computer mouse. As soon as I click on the internet, an icon pops up and it says, "I've got mail". I open it up and it's from Gangues.

Ghost,
Just to advise, those bastards have burned my Dragonslayer program! They fried it like it was nothing and almost got to me in the process. I don't know what this Air Force General and his unit are about, but they've got some serious juice! They apparently have some damn fine hackers working on their end, if you know what I mean? But I'm better. Bet your ass, I am! I'm going to have to approach it from a different direction at this point, but I will crack this thing! More as I get it,
Gangues

I e-mail him back, telling him he can back off, but I already know that he won't. I feel a smile tugging at my mouth as I type in the words anyway. Old Mark is a dedicated kind of a guy and once challenged with a computer problem, he can't let it go. He becomes obsessed and absorbed by it. He'll keep at now, no matter what, even if it's only on his own accord. I send the mail and then open a blank document. On it, I write my resignation as a Tribal Special Agent for the Pukaskwa. I copy it electronically, paste it to another e-mail and send it to Hennessey back at Wiitican, telling him that the island deal is done and that I am just not suited for the job. I tell him that I'm leaving the original resignation on the desk here at the boathouse.

Then I click print and sign the finished paper when it feeds out of the machine. After that, I limp over to the little refrigerator and take out enough hand-rolled cigarettes to fill my box and toss the remainder of the bag on the table to be packed up later. I then ease on my jacket, get another cup of coffee and begin hobbling out to the back deck to say my prayers, each and every step a new adventure in pain.

When I come back in, there're several lights blinking on the answering machine, but I know who the calls are probably from so I ignore them. I set about packing my gear, and in a short while have it all loaded into the Charger. I munch on cold pizza as I take one last look around the boathouse. Then I amble out to the idling Charger and slowly climb in to the heated warmth. I drive past the post office in town and after dropping the cassette tape in the mail, I'm cabin-bound and happy to be going home. The only thing that hurts more than the wounds I have on my body, is the fact that Nettie…isn't with me now and… is never likely to be.

The Stone Family Cabin,
Yellow Dog Point, Near Lake Superior,
Two days later.

I open the door of the old woodstove and stuff in another chunk of log, jabbing it around in the coals to catch it alight. The flames jump up and lick around the piece of maple greedily as I wedge in a few more pieces. After adjusting the damper, I limp back over and sit down on the couch. I'm smoking and nursing a bottle of Honey Brown beer, as the afternoon sun twinkles across the frosted windows. The beer is good. I'd stopped to pick up some Hamm's but the little store didn't have any. The gal behind the counter recommended this stuff and I'm glad that I tried it. An action at the window draws my attention and I look over to see snowflakes wafting down outside. I let my eyes go back to the bouncing flames of the wood stove. A few minutes later, I'm not surprised when I hear the sound of an engine grumbling up the drive outside. I'd expected someone to come and visit after I'd resigned. I work myself back off of the couch again and move over to the window. An old rusty-white '78 Ford pick-up pulls up to park alongside the Charger.

My car's parked next to the porch and so the truck pulls beside it, blocking my view of its driver. But I recognize the vehicle. It belongs to Amos Reddeer and I watch as, surprisingly, he gets himself out of the passenger side. I can't see who's driving, but it doesn't matter, anyway. I move over and open the door for my guest. He is the picture of an old-time Indian as the falling white flakes float downward. He ambles through the foot and a half deep snow, and up to the porch. He's wearing an old red plaid wool coat, faded blue jeans and lace-up mukluks. A brown, broad-brimmed hat, with a turkey feather poked from the band covers his silvery hair as it flows from his head like smoke from a cooking fire. He looks up at me, his wrinkled face smiling and his wizened eyes bright with alertness. "Booshoo, Raining Wolf!"

I return his smile. Booshoo. Pukaskwa for hello. I'm finding that I remember a lot of words and phrases that my mother taught me when I was younger.

"Hi Amos. What brings you out a wintry day like this?"

He steps up on the porch and keeps his smile while angling his head. "Oh, I think you know why I am here, eh?" He says that while squeezing my hand in a shake patting me on the shoulder with the other.

I nod at him. "Yeah, reckon I do." I step sideways and motion with my hand. He walks past and I follow him inside, turning to look back at his truck. "Uh, do you think your driver would like to come in?"

He flings his hand out like he's throwing away rotten meat and bends to unlace his boots. "Nawww! That is one stubborn Indian out there, eh?"

I nod then and close the door. I briefly argue with him about keeping his boots on but he pays no attention and removes them anyway. I point to a chair as he removes his jacket. Then I move over to the icebox. "Have a seat, Amos. You want a beer?"

He takes off his hat and flings the snow from it, while emitting a Yooper sigh. "Ehhhh, schee. That sounds good, eh."

I take another beer from the icebox, twist off the cap and hand it to him. I have to hold my side as I ease myself back down on the couch, and he sees that. He points with the bottle.

"So, is that where you got hurt then?"

I force a smile. "Well, it's one of the places." I pick up the bottle from the floor beside me and take a swallow before asking him. "So, I assume that you've talked to Annette then, I mean, if you know about me being injured, huh?"

His head gives barely a nod. "Yes, she told me you were hurt, eh. But she will not say more." His eyebrows move up quizzically. "Are you going to tell me of these things, Raining Wolf?"

I slowly shake my head. "No, sir. It's not that big of a deal. Really, it's not." I flick a hand in his direction. "I suppose you're also here about my resignation?"

He laughs then, a gentle old rumble. "Yes. That is one reason why I have come. John Hennessey is beside himself with worry about your resignation. He thinks that we can not go on without you now." Amos cocks his head at me, the mirth still evident. "He believes that you are what I have said you are… our Pathfinder."

My turn to laugh, but all I can manage is a chuckle. "Well, I ain't no pathfinder, Amos. I told you that before. I'm just a guy that did the best he could with the situation and circumstances." I look at him steadily. "The Air Force would've just taken the island for national security purposes if we hadn't found a compromise. So, all I did was waggle a deal where we got some other land in exchange for turning over the island to them for a year. That's it. No pathfinding. Just wheeling and dealing, is all."

Amos takes a long pull on the beer and looks at the bottle appreciatively when he takes it from his mouth. Then he shakes his head slowly at me. "No, you are wrong about that, my young friend. We have no business on this island when evil and other-world spirits are in residence, eh?" He points at me with his free hand. "And you are the one responsible for keeping the People from this danger. That… is what a pathfinder does. You need to either eliminate the "myanit maskiki" or keep us away from "Wazhashk Minis, eh?"

"Myanit maskiki." That means bad medicine. And "Wazhashk Minis" are the Pukaskwa words for Muskrat Island. I swing my head sharply and lean forward, a little too quickly, and pain reverberates through my side. I can't hide the look of pain that I know appears over my face as I bend forward.

"Amos, look. I probably shouldn't, but I'm going to tell you what they're after on the island." I look at the aged face across from me and believe that there's no other way here. "The objects that the Air Force are looking for on that island are not evil… they are some top secret documents, just papers, Amos. Important papers, yeah," I fling out a hand, "And dangerous… maybe… but evil?… I don't think so."

He sits back and looks at me curiously, his eyes now clouding in self-thought. "Papers?" he mumbles, "This couldn't be it, eh?"

I nod again. "That's what they said, Amos. Secret documents that are vital to our national defense."

He has his hand to his chin, stroking it gently as he looks at the fire, burning behind the glass door in the stove. After a bit, he shakes his head and turns back to me, looking intently into my eyes.

"That cannot be it, Raining Wolf. Papers cannot be the spiritual evil that lives out there, eh. You did not hear, did you? You listened, but... you did not hear?"

I'm confused and turn my head from side to side before looking back to his face. "Listen? Listen to what? Hear what?"

His countenance grows stolid. "The se se kwa."

I'm lost. "The what?"

"The se se kwa, Raining Wolf." He has a hand resting on his knee and he rolls it outward to me. "The se se kwa, the murmurings of the trees. I know they spoke to you, because I heard them doing so."

I feel my head drop downward as memories invade my mind. I snap my eyes back up to him. He can't possibly be talking about that stupid song, can he? Ghost Riders in the Sky? No, don't be ridiculous. There's no way he could know about that! But he's slowly nodding his head while looking at me. Now the shinkakee invades my being as I feel goose bumps rise along my arms and neck. I can do nothing but look at him. After a few seconds, reality takes hold, or the 'reality' I'm more comfortable with, anyway. I shake off the goose bumps and clear my throat.

"Well, anyway... you don't have to worry about it for at least a year. It's the Air Force's problem now, right?"

He looks at me steadily for awhile before solemnly nodding his head in the affirmative. "That is so. For now, at least." He sits back and eyes me speculatively. "I did not realize how close to the truth John Hennessey was until this very moment. He is right. We can not go on without you any longer, eh?" He twists an old hand on his knee. "Oh, he was speaking mostly of monetary issues, but without knowing all, he still spoke the truth, eh? We can not go any further without you, can we?"

Any further? Further where? Sometimes this guy's mumbo jumbo makes no sense at all. I emit another chuckle. "Well, even if that is true Amos, and I assure you, it isn't, you're still gonna have to find another boy. I'm all done trying to fit back into a world where I don't belong anymore."

He's nodding at me while pushing air with his hand. "Yes, yes I know. I told John Hennessey this. A warrior needs time to heal after a battle, both physically and spiritually. I have told him of these things, but he still fears that you will quit, eh?" He stands and drains the beer bottle in two big gulps and then smiles favorably at the bottle. "This is good beer, eh?"

I look at him from the couch. "Yeah, I like it. There's more in the icebox, help yourself." I scratch my head and try to think of a way to convey what I feel.

"Uh, look Amos, healing really doesn't have anything to do with my decision to resign from the job. I just can't do it anymore. Can you at least try to understand?"

He's nodding his head again and moving toward the kitchen. He opens the icebox and takes a bottle out, looking at me from there, and holding the brown bottle up. I nod and he takes out another one before closing the door and coming back into the living room. He hands a bottle to me and then sends his eyes questioningly around the room.

"Where is the bottle opener, Raining Wolf?"

I smile and say, "You don't need one. Watch." I screw off the cap as he watches with an amazed look. Then he unscrews his own, smiles broadly and takes a drink. For a guy who likes beer and especially a Yupper, it seems strange that he doesn't know how to open a screw-cap bottle.

"What kind of beer do you drink at home, Amos?"

He moves back over and sits down again. "Oh, I don't drink beer at home. The white doctor told me ten years ago that I can not have beer." He cocks an eye at me. "They say it is bad for my heart." He groans a bit and adjusts himself in the chair. "I didn't pay attention to them, but then Annette found out about it and made me promise to never drink beer at home again. So I don't." He turns to me with a mischievous smile. "But I didn't promise to not drink it when I visit someone though, eh?"

I smile in kind. I figure that if he's not allergic to it, then a beer every now and then probably isn't going to be too bad. I wink at him. "Your secret's safe with me." He holds the bottle up in a toast and I return the gesture before taking another swallow. This time when he looks over at me, he is serious again.

"I told John Hennessey that you only need some time to yourself, eh? He is happy to place you on half pay and by doing this," he gestures in a wide circle, "you still keep your job and have this time for healing and... what is the most important of all things... the People still have you as their Pathfinder."

My head is shaking even before I can tell it to. "No, Amos. I can't do this, anymore. I just can't."

The wrinkled man looks at me from across the warm room while holding up his hands in a "what's the big deal" manner. "What can this hurt, Raining Wolf? You have time to heal and who knows, maybe you will look at this differently when the healing has come. If you don't, you could always quit then, eh? If the Tribe has the money to keep white lawyers on what are they call," he twists up his face as he searches for the word, "… retainers, then we can surely keep our Pathfinder on such a thing, eh?"

I'm holding my side, pushing myself forward while voicing my negatives, telling him that I'm not a pathfinder, saying that I can't be out in the world anymore, but he continues on as if I'm not talking at all. Finally, his words stop me when I hear the sincerity in his voice.

"We need you, Ely-Raining Wolf. Your People need you. Please… just allow us to do this while you heal, and wait to see what happens afterwards, eh?"

I sit back, totally defeated. As I look at the old man across from me, I know it's a lost cause for now. The wizened old face is openly genuine. That face belongs to my Uncle's lifelong best friend. That face secretly loved my mother from afar, and that face is imploring me to do this simple thing. Okay…fine.

After what seems a long time, I nod and say, "Alright, Amos. Ya'all wanna keep me on the payroll after I've resigned, then go ahead." I cock my eye at him. "But as far as I'm concerned, the resignation stands. I'm not doing anything else for the Band unless I personally see the need for it. Fair enough?"

The old man smiles, then the smile turns to a huge grin as he sits back and relaxes. "That is good, eh? That is very good." He takes gulp of beer and fixes me with another look. Then he leans on his side while reaching into his pocket. He pulls out a small leather bag and leans forward handing it out to me. I get up and take the bag. It's newly- formed, but empty. It is stitched from a piece of deer hide. There are markings on it of dyed quillwork, three rows across the bottom, and they're beautiful. The little pouch is pulled shut with slender strings of rawhide. As I hold it up, it slowly twirls from the rawhide strings and my eyes go to the old shaman as he points to the bag.

"That's for your maskiki piwaka."

I feel my eyebrows rise and the drums begin to beat deep down Inside my soul. An uneasiness grips me like I haven't felt in ages. "Maskiki" is the Pukaskwa word for medicine. Everyone has their own personal medicine of some kind, if they care to anyway. And it's called a "piwaka". A pesik piwaka, to be precise. The word "pesik" mean's "one's own" or personal. The two words are usually shortened because everybody knows that it only pertains to one's personal medicine. It's just called a piwaka.

Some folks don't bother with piwakas at all. Others will keep theirs in a bag or box or wear it around their neck. Because of the jobs I've always held, I've carried mine mostly in my head. But when the two words are joined together, it's a whole different thing. To the Pukaskwa Indians, a "maskiki piwaka" is only used by a very spiritual person, like a shaman. What the white folks call a medicine man. Like Amos Reddeer, the old man sitting across from me. If you're not a shaman, then you have no business being near a maskiki piwaka, period. The power it contains is dangerous and deadly if used by the wrong person. Since I'm not a shaman, what can he be implying. The fear is thick and it pervades my being. The only other type of person that I know of who carries a maskiki piwaka is... I feel my eyes growing huge as I look across at the old medicine man and draw the only plausible conclusion.

I begin breathing in quick snippets, almost hyperventilating because I know that this only other person... would be a shape-shifter! An "Ig-qwir-ha-kazi"!... a witch! Holy shit! He thinks!!... my breath catches as I try to form the words and get them through my lips! After what feels like a thousand years, I finally stutter them out.

"Amos... I'm not a...I'm not a... a witch!!..."

He looks at me with surprise and sits back, his face showing confusion before he speaks. "No, of course not, eh?" His eyes turn thoughtful for a second, then he smiles, gently. "Ahhheee, I see." he lightly slaps his leg and chuckles softly while I stare at him bug-eyed from across the room. He lowers his head and slowly shakes it, as an understanding smile spreads over his wizened features.

"No, Raining Wolf. No, I know that you are not a witch, eh?" He brings those omniscient old black eyes back up to me, the smile still twitching at his mouth. "There is another spiritual person who is neither shaman nor witch, Ely." He's looking at my mystified face as talks with his hands, his palms turning this way and that.

"They, like me... have only "mino maskiki", eh? Only good medicine." The smile wanders around his face as he speaks and his mind seems to go back in time. "There have never been many of them and they are a combination of both warrior and spiritual leader. They are chosen by the Great Good Spirit to guide and protect the people in troubled times." His old eyes find me again and turn deep with seriousness.

"They are called the "Um-oya Ind-le-la Um-kho-keli." He turns hand and says the shortened version. "Ind-le-la Um-kho-keli. It is what you are, eh? A "way leader" and spiritual warrior. The one who protects the People by showing them the right path. This... is what a pathfinder is."

I'm still looking at him and can feel some of the fear subsiding. I change my focus to the small leather bag that I'm now holding up like a dead rat by its tail. I turn my eyes back to him as he speaks again. "You're time is coming, Raining Wolf. I know, for I have seen this, eh? We have made that for you because it is the other part of what you will need in this coming struggle. There is much more to it than this, but, for now, just know that you must fill it with things that are dear to you." He moves his head in speech as I take a darting glance at this voodoo-like bag that I still have ahold of.

"These things must have spiritual meaning and worth to only you. These must be things that you place a high value on, Raining Wolf, things that represent what you would fight and die for, eh? A warrior's pledges, eh? But most important of all," he turns his head for emphasis and rests both hands on his knees,

"You must put in it, that which represents the People to you. Our band of people. You must think of this one thing and put it in the piwaka. Then you must tell the Great Good Spirit that you will protect the People. Make a promise, eh? You must do these things, if the piwaka is to help you in this new fight."

He points a finger at the bag that I've now brought down to my lap. "That is simply the medicine pouch of a pathfinder. A "maskiki makak." Only a medicine container." He juts his jaw to stress the point. "But it is still sacred, eh? It belongs to you, our People's Ind-lela Um-kho-keli." Our Pathfinder."

I'm looking at him with a face that I know contains astonishment. Well slap me silly and stomp me into the ground! I let my eyes drop to look at the little leather sack. So that's what it is, huh. I didn't know that there were spiritual people other than shamans and witches. Great! I've learned something new today! At least he's not saying I'm a bear-walker, that's something, anyway. But what's this fight he's talking about? And why the hell is he so bent on me being this pathfinder? As I wade through this stuff, the old man's hand comes up in a pointing gesture at me.

"Up to this point Raining Wolf, you have fought only the warrior's battle and the Great Good Spirit has protected you. But from now on, you will be dealing with the spiritual battle as well. I have seen this! And now that you have arrived as a pathfinder, the evil ones will wage hard battle for your soul, eh, because you will carry the fate of the People with you." His old head wags again, the gray-streaked hair swinging to and fro.

"This will be spiritual warfare… other-world spirits. And the battle will not always be of the physical kind, eh? You must have more than quick reflexes and cunning to do battle here, Raining Wolf. You must have spiritual power as well, if you are to show the People the "way" out of this trouble. Do you see this?"

A million thoughts race into my mind in response. Do I see? Yeah, I have a view. I'm looking at him and trying to rationalize all of this. Down deep, I can feel a yearning in regard to all of these new things. But, the fear of unknown territory is also present. I think I'd like to buy into all that he's saying, but I just can't. As I arrive at this conclusion, I wonder just how far this old Indian expects me to go with the folklore. I can see that he's sincere, but, man... me? Well I'm just not a believer in this theological leadership stuff. I've seen too many adulterous preachers, pedophilic Catholic priests, abortion loving Jewish rabbis and murderous Muslim clerics to buy into anybody else's spiritual guidance, anymore. And I sure don't think I'm the guy to be showing anybody the right road either, ya know?

I mean sure, I know that there's a right way and a wrong way and hardly any other way. I see most of life that way. I always have. It may not be politically correct, but that's the way it is. I know God exists and I humbly pray to him everyday. And I know that spirits are here, too, both good and bad. I try to stay away from the bad ones and help the good ones to assist my fellow man. I think that's what's expected of me. But all of this pathfinder stuff... no, I'm not a cleric and I know that I don't want to be one, either.

I hand the bag back to him. "I don't think I can take this, Amos. I'm sorry, but I'm not a pathfinder. I'm just an ordinary man, not any kind of spiritual leader, boy scout guide or even a wedding usher, okay?"

No sooner do the words leave my lips than I get a feeling, down deep inside, that I may be reading this all wrong. I may be misunderstanding all of this. This old shaman is different and I know it! Amos takes my hand and folds my fingers up over the bag. Then he frowns up at me while tilting his head.

"Don't you want to know what all of the strange noises in your head mean... why they've always been there?"

The look of surprise must be too evident on my face, as I once again stare bug-eyed at him. It's a second before I regain composure and go back to sit down. He's smiling at me from across the room.

"Oh, I know that you have heard them." He angles his head and laughs quietly before looking down at the floor as he goes on. "Actually, you have heard these spirits most of your life, but you have not known their meanings, eh?" The eyes come back up to me. "They have often helped you when you were in battle or in trouble, but maybe... you just can't see that yet, eh? Well my young friend, like it or not, you will soon see that you have been chosen for this, Raining Wolf. You will now begin to "hear" and "understand" the noises that come inside your head." His finger jabs in its effort now.

"This is a truth that can not be changed, eh? That piwaka will be your most vital weapon and it will provide good medicine, if you use it, eh? The Great Good Spirit will guide you and help you in your journey, but you must fill the piwaka with your own personal medicine and that which you have a sacred duty to protect, eh… Your People…the Pukaskwa." He angles his head again in question form. "Can you understand this?"

I exhale a deep moan and look over at what I've come to accept as my oldest friend. He's touched a nerve about the noises that go on inside my head and he knows it. But how… did he know about them? That's a question I've pondered a lot. How does he know stuff like this? Somehow, this guy gets into my head… or maybe he really doesn't get in…maybe I just put him there myself. But still, he comes up with things like the noises in my head? Maaaaan, this stuff goes way beyond me. I might as well be sitting here drinking a beer and shooting the shit with Rod Serling. The Twilight Zone again, for real! I look at him and decide that just in case, I'll give him his due.

"Jeeze, Amos, I haven't understood anything about anything, ever. And it's only gotten worse since I walked into the tribal chambers for that job interview!"

His black eyes survey me from across the room, and finally, he smiles. A gentle smile, an easy smile. He squints his eyes and barely nods his head at me. "You will. You will begin to understand, eh? But it is a life-long journey, my young friend. It has taken me a lifetime and I am still learning, eh? When the time is right, you must fill the piwaka with your cherished things and the one thing that equals the Pukaskwa People to you. Then you keep it with you always until the battle is over, eh? We have already asked the Great Good Spirit to bless it for you. This had to be done before you enter battle with the other-world, eh?" His eyes turn serious.

"You must do this, Ely, before you confront this evil, or the Great Good Spirit will not protect you. He has chosen you and if you push this choice away… then you will be on your own. Remember, a warrior alone, battling the evil spirits without the Creator's help… will surely die." He slowly shakes his head and then looks down at the floor. Suddenly, the black old eyes shoot up to me again. "If this happens, then the People will die as well."

My eyes drop down to the little leather bag. Confront evil again? What the hell's that mean? And what's this other-world he keeps talking about? I don't plan on confronting anything! My turn to nod. I do so while asking a question, but my voice comes out hoarsely.

"Other-world? Spirits?" I ask with raised eyebrows.

He tilts his head and looks away for a second then back to me. "Yes. I do not know what exactly, but they are from the other-world. This much I have been told, eh?"

We hold each other's eyes after he says that. I'd like to just find a hole someplace to crawl into and die. I look over at the stove. I have no idea what's transpiring here between me and this old man but I know that's it's something. I just can't help but think that this whole thing is nuts. But somehow, someway, as my eyes come back and lock with the old shaman's again, I know down deep inside that he's right. I don't know how or why, but I think… ah crap! I don't know what to think. And… well, I don't know what to say, either… so I say nothing. I just nod my head. Over in the chair, he leans back again and exhales heavily, as if he's just taken a five hundred pound bear off his chest.

"Good. Now, for the next thing." He turns sideways in the chair and faces me more directly. Then he speaks. "Annette will not tell me of the problem between the two of you. But I know that your spirits have been bound together by the Creator. This is a truth that all of the three of us know."

His black eyes turn sincere. "The two of you must fix this problem between you, Raining Wolf. The Great Good Spirit expects this."

I nod and ease myself up off the couch, hand to my aching ribs, just glad to be out of the conversation about spooky things that I have no control over. Not that this new topic is much better.

"Yeah, well that one's out'ta my hands, Amos. Nettie saw something in me that she didn't like and," I look over at him, "I don't blame her a bit for not liking it. But I am who and what I am. I can't change that, no matter how much I want to." I point to the bathroom. "I've got to hit the head. I'll be right back." I say the last as I make my way to the bathroom.

When I come back into the living room, Amos is looking at pictures on the mantel. He jabs his thumb over his shoulder. "Annette is out in the truck. Why don't you go out and talk with her, eh?"

"Nettie's here!" I start quickly toward the door, my side crying out with the sudden effort. I stop myself short, and stand staring at the door in front of me. It takes me a second but I finally get the words out. "She doesn't want to see me… does she Amos?"

He answers from behind me. "Well… that is what she says but I do not think that is what she means, Ely."

I squeeze my eyes shut and force down the hurt that drives upward from deep inside. I slowly turn around and Amos is looking at me. I make a connection with his dark eyes. "No. I don't think so. She's a girl who knows her own mind, Amos."

His eyebrows and shoulders arch upwards and his voice is low and gravely. "Maybe she knows her mind, but… she has not met her heart yet… eh?" He motions his head toward the door. "Go and talk with her. Don't be stubborn like I was, eh?"

I smile then. "You're talking about my mother, aren't ya?"

A slow smile cracks around his mouth. "Yeah, maybe I am, eh? In any case, she's sitting out in that truck," he points his finger, "being just as bullheaded out there as you are in here."

I finally figure out that he's right. What can I lose that I haven't already lost? After a second, I grab my jacket, slip it on and pull on my boots, wincing at both the physical and emotional pain behind the efforts. I snap a glance at Amos who motions me out. Then I open the door and I'm wading through the snow around the Charger. I can see her as I approach. She's got her head resting against the window and her eyes are closed. I come to a stop by the door and stand looking at her. Her dark hair is folded angelically around her face and shoulders. My Lord, but she's beautiful. How did I ever think I stood a chance with her? After a heartbeat, I raise my knuckles and tap gently on the glass. Her almond eyes flutter open and then grow large as she realizes it's me.

She smiles tentatively as she cranks the window down. "Hello, Ely."

"Hi, Nettie. How are you?"

She continues to smile, but it's strained. "Oh, I'm fine." Her eyes turn serious and drop to my side. "How are you doing? How are your side and your leg?"

She asks with genuine concern and for a fleeting moment, I think that maybe… I nod. "Tolerable. They're sore, but I guess that's to be expected. Uh, listen," I motion toward the cabin, "would you like to come in, maybe have some coffee, hot chocolate, a beer or something?"

Her smile fades and she looks away before turning the light brown eyes back to me. "No, I don't think so, Ely, but thank you. I just came because Amos shouldn't be driving in weather like this."

I clear my throat, which has all but closed up. "Yeah. That's good of you, Nettie."

Her eyes drop to the floor of the old truck, her long lashes batting quickly. Her voice is meek. "So I understand that you're resigning from your job with the Tribe?"

I look at her, the pain in my chest welling up and dwarfing any minor distress caused by my cracked ribs. "I turned in my resignation."

She brings her face back up to mine. "I hope this isn't because of me, Ely. I…I…uh, well, Amos and John both want you to stay."

I keep her eyes and jut my chin out at her. "What about you, Nettie? Do you want me to stay?"

Her eyes fill with water then and she looks away. "Of course I want you to stay, Ely. I don't want to be the one to drive you off." She brings her eyes back to me then, wet with tears. "I... I...have feelings for you but I... just need some time...time to sort it all out. I mean, you frightened me, Ely. I just don't know what I'm doing anymore... I jus..." She breaks up then and turns away from me, her shoulders shuddering with her crying. This hurts more then anything, this seeing her cry. I swing away and plow through the snow back up to the house. Amos has helped himself to another beer and has his backside to the stove when I close the door.

He nods at me. "So, how'd it go, eh?"

I peel off the jacket and pull off the boots while throwing my head backwards, toward the door behind me, the fury of my inadequacy consuming all. "You better get her home, Amos. She's out there crying and I... shit! I'm sorry. I don't think I said anything, but she's scared of me now and ..." I let the rest of it fade off. Then I truck over and swipe the bottle of Jack Daniels off the mantel and unscrew the cap. I take a healthy pull off the bottle and offer it to the old shaman. He shakes his head as he pulls on his boots and coat. Then he stands erect and looks at me closely, that crackly old voice sounding thousands of years old in the wooded cabin.

"Getting drunk will not help, but you know that, eh?" He sends his old hand up to rub the bottom of his chin while he eyes me from across the room.

"You know, a woman's heart is much softer than that of a man. And a man's heart is often softer than that of a warrior's. But Winter Otter is as the Great Good Spirit made her. She is a woman and she will eventually see that you... are as the Great Good Spirit made you also, a man and a warrior. She is for you, Raining Wolf, and you... are for her. The only thing that can change this... is the two of you." He takes a deep breath and sets his face solidly at me. "Do not give up on her, eh?"

He smiles then and waves as he turns and opens the door. "Thanks for the beer, young Ely, and we'll see ya later, eh?" He places a firm hand on my shoulder and squeezes while looking into my burning eyes. "Bring me the piwaka when you know it's time, eh? And these love wounds," he winks, "they will heal like those of the body, eh? You trust me on that." Then the door closes and I'm alone.

I stand there stock-still, with the whisky firmly in my hand, even after I hear the old Ford start and see it back away through the windows. I look down at the bottle and know that the old man is right.

The Murmurings

Getting drunk won't change anything but my mental state. But shit man, right now… I could use a change of mind. I throw back the bottle and take a big hit as the snow begins falling peacefully outside.

|<<<|>::<|<<<|>::<|<<<|>::<| :+: |>::<|>>>|>::<|>>>|>::<|>>>|

PART TWO

Chapter Twenty-Four
"I've got the feeling that somethin' ain't right"

The Stone Cabin,
Yellow Dog Point, Near Lake Superior,
Six Weeks Later.

I sight down the barrel of the rifle as the rabbit hops from out of
the cover of the wild rose thicket and stands on its hind legs to look
around. A slight gust of wind blows against the turkey feather that's
tied to the forearm of the rifle, but the motion is both subtle and
natural and the rabbit doesn't notice. The brown fur of the cottontail
contrasts nicely against the whiteness. His dark coat stands out
starkly in the white blanket that surrounds him. His head is hidden by
the hanging branch of a jack pine. The snow is deep, now, and I've
spent the morning hunting rabbits.

My cold fingers are wrapped tightly around the .22 single-shot
Marlin, my uncle's old rabbit and squirrel gun. I wait out the animal
as I want a clean kill. The rodent drops back down and I snap off the
shot, seeing the rabbit plop over. I already have a couple of snowshoes
so three rabbits is enough for one day's hunting. I truck through the
deep whiteness, pick up the kill and quickly begin to field-dress it.
Thoughts meander around in my head as I work. I have made it
clear to Annette and everybody else in the Band, that for all practical
purposes, I am a non-participating member of the tribe. But that
doesn't seem to be getting through to Amos Reddeer or John
Hennessey. They both still consider me a bona fide employee
and genuine Pathfinder for the People. I am tired of arguing with them
over the title, and, jeeze man, as long as they leave me alone, what do
I care, anyway? There is one person, however, who would have been
more than happy to accept my resignation, even if his bosses wouldn't
and that was the honorable Captain Morse. The prick had called me
on the phone shortly after I'd returned to the cabin, and proceeded to
accuse me of being everything but human for hurting Nettie.

Obviously, I wasn't too happy with his tone or accusations, even if
I secretly agreed with him. The conversation ended with my invitation
to him to come up and kick my ass, or at least… give it his best shot.
He had just called me an asshole and slammed the phone down. I

missed him, but I was dealing with it. Sheeeeit! So much for my brief re-encounter with the outside world. I'm headed back to the cabin with bunnies draped across my shoulders when the familiar sound arrives. If you've ever been around one for any length of time, you never forget their particular noise. Like the military Jeep before it, the Hummer has its own distinctive sound. I have company coming and it is probably of the military persuasion. The sound makes me uneasy.

I'm not far from the cabin as I begin working back toward it, shinkakee lightly tapping my psyche. I thumb another .22 shell into the rifle as I move along, and check to make sure that the rest of the box is loose and in my jacket pocket. As I emerge from the thickets by the lakeshore, I catch the unique body lines of a woodland camouflaged Hummer passing through the trees along my driveway, headed toward the cabin. As I walk up from the lake, I watch the Hummer come rolling in to stop by the porch. I'm still walking as I see a black man in camouflaged BDUs exit the passenger side of the Hummer and move around to step up on the porch.

He hasn't seen me and neither has his driver, who was stepping out of the other side. She is a small girl, also in BDUs but wearing a sidearm over her field jacket and a blue beret. Security or Air Police. Air Force. The uniform makes her look like a small child. I look at the porch. Uh, huh. I'll bet a dollar that the man on the porch is Captain Peter Mussenberg. I continue on, making mental calculations and searching the ground for cover as I move ahead. Everything looks okay but I still, I thumb the safety off the rifle. One never knows… does one? I can see and hear Mussenberg knocking on the door as I approach. The little Airman is looking his way and doesn't see me until I speak. My voice startles her.

"I'd say come in but it'd be more logical to say "go in" instead."

The Airman is surprised but she doesn't take an offensive posture, So I rest easy as I walk ahead. Mussenberg has his hand up to knock again when he hears me. He steps over to the porch post as I traipse up, quietly easing the safety back on the .22. The rabbits bounce awkwardly off my shoulder as I reach the cleared snow of the drive. Mussenberg raises his hand and points with a smile. "Holy shit, Stone! You've gone native on me!"

He's referring to my hair, which I've let grow down to my shoulders. It was already long when I met him the first time. And now, I wear it parted in the middle and keep an inch-wide piece of deerhide around my head to hold it in place. Over the last weeks, I'd become more Indian than even I thought was possible, reverting to my roots, I guess. I'd noticed it in myself. Not only in the mirror, but in my everyday life. I nod up at him.

"So what's up, Captain? I thought I made it clear that I was out've the picture when you and I talked last?" I give him my best 'you better be leaving my ass alone' look and he seems to get the message and begins pushing air with his hands.

"Oh yeah, you did and that's fine. That's not why I'm here," he looks at me, but I must seem unconvinced. Good. That's what I am trying to convey. He's fanning the air with his hands now.

"No, really Stone! Our deal's fine and everything. It's just that I… I've come for something else."

I tip my head at him, keeping the little airman in my peripheral vision and my hand on the rifle's safety. "Uh, huh. Well, what brings you all the way up here to Injun country then?"

His face turns serious. I… needed to talk to you, and well," he rolls out a hand and smiles crookedly, "since you don't have or," he looks up wonderingly at the treetops, "can't get phone service up here, I figured I'd better come and see you." He puts both hands on his hips. "Actually, I needed to talk with you in person. You have any idea how hard it is to find your ass, Stone? We must've been up and down that road a hundred times before we finally stopped at a bar in Big Bay and they gave us some half-assed directions."

I step up on the porch, the motion being a practiced art when wearing snowshoes. I wink at him while pulling the rabbits off my shoulder. "Oh, I gotta phone. I just don't answer it because there's a 99.9% chance that I won't want at talk to the person whose calling."

Mussenberg shakes his head but continues the smile. "Well, why even pay the bill then, man?"

I hold up my finger to the air. "Because… I'm an optimist. As long as there's a tenth of a percent of a chance that somebody may call that I want to speak to… well you know, always leave that window of opportunity open. Right?" I look at him and he shakes his head grinning. I bend down and slip off the straps, and then rise up and kick the snowshoes off to the side. I open the door and motion with my hand.

"Com'on in and I'll give ya a cup of Indian coffee." I look over to the young girl. "You to, Airman. Come on in."

She smiles a "thanks anyway", then sets her jaw. "Thank you, sir, but I'll stay with the unit."

I look at Mussenberg who just shrugs. "Hey, what can I say? She signed the vehicle out, ya know? She's well trained." He points a finger at me. "Remember, she's in the Air Force, not the Coast Guard. She… takes her job seriously."

I nod. "Ahh, so that's what it is." I follow him in through the door, and then go past him and into the kitchen while telling him not to worry about his boots. I lay the rifle on the table and put the rabbits in a large pot of saltwater to soak. Then, I peel off my jacket and wash my hands. I tell Mussenberg to have a seat and he takes my advice. I put some coffee into the Bunn machine, and in a few minute, there's a pot of the hot brew. I take down three cups and pour the black liquid into them, stopping about two- thirds of the way full. I pour a tablespoon of honey into each cup then fill them the rest of the way with Jack Daniels before stirring each. I carry a cup into Mussenberg and after he takes it, I swing open the door and walk over to the Humvee. I hand her the cup and she moves up to take it as Mussenberg steps into the doorway.

"Mmm. What's in this, Stone? Whisky?"

I nod at him. "Yeah, whisky and honey. Just enough to take the edge off.

The Airman drops the hand that she has raised for the cup.

Mussenberg makes a favorable sound. "Hey, this is good man."

I look back at the girl in the oversize uniform. "Go ahead, Airman. The Captain doesn't mind." Her eyes dart to the officer before coming back to me. She slowly shakes her head in the negative.

"Ah, no thanks, sir. But, thank you, anyway." I look back at Mussenberg and he switches his eyes from me to her before getting my drift and motioning with his free hand.

"Yeah, it's okay Styles. Go ahead. Take it. It's good and it's cold out here. He's right, it'll take the edge off, too." He motions with his hand. "Take it and climb back in the Hummer where you can get some heat going."

The girl looks up at me and smiles. She takes the cup and demurely says "thanks." I return her smile and head back inside. We Coasties may not be well trained in vehicle protocol, but with us... everybody gets coffee... if anybody gets coffee - whiskey or no. I move back into the house and into the kitchen. I pick up my cup before wandering back into the living room. I look over at Mussenberg.

"So tell me Captain, does your dad know that you're here?"

Mussenberg is in the middle of a sip when I ask and I watch as his eyebrows go all quizzical for a second. "Dad?... Oh, you mean the General?" he asks with a half smile. "Yeah, he knows I'm here."

I return his grin and raise my eyebrows. "And your trusty sidekick, Major Shears?"

Mussenberg leans forward in the chair and nods his head. "Al's in the Middle East. He was put on another mission. It's pretty hot over there right now." He squints his face and looks to me. "That's about all I can say about that."

I have my hand up in a stopping motion. "I understand." I lean against the archway between the two rooms and address the other man. "So, tell me, Captain, what exactly did you think I might be able to help you with?"

Mussenberg eases back in the chair and eyes me. "We uh… well… we're not having any luck finding what we're looking for on the island and I just thought that maybe you might remember something. You know, seeing as how you had the interaction with these CHEE agents?"

It's my turn to be surprised. It's been almost two months and these guys haven't found that black bag, yet? Now that's a little strange. I know the military, and especially military investigator types. They should've found that bag within a day, easy. Mussenberg has his eyes locked on mine, as I try to keep the startled look off my face. I slowly shake my head and look around the room. I can barely hear the gentle rumble of a tune in the back of my mind. I can't make out the words, but I think I know the melody. Shit! I've got to keep this conversation moving for now. I look back at my visitor.

"I don't think so. At least, not that I can remember anyway." I turn my head slightly. "So those guys were Chinese, then?"

Mussenberg nods. "Oh yeah, CHEE agents, just like I told you they probably were." He rolls his eyes in an "I can't believe it" manner. "They had extensive plastic surgery, country of specialty saturation, extensive training… the works, man." He sets his gaze directly on me. "You cost the Chinese five really good agents, a bunch a money and at least one Chinese Navy Admiral, pal."

Goose bumps arise all over me as Ghost Riders in the Sky begins a slow-play in the recesses of my head. I'm mentally forcing the tune up into a corner of my mind as I try to hold the conversation together. But I can feel the shinkakee melting over me like a warm rain as I look at the man. I'm standing here in a state of astonishment and that damn song is getting louder. I clear my throat.

"Navy admiral? What's that about?"

Mussenberg angles his head. "He was their navy's chief of intelligence. He croaked himself shortly after you did-in all of his people over here." He sucks in his cheek. "The Chinese said that he died in a car accident but our intel says that he ate a 9mm round." The sucked-in cheek gives way to arched eyebrows. "That's usually the way things go over there when a major mission goes into the toilet. The brass in charge doesn't last long afterwards. They have to accept responsibility, and the Oriental way of acceptance is usually suicide." A grin breaks over his mouth. "Kind of makes you glad that you weren't in the Chinese Coast Guard, doesn't it?"

My head gives the hint of a nod. Wow. The shit that do go on. I've squashed most of the internal song noise and after another beat, I form my next question. "And the one guy, the one that had Oriental features? Was he the team leader then?"

Mussenberg crosses his legs and nods. "Yeah. That's what we figure. Name was Chin. He was a full commander in their Naval Intelligence branch. We have a file on him going all the back to Viet Nam. He was a nasty son of a bitch." He looks at me inquiringly.

"I've gotta tell you, man, these dudes were the best of the best that Old Mother China had to offer. And you…" he points a finger my way, "took them all out… all by yourself. To a lot of us, Stone, that's pretty unusual, ya know?"

I squint my eyes in disgust. "Yeah, well that ain't nuth'n. I also know my times tables, all way up ta ten." I twist my head angrily. "Shit! Those people almost killed me and I mean…killed-me-dead!" My hand goes up to touch my side before I even know it. "They damn sure hurt me bad enough. I was just lucky that the Great Good Spirit was covering me. Period!"

Mussenberg eyes me carefully and speaks quietly. "Okay. Good enough."

I push down the heat that's risen up inside me. Fellow-warrior-worship. I understand it and I respect it, but few men ever give the credit for survival and victory to the one who deserves it. And that's God! After a few beats, I take a breath and jut my chin toward the other man. "So your people haven't found the bag, huh? You guys've searched the lighthouse too, right?"

Mussenberg nods. "Yeah." He angles his eyes at me, trying I reckon, to see if I knew that the bag was in the coal chute. I see the resolution pass over his face as he decides that I probably already had that knowledge. "Yeah, well… we found the bag. But what we're after, wasn't there…" His shoulders give a little shrug. "We've been all over that damn island, and other than the dead bodies you left everywhere, and the shot up kitchen in the lighthouse, we haven't found zilch!" He scratches his jaw. "It's gotta be there though. I mean," he snaps his eyes to me again, "we know it's there… someplace."

My heart rate continues to slow as I look at him. Hmm. Now, isn't this a quandary? I remember seeing the papers in that bag, but I never looked at them closely. So, honestly, I don't know what they were. And the reason he's here is to poke around. I sense danger with this little visit 'cause I know the military mindset. If those papers weren't there, then right away, they're looking to see if maybe somebody else has them, namely… me. But if that's what's going on, then why did he say "it's got to still be there"? If I had them, then they'd be gone, right? It was probably just a slip of the tongue. What he probably means is… they know the papers were there but they aren't there, now. Okay. Time to put up some defenses here. I give him my best cold stare.

"I don't know what to tell you Captain. I never had those papers in my hands so… what more can I say?"

He's looking at me and searching my face. "No, and we don't think you have them either, okay? So just settle down, alright? I didn't mean any offence. And look," he stands and rolls out his hand, "my name's Pete, okay? I know we didn't get off on the best foot but I'm not here to jerk your chain or anything." He sways his head easily from side to side. "I'm just trying to complete my mission, that's all."

Uh, huh. Sure, pal. Whatever you say. I watch as the man shifts his weight from one foot to the other while trying to formulate what he's trying to say. Finally, he stands still and looks at me squarely.

"Look, can I call you Ely?"

I give it another beat while letting my eyes roam over his face. When I feel that he looks uncomfortable enough, I slightly tilt my head. "Sure. Why not."

That garners an uneasy smile. "Thanks. If you call me Pete, then we'll almost be friends." His look turns earnest. "What I said before… that's the straight skinny. No shit, okay? The General didn't send me up here, I asked if I could come and talk to you. He doesn't think you have what we're looking for and neither do I. But we're up against a wall here man and I just thought… that you might remember something," he bunches up his shoulders, "that's all. Square business. Okay?"

I continue looking at him, and after a minute I allow my head to nod. He seems sincere and shoot… who knows? "So, you got something specific to ask me then or was that it?"

He walks past and takes his cup in to place it in the sink. "No, not really. I was just hoping that you might've thought of something, that's all."

I walk into the room and pour myself some more coffee. I hold the pot out toward my guest and he shakes his head no, and then changes his mind and retrieves his cup. I pour and add the Jack and honey to both cups before stepping back outside and walking over to the Hummer. The Airman is already climbing out as I approach.

"If you'll give me your cup, Airman, I'll get you some more coffee."

She's holding the cup in her hands and looks down at it before back to me with a smile. "I'm all set, sir. I've still got half a cup. It is very good, though. Thank you."

I ask if she's sure and once she says she is, I wander back into the house. Mussenberg is still in kitchen, looking now at the old rifle on the table. He looks up when I enter. "Hey, what's with the feather?" I pick up my coffee and take a sip. "It's just a tradition. More for good luck than anything. That feather's probably fifty years old. The rifle, like this cabin," I make a sweeping motion with my arm, "was my uncle's."

Mussenberg fingers the feather. "Fifty years old, huh?" Then he looks around the room. "You like living way back here, don't you?" I step over to the sink and look out the window. "Yeah, I do." My eyes wander down to the lake and I see that one of the tip-ups has a flag up and waving. I'd placed two of them on the lake before going out after the rabbits this morning. I quickly finish the coffee and begin slipping into my coat as Mussenberg walks over and looks at me.

"What gives?" He turns his glance to the window, then back to me.

"I've got a fish on down there. I've got to check it out before the hole freezes over too much or else I might lose the fish." I gear up and head out. Mussenberg follows, grumbling behind through the deep snow on the path. But that changes when I finish hauling a three-foot pike onto the ice.

"Damn, man! That's a big fish! What kind is it?"

I look at him. Why would he be so... then I remember. He's from California. "It's a northern pike."

"Wow, man. That's cool. No shit. I've seen the guys in Escanaba out on the lake with these little wooden things with red flags on 'em but I didn't know what they were doing. What kind've fish did you say that was?"

"Northern pike." I unhook the fish and then reach into a billows pocket and pull out a nylon stringer. I thread the metal point through one of the pike's gills and out its mouth, hooking the end through a metal loop, effectively tying the fish to the stringer. Then I collapse the tip-up and walk across the lake to the other one I have set up over there. I check this one and find that the bait's been stripped off from the hook. I fold up the tip-up and trek back to where Mussenberg stands by the fish. I bend down and set the two tip-ups together, wrapping the vinyl strap over them and hooking the Velcro closure. Then I grab the stringer and both tip-ups and look at my new friend. "Well, you ready?"

Mussenberg nods in the affirmative and extends his hand. "Yeah. Here, let me carry something, the fish or those poles?"

I just smile at him. "Naw, that's alright. You better just concentrate on walking. That's hard enough to do in deep snow, if you're not used to it." I don't give him a chance to argue and start off. I hear him talking as he falls-in behind me.

"Pike, huh. I think my wife ordered walleye pike at the restaurant last night. Maaan, that girl loves fish."

That halts me. I turn back, and with my sudden stop he loses his balance and falls against the path of thigh-high snow. "You're married?"

He gives me a disgusted look. "Yeah. So?" he asks as he pushes himself up.

I turn back to the path and resume walking. "Just surprises me, is all. You don't wear a wedding ring."

"No. I can't get a ring on over my left knuckle. I broke it playing football in college and it developed a lot of scar tissue when it healed. If I get one big enough to go over the knuckle, then is it's too big for my finger. So, I just don't wear a ring."

I give a slight nod and then turn back and resume dragging the pike along toward the cabin. I hear him following again. That's funny. I don't remember him being married in the file that Gangues sent me. It would've said so, if he were. I turn my head and speak over my shoulder as we go along.

"How long?"

"What? Oh... not long. It's going on six months now."

Ah. That could explain it. Probably not enough time for the change is his status to've been entered into his record. I throw my voice over my shoulder again. "So, how's she like military life?"

He snickers. "She hates it. Can't stand the separation and all the rules. She's a graphic artist and has that thing about individuality, ya know? She wants me to resign my commission and get out."

I stop by the back porch and turn to him. "Are you considering doing that?"

He's catching his breath as he hikes up to me. "Well... no. I'm not going to get out've the Air Force." He wipes some sweat off his forehead and squints at me. "She knew what I did before we got married, and I explained how things would be, so... no, I'm not going to get out."

I unwind the stringer off my hand and look at the fat pike before bringing my eyes back to him. "Are you guys gonna to be able ta work it out then?"

He hikes his shoulders and looks around. "I don't know. She's here for a couple of days and then she'll head back home." He shakes his head. "She's staying with her folks in Ohio." He wrinkles his mouth in a "time will tell" attitude. "We'll talk some more before she leaves." His eyes resume their wandering of the area.

To paraphrase old Forrest Gump, 'Military is… as military does.' That's just the way it is in the service. I'd seen it a lot. I watch him for a second, and can't help but think that it's too bad. I've seen a lot of marriages fail due to the stress of military life, and well, it was always a shame. He steps up after me and begins brushing the snow from his legs as I set the tip-ups down and then heft the fish while opening the door. Mussenberg stops to look at the log with my knife stuck in it. He looks closely at the numerous "stick" marks in the wood before he switches his eyes from it back to me. A silent understanding passes between us. He'd no doubt been at the autopsies of the people out on the island. I open the door and move inside. I bump my head at the door. "Come'on, Mussenberg."

My visitor steps in after me as I lay the fish on top of two brown paper grocery bags on the floor. He closes the door and turns to me. "What's with this Mussenberg stuff? Can't you call me Pete?"

I rise up and pull out a hand-rolled. I light it and shift my eyes to his. He's trying hard to be my pal and yet, the shinkakee is bee-bopping all over me. "Yeah, reckon I can call ya Pete. As long as you don't think it means that we're going steady or anything."

He smiles. "Yeah, well you are cute, but like I said, I'm married, remember?" He smiles awkwardly. "And it's okay if I call you Ely then? Or," the smile weakens a bit, "would you prefer… Ghost?"

Nobody calls me Ghost. I won't answer to it, except from my team mates. And this guy… sure ain't one of them. "Ely, will be fine." I tilt my head at him. "I do hope that you and your wife can work things out. Are ya staying in Escanaba then, or what?"

He shifts his weight before answering. "Yeah. I rented a little apartment in town, but I spend most of my time on the island. We set up a staging area at the airport, and I chopper out of there, back and forth, to that miserable rock." He twists up his mouth and looks down. "I thought that I'd fix her dinner tonight, but maybe I'll just take her out again." He brings his eyes back to me. "The big thing between us right now is this mission. That's part of why I came to see you. If I can sew this one up, then I can head back home to Chanute." He rolls his shoulders in explanation. "That's where I was stationed when I got the call from the General to come up here."

I nod. Chanute Air Force Base in Illinois. But I thought I'd heard that they'd closed that one? I take a breath and cock an eye at him.

"Well, I'm sorry, buddy. The only thing I can think of is, to do a thorough search of the lighthouse and," I squint my eyes, trying to make the point, "that includes the whole lighthouse, from top to bottom."

He brings a hand up and rubs his chin. "Yeah, well like I said, we've done that but what we're looking for isn't there."

As I look at him, I hear another tune start-up in the recesses of my mind and my eyes drop to the floor. It's too low to hear the words yet, but it's playing and slowly getting more distinct. Huh? Now what's going on? Crap man, there's only so much room in my scull, for crying out loud! I bring my eyes back up and he looks at me squarely.

"You're sure, huh? You can't think of anything else?"

I raise my shoulders. "Nope." Then I take the rifle off the table and step into the living room and move quickly across the space to put the gun away. I'll clean it tonight, but this gives me the opportunity to unload the rifle while company can't see me doing it. I'm already working the bolt as I leave the kitchen. Mussenberg walks into the room as I close the door on the gun cabinet and pocket the .22 round.

"Well, okay then, I guess I better head back to Escanaba. It's another fun day of "seek and seek" on Muskrat Island tomorrow. I take a drag off the smoke and flick ashes into a tray on the table before addressing him again. "I wish I could be of more help." I arch my eyebrows at him as a disgruntling question passes through my mind. Why… is he here?

He nods and pulls the camouflage fatigue cap out of the shoulder epaulette of his field jacket and screws it down onto his head. He turns back to me as he moves toward the door.

"Yeah, I was just hoping, ya know? Well, anyway, if you think of anything, will you give me call?" He retrieves a business card from his field jacket pocket and hands it to me. "My cell number's on there and you can reach me anytime, day or night, by calling it, okay?" I take the card as the song is playing solidly in my head. While I can't put my finger on the name of the tune, it's very familiar. I watch as he rolls up his shoulders and then steps to the front porch. He speaks as he walks away.

"If I can find this thing, then maybe Pam and I can get our stuff together."

I follow him out and hear the gentle rumble of the humvee as it idles. The Airman at the wheel smiles and I return it. "Yeah, well like I said. I do hope you get it worked out."

He sighs and moves his head in understanding. Then he looks over to the patrol Jeep, parked next to my uncle's rusty Jeep CJ-7 that I plow the drive with. He points to the snow covered patrol Jeep.

"I thought you said that you were quitting the tribal job?" He turns to face me. "I called the Reservation in Wiitican, hoping to get your address. I told them that you used to be one of their employees. I was surprised when they said that you were still employed by them?" He says the last with arched eyebrows.

I hike my shoulders and lean against the porch post. The Airman's empty coffee cup is sitting on the deck by my foot. "Yeah, well for all practical purposes, I'm not employed. But this federal recognition is a brand new thing for them. They're still trying to get their act together and they wanted to keep me on, for paper purposes, I guess. They drove the Jeep up here and left it," I roll out my hand, "in case I need it, or so they said. It's been sitting there for two months now."

The officer steps down and looks back over his shoulder as he moves around the military vehicle "Are they paying you then?"

I finish the cigarette and begin field stripping the butt. "Well, there's some money being direct-deposited into my account so, yeah, I guess they are."

He pops open the passenger door and puts one foot inside the humvee while smiling up at me. "No shit! Well maybe I should get out and get myself a dick job with my own tribe, huh?"

I smile at him. "Sure, why not. But you'll probably have to go to South Africa. I think that's the only country giving anything to any of the native peoples from your neck of the woods."

He slants his head and looks thoughtful. "Yeah, you're probably right," he smiles, "and that sucks the big one, man, 'cause I don't want to move to Africa!" His smile fades and his face forms another thought. "Oh yeah, I almost forgot to ask. If we need more time," he twitches his mouth, "on the island I mean, then we'd have to talk to someone at the Reservation then, huh?"

I nod at him and give my best "you've been told" look. "Yeah, that's right. Probably Hennessey, but I don't know for sure. Maybe they have a lawyer now that's handling that kind of thing. But it won't be me," I sharpen my eyes at him, "and that's a fact."

Mussenberg has a smile back on his face and his hand is up in a "take it easy" motion. "Okay, okay. I was just asking."

As if my feeble little mind wasn't crowded enough already, another thought passes through it. I hold up a hand. "Hey, hold up a minute." Mussenberg stops and nods as I dash back into the cabin. I'm back to where he's standing pretty quickly. I hand him a freezer bag and he reaches to take it from me.

I point to the bag he now holds. "Those're northern pike fillets, just like the one we just caught down at the lake. There ain't any bones and if you stop by a grocery store and pick up a lemon & butter seasoning bag to cook them in, I'm sure your wife will like them."

He brings his eyes up from the fish and I have mine meet them.

"Do like you said, Pete. Fix your wife dinner and talk things out. The mission will wait awhile. Your marriage... may not."

He slowly takes that in and then nods with a smile, while climbing into the hummer. I look over at his driver. "Airman, would you care for some too? I've got plenty in the freezer."

She waves her hand. "Oh, no, thank you, sir. Neither my room mate nor I cook, so it would be wasted on us."

Mussenberg holds the fish up with a bright smile. "Hey, thanks, Ely, I'll give this a try tonight."

"Okay then. Ya'all take care." I step back before looking back at them. The Airman puts the hummer in gear and begins reversing the vehicle while I move back by the porch. Mussenberg waves as the humvee rolls past and I turn to go back inside. Then the new song playing in the depths of my head becomes clear. I stop and look at the camouflaged hummer driving through the snowy woods. The tune is an old "Stealer's Wheel" song and I whisper out the words effortlessly now. Then I say the words out loud, as I watch the military vehicle fade into the treeline.

"I don't know why I came here tonight. I've got the feeling that somethin' ain't right. Clowns to the left of me, jokers to the right... Here I am... stuck in the middle, yeah, stuck in the middle!"
Yeah, no shit, Sherlock. Something ain't right! The sound of the hummer is fading, before I move up the steps and into the cabin. Clowns, jokers... shit man, I cast one last look at the fleeting hummer. And here I am... stuck in the middle! Caaaarap! I shake my head to clear it, but it's no use. Oh well, I have a fish and rabbits to clean. Come to think of it, I've got mental cleaning to do, too. A tune about "ghost riders" and another one about "something not being right." Somehow... I've got to get that old mental victrola cleaned out, too, before I go crazy.

In the Hummer

Mussenberg lays the bag of frozen fish on the rear seat and opens his laptop computer as the truck winds down Stone's wooded drive. He checks several things on the machine, and then types furiously for an instant before finally closing the little contraption. The hummer rolls out to the main road and after looking both ways, Airman Styles pulls out and picks up speed. Captain Mussenberg looks over at his driver.

"So, what'd you think of our Indian friend, Styles?"

The Airman twists her head as she glances at the rearview mirror. "Seems like a nice enough guy, sir."

Mussenberg chuckles. "Oh yeah, he's a right nice fellow alright. But I don't think you wanna get him pissed at you." He turns to look out the window at the dense timber and brush along the road and the smile fades as he takes on a look of discomfort. "Actually, he is a nice guy."

Airman Styles clears her throat and keeps her eyes glued to the road ahead as she asks, "Uh, sir, I didn't know that you were married?"

The Captain grunts and shakes his head. "With good reason, Styles. I'm not married."

She takes a quick glance at him before returning her eyes to the road. "But I thought I heard him say…"

Mussenberg is nodding. "Yep. He thinks I'm married. In fact, I kind of used you as a model for my fictitious wife." He smiles. "I hope you don't mind?"

Mussenberg watches as her features grow more confused. "Look, Styles, in our business, that's called a little white lie. I think this guy has information that's vital to our mission on the island. If I'm right about that, he's being tight-lipped for some reason. I don't know what that reason is, so I explore different angles. A guy with wife problems may loosen him up. Do you see what I mean?"

Styles crinkles up her face, her confusion complete. "Not really sir."

Mussenberg sighs. "Okay, it's like this. You have to handle people in different ways sometimes. With this guy, my gut feeling is that he's kind of sentimental. So, I figured I'd give him a sob story about my wife and me having marital trouble, because of the mission, get it? So if he's holding anything and… if he thinks that I'm his friend… then maybe he'll break-down and pass that info on to me," he rolls out his hand, "in order to help me out, see?"

He shakes his head. "A guy like this, he'd die under torture before giving anything up so you've gotta explore different approaches. You have to be creative. Do you see how it works?"

Styles sets her face and continues to stare at the road. "Yes, sir. I think I do."

Mussenberg looks over at her. "Yeah. But you don't like it, do you Styles?"

She doesn't take her eyes from the road. She angles her head a bit as she responds. "It just seems dirty to me, Captain. I mean, if we have to lie to the man to get this information, then isn't it going to be tainted when we go to trial anyway?"

Mussenberg scratches his eyebrow and looks back out the window. Well, he asks himself, what else would she think? She's just part of the security detachment, not the recovery team. She's not a Detachment Four member, is she? Right. Her job is to secure the Air Force equipment at the base of operations at the Escanaba airport.

She's not involved in the search on the island, and thus, she doesn't have the "need to know" clearance. She, just like Stone, thinks that they're looking for papers from a black bag. Still, as an OSI officer, he can give her a little career guidance on the topic. He turns back to her.

"No, it wouldn't be tainted, Styles. This is a sensitive military operation, remember? Ordinarily, We function under the rules of the UCMJ, not the civilian courts, anyway. But when national security concerned, we get what we need and how we get it, is our business. You need to remember that if you're going to make a career out of the Air Force," he raises a finger for emphasis, "especially in the security branch."

Styles nods. "Yes, sir, I'll remember."

But Styles had no intention of making a career out of the Air Force. She had enlisted for the GI Bill and as soon as she got out, she was headed back to law school in Ohio. And sensitive or not, she didn't think it was right to lie in that manner to the man back there. Lying to play on someone's sympathies just didn't sit well with her. Besides, the guy was cute, in a 'Jeremiah Johnson'- Robert Redford -'Mountain Man' kind of a way. She kept quiet, though. She had learned that officers liked it best that way and she wanted to make sergeant before she got out. Airman Pamela Styles just gritted her teeth slightly and drove on.

The Stone Cabin.

After my visitors leave, I set about frying venison for supper. I complete the task the way my mama taught me and sit down. As I eat, I can't help but wonder why I had a visit from Mussenberg. Like the song says, "Something ain't right". Now the big question for me is... why am I worried about it? I'm not in this deal anymore, am I? No, I guess I'm probably not, but then again, I took the job, didn't I? So if the tribe's going to have difficulty over this, then isn't it still my responsibility? My head tilts in my silent conversation with myself as I try to answer that last question. Well, technically I'm not responsible, but personally, I still feel responsible, don't I? Yeah, yeah I do. So the answer is yes, I guess I am still responsible for the island and the mess that it's become, huh? Okay, so I'm still responsible. So what? I don't have anything here to be overly suspicious of, do I? Yeah, crap. Like heck, I don't. That boy wouldn't have been up here asking me questions about something that they should've found easily in two or three days, unless what they're looking for, is something other than what they said it was, huh? Yeah, that's right. So that means... that the bastards lied to me, doesn't it?

Okay, no big surprise there, is it? Shouldn't be. But how can this impact the tribe? That's really the big question for me, ain't it? And the answer to that one is… I don't know. Since I don't know what they're after, I don't know how, or if, it can come back and bite us. My head shakes as I realize that I'd used the word "us". I guess that I consider myself part of us, don't I? Yeah, I guess I do, and over the past couple of months, I've got to admit, that I've been doing more and more of that. Why? Well, that's a quandary all by itself, isn't it? I finish the last of the meal and tip up the glass to swallow the remaining milk. I tote the plate and glass into the kitchen and put them down in the sink. Then I lean on the counter and look out the window at the deer hide, stretched between the trees. My mind continues its arguments with itself, as I come to the conclusion that basically what this means is that I have to pursue this some more. I really don't like this decision either.

It's not been all that bad here since I left that damn job, ya know? Granted, missing Nettie hurts on a daily, almost hourly basis, sometimes, but there've been other pluses. I haven't been dreaming, and for me, that's a biggy, ya know? And I've been studying the Pukaskwa to English dictionary a lot. I've been utilizing more and more of the words, if only in my mind, and really enjoying that. No, enough of this trying to talk myself out of doing what I know is the right thing, here. I took the job and it's my responsibility to follow it through. I push away from the sink and look into the living room at the telephone. I need to get a hold of Gangues and see if he can help me again. But I'm going to walk lightly, here, like I'm stepping barefoot on broken glass.

If Mussenberg came here to talk to me, then there's a chance that my phone's bugged or shit… who knows what all? I have to contact Gangues from somewhere else. I silently wonder if I'm up to this, as my hand glides up to feel my side. The bruises are long gone and I only catch a twinge of pain on occasion. The ripped flesh on my leg has healed up leaving only a slight scar, so I figure I'm good enough to go. As I stand there, Amos Reedeer's words pop back into my head.

What was it he'd said the day he and Nettie had come here? Oh yeah, he'd given me that little leather bag and… my eyes dart to the top of the refrigerator where I'd laid the bag. I move over and raise my hand to grab the little leather sack. As I look at it in my hand, I rub it back and forth in my fingers. An uneasy feeling rolls over me and suddenly, I'm spooked. The shinkakee again. Amos had said on that day… that the time would come when I would be doing spiritual warfare and that I'd need this little… what'd he call it? A medicine bag. A medicine bag for my piwaka. Holy shit! I don't like this. Not at all, man. The phone rings then and I jump! It nearly causes me to go into cardiac arrest! As I make my way to the cordless, another thought blows into my feeble noggin. I don't get phone calls. I pick it up and say hello.

"Hello. Ely?...Ely? It's Gretchen. Um, Gretchen Cooper."

My eyes dart to the mantle and the crayon colored envelope, dotted with airmail stamps. I smile. "Yeah, Gretchen. How the heck are ya? How's your daughter... Carrie?

"Oh she's doing fantastic, actually." She takes a breath. "We've just returned from Zurich yesterday. I've been wanting to call you since the Foundation notified us that we had enough money to take her for the treatment." I take the cordless phone with me as I move over and pick the envelope off the mantle. "The doctors say her prognosis is excellent."

I feel my smile get bigger. "That's great, Gretchen. Really great."

There is silence for a beat and then she clears her throat, the long distance echoing the sound off the wires. "Ely, we got the check for Carrie from the Tribe, and, well...I, um, well, I know that you had a lot to do with that and I jus..." Her voice cracks.

I squeeze the phone in my hand as I look out the window to see a large black crow light in the white pine beside the house. "Hey, Gretchen, don't mention it, okay? The Band had the money to help her, and besides, your dad helped me with a case I was working on." I'm nodding to an empty room. "He really did. So, just consider it a tit-for-tat deal, okay?" I wait as yet another of the big black birds lights on a tree limb. I listen to her lightly sobbing over the miles. After a few seconds, she has it under control. I look at the ceiling. Man, I hate it when women cry.

"Well, maybe that's so. Anyway, Ely, I wanted you to know how much it means to us, to Carrie, to my father, to all of us. We'll forever be in you debt. Forever."

Another crow lands in the tree and I'm struck by an uneasy oddness as I turn back to the phone. To get her off that subject I ask, "What about your dad? How's he doing?"

She laughs then, that deep womanly laugh that I remember. "Oh, Dad's just fine, too. He's like a kid again, racing Carrie all over the place. He hasn't had any more medical problems and I'm honestly beginning to think that Carrie's cure was his as well."

"Well look's like you're batting a thousand there, kid. I'm happy ta hear it."

One of the crows drops and flies up to light on the porch. I pull the curtain back as the black bird hops up onto the handrail and turns to look me in the eye. The "ka-gak-shi" seems almost human as its head twists and it goggles me through the windowpane. The yellow beak opens and closes as if it is speaking. I shudder and… I don't know why. I gulp air and continue speaking as the bird and I eye each other through the glass. The meanwhile, in the back of my mind, I can hear Gretchen talking, saying something about how she would like to see me again. But I'm only half-listening as I mumble out, "uh…me too." My concentration is on the big black bird. She's saying that she has to go now as I shake my head, trying to clear the shinkakee filling it. I speak into the phone as I watch the bird through the window.

"Gretchen, uh, it was so good to hear from you. Thanks for letting me know how Carrie and your dad are getting along."

A shiver is slowly making its way down my spine as I stare at the black bird outside. I can hear her talking but the words aren't registering. I feel the shinkakee spooling through me as the bird twists its head from side to side and looks at me through the glass. This, my mother had once told me, is an omen. A black crow or raven, visiting your door, foretells that evil is near. Well that sucker's sure a "ka-gak-shi", ain't he? That's a crow, if ever I saw one!

There is silence on the other end of the line then she begins speaking again. I drop the curtain and leave the birds to themselves, forcing down a shiver. What evil? Come on? Geeze, man. Some of this Indian lore is just that. This has to be nothing more than what it is… just a black crow, landing on my porch. Okay… but then why is the shinkakee blowing through me like a hurricane? I need to think this through. I'd had a rough time with prayers this morning, not quite being able to concentrate on them before the rabbit hunt. Now, there was the Air Force visit. I have to think about this! I turn back to the phone to end the conversation.

But she's already saying goodbye and I answer, gently easing back the curtain. "Yeah, okay. Thanks for calling, Gretchen. You take care, okay?" There is another pause before she says," Please stay in touch… okay Ely?"

I nod at the window, watching the ka-gak-shi, feeling goosebumps rise all over me. The bird is walking toward the window now, foot over foot, like a man? Crows don't do that - they hop? Whoh. I'm not liking this. Not at all. I stutter out a reply to her, "Uh.. sure thing. Good-bye, Gretchen. Uhm, say hi to your dad for me."

She says she will and hangs-up. I fumble the phone down and pull back the curtain again to look into the beady eye of the big black bird. The crow is facing me, and suddenly, it rears up and spreads its wings, like a bird of prey. Then it jabs its head at me once before it leaps into the air, flying directly at the window before spooling off and away, its wings beating furiously! I jump back shaking and then crane my neck to watch it sail into the dense cover of the woods. It's swallowed up quickly and disappears. The other birds are all gone now, too. Well... yes'siree'bob! I got the feeling that somethin' ain't right! I feel my eyes enlarge to the size of oranges. No jooooke somethin' ain't right! I let the curtain drop and say out loud to an empty room as I turn around.

"I sure don't like that shit. Man, I don't like that at all! Not one little bit!"

Chapter Twenty-Five
"Holy Hiroshima, Bat Man!"

**The Denny's Restaurant,
Escanaba, MI.
The next morning.**

Mussenberg sat in the chair sideways with his legs crossed as he read the Detroit Free Press. He casually sipped his coffee as he perused the newspaper and nibbled on the last of his toast. The breakfast crowd wasn't too bad here and he enjoyed the quiet time. The Air Force officer drew some curious looks, but now that a whole cadre of them were in town, the interest didn't last long. The cell phone began chirping as he was folding up the sports section. He reached over, snatched the phone and glanced at the caller I.D. It was the General's Washington D.C. office. He placed it to his ear.

"Captain Mussenberg."

"Pete, it's General Kourn. I just gotta a call from Colonel Michaels. He's in a Blackhawk on the north side of the island and they just gotta hit own somethin' ouch'yonder in about twenty feet a water. He says it's about the right size, whatever it is, so git yer scrawny butt over'ta the field and head that way. This could be it!" Mussenberg tossed the paper on the table and reached for his jacket. "Yes sir! I'm enroute right now."

"Good. Give me a SITREP as soon as you have one. Now, what'd Stone have'ta say yesterday?"

Mussenberg slipped one arm through a jacket sleeve and spoke into the phone nestled into his shoulder. "He claims that he's not working for his tribe, anymore, sir, and that checks. He's just on a retainer of some sort. A check of his phone records indicates that he's only had calls in from the tribe and that he has only placed a limited number of calls. The only out-of-state call was to Tennessee to a number that we've determined to be his brother's home there. I didn't see a computer when I was inside his cabin and there is no apparent internet access. Other than that there's… well…"

"There's what?"

Mussenberg zipped his jacket and tossed a two-dollar tip on the table. Then, he took his bill in hand. He walked up toward the cashier while he spoke into the phone. "Well, sir, he's really gone native.

He's got hair down to his shoulders and is doing a lot of hunting and stuff like that." Mussenberg snickered. "If he had a wolf, General, I think the guy'd be dancing with it, if you know what I mean?" There's a patch of silence as Mussenberg waited in line to pay his tab. Then, Kourn asked him.

"Hmm. So you don't think that he's still involved here then, huh?" "No sir, not at this time, anyway. He wasn't happy to see me, but overall, I think that's because he thought I was there to mess with him some more. He stated that he was done and that he thought that we should know that. I suppose that we might've tipped him by showing up there yesterday, but I think I probably smoothed over well enough. I don't know, General, the guy seems like he's dropped off the face of the world, knows he has and... doesn't want ta be found."

"Hmm. Okay then, own ta question two, then. What'd ya find out about the other stuff?"

Mussenberg reached into his wallet and pulled out bills to hand to the cashier. "Oh, you mean the computer search? He did have some limited correspondence while he was in town here. And, well, sir, we've been able ta read all of his out-going e-mails during the time that he was at the boathouse, and some of 'em that came in. But there are several of 'em, that we assume came from this "Tenth Rubber" that he was mailing. And we haven't been able ta track those."

"And why is that?"

"Well, sir, whoever it is, when Stone mailed him, each message was sent to a different address before being automatically forwarded to the next one. Each time this happened, a part of the message was broken off and sent to totally different site, and shortly thereafter, automatically deleted." He took a breath and smiled at the cashier.

"And we don't know from that point if these fragments of message were forwarded before deletion or what. By the time we got to what was left of message's final destination, there wasn't anything left of the message to read. We don't know how this was done. It's new to my computer people, but we're still working on it. Whoever this Tenth Rubber is, he's really good, sir."

Mussenberg heard Kourn cuss under his breath. "Yeah, well I reckon that it's the same guy that was a hackin' into our files, here. I've got my people working own it at this end, too, but they's not been any more activity since we closed our little deal with Stone." Kourn sighed. "Okay, anything else?"

"Uh, well, most of what Stone asked this Tenth Rubber was in the form of questions about us. I assume that the responses to those queries are in the groups that we can't read. One of Stone's questions asked about somebody named Veeter. We've only done a cursory check on this guy, sir. He was hospitalized here. We ran the name through the DMV and Secretary of State's office here in Michigan and the info checks. Veeter lives in Grand Rapids. Nothing stands out about the guy. So, we haven't done anything more with it because we didn't want ta raise anyone's antennae."

Kourn sighed. "Uh, huh. Well, what about our boy Stone? Do ya think that he knows more than he's show'n? Any ole chance atall that he's a hide'n somethin'?"

Mussenberg took his change from the girl at the register and nodded his thanks before he headed out through the door. "Well, sir, I guess there's always that possibility. But my opinion right now is "negative" on that one, sir."

Kourn hesitated, but finally responded. "Well, okay, Pete. It's yer show, now. But ya better be keep'n at least one eye own that fella Stone 'cause he's a wild card as far as I'm concerned."

Mussenberg stopped at the driver's door to his car in the early predawn darkness. He turned back to face the restaurant as static fizzled over the phone. "Yes, sir. I will. And I'll get you a SITREP on the contact as soon I can verify it, sir."

The Blackhawk helicopter attached to Mussenberg's search team was utilizing a brand-new infrared search device, still in the testing and-design stage by the Navy. So far, the tests had proven solid so Kourn had ordered the equipment sent. They'd had the unit and two Navy operators flown to Michigan from Puget Sound, Washington and installed on the Air Force bird last night. Today was the first operational check of Muskrat Island and the surrounding waters using the new equipment. Mussenberg heard static fizzing in and out, and thought that he might've lost the phone signal. He asked the General if he was still there.

"Yeah, I'm here." Mussenberg heard as he turned to catch a better signal. "I said "good!" I wanna know the minute you know if that whirly bird's successful!" Mussenberg heard a paper rustle. "Oh, and by the way. I've gotta little message here that says ya've been promoted ta major. So I reckon ya can toss them old railroad tracks yer'a wearn', Pete, and pick-up a pair of gold leaves ta start a polishin'!"

"No, shit! Hey, thanks, General! Thanks for letting me know!"

"Yeah, no sweat, Pete. It ain't official yet, not even out ta all commanders. In fact, yer regler C.O. won't get the promotion list fer another month so keep this under yer hat. I had a word in ta let me know, is all. Anyways, I wanna hear the minute that ya'all know anything fer sure own this here contact and Pete... watch that Indian! I gotta feel'n he ain't exactly own the up and up."

Mussenberg smiled and unlocked his car door and then slid

behind the wheel. "Yes, sir. I will, and again, General, thanks!"

"Don't mention it, Pete. Talk ta ya later." And the line went dead.

The Stone Cabin,
Same time, Same day, Same channel.

I bend my knees and listen to my old bones crack and pop in the
cold. I'm standing on the porch and looking at the frozen lake below.
I move over to the post and rub my back against it to get at an itch
that's been irritating me. When the itch disappears, I move back over
and look upward at the blackish-blue sky cracked by alabaster streaks.
I finish my prayers, as the moon is chased further over the horizon by
the coming sun.

I stifle a yawn and sip the coffee again. Last night had been a long
one. The crow had put me over the edge yesterday. That omen of a
black-assed bird! When coupled with the other signs and the
shinkakee…well, I'd known that it wasn't over. I was back in it
again. And while I wasn't happy with it, I'd accepted my
responsibility. Yet, just because I had to do it… didn't mean that I had
to like it. That uneasy thing that's been bothering me has been around
ever since I got linked up with the island, hasn't it?

I sigh as I head back into the cabin for more coffee. As I pour the
last of the dark liquid into the cup, I continue pondering. What was it
Amos had said? What had he called these. He'd said "other-world
spirits". So… I guess we'll see, huh? It's just the not knowing that
bothers me. The worry that's been brewing is all about that. I'm about
to go poking around in this and I don't have all my ducks in a row.
And man… poking into things without being knowledgeable about
what that prodding will do, can be very bad. I ain't the brightest guy,
but even I know some stuff. You don't poke a wasp nest unless you
want to get stung, ya know? Geeeeze! I shutter involuntarily. For an
Indian, spirits are sometimes a spooky business. But, shit, man, these
otherworld spirits… whatever they are…can be down-right terrifying.

I shake my head at a blossoming sun as it crests over the trees.
Yep, it's just been great fun thinking about how this'll all turn out!
Oh, well. I twist my wrist and look down at the watch. I figure that I
might as well get started on this little junket. The first thing on my
agenda is to ask Amos Reddeer if I can use his phone. I no longer trust
mine. I reach down and slip a finger through the cup handle and make
my way into the cabin. As I dial Amos' number I look out the window
at the pale dawn. The snow that had been falling so hard yesterday,
seems to have given up for now. But it'll be back. The phone rings,
but nobody answers. It's almost 6:45 and I was sure that I would catch
Amos before he left, today. After several more unanswered rings, I
hang-up. He must've left early. I decide to wait until after eight o'clock
and then try catching him at Wiitikan. I peel off the sweatshirt and

head into the bathroom to shave and grab a shower.

At 8:15, I dial the main number for the tribal headquarters and the phone is answered after four rings. I recognize Hennessey's voice.

"Morn'n, John. I didn't know that tribal chairmen answer the phone?"

"Oh yeah, we do sometimes, eh, when the person that usually does it is indisposed." There's silence for a beat and then he asks, "Is this Ely? Ely Stone?"

"Yes, sir. It's me. I was hoping to catch Amos there. Has he shown up yet, do ya know?"

"Oh yes, he's here Ely! Boy, it's good ta hear from ya." For some reason, he's very jovial. "I hope you're calling to tell us that you're ready to come back ta work, eh? We could sure use ya around here, I'm telling ya, eh?"

"Well, as nice as it is to be wanted, John, I can't say as I'll ever be coming back. You know that, right? I mean, Amos did tell you that, didn't he?"

"Oh, yeah! Yeah, he did, and I wasn't pushing, Ely, really I wasn't. I just... well, I just want ya ta know that your job is here any time ya want it, eh? The Band needs ya, too. That's all."

I honestly don't know what to say to that, so I say nothing.

Finally, Hennessey says that he'll go and get Amos. He puts me on hold. Two minutes later, the line is picked up again and I know this voice, too. "Pukaskwa Tribal Headquarters, Can I help you?"

The voice is like a shot of peach schnapps, rolling down my throat. Warm, velvety and sweet all at the same time. "Hi, Nettie. I was on hold, waiting for Amos."

There's dead silence for a long few seconds and then she talks.

"Hello, Ely. It's good to hear from you."

"Is it?"

Silence and then, "Yes."

"Uh, huh, well don't get too excited." She doesn't respond to that and so I try to smooth it over a bit. "I'm happy to hear your voice, too. You have no idea. You really don't, Nettie."

"Ely... you... we... oh, here's Amos." The noise on the phone allows me to visualize the receiver being passed to someone else. Then Amos' voice barrels into my ear.

"Hello?"

"Hey, Amos, it's Ely Stone. I tried your house early this morning, but you must've left before dawn today?"

"Oh, hi ya, Ely. Yah, I did, eh? I had a healing ceremony to go to before the guy left for work. So I left around six this morning, I guess. Did ya need something, Raining Wolf?"

I can picture him looking at Nettie as he uses my Indian name, maybe trying to work on her still. Problem is, my friend, she ain't interested anymore. I decide to get to business.

"Yeah, well, when I called your house this morning, I was going to ask if I could use your phone. I think mine might be having some problems and I have to make a long distance call. But since you're not home, maybe you could tell me. Do you know, does that pay phone at the tavern there in Big Bay work? I don't know if you know the one I mean, but it's an old pay phone in the bar's parking lot?"

"Oh sure, sure. I know the one ya mean. But I don't know if it works or not. But, Ely, mine does. You go on over and use it, eh? The door's unlocked and the phone's in the front room, eh? You help yourself."

"No, Amos, I'm not gonna go over if you're not there. But thanks anyway."

"You shouldn't be so stubborn, Raining Wolf. The phone is there and I'm happy ta have ya use it, eh? Ya go ahead and make an old man happy now, eh?"

I think about it for a second. We are neighbors and I really don't have time to waste if I'm going to get started. I figure that if he doesn't mind, then why not. "Amos, if you're sure, then I'd really appreciate it. I have a long-distance calling card so there won't be anything billed to you."

"Sure, sure, Ely. The phone's in the front room, by my chair. I've gotta run now 'cause I'm late for a coyote clan meeting. I'll talk ta ya later, eh?"

"Yeah, okay, Amos." Then I remember something. "Hey, I need at ask ya something before I let you go. That little bag you gave me... the piwaka? What'd you say I was supposed to put in it? Things that're special to me, right?"

There's another silence before he speaks. "Ya know... I thought last night that maybe you might be getting close..." He emits a sigh. "It is a maskiki piwaka, Ely. And yes, you put things in it that are special to only you. Things that have spiritual worth only to you. But you must also put in it the thing that represents the People to you. Have you thought about this? Do you know what thing that would be?"

Truth be told, I'd run that conversation over and over again in my head. The one we had had the day he gave me the little leather bag with colored quillwork on it. For a long time, I couldn't stop thinking about our talk that day. But that was because it had been too bizarre to forget, hadn't it? And I think I now knew what was representative of the Pukaskwa People. Well, to me, at least. I turn my attention back to the phone.

"Yeah, Amos, I think I've got an idea." He emits another sigh filled with worry.

"Well, you'll know these things when you think about them, eh? And, Raining Wolf, you must then keep this piwaka close to you! Do this now, before you begin anything else! It is important that you do this thing now! I believe that you are already in battle as we speak. Promise me this?"

Battle? What battle? Geeze, it seems like every time we talk about this weird stuff, I get pushed further and further into the dark. I'm wishing that I'd never brought it up and I'm busy trying to get out of it. "Yeah, yeah, I will, Amos. I will, okay. I'll let ya get to your meeting now, and, Amos, thanks, I appreciate it.

There's that silence again before he talks quietly, in that age-old voice of his. "I will try to get done early so that I can come and see you, but if I do not, you must be careful on this journey. The People are relying on you. That black bird was sent to you for a reason. Remember this. I will be praying for you, Raining Wolf. Goodbye now." I hear him handing the phone back.

I wait, hoping that she'll say something else, anything else, but then, there's a click as she hangs up the receiver. Well... what'd I expect? She's not abou...then thoughts of Nettie are rushed quickly out of the way as Amos' words hit home. The shinkakee drips over me slowly, like warm, sticky molasses as I feel my eyes enlarge and I turn the phone over in my hand and look at it. "Bird!" Then I drop the thing like it's a viperous snake!... right back into the charger.
I shudder then as I bring my eyes back up to the icebox. I have no idea what's going on here but I think I'll hedge all my bets! I go over and get the little brown leather bag and take it with me into the bedroom.

As I finger the quillwork, I vaguely remember Uncle Mason telling us about these when I was six or seven years old. He'd given us each a cigar box and told us to gather stuff that we thought was special and put it together in the box. He'd said that then, the boxes would be our personal medicine. I recall that I had a baby turtle shell, some stones and clamshells in mine, but man... that was a long time ago. I can't remember anymore than that, and, of course, I have no idea whatever happened to the cigar box. But right now, I feel like any help I can get, even if it is superstitious nonsense... I'll take, ya know? On the dresser, I open a small jewelry box and look at the stuff inside. I have in it all of my military medals and other trinkets that I've accumulated over the years.

My fingers fiddle with the loose items, until they finally latch onto a small gold cross on a chain. It was my mother's. She wore it only on special church days. I hold it up to the light for a second, and then open the little bag and drop it in. I rummage some more and find my daddy's purple-heart ribbon from World War II. He was equally proud of it and wore the thing every 4th of July and to his VFW meetings. My brother has the actual medal. I drop it into the leather bag, too. Then I find my brother's Viet Nam service ribbon. He isn't proud of it, but I am, so I add it to the bag. There's a small Civil War pistol ball that belonged to my great grandfather and the next thing I seek is a tiny pocket knife that belonged to Uncle Mason. It's too small for my use, only as long as your little finger, but he'd been able to whittle and cut with it just fine. I pick it out of the cluttered box, and add it to the bag. I rummage some more until I find the set of dog tags that I'd worn, off and on, for most of my career. I take off one of the tags and let it fall into the bag. I close the box and walk back into the kitchen to set the bag on the table.

Now, I shift papers on the countertop until I find the Wiitikan Gazette. It's a by-monthly newsletter that the Band sends out with news on tribal happenings. I'd ordered my new version of the Pukaskwa Dictionary from it. I flip to the back where there are pictures of the Council members. I pull open a drawer, take out a pair of scissors and cut out the photos of Annette and Amos, and then push these into the bag and cinch it up. I hold the little leather sack up and it twirls around in the diffused light of the cabin. I'd thought about Amos's words a lot over the weeks, mostly because they troubled me so much. But I'd come to a conclusion about one of his questions.

He had said I would need a symbol of the People. I'd determined what I believed that was to me. So, I grab a plastic sandwich bag from a drawer and shrug into the field jacket before making my way out to the woodpile. I start unloading the split logs from one row, working my way down to the last one that rests on top of the dirt. I peel it off the ground, and the soil underneath it isn't frozen. The heat generated by the decaying wood has kept this dirt thawed at a time when everything else around is frozen solid two-feet deep. I sweep some decaying leaves away and scoop a small pinch of the soil up with my fingers.

I hold it up and look at it in the morning sunshine as little gray chickadees flit around in the trees beside me. This, I think, represents the Pukaskwa. We are from the Mother Earth and we return to the Mother Earth. It's both Biblical and Indian, and true on both accounts. Like the soil, we can't exist without all of the other things around us. Without the trees and their roots and leaves, we'd dry up and be blown away. Without the life cycles of the animals that live with us, we would gain no nutrients and become barren and produce nothing ourselves. We're dependent upon our Mother earth, to keep us alive and existing. We are as much a part of her, as She is a part of us. That's why I figure that this soil represents the Pukaskwa.

I turn into the sunshine and whisper my prayer. I'll defend this land and the Pukaskwa. I promise. I drop the dirt into the little plastic bag, zip it closed and fold it into the piwaka. In a nutshell, I believe that these things all have spiritual meaning to me. And as I look at the bag with the brightly colored porcupine quills, I sure hope that it matters. I slip the leather strings of the pouch through my jean belt loop and tie it off. Okay, it's time to get the show on the road. I quickly restack the wood and then move back up to the porch.

I walk over and open the little freezer, the medicine bag gently slapping against my thigh. I remove a plastic-bagged grouse breast and a rabbit. I take the wee-oss, or meat back inside with me. I'll leave it over at Amos' as a gift. I feel a smirk on my face. It is, after all, the Pukaskwa thing to do, the exchanging of gifts upon a visit. I stop by the window and look out. Funny, but I feel like I shouldn't have thought that. Even my own sarcastic thoughts don't ring true, anymore. Man… this is weird. Shaking my head, I stoke a couple of pieces of wood in the stove and then grab my little personal phone book and throw on my field jacket. Then I truck outside to the plow Jeep.

Amos' property adjoins mine and is a short jaunt down the road. As I steer down the twisting drive, his cabin comes into view. I'd seen it before, but only as I was making a quick plow pass while pushing snow out of his drive. I plow his drive every time I plow mine because it is the neighborly thing to do. But I hadn't really paid much attention to his cabin before. The last time I had, I'd been a kid. The place seemed a lot bigger, then. The recollections of youth, I reckon. I hadn't visited Amos here either, so I'm surprised as I look at it now. The cabin looks the same as mine. As I pull the Jeep up and stop, I remember that my great-grandfather and Amos' grandfather had helped each other build the two cabins. So I guess they should look alike. I get out, taking the meat with me as I move toward the steps. There's a hint of smoke still trailing from a fieldstone chimney and huge white pines that tower over the cabin hang heavy with last night's snow. His porch doesn't wrap all the way around like mine, but otherwise, the buildings appear the same. Same logs, same gray chinking between them. I step up and turn the knob and the door opens freely for me.

The dry warmth of the fireplace rushes at me as I come in, and there's a reminder of Amos' pipe smoke in the air. My eyes go to the large stone fireplace and mantle, and then drop to the weakening red embers of last night's fire. I remember that Uncle Mason once had a fireplace like this one, too. He'd taken it out so that he could put on the extra bedroom for my brother and me when we came to stay in the summer.

There are skins, bird claws, deer antlers and ceremonial clay-pipes on the walls, along with old pictures galore. As I visually survey the room, I am even more amazed at the stuff it contains. My sight is drawn to a bone chest-protector, treated with full-regalia and hanging from the back of a dining room chair. There are feathers everywhere, and on the side of the stone chimney hangs a chief's ceremonial head dress, decorated with quills and eagle feathers. On the front of the stone structure, centered above the mantle, there's an old hammerlock, double-barrel 12 gauge shotgun, resting on wooden pegs.

Turkey feathers hang off the forearm of the old scattergun. My sight wanders to the archway that, like my cabin, lets onto the kitchen. I can see reed baskets and painted turtle shells on the walls in there. I stomp my feet on the rug and ease into the room, shutting the door behind me. Boy, I could be back in time. The place reminds me of how I'd always mentally pictured a bark-covered 'Pukaskwa wagaahigan', or house, of four-hundred years ago. The thought passes that, maybe… Amos could really be that old, too? As my eyes continue to travel around the room, I realize, of course, that that's ridiculous. I pull off my jacket and slip it onto the hook of an old coat tree that stands by the door. I look around once more and can feel my eyebrows rising in question. Because then again… maybe it ain't so ridiculous.

I shake my head to regain some sanity. Crap, man! Next thing you know, I'll be looking around to see if he has a coffin in here someplace where he sleeps his immortal slumber like some old vampire! I curse out loud and shake my noggin again. Thinking that I have my stupidity in check for now, I place the wild game on the circular table that fronts the window by the fireplace. I look upward at the heavy timbers that form the roof and then to the lashed-together wooden ladder that leads to the loft. I don't have a loft in my cabin and as I stretch on tiptoes, I can't see up there, either. But I'm betting that it holds a wealth of really interesting stuff, just like down here. I won't go up to verify that, though. In police-work, that would be outside the realm of my "clear-view". I have no business up there, but my curiosity is piqued just the same.

Now, I look over to see an ancient, cracked, leather chair and ottoman, parked in front of a 1970s era television. There's an old black telephone on the stand beside it. I move that direction. The phone is at least fifty years old. It's heavy and black with a tall neck and a metal rotary dial. I'll have to call the operator, since I can't punch in the calling card numbers. I pick the receiver up and am somewhat surprised hear a dial tone. I feel the bulk and heaviness of the old phone as I tuck it into my shoulder and dial a zero. I watch with a smile as the dial takes an eternity to come all the way back to a stop. Then the antiquated old phone lines mesh and click in my ear before the operator comes on. I tell her what I'm doing and why, then read off the number I need to call from my book and follow it with my credit card digits. The line begins ringing and a few seconds later, it's answered.

"Good morning, Computer Creations, this is Sally."

"Hi, Sally. I'm looking for Mark Kersman. Is he in per chance?"

"Oh, no, I'm sorry. Mark stepped out've the office for awhile. I can take a message or transfer you to his voicemail, if you'd like?"

"Oh. No, ma'am, I really need to talk to him. Uh, it's urgent. He doesn't happen ta have a pager or anything like that?"

"Well… he has his Nextel. If it's really an emergency, then I suppose that I could call 'em on that?"

Nexttel? Oh, one of those new combination cell phones and two-way radios. I've seen people using them and am still amazed that civilians have them. That'll work.

"Yes, ma'am, I'd really appreciate it, if ya don't mind. Like I said, it's kind've urgent."

"Okaaay. Let's see if I can get ahold of 'em." There's a rustling noise then, a little Star Trek sounding "squeakity-squeak" noise, like Captain Kirk calling the Enterprise on his communicator. Her distant voice comes from her office and over the phone to me. "Mark?" A couple of seconds pass then he answers.

"Yeah, what is it Sally?"

"Uhm, I've gotta guy on the phone who says that he needs ta talk ta ya and that it's urgent."

"Yeah, well they all say that, Sally. I'm here at the cash register at "Chip World." Who is it, anyway?"

This is weird, man. Listening to two people holding a conversation on another phone while I'm a couple of thousand miles away. Ain't technology wonderful? I hear her voice in my ear again.

"Uh, I'm sorry, but I forgot to ask your name?"

"Sure. Please tell him that it's Ely Stone."

I hear her relay this and his reply. "No shit! Get his number Sally and tell him I'll call him back in about fifteen minutes, if that'll work for him? I have ta get through this check-out line and get this stuff out ta the van first."

She's back to me again. "Uhm, Mark says…"

"Yeah, I heard him. That'll be fine. Here's the number where I'll be, okay?"

I look at the antique dial of Amos' old phone and read off the number to her. I thank her and hang up the old hand piece. There's a scratch pad on the little stand so I take it and scribble a quick note to Amos, telling him that I left some wild meat in his freezer, and then tear it off. With it in hand, I move over, grab up the frozen game and go into the kitchen. His appliances are like his telephone. Old. They've got to be at least thirty years old. But, hey, I'm a firm believer in that adage, too, if it works, don't fix it. My own icebox was around when I was a kid visiting my uncle and it wasn't new then either. His freezer is almost bare, as I stuff the meat into it. I figure that he probably eats out or with people that he's constantly visiting as a shaman. Then I feel a little guilty for not inviting him over to my place before. Hindsight. I'll try to do better in the future. That is…if there is a future. I start to drift back into the living room when I look more closely at the work in progress on his table.

He has a small birch bark box that's about two thirds beaded in quillwork. My hand drops and I flip the medicine bag that dangles from my belt loop. So, Amos is the one who did the quillwork on the little bag, eh? A small carving knife, his brushes and dried stains are in the mix, as are the readied porcupine quills in the small wooden bowls. I pick up a pin-like quill and hold it up to the light, before returning it to the bowl. Then I dip my fingers into the dark blue powder in one of the bowls and rub them together. It's gritty, and I can see tiny pieces of dried skins of the polk berries that gave up their color for the dye. I look around at the work area. Some of the quills are already colored. Another large bowl holds those that are still natural and un-tinted, just as they came from "gaag" the prickly old porcupine. Wow, man. This is like visiting a museum. I meander back into what Amos calls his front room and begin looking at the pictures on the walls.

There are a lot of them, my uncles, my grandparents, Amos' mom and daddy, his sisters and brothers. The wall is replete with a photographic history of the two families. There's one of my brother in his tan khaki army uniform, a PFC rocker proudly on his arm. The dark green of the duffle bag that's leaning against his leg and the saucer cap on his head standing out against the blue of the lake by my cabin. I remember the day it was taken. It was when he came home from AIT and flew up here to meet us. It was before he shipped out for Viet Nam. His smile is genuine in the photograph but that was before he spent a tour as a "Track" driver in the heated jungles of that nasty country. He hasn't smiled like that since and probably... never will again. As I bend in closer, I remember how he described the smells of the jungle in the letters that he wrote me, hot, wet and putrid, like death itself. I'd only been there once, and then, only at night, but I'd smelled it, too. I step back and blink my eyes to wash the thoughts away. Then I work over to the picture that dominates the room.

It's the one that caught my eye when I first came in and it is centered on the mantle. It's a large photo of my mother and Amos. The two of them are very young. She's sitting on the fender of a 1938 Buick. He's standing by her side, looking at her with deep admiration. It was taken at least sixty years ago, going by the 1942 stamped on the license plate. Hmm. I rub a hand over the stubble on my chin. That would've been about two years before she met my father. I wonder what happened there? It's something I'm curious about. My gaze comes to rest on another woman's face that I know. She's older in the photograph, but I remember her. It's Sara, Amos's niece. She'd had a bad crush on me when we were growing up, but she was almost ten years younger than I was, all knees and elbows, a gangly kid. She was way too young for me to have returned her interest. As I look at her golden blond hair, bright smile and gray-blue eyes, I'm taken aback by her beauty. Boy, howdy! I'd say that she sure grew up well.

I step back and let my eyes continue their perusal of the room. Next to Amos' chair, there's a large old floor lamp with one of those heavy lampshades with the little tassels all around the rim of it. On the floor beside the chair is a pair of beaded and worn moccasin slippers. I move up to the lamp and slip my fingers to the tassels. The shade is old, the parchment faded and cracked. As I finger it, I'm moderately surprised. I'd expected it to be dusty at the very least, but the whole place is as clean as a whistle. These thoughts are slowly moving in my mind as the phone rings, bringing another smile to my face. The phone's ring is like something out of a 1950s movie. I step over and pick up the receiver. "Hello?"

"Hi. I was looking for Ely Stone?" I can hear sounds like those inside a moving car.

"Yeah, Mark, it's me. How're ya doing?"

"Well, shit, man and for crying out loud! I thought your ass was dead and buried Ghostman! What happened ta ya? Your fellow Indians scalp ya er what? It's like ya dropped off the face of the earth or somethin'?"

I move around and sit down in the chair, stretching the heavy black coils of phone wire with me. "No way, bud, you ain't that lucky. I'm still drawing breath. Hey listen, Gangues. Thanks for calling back. I know you're busy."

"I ain't never busy for a team mate and you know it. Hey, Ghostman," I hear concern in his voice now. "You ain't still messing with those Little Green Men, are ya?"

"What? Little green what? What're ya talking about?"

"Oh shit, that's right. I got that after you shut down your operation, didn't I?" He takes a breath and blows it out, the sound seeming like an echo over the distance.

"Yeah, m'man, those dudes you had me run checks on? Ah shit, what were their names? There was General and a couple a officers, all Air Force?"

I can hear big city sounds of horns honking and traffic and know that he's driving as he speaks. "Oh yeah, Kourn was the General and uh… Major Shears and Captain Mussenberg. What about 'em?"

A tire screeches and another horn blows close to him before he answers loudly. "Them're some bad ass dudes m'man, that's what! If you're still hooked up with them Ghostman, ya better get clear an I ain't shittin ya!"

"Yeah, I know. Thing is, Gangues, I don't really know what's going on here. I'd thought that I was clear, but now… I'm not so sure anymore." I squeeze my eyes shut. "And as bad as I feel about doing it, I was calling to ask your help again."

He hoots on the other end of the phone. "Sonavabitch! You are in ta some shit again, ain't'cha? Well ya got it, Ghostman! I'll be glad ta help! Just let me get to a secure line, I'll call ya back and then ya can tell me what'cha need, okay?"

I nod to the stone fireplace. "Okay, Mark, I appreciate it. When you get to a hardline, give me a call here. I'll stand by and wait, alright?" he adds the affirmative and we each hang-up.

While I'm waiting, I flip back to the newest entries in the notebook I'd brought along and dial Hank Scari's number in Escanaba. His wife answers and I hear her yell to him out in the garage to pick up the phone. Then he's on with me. We shoot the bull for a little bit and I tell him about life at the cabin and learn that he's rebuilding a rotor head for his helicopter out in the garage. It's a give and take, this and that kind of a conversation, before I finally inch into the questions I need to ask. What I find out makes me even more nervous.

Hank tells me in his Yooper-accent that it's really weird, the things that the Air Force have done in mounting this operation. Since I'd explained to him before that the Air Force is searching for some papers involved with national security, he is confused about why they brought in so much unusual equipment. He says that there're a bunch of Black Hawk helicopters outfitted with infrared search radar that he knows are only used to locate metal in the ground or underwater. Why would they be utilizing them? I have no answer for him and urge him further as to the goings-on in Escanaba.. I scribble notes as he talks. He says that the Air Force has established a no-fly zone around the island for a thirty mile radius, an unreal diameter for an aviator. He states that they're enforcing this perimeter with two F-16 fighters, based at the old Air Force Base up in Marquette, and a couple of bizarre looking helicopter gun ships like he's never seen before.

He adds that they're keeping the helicopters tightly guarded and Inside temporary hangers at Escanaba when they're not flying. He also says that the cadre of military people that has arrived keeps growing daily and is now getting close to battalion strength, in his opinion. The Air Force now occupies fully one-third of the airfield and their security is tight and rigid. A friend of his who was flying a twin-engine Cessna strayed into the no fly zone by accident and was told that he was going to be blown out of the sky by one of these new gunships unless he cleared the area ASAP!

I'm taken aback by these revelations and tell him so. Hank adds that, unless he's mistaken, these helicopter gunships look to him like the new RAH-66s, the Comanche. That's a new attack-helicopter just being developed. But we both know that that ship isn't even out of testing, yet. My mind is whirling a thousand miles a minute as this new information boils in. Then Hank says something that rings truer than any other idea I'd had. It makes the commonest and clearest sense of all. Hank says that it looks to him like they are looking for something other than a briefcase full of papers. Something big. He wonders if maybe… they might've lost a nuclear weapon out on Muskrat Island? He makes the comment with as much of a question as he can. I give him a "could be" - "who knows" type of an answer. But it sounds realistic as all get-out to me.

I say my thanks and goodbyes and pass my best to his family before getting off the phone with Hank. I light up another cigarette and move over to look outside as I try to fathom this new revelation. Yep, Hank is right. No two ways around it. I've been lied to by the Wild Blue Yonder boys. That thought is interrupted by Gangues' phone call. He's animated on the phone. He has that eagerness in his voice again, so I begin reading from my notes and passing my requests to him.

"Okay, Mark. I know you have no idea what I'm working on, but what I need is anything you can dig up an atomic weapon or anything associated as a top secret loss lately over the Great Lakes." I take in a deep breath and go on. "Particularly over Lake Michigan and in the northern part of that body of water, okay?"

I can hear his fingers flying over the keys, even over the antiquated phone line. He lets out a low whistle. "Okay, m'man, you got it! It'll take a few minutes 'cause it's all classified as top-secret stuff. But, hey, dude, like this is some heavy shit you're into, Ghostman? Should I be nervous here, man? I mean, am I gonna wake up inside a mushroom cloud, er what?" He snickers as I listen to his fingers fly over the keys.

I sigh and form an answer. "Gangues, you don't want ta know, okay? And trust me on this one, ya don't wanna be any closer to it than ya are right now."

"Okay, man. Ya know, I'll get all I can but you're worrying me, m'man. Next, you're gonna tell me that all this is connected ta them Little Green Men dudes, ain't'cha?"

"Little Green Men? You mentioned that before, Gangues, what the heck is that about?"

"Ah, sheeeeit, Ghostman, I told you, man, they're some bad-ass dudes. If you're tied up with them, then you need to get clear of this mission, m'man, and I mean it! I been trying to check on 'em, but every time I get close I crash and burn. But seems ta me like old Piranha said that he'd once had a run-in with some dudes had' a name like this before. Ya might wanna ask him about it, man. "And, Ghostman... you wouldn't believe how I had ta wire this thing, just ta get what I came up with, when I was inta them, ya know? When they came after me, they had some very, very heavy hitters there, m'man! They knew their shit, ya know? I mean some very savvy computer people working their end, dig?"

Well there's a thought. "You say Piranha might know who they are or something about them?" Piranha is Tom Murphy. He is a retired Marine Gunnery Sergeant now, but he'd been 4th Rubber on the Trojan Team.

"Yeah. It was, oh... I guess back during the Gulf War. I remember him saying somethin' about 'em, but I can't remember what exactly. He may have more."

"Okay. Maybe I'll check with him, then."

"Okay m'man. I'm in Air Force accident archives now... So what'chu need?"

"Any recent lost and un-recovered aircraft in the Great Lakes, especially Lake Michigan. That should turn up something. I'm thinking that these people are involved because there's a secret weapon of some sort... lost out on an island that the tribe owns."

I weigh just how much to tell him and decide that if my hunch is correct, then this is specifically an Air Force operation. I decide that I can pass on this much anyway, but I don't mention the Chinese. I explain my thoughts that maybe the Air Force is searching for a missing NBC (nuclear, biological, chemical) item of some kind out there and that's the reason for checking this out. I give him the latitude and longitude of the Muskrat Island and briefly tell him that I've been hired by the tribe as a special agent to watch over the island and that, that's how, I'd gotten hooked up with this Air Force Green Men Team, or whatever.

"Holy, Hiroshima, Batman!" he laughs out loud, "I don't believe this! No shit, Ghostman! You're work'n on a Broken Arrow?

I rub a hand over my face. "Broken Arrow" is the term used by the military for the misplacement of a NBC weapon. Nobody ever really loses one, they're only temporarily misplaced. The loss of a weapon of mass destruction would be catastrophic and certainly not the kind of a thing that the American military could possibly ever allow. Over the course of my career, I'd heard of only three such...misplacements. And I'd never learned if they were ever retrieved from the lost and found box or not. I drop my hand and turn back to the phone.

"Hey, I don't know, buddy, but yeah, as strange as it sounds Mark, that could be what this's all about."

"Okay, it'll take an hour or maybe an hour and a half ta get this. It'll be under lock and key but that ain't no big deal, man. It's a challenge ta git inta this stuff but it ain't nuthin like what them Green dudes have laid out, ya dig? So, I'll find out anything else I can on the other stuff and get right back ta ya when I got it tagether. Are ya gonna be at this same number?"

There's a mixture of relief and excitement in his voice as he asks the question, and I can't help but smile again as I answer him in the affirmative. After we hang up, I think of Gangues' Batman and Robin old TV show response to the Broken Arrow idea. He's right, I do get myself into some shit. And this whole dumb thing is running just like a corny 1960s TV series. All I need, now, is Albert the Butler, the Penguin, Cat Woman and the Riddler because we've already got Jokers and clowns in abundance with this show! I burrow my knuckles into my eyes and then pull them away and blink into the sunlight drenched room. I glance at the black face of the diver's watch and am surprised to see that it's already past noon. My head sways from side to side as I turn around. If this whole thing weren't so doggone scary... it'd be down right stupid! I think this as I walk into Amos's bathroom.

Chapter Twenty-Six
"Let It Be"

Muskrat Island,
Just Off-Shore, in a Black Hawk UH60.
1303 or 1:03 pm, Same Day.

Mussenberg caught a flash outside the window and strained his eyes to search. Then he saw the other helicopter. It was one of the Comanches, gun-ships that were providing security for the operation. It hovered quietly and death-like off their starboard quarter and seemed like a mystical spirit, floating in the air out there, all olive green and menacing. The attack chopper had taken up station beside their Black Hawk and was now hovering like they were, over this one specific locale.

These two RAH-66 Comanches were two of only six on active status in the whole U.S. Military, and all six of them were assigned to Detachment Four. But they weren't listed on any of the Air Force's unit rosters. Neither were the two F-16 Fighting Falcon fighter-jets that were based at the old KI Sawyer Air Force Base, up in Marquette. All of these aircraft, machinery and people that were assigned to Mussenberg for this retrieval mission, didn't really exist, as far as paperwork went. That was the way things went on DET 4 missions. He turned away from the window and looked across at the flight-Suited young sailor working the equipment. Then he stretched in his belt, to lean over. He peered at the small square box affixed to the bulkhead of the helicopter. The Navy Petty Officer that was working the equipment glanced up at the Captain in annoyance. It was bad enough, he thought, that they sent him all the way to Michigan on TDY, but this Air Force officer was driving him nuts with his questions every two minutes. While he waited for the next inquiry, he caught the flicker of the co-pilot's hand signal. He looked up forward and saw that the co-pilot was motioning him to get the Captain's attention. He quickly turned to the officer and spoke into his mike while pointing toward the cockpit.

"Uhm, sir, I think the co-pilot wants ya ta switch ta his freq."

Mussenberg shifted his eyes from the lighted box and looked at the Petty Officer before following the direction to look forward. He leaned back and turned that direction to see the co-pilot's hand signals. He nodded and switched frequencies, keeping his eyes on the man up front. As he clicked over the switch, the co-pilot's words came over his headset. "Captain, you've gotta call. Do you copy?"

Mussenberg maintained eye contact and nodded his head, the flight helmet banging against the bulkhead in the motion. "Yeah, Lieutenant, I copy. Put it through."

The co-pilot nodded his head "Roger that, sir. Here ya go." Then turned back to the front and his flying. Mussenberg noted that the helicopter noise was more evident on this frequency. He waited a beat then spoke into the mike.

"This is Captain Mussenberg?" He wasn't ready for the reply that boomed into his headset.

"MUSSENBERG!! WHAT THE HELL'S THAT FUCK'N INDIAN UP TO?!!," the voice bellowed into his ear.

Mussenberg's face took on a deathly pallor. He shook his head and turned slightly away from the men in the crew compartment. The Petty Officer across the deck stole unobserved silent looks at the Captain and noticed his dilemma, as the officer spoke over the radio. He'd seen the contorted look on the officer and knew innately that the man was getting his ass chewed. Then the Petty Officer, an aviation electronics technician or AT, by rating, stole a glance over to his Senior Chief, the only other member of the Navy detachment sent from Puget Sound. The Senior Chief, a black man with 22 years in the service, also watched the Air Force Captain. He noticed his partner watching him and switched his gaze to the other man before making a face and rolling his eyes upward.

The Petty Officer then snatched a quick look at the Air Force Technical Sergeant who was seated toward the rear of the aircraft. The Sergeant, who was the aircraft's crew chief, moved his eyes from the Captain's back and made contact with the Petty Officer. His face was already fixed with a smile, but when the two men looked at each other, the Sergeant's grin grew enormous inside the green flight helmet. The AT returned the smile and then looked back down at his scope. All three men were enlisted and had seen officers in trouble before. And for an enlisted guy, it was almost always a secret pleasure. He tried to hide his grin as he worked the knobs on the machine.

He was just grateful that the Captain was leaving him alone. All he knew was that the quicker they nailed down exactly whatever it was that the Air Force was looking for out here in this miserable place, the quicker he and the "Senior" would be on their way back home. The Petty Officer had a wife and new baby back in the Washington and that's where he wanted to be. He turned to his work with vigor. Meanwhile, Mussenberg, had nowhere to turn. He kept his back to the men as a shiver ran down his spine.

"Sir?" Mussenberg mumbled out the reaction as he recognized the General's voice. He was familiar with this tenor when the man was angry. And right now, the guy was really hot. The General's tone lowered an octave or two when he spoke again, but he still spoke in a very loud and very pissed-off voice that permeated Mussenberg's flight helmet and sent waves down his back.

"I said, Captain…,what's Stone doing? Somebody just broke inta our system again and made a copy of that damn F-89 accident report! Now I doubt that it was the Girl Scouts a sell'n cookies that knocked down 'are door and done this! So I say again… What's happening with that damn Indian?"

Mussenberg flustered. "Uh, sir, I honestly don't know. The last I have on him was what we talked about this morning."

"Well, I told ya, Captain…, that you'd better keep an eye on this asshole… didn't I?"

The General's voice had turned from hot to cold. Cold and threatening. Mussenberg squeezed his eyes tight before opening them and nodding his head. "Yes, sir, you did."

Kourn's voice lowered even more but the anger was still apparent. "Do you have anybody own him…? Is they anybody a keep'n tabs own this man or are we just not worried about mission security anymore, Captain?"

Mussenberg squirmed on the bench. "No, sir, we have no one on him at this time. Like I said, General, I don't believe that he's a threat. Sir, are you sure it was him? I mean… I just don't think he…" The General's voice echoed loudly through radio link again.

"Yeah… goddamn right you're not think'n. Now I don't know if it's him or not but I wont some SPs own his ass and I wont 'em there NOW! Do you read me, Captain?"

Mussenberg clenched his teeth before raising his voice. The higher voice level was unnecessary but years of military training took over anyway. "YES, SIR, LOUD AND CLEAR."

The General's voice dropped another octave but still held the tempo of his angst. "Good! See that you do. We've got some more own Stone too but not all. It waz all we could get before his file disintegrated."

Mussenberg broke in. "Disintegrated, sir?"

"Yeah, that's what the computer people say, anyhow. They was some kind of file virus attached ta his record an unless ya know about it first and enter the right access code er whatever, the file just self-destructs. Apparently, it's designed to do that. Anyhow, the thing's gone forever. It kain't be brought back. But from what they got before that happened, it appears, that our boy Stone, did some coursework at the CIA Farm and it looks like he also made it through some a the Army's Green Beenie's stuff, too. They waz more, but that's all my computer people got before they had the door slammed own 'em. Now this somebitche's dangerous. I wont a SITREP own that Indian as soon as it's available! Do you roger, Captain?"

Mussenberg nodded staunchly. "Roger that, sir. You'll get it."

Kourn sighed then went on, in a calmer articulation. "Good. Now what's the status out there?"

He'd quickly taken in the General's words about Stone, even as he contemplated their probable mistake in contacting the man. As he'd listened to his C.O. speak, he knew that this could end up bad. Very, very bad. Still, Mussenberg sighed in relief. He was just happy to change the subject.

"Well, we've definitely got something here, sir. We may have to go ahead and get that extension on the island lease though, General. According to the Navy, this thing is under about 20-30 feet of water and rock. There's rock all over the place under the surface, or, at least that's what I'm being told now, sir. But either way, there's snow and ice and no easy approach to mounting a large scale retrieval at this time of year."

"Okay. So, have ya figured own a way ta do this then?"

Mussenberg nodded his head while setting forth the retrieval plan that he had been laying out in his mind. "As it stands now, sir, I think we'll probably have to wait until the weather breaks. At least enough so that we can clear the large ice chunks out of the way so the divers can work." He bent his head over and looked out the door window to the area of water that they were hovering over.

"Then, sir, we'd have to remove all of the debris and get the hook-ups secured on it so we can heli-lift it out and fly it all the way up on top of the island." His shoulders shrugged, as he peered out the window. "The top's about the only place big enough to set it down and begin disassembly for shipping, sir."

"Uh, huh. Well, that sounds like a plan, I reckon. Time'll tell, won't it? Star Dust is our priority, anyway. So, what've they turned up? Anything yet?"

"Star Dust" was the code name given to the search of the island itself. Everyone involved in the operation was Detachment Four and Mussenberg was in charge. He gave Kourn an update – the island search was proceeding they had not found anything at this time – weather and terrain were making things difficult. When he'd finished, there was a long silence before the General spoke again. Okay, Pete.

Sounds like you gotta handle own it. But I wanna know what the hell's a going own with Stone. I mean it!"

Mussenberg jerked his head in the affirmative. "Yes, sir! I'll get right on that. Right away, sir."

There's a dead silence, and Mussenberg began to wonder if he'd lost signal, when the General speaks again. This time, the Air Force Captain has to strain to hear the voice because it's almost a whisper.

"You better, Captain. You damn well better... Out." Then the signal cut off.

Mussenberg sat staring at the overhead of the Black Hawk, listening to
the static of a dead radio frequency. Yep, he thought, this could be very bad indeed. If this operation were leaked to the media, from reputable sources, then the media would investigate. This was just too juicy to disregard. Between the Indian treaty, the recreational location and a thousand other things, running from radiation leaks to God's wrath, the media would eat it up and have a feeding frenzy!

And "we", he thought, just wouldn't be able to keep a lid on it this time. If the military tried, it'd just spur the investigation further, and then there would be congressional hearings with senators and congressmen, some of whom would not be privy to what Detachment Four was and... what they did. This could blow the whole country apart! Nope, there's no way to contain this one if that happens. Not a prayer.

And now, they'd probably goaded Stone into acting because he felt threatened somehow. And even if the guy didn't know anything, his actions might cause the same results. Why hadn't the old man listened to him when he told him Stone didn't know anything about Star Dust, the object they were looking for? They'd find Star Dust if the thing were here! It was just a matter of time. But the General just couldn't see that, could he? Now he had to sit on Stone and put a chain on the guy, somehow. Mussenberg squeezed his eyes shut and then popped them open, the brown irises blazing with decision. He quickly switched frequencies and leaned over to the Petty Officer and tapped the man's shoulder.

"Shut it down! We're going back in." He snapped over to the Navy Senior Chief and jabbed a thumb back toward land and Escanaba, even as the other man was leaning forward. "We're shutting it down and head'n back in!" Then he quickly twisted back toward the cockpit while switching frequencies yet again.

"Major, we've got to break off here, now! Tell everyone that we're headed in and let's get us back ta Escanaba in a hurry!" Mussenberg watched the cockpit as the white and blue striped helmet of the Major turned slightly and bumped up and down while the Lieutenant co-pilot looked back at him from the other seat.

The Major's voice came into his ear. "Roger that, Captain. Returning ta base." Several seconds later, the helicopter swung sideways and nosed downward as it powered up and began moving northward across the water.

The Escanaba Airport,
The Air Force Security Zone.
Thirty Minutes Later.

Mussenberg slid the door open on the Black Hawk and jumped down, ducking under the spinning rotors above his head. He ran across to the waiting Hummer and sailed inside, jabbing his finger toward the operations building across the field. A minute later, the Hummer slid to a stop in the slushy snow amongst a small group of airmen. Mussenberg bailed out, swinging his helmet with him as he trotted over to the small porch. He returned the airmen's salutes, on-the-fly, as he skipped several of the steps up to the door.

When he grabbed the door knob, it pulled off in his hand. He swore loudly and began banging on the door. An airman quickly opened it, and Mussenberg brushed by him in a hurry, highly agitated and still cussing under his breath. When he reached the desk across the room he dropped the knob on it and addressed a somewhat startled Technical Sergeant, who was seated there.

"Sergeant, get a hold of Airman Styles and have her report to me here, On-The-Double!" The Sergeant was nodding and already picking up the phone as Mussenberg swung back around to the astonished airman by the door who had let him in. He stabbed his finger at the doorway.

"Peels! I don't give a shit how you do it, but I want that fuck'n knob fixed right now! I don't care if ya have ta call a locksmith from town or what… but get it done!"

The distressed airman nodded quickly, "Yes, sir, right away, sir!"

Mussenberg watched the airman go across the room and pick up another phone. Then his eyes traveled back to the door as he uttered another oath. He shook his head and moved swiftly into his makeshift office, tossed his helmet on an empty chair and plopped down in a chair behind his desk. He pulled the zipper down a bit on his flight suit and then began rummaging through a mess of papers. He heard a knock on the open door. He looked up to see the Technical Sergeant standing there.

"Uh, sir, Airman Styles is off duty today," he held up the daily roster clipboard and waggled it, "and I took the liberty of calling her quarters, sir. She's not there, either?"

Mussenberg held the other man's eyes. "Does anybody have any idea where she is?"

The Sergeant sent his eyes to the ceiling before bringing them back to the Captain. "Not so far, sir, but I've got the word out. She's back on the roster for tomorrow, sir, if that helps any."

Mussenberg sat back, the chair bumping the wall as he stared at the enlisted man. "Well, fuck me!" He shook his head hard once, then scooted the chair ahead. "Okay. Keep looking for her. I need her found, Dick! Today! ASAP! She's been to this place and at least she knows the lay out."

Technical Sergeant Richard Canter had no idea what he meant. He watched the Captain grab up a yellow legal tablet and begin scribbling on it. The enlisted man could just barely make out a map that the Captain was sketching on the paper. The officer spoke as he finished the sketch and began writing out driving directions.

"And, in the meantime, I need a two-man obteam (observation team) suited up and equipped right now! Not DET 4 personnel, just SPs. They're gonna be work'n a stake-out. M-16s and a hundred rounds, in addition to side arms. Have 'em check out a Hummer with a cell phone, too. Then have 'em report here to me when they're ready to go and I'll brief them. And Sergeant…" he looked up at the man, "tell 'em to suit up with extreme cold weather gear and some MREs. They're gonna be in the woods on this one."

The Reddeer Family Cabin,
Near Yellow Dog Point, MI
Same Day, Same Time.

I'm still in Amos's bathroom when I hear a vehicle pulling into the yard. I open the door and catch a flash of tan stopping outside the window. It's not Amos' white pick-up, that's for sure! My hand subconsciously goes to the pistol in my back, but it's not there! I don't have the Glock with me! As my sight catches someone walking across the window outside, I realize that I don't have a weapon at all! I quick-step into the kitchen, swipe up the knife off the table and lightly step across the room to lean against the wall by a window! I ease back a crack of the curtain from the trim side and peek out of the glass. I can make out a tan and green SUV type vehicle in the drive, and a man walking around my old Jeep! My heart, which has been pounding like a bass drum, begins to slow in cadence as I recognize the man outside. It's a tribal cop, one with long hair, tied up in a ponytail, tucked under a tan Stetson wide- brimmed hat. Jason Treebird, one of the Tribal cops.

I'm resting easy now, the slight rush of adrenalin subsiding and flowing away. Holy smokes, man! How'd I get back into this mode? I grit my teeth as I watch out the glass. Geeze, I might as well be on an op in another foreign country. I blow away a breath and draw out the drapery a little more as I watch him circle my Jeep. He's carrying a couple of plastic bags in his left hand with some kind of branches sticking out of one of them. He walks as if he's used to the lay of the land here. Well-known terrain to him. He comes to a stop as he rounds the back of the Jeep and stares at the license plate for a few seconds. Then his gaze comes up to the cabin. He shifts the smaller bag to his left hand, also.

His right hand then drops to rest on the butt of his pistol as he begins to make his way up here. His eyes are searching everywhere as he approaches and I smile at his efforts. He's suspicious. Good man. Judging by his actions, I'd say that he's a frequent visitor to this place. And my Jeep is an unfamiliar vehicle here. I gently slip the curtain back and make my way over to the door. I turn the knob and open it to see him there with his hand raised to knock. I'm smiling at him as I swoosh the door open.

"Well, hi there, Officer Treebird, how ya doing? Long time no-see?"

It takes him a beat and I watch as the surprise floods over his face and then disappears. His smile is genuine when it comes. "Hi, Detective. "Booshoo." I didn't expect to see you here, eh?"

I nod and continue my smile. "Yeah, I can see that."

He turns back and throws his free hand at the Jeep. "I didn't recognize the truck there, or," he turns back and points at my head, "your new hair style either, eh?"

I return his smile. "Yep, they're both mine." I make a jerking gesture with a free hand. "My phone's on the fritz and Amos said I could borrow his. Uh, what brings you out this way?"

His eyes have remained on my hair, but now he looks down at the bags he's holding. "Oh, I told Amos that I'd drop these off." He points to the plastic bag with evergreen branches poking out of it.

"These're "schkop", eh? Cedar branches for ceremonial smoke." He points to the smaller sack. "And this is birch bark."

I nod. "Well, okay, you probably put those in here, don't ya?"

He hikes his shoulders. "Not the cedar, eh. I always leave that out here on the porch." He steps over and leans the bag against the wall and turns back to me while hefting the smaller sack. "This goes inside though, eh?"

I nod my head again and step aside as he enters and moves into the kitchen. I close the door and follow along, keeping the knife cupped in a covert manner in my hand. Treebird walks around the table and sets the bag on the countertop. While he has his back to me, I slip over and ease the knife back onto the table. Then I watch as he sets the drain stop and begins running hot water in the sink. He talks as he begins taking out pieces of birch from the bag, his uniform, cowboy hat casting an unusual shadow over the counter.

"So what have you been up to, Detective?"

"Jason, I don't work for the tribe anymore so you don't have to call me detective, okay."

He turns around and looks at me with a question mark on his face before dropping his eyes. When he raises them to me again, his expression conveys a decision. He shrugs his shoulders. "It's what you are, eh?" Then he turns back to the sink, his ponytail bouncing with the motion. "And whether you know it or not, you're still on our roster, too, eh?"

Hmmm. This guy's different, isn't he? I decide not to push the issue. "Well, I haven't been doing much. Just a little hunt'n... some fishi'n. Not a lot, ta tell ya the truth."

The water fills up the sink basin and he turns it off. I watch as he takes long sections of the birch and gently eases them under the warm water. He begins layering them on top of one another, taking care to see that each piece is fully submerged. He speaks with his head bowed to the business at hand.

"You know, I'm up here quite a lot and I was going to pay you a visit a couple of times. But Captain Morse has made even talking with you against Department policy, eh?" He speaks the words with a chuckle in them. "Oh yah, he even said that if any of us so much as uttered a word to you, he would have us up on disciplinary action." He nods his head to his own words and throws me humorous look over his shoulder. "What the heck did you do to piss him off so bad, anyway?"

I laugh, but it has a dead sound to it. "Well, Jason Treebird, let's just say that I didn't kiss his ass or shine his shoes and leave it at that, huh?" I motion to the sink as he turns back around. "So you soak the bark for Amos, huh?"

He finishes the task and moves around in about-face. He appears curious for a second as he looks down at the sink then back up to me.

"Oh, yah. I do bead and quill work, Detective. Amos makes birch bark boxes and things out of leather, eh," he motions to the bag hanging from my belt loop, "like your medicine bag there. He made the bag and I did the quill work on it." He moves over and dries his hands on a dish towel, his back to me again. "I also assisted in the prayer over your medicine bag, eh?"

He turns back to me. "I guess you can say that I'm a shaman in training." he waggles his shoulders, "or something like that, eh?"

"Hmm. I figured." I throw up a hand. "So tell me, do you think I'm a pathfinder or whatever it's called, too? Or is this just Amos' little mirage?" I send him my best teasing smile. "As a shaman in training, you should have a pretty good answer to that."

Treebird rests against the countertop, folds his arms across each other and looks at the floor. "Ahh, well, unfortunately, Detective, I'm afraid that I don't, eh?" He raises his countenance to me and his eyes have the sharpness of sincerity in them.

"You see, Detective, I'm just a novice in the ways of the spiritual world. Just a lowly pupil, eh?" He extends a hand toward the table. "I come up here in the evenings, and Amos and I sit around working. It's quiet, and, sometimes, hour an will pass with neither of us speaking." He tilts his head. "I do my bead and quillwork and he makes boxes and leather items. Between times, he tells me the old stories, eh? The ones passed down from our grandfathers." Treebird puckers up his mouth once before continuing.

"He teaches me things here and there, and, sometimes, I learn. But mostly, I have no idea what he is doing or saying, eh? He tells me that this will come with time." He furrows his brow. "I'm not sure about that. But occasionally, Detective, I do see the things he's showing me, eh?" He sends me a definitive look. "And I can always see the eternal depth and wonder to his wisdom." He gently shakes his head. "But as for me knowing how he knows all the things that he does, well… that's a long ways off for me, eh? I'm just happy to be learning from him."

I look at him from beside the table and nod. "Yeah, I can sure appreciate that. He does come up with some surprising things sometimes, doesn't he?"

Treebird nods, too. "Yes, he does. But in answer to your question, I can tell you this much. As far as I'm concerned, if Amos Reddeer says you're our "Ind-le-la Um-kho-keli", then I'll take his word for it." He angles his head. "I haven't seen this man be wrong yet, eh?"

Indlela Umkhokeli. The Pukaskwa word meaning "Pathfinder". We just look at each other from across the kitchen in silence, until, finally, I figure it's time to change the subject. "So… how're things going with the new casino? Anything new under the sun with the Band?"

He looks thoughtful. "Oh yah, the casino is being built fast," a sly smile creeps over his features, "but I think we've made some of the Chippewa pretty mad at us too, eh?" He winks at me in explanation.

"Their casino has been doing well for a long time over at "Baawitigong", eh? They think we'll be cutting into their profit a lot." He shrugs his shoulders again. "But Mr. Hennessy says that according to his figures, there'll be plenty enough to go around. So, I think that's just sour grapes, eh?"

Baawitigong. The Pukaskwa word for the town of Sault Ste Marie. The Soo, as it's called by everybody up here. I rub a hand over my chin. I'd been following the Tribe's progress through the newsletter and had thought about this, too. I have to agree with him.

"Yeah, Jason, I think you're probably right about that."

Treebird exhales a sigh and moves his head in a "what will be, will be" manner. "Yah, but other than that there's not been much…" He suddenly looks at me directly, some new realization there. "Well, we did have some visitors from the Air Force a few days ago." He sharpens his gaze. "It seems that they want to extend the lease on Muskrat Island, eh?"

He says the last with a look of expectation and question, like I have something to add to it. I don't, although I find that tidbit of info very interesting. I give him a dumbfounded look in return before phrasing my words in question, rather than answer form.

"Hmm? That's weird." I turn my head to the side. "Was it a General that was there running the show for them, then?"

He's watching me closely and slowly shakes his head. "No, "makte", eh? A black man. A captain, by his rank insignia. He seemed to be the one in charge."

I nod slowly. So Mussenberg was in command of their operation now, or so it would seem. That's right, he'd said that Shears had been transferred, hadn't he? That could be a break for me. I get along a lot better with him than I ever would've with Shears. I look over at the tribal policeman and decide to switch gears and move away from this topic. I snap my fingers.

"Hey, did you ever stop into the hospital down in Escanaba like I told ya to?"

A slow smile travels over Treebird's face. "Oh yah, I did. Back when I was down there closing up the boathouse, eh?" He shakes his head in remembrance. "I don't know whether to be mad at you or not for that one. I got a date with Wanda, one of the night nurses there, eh… for the next night and boy, she's a wild one."

We both laugh out loud at that. Then Treebird turns earnest and looks over at me squarely. "I know it's none of my business, but you do know that Annette Cole has a pretty serious thing for you, eh?" I sniff and feel the smile washing off my face as I look away. "Past tense, Jason. Past tense."

He fixes his eyes on me again and clicks his tongue. "Too, bad. She's a "winsakeeyahgo", eh?"

I smile faintly again and nod. Winsakeeyago means "pretty girl". Nettie is certainly that. He shuffles his boots on the floor and clears his throat.

"Well, you asked for my opinion before, Detective, and so I think I'll give it to you on this too, eh, even though you didn't ask for it?" I bring my eyesight back up to him as he continues.

"She and Amos are very close and so I see her a lot." Again he sends the sharpened look to me. "If I were you, I wouldn't be too quick to make a determination on how she feels, eh?"

That comment staggers me. "Has… has she said something to you?"

Treebird looks at me and smiles easily. "No, Detective, she hasn't." He cocks an eye. "It's what she hasn't said whenever your name is mentioned, that makes it so different."

He winks at me, looks at the clock above the sink and says that he has to go. I rally myself before he gets out the door and tell him I'm still waiting for a call and will probably be here until it comes in. I throw a wave and close the entryway. Then I put my palms flat on the wood and rest my forehead against the door. As I listen to his patrol Jeep back up and pull out of the drive, I ponder what he'd said. Nettie! I wish… man, oh, man… I wish! These feelings are overpowering me and it takes the ringing of the phone to jar me loose. I dash across the room to pick it up! As my fingers slip over the receiver, I hear "Ghost Riders" begin playing softly in the back of my mind. I don't have time to ponder that. It's Gangues on the other end.

"Ghostman? We still cool there?"

"Yeah, Mark, as far as I know."

"Hey, what'd I tell ya m'man? I was in there slicker than greased owlshit, dude! But the bad news is, Ely.. that they know I waz there, too."

A fear clutches at me. I'd wanted to keep him out of this as much as possible, and now, I've drug him right into it with me! I hear the worry in my voice as I phrase the question. "So you're compromised then, Gangues?"

"No, no man! It ain't nuthin like that! It's cool on my end, okay? They don't know jack about me, alright? Ya see, I waz supposed ta get in and out without them ever knowing I was there, okay? But shit man, they had the file booby trapped, ya know? I came in as quiet as mouse, found and attached the file, copied it and then, I noticed that it had an addendum attachment, another separate report about a different plane and crew er somethin'." He grabs a breath before continuing.

"So I thought, shit man, why not? And I waz gonna grab that file next, but as soon as I released the first file, man… the trip flares went up and claymores began blowing up everywhere, ya know!" He sighs mightily. "Anyways, I got away clean, but no two ways around it dude, they definitely know that somebody was there, ya know?"

I put a hand up to my brow and realize that there's sweat there.

Good old Gangues the Conqueror! He hadn't lost his touch. Thank the Great Good Spirit for that, huh?. I turn back to the mouthpiece.

"Yeah, well that part's no big deal, but Gangues… you're sure that you're okay?"

"Ab-so-fuck'n-lutley, man. Cleaner than a boot camp head but I'm really sorry about the mess-up, Ghostman."

I let a sigh escape and feel the worry leeching off. "No sweat, pal. So you got the file then, anyway? Was there another one or what?"

"Yeah, a separate report that was attached ta it, after this one was archived. The one I got is the original that was filed and it looks like this other report was a part a that somehow. I'm sorry I couldn't snag it, too?"

I smile to an empty room. "Gangues, I'm serious, okay? Don't sweat it. It's no big deal."

"Yeah, well, okay, Ghostman. But anyways, dude, the one I got here, well this don't make any sense, ya know? I got the accident report here, but it ain't about anything recent, m'man. This accident happened back in 1953? And shit, man, the plane was lost over Lake Superior, not Lake Michigan."

A cold chill sweeps over me as I hear that and the Ghost Riders song drones on quietly in the background. I clear my throat. "Ah, hem. Yeah, Gangues, what's it say?"

He begins reading information off the file as I mentally try to turn off the music in my head and deal with the sudden onrush of shinkakee. I'm able to tune him in better and begin listening in earnest. He says that according to the report, an F-89 aircraft was sent up on a search for an unknown radar contact at around 6:15 at night on November 23, 1953. The airplane was based at the now closed Kinross Air Force Base near Sault Ste Marie, Michigan. It apparently crashed out over Lake Superior, about seventy miles northeast of the Keweenaw Point. An exhaustive search turned up nothing. No sign of debris, no wreckage, no bodies… nothing. And then he pauses in the delivery to ask a question.

"Ghostman, this can't be what you want, is it? I mean, shit man, this thing's fifty years old, ya know?"

I mumble out an "I don't know" and Gangues resumes reading the file again. But I'm only half listening. A thousand questions are whirling around inside me, trying to dodge the shinkakee in there. Why would the Air Force be guarding this old file? How can an old accident with an airplane missing and crashed in Lake Superior, have anything to do with Muskrat Island? What, or who, are The little Green Men? How do the Chinese fit into this? Is Veeter connected to this at all? I hear that Gangues has stopped reading and is asking me a

question and I'm about to answer him when the final thought comes
flying in, knocking everything over inside my feeble little brain.
Wasn't November 23, 1953... the date that old man Veeter'd used in
his cock-a-maimie story about leaving the island? I feel shivers slide
down my arms as the song automatically goes up a notch inside my
scalp. I gulp and can't swallow. I try to speak a few times before I'm
actually able to respond to Gangues.

"I'm sorry, Mark, my mind was on something else. What'd you
say?"

"Yeah... well I waz just tell'n ya that I thought that I'd heard a
this before, ya know... this missing jet? Anyways, while I waz
search'n for the NBC connection, I did a little look'n around for this,
too. And sure enough, m'man, there's a ton a shit out there on the web
about UFO's taking this plane! The UFO crazies, man... they're firm
believers that a flying saucer snatched up this airplane an took it ta
Mars or someplace, ya know?"

I caress the back of my neck and sit down hard in the chair.
Thoughts crash through my head. That could be where Veeter came
up with his wild story. If the old guy's already sick, then the UFO
nonsense would factor right in, wouldn't it? Yeah, probably so. For
now, I dismiss Veeter as a party to this scenario. But there's still a
connection here for everyone else, ain't there? There's got to be, or
else, why did the Air Force pull this old accident report and secure it?
Maybe the missing plane was carrying something that it shouldn't
have been? Now that's a thought, isn't it? Again Veeter and his little
silver beach ball come into the picture. And again, I immediately
dismiss it. Whatever the little ball was, I don't think it's any type of a
weapon or top secret doodad from 1953. Too small, too light and
from too long ago, for any form of the new technology. I get back to
my friend.

"Yeah, that is crazy, Mark, but ya know, that could be it." I hear
his fingers clicking on computer keys again. "Okay," he says while I
try to explain.

"That could be the tie-in, this Air Force Base and its missing
plane. There's a connection here someplace. There's gotta be. Did
you come up with anything on the NBC stuff?"

He grumbles and the sound mixes with the sound of his computer
working. "Well, yes and no. That is, there's nuthin recent. But at
about the same time this plane disappeared, there was a real short
story that ran in the Chicago Tribune about an Air Force B-47 that
was flying over Lake Michigan on its way ta New Mexico and
supposedly dropped a payload of bombs by mistake. The writer
insinuated that the bomber was actually carrying some kind'a new

atomic bomb and not a regular payload." He sighs deeply before going on.

"But the guy didn't come right out and say that in the article either, ya know? Then, nuthin appeared after that first story until like five days later. Then, there's a an editorial comment stating that the paper'd made a mistake and had misquoted a source and all that kind'a stuff. They said that no plane had lost any bombs. Period. So I think that shows the original story ta be bullshit. Well, in my in my opinion anyways. Other than that, Ghostman, I got bumpkiss!"

My mind's racing now and the shinkakee is going deeper into the background. I think I have it with this. The early fifties? This was the heavy testing period with nuclear weapons, wasn't it? And most of that testing was in New Mexico, right? Yeah, it was. They could've come with something that was hot and that somehow... got lost. And maybe, whatever it was... still has a lot of value, even today, huh? If that's true? If that happened? Then the Air Force could've squeezed the Chicago newspaper to hush-up the story. Especially back in the fifties. They'd've of used the communist threat, McCarthyism and all that jazz. It was all going on about that time, wasn't it? And if they approached the newspaper with all of this...My mind snaps shut on the conclusion. Hell, yeah! The paper would've bought it hook, line and sinker and squashed the story flat.

"Gangues, where was that B-47 out've of?"

"Uhh... hold on a minute, I downsized it on another screen somewhere." I hear the keys of his computer go silent and imagine him squirreling a computer mouse instead. A blooping sound comes over the phone from his monitor

"Yeah, here it is. Yeah, the original story states that the plane left Kinross Air Base, Michigan after refueling and was flying ta an undisclosed location in New Mexico. Umm, it doesn't say where it was originally from. Shit man, like I said, it's a real short story, ya know, Ghostman?"

"Yeah, I do. No sweat Gangues. Uh, what about the reporter that did the story for the paper? Can you dig up anything on him?"

"Hold on and... okay. Guy's name was Arthur Krantz...," I hear computer keys again as he talks to me, "I'll start a search here... yeah, okay. That's work'n. What else, m'man?"

"Alright Gangues, can you also pull me up everything you can find on that base uhh, Kinross, right, and personnel who were assigned there in 1953?"

"Already done, Ghostman. I figured that was where ya wanted ta go next, m'man, and I've already gone back into the Air Farce's archives. Just let me get ta another screen here." There is the sound of a file blooping up on a screen, "and presto... So what'chu need first?"

That's what he'd been doing on the computer as we talked. There was nobody better at this stuff than he was. He did work for private investigators from all over the country. My man, Gangues! My euphoria at seeing light at the end of this crummy tunnel was showing. I almost holler at Gangues when I speak again.

"What kind of base was it, Gangues? I don't know much about what the Air Force did back in the 1950s or how their bases were setup or anything. Was it a Strategic Air Command Base? MAC? Fighters? What?"

"Well let me see here, Ghostman. Uh, the base was closed on September 30th, 1977. The base commanding officer in 1953 was... oh, a Lieutenant Colonel Nathan B. Hays. Um, it says here that they had both bombers and fighters assigned ta the base back in '53. Ummm... yeah, they had B-47s and F-89 fighters but it looks like the B-47s came in later..."

I'm chugging along nicely until he says that. Mark keeps reading off the info, but now, the shinkakee's cold hand is gripping my heart again. An F-89? Gangues had described the jet earlier, but somehow, I'd breezed right over that. I hadn't made the link. Hadn't Veeter said that he'd seen an F-89 that night in 1953? Yeah, he had. But I'm already starting to put it together now. I'm able to shove the shinkakee off to the side once more.

Was Veeter tied up in this somehow, too? How else would he know what kind of aircraft were based up here back then? Unless, the man really was a spy? I'm taking a big leap here and I know it. Anybody that's ever put model airplanes together could know military aircraft well enough to describe their number designations. I make a mental note to call his daughter and ask her if he builds model airplanes. Somehow, I think that'll be the answer here. My thoughts are pulled away as Gangues finishes relaying the base info to me and has something new.

"Okay, Ghostman, your reporter just came up here and I'm read'n his bio...and uh, oh," he takes a breath and blows it out. "If you waz plan'n on talk'n to 'em, ya can rule that one out. Says here, Arthur Edward Krantz, a career reporter who worked for the Sun Times, Boston Globe, uh... okay...bla, bla, bla and um...feature columnist for the Chicago Tribune until his death... in 1982. Sorry 'bout that, Ghostman."

Shit! I needed to talk to him, too. "Yeah, well ya can't win 'em all, Gangues."

"Yeah, ain't that the truth. Uh, listen, Ghostman, I can see by the old clock on the wall that I'm gonna have'ta break here, ya know?

Gimmie a few minutes and I'll call ya right back, okay? Ya gonna be around?"

"Yeah, I'll be standing by."

"Right, dude. It'll take about fifteen minutes for the system ta reset. While it's doing it's thing, I'll pull the unfo on the base personnel and have that ready. Be right back. Bye, Ghostman!"

I mumble a goodbye as my mind tries to place the pieces of this bizarre puzzle into place. I pull the heavy phone off my ear and reach over to let it drop into its cradle. Then I push myself out of the chair and stretch before lighting up a cigarette. I move over to the window and look up at a blue sky with highlights of a coming snow. It has been clear all day but we'll have snow by early tonight. I take a drag off the cigarette and blow it downward as my head drops in thought. This has to be what it is all about. The Air Force is looking for something of a very secret nature out on Muskrat Island. Something top secret and dangerous and highly desired by a lot of people. It is probably something nuclear, maybe some special type, I don't know. I move my head in a sing-song manner.

What I do know is that they were playing with all kinds of different things back then. Hydrogen, neutron… jeeze, it could've been anything. Maybe even some bizarre chemical agent, who knows? Whatever it is, the Chinese found out about it and wanted it badly enough, to send their best agents after it. And old man Veeter, well, I wasn't sure where he fit into this, if he fit into it at all. A sigh escapes from me as I realize that there's just too any unanswered questions here. I need to speak to somebody who was stationed on that base back in 1953. Somebody who would've been in a position to know about that B-47 and its loss of a bomb or bombs. I raise my eyes to the burning hand-rolled and watch the smoke chasing itself in twin spirals upward as my other hand drops to the piwaka at my belt loop. Why did I feel like this whole thing is spiraling up too? Ghost Riders is just finishing yet another play in my head. I feel the piwaka in my fingers and give it a squeeze. My head shakes of its own accord as I feel nature calling. I finish the smoke and head to answer the summons as I make my way into Amos Reddeer's bathroom again.

I'm standing by the window looking outside when the old phone sounds its ring. I step over and pick it up. "Hello?"

There's a moment's hesitation, then, "Ghostman. We still hands-out there?"

I sense a smile roll over my face. "Far as I know, Gangues, what's the scoop?"

"Ahh, m'man, well, I didn't have much luck on the roster dude. All I've got for you is four names, all of 'em stationed at Kinross in

November a '53 and all of 'em probably… in a job where they might'a known somethin' about that B-47. But shit, dude, I don't think any of 'em are close ta ya, ya know. Where are ya exactly… you're in the Michigan Upper Peninsula somwhere, right?" I hear computer keys clicking again in the back round. I ready the paper and pen and talk into the phone as I wedge it into my shoulder.

"Yeah, Mark, but listen, don't worry about where they're at, okay. I'll take it from here. Just shoot me the names and addresses, if you have them."

"Yeaaaaah… just keep yer pants on there dude. I'm look'n up somethin' here on the map and yeah… here we go. Okay, Ghostman. Do you know where Grand Rapids is?"

So he had pulled up a computer generated map on one of his screens. I let the notebook lower in my hand. "Yeah, it's down-state. Somewhere centered in the lower half, I think. Why?"

"Because, m'man, one a these dudes is there. At a Veteran's Home someplaaaaece… here!" I visualize him squinting at the small street names on a map the size of a 13" television. He's happy with himself now that he found it and the glee transmits easily over the line.

"Yeah, Ely, it's on some street called Monroe in Grand Rapids." He reads the rest. "This guy's name is Joseph Daren Markowski. Dude had an MOS as a radar operator, so I'm assuming that he was probably working in that job while he was there. Anybody with that MOS, would'a probably known the skinny on this B-47, ya know?

I'm busily jotting these things down as he speaks. MOS was the acronym for "Military Occupational Specialty". In civilian terms, it was just the type of job that he did while he was in the Air Force. Gangues is still going.

"Umm, let's see. He was assigned ta the 433rd Fighter/Interceptor Squadron on this November 23 of '53 date and was ETSd out've the Air Force on January 16th, 1955 with an honorable from Lackland Air Force Base in Texas."

I finish scribbling his ETS date. ETS was another acronym for "End-Termination of Service". The military's way of saying the date that you're discharged from duty. All it meant was the date that he got out of the Air Force. I smile as I write out the word "honorable". By honorable, Gangues meant that Markowski'd had a good or favorable separation from his military service, or at least as far as the government was concerned. For some guys, their separation wasn't too favorable from their own perspective. Mark passes me the man's home address which is in Indiana and explains that this guy, Markowski, is hospitalized at the Grand Rapids Veteran's Home for degenerative back disease.

He'd been admitted about two years ago, and he'd been there ever since. I catch up and tell Gangues to go on with the other names. There's one in Missouri, one in Nebraska and another in Florida. After I've copied everything, I scan the information. The guy in Florida had been a Master Sergeant whose MOS was air-traffic controller. Out of all of them, he would probably come the closest to knowing what-was-what, if anything, about this B-47 that I'm interested in. I turn back to the phone.

"Okay, Mark, that should be good enough for a start. Thanks, I appreciate it."

"Yeah, sure. Hey, I'm sorry I couldn't dig up anymore, Ghostman, but fifty years, dude, that's a long time, ya know. A lotta these guys ain't with us anymore, m'man. They're on the farm now, ya know." I sigh as I look at the first snowflakes fluttering down outside the window.

"Yeah, I know Gangues. This is alright though. I should be able to do something with this." There's a short stretch of silence over the line while neither of us speak. Finally, Gangues breaks it.

"What else can I do for you, man? What else ya need, Ghostman?"

I feel my head twist as my eyes drop down to the notepad. It looks like I'm going to owe Amos a new one because I used a lot of this one up. I'd never planned on this whole thing taking this kind of a turn, but then…once the game's afoot, you just can't ever tell where it'll lead. I say as much to Gangues.

"Nothing, Gangues. I've got no concrete idea what the hell's going on yet, ya know. I'm just following the current ta see where it leads right now." I nod my head at him over the phone. "I think I'm gonna be good with this for now. But why don't you give me your cell number. If I need ta get in touch with you, I'll call you on that and then we can set up a secure line at another location, okay?" Gangues gives me his number and I copy it down on the pad. Then he's asking again.

"You're sure, Ghostman? 'Cause like I said, dude, I ain't doing nuthin that can't wait, ya know? And like I told ya, m'man, I can give ya a physical hand here too, ya know?"

I smile as I drop the pad on the stand and straighten up, stretching my back. "No, buddy, I think I'm square for now. I should be…" then another thought runs across my mind. Why not? You never know, right?

"Wait a minute, I just thought of something else ya could check for me, Gangues. It's an obituary. An old one in Milwaukee, Wisconsin. Guy's name was…" I lean over to the stand and spin back the pages of my little book to my notes from the island and place my finger on the name… "Scheel. Albert Scheel. Supposed to have died in November of '53 too. And Gangues, this ain't a biggy either, ya know? It's just a detail I'm working. My hunch is that you won't find anybody by that name 'cause there's nobody ta find, okay?"

I hear computer keys clacking again. "Okay, dude, but… ahhh shit, man! Okay, I waz pull'n that up for ya right now but the server's down. I gotta get ta different screen. Just be a minute, okay?"

"No, Mark. Forget it for now, okay? I've got ta get going here. I'll give ya call and you can give it ta me then, okay?"

"Okay, Ghostman, I can dig it. I'll have that for ya when ya ring me up, dude. But you keep me posted on this shit, ya hear? I mean, I wanna know if the Air Farce starts playing outside the rules, dig?" I snicker. If he only knew, eh? "Yeah, Gangues, I dig. And again bro… thanks. I mean it."

"Hey, ain't no thing, dude. Keep yer powder dry, Ghostman! Toot-a-loo."

I say goodbye and toss the notepad into the chair. Then I press down the button on top of the old phone to clear the line. When the tone comes up, I dial directory assistance and ask for Grand Rapids and the number to the Veteran's Home there. The mechanical operator passes the number and I bend over and scribble it on the pad, resting it on the chair seat. Then I dial the number and when it's answered, I glance at my notes and ask if Joseph Daren Markowski is still a patient there. The receptionist checks her roster and says that, yes, indeed he is, and would I like to be connected to his room. He's in 407. I thank her and say I'll call back later Then I hang up the heavy old receiver and grab my small book from the stand.

I turn away a little too quickly and feel a jab of pain in my side. It's not enough to kill me but sharp enough to remind me that the ribs are still tender and haven't healed all the way, yet. I make my way into the kitchen and pull out a ten dollar bill from my wallet and lay it down. Then I add a P.S. to the note I'd left for Amos on the table, telling him about the long distance call and the tablet. Then I move back out to the front door. As I open it an turn back to survey the museum-like place, I casually wonder if I'll ever see it again. I hope so. There're a lot of things in here that I'd like to talk to the old shaman about. But I'm going someplace and I don't know exactly where… or if, I'll still be breathing after I arrive. I blow a long breath into the room. Oh, well, I know that the first place I've got to go is home. I've got to gear-up and get on the road to that someplace, wherever it turns out to be. I pull the door to and move down the steps and over to the old Jeep, covered with an inch of fluffy new snow. A few minutes later, I turn in my own drive.

Back at the Stone Cabin

As I idle the Jeep down my driveway, I let my eyes rove over the terrain, looking for anomalies. I'm positive now that I'm back in the game and my senses are working that mode. As I drive along, I see nothing that looks out of the ordinary. The other half of my brain is pondering the travel question. I've pretty much decided that my first stop on this little journey is going to be Grand Rapids. It's close and while the odds are better that I'll get the info I need from the guy in Florida, I figure I might as well cover all the ground I can, in the easiest way possible. From an investigative point of view, that means interviewing this guy Markowski first. Now the only question is, do I drive down there or catch a plane and fly?

I bring the Jeep to a stop by the front door and look around. Everything appears normal enough. I get out and make my way around the cabin, looking for sign. I don't find anything unexpected, so I enter the cabin and go through similar motions there. Again, I come up empty. That's good. Then I make a beeline straight into my room and the picture on the wall. Tossing my jacket on the bed, I swing the painting back and take the little Glock from its crevice. I remove the clip and work the slide, ejecting the shell that was in the chamber. It pops out to land on the rug covering the hardwood floor. I visually check the weapon then re-insert the clip and chamber a new round into the barrel. Then I bend down, retrieve the shell and pop the clip out again to feed this round into the clip. Finally, I snap the magazine back in place and slip the pistol into its holster and slide it into the small of my back.

There. For the first time in a couple of hours now, I feel comfortable again. Not carrying a weapon is fine as long as everything is alright in your world. In fact, having to carry one when everything is okay, is mostly a hassle. But once it isn't, once things turn wrong in my little universe, then not having a weapon worries me a lot. And I know for a fact, now… that things are not alright in my world. It may not be solid as far as proof goes, but everything I smell, sense and feel… right down to the marrow in my bones, tells me that I'm in trouble again. And I'm dragging the Black River Band of Pukaskwa right along with me, too. I nod my head to myself. I'll heed these feelings.

I walk back out into the living room and feel the coolness of the air. I go to the stove and open the door. Yep, it's almost out. There're only a few small pieces of the wood still holding flame from those

that I'd stoked before going over to Amos's. I wonder if I should add
more wood, or not? I glance at my watch and decide that I'd be
smarter not to. What I can do, though, is heat up the room and burn
out the creosote that accumulates in the stove pipe at the same time. I
step back into the bedroom and grab my field jacket off the bed.

I throw it on as I walk back out through the kitchen door and head
over to the wood pile. My eyes roam around and see nothing amiss out
here. I load several pieces of split jack pine into the crook of my arm
and make my way back into the cabin. I chock the light-weight wood
into the stove and the flames begin licking around it greedily. I shut
the stove's door and clamp down the handle before standing. Next, I
twist the damper in the pipe to fully open and the stove begins to roar
with the noise of flame inside. The room immediately picks up the
heat. That done, I head out the front door and go over to the old red
Jeep.

I pop off the hood latches on either side and raise the hood to
check the oil, water and belts. I'd changed the oil last week so it
should be good enough. The windshield washer reservoir is even full.
Everything else looks good, too, so I lower the hood and re-set the
latches. I walk around and bop my hand against the spare tire
mounted on back. It's solid and holding air and the other four are in
good shape too. The jack is under the hood, so… I stand back and
decide that the old Jeep will make to Grand Rapids. I take out a
handrolled and light it up in the gently falling snow. The old red CJ-7
Jeep was the first and last brand new vehicle that my Uncle Mason had
ever owned. He bought it new in 1985 and the thing only had thirty
thousands miles on it now. I could fly to Grand Rapids, but money, as
in currency form, would be a problem.

I'd have to use a credit card for a plane ticket and that, I figure,
wouldn't be too smart right now. I'll probably have to use a card a
anyway, especially since I don't expect the interview in Grand Rapids
to pan out. But not at the start. You never know, I might get lucky
down in "Trollville". One never knows, do one? I'm thinking about
this as I take my stuff from inside the Jeep and begin walking toward
the cabin. Trollville was what the Yoopers up here called anyone who
lived in Michigan's Lower Peninsula. Those folks were south and
hence, under the Mackinaw Bridge that connected the two bodies of
land. I always forget the simple little dumb things that can make life
enjoyable, don't I? I'm smiling in memory as I begin to pass the old
knife-stuck stump. I feel the smile disappear as I stop and wiggle the
survival knife out of the wood. I take it up the steps and into the cabin
with me. Yep. One never does know… does one?

An hour land a half later, I have all of my gear packed and sitting out in the Jeep. I'd pulled it up and disengaged the snowplow, dropping it off by the garage. An oldies station out of Marquette is Ghost Riders tune that's on "constant" play inside my head. I fix some eggs and potatoes and sit down. As I sip from a glass of milk, I look at the stack of money lying on the table. This is all of the cash that I have here at the cabin.

Four hundred and twenty two dollars. That's not much, but I can Only get to my other finances electronically. If somebody's watching me, then they're probably monitoring my accounts, too. My hand idly stacks the money as I eat at the table. I finish eating and look at the mantle clock in the living room as it strikes the quarter hour. I'd better get going. I hadn't slept much last night and I have a long, dark drive ahead of me. I also have to stop at a barber shop someplace in Marquette, before everything closes down there. I figure that there is a chance I might have to play policeman again. A cop would probably seem a little more authentic with short hair. So I'd cut most of mine off in the bathroom with the scissors. But a hack job is a hack job. I need to get it trimmed up better than it is. I take the plate and glass over to the sink and then head outside to start the old Jeep so that it can begin warming.

When I come back in, I stuff the money in my pants pocket and turn off the radio. Then I move at a brisk pace as I quickly wash the dishes and put everything away. After that, I move around the cabin, locking doors and windows and pulling curtains shut. I figure that there's no sense in making things any easier for my unwanted guests, should they come calling. I decide, at the last, to leave the table light on in the living room. I check the wood stove and see the bare traces of embers in the firebox. I move over and adjust the thermostat that controls the back-up heat for the cabin, two old wall furnaces, fired by a propane tank outside. I lower it to fifty degrees, just enough to keep the pipes from freezing.

I already have my flight jacket out in the Jeep. I think I've got it all here, so after a quick look around, I slip back into the camouflage field jacket and step through the front door, pulling it closed behind me. It shuts with click and locks. It's snowing steadily again. The rusty old red Jeep is purring in the drive as I snap my fingers in remembrance. I grab a push broom off the porch and move over to the Pukaskwa Patrol Jeep. I sweep the accumulated snow off and knock it free from the door so that I can gain access. When I finally get it clear, I find that the driver's door is frozen shut. I have to make the same effort on the passenger side before I can get a door open. Once inside, I rummage around until I find the wallet with my Tribal badge and I.D. Slipping it in the chest pocket of the field jacket, I close the door and trot back around the idling Jeep.

Twenty five minutes later, I'm close to my turn. I have to flip up the old Jeep's wipers to fast speed. The snow is coming in thick wads now and if there were any wind to speak of, it would be white-out conditions on the road. Folks seem to know it, too, because I haven't seen another car since I left the cabin. I'm approaching the turn off for State Highway 28. My eyes do a cursory security check of the mirrors every now and then as I ponder this trip. The travel route is laid out easily in my mind. I'll take State 28 down to County 77 then follow that road until I hit US 2. I'll take Highway 2 to the east, right over to Interstate 75 and head south that way until I pick up US 131. That interstate, will bring me right into downtown Grand Rapids.

As I slow for the upcoming turn at Thoney Point, I see a military Hummvee just slowing and coming to the stop sign with his turn signal on. I reach over quickly and grab the sunglasses off the passenger seat and poke them on my head. I brake for the turn and angle my face away. I crank the wheel over as the driver in the Hummer glances at me passing by him. I speed up and shift the Jeep as my eyes pop to the rearview mirror. The Hummer's not following. It's completing its turn and driving back toward the way I'd just come. Toward my place. I keep flipping my eyes to the mirror as I drive on, but nothing changes. No followers. I didn't get a good look at the Hummer. No way I could've made any registration numbers painted on the unit.

But it was camouflaged in woodland pattern. Well, yeah, but crap, man… so was every National Guard and Army Reserve vehicle these days, too. So it's possible that it was just a couple of Guardsman or Reservists, out doing whatever it is that they do? Yeah, but I doubted it. As that thought passes, my eyes dart to the mirror again and still they see nothing. The guys in the Hummer might not have made me either, eh? The snow is coming hard and I turned away as I passed them. My hand thumps the steering wheel as I give up on it. Just to be on the safe side, though, I decide to wait until I get to the other side of bridge to get my haircut. I'll stop someplace once I am across.

I shake my head to the flipping wipers in front of me. Worrying isn't going to help, is it? If they're looking for me and they made me, then they made me. So what? What's the worst that could happen? Ahhh shit! I smile as I think. Yeah, well, I already know the answer to that one, don't I? I reach over and turn on the radio. The oldies station comes in even better this close to Marquette and The Beatles are singing out, "Let It Be!" My eyes jump up to the mirror once more and I begin singing with them.

The Observation Team,
The road in front of the Stone Family Cabin,
Twenty-Five minutes later.

Staff Sergeant Steve Wilkes had the wipers going full blast and he still couldn't see anything. Shit!, he thought, why the hell were they out here? No one else was! The only other car they'd seen since leaving Marquette had been that guy in the red Jeep. He stole a quick glance at his partner, Sergeant Hector Ramerez. He was bent over the Captain's silly-assed map drawing, trying figure out if they'd taken a wrong turn somewhere. He squinted into the whiteness out the windshield and spoke to him.

"Well, what about it, Heck? Do we go back or not?"
Ramerez shook his head no and raised his eyes to peer out of the windshield. "No, mahn, I theenk thees is the right road." He jabbed a hand at the glass in front of him. "Slow down, hermano. I see a mailbox er something up ahead."

Wilkes applied the brake and the Hummer slowed. And sure enough, as he squinted through the beating wiper blades, he saw a mailbox, too. As the Hummer rode past it, both men could make out the faded lettering that said simply, "Stone."

"Tha's eeit, Steve. Le's go down and come back, eh? Tha' way we can eese up and park thee unit som'place', eh? An make our approach tha' way?"

"Yeah, okay, Hector. But you see how deep this snow is here, man? I told you we needed the snowshoes, didn't I?"

Ramerez smiled at his friend and held up his hands. "Hey, mahn, I tol' you, I don' kno' nathing about no snow, mahn. In Houston, we don' get any of thees stuff, you know?"

Wilkes was pissed. He didn't want to be here and he really wasn't looking forward to dragging his ass through fifty feet deep snow, either. He jabbed a finger across at Ramerez as he slowed, eyeing an old logging road off to the side.

"Yeah well next time, amigo, you listen ta me! In Pennsylvania, we get plenty a the shit and I'm tell'n ya, it's gonna be miserable as hell traipsing through this crap and lugging all the gear, too!"

Wilkes decided to pull the Hummer into the old abandoned road and eased it over the five foot high snowbank. Both men braced as the vehicle climbed up and came down hard on the other side. They parked the Hummer off in a stand of pine trees and pulled their gear out to the old logging road. It was snowing even harder as they began their trek into the woods bordering Stone's cabin. It took them almost an hour to get to the outskirts of the log structure by a frozen lake.

The temperature was falling almost as fast as the snow. Both men were cold and tired. Wilkes un-slung the M-16 from his shoulder, as Ramerez scanned the area around them, his weapon at the ready. It was fast going dark now and the snow was coming down relentlessly. Wilkes pulled out the binoculars and focused in on the cabin. He spoke to Ramerez as the other man looked over the terrain for the most suitable observation post.

"Yeah, I think we got'em Heck. There's some smoke coming from the chimney and I can see that Police Cherokee that the Captain said ta look for. It's parked right beside that barn-like building. There's a light on so he's in there, buddy boy." He dropped the glasses and turned to his partner. Ramerez nodded in the tween-darkness over to a clump of birch about two hundred and fifty yards from the cabin. The Mexican Security Policeman was shaking in the cold.

"I theenk we should set up thee NDP by thos' white treees, don't 'cha think?"

Wilkes looked where his partner pointed and shrugged his shoulders through a shiver. "Them trees are called birch, ya dumb taco vendor. But you're right, that's a pretty good spot for a night defensive position." He smiled at his friend as he re-slung his rifle.

"Let's go get one a them little stoves go'n before I freeze my nuts off."

Ramerez started gathering gear and replied through chattering teeth. "Hey, hermano. I don' geeve a sheet wha' thos' treees are called, mahn. An a woman like you... she probly' don' have no nutz, anyway. So don' woory abou 'em freezeen, huh?"

Wilkes chuckled as the two men began their exhaustive maneuver over to the clump of birch. He climbed out behind his partner and whispered a hushed response. "Listen, Airman Ramerez, that kind of talk borders on disrespect, even if it is true, okay?" Ramerez chuckled softly up ahead as they crawled along and Wilkes continued the light banter.

"Next thing ya know, you'll be making inappropriate remarks about my dressing in women's clothes, too. Remember, you no-green card little twerp, I outrank you, so if ya don't wanna get inta trouble for insubordination, I'd leave it alone if I waz you. Just let it be, Ramerez. Let it be." Wilkes smiled in the dark as he heard his partner guffaw in front of him.

They had to move slowly due to the weather, the deep snow, and the need to remain undetected. It took them another forty minutes before they were in position and were able to radio back that they had the subject under observation and status was normal. And it wasn't until then that they could break out their small stoves and begin to warm themselves and some hot cocoa. The snow came down in white clumps, with flakes the size of golf balls all around them. Both men hunkered down for a long night as they watched the cabin and some guy named Stone.

Chapter Twenty-Seven
"Midnight Cowboy!"

The Town of Naubinway,
Michigan's Upper Peninsula,
2030 hours or 8:30 pm, Same day.

I see an old telephone booth in a bar parking lot and slow down to make the turn. I'm sure now that I'm not being followed but numerous other things are rolling around in my harried little brain. Chief among them is what Gangues had said about these Little Green Men. I've decided that I'm going to give my old pal Piranha a call to see if he can tell me anything. Of course, he may not be home. It's Friday night, and unlike me he may have a social life. I roll the old CJ-7 up to the payphone in the tavern lot and shut it off.

I stretch my legs in the cramped space as I look back at the road I've just pulled off from. It's been snowing steadily all night and the traffic is taking its time on the snow-plugged and greasy thoroughfare. The county plows haven't been able to keep up with the white stuff. I switch my vision back to the phone booth. The snow certainly makes for great cover.

I climb out of the Jeep and the cold almost smacks me silly. I hunker down and scoot the short distance to enter the phone booth. I use my lighter to illuminate the touch pad as I look at the number in my book and press in the digits on the phone. I follow these with those of my long distance calling card. It takes a second or two and then I hear a female voice from the past.

"Hello, Murphy residence?"

"Hi, Dottie, how are you?"

"Oh… I'm fine. Who is … wait, is this? Ely that's you, isn't it? Ely Stone, is that you?"

I look at my reflection on the booth's glass. "Yes, ma'am. It's me."

"Well, for goodness sakes alive, how are you? It's been ages since we've heard from you!"

"It's good to hear your voice, too, Dottie. How're the kids doing? Geeze, I guess they ain't kids anymore, are they?"

"No. No, they're not. Charlotte is married now and has a little one. A boy named Tom, after his grandpa. Susan's is in college and

Frankie well, he likes to be called Frank now, he'll graduate from high school next summer."

"Wow. Time does fly, doesn't it, Dottie?"

"Yes, it does. So, Ely, how are you? Is there finally a woman in your life now?"

I smile then frown as I think of Nettie. Dottie was always worried about me being an old bachelor. Well, there was reason for her to fret, wasn't there? I clear my throat. "No, ma'am. Nobody's been brave or dumb enough to get that close."

She clucks her teeth. "You need to find a girl, Ely. You really do." I don't answer and she sighs in resignation. "Ah well. You military idiots are all the same – pig-headed. Uhm, Tom said that you turned in your papers and got out of the Coast Guard?"

"Yep. I'm just like your old man now. A crotchety, lazy old grump with a bad attitude."

She laughs. "Oh boy, old is right. But he's always been a crotchety Marine and you know it. But enough of this, you hold on and I'll get the Gunny."

I snicker and mumble an "okay" as she sets the phone down. I can hear her calling his name in the distance, as I glance longingly at the Jeep. I'd left my gloves on the seat and the wind whipping through the cracked windows of the booth is cold. I think about her comments in reference to Piranha's retirement. He wasn't happy being out of the Marine Corp but he was alive. So you have to be thankful for the little things, eh?

Piranha had received his nickname because, for some reason, mother nature had seen fit to supply him with an unusual mouth. All of his teeth, even his front ones, were somewhat pointed, like his incisors. He had a smallish, elongated head, that he kept shaved close, and a mouth full of pointy teeth. He kind of looked like one of those little carnivorous fish. In fact, when the movie "Alien" came out, everyone on the team had accused him of being the model for the monster. He didn't think it was funny but we all did. I hear Piranha ask Dottie who it is, and her answer my name. After Tom had retired, they'd moved back to his native Boston. The guy had never lost much of his accent anyway and when he picked up the phone, I knew I had a genuine 'Beantown' boy on the line.

"Hello?"

"Hey, Gunnery Sergeant Murphy, how's it hang'n?"

"Well sonavaaaabetch! It is you, ain't it? You slimy, shallow wateh sailah! How the hell ah ya?"

My smile grows broader in the darkness. Twenty-five years in the Corp and he talks that way to a Coastie. Some things never change and hopefully, never will. "Well, Thomas, I'm staying out've trouble and not getting caught on my good days, ya know?"

"Sheeeit Ghost! Yoah scrawny ass couldn't stay atta trouble on yoah bestest day an you know it!" There's a short silence before he goes on. "Hey, I got the package ya sent an Dottie knows waat ta do with it… just in case I ain't theah… ya know? Is that waat yoah call'n about?"

I switch hands on the receiver and blow warm breath on the free one. "Well, no, Tom, actually, it's something else." I switch hands back again and turn to scope the lot as I continue.

"So…you a'right?

"Yeah. My personal SITREP is good. I just need to pick your brain a little." My attention is drawn to a car pulling into the lot. "Uh, Gangues told me that back during the Gulf War, you had a run-in with some Air Force guys from some weird sounding unit?" My concentration is still on the lot as I watch a man and woman exit the old Dodge and begin walking toward the door of the tavern. They're both staggering a little. I decide that they're harmless and continue.

"Uhm, some unit called "Green Men" or whatever?" There's silence while I figure Gunny's rummaging around inside his memory. But when he speaks again, I know that he hasn't been doing that.

"Ely, ah you mess'n with these guys?" A short silence passes,

"Cause if ya ah, you betta be watch'n yoah ass. Theah some bad people, I shit ya not!"

That causes me to look away from the new arrivals for a second. "Bad how, Tom?"

He sucks in some air on the other end. "These guys've got clout like ya wouldn't believe. An, from waat I laahned, theah like James Bond, ya know? A license ta kill Amehacan citizens, even on U.S. soil. Know waht ah mean? Now national sacuahty uh not, that's some heavy shit!"

The newly arrived couple enters the tavern as I digest that. "What do they do, Tom? What's their primary?"

"Well, like ah said, theah woahk'n undeah national sacuahty. Some'thin ta do with downed NASA satellites and space junk that falls back ta eahth, I guess."

I'm getting a very bad feeling now and the cold seems a minor discomfort compared to it. The little song that's been playing quietly in my head goes up a notch in volume as I form my next question.

"Tom, how'd you happen to run into these guys, anyway?"

"Well, it's like Mach tol'ja. We waz in the Gulf an' I'd busted my ass ta get an infantry company hidden, so's they be able ta pop the

ragheads when they came past'em. Then this Aah Fohce captain
named, Sizzahs or Clippahs, something' like that...

My head does a quick jerk as I interrupt him. "Wait a minute!
What was his name? Could it've been Shears?"

He thinks a minute before responding. "Yeah, that sounds right.
Sheahs. An Aah Fohce captain."

I rub my free hand over my eyes as my stomach roils around.
Probably Major Shears now. I drop my hand and look at the dark lot.
Man...this sucks. I turn back to the phone.

"Yeah, okay, Piranha. Sorry to interrupt. Go ahead."

He waits a beat before continuing. "Yeah, well anyways, this
captain says that we gotta move the company cause a somethin' he's
doin'. An them command idiots... they waz gonna do it, too! Them
troops would'a got the shit shot ahtta 'em by that time... an so I told
this wingnut bastahd that I waz gonna cut his head off and pull his
spine out'ta the hole! Anyways, a Mahrine one-stah stopped me from
doing it an we finally got aiah support foh the grunt's withdrawhl," he
takes a deep breath. "An lateh on, I did some check'n with an old CIA
bud from the 'Nam an that's how I know what ah've told ya. Theah
called the Little Green Men."

There's dead silence on the line now as I take that in and it begins
to swim around in my world of shinkakee. A memory of old man
Veeter's face flashes in my mind for a second. Then I see a mental
picture of a B-47, dropping an atom bomb. Boy, I don't like this. Not
at all! I turn back to the receiver.

"Um, okay, Tom. Do you have anything else on these guys?"

He sighs. "Naw, that's all I know about'em. I dropped it aftah
that." He's concerned. I know that, and can hear it in his voice.

"Is theah somethin' I can do ta help, Ghost? Just say the wohd and
I'll be on'a plane ta whehevah yoah at in a heahtbeat?"

"No, but thanks. I'm clear of these guys now, so I think I'm okay.
I'm just tying up loose ends, is all. But, listen Piranha... if I don't call
you back in the next five days, you go ahead and expedite that
package that I sent... okay?"

He cusses, acknowledging the fact that I'm still in some kind of
danger, but am not accepting his offer for help.

"Shit! Affehmahtive! But you watch yoah six, okay? 'Cause the
next time my dress blues get broke out, I wanna be buerhed in 'em, not
weahing 'em ta yoah funerhral! Ya heah me, ya shallow watah squid!"

I smile, in spite of myself. "Aye, aye, Gunny. My best to the
family and I'll be in touch, okay?"

I hang up the phone after our goodbyes and quickly move back to
the Jeep where another two inches of snow has accumulated. I twist the

key and the starter bites, firing-off the engine. I reach over, grab the snowbrush and walk around whisking the accumulated snow off the old Jeep. I notice that the music's died in the tavern and can hear sounds of a barfight going on inside. Definitively time to scoot. I climb back in to await the Jeep's warm-up knowing that I have to leave before the cops show-up. My eyes move down to the heat gauge in the center of the dash as my mind wanders around in the sea of shinkakee inside my noggin. I force myself to find an island in the abyss. I finally do, and mentally climb up on it to try and sort things out. The first thing I see from this vantage point is that there's a lot more to my new Air Force friends that what I'd thought.

The Jeep's heat gauge is back on the quarter mark now, so I click the fan to on and pull out the defrost lever even as I'm moving, trying to get out of the lot. I switch on the lights and wipers and cruise out of the lot, swiftly going through the four speeds in the old CJ-7. Well, okay. So far - so good. I'm not a mile down the road before a County cruiser with rotating flashers passes me in a hurry from the other direction. I watch the cop car fade in my rearview mirror and think, yeah… so far – so good.

The song on the radio right now is "Rhinestone Cowboy" by Glen Cambell. And I can relate to what he's saying, too. "…get'n cards & letters from people I don't even know and offers come'n over the phone…" Yep. My little Air Force friends, eh. Something about the word…'cowboy'… bothers me. Huh. That's weird. If the weather doesn't get any worse, I should make the other side of the bridge by midnight. My eyes keep darting to the mirror as I move along. Those cops probably weren't looking for me. I'm almost to the little village of Gros Cap, before I decide that bars + drunks = cops. So, I'll be stopping at no more roadside taverns. I still haven't seen a tail and other than a nagging little cowboy thing … I'm beginning to think that I'm skating free. But then, I ask myself, when have I ever thought right?

St. Ignace, Michigan.
"The Straights of Mackinaw",
Between Lakes Michigan and Huron.
Almost midnight, The same day.

I stand drinking a cup of coffee and looking out the service station window at the Mackinaw Bridge. It's beautiful tonight. I bend my legs and twist my back, both of which have stiffened during the drive south. As I stare out the window and sip coffee, the snow is still falling. The bridge is fully lit, making is seem even bigger and more massive in the darkness. I remember that when it was built, it was the longest suspension bridge in the world. Five miles across. I idly wonder if it still holds the title as I head to the restrooms. Glen Cambell is moaning-out "Rhinestone Cowboy" again, this time from the station attendant's country station. I see that's it's almost midnight as I enter the 'Head' and the dumb song still bothers me, eh.

As I wash my hands, my mind ponders the new information I've gleaned. What Tom told me about the Little Green Men bothers me. All of this has to be about that Air Force bomber and a missing bomb, doesn't it? Everything comes back to this and it is making more sense all the time. And these guys, Shears and Mussenberg, are part of a nuclear recovery team of some kind, right? It's the only thing that makes sense.

But if that's what they are, shouldn't they have a name like Atom Ant or Atomic Assholes or something like that? I notice my furrowed eyebrows in the mirror, as I continue asking these questions. What's this Little Green Men deal? And Piranha said that their primary mission was supposed to be recovering space satellites, right? Why would that have a heavy national security application? Could it be something like this star wars missile defense shield that they're always talking about? Maybe, but in 1953? Crap! I shake my head at the reflection. Man, I don't like the way this keeps drifting around here. I see my face grow worried, as I subconsciously drop my hand and finger the piwaka hanging from the belt loop. I shiver out a shrug.

The chubby little guy behind it asks if I'm going over the bridge. When I answer yes, he tells me that the wind has died down, so crossing the bridge shouldn't be too bad right now. He explains that a few years ago a girl in a small car was blown right over the side in a gust of wind. She went all the way down to land in Lake Huron. She and her car fell the almost half a mile and crashed right through the ice. They say that just the fall probably killed her so she didn't drown or anything like that. I nod and go back outside.

As I leave the clerk behind and turn back into the driving lane, a following county snowplow's amber dashing lights are all that I have in the rearview. I can make out the lights ahead belonging to Mackinaw City. I have an oldies station from that city tuned into the radio right now. "Three Dog Night" is singing about Jeremiah being a bullfrog as I drive along. My thoughts go back to what the gas station guy said. There's something here for me but I don't know what it is.

I shake my head and tap the steering wheel to the song's beat. A part of the chorus rings true with me as I sing, "I never understood a single word he said, but I helped him drink his wine, yeah, he always had some mighty fine wine". I don't understand what it actually was that the guy at the gas station said that was bothering me, but it was something important. I know it is. Something underlying his comments triggered something else in my feeble little mind.

Was it that most people would think the female driver had drown when actually, it was probably the fall that had killed her when she went off the bridge? Something simply mistaken... for something else? I shake my head in dismissal. I'm tired. Oh, well. Until it comes to me, I decide to let my attention be drawn to the monstrous bridge that I'm driving over. It's illuminated with hundreds of snow-covered white lights that look like sparkling bright eagle feathers in the flurried night. It's pretty and causes me to smile.

**Interstate US 131, A Rest Area On The Southern Route,
Just North of Rockford, Michigan.
5:10 am, The Next Morning.**

I open the door and crab my way out of the Jeep, dragging my flight jacket with me. A gust of wind grabs the door from my hand and slams it shut for me. I'm too tired to care. The jacket is still encased in the plastic wrapping, like it has been since I'd picked it up from the cleaners in Escanaba. As I peel the plastic wrapper off, I feel every joint and bone cry out in protest. A cramped Jeep does not make for a pleasant dive, eh. I finally get the stretchy stuff unthreaded and swing the jacket over my shoulders. I wad up the plastic as I try to straighten my body out. I contort myself into a stretch and then roll my wrist up to look at my watch.

It's ten after five in the morning. I bring my sore eyes upward as a semi-truck goes roaring down the expressway in front of the rest stop, its tires and diesel making the commotion as it sails on past. I let my eyes wander about. There are several big trucks and trailers sitting around the rest area, their parking lights on and engines running while their drivers catch a few hours sleep. I envy them because I'm tired, too. No, maybe exhausted is an even a better word. Inside the brick restroom facility, I stop to look at a glassed-in state map with a "You Are Here" circle affixed near the town of Rockford. I'm just on the outskirts of Grand Rapids now. That's good, anyway.

My morning bath ritual complete, I amble back outside and quickly run through my daily prayers, facing the four directions as the sun begins to crack the horizon. Then I wander over to the Jeep. I weasel my way back in, lock both doors and stretch my legs across as best as I can, my head up against the driver's door and window. I draw up the old gray wool Coast Guard blanket that I'd liberated from someplace over the years, and finally adjust myself.   I have the Glock firmly in my right hand, resting on my chest, under the blanket. I drop my eyes down to the emblazoned, large "U.S." stamped on the blanket. It's resting over the top of the hand that holds the weapon. I've had the blanket a long time and fervently hope that I won't have to ruin it with a bullet hole. I'm hoping, even more, that some one else doesn't ruin it with a bunch of them. I'm thinking that as "Ghost Riders In The Sky" plays low and gently in my psyche. My eyes flutter once or twice before I drift off.

The Stone Family Cabin,
Near Yellow Dog Point, MI.
Same time, Same day.

 Airman Pamala Styles grunted as she dragged the pack through the deep snow. At least she and the other two airmen were able to follow the busted trail that Wilkes and Ramerez had broken on the way in. The heavy cold weather uniform didn't help matters either and neither did the damn dark! She was exhausted as she pushed along behind the men in front of her, every step driving a flash of cold between and around her legs as she sank down in the snow up to her crotch. She struggled along as she thought about yesterday. She and her room mate Trish Gardner, the only other female airman assigned here, had been in Sault Ste. Marie all day and all night. They had wandered around museums, gone to dinner, seen a play at the university, and then had stopped off at a local bar where they'd danced and flirted with the college guys. It had been great, and since neither of them had been scheduled for duty until noon today, they had planned to sleep in, too.
 So much for that, huh. When she and Trish had driven into the gatehouse at one o'clock this morning, she'd been told to report to Captain Mussenberg's office immediately. He had all but accused her of dereliction of duty for being out of touch all day. But that, of course, was ridiculous. He then told her that he needed her to verify this OP (observation post) tonight. So here she was, dragging this stupid pack and rifle in snow almost over her head, and freezing to death. Well, at least they didn't have to carry that stupid satellite phone from their hummer, too. The guys already had one out here and that was how they were able To contact Mussenberg. Her new unit had communicated with Wilkes and Ramerez by radio while on the way. They had parked their own unit right beside the other in the pine trees. This snow was murder, as she sank down past her crotch with each step. She was sweating and freezing all at the same time. A few seconds later they stopped, and the lead airman whispered an answer to the hushed challenge that

came from observation post up ahead. Then she and the other airmen resumed their trek and eventually waded their way up to where the other two men waited. She slid into the makeshift hole they had dug that had a white poncho caped over it. She could feel the heat from the little stoves as soon as she got inside.

The two replacements, Airmen 2nd Class Barnes and Airman 3rd Class Conners, were there to relieve Wilkes and Ramerez on the OP duty. For now, they remained outside and covered the position with their weapons. Captain Mussenberg had told her that her job was to verify that everything was the same as it had been when she was here a few days ago. If everything were as it should be, then she'd be able to ride back with Wilkes and Ramerez. A hummer doesn't have the best ride, but as tired as she was, she figured she'd catch a few winks with no problem. Wilkes looked at her as she leaned her rifle against the snow. He smiled as she pulled off the pack that was almost as tall as she was.

"Well, Styles, what's the matter? Ain't ya glad ta be here, er what?"

She looked at him as light from the dawn began making its way across the land. "Oh yeah, right, Sarge! I'm really happy to be here with you guys!"

She finished shrugging out of her pack and slithered in the snow up to the little window made from forked sticks and packed snow. She looked across at the cabin she'd visited a few days ago. There was a light on, but, otherwise, no sign of life yet. "So, I take it he's still sleeping, huh?"

Wilkes took the binoculars off from over his head and passed them to her. "Yeah, that's what we figure. By the time we got set-up, it was almost dark. But there was smoke coming out'ta the chimney and that light was on. Nobody's stepped outside all night."

Styles adjusted the eyepieces down to fit her, then focused the Glasses in on the cabin. Wilkes and the Ramerez began whispering to the new guys, explaining about the OP layout and other pertinent information for their relief. She had the low light glasses up and searching around the area below. Everything looked like it had the other day. She continued to work the glasses over the scene and then suddenly stopped. Ramerez was whispering to her about how cold it had gotten last night. As he packed his personal gear, she turned around quickly and cut him off. Looking directly at Wilkes, she said, "Where's the little Jeep?"

Wilkes finished packing his stuff as she said that. He pushed the words out in hushed tones. "What little Jeep? What're ya talking about? The Jeep's parked right there, by that barn er whatever it is."

Styles threw the glasses back up to her eyes again. "No, not that police Jeep, the little red one. The one with the plow?" She dropped the glasses again and looked over to Wilkes. He, in turn, looked at Ramerez. His partner's face showed confusion as he hunched his shoulders. Wilkes turned back to her.

"Hey, that's the only Jeep that we've seen, Styles. Are you say'n that there's supposed ta be another one 'cause if ya are, then we gotta problem!"

The woods around them were beginning to take on shape and texture as the dawn broke over the treeline. She brought the glasses back to her eyes once more and scanned the roof. "Shit! There's no smoke coming from that chimney!"

Wilkes slithered over by her and spoke in a harsh whisper, close to her ear. "Yeah, but that don't mean nothing. We wondered about that, too." He pointed a gloved finger out of the opening. "Ya see those little silver pipes sticking outta the roof? Well, those're furnace pipes, okay? So he might've let his wood fire die, but he's still got heat in there."

Styles was still scanning the area below when she uttered an oath. "Shit! There's the snowplow!" She quick pulled the glasses off her head and passed them to Wilkes. He put them up as she pointed to the garage in a soft voice. "See it? Right there by the garage, just in back of the police Jeep?"

"Yeah, I see it now." He lowered the glasses and looked at her in the brightening woodlot.

"So, there's supposed ta be another Jeep, another cop Jeep down there then? The Captain didn't say nothing ta us about two cop Jeeps, Pam!"

He's digging in his field jacket pocket and comes out with a folded piece of paper. He quickly reads it over and then hands it to her. She unclips her red lens flashlight, and keeping it down, reads over the hand written instructions that Mussenberg had given to the observation team. Sure enough, only the police Jeep was mentioned. She rested her weight on her knees now. She looked at Ramerez and Wilkes, refolded the paper and gave it back while speaking.

"Well, whatever, Steve. But this guy might not be home down there, 'cause there was another Jeep when I was here last time and it had the snow plow attached to it."

Wilkes shakes his head and looks back to the cabin. "Oh, that's just marvey! Alright, well," he wrestled around behind him and pulled over the cell phone, "ya better call 'em then and see what he wants us ta do."

Styles looked at him incredulously. "Me? Why me? You're the

senior NCO here, Steve."

Wilkes nodded as daylight washed bright and sunny all around them. "Maybe so, Pam, but I ain't the one that was supposed ta be here last night either, ya know, and right or wrong that's the way the Captain is look'n at it, okay? Besides, he said ta have you report ta him right away, and that, little lady... is what I'm gonna do."

He jabbed the phone toward her. Styles returned his look, cussed softly under her breath and then took the phone. She pushed the memory button and then selected a number from the list. She pushed it and then the send button. It rang twice and was answered. "Captain Mussenberg?"

"Good morning, Captain. This is Airman Styles. Uhm, sir, I'm up here at the OP in Yellow Dog Point, and I, well.. I think we may have a problem here, sir. I think Mr. Stone may not be at home."

"What? Well, did Wilkes or Ramerez see him leave? What's going on?"

Styles looked over at the two men who had been there all night long and swallowed hard. "Well, no sir, they haven't seen any activity at the cabin. It, uhh... it seems that they didn't know to look for that little red Jeep, sir, you know... the one with the plow?" She waited a second before going on, to give him a chance to remember its presence and his mistake in not mentioning it to the team. That done, she hurried on with her report.

"Anyway, it hasn't been here since the team arrived, sir. And the snow plow, well it's sitting off to the side of the cabin now, sir."

There was dead silence as Styles chewed a gloved finger and waited. When the response came, it was as nasty and loud as she'd expected. "You've gotta be fuck'n kid'n me! Those guys've been there all night and we don't even know if Stone's in the fuck'n house? I don't believe this shit!"

Styles grimaced and sent her eyes back to the cabin through the woods. "No, sir, that's about the size of it." She held her breath, waiting for the next tirade, but it didn't come. He was calm and collected when he spoke again.

"Okay, fine, Styles. That's my fault. I'd forgotten about that other Jeep. Alright, here's what I want you to do. I need you and Wilkes to go down and see if he's there. Stone has seen you, so he'll remember that, right? Just try knocking on the door, and if he answers, tell him you need to use the phone or something like that. Say your humvee broke down. I don't care. Just verify whether or not he's there. If he doesn't answer, I want you to gain access and report back right away. Are we clear, Airman?"

Styles eyes shot to Ramerez and Wilkes as she heard this. These two exchanged looks when they saw the shock in her eyes. She stumbled over the words as she barely choked them out. "Uhum… ahh sir, even if he's not home, we still don't have probable cause to gain access. That would be an illegal entry, sir, and sir… this guy's not even in the military."

"Ahh for fucksake, Styles, I don't have time for this shit! Put Staff Sergeant Wilkes on this line, NOW!"

She mumbled a "yes, sir" and passed the phone to Wilkes. He listened and looked sharply at Styles before signing off. He put the phone away and called out softly to all of them.

"Okay, people, listen up. Styles and I are gonna go down and knock on the door ta see if anybody's home. If he ain't, then I've been ordered to gain entry. So here's the drill. Barnes, Conners, Ramerez, I need you guys ta fan out and grab cover around the front of that cabin. Keep yourselves hidden, but be sure that you're in a position ta give us cover'n and supress'n fire if things go wrong down there. We clear on that?" He looked at each man as they nodded before continuing.

"Okay, then. Radio when you're in position and watch for Pammy and I ta come down. Like I said, if the guy ain't home, then we'll find a window ta climb in er somethin. Okay, let's get it done. You guys move out and Styles and I will wait 'till ya call." The other men had checked their weapons begun crawling through the snow toward the cabin when Wilkes called softly to them again.

"Oh, yeah, you guys, I almost forgot. The Captain says that this guy Stone is some kind'a bad-ass, too. He's former SPECOPS, SEAL or something like that, so keep it in mind." He watched again as each man nodded and then resumed their crawling. Wilkes turned back to Styles, whose face was wrinkled up in exasperation. He raised his palms up and said, "What?"

"Stone's not a SEAL, he was in the Coast Guard. Mussenberg said that he was retired."

Wilkes snapped his head in a dismissive gesture. "Well, good. Last thing we need is some burned out SEAL trying ta blow us all away. Besides, a Coast Guard guy should be kind'a laid-back, right?"

Styles shook her head as she reached over, grabbed the glasses and brought them up for a quick look at the cabin. "Yeah, well, you haven't seen this guy yet either, Steve. He doesn't look like a laid-back kind've a guy." She lowered the binoculars and looked at him directly. "Are you going to break into the cabin if he's not home?"

Wilkes puckered his lips and blew air through them. "Yeah, I am. Those're my orders."

Styles sat back and displayed a "Come-on" look as she angled her head. "Yeah, but they're not legal orders, Steve." She jabbed her hand toward the cabin. "We don't have any right or authority to break into that guy's house and you know it!"

He just looked at her, "They're orders, Pam. I follow orders, period."

She was animated and beside herself with this injustice. "Come on, Steve, you don't have to obey an illegal order and you know it!"

He leaned forward then, a little anger on his face and heat in his voice as he put two fingers to the rank device on his collar and pulled it out.

"You see this, Pam? I've worked seven years to get these stripes and I plan on having a lot more before I walk away from the Air Force. Now, I'm not get'n out and going to college or law school, okay? I'm a lifer and this is what I do! I follow orders!" He sat back hard against the snow and continued in a hushed tone.

"I don't like this, either. It probably ain't right. But if the Captain wants me ta creep this guy's house, then I'll do it 'cause that's my orders." He pointed a finger at her. "Ya know, Pam, when you're in the military, you take orders. That's our job. We don't have ta like it… but we do have ta do it." He appeared to waver for a second as he continued. "There's a lot a things that people don't like ta do in this world, but if it's yer job, then ya do it." He took a deep breath and blew it out along with whatever anger he had left.

"Creep'n this guy's house is a little thing, Pammy, and you know it. But, if you don't like these orders and wanna change things, then point that weapon at me and call the team back. We'll tell 'em that you're mutinying and we'll all go back to Escanaba, just sweet as ya please! Otherwise, Airman, we're gonna follow orders! You clear on that?"

Styles returned his look, sadness and disgust filling her being. Finally, she nodded and looked down at the cabin. She didn't like it, but she had no choice.

The Escanaba Airport,
The Air Force Security Zone,
Same Morning, Forty Minutes Later.

Stone wasn't there. The team had searched the cabin and learned that Stone hadn't been there all night. Mussenberg finished telling Staff Sergeant Wilkes to leave the relief team in-place at the Stone cabin just in case the man came back. Then he told Wilkes that he, Styles, Ramerez could pack it up and head back to the base. He flipped the cell phone closed and stared out the window as fresh morning light washed in. He would keep a team of security police on the cabin because that's what he'd been ordered to do. But he didn't think the man would be back. Nope, not for awhile. He picked up a pencil and began idly tapping it on the desk. So, he thought, Stone was in the wind. This wasn't good. Not good at all. Mussenberg's head was in a vise on this one and he knew it. He stood the chance of being severely kicked in the ass or maybe even transferred. And if things went as badly as he secretly thought they could… the whole country could be rocked. He shook his head hard at this turn of events.

He had advised the General against his visit to see Stone. He'd figured that any further contact could possibly alert the guy about them. But noooo, the old man wasn't finding this thing fast enough and so he'd sent Mussenberg to speak with Stone. And while Mussenberg had knew it was a risk, he'd still walked away from Stone quite sure that the guy was no threat and knew nothing about their mission, or where the item they sought could be found. Well, he'd been right and wrong, hadn't he? Yeah, well it didn't make a hell'va lot of difference anyway, did it? The General was going to be asking what was happening with Stone soon. Very goddamn soon!

The only break he had was that Kourn was going to be in high level meeting all day with the president and then his security advisor, the Secretary of Defense, all of the Joint Chiefs and a bunch of similar types. The General had told him that unless it was an emergency, he would be out of touch until after 1700 hours. And the General had said that he wanted a situation report promptly at 1700. That meant that he had to have a SITREP on Stone, as well as everything else, by five o'clock this afternoon. He got up from his desk to walk around it and over to the state map, pinned to the wall. He looked at it and wondered where the guy would go? What was he doing? Did he know something that he wasn't telling or… was he really just a reverted Indian who had stepped out and gone to the local library or something? Mussenberg shook his head. Uh, uh. No way. Not all night long! This guy was up to something, moving for a reason, acting on intelligence that he had. And he probably knew that they were looking for him, too. Shit! He walked over to the door and flung it open.

"Sergeant Canter! Would you step in here, please?" Mussenberg moved back to the map as the Technical Sergeant walked in. Mussenberg looked up and motioned for the other man to close the door before speaking.

"We've gotta mission threat, Dick."

The Sergeant nodded at the officer. "Yes, sir. Stone again?"

Mussenberg blew out a long breath. "Yeah. He's not at his cabin." He hiked his shoulders. "My mistake, but the team sat on an empty building all night. Wilkes says that it looks like he's been gone since yesterday sometime." He turned back to the map.

The Sergeant stuck his hands in his pants pockets. "You want me to get the HEAT team on it then, sir? Advise them that they'll have wet work here?" He watched as he waited for a response and the officer shook his head before looking up from the map.

"No. I don't wanna do that yet, Dick. Not for awhile yet, anyway." His eyes went back to the map as he continued. "Now the old man's gonna be tied up in meetings all day, so we have," he rolled up his hand and looked at his wrist, "roughly twelve hours to find this guy. I wanna give it all we have until I have to call in HEAT." He looked back at the enlisted man, the acronym spelling out in his head. 'High Energy, Apprehension or Termination'.

"I need to find this guy before the General knows that he's missing, Dick. Because if I don't, the General's gonna institute HEAT right away and you know it. And I've gott'a feeling that this guy's already covered his bases and probably left intel out there on us, ya know?" Mussenberg cocked his head as he looked at the map. "Shit, man. I wouldn't be surprised if that fucker didn't have is own HEAT team or, its equivalent, that would be on our six two minutes after we dumped him."

Mussenberg walked around and sat behind the desk.

"He's not your regular kind of a guy, Sergeant, ya know what I mean? He's got a history of making things happen that aren't all that pleasant." Mussenberg laughed sardonically. "Shit, Dick. The guys he served with when he was in the Coast Guard... they called him Ghost, man!" Mussenberg made a face then established eye contact with the Sergeant again.

"I've seen what he can do and while I know that our HEAT could handle 'em, he'd probably get a couple of them before it's over, too. And the guy has friends that're players." He snapped his head in a quick shake and made another face, a worried one, before continuing.

"So what I'm thinking is that it would be ironic as hell... if we had our asses blown up by this guy, ya know what I mean?" he sends a dedicated look to the Sergeant. "And I think the fucker can do it, Dick. I really do. So, I wanna move easy here. Not rustle the brush too much, okay?"

The sergeant looked surprised then asked, "Okay, sir. What's the plan then?

Mussenberg was looking at the map again. He slid a tablet of paper across the desk and the Sergeant picked it up as Mussenberg began speaking.

"I want a BOLO sent to every police agency in this state and

Wisconsin. We'll concentrate on these two states for now. If he's driving, that's about as far as he could've gotten. Contact the DMV, or whatever it is here, and get the license plate number on this Jeep he's driving. It's an older one," he flung out a hand. "I don't remember what you call them." Canter interrupted him.

"It's the Secretary of State's Office here in Michigan, sir. They handle the vehicle registrations. Sir, before you go on, are you sure it's a good idea to put out a BOLO? I mean, isn't this guy a tribal cop? Wouldn't he have connections with local law enforcement people?"

Mussenberg rubbed a hand over his course hair and thought. A BOLO was just an acronym for 'Be On the Look Out'. Law enforcement people seeing a vehicle or person matching the BOLO description simply did whatever the BOLO asked them to do. On this end, he could tailor the BOLO message any way he wanted before sending it out. But Canter was right. As resourceful as Stone had been up 'til now, they might be giving him just one more edge. He stole a glance at his watch. No, they didn't have the luxury of time here, edge or no edge. He turned back to the Sergeant.

"Yeah, you're right, he may figure out that we're looking for him by sending the BOLO. But my guess is this guy already knows that. Besides, we don't have the time and we need every piece of support we can get. So go ahead with the BOLO. Make it short and sweet. Something like," Mussenberg looked up at the ceiling, "Observe Only and Immediately Report Subject's Location to the FBI office, at the number listed." He brought his eyes back to Canter who was now taking notes furiously. "Then expedite the installation of a toll free number. Set it up here and man that phone with one of our DET 4 people. Instruct them to answer the line, "FBI"," he flung up a hand, "agent whoever". Clear on that, then?"

Sergeant Canter mumbled a "Yes, sir" and continued writing.

Mussenberg took a breath. "Okay then, lets get some people to the airports in Marquette, Sault Ste. Marie and Houghton and any others with out-bound flights to see if maybe he bought a ticket and paid cash. We know that he hasn't used a credit card, yet. I want an OSI agent covering the reservation. Usual profile procedure and quick reports back here. I want another one following leads around here in Escanaba. See if he left any kind of a trail at all around here. Next,... next?... oh, shit, Dick..." Mussenberg rubbed a hand roughly over his face and looked up at Canter, "I can't think of anything else, can you?"

Technical Sergeant Canter flopped the paper back over and dropped the tablet to the side of his leg. He thought a minute before answering. "No, sir. I'd say that's about all there is for now. I guess I better get started on this stuff then." He winked at the Captain as he turned to leave. "I wouldn't sweat it, sir. I think we'll get him." He stepped out and closed the door behind him as Mussenberg watched. Then the Captain spoke in a lulled voice. "Yeah, sure we will... if he doesn't get us first."

Interstate US 131, The Rest Area,
Just North of Rockford, Michigan.
0708 or 7:08 am, The Same Day.

    I blink my eyes at the noise and sit up as a group of kids, junior high age, go running past yelping and hollering in glee. They're clambering into a small yellow school bus parked next to the Jeep. I slip the pistol into my pocket and uncoil myself from inside the vehicle before popping the door open. Outside, I look quickly around and see no immediate threat. I stretch and look at the lettering on the bus as the kids load into it. It has the words Hart Public Schools printed on its side. I look over as the last child boards the bus and see the words "Hart Pirates" sewn across the back of his jacket. As the bus backs up and kids fill every window, I figure that they're on their way to some sporting event. The yellow bus drives past me as I begin a survey. My eyes flow over the Rest Area, and some of the semi trucks that were here earlier, are gone now. But new ones, with the same plan, are now parked around, their engines idling in the morning air. I see nothing out of the ordinary and I'm surprised at the weather.

    The air is almost balmy here. The temperature has to be close to Forty degrees and it's still early in the day, yet. I yawn and try to stifle the next several that come in quick succession. Sleep had been fitful and elusive. I know that all I'd really done the past couple of hours was rest a little. I didn't get any real sleep, but then, I hadn't expected to either. I feel nature's call and make my way up to the brick restrooms. As I'm opening the glass entrance, a reflection catches my eye. In the bottom half of the door that is showing the rest stop off-ramp, I see the royal blue and red bubble flasher of a state police cruiser as it glides in off the expressway.

    My heartbeat immediately jumps upward as I release the handle and turn around to face the new arrival. I pull out the cigarette box from my shirt pocket and shake one out, even as my right hand goes back in my jacket pocket, closing around the pistol. I see the car braking now and taking a good look at the trucks that're parked around the facility. I light the cigarette and step around the building, as my eyes follow the cruiser's progress. It's closer and I can see that it's rolling slowly past the semi-trucks, the single officer driving giving each a good once-over. I blow out a breath as realization sets in. I can now see the logo on the car's door. He's a state weigh master, not a regular state trooper. This guy may have police powers, but his primary job is regulating the trucks. He's just checking out the semis that're parked here. My heart rate is returning to normal, so I butt the smoke and grab the handle to enter the bathroom. I desperately need to relieve some extreme pressure on my bladder right about now, and that dumb blue car almost had me doing that right here in my pants!

Escanaba Airport,
Air Force Security Section,
Operations Building,
Twenty Minutes Later, Same Day.

Sergeant Canter rapped his knuckles against the door as he turned the knob. He pushed it open and closed it tightly and whisked into the room in one fell swoop. He stopped next to Mussenberg, who was on the phone by the map, the cord stretched across the small office. The officer looked up as Canter waved a paper. Mussenberg quickly finished up and turned to the Sergeant. The other man spoke.

"We've gotta hit, sir! A motor carrier officer down-state just called in Stone's vehicle. It's parked at a rest area on US 131!"

Mussenberg broke out into a grin and clapped his hands together. "Hotdamn, Dick! Alright!" He quickly moved around the desk and jerked a drawer open. "Where down-state?"

Canter glanced at the paper. "Someplace called Rockford, but actually, it's right by Grand Rapids. That's a pretty good-sized town, sir, about half-way down the Lower Peninsula."

Mussenberg pulled out the Walther PPK .32 caliber pistol and worked the slide on the weapon and checked it all over. He found it to be in working order and fully loaded, so he slipped it into the holster and then tucked the small gun into his side between his shirt and his pants. He was in civilian cloths today and the little gun was barely noticeable. He looked up at the Sergeant.

"Well, can this unit sit on Stone until we can get somebody there?"

The Sergeant's eyebrows twisted and the man dropped his head a bit. "Well, Captain, the guy didn't stick around 'cause all we had on the BOLO was for anybody seeing the vehicle to notify us immediately, and that was it, sir."

Mussenberg's hands went to up to his hips and his eyebrows arched menacingly. "Okay, Dick, what the hell's a motor-carrier officer? And can he get his ass back to wherever Stone's at and sit on 'im or not?'"

Canter turned his head sheepishly. "A motor-carrier officer is a semi-truck weigh master, sir. You know, they regulate civilian heavy trucks on the roads, that kind of thing."

Mussenberg just stared daggers at the Sergeant and waited. The enlisted man swallowed and went on. "Yeah, well sir, I already took the liberty of checking on having the weigh master go back and I made the request. And well… the officer did go back but Stone's vehicle was gone by then."

Mussenberg let a curse escape under his breath and then rolled his eyes up to Canter. "Okay, Sergeant, so do we have any idea where he's headed then?"

Canter shook his head. "Yes, sir, some anyway." He stepped over to the map and pointed at Grand Rapids. "He was on the southbound side so that would put him here, heading toward Grand Rapids. But there're interchanges there, sir, that could have him going east to Detroit, west toward the Lake, here, or even further south, down this way."

Mussenberg had both hands locked behind his neck now, his elbows protruding past his face, as he studied the map with wrinkled brows. He knew that there was little else they could do right now, until they received another call. They couldn't put out a pick-up order and they couldn't know where Stone was exactly. It sucked, but that was the way it stood. He nodded his head sharply, one time.

"Very well, then. I want a Hawk put on stand-by and ready to go as soon as we get a firm location on Stone. I also want two DET 4 operatives in civies geared up and ready, too. So set that up, will ya, Dick?"

Technical Sergeant Canter cleared his throat. "Well sir, that'll be a bit of a problem, too. No problem with the men, but we've got two birds down on mechanicals and one that's still working the island. So, unless ya want me ta pull that bird off the island search, we don't have anything available right now, sir." He hiked his shoulders. "That is, unless ya wanna ride second seat in one of the Comanches, sir? Or, depending on the circumstances, maybe take one of the 16s? You're checked out in them, ain't'cha?"

Mussenberg looked away from the Sergeant, his eyes welled in thought. No, he couldn't take one of the F-16s. He would need the versatility of a helicopter, because he would be taking an arrest team to wherever he was going, just in case. And he couldn't take the Black Hawk away from the island, either. The General'd shit a brick over that one. That aircraft was mission critical and had to keep working. He snapped his fingers and looked back at the other man.

"What about Major Luce and his bird? Have they left yet?"

The Sergeant rolled his eyes. "Well, no sir, they're still on-site. But those guys're planning on going home, Captain. I have their national secrets briefing scheduled for this afternoon." He twisted out a hand. "The whole crew was up late last night, too, sir, because they spun a main rotor bearing on their last sortie and had ta have it fixed so they could leave today."

Mussenberg raised his eyebrows in question. "What's the status on their aircraft, now?"

"The bird's green tagged now, sir. But, Captain, uh, beg'n yer pardon, sir, but remember? The Major and his crew, well, they're not DET 4, sir. They got pulled off their regular station to pick up those Navy guys for us, kind've outta the blue. And these guys... well they didn't have a chance ta go home or nothing, sir, before they were routed here. They don't know who we are or what's going on here, Captain, and they aren't gonna be happy about not going home."

Mussenberg shook it off. "Too bad. He and his aircraft are attached to me until I release them, and I'm rescinding the release order I signed, as of right now. This," he threw out a hand at the map, "can't be helped. Tell them that I said to suit up and be ready to fly." He looked directly at the Sergeant and sharpened his eyes. The sergeant held the look for a second and then gave a quick nod, dropping his attention to the next agenda item that the Captain was setting forth. Mussenberg went on.

"If we get a location on Stone... then that'll start the mission sequence. The mission call-sign will be "COWBOY", got that?" Canter straightened slightly to attention, mostly to show respect and his attentiveness. He looked at the Captain. "Yes sir, I understand. The mission, once initiated, will be entitled, "COWBOY".

Mussenberg slowly nodded. "That's correct. I want you to brief the two DET 4 guys on Stone. Tell 'em to be ready for anything. This guy's cagey and very capable. This mission could turn into "wet work". Mussenberg shrugs. "If that's how it's gotta be, then that's how it's gotta be." He looked directly into the Sergeant's eyes.

"I will be contacting you every hour on the hour, once this operation is in-play, alright? And Dick, if for any reason you don't hear from me at a scheduled interval, then the mission name will immediately change to, "MIDNIGHT COWBOY". If that should come to pass, you will obviously notify the General immediately. Even before you do that, I want you to activate the HEAT team and give 'em everything we have on Stone. From that point on, they'll have my directive to terminate the subject with extreme speed and prejudice. Now... are we clear on all of this, Technical Sergeant

Canter?"

Sergeant Canter's eyebrows formed flat lines as his face took on a deadpan, knowing look. He nodded his head. "Yes, sir. If you miss a check-in, the mission will change immediately to call-sign MIDNIGHT COWBOY and HEAT will be initiated ASAP. Will do, sir. And perfectly clear." He shot a reverent look to his captain. "Anything else, sir?"

Mussenberg looked calmly at the Sergeant. "No, that will be all for now Sergeant, thank you."

Canter assumed the position of full attention. "Very well, sir." He angled his head slightly. "By your leave, sir?" Mussenberg smiled and nodded respectfully, in kind. The Sergeant spun around in an about face and exited the office, again closing the door behind him.

Mussenberg had just told the Sergeant, in not so many words, that He fully expected that he could be killed on this trip. The callsign for the mission had been decided as soon as he knew that Stone was onto them and had skipped. A jagged smile rolled up around his lips as he sat looking at the map. What else would you call this little game but Cowboys and Indians, eh? As he stared at the map, he spoke to an empty room. "Come on Indian, we're running out've time here, man. Just stick your head up...once more... for this 'lil ole cowboy!"

Chapter Twenty-Eight
"Turn The World On It's Ear"

The Motel 6,
Grand Rapids, MI.
0816 or 8:16 am
The Same Day.

I step out of the bathroom, still toweling off my hair and sit down
on the edge of the bed in my underwear. I fight the strong urge to just
flop back and sleep for a million years. I finish my hair and then wipe
down the Glock. I'd brought it into the steamy room with me while
I'd showered and shaved. It needs to be cleaned better, but this will do
for now. I start mentally ticking off the things that I have to make
happen before I can close my eyes and sleep, and there seems to be
way too many and they seem to stretch way too far into the future. I'd
called the Veteran's Home from a payphone before leaving the rest stop,
and had spoken to a nurse who worked Markowski's floor. She'd said
that if I really wanted to come visit, I'd probably be smarter to come
after noon, sometime after they'd eaten lunch.

I thread on a pair of clean socks as I ponder my options here. I've
checked the phone book, and there's a place called "The Hair Port"
just down the street. I can get a haircut there. If I'm gonna be a cop
again – I better look like one. Another couple of blocks down, there's
a cellular phone dealer, too. I need one and would have to spend cash
to acquire it. I'd paid cash for the room when I learned that I had to
wait to visit Markowski. I'd needed the shower and change of clothes,
but now my cash is in short supply. I'll have to be careful on my
expenditures or I'll be forced to use the credit card that's riding in
my wallet. Once I do that I'll be real easy to find, if someone is
looking for me. And between me and the bedpost here, I don't think
that there's any "ifs" about it. I can feel them out there.

I put on a red and black flannel shirt. I've been the pursued before
and know the feeling. I know that the "Wiisagi-ma-iigan" is following
me. I can feel the coyote out there, sniffing, checking sign...looking
for me, his yellow eyes vibrant and intent. I sit and wrap the watch
around my wrist and secure the Velcro. Then I yawn and stretch before
I stand again. I pull on a clean pair of jeans and transfer my keys,
change, wallet, comb and pocketknife to my pants pockets before I tie

the piwaka back on the belt loop, and then slip it into my left pants pocket. I poke the Glock into my back and wander over to pour a cup of the motel coffee self-brew. I ease across the room and pull the heavy drapes back slightly. The sun is cascading across the parking lot and I can see cars traveling fast, up on the US 131 as it snakes past the motel. I watch and sip the coffee for awhile. Shortly, I have the java finished and yawn again before checking my watch. It's time to move. I pull on my boots and cord my arms into the old G2 flight jacket and take one last longing look at the bed, and then head out the door.

**Downtown Grand Rapids, MI,
0931 hours or 9:31 am.
The Same Day.**

 I creep along in traffic while scratching the back of my neck. A fresh haircut always leaves little pieces that cause an itch back there. I slam on the brakes as a car shoots into the lane in front of me. Man, I hate big cities! But at least the roads are clear. I can't get over how warm and dry it is here. Where I'd just come from the snow was plenty deep and the cold, equivalent to a deep freeze. I gradually move ahead in the snarled traffic as numerous people pace the sidewalks and cross intersections. It's stop and go and my fatigue level isn't helping any. I take a quick glance at the cell phone on the seat beside me. But I see that I still have a red light, meaning that I don't have a signal yet. After my haircut, I'd stopped to buy the cell phone. From what I'd been able to gather from the salesman, my name wouldn't appear on any lists out there for about 24 hours. It takes that long for the owner's name and address to appear on the records.

After I got the phone, I'd decided to tie-up loose ends while I was waiting to see Markowski at the Vet's Home. One of those ends was Veeter. I wanted to ask him about that black bag and maybe the little silver ball, too. Somehow, the Air Force knew about the bag and while I was almost positive now that this whole thing was about a missing nuclear bomb or something like that, there were still these little nagging anomalies. I'd gotten directions from the cell phone salesman. But, somehow, I'd taken a wrong turn and now, I was downtown in this mess.

I hadn't called Veeter's house because it's always better to approach people from out of the blue when you're going to question them. That way, they don't have time to get their story straight before you arrive. Now, I'm wishing that I would've just called him. I'm lost and need to find someone to ask directions from, again. Then I see a little enclosed traffic scooter up ahead and a meter maid walking the sidewalk. I gun

the Jeep forward as I see a car pulling out of a space. I slide the Jeep
into the slot in front of a large bank and turn off the key. I have the
door handle partly pulled when the little phone rings beside me. I
notice that the light's green and find that amazing. I've had no signal
since I got into downtown Grand Rapids. It's got to be the salesman,
checking the phone to see that it works. He said that he'd call.
Nobody else has this number. I flip it open and jab it to my ear.
"Hello?"

"Hey, hello, Raining Wolf. It's Amos Reddeer, eh?"

I'm momentarily confused and take the thing away to look at this
phone that I've only had for about fifteen minutes. Then I place it
back to my head.

"Hi, Amos. Uh, Amos…how did… how did you get this number?" He
chuckles softly, the radio waves echoing the sound.

"Oh, yah, that's kind've funny, eh? Last night, I had a dream, and
in this dream I had to talk to you. And, well, then I just called this
number and you answered. So today, when I had to talk to you, I just
did the same thing 'cause I remembered the number from last night, eh?"

My mouth goes dry and the Ghost Riders song that's an ever-playing
melody in my head, goes up a notch. I try to swallow and can't get any
spit as my eyes go up to the mirror and see that the meter officer is looking
at a car three spaces behind me. Then Amos speaks again, but static
begins fizzing in my ear as the signal fades.

"Yah, well Ely. The reason I called, eh, is that it came to me in the
dream last night… I…ow …wh.. thes.. oth.. rld spirits are. They… be
"Wajakosh Umoya", eh? That is what I didn't know before. We have
many old stories …bout …em, …eh. And…" Then… nothing.
I'm raising my voice, asking Amos, "What?… What?… I can't
hear you, Amos!" But the signal fizzles away as an armored truck
rolls up beside my Jeep, almost clipping off my outside mirror. Its
flashers are blinking in a double-park mode and its sides are stenciled
with the words, Wolverine Armored Services.

I twist the phone over and see the red light again. I unsteadily fold
it up as the shinkakee spreads like wildfire. I make a conscious effort
to shake it off and start to get out but realize that I can't. The armored
truck is so close, that I can't get the door open. My eyes dart up as the
courier who goes in and gets the money, hops out of the side of the truck.
He runs into the bank, dragging a dolly with him. My internal defense
mechanism switches rapidly into gear, and my conversation with Amos
fades instantly for now. Something causes me to look up to the review
mirror then, and as I do, I see the meter officer, now standing behind
the Jeep and looking down at my license plate, her ticket book in-hand.
My hand is already on the pistol and I have it pulled and held tightly,

under the gray Coast Guard blanket. My survival instinct in full mode now,

I quickly lean over and roll down the passenger window with my left hand, calling to her as I do. She steps over and I explain that I was just stopping to ask directions when I got blocked in by the armored truck. She's gracious and folds up her ticket book. Then I ask her how to get to where I'm going and she explains the easiest route. I thank her, and by that time the armored car guard is back out and stuffing bags into the truck and then hopping into the back with them. A few seconds later, the heavy truck pulls ahead and I swivel out into traffic behind it. I look down and see that I have a red light on the cell phone again. A light that's been red since I drove into the downtown. Well, all except for when old Amos called. It was green for him, by golly. I can't help it as a shiver runs down my spine...

**The Escanaba Airport,
The Air Force Operations Building,
Thirty-Five Minutes Later,
The Same Day.**

Major Randy L. Luce, helicopter aircraft commander, eleven-year member of the United States Air Force and a graduate of its academy, stormed into the operations building and headed straight toward Mussenberg's office. He was met, two-thirds of the way there, by an armed security policeman who blocked his travel and stood menacingly with his hand on his sidearm. Luce spun around and bellowed to Technical Sergeant Canter, who was just coming from the telephone room down the hall.

"Sergeant, you better get this man outta my way... Right fucking now!"

Mussenberg appeared at the inside of the office door. "It's okay, Airman Peels, I'll see the Major." He looked over at Sergeant Canter and nodded as the Major nudged rudely past him and entered the office. Then Mussenberg stepped back inside and closed the door. He walked around the desk and sat down while the Major stood in front of it fuming. He calmly brought his eyes up to the man. "Now Major, what did you need?"

Luce was livid as he spit out the words. "Just what kind've a clusterfuck is this, Mussenberg?" He swung his arm back. "You've got a fuck'n lightbird colonel out on that damn island taking orders from you... a fuck'n captain!" His eyebrows formed incredulous peaks that were in danger of pushing his blue garrison cap right off his head as he spewed out the words.

"You've got two F-16 Falcons setting on the tarmac, armed ta the teeth, up at old Sawyer! And two Comanches, flying a combat air patrol out there! Those birds don't even exist in our inventory yet, for God's sake! They won't be operational until 2007! And you..." he jabbed an index finger, "you're running this show?" Again, his features took on a look of disbelief. "Now you tell me that we have ta be ready ta fly on a minute's notice? After my crew's been up all fuck'n night... And have been fly'n day-long sorties every day for the week since we got ta this shithole! What the fuck's go'n on around here! What kind'a fuckfest is this, for cry'n out loud! Who're you reporting to?"

Mussenberg waited quietly through the barrage. The man's anger was understandable, if not acceptable. He raised his eyes to the other man. "Major, have you been trying to get in touch with your parent command?"

Luce drove his head up and down. "Yer fuck'n A right I have! I've been try'n ta get a hold of my squadron commander since that asshole sergeant of yours told me that you rescinded our departure order and we couldn't leave taday!"

Mussenberg nodded. "And you haven't been successful in contacting them, have you?"

Luce leaned forward and rested his palms on the desk, giving Mussenberg a satisfied look "No Captain, I haven't. Not yet. But when they call back, I guarantee you that the shit's gonna hit the fan! I don't know what's going on here, but you're sure as hell not gonna keep me and my crew locked up and on a 24 hour flight status!" He straightened and threw a daggered look at Mussenberg. "Maybe you don't know it, but there is a little thing called regulations, Captain, and by God... you're gonna learn about 'em, and then, you're gonna abide by 'em!"

Mussenberg merely nodded again. "Yeah, well Major, when you received your orders assigning you to my command, you were told that you, your aircraft and your crew would be attached to my command until I released you, period. You were also told that there was to be no contact with your home base until you had been released." Mussenberg allowed his features to form a question mark before he went on. Then he picked up a copy of Major Luce's orders, assigning him to Escanaba and began reading.

"Also in those orders, were the words, "Above Top Secret". Mussenberg held the paper up and pointed to the emboldened lettering as Luce's eyes followed, his face already showing the barest semblance of defeat. "They go on to say, and I quote here Major, "Aircraft, commander and crew are to acquiesce all domination of command, including control and conventional chain of command procedures, to Captain Peter Mussenberg, USAF, Detachment Four, 696th Air Intelligence Group, currently in command of DET 4 Detail to, the Escanaba Municipal Airport, Escanaba, Michigan. Above personnel and aircraft are to be made available to assigned command until released by Detail Commander. Note, No comms. with normal assigned command are permitted on the TDY transfer."

Mussenberg then pointed to the signature and title of a major General, commanding the squadron that Luce came from. He dropped the papers on the desk and shook his head gently.

"You know what that means Major. I don't have to spell it out for you, do I? I was the person you were told to report to and that acquiescence of command," Mussenberg drove a thumb into his chest, "stops right fucking here! Your squadron C.O. isn't going to return your call because, until I release you, you don't exist. Your aircraft and all personnel attached to it have been completely turned over to me. In fact, from the time those orders transferring you were cut, your designator ceased to exist on your unit roster back at Nellis Air Force Base, and your records, as well as your crew's, were transferred to Me." Mussenberg took a breath and continued, even while the Major seemed to deflate before his eyes. "Now, you were told all of this when you arrived. And you very well know, from your initial arrival briefing, that I am in command here. Who I report to, is none of your goddamn business. You also know that this operation is a of a highly secret and sensitive nature. It's vital to national security and Major…" Mussenberg looked directly at him and drove the words home. "YOU WILL COMPLY WITH ORDERS!" He raised his hand and drove a pointed finger at Luce. "Either that, or I'll put your ass in a cell at Leavenworth!"

Mussenberg watched the fight drain out of the Major, the man's eyes taking on a subdued look. He let go a sigh of his own. Major Luce, meanwhile, had been afraid that it might turn out this way, and as he looked at the Captain he knew it was true. Now Luce looked away as he quickly ran this stuff through his head. He just couldn't believe it. But, there was too much power here for it to be anything else, wasn't there? No one from his former unit or command would return his calls, just like Mussenberg said. So he'd called an old academy classmate who was in Air Force Intelligence at the Pentagon.

After explaining what was going on here to his friend, his buddy had said that Mussenberg and his whole entourage here, were quite possibly something called, "The Little Green Men". He'd then listened in awe as he friend had told him all that he knew about them, which wasn't much. Luce just couldn't accept that it was true. That kind of authority and power? He'd never heard of anything like this before. He'd decided that he would just come over here and brace this pissant little captain, and get this shit straightened out! But... maybe, he thought now, he just hadn't wanted to accept it. He brought his eyes back to the to the black officer and knew, down deep inside, that this little fight was over. Finally, he just nodded from across the desk and as he did, the fire left the Captain's eyes. Mussenberg spoke again.

"Good, Major. I promise, as soon as we can, we'll release you and your guys will be back in Nevada before you know it, okay?" As he was finishing that sentence, there was a knock and Sergeant Canter raced through the door, waving a paper, capturing both men's attention.

"Captain, we've got another sighting." Canter looked down at the sheet then shot his eyes up. "It's in Grand Rapids, sir. A traffic officer wrote down his plate in the downtown area, somewhere called Pearl Street."

Mussenberg broke out into a grin and slapped his hands together and wrung them in a washing manner before he turned to Luce.

"Okay, Major, that's your cue! File a flight plan and wind that baby up! We're going to Grand Rapids!"

The defeated major nodded and sulked out of the room even as Mussenberg was turning back to Sergeant Canter. "Okay, Dick! Is this traffic officer still on 'im then?'

Canter shook his head. "No, sir. Didn't even see the BOLO until she was back in her unit, I guess. But the dispatcher down there states that Stone asked the meter officer directions to I96."

He stepped over to the map table, sifted around and pulled up a map of urban Grand Rapids and then laid it out flat. He traced his finger around with Mussenberg watching until he fingered an area where the lettering of the street name "Pearl" was indicated. He looked up at Mussenberg. "This puts him right smack-dab downtown. There, sir." Canter's finger jabbed the map as his eyes shone with discovery. "Probability says that he's still in that area."

Mussenberg was running a hand over his jaw, his eyes clouded in thought. "Yeah, I think so, too. Either way, it's a starting point and that's where I'm going."

Kentwood, Michigan,
A small suburb, outside of Grand Rapids.
10:03 am, The Same Day.

I pull up along the curb and look across the lawn at the address on the house. It matches the one I have in my notebook for Veeter. I stifle another yawn as I climb out of the Jeep and walk up to the door. I note that my balance is off as I move past a snow sculpture and wade the light snow that covers the ground here. I raise a hand to knock left handed, my right one in the jacket pocket, holding the Glock. I stop my hand from tapping the door, as I take a moment to look around. I'm still running in the "safe mode", but there're no bad vibes here.

The exhaustion is dulling my senses and causing me concern. I hold off for a second and look around more intently. My eyes feel like somebody did a job on them with sandpaper. I blink hard several times, and then look closely. The house is in an upper middle class neighborhood. As I switch back and look behind me to the Jeep in the street, I see the snowman that I'd passed on my way up to the door. He's a happy looking soul, holding a broom. If the weather keeps warming here, that snowman is going to loose a lot of weight. I don't sense anything wrong, so I turn back and rap my knuckles against the door. No answer. There may be nobody home. I see the doorbell and push a finger to it as my eyes go back up to the windowed front door. I'm about to leave when Gretchen opens the door. She's in a white bathrobe and has a towel wrapped around her head.

She smiles as she opens the door, and she seems embarrassed, a bashful grin tweaking at her mouth. She has her hand up to the towel again as I speak. "Hi, Gretchen."

"Ely? It's so good to see…um… please, please come in?" She swings the door wide and I step inside.

She fusses with the towel, her embarrassment evident as she speaks, telling me that she's sorry, she's just gotten out of the shower. She's saying how disappointed she is that Carrie isn't there to meet me, and a multitude of other things. She has me remove the jacket, and I do, but keep it and the Glock, close at hand. Once seated on the couch, she stops talking in mid-sentence and looks at me. She stands barefooted, droplets of water still clinging to her face and arms, and a concerned look on her face.

"Oh, Ely, I'm so sorry. I must look a fright to you, don't I?" her face smiles shyly and her hand goes back to tuck in the towel where it has pulled loose.

I gesture dismissively. "You look fine, Gretchen. Most women

I've known wear a towel when they get out of the shower, and you do a bathrobe justice." I wink at her.

She smiles more genuinely before moving over to sit near me in a large easy chair. She explains that she was up very late juggling bills. She hadn't got much sleep. Even though Carrie is healed, she explains, and is doing much better, she still needs therapy, medications and other things that are taxing their meager budget. The money just doesn't stretch far enough. I mumble an understanding as she fixes me with those jade eyes. Then she points a feminine finger at me.

"Well, Ely, at the risk of insulting you, especially after you having given me such a nice complement a few minutes ago, I have to tell you that you look like hell. Your eyes are as red as cherries!"

I quickly raise a hand to my mouth to simultaneously smother and hide another yawn. I shake it off and answer her while nodding goofily. "Yeah, I don't doubt it. I uh… drove all the way through from Yellow Dog Point last night, and well…," I roll up a hand and look at my watch, "I guess I haven't slept in probably thirty-six hours or so."

Her hand raises up to her cheek. "My gosh, Ely!… Why?"

I shake my head and shrug shoulders in an attempt to blow it off. "Oh, well, that's just the way things worked out, I guess. I've got to go to the Veteran's Home here in Grand Rapids to interview a guy later this afternoon."

She's shaking her head. "That's crazy, Ely. You can't do this. It's not good for you. Can't you see this man tomorrow?"

"Nope. I'll have ta do it today. It's kind've important."

She's nodding her head again, bringing her knee up to cross a leg. I watch in fascination as the robe drops downward and exposes a good deal of her thigh, her bare foot dangling and the curve of her calf very enticing. I quickly look up at her as she speaks, feeling my own embarrassment. There is concern in her voice, "Well okay, what time do you have to be there then?"

"Around two, I guess." I start to bring my eyes back up to hers, but they stop for a second at the V formed by her robe crossing over her breasts. We make eye contact and again she smiles. I don't know if her smile is because she knows what I'd been looking at, or if it's for another reason. I feel the shame again as I look away.

She takes the towel off her head and begins gently buffing her hair as she looks at me. I lean forward, the motion making my head swim a little. My exhaustion is overwhelming. I look at her and catch her eyes. Once again, I'm reminded of what a handsome woman she is. I tip my head at her.

"So, your Dad's not here then?"

She continues looking at me, her face still affixed with the pleasant smile as she lowers the towel. Her damp black hair cascades around her face now, forming a very lovely picture. Her skin has the tone of stark white porcelain. And her coal black hair, accentuated by the slender strands of silver in it, are extraordinarily appealing. All of this set off by those fiery emerald green eyes. And those vibrant eyes are searching me now, in what I assume is a look of happiness, for lack of a better word.

"No, Dad took Carrie and several of her friends to see a movie. I was headed to bed when you knocked." Her face forms a disappointed frown. "They won't be back until later this afternoon?"

She says the last in question form and I nod at her. "I was hoping to see him," I roll out a tired hand, "I just had a question about the case I was working when we met. It's no big deal."

Her face changes to what? Disappointment? Her green eyes are alive with inquisitiveness. "So… you didn't come to just see me then?"

I look over at her and can feel the strong attraction, even through the haziness of my fatigue. It's been a long time since I'd been with a woman and the sexual impulses that this lady was setting off in me, are real. Very real. Even in my weakened physical state, with the music playing lowly in my head and the trouble I'm in, I can still feel the sparks and shocks that she ignites in me. I look at her and know that I have to be truthful here.

"Well, to be honest Gretchen, no, I didn't. I am attracted to you but I kind'a still have an emotional hang-up with another woman." I shake my head in an "Aw Shucks" manner. "But you are a beautiful lady though," I wink, "and that's no lie."

She sits and looks at me thoughtfully. I can feel the sexual pull of her as she seems to make up her mind. Then my eyes are drawn down to her hand, that she's lowered to her crossed calf. She is gently stroking her leg, sensually rolling her fingers over her ankle as she begins speaking again. I have to force myself to look up and meet her eyes.

"You know, you're the first man I've been interested in since I lost my husband." She nods, taking her leg off the other as my sore eyes follow the action. Then she leans forward, closing her legs together and lacing her hands around her knees, her feet going up on her toes. Her green eyes turn serious as she continues.

"And Ely… I'm lonely. I think you are too and well… I'd like to just be with someone again, to feel that closeness again." She twists her head, the onyx-like black hair, with its slim streaks of premature silvery gray, falling lightly around her shoulders.

"I know that this probably won't work for me and you," she gently bumps her head, "because I have Carrie here and she has to go to therapy. That's not anything that can be done up there, where you live. And I don't think that you will ever come here to live either but can't… can't we at least try to… oh, I don't know… give it a chance, anyway?"

My head is swimming now with a mixture of the heated room, shinkakee, utter exhaustion and sexual thoughts that are bombarding me constantly. I turn tired eyes to her and see the earnest face she displays. We're both lonely, I know that. But satisfying that craving that this emotion draws, is often the thing that causes even more pain. I'm not in love with her and I tell her so. She drops her hands and looks deeply into my eyes.

"I know that Ely. And maybe… I'm not in love with you either. I'm just asking for a chance to find out?"

I feel drowsy as I look into the pools of green that are her eyes. I start to get up. "I better go."

She places a hand on my leg, an action that sends a shock of sexual energy through me. I look up at her open mouthed as she stands and I see a conclusion go across her face. She raises a hand to point at me.

"Okay, Ely. But why don't you just sleep here for a few hours. I'll get you up in time to make your appointment?"

I waggle my head back and forth. "No, I better not Gretchen. I might not be able to get up and I need to make this interview."

She looks at me, a concerned frown on her face until she nods. "Okay then, have it your way. I think I better get some coffee into you though. Does that sound like a good idea?"

I look up and send her a droopy smile. "Yeah, that would be nice. It'd probably help. Thanks."

She says it'll only take a minute and goes into the kitchen. I watch her walk away, the sway of her walk arriving in cascading rushes, inside my body. I listen to the noises from the kitchen as she makes coffee. I try to focus on all the things I have going on and then…blackness comes.

The next thing I know, someone has my left arm and is pulling me! My eyes pop open and I pull my hand free of the jacket pocket! Then I'm swinging my right arm up and over, grabbing the arm holding me and turning it over their head, swinging their body around and back down, into my chest!… my left fist doubling for a strike! There's a feminine squeal, as Gretchen bumps roughly against me and I blink into the room! I realize what's going on and release her. She quickly regains her feet and steps away. She looks at me in an expression of awe and fear as I stammer out an apology. After a few beats, she smiles.

"You are exhausted. Here," She extends a hand and takes mine in hers. "Come on. I'm going to put you down in the spare bedroom. I'll get you up in time for your appointment, I promise. Now, come on! I'm not taking no for an answer!"

She's pulling me forward and I have so little strength, that I can barely halt her progress. I stumble along behind her, dragging the flight jacket as she leads me down the hall, into a room and over to a double bed. She pushes me down onto it and I fall flat on my back. I watch her through foggy eyes as she lays my jacket on a chair then goes to a closet. She takes out a blanket and brings it back and covers me. Then she sits on the edge of the bed by my side and leans over me to situate the pillow around my head. As she does, her robe spills open and I am looking at one of her breasts, a large dark colored nipple prominently hardened and bouncing freely inside the material.

I feel the rumblings inside of me and squeeze my eyes shut. She finally sits back and I open my eyes. As I look up at her, she brings up a hand and folds her fingers over my eyes, closing them again. Then I feel her lean forward and gently touch my lips with hers. My eyes open again and I see her dark eyebrows and eyelashes, the green irises obscured now, by her closed lids. I close my eyes too and gently return the kiss. As I feel her lips leave mine and her weight begin to leave the bed, I want to thank her. As she gets off, I snatch out a hand and catch her forearm.

She stops and turns back to me. I hold her arm and look up at her with all of the pent-up excitement in me. My thumb caresses her arm as I'm looking at her through what seems like an alcoholic haze. I mumble out the words, "Thank you." and I see her smile. She unfolds my fingers from her arm and looks at me steadily. I think that she's going to leave and begin to turn my head away when she brings a hand up and unties the white robe and lets it fall to the floor. Her skin is milky white in the sun-filtered room. My eyes drop to the dark triangle below her belly, then journey down her long legs to succulent ankles before slowly coming back up again all the way to her breasts. They are large and have big hardened raspberry colored nipples on them. I force my gaze away from these delights and up to meet her radiant green eyes. She's a strikingly beautiful woman! I'm shaking my head no, but inside, inside…my body's screaming, Yes!… please, yes!

A picture of Nettie comes into my tortured mind, but… a voice screams out just as quickly, "She doesn't want you though, does she?" Mixed emotions and sexual desires fill my being in explosive blasts as Gretchen pulls back the blanket and steps near the bed. Her breasts bounce lightly and I feel the blood begin pounding fiercely in my temples and lower regions. My exhaustion is blown away by sexual desire as I struggle to hoarsely bleat out my words.

"No Gretchen... we can't." I look at her with all of the pleading I possess. "You've got...you've got to believe me... I want to! Oh, sweet Jesus in Heaven... you don't know how much! But please... don't! It's not right and we'll both be sorry!"

She stops then, an astonishing look flowing across her features. Her voice is husky and timid all at the same time. "Why, Ely? What can this hurt?"

I'm shaking my head, stumbling over the words that are choking in my throat. "This isn't right Gretchen...I'm...I'm not in love with you. Don't you see? I'm in love with someone else."

She brings a finger up to touch my lips, and then lets it linger on the side of my face. She whispers in a soft voice, her emerald eyes dancing with fire from the sunlight. "I know. And I... I don't know if I'm in love with you, either. We don't even know each other, and yet... I feel like I've always known you." She sighs.

"But we both need somebody now. You know that's true, Ely. And I do want this. Please Ely, let's just have this for now... please?"

As I look up at her, I'm fighting primordial instincts and urges that are driving me to respond. I want this so bad! Need this!... Need her body so much! The delirium and frustration of exhaustion is fast being displaced by the heat of unbridled passion! I'm losing it and know it! If I can't stop this quickly, then I won't be able to! I try one last time.

"Gretchen... You're beautiful. But we can't do something wrong just because it feels good or... right. If we... if we do this... it will destroy whatever we have between us, whatever friendship or..." I'm scared to touch her, afraid that the mere feel of her will cause me to loose whatever resolve I have...what it will lead to. But I have to touch her. It's the only way to covey my sincerity. I take her hand and squeeze it gently. The sexual shock and electricity is blinding and flashes over me as I stumble out the words.

"Look, what I'm trying to say is that... this coupling is a special thing, a God given..." My nose picks up the scent of her sex and I squeeze my eyes tightly shut, struggling to go on, to just hold on. I release her hand but I know it's over! My resolve has crumbled to dust. I'm going to take her as long as she's willing!

When I open my eyes again, she is standing there, a gentle smile and a look of marvel on her face. After an eternity, she tilts her head and speaks. "You are an unusual man, Ely Stone."

As I look at her, I avert my eyes from her body and push down the urges that are raging wild inside of me. Maybe there's still a chance... I take a deep breath and catch her eyes again before croaking out my words.

"A lot of people tell me that, but... uh hum... considering what I'm doing now, I'd say I'm a very stupid man! I know I'll think that later... when I relive this moment."

She laughs then, gently with the resounding sound of womanhood. "Some things never change, do they? Men are still men." She tenderly shakes her head as she takes my hand in hers.

"You're not stupid, Ely. But you are special." Her eyes turn serious and now search my face. "Would it... would it be alright if I just laid down with you?"

The passion that had welled in me is still present and she has no idea what she's asking. To have this fine-looking woman lying next to me after what I've just been through...am still going through, well... but she's right. Some things never change. Women are still women too. I smile up at her.

"That would be nice, Gretchen." She returns the smile and bends to pick up her robe. My eyes follow her dangling breasts and I have to force them to go elsewhere in the room. She dons the robe and climbs in next to me, pulling the blanket over us both. She turns on her side and eases her rear against my pelvis. I reach down to try to pull the jeans material away from my crotch where the pressure is very discomforting there. I feel my eyes wander over to see the curve of her hip beneath the blanket. A picture of her recently standing naked before me flashes brilliantly in my mind. I know that I can still take her! All I have to do is reach over and... No! I snap my head away! Think of something else! Nettie. Think of Nettie! I try this but the picture that forms is her horrified face as she looks at me that night in the boathouse. No, that won't work! Think of what's going on. Think of other things.

Anything. But as fast as the passion began, it seems to be dissolving, convalescing with the tension and sheer exhaustion. As I begin to fall away, I hear Gretchen's breathing change. She sleeps quietly. Her breath comes easily as her chest rises and falls in gentle rhythm and I fall hard into heavy slumber. How long that sleep lasts, I don't know. But at sometime, the deep sleep ends and I fall off from it, and roll into the cavernous abyss of tormented remembrance. The abyss of my dreams. I'm dropping down from the thick darkness, going through layers and layers of lighter haze, almost like black, then gray then white smoke until suddenly... it's bright sunshine...

**Barranquilla, Columbia,
The Old Ocean Wharf,**

The War On Drugs,
The Recent Past.

It is siesta time, and what few people had been around were long gone from the area by the time we come running into it. Now that the police are here, they will surely stay clear, too. We're crouched on the deck of an old freighter that's tied up against the wharf, using the rusting old hull for cover. The afternoon sun is beating down all around, causing heat waves to bounce everywhere, and sweat to roll off in streams. I look around and know that we're out of options here.

Four minutes earlier, we were talking to an informant, a guy who worked as a stevedore. Then the National Police Jeeps and trucks came blasting to a halt in front of the café. We knew they were looking for us as soon as the policemen began asking the dock people if they knew of the "Coasta Guardia de los Estados Unidos"- Spanish for United States Coast Guard. We'd left in a hurry out the back way that opened into an alley. Then a kid screamed, "There he goes!" And they'd chased us. We'd wound up here, with no place else to go; our backs to the water and our fronts to crooked cops with M-16s. Both of us turn our heads when we hear the mixture of Spanish and heavily accented English from the dock.

"Ehhhh, Americano! La Guardia, eh? Leesin amigo, nobody has to die, eh? Jes come out weeth yor hans ap an we can talk, eh? Eef yor who you say you are, then weee're amigos, yes? But I don kno eef yor who you say you are. Comprende?"

We both recognized the voice. It belonged to Lieutenant Santiago Barcas. I look over at Coast Guard Intelligence Agent Danny Vas Quez, my partner, and senior in both rank and experience. We called him, "Danny Boy" because he was Black Irish on his mother's side. He knew a lot more about this stuff than I did. This was only my second undercover mission since being assigned to CGI. I hunch up my shoulders and whisper to him, "What d'ya think, Danny?"

He's looking around the freighter, holding up his little Colt pistol and trying to get a take on how many men are out there. He whispers to me over his shoulder. "Yeah, shit Ghost... I don't know. It... it could just as easily be a trick as legit... know what I mean? You can never trust these guys."

I nod then and bend down to look through the ship's old superstructure, trying to see any of the policemen across the boarded dock. I'm situated against an old rusty hatch as I peer across the chipped and beaten old ship's deck. We had been working this undercover mission for the better part of two months. We were assigned to a DEA investigative sting team, down here to add a little more fuel to President Reagan's fire on drugs.

The DEA had given us the waterfront, as waterborne smuggling was our forte. The Columbian guy talking and inviting us to come out was a Lieutenant in the Columbian Police. He was the gentleman we had targeted. He was one of the Cartel boys and he was dirty. And while it was not publicly known, a lot of the other cops down here were, too. Everyone knew that, at least everyone in the U.S. narcotics law enforcement community. This guy's particular police job was vessel inspection before it left port. But since in his primary job he worked for the Columbian Drug Cartel, he didn't see anything wrong with sending a ton of cocaine, mixed in along with a shipment of bananas, up to Charleston, South Carolina.

Danny swiveled back around to me. "Have ya noticed that he keeps say'n one, like "amigo" as in singular, rather that amigos?" He tilted his questioningly. "Sure sounds like the bastards only saw one of us, doesn't it?"

I hadn't thought about it, but now that Danny said so, I did realize this too. I bump my head at him. "Yeah, he has, hasn't he?" I shift forward and look at him, my decision already made.

"Okay, Danny Boy, how about if I go ahead and give myself up, and then you beat feet back to Weller and tell'em I'm in trouble down here?" Derrick Weller was the DEA agent in charge of this operation and the guy that Danny and I reported to. But Danny was already shaking his head no.

"Uh, uh. Not gonna happen that way, buddy." He narrows his eyes. "Now, while I have some clout because they'll know my name, you," he pointed at me, "they won't know from Adam. If they take you ta their jail, they'll beat the shit outta ya and maybe throw in a little torture, just ta see if ya know anything useful." He swung his head adamantly when I started to protest and pushed his free hand at me in a stopping motion.

"No! Now that's all there is to it, Ghost." he said in hushed voice while he pointed a finger at me. "Make no mistake, if ya don't have some kind'a reputation, then these dudes just think yer a nobody and will kill ya at the drop of the hat. Now that's it. I go, if anybody goes. That's an order! We clear on that?"

I look at him as he's staring daggers at me with his black eyes. I know that the shinkakee feeling I have is rampant inside me. I don't like this, but he's senior in rank and has a lot more experience than me. On top of all that, he's given me a direct order. Shit! I finally nod. Danny heaves a sigh and turns back to look around the freighter's bulkhead. Then he quickly snaps back to me and looks at the hatch I'm leaning against, pointing to it. "See if that'll open!" Then, he's looking back toward the Spanish speaking voices over on the dock.

I jam my weapon, a small Colt .380, the same as Danny's, into my waist and swivel around to lift the old lever on the hatch. My hands are slippery with sweat and I have to strain to make the lever move. It squeaks as I pull it up and scoot sideways so that I can drag the door open onto the deck. The noise from the old hatch is covered by the seagull chatter as the birds fly all around us. Danny takes rapid looks back over his shoulder while keeping his weapon covering the dockside. I peer into the opening. It's an access to the spaces below and a short area, maybe three feet square, is available before a ladder drops downward. I look back to Danny and he's motioning me to go in. I scamper into the void and reach for the hatch as Danny scoots back and helps me close it. He flips the Colt to his other hand as he speaks to me.

"Here, they won't need this." he cranks up his knee and un-straps the holstered little Beretta around his ankle, handing it to me. "You can get it back to me when we meet up again." He takes another quick look around and turns back to me.

"Look Ely, I have no idea how this'll go, okay? They could deport me, alright? That means that you'll be on your own 'til the Guard gets somebody here ta replace me. If that happens, you just lay low and don't give these assholes any reason to start look'n at you, okay?"

I nod and he continues. "Okay, if they let me go, then we'll meet up at the hotel in Medellin at say," he rolls his hand up and peers at his watch, "fourteen hundred tomorrow, okay?"

I nod again, but this time I add my disapproval, too, the shinkakee splashing everywhere in my being. "Yeah, okay Danny, but look, I've got a funny feeling about this, okay? I don't think it's such a good idea!"

"Well, if I'm right, then they won't be look'n for you." He hikes his shoulders. "And if I'm wrong, then you may get deported with me, either way… it's worth a shot." He reaches over and pats my shoulder then turns away standing up and walking with his hands held high, pistol held threat-free, even as I'm whispering in hushed and heated utterances, "No! No Danny! That's not what I mean!" But he's too far away to hear.

He's talking to them now, all in Spanish, as I curse under my breath and heave and drag the door closed, pushing down as hard as I can on the rusted old latch. I step over quickly to peer out the dirty porthole in the door, my pistol at the ready. I can see Danny standing there against the handrail at the ship's side. Then I can feel slight movement and sounds as a number of men come aboard the rusting old hulk. And I hear commands, ordering Danny to put his gun down. I watch as he bends forward and does so. Then I hear Barcas's voice, speaking in Spanish, the pronunciations and words easily translating in my head. They're probably standing in front of Danny now.

"Well, well. So it is you, Lieutenant Commander Vas Quez. I did not expect such a distinguished and notable visitor as yourself, eh? from the American Coast Guard."

I can see Danny, a goofy smile on his face, his hands still held in the air as he replies. "Ah, well, you know how it is Lieutenant Barcas, I am short on time and long in tooth. So my superiors say, why not send the old man, eh?" He inclines his head toward them. "I did not know it was you, Lieutenant, the Honorable Commander of the Port Police forces, that was pursuing me out here, or I would have come out sooner, eh? I thought it might be Cartel men who were chasing me."

I have that old feeling again. The one I always have when things are going to shit. Man, I don't like this! In the confined steel room, I have to turn my head to hear Barcas's responses but I'm getting them.

"Hmm, this is a coincidence, Commander. A friend of mine was just telling me that you have been down here asking specific questions about my alleged association with the Cartel?

The little room is like an oven, and I'm sweating profusely as I see Danny's face change, worry appearing on it as he begins talking again. "No, Commander. I think you have been misinformed. I am here to investigate drug smuggling, not respectable policemen, eh?"

Barcas laughs. "Ah, yes and you would never suspect me, would you Commander? But you, my good friend, are a well-known and accomplished policeman in your own right, eh? So given this, I feel that I must err on the side of caution here. I have interests to protect and my information suggests that you know… that I am an employee of the Cartel. And it appears to me, sir, that you have come here to our fair city to arrest me, eh?"

Danny's voice is edged with concern as he speaks. "No, Lieutenant, I can assure that you are wrong in this regard. I do not believe you to be of the Cartel. I have only the belief that you are an honorable and respectable policeman, yes?"

Barcas laughs again, heartily this time. "Yes, I think that you, Commander, may add the fact that you are very accomplished liar to your list of other achievements, eh?" Barcas emits the guttural laugh again before finally speaking once more.

"Well. Mr., the irony here is that I am indeed one of the former but alas, I am no longer one of the latter, eh. And, since I do not wish to go to prison or to be executed, I am afraid that you will have to disappear from our fair village. I am sorry. Fire!"

I realize what he's saying about the same time that Danny does, but it's too late for either of us by then! I hear the deafening sound of rifles firing as I see bright red splotches appear all over Danny's body! In slow-motion, I see the hits from the M-16s registering all across his chest, little puffs a meat and blood exploding out of his back, his face registering shock as he's blown backwards, over the rail. I'm lifting on the handle as hard as I can, my hand slipping because of the sweat! Then I see tan uniformed policemen hopping down to the deck all over the place. There has to be at least twenty-five or thirty of them. I watch in terror as I see them at the rail, firing down into the water where Danny disappeared.

Then more Spanish is being shouted outside. Someone is saying not to worry about the body, as it will contain no identification. Then Barcas is ordering the policemen to make a cursory check around before returning to the station. As I peer out the dusty window, sweat streaming down my face, back and legs, I see the cops beginning to look around outside. A helmet suddenly appears at the glass and I hurriedly step aside, my free hand and weight holding down the lever. I feel it being pulled upon, but shortly, another order is called. A face appears with hands shading the porthole for a moment, and then the cop gives up and leaves to join his friends.

I crouch there, my weapon ready in the heated box, for another ten minutes, and then I venture out. I see nobody around the dock, but then after what just happened, I don't expect to. I finally make my way to the rail and look down. Danny's body is floating face-up, his eyes still registering surprise. He bobs in the gentle waves down there, in amongst a dirty white bleach bottle, the seaweed and flotsam of this nasty harbor. His youngest son will graduate from high school next month. But Danny won't be there. I wipe a hand over my face, smearing the accumulated water from sweat and tears that have formed there.

I know how this will go when I report it. They'll issue a warrant for Barcas. If he doesn't skip to the deep jungle, then he'll be extradited back to the USA. Then he'll probably be tried and convicted and maybe spend the rest of his life in a nice cozy federal prison. I don't like that idea. Nope, as I look at my friend and mentor floating in the dirty water, I decide that I don't like that idea one little bit. I make my way off the dock and fade into the village up ahead.

A week later, I sit against the hillside surrounded by jungle bushes. I have been here all night and it is mid-day now. I look through binoculars into the open window of a small earth brick home in the clearing below. Barcas just finished having sex with a young girl in the dwelling. Danny and I had followed him to this isolated place twice before. He apparently kept one of his young mistresses here. I'd watched her face as they had had intercourse, and while Barcas never saw it, it was obvious that she didn't enjoy the act. I doubt that he would've cared anyway. As I look now, I see her force a smile as she climbs off from him, her small breasts bouncing in the lenses.

She says something and then pads into the only other room in the small house, a small kitchen area. When she comes into sight again, she's carrying a small child, propped deftly on her hip. I find this very sad because she's only a child herself. My attention is drawn back to Barcas as he sits up and pulls on his uniform pants. He stretches and yawns, then apparently tells her he'll be right back. He takes his pistol holster and goes across the room. Next I see the side door open and Barcas steps out. I hope he doesn't go around front where his Jeep is parked. He doesn't. He's barefooted and wearing no shirt as he begins picking his way across the clearing to the wooden outhouse. I adjust the focus and follow him as he enters the potty. Then I lower the weapon. Why not, eh? I grab my bag and make my way down there. Three minutes later, I jerk the door open and see the startled face of Barcas looking up at me! His Playboy magazine falls from his hands! His eyes dart to the holstered pistol hanging on the wall then back to the little .22 caliber Beretta I have pointed at his chest! He begins speaking quickly in Spanish as he tries to bluff, but I can see that he's scared and I like that. I smile at him.

"Who are you? What is this? Do you know who I am?"

I nod and continue my smile as I answer him in Spanish. "Yes, Mr., I do know who you are. But apparently, you do not know who I am, eh?"

He slowly shakes his head, so I go on. "I am an American Coast Guard Agent."

He smiles then, relief washing over his face. "So... Mr. You are here to arrest me then? I understand this." I see the fear leeching away from him as he points a stubby finger at me. "What is wrong with your face, Mr.?"

I answer him softly. "I am also a North American Indian, and this... is my war face."

I let that soak in a second, his confused features staring back at me, and then quickly move the pistol up and fire! The sound of the .22 is deafening in the little wooden house and he screams and throws a hand up to his ear that is mangled and bloody. His horrified eyes find mine and I speak again, this time without the smile.

"Mr., I was also a friend of Commander Daniel VasQuez."

Now he knows... and he begins pleading and begging with me "Please, Mr ... Please? I have a wife and children, Mr. ... Please?"

"Yes, yes, I know Santiago. A wife and three little ones back in Barranquilla, eh? But you also have that fourteen-year old girl up in the house, too? And her baby, that's one of your children, too, is it not?"

He nods his head as he looks up at me, and I smile again. "Yes, well, Commander Vas Quez had a wife and children, too, Lieutenant. Yet, you thought that made little difference to him, so I don't see why it should matter now, eh?"

He's crying now as I look around the small room and smell the odors it contains. I keep speaking as my eyes travel about. "Now Santiago, this is a fitting place for you, is it not? You are nothing but a piece of shit, and as you know, shit is sometimes sticky." I bring my eyes back to him. "I think you should meld with this shit, eh? Stick to it and become one until it's time for you to go. I'll leave you here to contemplate that." He stops the sniffling and looks at me directly.

"Yes Mr. You have others coming for me, yes? I understand and will comply, Mr. I give you my word on this! I do not want to die here!"

I nod my head at him. "Good, Santiago. You should stick with this shit, blend and meld together, become a part of it, Santiago, because... you are the same, eh?" I smile and step back, taking his pistol belt with my left hand as I do. "I am giving you this small time to expand and change yourself amongst the shit. I must go and check on your driver now. So do not try to leave here, Santiago. You just stay here, and...get your shit together, eh?"

I chuckle at my own joke as he looks at me gratefully. I close the door as he's thanking me over and over again through sobs. There's a heavy metal hook on the door, to keep it from banging in the wind, and I fix it in place. I say loudly over my shoulder, "If he tries to come out - shoot him!" Then, I throw his pistol belt up into the jungle as hard as I can, before stepping around the side of the old outhouse. I reach in the bag I have slung over my shoulder and pull out a white phosphorus hand grenade.

My original plan had been to affix the grenade to the underside of his Jeep with a remote detonator, but then I'd changed my mind. I'd decided that I wanted to tell him why, and see his face as I shot him with Danny's gun. But heck man, this'll work just fine, too. In fact, it's kind of poetic. I pull the pin and do a four count before I drop it into the ventilation gap that runs all along the roof of the building. A second passes, and then Barcas begins screaming maniacally. But by that time, I'm running hell-bent for the front of the house and rounding the tree line as the building explodes behind me!

I hit the dirt as pieces of debris fall all around behind me. I look back to see the littered mess and a large fire and chunks of burning wood everywhere. The gases in the building made a lot larger explosion than I'd thought they would. Then, I'm up and running again, coming up to the front of the military police Jeep parked in front of the house. I'm slightly worried about the girl. I know that there aren't any weapons inside because I'd searched the house when she'd gone to the market earlier. Barcas had only taken his sidearm in with him. I slow to a walk and look around as I come up to the dead driver, lying face down beside the Jeep. I place my boot on his back and pull my survival knife out from between his shoulder blades, wiping the blood off on his shirt.

It's then that I see her, standing inside the house, holding the child with fear emblazoned on her young face. I just eliminated her meal ticket, and life would be very rough for her now. I did this to her. I hold up a hand and speak to her in Spanish. "Please, little girl, do not fear. All will be well." I sheath the knife and look back at her before leaving. Her face is a mixture of child-like innocence and anguish, and I know that what I've done here will only make that worse. My head drops, and then I look back up and across the Jeep's seats to her.

"Tengo simpatico, nina." I am sorry for you, little girl.

Then I'm running back into the jungle and up to where I have my old Toyota truck parked. As I go, I'm wiping the camouflage paint off with a towel from the bag. My face was divided in half with it. One side olive green, the other white – Dog Soldier style. But now I am off the warpath for awhile. There are noises as I get closer to my truck and I don't understand this. I'd been here before, many times to this place, and there are never any noises here? Not by my truck? What's… why? I keep running, pushing brush out of my way, going forward, the bag slapping against my side, the noises getting louder and louder! What is this?

Then I'm breaking through the jungle and there's my truck! I'm still running and I hear the noise overhead! I look up and there's an F-16 fighter flying low, causing me to dive to the ground! I raise my eyes up and the jet turns into a black crow, its wings beating furiously before it changes into some funny-looking helicopter!

I'm up and running again toward the truck, but there's someone sitting in the cab! Who? There's not supposed to be anyone there! I know better than this as I race up to the truck! There's never anyone there! There never is! Whoever they are, they're sitting stock-still, not moving! The noise comes again and I involuntarily duck, searching the sky for the jet. It's not there. I reach out and jerk open the door and… Mussenberg turns and smiles at me! His already dark face is in the shade of the cab and his white teeth gleam outrageously! Then he shifts and changes... becoming a coyote! His eyes... his yellow eyes are mocking me!

I come awake disorientated and confused, my eyes enlarged and glaring at the stucco ceiling. I'm sucking breaths down in huge gulps! I hastily look around the sun-lit room, my eyes darting everywhere. The noise is just outside! I'm sweating profusely and can feel my heart racing in my chest as I look over and see Gretchen beside me, my jacket, beyond her, on the chair. I roll off the blanket and ease out of the bed looking back but she doesn't stir. I inch over, pull the Glock out and make my way back to the window. I slightly pull back a curtain and peek from the side. Next door, two men revving up a snowmobile in their driveway.

That's the noise. A dumb-ass snowmobile engine. I drop the curtain. Holy shit! Who needs LSD when you can have dreams like that! I look at the luminous dial of my watch and can see that it's 12:45. I have to get moving here. I quietly slip into my flight jacket, then sneak out. Pistol in hand, I make a quick check of the house. Nobody's here. I crack the door open to look in at her before I leave. She's still sleeping peacefully, her dark hair flowing over a pillow. Her left shoulder and a bare breast are exposed, the raspberry nipple dark against her white skin.

As I look at her, I pull my pants fly away from my body. I mentally kick myself for standing here looking at her nudity in my masochistic tendencies. I remind myself that this is like a diabetic looking longingly at a piece of chocolate cake. Something you want so bad but know... you can't touch. I don't know about other guys but I've always been the type to be easily aroused by sexual desire, whether dead-tired, blitzed drunk or out of a four-year coma. I force my eyes to avert to her face. She sleeps soundly as I watch. I figure her dreams must be good ones. I feel a strange mixture of pride and dissatisfaction that I guess is not too hard for me to define.

I know that the pride comes from managing to hold myself away from doing wrong to this woman, whom I do not love. I suppose that the dissatisfaction I feel, probably comes from the non-release of pent-up lust that we could've shared with each other. But that's all it would've been on my part though, lust. No sincere emotion, no soul connection, just sex. But with her... well I doubt that would've been the case. I silently thank the Great Good Spirit for helping me through this while at the same time... I kick my mortal self for not tasting the sweet nectar of her offerings. Oh well, I think as I quietly close the door. Such is the paradox of Ely Stone.

The Kent County International Airport,

Mussenberg paced back and forth across the uncarpeted floor. He and his men were in a large lounge, which was shutdown for remodeling. One wall was adhered with new gypsum panels and taped plaster joints. Pieces of 2x4 and building scraps, and other debris of construction, littered the room. After the hour and a half flight down here, it had taken almost twenty minutes to find the airport manager. They needed to get permission from him so that his two men and Luce's aircrew could inhabit the vacant room for the interim, as well as to permit the helicopter to be landed and parked close enough for easy access. He looked outside at the Black Hawk sitting within spitting distance from the window.

The airport manager had been an easy enough man to control. He'd simply showed him his I.D. and explained that he was on operating under national security, having to do with terrorism and the fellow had complied. The guy had accepted that at face value, given the men and their aircraft. His face made a smirk. It wouldn't've been so easy with a cop. Police officers were a nosy breed and while they would initially go along with any request he made, they would almost immediately start asking questions, too. And while Mussenberg had the authority, if he decided to invoke it, that whole happenstance would inevitably lead back to informing the General. And that was something he couldn't afford to do just yet. He shook his head in disgust at his predicament.

It was ironic, he thought. All he had to do was say the word, and he could have every police department, state, city and county agency, as well as any and every piece of military equipment and manpower that he wanted, out looking for Stone. And they'd have him in short while, too. Of course, in order to do that, he would have to contact the General and give him the situation-representation. That SITREP would certainly do the trick, alright. But it would definitely end his career association with DET 4, too. And if Stone managed to leak things vital to DET 4's primary mission, then Mussenberg could probably kiss his own personal butt goodbye, as well. He would no doubt have a very unfortunate accident of some sort. He sighed as he turned away from the window.

This was his first "command" retrieval mission. There could be no fuck-ups in a retrieval mission. That was the General's standing order. Then he looked at his watch again. Almost 1400. Time was running out to save both his ass and Stone's. Almost 2 o'clock and still nothing. He'd have to call Sergeant Canter again, shortly. And since the man hadn't contacted him, it meant that they still had no word on Stone. They didn't have even the slightest idea where the man was. Mussenberg gritted his teeth. In less than three hours, he was going to have to call the General and tell him about this. That really wasn't going to be good.

He cast a glance across the room at Luce and his crew. They were all camped out, sleeping or trying to, on chairs that they'd drug together. He didn't blame them. His eyes went over to the two DET 4 agents. Those guys were drinking sodas and playing cards, bought up front in another lounge. He switched gears and began thinking of other things. He hadn't thought much about what he was going to say to Stone, if and when they caught up with him.

He knew that he could no longer just keep the man under observation, that was a given now. Stone knew something about Stardust. He had to, otherwise... why run? Of course, it was possible that even Stone didn't know what he knew. And maybe that was why he had rabbited. Well, if Stone didn't tell him what he knew outright, then that meant that they'd have to take him into custody to try and find out. Time to check in. Mussenberg pulled the phone out of his pocket and punched in the number for the Escanaba Operations Building. As the connection clicked and clacked, he returned to his previous thoughts. Now since he didn't think that Stone was going to permit himself to be arrested, it meant that Stone would probably die. A more plaguing question though, as Sergeant Canter answered the phone, was just how many of the men in this room would the guy take with him?

En-Route To The Grand Rapids Veteran's Home.
Grand Rapids, Michigan,
1330 hours or 1:30 pm,
The Same Day.

As I drive down 28th Street, I fumble with the city map that I just bought at a Quick-Mart. I glanced at it before heading out into traffic and remember that the airport is up ahead someplace, too. So I decide that I'll go past there, then hit Interstate 96, to go west and over to the Vet's Home. I flick ashes from the hand-rolled out the window and marvel at the sunny day. The weather is beautiful, at least forty degrees outside. Although the sleep I'd gotten at Veeter's home wasn't enough, I am at least coherent and able to function again. In spite of that crappy-assed dream.

Anyway, I know that my new energy is not going to last long, but I figure that it will be enough for me to do this interview. I also figure that I'll have to go see the guy in Florida. I just don't hold out high hopes that this former radar operator in the Vet's Home will know anything about a possible missing nuclear bomb, or whatever. So driving past the airport is my way of getting a handle on where it is for the flight I'll probably have to take tomorrow. Soon, I see signs along the road and big jets overhead.

Then I pull into a Citgo gas station right before the interchange for I-96. As I fill the Jeep's tank, I rub sore eyes and look around. The airport access road is just back to the east from here. I can see it from where I stand. I twist back and see the expressway behind and above me. The traffic is howling overhead as it continues on over 28th Street. At least I won't have any problems finding this place tomorrow when I leave the Motel 6. It's almost a straight shot to here. I let my eyes wander around until I hear the gas nozzle click off. A few minutes later, I'm back in the Jeep and climbing the on-ramp of West-bound I-96, the city map spread out on the other seat. Shortly after that, I'm exiting again and driving toward the hospital. And before long, I pull into the visitor's lot.

I shuffle around in my bag and find my Pukaskwa Police I.D. Then I pop the door and begin walking across the lot to the building's entrance. The elevator opens and I walk down the hall, looking at room numbers until I find 407. Someone's just wheeling a man out in a wheelchair from the room as I come to a stop. I look down at the old fellow in the chair and smile.

"Uh, excuse me, sir, you're not Joe Markowski, are ya?" The old man looks at me and shakes his head as the nurse, a large black woman, answers.

"Nawwww. This here's Mike Delbert," she taps his shoulder, "ain't that right, Michael." The old guy smiles and nods as the nurse turns to face me, tilting her head behind her toward the room, even as she's wheeling the chair around.

"Joe's in there. His bed is over by the window, but I think he was going to the bathroom as we were leaving. You can go right on in. He shouldn't be but a minute."

I thank her and walk into the room, easing over to the window. The view overlooks the grounds and the Grand River. There's a monument center with a group of flag poles situated inside. All five branches of the military's flags are flying from the flagpoles, along with the U.S. and state banners. The grounds are pretty and I assume that in the summer, they make a nice place for these guys to go, when they can get out there.

I look around and see family photos and greeting cards on top of a chest of drawers. I step over and look more closely. These are probably the kids and grandkids. In addition, there is a black and white wedding picture, probably from the 1950s. Then, I spy a service picture of a guy in an Air Force blue Eisenhower blouse and saucer cap. My head nods to the photo. Definitely vintage 1950s Air Force. The "Ike" blouses weren't worn by 1960. At least I probably have the right guy. I hear a toilet flush noisily, and a few seconds later the side door opens and an old man with a walker slowly makes his way out of the bathroom. He's kind of obese, not at all like the skinny youth depicted in the service picture and wedding photograph. But the features are the same, only older. He sees me and blinks a smile. I return it as I speak.

"Mr. Markowski? Joseph Markowski?"

He keeps stepping slowly toward the bed as he nods, his weight and the walker a cumbersome addition. "Yep, that'd be me." He's looking at me curiously, trying, I reckon, to figure out who I am. I pull out the badge I.D. as he gets to the bed. He's got it down to a practiced art as he sits down and quickly moves the bulky walker to a place beside the night table. I step forward and hand him my I.D. He takes it, adjusts his glasses and gives it a good look before handing it back. I reach over and retrieve it, slipping it into my jacket pocket.

"My name's Ely Stone, sir. I'm a special agent with the Pukaskwa Tribal Police, up in the Upper Peninsula and I was…"

He interrupts me and points to my flight jacket. "That's a Navy G2 you're wearing, ain't it?"

I nod and smile. I'd forgotten for a second that he was prior Air Force. All of his friends up here were prior military too. This was a veteran's home, wasn't it? These guys probably talked military a lot.

"Yes, sir, it is."

He nods as he swings his feet up, his face and voice showing pain at the effort. "Yeah, I thought so," he says, as he finally gets situated. He sends inquisitive blue-gray eyes over to me and raises a wrinkled finger toward me. "So, you were in the Navy then?"

I twist my head slightly. "No, sir, Coast Guard."

His eyes light up and he slaps a heavy thigh lightly. "Aw, really? Geeze-o-peets, my roommate, Mike Delbert, was in the Coast Guard! At Pearl Harbor when the Japs bombed it, no less! Damn," he shakes his head, "He's gonna be sorry he missed you! How long ya stay'n? He went down for some x-rays, but then he has physical therapy afterwards, so he'll be gone awhile."

I shake my head in answer. "I don't know, Mr. Markowski. I'm kind'a pressed for time. It depends on what you might be able ta tell me more than anything else, sir?"

He flings up an arm. "Well, go ahead, sonny, I got nuthin but time here. Shoot, I'm probably not ever get'n outta this place. I got degenerative disk disease in my back." He waves a hand, "An old C-47 crash back when I was in the service. So go on, ask away."

I nod, happy to be able to ask the question that I'm pretty sure he doesn't know the answer to. "Okay, well I'm working an old case, from back around 1953. I understand you were a radar operator, stationed at Kinross at that time?" His eyes are solemn now as he stares at me, gravity spreading over his features. Then I see the barest hint of a nod of his head, his eyes locked onto mine. So I nod, too, and go on.

"Okay, good. Ah, Mr. Markowski, this has something to do the old Kinross Air Force Base and maybe a missing…"

He cuts me off, leaning over his bed and looking at me intently, his eyes a combination of dread and astonishment. "Did they find it then? Is that what this is about? You people have found it?"

The old man's animated and excited all at the same time. "Sir?"

He's sitting back on the bed now, looking straight up at the ceiling and slowly shaking his head. "Boy, I had a feeling that if they ever found it… it'd turn the world on it's ear, and I guess that's so… ain't it?"

Chapter Twenty-Nine
A Tangent For The Ghost

**The Kent County Airport,
Grand Rapids, Michigan,
1407 hours or 2:07 pm,
The Same Day.**

Mussenberg stood in the lounge, staring out the window at the bright sunshine. He couldn't get over how warm and dry it was here, compared to the cold and snow he'd just left in the U.P. He was pondering this when his phone rang. He flipped it up and saw the number as he brought it to his ear. He had just spoken with Sergeant Canter. He'd called him for his hourly check-in and now he supposed that the man had forgotten to tell him something about the island operation during their recent conversation.

"What is it, Dick, you miss my voice already?

"No, sir. We just gotta report from the Kent County Sheriff's Office there in Grand Rapids, that one of their deputies copied Stone's plate a little while ago. And, Captain, Stone was on 28th Street. That's right by the airport - where you're at now, sir!"

"No, shit! Okay, does this deputy still have him under observation?"

"No, sir, but he stated to his dispatch that he observed Stone's vehicle traveling east on 28th Street at around 1335. That's only half an hour ago, Captain."

A thousand things entered Mussenberg's mind as he ran a hand over his head. The other men in the room had all looked up at his excited voice. He assessed the situation and still found himself stuck. He couldn't request that the cop go back and look for Stone without going through the officer's command. If he did that, then the questions would start coming. No. He couldn't use any local, county or even state police. But federal cops, that was a possibility. While he'd still been in the air, flying down here, he'd asked Canter about any federal assistance that might be available. While he couldn't stop the locals from being curious, other feds would probably cooperate and keep the lid on.

The Sergeant had told him that there was a federal building in downtown Grand Rapids that he'd already checked into. There is a

Deputy U.S. Marshall's office as well as a FBI sub-office located there. But Canter had also said that the offices were closed on the weekends and had very limited staffs. So, since it was a Saturday, the odds of getting them to provide assistance was slim. His thoughts landed back on Stone. He still didn't know where Stone would stop, if anywhere. But the man was in the vicinity and that was something at least. His best option was probably to sit tight. He turned back to the phone.

"Dick, is there anyone else, any other people on the federal level that we can tap for assistance here?"

"No, sir, I've checked. Nothing. The only other thing I've come up with is the Recruiter's office. We have an Air Force Recruiting Office there and I've got home numbers on those guys?"

Mussenberg threw his hand up in the air and spun around, speaking sarcastically. "Oh, shit! Yeah, that's a great idea! We'll just get Stone to enlist in the Air Force and that'll solve all our problems, won't it?"

"Yeah, I know sir, but that's all I got. I can't think… wait a minute! There's got to be federal police officers that guard that building, sir! Most federal buildings have them. I'll try to raise their supervisor and see if we couldn't get someone cut loose from there, if ya want?"

Mussenberg dropped his head and slowly shook it. "Yeah, go ahead. That's something. Let me know what you come up with. Now, about that deputy sheriff, could you glean anything from his dispatcher about Stone's direction of travel? Anything the deputy might've thought? Anything like that, at all?"

"No, sir. The dispatcher stated that the cop had just said that Stone was pulling into a gas station by the I-96 interchange when he passed 'em. But accord'n ta the map I have here, Captain, that's right where you're at."

Mussenberg nodded as a mental picture of the surrounding area popped up in his mind. He had the same map in his briefcase and had spent time studying it since his arrival. The frustration was mind-boggling and extremely infuriating. He screamed into the phone.

"Yeah, well that doesn't help us very fuck'n much, Sergeant! I still don't know where the hell he's going, do I!"

There was a brief silence before the Sergeant answered. "No, sir, I guess you don't. Are you going to be on the move then, Captain?"

Mussenberg rubbed his fingers across his brows and sighed. "No, we'll be staying here for awhile. We'll see if we can't get a positive or at least a better location on him before we move. I'll notify you when we decide to reposition and we're in motion. And, Dick… I'm sorry for that… it's just well… shit, I'm sorry, okay?"

"No problem, Captain. I understand. I'll keep you informed and find out about the federal cops. I'll look for your next check-in at 1500, if I don't speak to you before, sir."

Mussenberg nodded. "Okay, roger that. Out."

He flipped the phone closed and glanced around at the curious faces looking at him. "Well guys, we know our boy's here. He was out in front of this very airport about thirty minutes ago." He took a deep breath before continuing.

"So what we're going to do is wait a bit longer, see if he doesn't come to roost someplace for more than two seconds. If that doesn't happen soon," he looked at Major Luce and his flight crew and bumped his head, "then me and my two guys'll get a car and do a little driving around, see if we can't spot 'em. 'Till then, we just sit tight."

The Grand Rapids Home for Veterans
Grand Rapids, Michigan,
Same Time, Same Day.

I sit on the window ledge of Markowski's room, looking at the old man as he stares at the ceiling. His eyes are wide and lost in thought. Some remembrance is passing over them, and as I sit here, I know that I've initiated this process for him. Something I'd said upset him and gave me hope all at the same time. I think he knows about the B-47 and the missing weapon. Something sure has to explain his reaction when I'd mentioned Kinross and a happening back in the early 1950s, didn't it? I set the small notebook down and lean forward, rubbing my hands together.

"Mr. Markowski, you know something about this bomber, don't you?" It takes a second, but then he turns his head to me, his gray eyebrows furrow into question marks behind the glasses.

"Huh?… What did you say?… What bomber?"

I nod. Okay, it'll take a little coercing, I reckon. He was probably sworn to secrecy when the event happened. Whatever this thing was, it was big enough to stay hidden for fifty years so it'll take more than just some guy walking in out of the blue, to make him speak what he knows. I've got to put his mind at ease somehow, if I'm going to get the information. I turn my head and begin.

"The B-47, Mr. Markowski. We know all about it and… what happened." I wave a hand. "I'm just here to get some follow-up stuff for the report, sir. Nothing more than that, okay?"

He still looks puzzled. Then his expression changes. "Are you talk'n about that 'Strat back in '52? The one that supposedly lost an A bomb? Is that what ya came all the way down here ta ask about?"

It's my turn to be puzzled. I don't know what a strat is but an A bomb has my undivided attention. I look at him curiously. "Strat?"

He's nodding. "Yeah, 'Strat. That's what we called 'em, "Strats". They were B-47 Stratojets and most everybody just called 'em Strats. Is that what ya want ta talk to me about?"

I unfold my hands and lean back, a good but tired feeling coming over me. I don't think I'm going to have to fly to Florida after all. I nod at him.

"Yes, sir, Mr. Markowski. We're aware, due to information from that time, that a B-47 did lose a weapon over Lake Michigan and well… I just need to hear what you know about it."

He "ha-rumps" and throws me a disgusted look while pointing at me again. "Hey, I was there and that was just a bunch a B.S.! He throws a hand up in dismissal.

"That never happened. No '47 ever lost no A bomb out over Lake Michigan or any other damn place, at least not while I was stationed up there, it didn't!"

Now I'm taken aback and am leaning forward. "But… there are eye witness accounts and newspaper stories of a B-47 losing a nuclear bomb out over the Great Lakes. I don't…"

He cuts me off with an furiously jabbing finger. "Ya wanna know what happened? I'll tell ya, 'cause I was there. What it was was… we'd just got these new birds in, ya see? And the B-47 was a new bird at that time, okay? The crews were green on 'em and they didn't know everything about the planes yet, see?" He's expecting an acknowledgement and I give him one by nodding.

"Yeah, well one of 'em was out over Lake Michigan and went ta test their bomb bay doors and when they opened 'em, one of the damned weapons wrappers blew out've the bay! The weapons wrapper was a light weight piece a aluminum with the wording on it, "DANGER - ATOMIC WEAPON", okay?"

I nod again and he continues. "Those thing's're supposed ta be removed by the air crew and given ta ground personnel, once the ordinance is loaded. But somebody screwed up and the damn thing got left in the bomb bay. That's all that happened. That plane wasn't even carrying any bombs on that flight, for cry'n out loud!"

I'm perplexed and confused now as my eyes drop to the floor and search the plastic tiles there. What's the deal here? I bring my gaze back up to him. "What about the newspaper story? Do you have any idea how that came about?"

He's already nodding. "Hell, yeah, I know. This reporter, a guy from the Chicago Tribune, I think it was…" He stops, his mind clouded in thought. Then he expels any concern and goes on.

"Well, anyway… wherever he was from, that's how the whole thing got started. Some fisherman found the weapons wrapper and called this reporter. Then he came up ta the base and started poke'n around, talk'n ta airmen in town, ya know, just ask'n questions. Well, anyway, he found out what a weapons wrapper was and just jumped ta the conclusion that we'd lost one, see? The newspaper ran the story without even talk'n ta the brass or nothin! Then they had ta end up eat'n crow and doing a retraction and everything." He finishes with a flurry, satisfied that he and his outfit weren't responsible for losing an atomic bomb.

I'm sitting back now, the wind sucked from my sails and disillusionment filling my being. Where do I go from here? I'm looking off into space and thinking this over when I catch movement, and see Markowski getting off the bed and taking his walker. He looks over at me as he moves along,

"I'll be right back. I gotta hit the latrine again. They've got me on water pills and I'm piss'n every five minutes, seems like."

I nod and return to my misery as he ambles into the tiny room and closes the door. I can feel the fatigue in my body, and the dullness in my wits, too. So what gives now, eh? This was the one solid lead I've had and now, if I believe Markowski, then it's a dead end. And I might as well believe him 'cause it jibes, doesn't it? This is probably the accurate picture of the news account, too, isn't it? I hear the toilet flush and look up before continuing the thought.

Yeah, Markowski here, is probably telling the actual tale. According to what Gangues said, the Tribune ran a retraction of the first story, shortly after it appeared. Good gravy, man! Oh well, I'm lost and can't do didley-squat about it. I decide that I'm a physical wreck and am too exhausted to care anymore. I'll head back to the motel and get some rest. There's no big rush to get to Florida now, is there? I'll get into it again tomorrow. I'm thinking this as I watch Markowski shuffling back onto the bed. I pick up my notebook and pocket it as look over to him.

"Well okay Mr. Markowski, I think that takes care of all I needed. You've been very helpful and I want to thank you."

He's looking at me with the face of a disbeliever. As I stand on tired legs, he asks me. "Did you really come all the way down here just ta ask me about that dumb newspaper story?"

I look at him and try to decide what to say. My mind's foggy and it's a feeble mind to begin with, so this is really a dangerous condition to be in. Ah what the hell, what've I got to loose here. I angle my head and stick my hands in my pockets before speaking.

"Ya know, Mr. Markowski, I really don't know what I expected to find out here. I've got something going on up on reservation lands and it has to do with the Air Force and something that I thought might've happened back in the 1950s. But now... I just don't know?"

He looks at me thoughtfully over his glasses and slowly nods his head. I begin making my way around his little meal table when the music that's an on-going melody kicks up a notch in my head. Johnny Cash is singing out loudly, "Ghost Riders in the skyyyyyyy" and I stop dead still. My head snaps over to Markowski and I suddenly remember his astonishment when I mentioned Kinross and the early 1950s. Something set this old guy off when I'd said that, hadn't it? Then I remember Gangues telling me about the crashed F-89! Old man Veeter's face flashes in my brain as the music goes up one more click! Noooo, I say to myself! But I have to ask. I have to! I take a swallow and form the words.

"Unless..." I clear my throat and try again. "Unless, you happen to know anything about an old accident, involving an F-89 from Kinross?"

I see his features change and go blank a second, his mouth drooping and his eyes enlarging. He raises a hand and fits his glasses closer to his nose, an act of nervousness. He tries to speak, but finds his own mouth dry, too. He holds up a hand for me to wait as he picks up a water glass and sips from a straw, his eyes elsewhere, searching for something, possibly a way to answer me. He finally sets the glass down and looks over to me while raising up a hand.

"How much do you know about it?"

I shrug. "Not much. I know that the plane went missing over Lake Superior and that it was never found."

He takes that in and I see his eyes make a decision and it's not a positive one for me. He doesn't think I have enough information of my own so he's going to lie. I can see it in his body language. Basically honest people can't hide it. That's because they have little experience at lying, and thus, can't control their bodies or how they give away messages to someone like me. I've seen this a hundred times before. So I say the only thing that I can that may break his decision and allow him to talk truthfully to me. Before he can get his rebuttal words out, I hurriedly add my own.

"But I also have an eyewitness who says that... that plane actually crashed over Lake Michigan, not Lake Superior."

That stops him cold. His posture weakens and I think that he's going to talk with me. I think he'll tell me what he really knows. Again, I see it in his body language. He peers at me through his blue-gray old eyes. "An… an eye witness, ya say? You have somebody that actually seen it?"

I nod at him, and then wait. He stares at me a beat and then turns away from me to look out the window. "Ya know, when ya first said that… about something missing from Kinross back in the fifties… I right away thought about that Scorpion and her crew."

He turns back to me with wet eyes. No tears, but definite emotion there. I watch as he holds his glasses up and wipes away the wetness with his free hand before readjusting the bifocals again and turning back to me.

"Ya know, "Scorpion" was the given name of the F-89, just like an F-14 is a "Tomcat" and a P-51 is a "Mustang". He nods once, solidly to himself, then raises a hand, "Go close that door."

It's a command and I do as ordered. I kick out the stop and let the heavy door swing slowly closed, shutting out all of the noises out in the hallway. Then I walk back over to his bedside and wait. He motions me back to my former place at the window ledge, and again I follow instructions. I ease back down, and as I do, I notice that the ever-playing song in my head has dropped back down in volume. I have no way of knowing if that's good or bad as I turn my attention to Markowski and he begins speaking.

"What I'm gonna tell you…I've never told another soul." He sends a look of sincerity to me, "Not even my wife, God rest her. They made us sign National Secrecy Act papers and swear that we'd never divulge what happened that night. But… I'm gonna die soon. I know, 'cause I been diagnosed with cancer and the doc's say I've got maybe six or seven months left. And this plane and those two guys… have always haunted me."

I feel the shinkakee swirling around me as I watch him. Somehow, I know this is it. What he's about to say is my tangent, the link in this sick, sorry mystery. I watch him shake his head and lower it. When he brings it up again, he's not here in this room. His eyes are clouded in far away memory of another time.

He looks past me, out the window, and I turn to look, too. Both of us are staring at the gray sky overhead as he begins speaking, and all of a sudden, the two of us are not here in the present anymore. We're off on a journey back in time. Back into history. We arrive at a cold and snowy night in the Upper Peninsula. He's describing the scene as he knows it to be and heaven help me…I'm there, too.

A "Tangent" For The Ghost

Kinross Air Force Base,
Sault Ste. Marie, MI.
433rd Fighter /Interceptor Squadron,
4706th Air Defense Wing, USAF.
23 November 1953 - The Remote Past
The 1st Alert Runway, at Kinross AFB 1822 (6:22 pm, EST)

The crack of thunder and white-hot fire from jet afterburners lit the dark sky as the first "Ready Alert" climbed off the runway. Meanwhile, ground crew airmen in green uniform fatigues finished chocking the wheels on the second "Ready Alert" and then hurried back into their shack to escape the cold. The two replacement F-89c jet fighters now sat idly on the cold runway as the sounds of kindred jet engines crackled into the distance. The airplanes were used to the cold though, even if they were away from home.

They were just visiting, lending a helping hand here at Kinross. Their real home was Truax Air Force Base in Wisconsin. They had been sent here to cover for the Kinross planes that were away in Arizona, performing gunnery practice. So in spite of their namesake, the "Scorpions" didn't seem to mind the coolness of the night air. These sleek silver jets were America's premier all-weather, day or night fighter/interceptors. Their wings stretched almost 60 feet across and their bodies were over 53 feet long. Their rear fuselages swept upward as they neared the back and the overall appearance was that of "Scorpion", with its tail stinger poised to strike.

Carrying a pilot in front and a radar operator behind, the "Scorpion" came armed with six 20-millimeter cannons and various missiles. These aircraft were our first, best defense in 1953. They had a top speed of 627 mph., and for the day and time, were probably the fastest and most advanced fighters in the world. They could easily out-fly anything their enemy could send their way. Well, most enemies anyway. The Cold War was at it's beginning, and the USA fully expected a flight of Russian bombers to come over at any minute to drop their atomic bomb loads. On similar Air Force bases all over the country, jet fighters sat at the ready, just like these two. They often took off in a hurry to intercept an aircraft that looked suspicious, especially if it was in one of the northern states. The belief was that a Russian attack would most likely come from the north.

In late November, darkness comes early in Upper Michigan and only moments before, the replacement jets had rested inside their heated hanger. The reason for their move was that the first "Ready

Alert" had just left the base on such an intercept mission. Now these two jets, occupied the place of "Ready Alert" to continue to be on guard. The jets seemed quiet and docile. In the dim light cast by the hanger windows, they certainly didn't look menacing. And in spite of all of the advanced technology, maybe they weren't that threatening anyway. After all, before the hour was up, one of their sisters would find it really difficult just staying in the air.

Fighter Operations Bldg, C.C.C.
The Combat, Command & Communications room,
Kinross AFB, 1858 (6:58pm, EST)

The room was full of men in olive green fatigues or flight suits, all busy at different tasks. And if the furnace hadn't been working, the tension and sweat that existed in the air would've formed clouds. It was that thick and everyone could feel it. The Captain was bent over the radar operator's shoulder and stared at the screen with a look of consternation, mixed with shades of fear. The lighted hand of the radar swept around and around but nothing else appeared on the oval glass. The Captain straightened up.

"Nothing? I mean, Naples hasn't got'em now, either?"

Airman Second Class Joseph Markowski turned up from the screen and shook his head. "No, sir. No targets registering."

"Shit!" The Captain whirled around to look across the room. There was an Airman by the Communications Office.

"Kessler, get me the walky-talky and tell communications to patch me through to the Squadron Commander ASAP! Then get the Squadron Exec (executive officer) on the horn and tell him we need him here right away, too."

The Airman quick-jabbed his head and turned to enter the office as the Captain swung back around, just in time to see the star-winged patch on his Master Sergeant's arm as it extended two manila files outward. The Captain saw the files with the names Moncla and Wilson across their tops. He then let his eyes wander up to those of the gray-haired Master Sergeant.

"You're way ahead of me aren't ya, Chuck?" The Captain let his eyes search those of the older man. He could see that the same things he thought were going on in the Sergeant's mind.

"I'm trying, sir, but I gotta tell ya, I've seen shit like this before and it always scares me more than any fight'n I ever seen over Europe or Korea. Them foo-fighters are some dirty bastards, sir."

The Captain nodded and sat down at a desk beside the radar operator. Yeah..., he thought, Foo-Fighters... shit! "Foo-Fighters" are what American airmen called flying objects that they had seen while flying combat missions. The craft aren't ours and they're not the enemy's and they're sure not airplanes because they're as unconventional as hell. He had personally never seen one, but men he knew and respected had, and therefore, he didn't doubt their existence one bit. Over the years, the bizarre antics of these foo-fighters had resulted in several crashes of military aircraft. The Captain closed his eyes and squeezed his fingers tightly to the bridge of his nose. He opened them and thought, well… it sure didn't look like this one was going to turn out to be a crash. He let a sigh escape as he ran fingers through his already thinning hair. He had better get his shit together quick because the brass were going to want to know what happened and they'd want it all "Right Now!" He opened the files and quickly scanned them before the Airman approached and gave him the walky-talky. He nodded to the man and did a once-thru in his head, and then put the bulky phone to his ear and pushed the button. He listened as the switches clicked and clacked. The sea of olive green uniforms maintained the brisk business as before, but now… every ear was listening.

"Good evening, sir. I'm sorry to bother you at home, but we've lost a plane. Yes, sir, it was working an intercept. Yes, sir… sent up after an unidentified aircraft. Ah, no, sir, nothing on the UA. Right. Nothing other than radar. No, sir, no visual reported, sir. Uh… yes, at this time I am classifying it as hostile action, but let me qualify that, sir. The UA, well, I don't think … well it probably wasn't communist or even… civilian. Uh.. as for the particulars of that, sir…uh, I'd rather not broadcast over the air. Yes, sir. We re-routed the wingman to Truax – they're both shook-up, sir. I agree. Uh…hold one."

He covered the mouthpiece and pointed at a Lieutenant, just walking through the door, "Phil, stand-up the second "Ready Alert" flight and advise them that we've lost a plane. This is a combat-mode RED Stand-Up!" He saw the officer's eyes widen in surprise as he nodded and hurried to the communications office.

Then he uncovered the mouthpiece. "Okay, sir, the second Ready Flight is standing-up. Uh…yeah… the UA went off the scope and none of the ground stations have tracked it since then." The Captain's eyes shot up to the clock on the wall.

"Yes, sir, I'll see you in exactly five minutes and we'll go ahead and contact Search & Rescue. Uh, sir, will you notify the Base Commander? Ah… yes, sir. Thank you, sir. Over and out." The officer sat the walky-talky down. The perspiration was beaded heavily on his face. He turned to the Master Sergeant.

"He'll contact the Base C.O. and then the C.O.'ll contact the Air

Defense Command. He said that he's throwing on a uniform and will be here five minutes. We've also gotta initiate SAR and contact Wing Command to advise them about the UA and our lost plane. Can you get that moving, Chuck?"

"No problem, sir", the older man replied as he swiftly moved over to a bank of phones. The Lieutenant came out of the Comm. office and caught the Captain's attention.

"Sir, I got a hold of the Exec. He was in the 'Soo having dinner. He's on his way back now and the second Ready Flight is warming up on the flight line, Combat Mode-Red."

The Captain nodded. "Great, Phil. Thanks." Then he turned to the radio operator seated in a cubbyhole off to the side of the room and raised his voice while waving. "Higgins, anything else from Naples or Pillows?"

The airman on the radio shook his head. "No, sir, they're saying the sky's all clear except for a couple of Royal Canadian Air Force aircraft, but they haven't been in the AO and are still outside of it. Their pilots are asking if they can help with the SAR?"

The sweat was forming huge dark rings under the arms of the Captain's green flight suit as he nodded his head. Yeah, he thought, the Canadians hadn't been in their A.O., or Area of Operations, at all. But he had a sinking feeling that it might end up differently on paper. He shot a solid glance to the radio operator in the cubbyhole.

"Yeah, tell'em thanks, Higgins, and that we'd appreciate that." He jabbed a thumb toward the Master Sergeant working the phone bank across the room. "You can have 'em coordinate with master Sergeant Stribley, okay?"

Airman Higgins nodded, "Yes, sir, will do," and turned back to his equipment and began broadcasting.

The Captain angled up his head then and glanced at the clock. He had better get snapping here. First things first, he thought. He had to talk with the radar operator first. "Pillows" and "Naples" were the code words for two separate ground control intercept radar stations, or CGIs, that direct the fighters to their targets. And Airman Markowski needed to be cautioned about what he said about them. He turned to the radar operator beside him, touching the Airman on the arm. He knew that the earphones the man wore would require him to speak louder than he wanted to. The young Airman turned to the Captain as the officer made motions to remove the headset. The Airman took off the earphones and appeared curious, but nodded as the Captain brought his index finger up to his mouth in a "shooshing" motion.

"Okay, Markowski," the Captain whispered, "now you said that right after the two contacts merged, Pillows lost them, right?" The

Airman nodded so the Captain continued. "and that was over Lake Superior, right?", whispered the Captain.

Airman Joe Markowski nodded again and responded in a trace voice. "Yes, sir, but Naples picked up the UA again over Lake Michigan for maybe… ten seconds, then it vanished off their screen, too."

The Captain frowned as he looked at the Airman. He finally gave his head a single nod. "Okay, Markowski, here's the drill. Until we know how the brass are gonna play this, you keep everything that's happened on this mission to yourself. I don't care if a guy was here in this very room and witnessed it all and asks you a simple question about it, you just clam-up about your end, okay?"

The Airman slightly braced in his chair. "Yes, sir."

The Captain nodded once more then broke eye contact to glance again at the clock. He picked up a clipboard and began writing. Exactly four minutes, thirty three seconds after the captain had set down the walky-talky, the Squadron Commanding Officer came into the room carrying his uniform jacket and cap. He was a gruff man and he was clearly agitated. The Lieutenant Colonel saw the Captain and walked directly to him.

"Okay, Tom, do we have the second Ready Flight stood-up?"

"Yes, sir, they're on the field, warming up now, Combat Mode-Red.

"The Colonel shifted his weight. "What about other contacts… anything else going on?"

The Captain shot his eyes over to the radar operator and touched the man's arm again. When the Airman looked up, the Captain gave him a hand signal asking "Anything new?" The Airman shook his head before returning his gaze to the lighted screen in front of him. The Captain turned back to his Commanding Officer.

"No, sir, nothing airborne but a few RCAF aircraft. And sir, according to both GCIs, they've been well outside of the incident area from the beginning."

The Colonel was a bit relieved. You never know in a situation like this. He jutted out a cleft chin. Okay. Weather conditions?"

The Captain checked his notes. "Light to moderate snowfall, winds southwesterly at 10 knots, viability about 10-15 miles at this time… uh, let's see, the plane went off the screen when it was at about 8000 feet and the mean temperature at that altitude would have been around minus 7 degrees."

The Colonel straightened his back and lowered his voice. "All right then, let's have the rest of it in a nutshell, but quietly, okay?"

The Captain nodded. He raised his clipboard and began, his voice hushed. "At approximately 1815 (6:15pmEST.) we received a call from Naples to scramble a fighter intercept on a UA that wasn't squawking to radio calls. The UA was exhibiting very high speeds and erratic flight patterns." The Captain looked up to the Colonel.

"Both GCIs say that the UA had speeds in excess of 500 mph and was bopping around all over like a big ping-pong ball. They say the speed buried their readings on several occasions, too."

The Captain saw the Colonel cinch his teeth tightly as he pulled out a cigar and began fiddling with it. The Captain dropped his eyes back to the clipboard and went on.

"Uh.. let's see. Missing jet is aircraft number 5853, commanded by First Lieutenant Felix Moncla. Umm, his Radar Operator was Second Lieutenant Robert Wilson. The 5853 was airborne and went feet-wet along with aircraf..."

The Colonel held up his hand to stop the officer. "I don't want to hear about the wingman right now, I'll debrief them when they get in. Just tell me what happened to 5853."

The Captain's face tightened. "Yes, sir. Um... let's see...okay, Aircraft 5853 became airborne from Kinross at exactly 1822 hours. Naples held GCI until 1841 hours, when control was passed to Pillows. Aircraft 5853 was directed by Pillows to an intercept point with the unidentified aircraft over Lake Superior at 1847 hours. Then Pillows advised 5853 to drop to 7,000 feet. At 1851 hours, aircraft 5853 was advised by Pillows to turn to a heading of 20 degrees to the cut-off vector with the UA. After the turn was completed, Pillows advised 5853 that the bogey was at his eleven 'o'clock position, ten miles distant.   "Then..." the Captain's eyes come up to look squarely into those of the Colonel before saying the next part.

"The Pillows radar operator says that all of a sudden... the UA seemed to turn into aircraft 5853 or something... because the UA shot across the screen and the two radar contacts "merged" into one in a split second, and we lost all radar and squawk from our plane." The Captain swallowed and looked closely at his Commanding Officer, who was now chewing nervously on the unlit cigar. The colonel held the Captain's eyes for a second or two before dropping them, and telling the more junior officer to "go on".

The Captain scanned the notes again. "Well, anyway, sir, the Pillows operator said that all of this, well... it happened in an instant, sir. Too fast for a normal turn by a conventional aircraft or...um..or whatever."

The Colonel chomped on his cigar as he slipped into his blue "Ike" jacket. He addressed the Captain as he buttoned the heavy silver buttons on the jacket, his voice barely audible. "Okay, so what happened to the UA after the hit? Did it go down or what?"

A military guy is a military guy and the Captain's eyes were diverted to the numerous rows of ribbons and heavy silver combat wings on the Colonel's blue Ike jacket. He slowly shook his head no, while dropping his voice an octave or two and again meeting the other senior man's vision.

"Pillows had the UA disappearing after merging with 5853, sir. But Naples picked up the UA for about five to ten seconds before it disappeared off their screens, too. It wasn't losing altitude, sir. Not at all. And, sir...," the Captain slanted his head as he looked at his Colonel.

"Naples had this... this "merged thing" headed straight south, out over Lake Michigan, when it went black on their scope." The Captain was watching the Colonel, who was now stepping back with a look of shock on his face. The Captain dropped his voice to an even lower undertone and spoke his next words carefully.

"Yes, sir, that's what I thought, too. If I've done the math right Colonel, then that UA was cooking at about 900 miles an hour when it left the area", he whispered.

The Colonel was staring at the Captain. He was astonished and... frightened. Cocksucking foo-fighters! he thought. He had seen them before and he sure as hell hated the little pricks! Although... some of them weren't that little. He couldn't let the Captain see this though, could he? He turned back to his subordinate.

"Okay, Tom. Where was it that the two aircraft met again...?"

The Captain flipped a page on his clipboard. "Out over Lake Superior, sir maybe...70 miles off the Keweenaw Peninsula."

The Colonel ran his fingers over the white scrambled eggs on the bill of his dress blue cap, then tossed it on the desk. His hand rubbed his darkened beard as he spoke.

"For now, let's just give those coordinates as the accident site." The Colonel swiveled his head around the room, then back to the Captain. "And where exactly is the last fix we have on the UA before it went off the screen?"

The Captain scanned his papers again, then met the colonel's Eyes in a whisper. "Lake Michigan, sir," he whispered, "due south of Escanaba before it cleared Naples' scope."

The Colonel nodded. "Okay, let's keep that quiet. In fact, I want this staff buttoned-up tight on this incident." He pointed his hard eyes at the Captain. "Got that, Tom?"

The younger man studied his Commanding Officer and finally, gave a trace nod before replying with, "Yes, sir."

The Colonel could see the disapproval in the young Captain's face, but there probably wasn't much he could do about that. He determined to give the more junior officer his reasoning. He lowered his voice even more and looked at the Captain.

"Look Tom, all I know is that back in '47, there was that big bruha-ha down in New Mexico and the brass… well they're touchier than shit on these things. So we'll just tighten things up until we're told different. I bet you dollars to donuts that there'll be some hotshot intelligence officer here before 0100." The Colonel swung his head in dismay and sighed.

"So when our illustrious Executive Officer gets his ass in here… well, you fill him in and keep it locked down, okay?" The Colonel pointed his index finger at the Captain for emphasis.

"Yes, sir. I'll get right on it now." As the Captain turned to leave and the Colonel stopped him.

"The crew of 5853, how's their record look?"

The Captain nodded and flipped open one of the files given to him by the Master Sergeant. "Let's see, uhm… okay, Lieutenant Moncla has over 800 flight hours, uh… good fitness reports and especially high marks for aircraft commander. Over all, no problems in his record. Lieutenant Wilson looks good too, sir. Good marks, an up and comer." He closed the files and looked at the Colonel. "And according to the crew chief, the aircraft seemed to be flying fine before it disappeared."

The colonel gritted his teeth. "Yeah, well… not fine enough Captain! Those poor sons'a'bitches couldn't fly 900 miles an hour…now could they?"

The Captain returned the Colonel's agitated look with one of understanding. He knew that the senior officer was feeling the loss of the men. The burden of command. He had felt it too and regardless of the circumstances, you always felt their loss.

"No, sir. I guess they did have the odds against them, didn't they?"

"Goddam right they did! Now when that wingman touches down, I want him and his RO on the secured radio net to me before the fans wind down on his engines… Got it?"

The Captain saluted and replied in the affirmative before hurrying about his business. The Master Sergeant came over by the Colonel and leaned against the other side of the desk. Both men had served in combat during World War Two and Korea and had talked honestly about their experiences. They were friends, in spite of the difference in rank. The Sergeant folded his arms then cocked his head at the officer and spoke in whisper.

"I checked, and the only thing flying up north of the Lower

Peninsula was a couple of Canadian planes. But both of them were way outside the incident area. And the Canooks say that none of their aircraft were involved. They said that they monitored our radio traffic though and… a couple of Ham radio operators called in to say that they heard it all, too."

The Colonel listened, and when the enlisted man finished, merely nodded his head. He had been down this road before in similar situations with missing planes and he had told the Sergeant about it. He kept his speech in low tones as he responded.

"Well, that means that if this goes like the others and we don't find any wreckage, then they won't be able to keep a lid totally on top of this. And somebody," the colonel gestured with his hand, "maybe those Canadian planes, are gonna be the bad guys. I can almost guarantee it."

It was the Sergeant's turn to nod his head while casting a sideways look at the officer. "Ya ever wonder Colonel… if maybe we're worrying about the wrong enemy here… being concerned about the Russkies like we are?"

The Colonel took the soggy end of the cigar out of his mouth and looked squarely at the Sergeant. He spoke in a trace voice.

"Yeah, Chuck, and I agree with you, okay? The fuck'n foo-fighters are some dirty bastards. But who's dirtier, huh?" He jabbed the wet end of the stogie for emphasis.

"I'll lay ya odds that once the big brass get wind of what happened here, I'm gonna end up bending the truth something fierce to those dead guys' widows and families about how, where or if these guys actually died." In a sudden fit of irritation, he flung the cigar across the room, causing several men in the room to look over at him.

"And you know what, Charlie?" the Colonel asked in a hushed voice. "I'll do it because they say I have to. National security, an officer's oath and all that bullshit!" The words sounded especially harsh in the hushed whisper. "But any way you slice it… I'll do it. *Now you tell me… who's really dirtier!…*

There's a knock at the door and suddenly…we're back in the room again! The spell is broken. Both of us are shocked at this abrupt withdrawal from the past. We look over as the door swings in and voices, commotion and the reality of the present, blast into the room from outside. I think I'm going through menopause, as I'm sure getting plenty of hot flashes right now. The song is blaring in my head and I want desperately to crawl away somewhere and just die.

Somewhere during the course of our time travel, I'd removed the piwaka from my pocket and now held it tightly in my hand. I look at

Joe Markowski and he seems almost as disturbed as me. But judging by his face, he may be coming back quicker. Well, hell yeah, he can do that! He doesn't know what I know! Neither of us speak, the trance still a fresh reality for the two of us. A nurse walks in, speaking over her shoulder to someone out in the hall, and places a small paper cup on his dinner stand, with pills in it. She nods her head at the old man.

"Your afternoon meds, Joe." She turns, smiles at me, says "hi" and exits the room, letting the door close behind her. Markowski and I both watch her leave and say nothing. We're still captured by the trance of time travel. The door comes to a close, before we turn back to each other. I can feel my eyes bulging with this new reality as I finger the piwaka and he speaks to me.

"Hey, are you okay?"

I just look at him and whisper out the plainest truth I know. "Nope."

He leans forward and looks closer while I sit there, frozen in place. "You look kind'a pale and your eyes are all red and wide."

I rumble out a groan and poke my thumb into my chest. "Yeah, well trust me. All of it looks better out there than it does in here." I lean back and shake out the tension before looking at him again. We sit here, just looking at each other for at least thirty seconds before he speaks again.

"Those two guys, Moncla and Wilson, the pilot and back-seater in that F-89… they weren't even from our base. They were TDY from Truax, in Wisconsin. Our regular fighter jocks were off at gunnery practice somewhere out in Arizona. And all these years…" He shakes his head again before going on.

"All these years, their families have never known what really happened ta them." He wipes his eyes once more then, looks at me intently. "I don't think that's right, but… I don't know what can be done or if anything should be."

His face rumples up in confusion. As for me, well over here on the window ledge, I'm still going through my little change of life. I've gone from flaming hot to freezing cold in my little world. The shinkakee flows over me now, like hot lava. As Markowski keeps talking, I drop my eyes and squeeze them shut. When I open them, I can only see him peripherally. But I hear him well enough.

"All I do know for sure, is that there's not too many of us left alive… that know what really happened that night back in '53," his head bumping up and down, "and I wanted ta at least tell someone, so the truth would still be around when I'm gone! Do ya see what I mean?"

I mumble out a "yes" and look up to him. He stares at me for a long minute. Then he sets his head, as if his mission is completed now. I clear my throat.

"So, according to what you just told me... about that night... the plane actually disappeared over Lake Michigan, right? Not Lake Superior?"

"That's right. I knew both of the guys who were working the GCIs that night. We were buddies. They're both dead now, but I knew them when I was stationed up there. Bernie Karlisle was the operator at Pillows that night and I knew George Kinnesten, too. George was the radar operator at Naples, on that night in '53." He points a finger at me.

"Now George swore that he saw the UA right out over Lake Michigan, for at least ten seconds, maybe even twelve seconds before it just vanished."

I feel my eyes wander away. We both sit in silence for another beat. Now, my world changes again. It's a frigidly white-cold storm of emotions coming together in a hurry. It all seems to fit now, but sweet Jesus... my Lord! Then the old guys grumbles and I look back at him.

"Ya know, I've felt guilty and ashamed about this for almost fifty years now. The thing's haunted me all my adult life." He raises a finger and thrusts it at me. "Now, I'm passing you the truth about it. But...if it's all the same ta you," he looks at me sincerely, "I'd like ta just not talk about it anymore, now."

I nod, mostly because I don't know what else to do. Then he says he has to go to the bathroom again. He works the walker over and closes the bathroom door. I sit there, the full realization of this hitting home, and find that I can't move. But shit. I don't want to move anyway. I want to just stay perfectly still and never move again. But as I sit there, even in my weakened physical state, I can see it. I can see it all now, as the answer to this riddle is unfolded and laid out cleanly.

Everything is falling into place in the puzzle, but it's a nasty, creepy and disturbing picture too. At least for me. I don't like this kind'a stuff. Not at all. But at least I know what it is now, and how I'm going to deal with it. As I caress my piwaka, I think... that's something, anyway. The toilet flushes and Joe Markowski emerges from the room, his pajamas flapping as he hooks his robe on the edge of the walker. I catch his attention and he stops his forward motion to look up.

"Mr Markowski... Thanks for talking with me today, and I'm sorry. I'm sorry about the cancer."

A slow smile creeps over his face and he throws up a hand, dismissingly. "Hey, this's fine with me. I've lived a good life, was married ta a good woman for thirty five years and well, I'm ready when the time comes."

He maintains the smile as he starts forward again. As he does, there's another knock at the door and he stops the walker's motion once more. The door is opened by an old, gray-haired black guy, who pokes his noggin in to look around. He sees Markowski and motions to him.

"Hey Joe, they're gonna start the movie in a few minutes. You coming?"

Markowski smiles and nods. "Yeah, Benny. I'll be along in a minute." He waves to the guy and the other man closes the door. Markowski turns back to me, pointing over his shoulder.

"On Saturdays, they have a movie down in the recreation room and I usually go." He shakes his head. "I think I'm gonna head on down there unless ya have some more questions."

I just look at him. His face is drawn and seems sucked of mirth. I figure that's because of our little visit here today. Meanwhile, my world is upside down. My poor little mind is so crowded with things, I don't think there'll even be room for the headache that's trying really hard to get in. The shinakee is a whirlwind inside of me, like a tornado, but I feel it winding down as I accept the truth here. I know that Joe Markowski wants to get away from this room, these memories and me. And I'll oblige him. But I do have one more question. So, I go ahead and ask it. But the really scary part…is that I already know the answer. I form the words as "Ghost Riders In The Sky" belts out an anthem in the privacy of my pathetic cranium.

"I do have one more. I don't suppose you happen to remember the longitude and latitude, out over Lake Michigan… where the jet vanished… do you?"

Markowski's face takes on an omniscient look. "You bet I do. I'll never forget it. Coordinates, 45 Degrees, 00 Minutes North - 86 Degrees, 49 Minutes West."

I nod and throw up a feeble wave in goodbye. He gives barely a shake of his head and then works the walker out the door. I sit on the window ledge, squeezing the piwaka and stare at the wooden entryway as it slowly closes behind the disappearing back of Joe Markowski. I run the coordinates through my head again. 45 Degrees, 00 minutes North - 86 degrees, 49 minutes West. How silly of me. That's my tangent, isn't it? That's right where Muskrat Island is. Uh huh. I just want to scream.

Chapter Thirty
"We're Sure Not Gentlemen"

The Kent County Airport,
Grand Rapids, Michigan,
1534 or 3:34 pm, The Same Day.

Mussenberg pulled the phone from his pocket and snapped it open, even as it was ringing.

"Captain Mussenberg."

"Captain, we got him! He just called here from a pay telephone on Monroe Street. I had time for the trace and I've got a cop from the Federal Building on way there now!

Mussenberg almost pissed his pants in his excitement. "Okay, where's this place at? Is Stone stationary?" He shot a look at his two officers who were already up and moving over by him. He motioned for them to check the map. As they did that, he turned back to the phone.

"Okay, what's the name of this street again?" Sergeant canter told him the address and he repeated it to his men. One of them found it, jabbed a finger at the map, and brought it over to Mussenberg. He showed it to the officer while shaking his head and hiking his shoulders. The Captain nodded and spoke into the phone.

"Do we know what this place is, Sergeant?

"No, sir, no idea. I just ran a check through our system and got the address. The cop should be there in a minute though."

Mussenberg quickly weighed the options again while he scanned the map. Stone could still be there, or on the move again. Shit! He had to wait. "Okay Sergeant, we'll sit tight and wait ta hear from you. What's the ETA of that officer?"

"Can't be more'n a couple minutes now, Captain. This address is close ta downtown and that's where the Fed Building is."

"Right. Hey… what did Stone say when he called?"

"He was looking for you, sir. I had ta fight ta keep him on the line long enough for the trace but we nailed it!"

"Okay, good then! As soon as you hear! Out!"

He snapped the phone up and looked at the men in the room. His eyes found Major Luce. "Major, you might wanna go get that bird wound up. We'll be leaving here, one way or another in the next half hour."

The flight crew ambled out to their helicopter as Mussenberg and his two men, quickly packed their gear. Then they waited. Again.

Grand Rapids Orthotics & Prosthetics Supply,
18784 S. Monroe Avenue,
Grand Rapids, Michigan.
1545 hours or 3:45 pm.

I roll into the parking lot and brake, as a UPS van backs across my path and up to the building. Then I tool around him and park close in the only available spot left. After switching the Jeep off, I take a deep drag off the hand-rolled and blow the smoke hard, while lightly pounding the wheel with my fist. I'm pumping now and can feel it. Coyote's after me! I take another drag off the cigarette and crank down the window farther. After that rollercoaster of a ride with Markowski, I was freaked. Scared shitless, is a better term, and while that feeling hasn't dissipated much, I'm working on pure, 100% adrenalin now. My physical weariness and exhaustion has been supplanted by the new facts I've learned, and to top it all off, Coyote is after me! I turn to the cassette player I have sitting in the other seat. I lift both lids up on the little machine, the same one that I'd bought in Escanaba, and remove the two cassettes that I'd just recorded.

After leaving Markowski's room, I went back to the Jeep and dug out the recorder and remaining blank tapes, as well as the ready-mailers, that I still had. This little plan of mine wasn't much, but it was all I could do at the present. Then I'd sat there in the Veteran's Home parking lot, the window rolled down, smoking a cigarette and speaking into the little device, as it wound upon my words. I mentioned every fact I could think of, and everything... that I now believe about Muskrat Island. The tape included Veeter, the Chinese, the Air Force and... what I think is still out there. Then I'd grabbed the tablet and scribbled notes, explaining my wishes. I tore them off the notebook; I would send these tapes and notes, as I had sent the others weeks ago, but to different people this time. That way, a partial story and cast of players would still be available to many different people, if necessary.

My friends would receive and hold them, just in case something happened to me. If it did, then they would follow my instructions about what to do and who to get the tapes to. This was a team practice and we all did this for one another, whenever the situation demanded. Nobody would open the mailers as long as I was alive. But if that changed, well then... everything changed. All I ever had to do to stop the process was notify them and say so. The packages would be destroyed without ever having been opened.

I have several people listed, to whom other newly made copies of the tape would be sent. These others were people in the media, congressmen, senators and a few in the military. I hoped and believed that any one of them would take what the tapes held and run hard with it. And that, I figured, was probably the best I could do.

I begin addressing the ready-mailers. One of the names that I scribble in the appropriate place was a former team mate. Odds were good that if I die here, then he and other team members will come seeking revenge. I can't stop it, no matter how hard I might want to. It's our code and we all live and... die by it, too, I guess. I figure that supplying them with some names and a story to start with, might make their endeavors easier. It's the best I can do for them, too.

As I finish the smoke and think about it, I'm sure my voice on the tapes will show my alarm and dread at the newly revealed information. This is the puzzle's bizarre conclusion. Indians, at least those that aren't shamans or witches, just don't cotton much to spirits. And they especially don't like the weird ones, ya know? I take a final drag of the hand-rolled and butt the smoke. I'm doing all of this now, because I know that the Coyote is after me. Coyote is what I've named my old pal, Mussenberg. When I pulled out of the Veteran's Home lot, I drove this way looking for two things. I needed a pay phone and a mailbox. I found the phone first, and pulled into a drive-up pay phone about a block down the road from here.

I'd needed to talk to Mussenberg. So I called his office number up in Escanaba. And what do I learn... old Uncle Pete's not there. The noncom I talked to said he was here, in Grand Rapids. The Sergeant also said that it was urgent that I get in touch with the Captain, because he needed to speak to me right away! A topic of great importance, the guy'd said. The captain, he'd told me, was at the airport right now! Well, if that ain't ever peculiar? Nope, I don't think so. I told the Sergeant that I'd give Mussenberg a call and hung up. I'm cooking in survival mode now. I've got the Air Force on my trail and I've got a gut feeling that if I don't shake them soon, they're gonna tree me. Once they do... my ass is grass.

I place the cassettes into the separate little compartments of each ready-mailer and close the plastic flaps. I bought them up in Escanaba. The little self-sealing envelopes are made of bubble wrap and already have pre-paid postage on them. They're made specifically for mailing cassette tapes. I can feel the adrenalin working with all my other emotions, as I begin softly singing an old Buffalo Springfield song. I climb out of the Jeep next to the brown UPS delivery van. I make my way around it's front and keep moving over to the blue mailbox. I spied the box after leaving the phone. It's sitting in front large glass windows. My eyes travel the street as cars go back and forth. Nothing. Good enough, so I bend to my task.

"Still emotions run deep..." I quietly sing the words, then put my teeth to one of the adhesive stickers, to get the thing to pull loose. I tear it off and seal one envelope, dropping it in through the metal door of the box. I pick up the song again. "Stop, say what's that sound, everybody look what's going round..." I seal the next tape and slide it down the chute as a police car slides past reflected in the glass windows. I turn back and see the Ford Crown Victoria slowing as it passes the pay phone that I visited only minutes ago. The car has a white license. Strange plate, eh? For some reason, I keep singing the song almost unconsciously, and under my breath I watch the car's brake lights flash further down the road.

"Something's happening here... what it is... ain't exactly clear". I watch and sing, as I see the car make a u-turn and swing around to come back. "There's a man with a gun over there... a'telling me... I gotta beware..." The cruiser comes to a stop and the officer on the passenger side bales out and runs up to the phone looking all around.

"So, stop... hey... what's that sound... everybody look what's going round..." The car's a federal police unit. Not a Grand Rapids cop. A federal cop? They only have jurisdiction on federal property? And the bastards are checking a phone that I just called from. They traced the call. Yeah, shit. "Everybody look what's going round" is right! I have to get away from here, fast. I don't want them seeing me anywhere near this mailbox. No where's close to it at all.

I make it back to the Jeep and manage to back it out under the cover of the UPS truck without them seeing me. Then I ease it around the side of the building, and gun it back to the alley. I drive down and out of the alley that backs the store. A few minutes later, I'm gone, leaving the federal flatfoots still watching the dumb phone. As I drive in an easterly direction, my mind's flying, adjusting to these little nuances and anomalies.

Number one, Mussenberg's here and he's here for me. Number two, if they traced that call that fast, then there's a reason why only a pair of federal police cops showed up there. If Mussenberg has the kind of clout I think he has, there should've been sixty local cops at that stupid phone. Why only two federal cops? Why no other kind of cops? In fact, why have I been able to drive around so easily here? My head begins nodding. Yeah, that old Buffalo Springfield song. Something's happening here but what it is - ain't exactly clear. The prick's keeping a lid on this, isn't he? He's not going outside his immediate control, right? I slowly shake my head. Shoot, I don't know if that's it or not, but it makes the most sense right now, so, that's how I'll classify it. I mean, what else am I gonna do?

**Kent County Airport,
Grand Rapids, Michigan,
Same Time, Same Day.**

Mussenberg jammed his hands into his pants pockets and
exhaled loudly. Then he quickly pulled out his hand and looked at his
watch. He was about out of options here. He had an hour and a half
before his world collapsed. He jammed the hand back into the pocket
and fingered his pocket change as he looked out the window. He was
standing in a little foyer that led off the side of lounge. He cursed
under his breath as he thought for the millionth time today, where the
hell was Stone? Canter just called and told him that the federal cops at
the pay phone within ten minutes of him hanging up, but Stone was
gone. Where the hell was he? It was like he just disappeared, every
time they got close. Maybe the bastard was a ghost.

What was it that Army General had said about him? He said that
he believed that Stone was just like a ghost, able to fade in and out, or
something like that. Well, damned if he wasn't becoming a believer,
too. As that thought was passing, his phone rang. He rapidly yanked
his hand free, ripped the phone from his pocket and flipped it open in
one fell swoop.

"Sergeant Canter, I'm in world of hurt here. You better have some
news on where this asshole is!"

There was a second of silence. Then, "Well my guess is, that you
should try looking about twelve inches up from your shoulders there,
pal."

Mussenberg was struck silly by the remark and it took him a
microsecond to get it. Then, holy fuck! He immediately knew the
voice and began pounding on the glass window of the lounge. His two
men saw his pointing motions to the phone and quickly ran to the case
that carried the tracing machine. He turned back to the phone as he
saw his guys give him the "thumbs-up" sign.

"Stone, is that you? Hey, how ya doing?"

"I've been better."

Mussenberg watched the men working the dials on the "tracer" as
he spoke into the phone. "Yeah, well I need ta see ya? I stopped by
your house yesterday but ya weren't home. Where ya at now?"

There was a stretch of silence then, "Grand Rapids."

"Grand Rapids, no shit. Hey, that's where I'm at, too. Wow, what
a coincidence, huh?"

"Ya know, Mussenberg, coincidence is the same thing as the tooth
fairy. If you want ta believe in it, then be my guest. I think I'll just
stick with the truth on this one and go with the fact that you being

here ain't no twist of fate, okay?"

Mussenberg watched the men as one turned to him and shook his head. "I don't know what you're talking about, Stone. But listen, as long as we're here together, we need to talk, ok? I mean like right now, the sooner the better."

"Uh, huh. What's the rush?"

Mussenberg weighed the choices he had, and basically, they were few. Add to that the fact that Stone knew that something was up and the time drain, and the alternatives faded into nothing. He either made this happen now... or it probably wasn't going to.

"Okay, Stone, I'm gonna level with you, okay? The General thinks you know something about that island that you're not telling us. So, do you? Do you know something? Because if you do, then we've gotta meet."

Silence again, and Mussenberg wondered if maybe he'd lost him. Then the voice came back. "And if I don't?"

Mussenberg snapped his eyes back to the men in the room. They were both nodding at him now. He went back to the mouthpiece.

"Okay, Stone, obviously, you know that something's going on here. So let me give you the straight skinny. It's like this. At seventeen hundred, the hounds are gonna to be let loose on you unless you and I have a little chat, alright? And there's absolutely nothing I can do to stop it, unless we talk. Even if ya don't know anything, that's what's gonna happen. The full weight of the U.S. Air Force is gonna come down on ya, Stone. So we'd better get together here fast, and I mean, quick-assed-fast!"

Mussenberg heard a chuckle. "The full weight of the U.S. Air Force, eh? Well we wouldn't want that now, would we? Not with me out of popcorn. That sounds just like a line from a B grade movie, Mussenberg. Geeze! My, but you are a card." He heard a sigh on the line. "Okay, good enough. You're at the airport, right?"

Mussenberg nodded his head. "Yes, that's right. Just tell me where you are and I'll come to you."

There's silence again. "I'll call you." The phone clicked off. Shit! Mussenberg ran into the room even as one of the men was coming out to him. "Well, did we get 'em?"

The man stopped and grimaced. "Yes, sir, we got him but he was on a cell. He's moving."

Mussenberg's face bunched up into a knot of rage as he turned to the door and pounded the heel of his fist into it.

By The Airport,
28th Street & Interstate 96
Grand Rapids, Michigan.
Eleven Minutes Later.

I pull onto Patterson Street and follow the road past the Citgo gas station where I'd stopped earlier today. I drive around and come to a large lot, circling until I find a spot next to the trees. If my guess is right, they'll make the Jeep right away from the air. But that doesn't matter too much. It'll end here today, one way or another. I wrestle around in my gear and find the binoculars before climbing out. I loop them over my neck and look at the large prominent building that owns the lot. In big letters across the face of it, are the words, "Robert Groters Development Company."

I noticed the building when I stopped for gas, and considered it a landmark for this airport exit. I don't know what a development company does, and I don't really care. I just want to borrow their roof for a few minutes, if I can. I cross into a grouping of scrub trees and brush. The little thicket of woods backs the building and it's lot, and parallels the two. I work to stay out of sight of the building's windows, but I move quickly along.

Shortly, I'm at the rear of the building. I watch it silently for awhile. There's no activity and like most structures akin to this, there's an access ladder. It's about twelve feet off the ground, attached to the side of the building. There's no easy way up, but I think I can reach the ladder by climbing on the dumpster. At least there's no snow. The weather is gorgeous today. I watched long enough for my satisfaction.. I haven't seen anyone back here, so I move out and over to the big red dumpster. I hike my way up onto it and stretch my arms. I can reach the bottom two rungs of the ladder easily, and after looking around quickly, I haul myself up. My side sends a slight reminder that it's still there and still sore.

A few minutes later, I'm on the far side of the roof, five stories up. The view is panoramic, as I figured. I bring the binocs up and scan around. Behind the gas station, on the hill of the overpass, I see the large scrub pine. I noticed that when I was pumping gas earlier today. As I work the glasses around, I have a clear shot in almost all directions. But best of all, I can see most of the airport from here. I'm also overlooking 28th Street and the Airport access road. The wind is biting up here, and once again I'd left my gloves in the dumb Jeep. I call Mussenberg.

"Captain Mussenberg."

I turn into the phone. "Okay, Captain. Time to get the show on the road. Now, I'm going to meet with you and you alone. So you will be arriving at our little rendezvous all by yourself. So far, so good?"

"Stone, what is all this? We really don't have time for games here, man."

"Humor me, Captain. I'm an Indian and ya know ta us, ya'all speak with a forked tongue."

"Hey, Stone, ya can call me a lotta things, but white's not one of them!"

"No. No you're not. You're just a modern day buffalo soldier, bud. Now, if you and me are gonna talk, then we're gonna play this little event my way. So…what's it gonna be?"

He answers back flustered and agitated. "Fine! How do we do it?"

I have to phrase my words just right here to make sure that my nuances convey different meanings. "Okay. Get yourself a yellow cab and tell the driver to bring you out to 28th Street on the access road. Then pull off to the shoulder at the light and wait. And, Captain… keep your aircraft on the ground. I'll call once you're underway."

I close the phone, even while he's yelling on the other end. My goal here is to make him think that I have someone there watching. I don't know if it'll work, but heck, what've I got to lose? I focus the glasses on the access road and think that it might just work, at that. He's a pro, used to a lot of power. But his voice on the phone is anxious. He's nervous and maybe even a little scared. I've gotta notion that those kinds of feelings might just be rare enough to him to set him off balance. I bring the glasses up and focus them on the airport. Sure enough, three minutes later, I see a dark green helicopter lifting off from behind the facility. I drop the glasses and pick up the phone.

"Captain Mussenberg."

"I bet you got spanked a lot when you were a kid. My friend says that your chopper just took off. You better get that bird back on the ground, Captain, and I mean now!" I close the phone.

I have the glasses up again and can see the helicopter, a Black Hawk by the looks of her, just gaining some altitude. I watch as the helicopter continues its forward motion, and then hangs a moment in the air before spinning around and moving back toward the airport. I look through the glasses as the helicopter begins dropping down. It disappears behind the building in about the same General area it took off from. I drop the glasses down in time to see a yellow Chevy Caprice taxi, pulling off to the shoulder by the intersection at 28th Street below. I switch items again and push the phone button.

"This is Mussenberg. Alright Stone. I had the chopper return, are ya satisfied?"

"Well, let's just say I'm content enough for now. Tell the driver to turn right and bring you over to the Citgo gas station across the road. You get out there, way out front in the lot. Stay away from the building and send the cab clear. There're bathrooms on the left side of the station, as you face it. That's our spot, Mussenberg. You wait until I call." I hang up.

I have the glasses up and can see the taxi turning out now but it's the other cars around it that I'm most interested in. There's one person in the back of the Caprice as it turns into the station lot and I see three other taxies driving past it. He's probably got help in one of those, or any one of the other hundreds of cars down there. I focus my attention back on the Caprice. Mussenberg gets out and leans in to pay the driver. Then he turns around and faces the station. There he is. Old "wiisagi-ma-iinagan"- the coyote. I've named him coyote because that's how I see him. A coyote will sometimes pick up the scent of a tired or wounded deer and pursue it. They could not bring down a healthy deer but a tired or hut animal is different. A coyote will tenaciously stay on the exhausted animal's trail until the deer, out of energy and too weak to go on, stops and holds up. Then and only then, the coyote will have the opportunity to kill the deer. I am the deer to this coyote. I dial him up.

"Well, Stone, are we gonna get this show on the road or what? We're run'n out'a time here, man!"

I smile as I make my way back across the roof to the ladder. "How'd you know it was me? Hey that's cheat'n. You have caller I.D., don't'cha?" I say in a mocking voice. Then I add this last before closing up the phone. "Okay, you just stay put. I'll be there in a minute."

I hurriedly step my way down the ladder and off the dumpster. There is still nobody around. Then I'm trucking back into the woodline. I call him again. After he answers, I tell him to go in the men's bathroom and wait. Then I hang up. I figure that he heard the walking noises and vibration in my voice as I spoke, but that can't be helped. I need to keep moving. It takes me almost four minutes to get to the big pine. I push my way into it and let the branches flow back over me. Then I look around. I've kept a vigil on the sky, and other than the taking off and landing big jets, I've seen no other suspicious aircraft. I flip up the phone and call.

"Where the hell are you, Stone! Maybe I'm not making myself clear here! We don't have time for this shit, man! I mean we just don't have time for it!"

The cars howling over behind me make it hard to hear on the phone. I elevate my voice. "Yeah, well I'm a cautious kind of a guy,

Mussenberg. I really don't wanna take a round in the head until I've talked ta ya. 'Cause pal, I have something you may need? Now, come out of the bathroom and walk around behind the gas station. Directly behind it, you'll see a big pine tree, about a hundred yards off. Walk toward it and I'll see you there."

I hang up, even while he's talking on the other end. I look around. I have the overpass hill behind me and the needles of the pine to break up my silhouette. The high- speed cars are making quite a racket as they zoom over. For most of the area before me, I have open ground, broken with scrub brush. I've been expecting a bullet to end my existence at any time, but now the moment is closing. I finger the piwaka as I switch my eyes over the place. I decide that my little position here… is as good a place to die as any.

Then I cast my eyes forward again. I can plainly see the rear of the station building from here. Then I see movement. It's Mussenberg. He's wearing a sheepskin coat and blue jeans, and I can see him as he makes his progress toward me. The snow is almost non-existent here and he has no trouble traversing the distance. He sees me as he nears and comes to a stop in front of the big jack pine. He has his hands free and at his sides, as I move out of the tree's cover and away from most of the traffic noise.

My left hand is loose, but my right one is in my jacket pocket, holding the Glock. He looks at me and turns slightly this way and that as he speaks. "What is all this, Stone? What's the deal?"
I raise my eyebrows and splay out my free hand. "Stone? I thought we were on a first name basis here, Petey? Now I'm all hurt inside, my inner child is all emotionally fractured, here."

He makes a face and swings his head around, looking at the area as he talks. As he does so, I think I see a brown, flesh colored device in his left ear. "What's with all this cloak and dagger stuff, Stone?" Again, I raise eyebrows and tilt my head. "Hey, I've got my dagger - you bring your cloak?"

His eyes go hard and he jerks his hand up rapidly, to look at his watch. As he does this, I shift my weight and draw the weapon from my pocket in pretty quick fashion for someone as delirious as me. He freezes, his eyes on the gun, his wrist in the air. I can feel the juices flying fast in my body as I begin to ease off a little. I nod at him.

"I don't think it'd be a good idea to move your hands fast like that again." His eyes come up to me.

"Are ya gonna shoot me now? Is that why ya drug me all the way out here?"

I slowly shake my head. "Nope. Not unless you make me." I feel my brows crease. "Look, you and I don't know each other, so I'll give you a couple personal things about me. I consider myself kind of a quasi-heart surgeon, okay? Now if I get any indication, even the slightest notion what-so-ever, that our little SITREP here is changing… then I'm gonna do my best to give you a brand new forty caliber heart valve." I let my eyes convey my sincerity. "Hear what I'm saying, Captain?"

He gives me the barest hint of a nod, but his eyes have turned tough and mean in response. He's not scared, just determined. The man's a pro and I can appreciate that. I say the rest as a semi blasts by behind me. "Now the other thing you should know about me is that I get really cranky when I don't get enough sleep." I fling out my left hand.

"I sometimes do things too quickly, ya know, kind'a shoot from the hip, as it were. And Captain… I haven't had enough sleep lately. So it's up to you, pal. But if I was you, I'd tell the people you got listening to back off, so we can conduct our business in private here."

I wait to see what will happen now. And as I do, my eyes dart from place to place over the frontal terrain. I can do nothing about what's behind me and expect that this is where the attack will come from. As my sight settles back on him, I see that a distinctive thought process is going on there. His face is conveying a pattern of changes that're subtle, but there, none the less. Well, this is interesting, isn't it? I have a question, so I ask it.

"What's the big rush for time here, Mussenberg. Why this big hurry? Does the world come to an end at five o'clock, or what?" He's eyeing me now, his face a big question mark, as he seems to settle on a decision of some sort. Then he speaks, but it's not to me. He seems to be talking to the air.

"This is Captain Mussenberg. Tanner, Crocker. You guys hold off. You've heard our conversation and the subject is requesting discretion here. So I'm making a command decision and granting that request." His eyes flit to me. "I'm going to be out of contact. I'm removing the com-mike. Once you're in position, just cover and monitor. If you see me go down, then take appropriate action. I need to hear acknowledgements, gentlemen."

Keeping his eyes glued to mine, he slowly brings his left hand up to his ear. He angles his head slightly as he seems to listen to something. Then, he speaks again. "Okay, roger that. I'm removing the comm-mike now. Out."

Now he works his fingers in his ear and pulls out the little plug that I saw earlier. He brings his hand back down and opens his palm, the little hearing devise rolling around there. Then he slowly takes his other hand and unscrews the tiny mechanism, turning it upside down.

The little workings fall to the snow-spotted dirt. He crushes them with his hiking boot. Then he pulls out an ink pen from his shirt pocket, puts his fingernails to the top of it and pulls up a tiny, micro-thin antenna. He snaps this off and then drops the pen, crushing this with his foot also. He brings his gaze up to mine.

"Okay, Stone, nobody can hear us now. I'm gonna tell you the straight facts as I know them," he turns out a palm. "Fair enough?" I adjust my weight and nod at him. He points to my gun. "That thing may go off. Mind putting it away?"

I look down at the pistol, and then move my hand holding it back into my jacket pocket. My hand stays in with it as I answer him. "It won't go off unless I want it to. But my hand was getting tired, so thanks for caring." I angle my head. "So, what's the big hurry?"

Mussenberg's eyes stay on my pocket as he frowns. Then he nods and shifts his weight a little. "Okay. General Kourn thinks that you know something about Muskrat Island and what we're looking for out there." His eyes form an inquiry. "So do you? Is there something about the island or what it contains… that you're not telling us?"

I grimace. "I thought you were going to tell me something, not ask me something? So let's try again, Mussenberg, what's the rush to speak to me all about? Why before 1700?"

Mussenberg gives a nod of acquiescence. "Okay. You're right. Let me lay it out for you then. We know all about you and the Trojan Team, okay? And I'm guessing that you've picked up enough info on us, to know who we kind'a are, too, correct?"

I angle my head. "I'd say that's a reasonable assessment."

He nods solidly. "Right. Well the thing is, Stone, this is my mission. Muskrat Island and what we're doing out there… that's my baby. I'm between a rock and a hard place here." He brings hardened eyes to meet mine. "Because basically, I fucked up. I underestimated you."

I just look at him, silently urging him to go on. When he sees that I'm not going to respond, he does.

"We're looking for something out on Muskrat Island that is of vital importance to our national security. Up 'til now, we haven't been able ta find it out there. Now that said… the General thinks you know something about where it might be. So, if you know and don't tell me now, then we'll try to take you into custody to be interrogated." He says the last like he already knows that this isn't gonna happen. But I assure him anyway, just in case he's confused.

"I'm not going to be arrested, Mussenberg. You know that."

He nods his head furiously now. "Yeah, Stone, I think I do. But then the next thing that's gonna happen, is that a hunter-killer team will be given your name as a wet work assignment. And that will automatically happen," he eases his watch up, "in about twenty-eight minutes." He lowers his hand. "They take their wet work seriously and they will kill you. That's an honest to goodness fact, Stone, and after 1700 they can't be called off. Not by me, anyway."

I feel my eyebrows nearly pop off my head. "Huh. Well, reckon ya gotta do what'cha gotta do, Mussenberg. But let me just tell you what I've done, so you'll know that much, anyway." I shift my stance so I can get a better view of the brush beside the station below. Then I continue.

"I've gotta notion about what you're looking for out there and I've put it all into words and historical context. I've explained it all, at least what I know about you people, that jet in 1953, and... the thing it was chasing when they disappeared over our island. Now I've given that much information to a number of people, and it will remain sealed unless I say it should change, or... unless I die."

I blow out a long piece of air and look at him, his eyes tell me that he's followed my meaning. I finish the rest. "In either case, the mission you have on the island, and what and who you people are, will become public record. I can almost guarantee it. So that's my response to your little death squad, I guess." I shoot him an inquisitive look. "So, does that mean we're at a stalemate, now?"

Mussenberg rolls his shoulders, his eyes and face expressive. "Did you find it, Stone? If you can tell me anything that will help us to find we're looking for, then maybe we can both live through this."

There's an imploring look on his features as he stands there. The heat of adrenalin, physical exhaustion and shinkakee are all fighting for space in my being. My left hand fingers the piwaka. The Ghost Riders song that's been playing ever so softly on my mental turntable, goes up a scoash in volume. This is what I have to do in any event. No matter what, the government will take control of this thing, and even if I'm right in my hunch, I can't help those poor pilots or their families. I doubt that anybody can anymore. Too much time has passed. But now, this is my job, to protect my people. I position my head at an angle.

"Do you go to the beach much, Mussenberg?"

His face wads up in dismay. Then he speaks in a snarl. "What the hell...? What're ya talking about?"

"I know where there's a little silver beachball on Muskrat Island."

I see the look of wonder and enlightenment wash over his face as he takes in my words. His own voice comes out in almost a whisper.

"Sonavabitch!" He looks away then back to me. "It's real then? Wow! Where, Stone? Where on the island?"

Based on a true 1953 Michigan Mystery 475

"It's in the lighthouse. In the light itself, up in the tower."

Mussenberg nods solemnly. His face is fixed with a contented smile. All of a sudden it changes to one of suspicion. "How did you find it?"

I crinkle up my face in a false silent smile. His just turns darker with anger. "I'm asking you again, Stone! How did you know about this?"

I feel my temper bubble up a notch and then mentally squash it down before tipping my head at him. "The young agent? The Chinese with a neck wound that you found by the light house?" He nods and I go on.

"It's what he was after. I didn't know what it was, but… well, since he wanted it so bad… I just kept it from him." I hunch up my shoulders. "Nothing more than that."

Mussenberg searches my face for an eternity and then finally comes to a decision. He's buying it. I can tell. He points a finger and speaks. "You know, this whole thing could've been avoided if you'd have just told us about this?"

I angle my head and flex my brows. "Hey, partner, when I pulled onto the road with ya'all, I didn't see any one-way signs. If you people would've been up-front with me about what you were looking for then maybe…"

He's nodding. "Yeah, yeah. Touché. I deserve that, I guess." Then his face weaves askew and suspicion rolls over it once again. "Okay. But who else knows about this now, Stone? Who've you got working with you?"

I just look at him. "No one."

He's incredulous. "Bullshit! Someone told you about our "Hawk" and you knew my every move coming over here."

I hold up the binoculars and point to the building across the way. "I was up there."

His eyes drop to the glasses, and then follow over to the building and all around as he surveys the area. He's smiling as he turns back to me. "All by yourself, huh? Well, sonavabitch! That was pretty slick. I'm impressed." We're each silent for a beat then his features turn thoughtful. He raises his chin a bit, his eyes boring deeply into me.

"Do you know what this little ball is?"

I give him my most noncommittal stare. "Nope."

His eyes continue to rove over me as I make my countenance a mask of concrete. He continues to speak while probing me from across the way. "Yeah, well just suffice ta say that it's a device to a secret weapon." His eyes lock on mine then.

"We lost it a few years ago and have been looking for it ever since." I think he sees the disbelief on my face and I watch as his features do a mental dance, forming a resolution before finally deciding to let it go. Then he looks down at his watch and curses. He hastily reaches for his phone, his fingers slipping and fumbling as he finally gets it open and presses a button.

"Sergeant Canter, this is Captain Mussenberg. I am giving the order to cancel "Cowboy". Do you copy?… Roger that. The comm-link was shutdown due to mission priority. Yes. Right, so I need you to notify my team here, since we don't have the comm-link anymore. Uh huh. The mission is scrubbed on my order. My confirm is "Green Card Forty-Three", Tango, Delta, Zulu. I need an acknowledgement number from you now?… Roger, standing by."

As he talks, I listen to his words and while I don't know for sure, I think I know their meaning. "Green Card" is the euphemism for an illegal immigrant or alien. And an alien is also space man - a "Little Green Man". The 43, meant that he was forty-third on his team, maybe? Could be, couldn't it? He's getting his answer now as I continue to listen.

"Roger. I copy, "Cowboy" Cancellation, 147 at," he rolls up his wrist and sees his watch, "1651 hours. Good enough. What?"

Mussenberg rolls his eyes, "Yeah, Dick, no joke. It's cutting it a lot closer than I like to, too. Right. We'll be heading back to Escanaba within the next thirty minutes. Oh, and notify Colonel Hendrickson out on the island that I'll be calling him once we're airborne. Yeah, I think I've got good news for him. Ok, roger – out."

Mussenberg snaps the phone closed and turns to me with a grin. "Okay, Stone, I guess we're done here then, huh?"

I blink and feel lost as I rub my hand over the piwaka. The song just stopped. The "Ghost Riders In The Sky" melody, that's been a reoccurring theme in my head for so long… has disappeared. I realize that Mussenberg's said something, so I answer.

"What? No, not quite. I need you to get that thing and anything connected to it… off our island. And Mussenberg, if you don't do this…," I fix my gaze on him. "Then I will go to "me-gat-ki-win" with you and your people. That's our word for war." I feel my eyes grow onerous and my stare become icy as we look at each other. Then I set my jaw and slowly nod my head. "I promise you this bud. My solemn oath."

He stares a moment longer, and then nods, a look of understanding, tempered with wonderment on his face. He clears his throat, his eyes still searching me. "Will do." Then he nervously changes the subject. He smiles and points, his voice slightly subdued. "I see you cut your hair?"

I nod while holding his eyes. "Yeah. And I understand that you lost your poor wife?"

Mussenberg smiles broader. "Okay. I deserve that. But tell me something." He looks up. "If we would've killed you, would your old team members have come looking for us?"

I rumple up my face in uneasiness. "I don't know… Probably."

He brings a hand up to his chin and studies me thoughtfully. "We don't have that kind of loyalty." He tips his head. "Are they all as good as you?"

I shake mine in response. "Better. Much better. I'm not good, Mussenberg. I'm just lucky."

He continues to examine me appraisingly, and then shakes his head. "No, I don't think so. Well, I guess I better get going. My guys'll be looking for me. He extends his right hand. "I guess you can say we have a gentleman's agreement then, huh? This'll just stay between you and I, okay?"

I look at the offered hand but don't remove mine from the pocket. Then my eyes find his again, and I anchor them with a cold, joyless stare. "I just want that thing and anything connected to it… off our island and away from my people. You do that…, and we'll have an understanding." Then I feel my head shake.

"But we're not gentleman, Mussenberg. Blackhearts? Maybe. Warriors?" I sigh. "Probably. But we're sure not gentlemen. Leave it go at that."

Epilogue
"I've Heard You Se Se Kwa!"

The Motel 6,
Alpine & US131,
Grand Rapids, Michigan.
1758 Hours or 5:58 pm.
The Same Day.

I **walk** into the room, close the door and apply the lock and chain. I set my stuff down and peel off my jacket. I haven't been this weary in years. My physical state, after the drain of adrenalin, has only deteriorated. On the drive back here from my meeting with Mussenberg, I'd stopped to call Gangues. I'd pulled into a gas station, gone inside, flashed my badge and borrowed their telephone. I called him from the rear of the store by the potato chip rack, where I had a good view of the lot and some concealment inside the store. I was pretty sure that nobody saw me on the phone. My old pal Gangues had information for me. According to the Milwaukee Journal-Sentinel newspaper archives, an Albert Scheel, no known relatives and an indigent, was buried at county expense in November of 1953.

Well, nothing like putting a pretty little bow on when you're tying up a problem, huh? I already knew that there had been a robbery of the Air Force Base in Marquette back in the '70s. Gangues had verified that. But it bothered me that Mussenberg and his group had been looking for a little black bag and that Gretchen's father'd had just such a container out on the island. I wanted to know how those two things connected. But I think I've already guessed the answer. I flip my notes to the right page, pick up the motel phone and dial the number. I burrow the fingers of my free hand into my red eyes as the phone begins ringing. It takes four of them to be answered.

"Hello?"

"Mr. Scheel? It's Ely Stone."

There's a long stretch of silence from the telephone and I hear children's muted voices in the background. A little girl asks, "Mommy, can we have popcorn?" That's probably Carrie. A woman's voice answers, "Yes you can, honey." That would be Gretchen. Then a voice speaks into the mouthpiece in a harsh whisper.

"Why are you doing this? Why did you come here today? Our business is completed now, you and I. Leave us alone!"

I sigh as I look around the room. "I will. I won't bother you anymore after this, but I have to ask you a question. That black bag... the one that held the item? Where did you get it?"

Another quiet moment passes, and then he answers. "It was in the mine when I arrived there. I do not know where it came from. It was not there when I left, all those years ago. I just assumed that some hiker had left it behind up above. I thought that perhaps it had food in it, and that an animal had drug it down there."

Well... that takes care of that little detail, doesn't it? That was the last tie-in to this little mystery of horrors. Both the Air Force and the old man had knowledge about this bag, and now I see how they did. The thieves must've used the bag in their robbery and somehow, it ended up in the mine. The Air Force had found out that much, even though the money was probably long gone. And the old man, had simply used it to tote that spooky beach ball. I turn back to the receiver.

"Okay. Thanks. I won't bother you again."

There's more stillness before he talks. "You called me Scheel? You know, don't you? You know the truth now... don't you, Officer Stone?"

My turn to leave a long spell of silence. "Take care of yourself and those two girls. Goodbye, Mr. Scheel."

A beat passes then, "Goodbye, Officer Stone, and... it's Veeter... now."

There's a gentle click, then a dial tone. I hang up the phone and weave a little as I stand there. It all fits. There may never be any proof... but it fits, just the same. What did Amos say this morning on the phone? "Wajakosh Umoya" - Star Spirits. Maybe that's what the "Murmurings" were trying to tell me. My head shakes of its own accord, but I no longer feel the shinkakee or hear any music.
I send my sight over to the door and try to make some thoughts about protection as I look around the motel room. It doesn't matter. I'm done and I know it. Even if the Air Force or someone else is still after me, I'm too fatigued to handle it anymore. I look at the bed dreamily and notice the cell phone that I'd tossed on it. The little light is blinking, indicating that I have a voice message. That's odd. I enter the code to retrieve it. It's from Nettie.

She says that Amos gave her the number, and that well... she needs to talk with me... to be with me. Whatever the problems are, she says we can work them out. She says that... she thinks that... she loves me! And to please call her tomorrow! My euphoria is probably

heightened by my exhaustion, but I fall across the bed laughing hysterically. I yell out loud, "I have heard you, se se kwa! I have heard you!" And I know that there will be no dreams tonight.
Sleep is a monster, crawling up over me, its jaws ravenous and devouring. I manage to pull the Glock out of my back and get it to my side before sleep hungrily consumes me. I fall blissfully into slumber, one hand on a pistol, the other on my medicine bag, a smile emblazoned on my face with merriment in my heart and spirit.

Postscript:

**The Guadalupe River,
Kendall County, Texas,**

Soon to be retired, Command Master Sergeant Cory White whipped the fly rod back and forth, allowing a limited amount of line to flow from his finger with each movement as he worked to land the tiny fly in the deep hole. He effortlessly maneuvered around the broad brimmed cowboy hat that he wore and several small trees that surrounded the riverbank as he worked the rod. He wore a white tee shirt, tucked into Levis and a netted fishing vest. His dark tan subdued the bright colors of the Air Force Para-Rescue tattoo on his heavily muscled right arm. He had just landed the fly in his intended locale when his wife Maria, called his name.

He turned to see her walking down from their retirement home on the hillside. Her short black and silver streaked hair bounced lightly in the bright sunshine and her brown skin still looked radiant, even after almost thirty years of being a military wife. He was at his last duty station and would retire out of Randolph Air Force Base. He was going to like being around her all of the time. But right now… he was trying to fish! She was carrying a package and as she approached, she extended to him.

"This just came in the mail, Hon. I thought you might want to see it right away." He gave her an aggravated look and her eyes went hard.

"Hey hombre, look at the return address before you get mad at me, eh?"

With that, she thrust the package at him and he had to switch the rod quickly to his other hand in order to take it. He watched as she spun around and began heading back up toward the house, speaking unknown Spanish words, just under her breath as she went. He watched her for a second then turned the parcel over to read the address. Then he uttered out a "Holy shit!" as he looked at the sender.

The package was from Fifth Rubber.

The big trout in that hole forgotten now, he carelessly leaned the pole against a tree and opened the package. He had no way of knowing that just a day earlier, an old comrade of his, Brigadier General Juan Sanchez, had received an exact duplicate of this parcel and letter. That man's package and copied cassette tapes were already recorded, re-packaged in mailers and stored in a cardboard box in the man's garage in College Park, Virginia.

White saw that his parcel contained two cassette tapes before he pulled out and unfolded the note that was also inside. His eyes immediately went to the prominent hand scrawled lettering at the top. PLEASE PALM THIS AT THE TIP.

Well, he knew what that meant. It was code. "Palm" was short for napalm meaning, fire or burn. "Tip" was code for "end", as like the tip or end of a flagpole. It meant burn this correspondence at the end or as soon as he finished reading it. Damn. He dropped his eyes to read the rest.

Dear Mr. White,

I hope all is well with you and yours. I know that you are about to depart from playing anymore and I wish you well in your new pursuits. We did have many challenging games of our own, didn't we? Well, as fate would have it, I've stumbled into some controversy lately. I've had several realtors trying sell me a local farm and have almost succumbed and bought one. There have been times that the temptation was very great, but thus far, I've avoided a purchase.

At this point, I think that I have assured the realty company that I do not want to buy. I think they understand and will leave me in peace. But should I become weak and purchase a farm anyway, would you be so kind as to listen to, then copy the enclosed tapes and then send them to the folks I have listed below? These are legal matters having to do with the realty agency and their real estate. program. I'm sure that you'll understand, should you hear them. Thank you so much and take care. Hopefully, I'll be in touch soon. Your friend and former partner,

5th Rubber.

White's hand subconsciously caressed the Trojan Horse tattoo that he had on his right hip. He quickly folded the paper and creased it above the list of names then tore the paper in two pieces. He pocketed the names and held the remaining letter loosely as he fumbled in his

fishing vest for the Bic lighter he kept there. He didn't smoke but he
used the lighter to melt monofilament fishing line. Shortly, he had
it out and set the note afire and watched it burn away before dropping
it and crushing the ashes with his boot. He grabbed the pole, wound up
the line and began climbing the hill. He and Maria had to drive to town.
He didn't own a tape recorder and he had to buy one fast.

I<<<I>::<I<<<I>::<I<<<I>::<I :+: I>::<I>>>I>::<I>>>I>::<I>>>I

Statements from the Past... for the Reader to Discern

Quote-October 9, 1955: "The nations of the world will have to unite – for the next war... will be an interplanetary war. The nations of the Earth must someday make a common front against attack by people from other planets."

General Douglas McArthur, US Army

Media-May 28, 1975: Barry Goldwater, Senator from Arizona, states that he has been trying to get into Hanger 18 at Wright-Patterson Air Force Base, Ohio, to view the UFO artifacts there.

Media-October 19, 1981: Senator Barry Goldwater declares that he is giving up on ever gaining admittance to the "Blue Room", located at Wright-Patterson Air Force Base in Ohio.

If you wish to view the actual US Air Force Accident Report on this missing F-89 jet, go to: www.cufon.com/kinross/kinross_acc_rept.htm

Please visit the author's website at: www.Walks-As-Bear.com
There you can view "The Murmurings Photo Facts" page for more info.

I<<<I>::<I<<<I>::<I<<<I>::<I :+: I>::<I>>>I>::<I>>>I>::<I>>>I

Author's Note

The Murmurings is a story of fiction. However, what is depicted in Chapter Twenty Nine, *A Tangent For The Ghost,* did indeed actually happen. On the night of November 23rd, 1953, a U.S. Air Force F-89c jet fighter bearing the number 5105853A and carrying US Air Force Lieutenants Felix Moncla and Robert Wilson did... disappear in the ominous dark sky over the Great Lakes. This incident was early in the fight against communism. Since this date, many other military aircraft have disappeared similarly. But what happened that night, set the pattern and military response measures that changed the way that the US Air Force and NATO fought the Cold War. Thus, this true mystery... ultimately changed the course of the world.

That November night in 1953, the fighter jet was sent up on an air defense mission to intercept an unidentified aircraft of some kind – quite possibly a Russian bomber – over Lake Superior. So this was a combat mission. The whole scene was watched on radar scopes by numerous Air Force personnel on the ground. They watched stupefied, as the unidentified flying object... shot across the sky to merge with the approaching Air Force fighter. Right after this merging, all communications with that fighter jet ceased. And while the Air Force plane disappeared off radio and radar... the unidentified aircraft... kept flying as if nothing had happened. It was last seen on radar, shooting down across Lake Michigan before it too vanished. This was much too far of a distance for the thing to have traveled, had it been in an air to air collision with the jet, eh.

An exhaustive search for the fighter jet and missing aircrew turned up nothing. No wreckage, no bodies, no parachutes... nothing. Of course, that search was conducted over Lake Superior – not Lake Michigan. According to prior-service witnesses, that same night, there was another F-89c that crashed at Truax AFB in Wisconsin, about 30 minutes after the first one disappeared. There is no official AF accident report on that particular crash so...could this have been Lieutenant Moncla's wingman? The military does keep their little secrets, eh. Still, not one thing has been brought to light about Lieutenants Moncla and Wilson or their missing jet in all these years. That, too, seems odd, but then who's to say?

The F-89 Scorpion and her crew may be hidden on the dark, cold bottom of Lake Superior. Or, perhaps it's resting on the white sandy floor of Lake Michigan. Maybe she's blended into the dense forests of Michigan, Wisconsin or Canada. Or, then again… she may no longer reside anywhere at all…here on our Earth Mother, eh?

CPSIA information can be obtained
at www.ICGtesting.com
Printed in the USA
LVHW111514091019
633689LV00001B/19/P